FRAGMENTS

NYLA K.

Paperback ISBN: 979-8-9869189-5-2
Cover Design by Ashes & Vellichor
Photography by Michelle Lancaster
Model: Andy Murray

Interior formatting by Champagne Book Design
Proofreading services by Nice Girl Naughty Edits

To *sluts*.

Seriously. Loving sex isn't a bad thing.
And don't ever let anyone tell you it is.

Fragments

Alabaster Penitentiary, Volume 4

Survival is all that matters in here.

Still, it gets tricky when evil lurks around every corner, wanting to play.

To the arsonist, everything is a game.

Warren Xavier is Alabaster Pen's resident manipulative liar. The former pretty boy prince of Manhattan's elite is now locked away with the rest of us. Nothing but time to sit and stew… Scheme and obsess. And I'm the unlucky soul he's made the object of his cunning affections.

On the outside, I would never entertain the kinds of things Ren wants from me… Unfortunately, being trapped for so long in such a hellish place can wear down even the strongest of minds.

I'd be a fool to fall into his mess of lustful deviance again. After all, I've been burned before.

But that silver tongue is wrapped right around my heart. The next time his flames engulf me… I might let them.

Prison life can be fun when you hold the handcuff keys in your sullied hands. My *skills* give me power over guards, prisoners… Pretty much everyone. I control these men without lifting a finger. *Maybe bending at the waist…*

But not him. Not the one I truly *want*.

Lex "Luthor" Deon is too perfect to be rotting in this dungeon. He's a hacker, a *genius*; a shimmering diamond lodged in a dreary black pit of decay. Sweet, loyal… inexperienced.

In short, he's *way* too good for me.

But I'm too stubborn and volatile to ever let him go.

I won't allow fragments of the past ruin us. When it all comes crumbling down, Lex will have to make a choice… Risk everything, or play it safe.

Whether he likes it or not, he wants to believe me…

But sometimes even *I* can't tell when I'm lying.

FOREWORD

Well, well, well…

Look who just couldn't *resist coming back to the Isle.*

I have to assume you're here because, despite how treacherous Alabaster Penitentiary is, there's something about its darkness that's sucked you right in. Hopefully, you're returning after The Carver and Dr. Love left you bloody and satisfied. Which would mean you're more than okay with the pitch-black lack of morality, the depravity, and the nefarious goings on of this *prison*.

But if, for whatever reason, you're picking this book up without having met Dash, or Velle, or Felix, or any of the other broken boys, lovable narcissists, and cute, cuddly psychopaths from this series, I just need to make sure you're aware of a few things.

First, while this series does follow a new couple—or throuple—each book, the storyline itself is very much overarching through them all. Each book will end in a *happily ever after* for the characters, but that doesn't mean the general storyline will be wrapped up. In each book, questions are answered, but more are presented, all sides to this saga of mayhem culminating in a giant, explosive grand finale in Volume 6—*Ivory*.

That means it's strongly recommended to read the other three books before this one, to get the entire feel of what's happening. Because it's a lot. If you try to read *Fragments* first, you'll definitely be lost. It just won't hit the right spot.

We follow the same timeline in each book, seeing familiar dramatic events unfold through different eyes. *Fragments,* in particular, includes a crap-ton of pivotal scenes from *Distorted*, only from the POV's of our main characters, Luthor and Ren.

There's no other way to say it... *Fragments* will spoil the *fuck* out of *Distorted*. So definitely read that first. Then read *Joyless*, so you can familiarize yourself with Officer Chevelle and his team, who are also *majorly* involved in this book. And after that, I mean, come on... You're gonna want to spend some time with Felix Darcey.

Which brings us to Dash's cellmate, the hacker, and a certain arsonist who's been *pining* for him throughout the series thus far.

Don't go into this book expecting it to be like the others, because it certainly won't be. It's unique, and infinitely more dramatic, with boatloads more *action*. Of course, it's a complex love story between Luthor and Ren, but it's also a deep-dive into their pasts and what brought them to this point. It's a tale of found family—in the most unexpected of places, which sets the tone for the finale. (Something I'll definitely discuss more in the author's note.)

Just know this isn't simply a *romance novel*. It's a dark and devious world of secrets and lies, warped reality, unexpected love, self-discovery, and sex—lots and *lots* of filthy, illicit sex—all taking place on a mysterious island. If you're looking for a standard dark romance plot, you won't find it here. Alabaster Pen requires an open-mind, and a severe appreciation for detail.

So... if you've made it this far, let's move onto the next point. The *warning*.

Undoubtedly, you're aware that this entire series is dark. Some of the books more than others, and of course, the level of darkness will vary depending on each reader. *Fragments* has no shortage of sensitive subject matter that could definitely make some readers uncomfortable. Should you wish to check out the specifics before diving in, they can be found on the content warnings page of my website.

Hopefully, getting to know Luthor and Ren a bit in the previous books has somewhat prepared you for what to expect... But still, that was just a surface scratch. It'll get pretty heavy at times.

Let's face it, it's been fun laughing about Ren's sluttyness, but seeing it through his eyes, experiencing it firsthand *with* him, and with the man who's trying to love him… It might be a tough pill to swallow. But I urge you not to let that deter you.

Yes, there will be *"cheating"* in this book. Yes, there will be on-page—*and, quite frankly, off-page*—sexual interaction between them and people who are *not* each other. But it's just the nature of this story, and the crucial development of their painful, obsessive, undying yearn for one another over years and *years* of forced proximity.

This book won't be for everyone. I know that, whole-heartedly. But it's *their* love story, highs and lows and everything in between. And trust me when I tell you, Luthor and Ren earn the fuck out of their happiness in the end.

There you have it. *Finally*, the moment you've all been waiting for, wondering about, desperately craving to get inside.

This burn is long… and *deep*.

So cozy up in your cells, inmates. Dim the lights, grab some supplies, and get ready…

For fireworks ;)

Scan for content warning

FRAGMENTS PLAYLIST

Heathens (feat. MUTEMATH) – Twenty One Pilots
Kickstart My Heart – Mötley Crüe
Stay Away (Piano Version) – MOD SUN, Machine Gun Kelly
superdeadfriends – YUNGBLUD
White Iverson – Post Malone
A.D.I.D.A.S. – Korn
Fire – Two Feet
Waste Love – Machine Gun Kelly, Madison Love
MONTERO (Call Me By Your Name) – Lil Nas X
Blue and Yellow – The Used
Chills (Dark Version) – Mickey Valen, Joey Myron
BACK2YOU (feat. blackbear) – nothing,nowhere, Travis Barker
18 and Life – Skid Row
Seize the Power – YONAKA
Arsonist's Lullaby - Hozier
Thinking of You (I Drive Myself Crazy) - *NSYNC
bad guy – Billie Eilish
World Keeps Spinning – Theory of a Deadman
Headcase – Crystal Tides
Like A Virgin – YUNGBLUD
Kiss It Off Me – Cigarettes After Sex

Baby – Elvis Drew, Avivian
Sooner Or Later – Years & Years
Toxic – A Static Lullaby
Let Me Go (Acoustic Version) – 3 Doors Down
WILD - Troye Sivan
Not Enough – Elvis Drew, Avivian
Cry – Cigarettes After Sex
Bad Drugs – King Kavalier, ChrisLee
Love Songs – Maggie Lindemann
Gaslight! – diveliner
Thousand Miles – The Kid LAROI
Chemical - Post Malone
Blurry (Acoustic) – Puddle Of Mudd
forget me too – Machine Gun Kelly, Halsey
Tidal Wave – Chase Atlantic
Tell Me The Truth – Two Feet
unrealistic love – Jet Black Alley Cat
toxic energy (with Bert McCracken) – blackbear
California (Unplugged) – YUNBLUD
twin flame – Machine Gun Kelly
Firework – Katy Perry
hurricane – 44phantom
Forever – Labrinth
Home Sweet Home – Mötley Crüe
More Than Words – Extreme
Kryptonite – Flight Paths
Firewalk – Morgan Page, Lissie

"Yes, I'm still by his side.
Yeah, I'm Bonnie. He's Clyde.
I'm holding it down on the outside.
Hand in hand, that's how we ride."

—Bonnie Parker

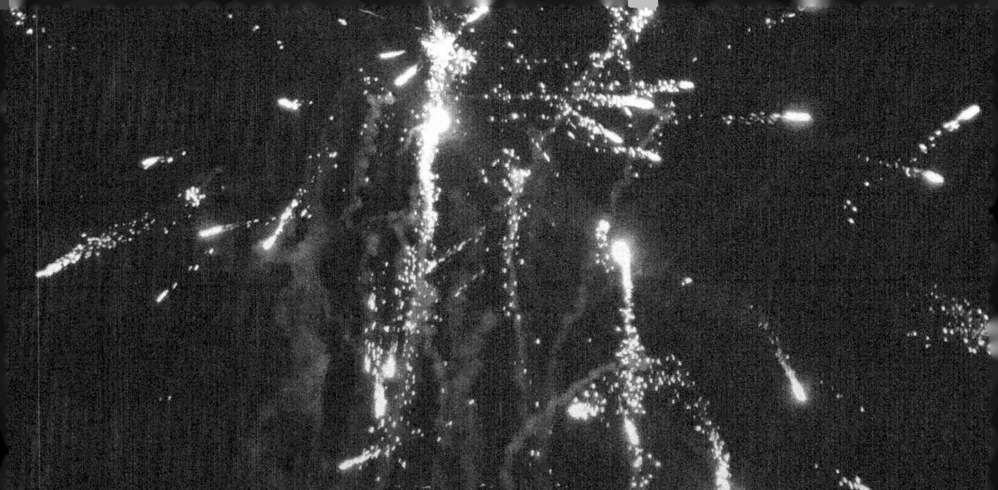

PROLOGUE

Ren

4 years ago...

“I NEED A HIT.”

He grunts, acknowledging that he heard me. But he makes no immediate moves to give me what I want. It irks me.

But then he pushes up into me and my eyes roll back. *Sure, yea. That’s much better than the line of coke.*

Positioning myself, I remember the angle, making sure to slope my neck and bite my lip, because they like that. Of course what’s happening feels good, it always does, but I also need to focus on making this *look* good for them.

It’s what they’re paying for.

A strong hand runs up to my throat where it stops, tightens, and squeezes. My face burns, and I clench my teeth. *If he’s gonna get rough, I need more drugs.*

“I need a—” My choked voice fades into a groan when his dick brushes my prostate again. “*Hit.*”

He breathes warmth on the back of my neck, and chills sheet my flesh, nipples bunched up and sensitive. Which reminds me…

My eyes open and I lock down the man across the room, who’s sipping scotch and staring at me, a giant, visible erection showing itself through his tailored dress pants.

"So you're, like, the silent partner?" I murmur in his direction, my lips quirking at the *oh-so serious* look on his face.

He looks like he wants to ignore me, or even call me a *disgusting faggot slut*—the usual MO of guys like him—but he can't even try to act like he isn't interested in what's happening on this side of the room. Not only can I see his whole cock right now beneath the measly fabric he's wearing, but the heat in his gaze is scorching me alive.

My mind sweeps up instantly, in thoughts of what he probably wants to do…

Drop that glass on the fucking floor and come over here. Whip out your huge dick and shove my mouth down onto it. Fuck my face until I'm crying while your friend tears up my ass.

Ravage me, stranger.

I guess I'm not the only one having these thoughts, because *John Doe* pauses his meticulous thrusts and pulls out, a shivering groan leaving his lips, audible to my eager ears even over the pumping bass of the music coming from downstairs.

He taps my thigh. "Up, baby. Let my boy sample some of this sweet cunt."

His filthy words in that hushed, growly voice send a zip up my spine. But I blink myself out of it, standing up slowly. "Set me up. I won't ask again."

I catch a glimmer of impressed amusement on the friend's face while John Doe chuckles. "I told you. This one's a live wire."

He reaches over, grabbing a sterling silver tray, cutting up some white lines with a black American Express while I watch anxiously. Using a rolled-up hundred, he snorts a line, whipping his head back and wiping his nose. Then he hands it to me.

When I bend to do my line, he smacks my ass. *Hard*. The sting feels good, and my balls throb. But still, I can't fight the irritation I'm feeling. *These guys are always the same.*

I think maybe that's why I'm so often annoyed by my clients. It's the unoriginality of it all. I can predict their moves, anticipate what they're going to do or say next. Just once, I wish someone would do something different.

I wish *anything* would change. Because I feel like I'm drifting…

I'm always drifting.

With the drugs in my system, I'm shivering with need. Everything is fast and in high definition. The thumping music of the club just downstairs rattles my veins, darkness and shadows surrounding us. I'm bathed in red light as I stride, naked, to the center of the room, approaching the quiet stranger. He's fiddling with his video camera that's set up off to the side.

Things like this are allowed in here… For a price. Only high rollers are allowed in these rooms. And I don't come up here for less than five-grand an hour.

Not that I need the money. It's the *principle*.

I like to get fucked, and I like doing it with strange men. *Bonus points if they're straight, extremely wealthy, and powerful government officials, like ol' John Doe over there.*

Sparse light catches the shimmer of glitter on my skin, highlighting the curves of my muscles. The stranger likes it. I can tell, because he isn't messing with the camera anymore. Now he's practically drooling while his hungry gaze slides all over me. Sidling up to him, I reach out hesitantly to play with the open collar of his white shirt.

"Whatever you want… it's yours," I whisper over his lips.

He's keyed up tight, holding firm. He doesn't do this as often as John Doe, that much is clear.

Something vulnerable flashes in his dark eyes as his head cocks to the right. He assesses my face closely, like he's looking for something. I can't help but wonder what he's seeing when he's looking at me.

The image… The *portrayal*. That's all they ever see.

The shell of Warren Xavier.

No one knows what's hidden underneath.

Uncharacteristically, Stranger's hand travels up, his fingers dancing tenderly on my jaw. He remains silent while his thumb grazes my bottom lip. His softness, the gentle way he's touching me, is a resuscitation to my dead heart. It tickles in the pit of my stomach… like an itchy frisson I can't shake.

It feels so strange… *affection*. But I don't… I don't think I hate it.

Unfortunately, before I can even process what I'm feeling, Stranger shoves his thumb into my mouth.

Things become fast and foggy after that.

He pushes me onto my knees, spearing my throat with his long dick while his friend snorts coke off my ass and jerks off in the background. I'm in a haze when he drags me back to the couch, and they sit, side by side, passing me back and forth. Using me like nothing but a sex toy.

But this is what I'm used to. This *makes sense.*

Being fucked hard, aggressively, by men who see me as an object. Their angry fists in my hair, pushing my skull in the dark.

The whirlwind of drugs and cum. Growling and bruises and control… The give and take.

They give. I take.

By the end of it, I'm numb. I know I've gotten off. I usually do, but I can't even remember the orgasms after a few seconds, and I'm not sure what that means.

They leave me with my wrists bound by their expensive ties, covered in cum, and a little blood, surrounded by a pile of sweaty cash.

Typical Friday night.

Once I'm cleaned up and dressed, the sun is rising slowly over this island we call New York. I leave the club, fighting the urge to limp and trying like hell to leave the cut on my lip alone. The black Town Car is parked along the curb, as usual. But I don't take it.

I never do.

In fact, I flip it off, walking the two blocks to the nearest subway station. The ride is sobering, as usual. I put in my headphones and listen to my favorite playlist, zoning out amongst Manhattan's walk-of-shamers and people who work at this ungodly hour, even on weekends. The city is broken, and lonely, just like the rest of us.

When I arrive at home, I can't help but gaze upward, eyeing the giant Upper East Side townhouse with a sigh.

I would love to watch it all burn…

Inside, the house is still quiet, shy of the staff who are already up, cooking and cleaning as quietly as possible. Not that it would matter… My parents are in their wing, which feels like miles away from this side of the house.

I ignore the looks they're giving me while I climb the stairs and go directly to my bedroom. *This is only a transitional period*, I tell myself while I strip down and go for the shower. My reflection in the mirror catches my eye, all the bruises covering my flesh sticking out amongst my scattered ink.

I like them. Bruises remind me that I'm alive and susceptible to hurt. Like when I was twelve and I used to cut myself.

Just to *feel*.

While I shower, my mind flicks through images. Memories of tonight, with John Doe. I'm contractually obligated to pretend I don't know who he is, although I definitely do. My parents donated to his congressional campaign. And the new stranger… he also looked familiar.

They always do. *If I gave up the names of all the high-powered men I've bent over for, I could take down the city of New York singlehandedly.*

I enjoy it, I do. I can't act like I don't, but that teeny, weakened little voice inside tries shouting up to my brain. *I don't want to be here anymore.*

Get me out.

Get… me… out.

After my shower, I get into bed. And I pass out for hours. *Many* hours.

When my eyes open again, it's dinnertime. And no surprise, I can hear my mother shrieking up the hall. I open my bedroom door, rubbing the sleep from my eyes and preparing myself for another installment of *'scream at Ren until he realizes the error of his ways.'*

"Rosa, I've told you *one hundred times…* If Mr. Xavier is due business visitors, we cannot have you all mulling about. It's distracting and unprofessional." My mother pauses her berating of the housekeeper for long enough to glance up at me. "Well, look who's decided to grace the world with his presence." Her gaze falls over my shirtless torso for a moment before she rolls her eyes and scoffs. "You're unbelievable." Then fixates back on poor Rosa. "Get everyone out of sight, right now!"

"Yes, Mrs. Xavier," Rosa trembles, scurrying off to go shit herself. And I get it. My mother is definitely scary… to people who give a flying fuck about her bullshit, which I certainly do not.

"What the fuck is wrong?" I yawn and stretch my arms over my head. "I need my beauty sleep and you're out here squawking like a demented bird."

"Warren, enough," Beth, my *mother*, shrills. "Your father is expecting company and you're standing around looking like the epitome of a disappointment. Put some clothes on."

I can't help the *huh* look I'm giving her. "Dad's company isn't my problem. Now, if you'll excuse me, I'm going back to bed. I have work in a few hours."

"Warren! I swear to God, we're not doing this again!" She rushes me, grasping me by the arm so hard her acrylics are breaking the skin. "It's bad enough the entire community knows you were kicked out of school for inappropriate conduct. And now you're flouncing around the city like a common whore! It's disgusting. Get your shit together, or we're sending you to back to rehab!"

"Blah blah *BLAH*!" I shout in her face, and she flinches, gazing up at me like I'm the spawn of Satan. *If the shoe fits, Mom.* "You sound so boring and stupid. Listen, I don't give a fuck about your yammering." I rip my arm out of her grip. "If you wanted a normal son, you shouldn't have fucked me up so bad."

My mother's blue eyes are wide, burning with unkempt rage in my direction as she goes quiet. It's that silent fury that lets me know she means business. But sadly for her, I still don't care. I *physically* don't possess the piece of my chemical makeup that allows me to give a fuck what people think—especially my parents.

And that's actually not the only part I'm missing.

"You're living in this house," she seethes. "We're *paying* for your lifestyle—"

"I don't need you to do that," I growl. "I'm making my own money."

"We are *not* speaking about that, Warren," she hisses, her Botox not allowing for the facial reactions trying to tug at her skin. "What you do with your time is disgusting."

"Why… because I'm a *man* doing it with *men*?" My arms fold over my chest. "Meanwhile, you slutting your way across the Columbia campus wasn't a big deal…"

"Kenneth!" my mother shouts at the top of her lungs, making my ears ring. She storms away from me in a huff, darting down the stairs, likely toward my father's office. "You need to get a handle on your son! I swear to God, I'm going to blow my brains out."

"Don't do me any favors, mother dearest," I grumble under my breath, spinning back into my bedroom.

I would love to go back to sleep, but after that, I can't. So instead, I get changed and go for a run. And when I come back, stomping into the foyer with my music turned up to full volume and the end of my water bottle in my mouth, I come face-to-fucking-face with the guy who fucked me and slapped me in the face last night…

John Doe's friend.

In my house.

What kind of cosmic bullshit…?

Upon noticing one another, we both go completely still and stare for a solid ten seconds. His eyes fall to what I'm wearing… my skin-tight running pants and a sleeveless mesh workout top that shows off all my side tats.

I witness him gulp, and my gaze narrows.

My father's business acquaintance, I presume.

His eyes shift around before he whispers, "What are you doing here??"

"Uh, I live here, Sherlock." I sip from my water bottle again. "What are you doing? Let me guess… investing. Or were you just so taken with my *skills*, you couldn't help but track me down? Wouldn't be the first time…"

His face goes ashen, while simultaneously morphing into appall, disgust, shame, and rage. So many things I'm used to seeing on men's faces. It's boring.

"You signed an NDA," he growls. "Don't forget that, *Ren*."

I can't help but grin at him. "But if you were to sue me… who do you think would be footing the bill?" I glance around the giant, lavish and opulent penthouse we're currently standing in.

His jaw ticks, eyes igniting a fuse of wrath as he steps closer to me. "You are such a worthless little slut."

"Ooh, *Daddy*," I hum. "Talk dirty to me."

I swear to God, it looks like he's about to lay hands on me. And I'm *praying* for it.

I need it, like a winding up that's been happening inside me for days, weeks, months, years… All the time blending together like a suffocating gray nothingness. The need to break *free* from the chains of this life, stretching me thinner and thinner…

I'm about to snap.

Hit me, motherfucker. I dare you.

"What's going on over here?" My father's voice breaks the spell, and Stranger falls back, instantly reacquainting himself with reality and his surroundings.

"I'm so sorry, Kenneth… Unfortunately, I won't be signing the deal." His surly gaze narrows at me. "I've had a change of heart."

He turns and stalks toward the front door. The palpable shift in the room is strong, like a sudden leak of noxious gas in the air. My father shoots me a withering glare, chasing his potential business partner to the door, pleading with him to reconsider.

My mother steps out from the dining room, simply shaking her head. "What have you done now?"

I lift my shoulder in a bored shrug. *Who cares?*

When my father comes back, he grabs me by the arm and hauls me to his face. "Do you have any idea what you've done?!"

My muscles stiffen in anger as I snarl in his face. "Do I look like I give a *fuck* about your business ventures??"

He shoves me away from him. "You're disgusting."

"Listen, Father, if you're no longer accepting funds from men who have ridden me raw, I'm sorry to say, but your accounts are about to be dryer than your wife's pussy."

He slaps me. *Hard*, right across the face. Like a bitch.

A laugh bursts from my throat, loud. A deranged cackle.

I spit blood onto the floor. "Fuck you."

"You think you can just get away with this?" My father glowers at me, and while I've always loved the way I look, in this moment, I despise it. The similarities between us. "Ruining our lives, our reputation with your sickening lifestyle?? You can't. I will burn you to the *ground* before I let you destroy everything I've built."

Burn.

A flicker of elation sparks inside me.

Like the strike of a match…

"Don't worry, Dad," I whisper with a curl to my lips. "I'm way ahead of you."

The shouts blur in my ears as I walk away from him. The threats I've heard since I was a child. The hatred I've built for these people, this home, it stacks up inside me like bricks. The final nail in the coffin.

The last straw.

Burn it down.

And later that night, when the castle is quiet, I'm surrounded by the scent of kerosene.

And I light a match.

CHAPTER ONE

Luthor

Today...

"Fuck yea... That's good. Hold still."

Squeezing my eyes shut tighter, I flop onto my side, yanking my pillow over my head.

"Stop squirming. Just take it..."

Muffled grunting and groaning still assaults my ears, framed by the incessant creaking of a rickety bunk bed. My teeth grind together.

"I'm gonna bust... Fuck, I'm gonna... *come* in you."

Whipping the pillow off, I shoot up in my bunk and roar, "Shut the fuck up in there! Some of us are trying to sleep!"

The obvious sounds of Cooper, my next-cell neighbor, having an orgasm, trail off into some grumbled curses. Then he shouts, "Sorry, Luth! I thought you were already out..."

"It's barely nine o'clock..." another voice mutters.

It's Simmons. *No surprise there.* They're cellmates. And despite the fact that he didn't sound too keen on being fucked when they started this rendezvous that's currently disturbing my beauty sleep, Simmons is now just raggedly conversing with his rapist, which has me scoffing and shaking my head.

This place, man.

"That don't matter," Cooper grunts to his roomie-slash-reluctant-fuck-buddy, hoarse and now audibly up and moving around. "It's about respect, bitch. Next time I push in that hole after lights out, you need to be a little more quiet. For *Luthor*. Got it?"

I hear a smack, and a groan. *This is entirely too much.*

"You were the one talking!" Simmons growls. "I couldn't even breathe. Your whole fucking fist was in my mouth..."

"Guys... *please*," I grumble-cry. Real petulant, whiny shit.

But these dudes aren't new. Everyone knows the rules on this end of the row:

Luthor loves to sleep, so shut the fuck up after lights out.

"Shhh! Shut that pouty li'l mouth," Cooper scolds Simmons in a whisper.

Truthfully, it's not their fault. I can usually sleep through the noise... Or at least, if I'm *already* asleep, I can. But tonight, I'm having trouble drifting off.

I always know why... *But I don't want to think about it.*

Now that Cooper has completed his aggressive exploration of Simmons's nether regions, the loud noises have stopped, and I can let out a breath of relief. Sure, there's still *noise*. There always is. But it's off in the distance, not next door. I can work with that.

My eyelids are finally beginning to droop, when a familiar voice yelps up the row. And they spring back open.

Fucking motherfuck.

I'm gonna be exhausted tomorrow, thanks to him.

I roll my eyes, flopping around on the top bunk, in the cell I've had to myself for the last few months. My frustrated gaze sets on the concrete wall beside my bed, and I just stare.

Listening...

Not actively trying to block it out, like I was with dumb and dumber next door.

I recognize it so well, *this* sound. Every dip and hitch and cadence... Shuddering breaths, raspy groans, jagged sobs. I've been listening to them like a soundtrack for years. I've come to expect them.

Sometimes I hear my name. And I refuse to admit it, but more often than not, I hope to hear it.

Slamming my eyes shut, I shake that thought away. *No... I don't want to hear my name from his lips while he's doing what he does.*

I don't *care* what's happening just up the row, in that cell I won't set foot in again. It's just another thing I have no control over; something I have to grin and bear, living where I do...

In Alabaster Penitentiary.

And I've been here long enough to understand the facts. I took hold of reality way back when. In all honesty, it didn't take me that long to swallow this jagged pill. After all, I'm a realist. I know there are certain things that won't change, and I've made my peace with it. *Unlike some other people I know.*

I've been locked up, on an island in the middle of the ocean, for nearly five years now.

And I won't *ever* be getting out.

So what happens now? you might be asking.

It's all about finding some semblance of life here. Living each day as best I can, not thinking about the future, and sure as shit not dwelling on the past. It's all pointless, anyway.

I'm here, forever.

So these fuckers need to let me sleep.

I do eventually get a few hours of decent shuteye, but it's nowhere near as satisfying as I usually find it to be. When the lights come on in the row, I grumble, stuffing my face into the bed. There's no rhyme or reason to the schedule of events in Alabaster Pen, but being here for as long as I have, you start to gain a sort of *intuition* for what's coming. This morning feels like a breakfast, then immediately to the showers kind of day.

Drifting in and out of consciousness, I feel a dream lingering on the edges of my mind, but I can't really remember what it was. The noises up the row grow louder once more as inmates wake up and begin their own daily routines. Mornings tend to be quieter than nights. Still, there are things you'll always hear… Shouting is a staple. Cursing, screaming, fucking, and fighting.

I barely notice it anymore. Unless it's interrupting my sleep. *Or coming from a certain cell up the row…*

Sitting up slowly, I rub my eyes, waking myself up fully. I hop down from my bunk, grabbing my toothbrush and toothpaste to begin my *regimen,* if you will. Take a piss, brush my teeth, wash my face. I still have more than half my tube of toothpaste left. *That's good.* I'm not looking forward to trying to get more… or the knowledge of what has to happen in order for me to get it.

Shaking it off, I go to my bunk, tucking my things back under my mattress and grabbing a fresh pair of boxers and socks. I change into them, beneath my standard dull gray jumpsuit, and my pair of Adidas I've had for years.

Folding up my dirty clothes, I place them on the bottom bunk. It reminds me of my last cellmate… And the fact that he's been MIA for months now. I swallow hard, remembering the day Henry Landon was ripped out of here, kicking and screaming…

Memories fade to the back of my mind at the familiar footsteps and chatter associated with Alabaster Pen's resident female. Joy Jameson peers in through the bars, and I offer her a cheeky grin.

Her brows furrow as she pushes open the door to my cell. "You're already up?"

"Just getting a head-start on this beautiful day," I mumble sarcastically, though I'm grinning as she chuckles, stepping up to me with cuffs in hand.

Fastening them loosely, she gives me a little shove toward the door. "Oh, Luthy. Why can't all the dumpster fires in this dungeon be like you?"

I laugh. Her raspy voice is laced with humor, but of course there's truth and fondness in there. Call it one of the benefits, if there really are any, of having been here for so long. I have a good relationship with most of the guards, and believe it or not, it's something I've earned *without* getting on my knees. But Joy is definitely my favorite. She's cool, and she respects the fact that I'm not here to cause rifts or get into trouble.

Sure, I freaked out a little when I first arrived, all those years ago. You'd have to be a total psycho not to…

Being tossed into a concrete tomb under the guise of rotting away for the rest of my life sent me into a spiral of epically freaked-out proportions. But I got over it quickly enough when I realized there was no point. Spazzing wouldn't change the reality of my situation.

And so, ever since, I've just been *existing* here. Doing my best to get by while still trying my hardest to smile. It's the one thing they can't take from me.

The last remaining piece of *Lexington Deon*.

Trudging up the row, Joy stops us to grab Kang and O'Malley. Once they're out in the hall with us, her hand stays planted on her Glock. Because while *I'm* a truly Zen motherfucker in this place, and Joy and Kang have their own little thing going on, Kieran O'Malley is still a wild card.

He's coming up on his one-year anniversary, and he's still just as crazy as he was the day he got here. I like him enough, but I'm not a huge fan of the unpredictable. I get enough of that from the cell on the other end of the row.

Glancing at Kang and O'Malley, I nod to them, and they nod back. O'Malley looks tired, as usual. He suffers from night terrors, when he's not actively freaking out, which makes him a pretty obnoxious cellmate to Kang, who's probably the quietest of our little group of prison pals. But still, Kang likes O'Malley. They get along, when they're not beating the shit out of each other.

It's a bizarre friendship.

"I owe you a bitch-smack," I grumble to O'Malley while Joy brings us farther up the row.

He gives me a look, then rolls his eyes. "Yer a real baby about yer sleep, brother."

"You know the rules, Shamrockstar." Kang grins, elbowing him.

I can't help but chuckle at the nickname. Velle started calling O'Malley that a few months back, and we all get a kick out of it. O'Malley hates it, which makes it even more fun.

"It's fine. It wasn't just you," I huff. "Cooper was being a bigger rapist than usual last night."

"Yea, I heard," Kang grunts, shaking his head. "I feel bad for Simmons's asshole."

"He liked it." A new voice joins our conversation.

And my eyes lift slowly, finding the familiar sky-blue gaze right on mine. As usual.

He looks at me more than anything else.

"You'd know," O'Malley says to Ren, smirking.

Ren weasels in between the other bodies to get closer to me. I back up. "Morning, Lex."

"Mhm," I grunt, refusing to make eye contact.

"You look tired." His voice is suddenly quieter, and that gets me. I peek at him. "Are you alright? You're not getting sick, are you? There's something going around..."

No, there isn't.

"I'm fine, Ren," I cut him off on a growl as Joy brings us through a door, meeting up with one of the other guards, Hancock, who's herding more inmates from a different row. "Leave it alone."

"Tell me who's been keeping you awake," he hisses, tone taking on a stern darkness. "I'll fuck 'em up."

My lip quirks, but I force it away. "You might have to fuck yourself up, then." I glance at him. "Since you're partially responsible."

He lets out one of his bright-white, charming smirks. "Dreaming about me?"

"You wish," I rumble.

Joy and Hancock bring the group of us through the long, dingy corridors until we reach the cafeteria, where we're met by Velle, aka *John Chevelle*—the head asshole in charge—and the newest guard, Harley Samuels, whom everyone refers to as *Rook*, already posted up inside.

We wander together up to the chow line, grabbing our trays in bored silence. It's the breakfast mood. Showers first is the ideal schedule, because the lukewarm water wakes you up. That said, we're all *hungry*.

Hunger is a permanent symptom here in Alabaster Pen.

Only three of us shuffle to our usual table by the wall, my gaze searching for the missing fourth. Ren is whispering something to Rook by the door, and when he's done, he struts over to join us. I squint at him, but choose to ignore it, taking a seat next to Kang. Ren plops down across from me, frowning. I ignore that too.

He always either sits next to me or across from me, crowding me with his insistence. But I'd prefer to have him across, rather than constantly trying to wedge his body closer and closer to mine.

He's fucking insufferable.

Eyes falling to the dry Egg Beaters and stale bread, I fork a bite and lift it to my mouth. It's bland as fuck, as usual. No salt, no flavor.

I'd kill for one of my mom's fancy omelets right about now.

Chewing and swallowing, I imagine that's what I'm eating. My mind tries to fool itself into thinking this is good; that I can taste the sweetness of caramelized onions, the crunch of the broccolini, the tang of feta cheese... the creaminess of the avocado. *God*, the avocado.

I'm a Cali boy. I miss my 'cados.

"Yo, Ren..." Kang's voice interrupts my drooling memories. "You think you can get another one?"

My eyes close, jaw clenching as I shake my head.

"Uh, no." Ren's eyes spring around the room before he lowers his voice. "I can't believe you got it taken away. What are you? *New*??"

Kang rubs his face, clearly still remorseful, even weeks later. "It wasn't my fault. If this asshole hadn't started shit with Brenner, he never would've found it." He points his thumb in O'Malley's direction.

"That preck had it comin'," O'Malley grumbles.

"Doesn't matter," Ren hisses. "Why the fuck did you bring it down to the rec room, anyway? It wasn't even yours. You fucked us all over." He peeks at me.

I roll my eyes. "You guys are idiots. What did you think was gonna happen?"

Ren's head lolls backward for a moment. "Do you have any idea what I had to do to get that fucking phone??"

"Stuff you would have been doing regardless…" I mumble under my breath.

He shoots me a wounded look, but covers it up and sighs. "I think Jasper bruised my esophagus." He rubs his sternum.

Kang lets out a laugh, and Ren's lips curve. I can't help but scoff a chuckle myself, which widens Ren's smile. He likes making me laugh, even when it's at him and his whorish ways.

"I barely even got to use the damn thing, Byron," Ren murmurs, side-eyeing Kang. "So you owe me. Like I said, it wasn't for you."

Blue eyes slide to me once more, and my gaze at him narrows.

His foot brushes mine under the table. I kick him, and he chuckles.

"I have something else I'm working on getting." Ren grins at me.

"Don't care." I shovel more shitty eggs into my mouth.

"Yeh got any more butts?" O'Malley asks him.

Ren pries his gaze off of me to peer at him, offering a quick nod. "Hancock made a nice deposit last night. He gave me a bag of snacks too. If you're still hungry, Lexington." My eyes creep up to his. "Something special, just for you." His foot taps mine again.

"Fuck off, Ren."

"Smartfood popcorn and Mountain Dew…" he sings, wearing that damn smirk to death.

My favorite.

My stomach grumbles, betraying me. But I scowl at him. "Not interested."

Ren leans in on the table and whispers, "Anything you want, Lex. *Anything* at all, I'll get it for you."

My blood is boiling in an instant. Memories assault my mind, flashes of a slideshow, from years up until this moment. The Luthor I see in them is a very different person from the hardened shell sitting here right now.

The showers running…

Echoing moans.

Biting down hard on the inside of my cheek, I glare directly at the topaz in his irises. "I don't want anything from you, *Warren*. You should know that by now. Every move you make comes with consequences."

He flashes me vulnerability; the same look of longing regret I saw all those years ago.

But it's a lie, just like it was back then. He covers the look with a casual flippancy that doesn't quite reach the pain and rage just beneath his lace-thin surface.

And he shrugs. "Fine. Your loss."

Right.

Always my *fucking loss.*

The cold is easing up.

Alabaster Penitentiary is like an icebox. The concrete holds in the cold, even when it's not necessarily that cold outside. When it *is*, it's brutal.

The winters here are purely awful. In times like the dead of January, even those of us not prone to cozying up to guards for goods consider getting on our knees for a goddamn electric blanket or something. Thankfully, it's never come to that for me.

But that's just because of Ren.

I *hate* accepting gifts from him, because I know exactly what he does to earn all the excessive crap that litters his cell. Something he enjoys doing way too much as it is.

Still, when temperatures drop on this island, you feel it in every breath you take. It aches your bones, dwindling what little energy you already have.

I can swallow just a spoonful of my pride if it means survival.

Anyway, the frigid cold has slowly been melting away. And though I have no idea what the weather is like outside, my calendar tells me spring is upon us.

Our group is in the showers. Kang, O'Malley, and I are lathering up, side by side, and I'm trying not to focus on how much smaller my Dove For Men soap bar is getting when Ren swings around the corner, padding over to us. Completely naked, and no fucks given.

Warren Xavier has no humility to be found. I'm convinced there are a lot of emotions he's lacking, but shame is certainly a big one. Where other people's brains ping those pesky insecurities around, Ren's just thumps all things sexuality, like the nonstop bass of endless techno music.

I swear, the dude's frontal lobe is like a club in Ibiza.

"I just heard something," he says, easing up close to me.

Kang and O'Malley turn to face him while I back up, because he's crowding me again.

"Ooh, *goody*," I mutter sarcastically, rinsing off. "Gossip."

"A new inmate is coming in," Ren goes on, ignoring my admonishing tone. "He's a bank robber from Brooklyn. *Dascha Reznikov.* I guess he's been, like… crazy successful robbing all these banks all over the place for years, rocking machine guns and rubber masks."

Ren's eyes are lit up. He clearly loves the tea, and I can't say I don't get it. Talking shit is a great way to pass the time in here. It's pretty much our television.

"Can't be that good," O'Malley grumbles, running fingers over his head of short black hair. "If he got scooped up."

"He killed the governor's niece," Ren says.

My eyes widen. *Shit… That kid is fucked.*

Governor Russo is a top source of funding for Alabaster Pen, and a close, personal friend of the Warden, Manuel Blanco. If this *Dascha* person really killed his niece, then he can damn-well expect never to see the light of day again.

"He just *killed* her?" I ask Ren, becoming immediately more invested. "Like, for no reason?"

"During a robbery," he replies.

My eyes flit to Kang, who's giving me a familiar look adorned with unspoken words.

He might be lying.

Turning back to Ren, I give him a once-over, eyes narrowing. "Where'd you hear all this?"

"I overheard Kemper talking to Peters," he says casually.

His pupils look normal, and he's not fidgeting at all.

Could be true…

"Kemper? The guard from solitary?" I raise my brow skeptically. "Why would he have been up here?"

Ren shrugs. "Not sure. But he was. He said this Dascha guy was just picked up, and the way they were talking, it seemed like he was on his way."

I peek at Kang again, and he purses his lips, head bobbing in a quick nod.

Alright… Maybe this is legit.

Still, with Ren, you can never be sure. I've known him longer than the rest of them, so I've picked up on a lot of the subtle cues he gives away when he's lying. But he's pathological, so sometimes, it's still nearly impossible to tell.

"Russo's gonna want him here, if that's the case," Kang says.

Ren nods, his eyes flitting to the doorway when Rook walks by.

"To be continued," Ren murmurs, grabbing his clothes and rushing out of the showers.

My stomach churns, but I push past it, finishing up my shower.

Minutes later, Joy is walking us back to our cells. Just as we're approaching the last door, it opens and Rook pushes through, stalking past us. His cheeks are pinker than usual, and he's adjusting his holster. Joy gives him a knowing smirk, shaking her head.

Unease settles beneath my skin, making me a little squirmy. And I *hate* it.

Joy brings us into the row, and despite how much I'm trying to fight it, I peer into Ren's cell. He's scooping himself up off the floor, flushed and rumpled. I recognize the look right away… the same way I recognize his sounds at night.

This *anger*… I don't understand it, and that just pisses me off even more. I fucking loathe this goddamn reaction…

I've been down this road, and it's a goddamn dead end.

Ren's gaze finds mine, from between the bars. And I remember it again…

Sounds of running water…

The grunts and wet slapping.

Stepping around the wall…

And then pain. Like a knife, slicing right in between my ribs.

CHAPTER TWO

Luthor

5 years ago…

"ALRIGHT, I'M BACK."

"Have a good pee?" The gruff voice gives way to a smirk I obviously can't see. But it's audible.

Laughter pings in my ears, and I chuckle. "Why are you interested in my bathroom habits? I gotta say, that's a weird fetish, even for you."

Eyes on the giant screen before me, I grip my controller, thumbs working on the joysticks to move my character across the post-apocalyptic terrain.

"What's that supposed to mean?" my friend Tony, or **DamnDatTony** as his username reads, grunts, and a few more bouts of laughter follow.

"It means focus on your own piss, R. Kelly," I tease into the mic of my headset.

"Snap!" Our friend Reno, aka **LuckyShot**, cackles.

"Jeez, fine," Tony grumbles. "I was just trying to be supportive." I laugh out loud. "But no more! I'll express *no* concern for your health." He launches into some chewing, and I roll my eyes.

"Crazy bastard."

The controller in my grip rumbles, vibrations signaling that a nuke was just dropped.

"Radiation rumble!" Reno chants.

"Yo, Luthor, stop messing with your house and come join us!" Tony says in between crunching.

"I will if you stop eating in my ears."

"What are you having?" Reno asks him.

"You even need to ask?" I tease some more. "Frito fuckin' pie, as usual."

"You know it," Tony replies, that southern accent and the fact that he's mowing down a Texan delicacy giving away his obvious location.

My eyes flick from where I'm finishing up my stockpile, to the new screen name that just popped up as *active*.

"No need to fret, boys. The queen is here!" **KillaClam25** shouts in our ears, and we all cheer.

"There she is!" Tony says between bites.

"Hurry up, Leah! Let's kill this bitch!" Reno exclaims.

Leah laughs. "How's it goin', kids?"

"As good as it can without you around," I tell her, stomping up to her character and giving her some love. My character makes a heart with his hands, and hers gives me one back. "Missed you, Leez. Where have you been??"

Leah doesn't answer right away. *Pretty standard.*

Of our little group of online friends, she's definitely the most… private.

But eventually, she sighs. "Oh, you know. Around."

I frown at the screen, because I have very little idea what she actually means by that. But I don't push it. I just jaunt past her—well, my *character* does—heading in the direction of the giant beasts we're about to battle for goods and level points.

"Come on, Clam." I grin, and she giggles. "Good to have you back."

I'm a gamer. I think that much is clear, but honestly, it's a hard thing to explain to people who don't get it. Video games have always been my *thing*. But when I discovered the vast world of online gameplay, well… suffice it to say, it changed my life.

I came up an introvert; a quiet kid who took to tech right from the start. I was twelve when my parents got me my first laptop, and even before then, PlayStation and Nintendo were where most of my interests lied. *I'm sure now they regret the gift, though…*

My Turtle Beach headphones block all noise outside of the game, so I don't even notice my father's presence in the room until he's standing in front of me, waving at my face. Pushing one off my ear, I glance around his body, which is blocking half the screen.

"What's up?" I ask, though I'm paying more attention to the *legendary* we're all trying to slay.

"Your mother wants to know what you want for dinner," he says in a stern tone, giving way to his underlying dissatisfaction.

I shrug. "Not really hungry."

My dad's eyes fall to the giant bag of Smartfood popcorn next to my chair and the open can of Mountain Dew in my cupholder. "Because you spoil your appetite snacking all day."

"What's the big deal? She said she wasn't cooking..." I huff, fingers going crazy on the buttons, shooting hundreds of rounds of my Gatlin Plasma at the huge monster.

"Regardless, we're eating dinner as a *family*," he goes on, wandering around the room, assessing the setup of my ultimate gamer lounge I've created in our garage.

Thing is, it's not *just* for gaming. My computer is in here, the one I built all by myself; a modification of a machine and software that I undoubtedly made a hundred times better. And maybe not entirely *legal*... But we won't focus on that part.

"Lex, it's a beautiful day," my father says. "Why don't you go outside and get some fresh air? It's too dark in here..."

"It's always beautiful in California," I argue. "I can go outside any time."

"But you don't," he gripes, and I finally peel my eyes off the screen to peer up at him.

"I will tomorrow." My brows lift petulantly. "I have class."

"Great," he mumbles. "From the house to your car to your classroom... that's not exactly what I'd call being *outside*."

I groan. "Why are you hassling me?"

"Because I just don't understand why you have to spend all your time online." He starts with the berating, this god-forsaken conversation I've heard so many times, I have the damn thing memorized at this point. "It's not *real*, Lexington."

"It's real to me," I bark, muting my mic so my friends don't hear us fighting. "This is what *I* like to do, Dad. Seriously, lay off."

"Excuse me?" he seethes, folding his arms over his chest. "You're living under my roof, young man. Please don't speak to me that way."

"So I'm not allowed to have a voice just because I live here??" Frustration rises in my limbs, making me shake. "I just turned eighteen. I'm not doing drugs or partying or getting arrested... I'm a sophomore at Berkeley with a 4.0 GPA! Honestly, what more do you want??"

"I want you to actually *live*, Lexington!" he hisses. "In the real world, with the rest of us!"

"I'm not having this conversation again," I mutter. "Tell Mom to get whatever she wants for dinner, and I'll come eat with you guys. But until then, I'm gonna play this game with my friends, and I'm gonna be online because it's what *I'm* good at. And if you think it's a waste of time, well… that's on you."

My dad scoffs out loud, but I push my headphones back into place so I don't have to listen to him anymore. Eventually, he stalks away, and I let out a breath of shivering anger before un-muting my mic.

My friends don't say anything. They just continue chatting about the game, and I have to appreciate it.

These guys, and girl, have been my closest friends for years now. I know it's a hard thing for people like my parents to understand, but it *is* fully possible to become genuinely close to people you've never actually met IRL. It's the way of our generation, after all.

And that's exactly what's happened with my Fallout crew.

I don't need them to be standing in front of me to feel a connection. *Online relationships are every bit as real as in-person ones, and I don't care what anyone says.*

We go on playing for a while longer, until my mom texts me that dinner is ready. I head inside from my garage lair, and I eat sushi with my parents, remaining quiet for most of the meal. The only things they ever ask me about are school related anyway, and it is what it is.

I like school too, because I'm good at it. I'm smart, like genius-level intelligent, and I'm not saying that to be boastful or brag about myself. It's true. I have an IQ of one-sixty-seven. I graduated prep school at fifteen and started my first year at the University of California Berkeley when I was sixteen years old.

Sharing an alma mater with the Great and Powerful *Woz* was always the goal, but even *I* hadn't expected it to happen so early.

And because I was born and raised only fifteen minutes from the Berkeley campus, I chose to live at home and commute to save money. A decision I tend to regret more often than not because of how annoying my parents can be.

They just don't get it, and I guess that's fine. Maybe they don't need to. I just wish they'd get off my back sometimes. I wish they understood that socializing has never been my forte, and I have plenty of other fortes, so it's really not a big deal that I'm kind of socially awkward and weird.

When I'm online, I can be me. The *real* me; the me I was always meant to be.

To the people outside, I'm just Lexington Deon. But on the web, I'm **BerkeleysLexLuthor**.

Yes, I'm also a comic book nerd. Is anyone surprised?

At least I'm in my parents' garage, not their basement. So… a little less cliché.

After dinner, I migrate right back into my cave, settling into my comfy chair to watch a friend of mine on Twitch. He's playing a new game we're all into, and myself plus a few friends are chatting as he does.

Cyclops180 is my friend Cyrus. I've known him in the online world for a while, and he's a cool kid. A quiet loner from Cali, just like me. We bonded over a mutual love of comic books, and much to the chagrin of many others, we both have a thing for the original DC universe.

The conversation quickly turns from the game to a discussion about superheroes, as it tends to. And because we're all nerds with a lot of opinions, it naturally morphs into a spirited argument.

"You just sound foolish," I grumble at one of our friends, **AshKetchup**, who's trying to tell *me,* of all people, that Lex Luthor isn't the most powerful Superman villain. *Sit down, lad. The grown-ups are talking.* "Doomsday can kiss my nuts."

Cyrus chuckles, and even though I've never actually seen his face outside of the occasional Insta-pic, I can imagine him grinning and shaking his head.

"And Zod?" Ash asks, almost triumphantly.

I roll my eyes at the screen. "Zod is a cog, my friend. Don't trust what the military industrial complex wants you to believe."

"Wait, we're still talking about comic books... right?" Cyrus chirps, and I laugh out loud.

Before I can launch into another tirade, my phone starts ringing. Picking it up, I note the name on the screen and murmur, "I'm stepping off, homies. Stay fresh."

Swiping the screen to accept, I immediately ask, "No FaceTime?"

Leah sighs out a giggle. "Desperate to see my face, are we?"

I recline in my chair, propping my feet up on the desk. "You know you just brighten my day up, woman."

She laughs again, my stomach twisting a little at the sound. "Lex Luthor, the sweet talker."

"To what do I owe the pleasure of this late-night booty call?" I tease, grinning while she chuckles some more.

But it fades off, and she murmurs, "I just wanted to check on you. After... earlier."

My own smile falls as I stare up at the ceiling. "Thanks. I'm fine."

She's quiet for a moment before asking, "You sure?"

"Yea," I breathe. "Just the usual... parents not understanding me, wanting me to be someone I'm not bullshit."

"I feel you," she says quietly.

"Do you?"

Leah goes quiet again. And I desperately want her to open up. Give me something more personal, something *deeper* to work with here.

We've been talking online for years, and I still barely know anything about the girl. She knows everything about me, along with the rest of our little crew. None of us are shy when it comes to spilling our guts. We talk about where we're from, our family lives, school, and work. It's like I said, these are honest to God *friendships*, and Leah is a big part of that.

But she's the mystery man of the group. *The Phantom Stranger.*

We've seen her face. We know she's real... But that's pretty much the extent of it.

"Don't take it to heart, Luth." She ignores my question, keeping the focus of conversation on me, as usual. "I'm sure your parents are proud of you." I scoff at that, and she mumbles, "At least you know they love you. At least you... have them."

My stomach wrenches. I really want to ask what she means by that.

Is she an orphan? Are her parents gone? Is she... alone?

But instead, I nestle up in the softness of my chair and sigh. "Leah... have you ever been in love?"

"Wow. Way to get super heavy on me," she snorts.

I grin. "I'm serious. Have you?"

She pauses, as if she's thinking about how to answer. And now maybe I get why she didn't FaceTime. It's probably harder to disguise the truths she doesn't want to tell with me looking at her.

"I don't know if I believe in love," she speaks softly. I *feel* the emotion in her tone. "What about you?"

An odd sensation of longing sets in my chest, and it confuses me.

I don't do relationships. At least, I never have before, and I don't think I necessarily care that much that I haven't. Granted, I'm a guy in his teens, so the hormones are definitely there, but with technology these days, getting off is much easier for us hopeless nerds.

I've had phone sex before. Sometimes I do the sexting thing on Snapchat. But when it comes to being able to express *real* interest in someone, face to face, I guess I'm as inexperienced as they come.

It might just be the way I am, like the social anxiety thing. Maybe I'm not meant to experience being with someone for real... *Surely, physical relationships aren't for everyone, right?*

But right now, there *is* something there. And it's unfamiliar.

Is it love? Do I feel it for Leah?

Or am I just wishing I could feel it with someone else?

"I'm not sure if I know... how to feel it," I stammer. "*Love*, I mean. It should feel obvious, shouldn't it?"

"Yea, it probably should," she sighs in my ear.

"Maybe I love you, **KillaClam**." My lips twist, and she laughs softly. "I mean it. We should... love each other. Just as friends, or whatever. Because I think love is... important. Even if I don't really understand it."

"Is this your cheesy, cornball way of asking me to go steady, Lex Luthor?" I can hear her grinning, and it flutters my chest with glee.

"Please. I know better than to try to lock you down," I tease, and she giggles. "You're a wild stallion."

"And what are you? A donkey?" She cackles.

"I don't know. Maybe a zebra?"

We both start laughing.

But then I hear something over the line. A voice that sounds male, maybe more than one. And they're shouting something.

"Oh, fuck..." Leah mutters. "Shit shit shit..."

My brow furrows, and I sit up in my chair like a reflex. "Is everything alright?"

"Yea... uh... it's fine," she breathes, sounding suddenly frantic. And a little scared. "I gotta go."

"Are you sure...?" I ask. The noises on the phone are getting louder.

Someone is *yelling*, and they don't sound happy.

"Bye, Luthor," Leah whispers, her voice shaking. "Hold out for the real thing, okay?"

"What?? Leah, wait!" I bark into the phone.

But it's too late. She already hung up.

My stomach is churning with nerves. I want to call her back and check on her, to make sure she's okay. But then I don't want to get her in trouble...

I know literally nothing about her situation.

Who were those men? Why were they shouting?

Where the hell even is she??

Instead, I pull up a text to her number.

Me: Leah, just let me know you're alright. Please.

Of course, I get no response.

Not for the rest of the night. Not for a while.

Not until I finally hear from her again, months later...

When everything gets way too real.

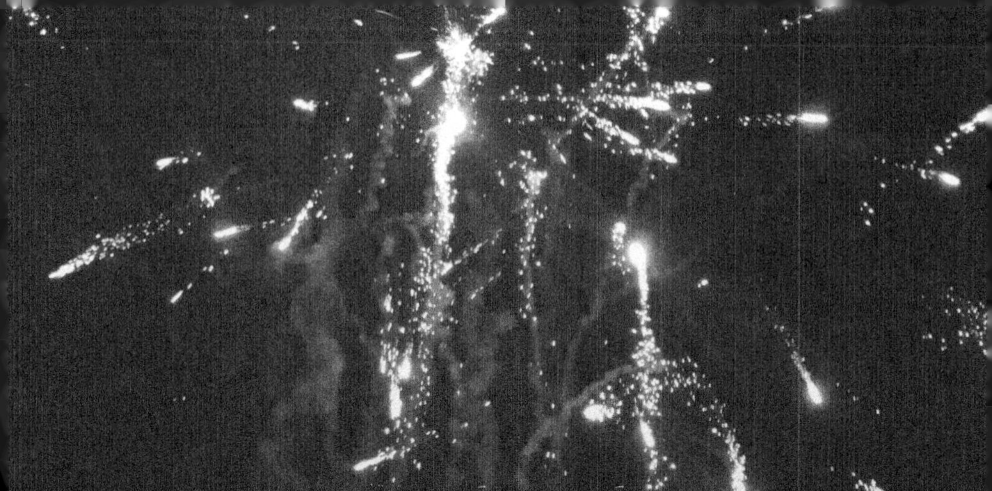

CHAPTER THREE

Ren

Meanwhile…
(Also 5 years ago)

DISGRACED.

It's not a word that means much to me. In the grand scheme of things I've been called, this one actually has a pretty nice ring to it.

I've officially been kicked out of college, after two faculty members walked in on my ethics teacher screwing me in his office.

I know. Ethics. The irony was not lost on anyone.

Professor Kensington—*who, let it be known, was way too hot to be a teacher*—was immediately fired, though I think his wife finding out he likes to fuck guys might have been the more detrimental consequence.

And I was expelled, just like I knew I'd be. All the money and sweet-talking in the world from my parents couldn't undo the emotional damage I'd caused. The tarnished stain I apparently made on the good name of Columbia University.

Dramatic much? I mean, come on. They act like they've never seen a professor raw-dogging the life out of a student on his desk before.

Do I regret ruining Professor Kensington's life like that? *If I say yes, will anyone believe me?*

Sure, he didn't *have* to fuck me… In his office. With the door unlocked. But still, *I came onto him*. And I did it for no other reasons than to sate my infinite, unwavering boredom, to get a rise out of my shithead parents, and play the part of exactly who the hell I am; who they all *expect* me to be at this point.

A willful worshipper of chaos. *An American Psycho, if Patrick Bateman was just* pretending *to give a shit about his lavish lifestyle and stupid fucking business cards.*

At least, I said the words. *I'm sorry* did leave my lips while I was seated in the dean's office, beside my irate, ashamed parents. But they were just that. *Words.* With exactly zero substance to back them up, and my parents could obviously tell. In the Town Car on the way home, my father told me I'd *disgraced* our family.

I felt nothing from that either.

That was six months ago, and while I was successful in getting myself out of school, it kind of just brought me back to square one. Living at home, in the same giant Upper East Side townhouse I grew up in, with my parents who actively despise me, and absolutely no *clue* what I want to do with my life, or even how to spend my time.

For months, I've been drifting, like a well-dressed tumbleweed, and unfortunately, the constant uncertainty, paired with nonstop indifference and loathing from my parents is guiding me back into old habits.

Staring at the orange flame, I watch it drifting closer and closer to my fingertips as the match burns. The heat warms my skin, then stings as it begins to singe me, sheeting my body in chills. It burns out and I drop it onto the floor of my bedroom terrace with the rest of them.

A sweet breeze of early summer rustles through my hair, brushing it in my eyes while I strike yet another match. My eyes stick to the little burst of fire, though this time, I use it to light my cigarette. Taking in a long drag, I hold the smoke, puffing it out into the air and watching it swirl. Floating away… into nothing.

What am I supposed to do now? I think to myself while I smoke and sit and stare. Yes, I hated school, but at least it was *something*. It got me away from this home of unmet expectations and bitterness. Now, there's nowhere else to turn. It's all blending together.

Days spent in the gym, flirting and hooking up more than actually working out, followed by nights spent bouncing from club to club, doing drugs, getting fucked, and passing out just before five, only to wake up and do it all over again.

The lifestyle of a rich, gay sociopath.

At least if I could find a way to earn my own money, I wouldn't be stuck under the thumb of my parents. The insufferable pricks who brought me into this world, only to show me nothing but loathing from the moment I popped out of that waspy cunt.

They wanted a good son, a clone of my father. A quiet, preppy, future conservative entrepreneur, who plays polo and wears slacks, to discuss the market with over brunch. Who would graduate from Columbia and climb the ladder of the wealthy Manhattan elite, marry a boring, pedigreed girl just like my mother, and make more clone babies to continue the bland bloodline in an almost incestuous fashion.

Instead… they got me.

Their only offspring is a gay, mentally marred narcissist, with no earthly desire to partake in any of their esteemed bullshit.

Even if I'd had the potential to be the son they wanted, how would they have known? I was raised by au pairs and miscellaneous staff straight out the womb. No kidding, I actually thought my nanny, Tabitha, was my mom until I was three years old. My parents only ever showed up to pluck me out of the comfort of *the help* when there was an event, or an activity that required them to portray that rich, successful, *perfect* family image. So naturally, when I began acting out, they blamed everyone but themselves.

When I was eleven, I took a razorblade to my wrist in the middle of one of my mother's charity functions. And then the therapy sessions and over-medicating started. Coincidentally, at the same time, I realized I *liked* to inflict pain on myself.

It was also when I discovered that lies roll from my mouth much easier than the truth.

Cigarette pinched between my fingers, I take another drag, then bring it down to my arm. I flip my left forearm over, revealing the tattoo I got last year; the wilted rose covering thin raised lines of jagged skin.

I press the ember into my flesh and breathe out slowly from the pain, the sting of searing heat unearthing a shivered chuckle. Hurt awakens sensations within me. I feel *alive*, if even just for a moment. It's a fleeting ache of pleasure, but I'll take what I can get to feel something. *Anything*.

Pushing past the baser human instinct to drop the cigarette and stop the pain, I keep it there, my toes wiggling as I burn myself until the cigarette goes out.

Nothing ever lasts.

There has to be something else; a more powerful *punch* to feed my emptiness.

Tossing the butt away, I stand up and saunter back into my bedroom to get dressed. I guess I'll go for a run. Maybe shoot a few hoops.

Basketball is the only sport I've ever enjoyed playing, and I'm actually pretty good at it. I used to hook up with a guy I met in the park, and he taught me his moves... *in exchange for me teaching him a thing or two about how to properly push past a gag reflex.*

It was fun for a while, but now I prefer to just shoot alone. *Not a euphemism.*

Dressed in an only mildly ostentatious workout ensemble, I head outside, jogging toward the park. I run around for a bit before stopping by the court. There are some guys playing, and while I'm not really feeling that social, they notice me watching and call me in. One of them is openly checking me out, which is probably the only reason he invited me to join.

The fact that I end up unexpectedly schooling them seems to make homeboy even more interested. So we exchange numbers before I leave, and I'm barely out of the park when my phone vibrates with a text from my new basketball buddy.

He's asking if I want to hang out later, and I'm tempted to say *hell yes*, since he's hot, and I could use some good dick to take my mind off the *vacancy* sign flashing in my chest. But because I'm *me*—an epic tease and a huge pain in the ass—I simply reply with a *maybe*, followed by a winky face.

I'll probably end up handling his balls at some point. The way he was not-so-subtly rubbing his dick on my ass while he was covering me was promising. And the desire to fill the silence in my head with grunts and aggressive slapping is a strong one.

I can't be *alone*. Loneliness leads to quiet, quiet leads to questions, questions that need answers I'm not equipped to give... And lying to myself will only get me so far.

Avoiding going back to the dreadful place I call home, I end up jogging for a while, in the opposite direction. And when I can't run anymore, I walk, letting the hustle and bustle of the city swallow me up. It's odd, to feel completely alone when surrounded by so many people. Probably something only New Yorkers would understand.

Four million people, all in our own little worlds. Fully separate from one another.

The sun is setting, and my depression is taking a turn for the tragic when I find myself in Hell's Kitchen. I spot two guys holding hands and laughing as they wander around the corner onto 51st Street. Trailing behind, I watch them, an uncomfortable tightness squeezing my chest.

They look… *happy*. They're cute together.

I wonder what that's like…

I've never had a boyfriend. I can't tell if it's because I've never wanted one, or because I'm too much of a self-destructive mess to deserve one. *Probably both.*

The whole thing with Professor Kensington just confirmed what I already knew about myself… I pick the wrong guys, and I'm way too much of a headcase to do relationships. None of the men I've slept with have ever even alluded to wanting something more than a diesel fuck sesh, and because I *love* sex, I've always been fine with it.

What would I do with a boyfriend, anyway? How would that even work?

Those guys make it look effortless…

Without even realizing it, I'm following them up the block, gawking at their blatant affection for one another. The smiles on their faces, sweet little touches, and illuminated gazes for only *each other*.

I wonder what it would feel like to have someone look at me like that. To hold someone's hand…

Would it give me butterflies in my stomach? Would I feel anything more than just the lust of arousal?

Am I even capable of such things?

My thoughts are interrupted when the couple I'm stalking passes a man who's walking up to the entrance of a small club. Kind of a hole in the wall, but just from the look and where we are, I'm assuming it's a gay club.

Regardless, that's not the part I'm focusing on. The man is familiar. *Very* familiar.

My eyes widen, stomach immediately cinching into a tight knot.

Oh my God… Is it really him??

As he turns, my heart jumps, and now I'm completely certain it's him, without a shred of doubt. Lingering on the sidewalk, I'm no longer focused on the cute couple.

All I can see is the man who took my virginity when I was fifteen.

But he disappears inside the club, and I'm filled with sudden desperation.

I *need* to see him… *I need to…*

Striding up to the door, I pull it open and slip inside.

It's ridiculous that I'm doing this. I'm not dressed to be out in any sort of social situation, let alone come face to face with *him* in some gay club. But it's barely eight on a Wednesday. *I'm sure the place will be empty.*

Why is he even here?? This makes no sense.

The front entrance leads me into a small hallway, where a bouncer is sitting, checking IDs. I show him mine while he gives me a quick once-over. His eyes fall to something on his desk that looks like a screen. And he just sits in silence while I shift on my feet for a few awkward seconds before he hands my license back and nods.

Okay. I guess that means I'm in…

Following the direction my old pal went, I wander inside the dark club, my face tilting all around to take in my surroundings. It's a bit larger than some of the other clubs in the area, and every bit as deserted as I assumed it'd be. Still, there's music playing, deep bass thumping, and the dulled glow of teal lights creating a strange ambience.

My eyes lock on the familiar body, dressed in his usual tailored business attire, as he makes a beeline toward the back of the club. He goes through another door, but it closes before I can get there, cutting off my view. I reach, but someone steps in front of me.

"You lost?" a guy asks, raising a dark brow at my face.

He looks to be in his late thirties, early forties, attractive, with a tanned complexion and light eyes. He's wearing an expensive suit, oozing attitude, which leads me to believe he must work here.

"No," I grunt, matching his snark with my own. "I'm meeting someone."

He glowers at me, clearly not buying my bullshit. "Really? Who?"

"None of your fucking business," I reply calmly.

"Actually, it *is* my fucking business," he says, tipping his chin. "That area's for members only."

"My boyfriend is a member," I state with confidence. "And he's going to tear you a new one when he finds out you're holding me up with your meaningless power trip."

The man's gaze narrows, lips quirking subtly. "What's your name?"

I pause for a moment, holding his eyes. "Ren."

His gaze slides over me, slowly, then he places his hand on my waist, guiding me away from the door. "Let me buy you a drink, Ren."

"I want to go back there," I mumble, swallowing the yearning clawing me inside as I allow this stranger to walk me in the opposite direction of the mystery door.

"In due time," he sighs, bringing me to the bar.

I take a seat, and he sits down next to me, addressing a bartender I definitely didn't notice when I first walked in. He's gorgeous—*muscles for days*—and dressed in only some tiny black shorts. It's pretty standard attire for employees of the clubs around here, but with one key difference… The black leather cuffs around his wrists. My interest is instantly piqued.

So it's some kind of BDSM club.

I suppose it would make sense… Mr. Kade did like to do bad things behind closed doors.

Before I can even tell the bartender what I want to drink, he returns with two cocktails of a vibrant teal color, garnished with cherries.

I stare at the glass for a moment, and the man slides it closer to me. So I carelessly pick it up and take a sip, while he does the same. The drink is actually delicious, though I still can't decipher what kind of booze it is.

Likely noting the confusion on my face, the stranger says, "It's our signature cocktail. Pretty good, right?"

"What is this place?" I ask, wanting information more than I want to chit-chat about the fucking drinks. "A sex club? A bathhouse?"

The man smirks at me, settling into his seat. "I thought you said your *boyfriend*—"

"Just tell me," I cut him off with a huff.

His smile widens. "Why do you want to know?"

"Because…" I murmur. "I'm interested."

He blinks at me. "How old are you?"

Jesus Christ… answer a fucking question already.

"Twenty-two," I lie effortlessly. *No surprise there.*

His eyes travel over me again. "Did you come from the gym or something?"

I purse my lips. "I was working out, yes."

"And you just decided to pop into a club you've never been to before?" Amusement lines his features.

I can appreciate that it seems strange, because it is. But just being in here, especially knowing *Mr. Kade* is here too, is giving me the jolt of excitement I've been craving. The same thrill I had the day I followed Professor Kensington into his office.

It's like the sting of fire against my skin… The slice of a sharp blade into my flesh.

Strike the match.

Burn burn burn.

Taking a sip from my drink, I swallow and puff out a tired breath. "Okay… I'll be honest. I came here looking for a job."

The man's head slants. "A *job*?"

I nod, solemnly. "My parents kicked me out. I've been crashing on a friend's couch, but I need to find my own place and I'm completely broke. I barely have twenty bucks to my name..."

Chewing the inside of my cheek, I peer up at the stranger, who's watching me intently. I can read his face like a book... The not-so-subtle cues given away by men.

They can be so obvious sometimes.

And whether it was his intention or not, the man I followed in here taught me a lot more than just how good it feels to be held down and fucked into submission...

When people see you as bad, *they stop expecting you to be* good.

"And what makes you think this is a place you'd like to work?" the stranger hums, his eyes falling to my mouth when I swipe my lower lip with my tongue.

"Because I'm desperate," I whisper, then lift my hand, dropping it gently on his thigh. "I'll do anything... Serve drinks, if that's what you need. Or I can do more." My fingers inch up to his crotch. "I'll show you... if you want."

A hitch in his breathing squeezes my stomach with uneasy delight. He stands slowly, gaze darkening as he reaches out, running his fingers over my lips.

"Well, Ren... I think you'll fit in perfectly here," he rumbles, brushing them down my throat. "Welcome to Club Edge. I'm Dom, the manager." He takes my hand in his to stand me up, then he runs it along my hip, down to cup my ass. "Follow me to my office... for your *interview.*"

CHAPTER FOUR

Ren

Today…

CONSIDER THIS…

My life now isn't all that different from back then.

I know what you're thinking. *You're in prison, Warren. How could you* possibly *think it's similar to the life you led as a rich boy living in Manhattan?*

Well, here's how. It's the fucking *same.*

Take away the penthouse in the Upper East Side, and some of the luxurious amenities I definitely miss, and I think you'll find that I'm living pretty much the exact same lifestyle I did four years ago.

I'm still being constantly nagged and berated by annoying people. But now, instead of my parents, bosses, the dean, and teachers at Columbia, it's prison guards and the Warden.

I'm still an *escort…* I'm just selling my body for goods and information rather than money and designer drugs.

And I still feel empty doing it.

But it's *still* what's expected of me, regardless of whether people want to admit it or not.

I'm just a body, albeit a fucking tight one. I still look good, even in prison, because I know how to take care of my shell with what limited options I have, to make it nice for the men who want it.

My exterior is stunning. An almost ethereal creature with gem eyes and perfectly chiseled features. On the inside, I'm decaying and rotten. *But no one sees that part, so it's okay.*

I've always been this empty husk, with the sole purpose of being used up and discarded by whomever needs to do so. And just like it was before my arrest and arrival in Alabaster Penitentiary, it's my source of power.

It's unwise to assume that getting on my knees makes me powerless. If you're giving it, it means you're giving up your control to *me*, and in that moment, while you're fucking my throat, or my ass, or wherever you're trying to stuff it, I *own* you.

Truth be told, I rarely felt as powerful before I came here. Men are always easily manipulated, but these guards and prisoners are truly something special. They're infinitely more susceptible to my skills than the high-powered guys I used to bone in the city. That's not to say those men weren't easy to control. They definitely were. But in *here*, it's a matter of boredom.

Sex is the *only* escape. There's nowhere to go, nothing else to do. We're all trapped, guards and prisoners alike. So my body becomes like a vacation home.

A nice little bungalow in Mykonos, or St. Barth, or Tulum… here to whisk you away from your problems. For a price, of course.

I'm scribbling on a notepad, sketching a new piece Byron asked me to do for him, when the familiar sound of the door opening at my end of the row catches my ears. Anyone else would probably stuff their contraband away, hide it somewhere under their mattress just in case a guard—*usually Velle*—is feeling particularly grouchy. But not me.

I've more than earned everything I have. By doing something, as Lexington so kindly put it yesterday, I *probably would have been doing regardless.*

I scoff at the memory, but my lips curve into a satisfied smirk. He's just so… *upset* with me. Still, even after all these years. I don't know how to feel about it.

Should I take heed of the fact that he still holds it against me, even after so much time has passed? Because I think it means he cares… *right?* Despite what he's always saying, if he's *still* mad at me for being the way I am and dragging him into it, then that must mean he's affected by me… *Otherwise, he'd just get over it.*

Or should I be more concerned? Because if he's always in pain around me, then he could never feel *pleasure* with me.

Clomping footsteps make their way over to my cell, and I peer up to the surly face of Officer Jasper. He pushes the bars open and steps inside, tossing a backpack at me. It lands on my bunk next to my feet, and my eyes light up because the thing looks stuffed to the brim.

"Took you long enough," I grumble, unzipping the bag to peek inside.

"Spoiled fucking brat," he sighs, shifting on his feet. My gaze slides up to him, and my eyebrow quirks. "There's something in there from Rook too. He said you've been waiting for it..."

Fuck yea.

Reaching in, I push clothing, food, and a few magazines aside, my fingers brushing a case.

Well, if this doesn't get Lex to come over, then I'm not sure what will.

"He couldn't bring it himself?" I murmur in a teasing tone that's only fifteen percent serious. "What, he doesn't like me anymore?"

Jasper scoffs. "We're busy. New inmate coming in."

My ears perk at that. "The bank robber kid?"

Jasper says nothing, but the way he's staring at me confirms my question.

Nodding, I think about that conversation I overheard yesterday between Kemper and Peters. It was... interesting.

Officer Kemper is the fuckhot guard who primarily works in solitary, so he's not usually up here just wandering around, conversing with the guards in general population. He's also the *only* one who doesn't fraternize with us inmates, which is crazy since, from what I understand, he's been here almost as long as Velle and Joy. And it's a real bummer too, because the dude is fucking *fine*.

I touched his dick once. Over the pants, but still. I was *so close* to crumbling him, but apparently, he spooks easily, like a horse. He scampered away, and I've barely seen him since.

Naturally, he didn't notice me eavesdropping on his conversation with Peters. Which is good, because I was able to overhear all these details he was spouting off about *Dascha Reznikov*. The way he was rambling made it seem like he's super invested in the Russian bank robber. Almost to an... unhealthy obsession level.

I'm familiar with the notion.

"When's Dascha getting here?" I ask Jasper, wondering if this elusive kid from Brooklyn will be the one to finally crack the hard-nut shell of Officer Kemper.

"Soon," Jasper replies, inching closer to where I'm sitting.

I can tell right away, by his tense movements and the fact that he's still just lingering in here, that he wants an orgasm. Gazing up at him, I lick my lip.

"I want a lighter," I demand softly, reaching out to run my finger up his thigh. "Or some matches. Something to light my fucking cigarettes."

Jasper chuckles wickedly, shaking his head, deep eyes glistening with an instant dominant desire. "Nice try."

I tug my hand away and shrug. "Too bad. I'm feeling extra *thirsty* this morning..."

Jasper growls, gripping the edge of the top bunk as he leans before me. "You think I was born yesterday?"

I roll my eyes in dramatic fashion. "I'm not gonna burn the place down, *Jacob*. I just wanna smoke."

"It's the one thing I can't give you, Ren," he rumbles. Then his fingers glide across my shoulder. "Unless you give me something *really* good in exchange..."

A flicker of excitement warms my gut, like a strike of the matches I'm not allowed to have.

Pushing my stuff out of the way, I slither out of my jumpsuit pants and my Calvin Klein boxer briefs. Rolling onto my stomach, I bend at the knees just enough, putting my ass on display. I reach behind myself, running a taunting finger between my cheeks. I hear him release a breath behind me.

"Raw?" I ask on a shivering whisper. "Or slippery wet?"

I hear the sound of his belt unbuckling, holster jostling out of the way. It's such a familiar noise, I hear it in my sleep sometimes.

"No time," he grunts, dropping to his knees behind me, his weight dipping the flimsy mattress. "Gotta make this quick, baby."

He spits on his hand, rubbing it over my hole while I clench beneath his fingers. His big hands grip my ass, spreading me open to spit some more. And before I know what's happening, he's barreling his way inside me.

It burns like a bitch, obviously, but I won't even say it doesn't still feel good. I always like it. No matter how detached I am, no matter how painful it is... it always does what my body needs it to. This physical response I've had since the first time. *Every* time a man puts his body inside mine, it lights me up. Even when I don't want it to.

Especially when I don't want it to.

I don't know why I'm like this. It's the way I was made.

I can't... help it.

"Fuck me, Lex," I whimper into the bed with my eyes shut tight, Officer Jasper's palm on the back of my skull, aggressively stuffing my face into the blanket while he rides my ass deep and rough. His pelvis is slamming against my cheeks and my eyes roll back in my head. "*God*, I fucking *love* how you fuck me."

Only about four minutes of him tearing me open later, his breathing becomes uneven. "I'm gonna come in your ass..." he growls.

"You're the only one who gets to come inside me," I purr, knees shaking as I push back against him, baring his weight to get him as deep as possible.

"That right?" he asks, fisting my hair hard enough that I yelp.

No. "Yes... Only you. Fill me... *fuuuck*, fill me up."

Jasper's familiar orgasm sounds slither into my ears as he hisses a stream of curses, his big cock pulsing inside me. The feel of the scorching heat he's pumping into my body sets me off.

"Lex... *Lex Lex Lex*, baby, you're making me..." A choked sob leaves my lips, my dick throbbing slickness all over my abs and my blanket.

As soon as Jasper's done, he pulls out of me slowly, playing with my hole while his cum drips out. Then he rolls me over, dragging my body down to kneel over my chest.

I know what he wants without words, and I open my mouth, letting him shove his cock inside. I suck on him, pulling out a few extra little pulses of salty flavor while he grips my hair, flicking his hips. His dick is really nice, just like his face. Jacob Jasper is a sexy, cocky asshole, rough in just about everything he does. And being that I've been letting him inside me for years at this point, I know what to expect from him.

Like the fact that his dick doesn't immediately soften after he gets off. So sometimes he does things like what he's doing right now...

Pushing my legs open, he shoves his cock back into my ass. His hand comes up around my throat, squeezing tight while he fucks into me again and again. Most of the time, he can get off again. Usually, I can too. But I'm not sure if that's what he's driving at right now.

It just seems like he's lost in something... and I don't give a single fuck what it is.

Because I'm thinking about...

"Lex..."

Jasper's thrusting slows, a sated breath fleeing him as he leans over me, capturing my lips with his. It's not really a kiss... more of a bite. He chews on my bottom lip while he liquifies over me, releasing my throat.

His hand drifts between us, the touch sort of cherishing as his fingers graze my nipples, down my abs to play with my cock.

Mmm… This is nice, Lex.

Touch me more, baby.

I'm in a bit of a fog as Jasper finally stops, pulling out for good and getting up without a word. I curl up like a satisfied kitten, reveling in the sensation for as long as I have it. No more than a few seconds.

My eyes creep open, eyeing the man who just fucked me. Who is *not* Lexington Deon, unfortunately. I observe him as he redresses, fixing himself up.

"Fire," I sigh with a smirk.

He shoots me an admonishing glare and grumbles, "I'll give you one match."

Stomping out of my cell, he slams the bars as I hum, "That's all I need."

I'm playing with the iPad I got from Rook when the sound of the door opening catches my attention once more.

I kind of enjoy having a cell near the door. It makes it easier to hear things that are happening on the other side. Of course, it would be nice to be closer to Lex… He's all the way at the other end of our row. But as much as I hate being away from him, I know it's for the best.

I wore him down once. *Clearly, it didn't go over well.*

The real bummer about my current living situation, aside from the obvious fact that it's in a disgusting prison, is that I'm alone. There are positives to it, sure. Like having extra space, and privacy when I'm using the bathroom, or giving myself enemas, which, yes, happens a lot. Not exactly something I'd wanna do in front of people… *Been there, done that.*

Some of my old clients back at The Edge were real perverts.

But the drawback is a lack of companionship. Parker, my cellmate and probably best friend, aside from Lex and Byron, has been gone a while. He was a good dude. Fun to talk to, and believe it or not, one of very few people in this establishment I never fooled around with. Mainly because of his condition, but also, because since the moment I met him, he felt more like a brother to me than a potential sex partner. I've never felt that before…

I'm an only child. When I was a kid, I desperately wanted a sibling, but I knew it'd never happen. My parents barely wanted one, and they were more than disappointed when the one they had turned out to be a worthless mistake.

I suppose it's a good thing I didn't have a sibling...

One less body found in charred rubble.

Parker was a cool, though. He was troubled, like most of us are, but he didn't make it anyone else's problem. He was just kind of... sad. But he had every right to be. Because he was like me; another body, used and discarded. Only his was ultimately saddled with something permanent and devastating.

I miss Parker. A lot. I wish this place hadn't taken him before his time. I wish I'd... been there to help him.

Guilt and sadness claw at my insides as I wander up to the bars of my cell, gripping them in my fists. I watch through them as Rook and Joy stomp into the row, tugging along a new sad soul, shuffling in his shackles.

This must be Dascha Reznikov.

Hello, candy-coated sex god. He's fucking gorgeous.

I mean, really, *truly* stunning. Tall, all lines and angles of sculpted beauty, with fear and anguish decorating his perfectly symmetrical features in a way that makes him a million times sexier. I can imagine him in a thong and glitter, dancing on one of the platforms at The Edge. Or maybe on a stage, draped in leather and mesh, singing emo songs.

His head is recently shaved, as is to be expected, hair color very similar to Lexington's. Light blonde, although his is more of a more platinum shade than Lex's California surfer palette.

The new inmate is being pulled down the row, and I call out a quick comment to Rook, earning me looks from him and Joy. But not the pretty boy bank robber. His gaze is stuck on his shoes, shoulders visibly slumped in despair.

Shackle up, Dascha. This is just the beginning.

They keep moving, and I peer through the bars, watching them bring him all the way down to the end of the row. I gulp, squeezing the rusty steel so hard, my hands begin to hurt.

Is he going to Lex's cell...?

Is he... Lex's new cellmate??

My stomach tightens in distress, a palpable wave of jealousy crashing through me. It reminds me of when Lex got his last cellmate, Henry.

I might need to have the same conversation with Dascha that I had with

Henry Landon... Let him know if he lays a finger on Lexington Deon, he better be prepared to lose it.

I spend the next few minutes pacing, yanking at my hair and mumbling to myself. I don't like this... *I hate it.*

I hate him being so goddamn far away from me. I can't even hear what he and Dascha are talking about down there. I have absolutely no *idea* what's going on in that cell, and it feels like blazing torture.

I know it's hypocritical for me to be so possessive of Lexington, when I spend ninety percent of my existence in this prison getting railed from both ends by everyone who isn't him. I *realize* that, but it doesn't change how I feel. And believe me, if Lex ever allows me anywhere near him again, I will not hesitate to take another stab at making him blissfully miserable.

But he never does, and I get why. And while I don't necessarily consider the hurt I inflict *intentional*, he doesn't see it that way. He just hates me, forever throwing roadblocks between us that feel like an infinite itch in a place I can't scratch.

My mood is spiraling. Plopping down onto the floor, I decide to distract myself with a workout. I do a hundred sit-ups, and I'm shaking, moving onto push-ups, assisted with my feet on my bed. Between the grunting and sweating and muscle strain, my mind is weaving through the past, a scattered slideshow of memories winding me up into a frenzy.

Eventually, I collapse onto the floor, breathing hard. Squeezing my eyes shut tight, I curl up into a ball and cover my head with my arms. A scream leaves my lips.

Burn burn BURN.

Burn it all down.

When my eyes reopen, I think some time has passed, though I'm not certain how much. My lids are heavy, body stiff and achy as I pull myself up off the floor. Sounds from the opposite hallway alert me to someone's presence. I don't care who it is, I need them.

Shaking my bars, the door makes a subtle clanging noise as I shout, "Hey! Get in here!"

The door to the row opens, and Officer Hancock strolls through, casting me an annoyed look. "What's with all the banging, 48?"

"Will you bring Byron over here, please?" I ask him, batting my eyelashes at his pretty face.

He's good-looking too. Believe it or not, most of the guards here are attractive, which is kind of fascinating. Maybe it's just prison goggles, but still… it's nice to be surrounded by hot dudes, especially when the rest of this setting is beyond fugly.

"You're high," Hancock scoffs, turning away from me.

"*Please*, Simon," I beg, using a salacious tone I know he likes, because he stops moving. "I just need to talk to him for a second."

His face tilts in my direction. "What's in it for me?"

I'm sighing inside. *These guys are all so predictable.*

"Whatever you want, gorgeous." I wink at him.

He seems grumpier than usual, but he gives in and stomps up the row, two cells over.

Walking in a circle, I chew on my lower lip, considering how to make this work.

It probably won't. Seriously, it's so far-fetched, it's in Canada. But I have to try.

Hancock returns with my pal Byron Kang in tow, cuffed. "You have five minutes." He opens my cell and shoves Byron inside, closing the door and standing guard outside.

Byron shoots me a puzzled look that has me grinning.

I like him. He's one of my favorite people.

"What do you want?" he rumbles. "O'Malley and I are playing poker, and I'm winning."

I chuckle. But then my amusement slips away, and I gulp.

"I need him, Byron," I whisper. His face falls a bit, but he covers it with a scoff. "Please… I just need your help."

"Ren, why do you keep torturing yourself?? And him. Both of you," he grunts. "You're *torturing* both of you with this incessant bullshit. Just let it go."

"I can't, you know that." I rub my eyes. "He told me not to give up on him. He *told me* he's in love with me…"

"*No*, he didn't," Byron growls. "Cut the shit, Ren. I know he didn't say any of that…"

"He did! He did, I swear," I gasp, crowding him. He backs up into the bars, blinking at my face, dark eyes shadowing something I can't quite place. "Tomorrow… in the showers. We can play…" My voice trails, fingers sliding along the waist of his pants. He swallows visibly. "And he can be there. He'll like it. It'll feel *good*, I promise."

He looks like he wants to protest. But he won't.

Byron's been clinging to his hetero status for as long as I've known him. But he likes it with me. *I know he does.*

"Why do you need this...?" he murmurs, gaze narrowing. "*Why*, Ren?"

My jittering evens out. And the confidence in what I'm about to say straightens my spine. "Because he's mine. Whether he wants to be or not."

My friend is gawking at me like I'm nuts, but before he can argue any further, the door to the row flings open. Rook peeks through, eyes landing on Hancock. Our attention is on them now.

"Hey... you gotta cover me for dinner," Rook huffs.

Hancock's forehead lines. "Why?"

"Kemper quit," Rook breathes, looking and sounding frazzled.

"He *quit??*"

Rook nods. "Bounced. He's just... gone. I gotta run down to solitary and help Brenner."

Rook's eyes dart behind Hancock, to me and Byron. Then he turns and storms off.

Hancock rakes his fingers through his hair. "Jesus fuck, I hate this fucking place..." Flipping his wrist, he checks his watch. "Fuck it. We're going now. Come on, assholes. Bitch-boy therapy session's over. Dinnertime." He yanks the bars open, nodding at Byron. "Against the wall."

Byron does as he says while Hancock cuffs me, bringing us both out into the row. But as soon as he does, the door bursts open, *again*. Joy and Peters clomp past us without word, heading for Byron's cell.

"What the fuck is this now??" Hancock barks. "This place falling apart or something? *Fuck...*"

"Don't worry about it, princess," Joy grunts at him while Peters enters the cell, striding out with Kieran O'Malley, cuffed and shackled.

"Wait... where are you taking him??" Byron shouts as they haul O'Malley away, struggling against their hold.

Hancock backhands Byron across the face. "I've had enough of this bullshit! Shut the fuck up and fall in line, inmate." Byron is raging as he squares up to Hancock. Hancock's hand falls to his taser, and he smirks. "Go ahead, 62. Make my day."

"Alright, alright," I mutter, shoving my friend away with my shoulder. "Let's just calm the hell down."

"Fook yeh!" O'Malley hollers. "Let me go! Yer all rats!"

Our heads whip in the direction of the door as Joy and Peters drag O'Malley off kicking and screaming. *Literally.*

I'm not sure where they're taking him, but I know for a fact it won't be a positive excursion.

Still, my friend Byron looks worried, and I don't want him to be. So I grab him by the shirt with my cuffed hands. "Focus," I tell him quietly. "Head in the game, remember?"

He lets out a long breath, trying to calm himself down as he nods. But not without first shooting a seething glare in Hancock's direction.

"By all means, inmate..." Hancock grunts, shoving us both through the door. "Keep looking at me like that."

CHAPTER FIVE

Luther

A little while later…

MY NEW CELLMATE IS A WEIRD GUY.

Truth be told, when I first heard about Dascha Reznikov, I wasn't sure what to expect. Admittedly, the idea I had in my head was *way* off.

I didn't expect him to be so young. I mean, he's older than me by a couple of years, but still. He's apparently this world-renowned bank robber, and from looking at him, you wouldn't guess it. In fact, he kinda looks like he should be a model, or a rock star or something.

He's got that frightened, deer-in-headlights thing going on right now, which makes sense, what with the circumstances and all. And his guard is way up, also to be expected. It's his first day in prison… and not just *any* prison.

Arrival in Alabaster Penitentiary is like being whacked in the face a bunch of times with a pillowcase filled with bricks, especially if you've never been in jail before. Even for those who *have*, being dumped in this place is a shock to the system.

I remember my first few days here…

Dash is gonna need some time to adjust.

Regardless of his wariness and the lack of trust, he seems kinda cool. And I know it's strange to say that, knowing he's killed someone. But you'd have better luck counting the people on this island who *haven't* killed people than those who have. It'd be a short list... Might even be just one name.

Mine.

Dash is alright so far. He's scared, trying desperately to act like he's *not*, and I feel for him. I wasn't exaggerating when I told him I'm probably the best cellmate he could ask for. It's true. Because, unlike many others, I won't try to fuck him, or fight him. I won't expect anything from him other than mutual respect, and if I can watch out for him and help him learn the ropes of this shithole, having the experience and seniority I guess I have here, then I'll do just that.

At the same time, I should try not to get... *attached*. I've been through too many cellmates already. I hate forming a bond with someone, only to have it ripped away.

It's happened way more than I care to think about right now.

We just got back from dinner, and Dash is fidgety. I can't tell if it's just the way he is, or if he's still coming down from the crazy drugs they pumped into him to get him here. Really, he could be the most self-aware dude in the world, but it'll take more than a few hours to get acclimated to Alabaster Pen.

Up on my bunk, I nestle into the stiff mattress, pulling a worn copy of *1984* out from under my pillow. I love this book, and it's one of only a few we've managed to scrounge up over the years, so I force myself to read slowly. My last reread was over a year ago, meaning I'll get some enjoyment out of it now.

Opening the book to my dog-eared page, my mind drifts to what Ren was offering earlier, in the cafeteria. He implied that he got something pretty good from Rook... *I wonder what it was.*

No... I don't care. He's just trying to manipulate me again. Using me as an excuse for more bullshit lies he spouts, easier than breathing.

I'm doing this for you, *Lex.*

If I let him fuck me, I can get you whatever you want.

Huffing out loud, I shake my head. *What a crock of shit.*

A raspy voice grumbles from beneath where I'm lying, reminding me that I'm not alone anymore.

Right. I have a cellmate again.

"You okay down there?" I ask Dash, feeling the bunk bed shift with his obvious tossing and turning.

He doesn't respond, but rumbles some words, kicking off his sneakers. They clunk to the floor, and more movement follows. Setting down my book, I lean over the edge of the bunk to peer at him upside down. He's doing crunches in bed.

My brow lifts. "You like working out?"

His breathing puffs raggedly as he counts to himself, stopping to mutter, "Huh?"

"Is that something you… enjoy doing?" I ask, just making conversation. Getting to know him and such. "Or are you doing it because there's nothing else to do?"

He does a few more crunches, then pauses once more, hazel eyes drifting up to my face. "I, um… I like doing it. I mean… I think I do?"

My lips curve into an amused grin. "You don't know if you like it or not?"

He blinks at me, wide-eyed and reticent, biting down on his lower lip. His fingers rush over his scalp and he frowns. "It helps me burn energy. I don't like to sit still. I hate being *confined*… I just gotta move."

I roll my eyes, swooping back up to my bed. "Great. Another hyperactive asshole I'm stuck dealing with. Just remember, man… after lights out, I'mma need you to keep it down. And don't be rocking this thing around all night. I like my sleep."

He's quiet for a second before he murmurs, "Sorry."

"It's okay," I sigh. "I get it. It's not easy being trapped like a rat in a cage."

"Despite all my rage…" he mumbles.

My smile returns. "Smashing Pumpkins. I like it." Shifting, I grab the bars, peeking back down at him. "You're alright, Dash."

His lips quirk into a small, satisfied grin. I have to say, it's quite the difference from that scowl he seems to love rocking. I'm guessing the resting bitch face is like a mask, to keep people from seeing the real emotions underneath.

But hey… what do I know? I used to smile much more, too.

Dash flops onto his back, still rubbing his head, likely in search of some newly missing hair. "Aren't you too young to like the Smashing Pumpkins?"

I chuckle, and his eyes spring to mine, smile becoming a little less strained. "My dad listens to them. Rock music is his favorite. Grunge, alternative, the classics… You name it. He used to play it while working on his old muscle car in the garage." I pause at the memory. "And then the driveway, after I took over the garage."

Dash's face flings. "You work on cars??"

"No way." I laugh, shaking my head. "No, I needed more space to build this badass computer I made."

His eyes narrow. "I've never heard anyone describe a computer as *badass*."

Grinning, I murmur, "Well, you obviously never saw mine."

"What did your dad have?"

"A sixty-seven Shelby GT…"

"Mustang," Dash finishes. "Sweet. *Eleanor…*"

I chuckle. "From *Gone in Sixty Seconds*. Yea. My dad used to say that too." My brow cocks. "So you're into cars?"

"I'm not much for repairs, but I like to paint 'em," he says, and I can see how he lights up talking about it.

It must be his passion. *Like tech is for me.*

"That's cool. Did you go to school for it, or…?"

"Nah. Self-taught," he explains. "It started as a hobby, and when I got a job doing it at a shop, it was supposed to be a cover. You know, for the robberies. But I got pretty good at it. When I'd get into my zone, all the noise would fall away, and I'd just concentrate on the project…" His voice trails, and I watch him staring off into space.

He's an oddball, for sure. But I like it.

I've always found the misfits of the world much more interesting.

Dash shakes himself out of whatever nostalgia he was lost in, then peers up at me, his voice suddenly softer, more vulnerable. "How do you… do this?" I blink at him. "I mean, like… how do you *live* here? How have you done it for so long without going completely nuts?"

My gut grows heavy while I stare at him for a few moments in silence.

"I just… do," I tell him quietly. "It's survival, Dash. I guess living here is like living with a chronic illness. You just do whatever you can to overcome it. Find some way, *any* way, to live with it. To *live*… in spite of it."

Something strange passes over his features. It's like part terror, part blinding realization. As if profound awareness just smacked him in the face, and he's horrified… but also relieved.

Dash clears his throat, his lips parting like he might say something else. But before he does, the lights in the row switch off, leaving only the dull glow streaming in from the door at the other end.

Inmate noise begins to taper off, and I cast the shadow of my new cellmate one last comforting glance before reclining back onto my bed.

I hear Dash let out a breath. Then I feel him slither out of bed.

"Goodnight, Luthor," he whispers. "I'll try to keep it quiet."

A small smile crosses my lips as my eyes close. I think he's working out some more, and I drift off to the sounds of him breathing and counting. Something about it is comforting.

Maybe it's just having a cellmate again. The solace of human interaction... Even an introvert like me needs it. Loneliness is a curse, after all. Especially in here.

Or maybe it's more than that. Maybe I'm pacified by Dash's presence because I think he could be a friend.

Would you look at that. Friends... in real life. And all it took was coming to prison.

My parents would be so proud.

I wake up in a decent mood.

I slept well, though I would've liked a few more minutes, but Joy is already banging on the bars to get us up for first shower. Fortunately, I'm able to sweet-talk her into giving us some more time, during which I let Dash use my toothbrush.

He doesn't have one yet, and he's being extremely whiny about it. I won't say I don't understand. I also love brushing my teeth, so I can sort of sympathize with his obsession. It's pretty much all he's been talking about.

We get to the showers as Velle is herding in a bunch more inmates. And before I can even look around, I feel fingers grazing my side. I flinch and turn, meeting light blue eyes.

"Missed you," Ren whispers by my ear, sauntering toward our usual section of showers while lifting his shirt over his head.

My teeth grind together, and I blink hard, following after him.

Kang falls into step beside me, nudging my arm. "Morning, Luth."

"Hey," I sigh, whipping my shirt off.

Turning over my shoulder, I look for Dash. But I don't see him. He must be attempting to get some privacy by using one of the empty showers. *Rookie mistake.*

See, you'd *think* going for privacy would be the best option. Less eyes on your junk, less proximity to other naked dudes. It's certainly the default choice for newbies trying to prove how *not gay* they are. But ultimately, it leaves you alone and unprotected, which isn't how you want to be standing around with your ass on display in this place.

Stepping up to the shabby concrete wall, I place my folded clothes on top and slam my fist onto the rusty button. Water flows from the shower head, and I let it hit me right away. The freezing cold water gives me a jolt that wakes me right the fuck up. Most other guys will stand out of the spray and wait for the water to warm up a little.

Not me. I like the sting of it first thing in the morning. It's like a cup of strong coffee.

Peering right, I watch Ren dunking his head under the stream of water. It tumbles over him, drenching his hair and turning the typically very dark brown into black. He runs his fingers through it, lathering up some shampoo and washing thoroughly.

Not that I want to pay him any compliments, because he doesn't deserve them, but he has *really* nice hair. I'm glad Joy doesn't make him shave it that often. He definitely looks better with hair.

And even that rugged stubble he sometimes gets on his jaw in between shaves...

Closing my eyes, I redirect my thoughts to my own showering, which is where they should be. But showering doesn't require any real *thought*, so they just keep wandering... back to the body over there, and the one in between us.

Kang is directly to my right, as he tends to be. Because I try to keep as much distance between Ren and me as I can in here. It almost feels like Kang showed up in Alabaster Pen just in time to become a buffer between me and Ren. Sometimes, I wonder if he keeps us *together*, or holds us *apart*...

Glancing at the two of them, I shake my head. *Apart. It's definitely best to keep us apart.*

As I'm rinsing off, I can sense Ren moving closer, and my pulse speeds up like a physiological reflex. My gaze follows him as he slinks out of his own water spray, pushing himself beneath Kang's. I swallow a lump in my throat.

Kang gives Ren a look, shaking his head subtly. Then Ren's eyes move to mine. His head tilts, tongue sliding over water droplets on his lips. He doesn't say any words, but I can *hear* him. I fucking hate it, but I can.

I miss you.

I miss you so bad every second I'm around you...

"Cut the shit, Ren," I growl, just loud enough that they can both hear me.

"It'll be fine," he says with a hand on Kang's chest. He shoves Kang up against the wall with a soft grunt, eyes on mine the whole time. "It'll be *fun*."

Without another word, Ren falls to his knees, his dark head of wet hair right in front of Kang's crotch.

"Why are you letting him do this?" I snarl quietly at Kang, though my wide eyes won't stop watching Ren's tongue flutter over the tip of Kang's rapidly hardening cock.

"He... he asked me to," Kang stutters, eyes drooping shut, head tipping back against the wall as Ren's plush lips suck him in. "*Fuck...*"

I gulp down a mouthful of saliva, my stomach twisting into a tight knot. "So, someone asks and you just... do?"

Slanting my head, I can't stop staring as Ren bobs in front of Kang's waist, sucking and *sucking*. It's not even close to the first time I watched him do this, but it still looks every bit as fascinating to me. And I don't know why... It's not like I *care*.

I honestly don't think I'm gay. Despite everything I've been through here, despite the tension between me and Ren and the things I remember that put it there, I still don't think I'm interested in men sexually. I just don't... know.

But I recall what I said to Dash earlier. *Lines get blurry in here...*

Fuck that. Blurry *is an understatement. They downright vanish at times.*

Ren slurps off of Kang's dick, fisting it as he locks our eyes from the floor. "Why does it matter, Lexington? You don't care who I fuck... *Remember*?"

My jaw strains in irritation and confusion and fucking hatred for this asshole who's supposed to be my *friend*, with all his bullshit head games. "You're right. I don't."

I turn away from them, ready to storm off and never look back, *again*. But Ren's voice stops me.

"Mmm... *Lex*. You taste *so good*."

Fuck this.

Fuck you, you evil, beautiful, slutty little liar.

Spinning back around, I inch up to them, crossing my arms over my chest. Ren's rampant sucking slows, dark lashes fluttering up at my face.

Kang grumbles, "Ren, maybe you should—"

"What's the matter?" I cut him off with a hiss, my words and furious glare aimed only at Ren. "Not as much *fun* with me here watching?"

Ren pulls his pouty mouth slowly up the length of Kang's cock, and I do everything in my power not to react to the sight. He replaces it with his hand, fisting and jerking as he hums, "I always see you, baby. Only you."

Sucking in a breath, my limbs are vibrating with the most blinding rage I've ever felt, an anger I never would've known I was capable of feeling if I'd never met Warren Xavier.

"Lies, lies… Bullshit and lies," I whisper. "Have you *ever* spoken a word of truth to me, Warren?"

"Here's some truth for you, gorgeous." His left hand reaches out, crawling up my naked thigh. I shiver, disguising it as best I can. "I wanna suck you so bad, I'll probably come the moment you touch my lips."

"I'm not doing this again, goddammit," I snarl between clenched teeth. I can't even tell if I'm talking to him or myself at this point.

I'm fucking *furious* for even still being here. For standing here, my body huddled in next to Kang's, the heat of his slippery wet muscles melting into me.

My cock jerks and fills before Ren's face as he leans in closer and closer, like it *remembers…*

Fuck, why does it have to feel like this??

Why does it still feel like this? I don't get it. I fucking hate him.

The problem is that my body has never caught up to my brain where Ren is concerned. That's always the issue. He fucking corners me, and turns me into a stuttering, bumbling idiot.

If I was really straight, I'd have no trouble leaving…

"You can hate me all you want, but you know it's true," Ren purrs, warmth dancing over the inches pumping my erection full. "I fucking *miss you*, baby…"

"Shut… up…" My words tumble out on shuddering breaths as his lips run gently along my firm flesh. "God… *fuck*… not again…"

"Mmm…" Ren hums, tongue sneaking out to graze my shaft.

I press my lips together to disguise the groan, eyes falling shut as my head lolls onto Kang's shoulder.

"Baby… *Lex*," Ren rasps, his voice crumbling, though his actions remain confidently driven. "Fall apart for me, love…"

"S-stop," I whimper, eyes creeping open.

He's stroking Kang's dick in his fist while kissing my erection over and over, so soft and so goddamn *warm…*

I want to slip inside. I want to… *push* inside, hard. Shove deep into him, to remember how fucking euphoric he makes it feel.

But I can't. I won't.

I'm not… doing this… again.

"*Uhhfuckyess*," Ren whines, with his mouth gliding up my dick, tongue fluttering under the head. His eyes roll back, chest pumping heavy breaths.

I swallow and glance between his legs. I think… maybe he *is* coming a little.

Fuck me…

Fuck fucking me.

He's not even touching himself, but his dick is bobbing, twitching and throbbing while he slopes his lips around my crown to suck out a pulse that feels like heaven *and* hell, sheeting me in wicked tingles.

"N-no…" I pull myself away from him. His eyes spring open, glistening vibrant blue staring up at me. I shake my head. "No. You don't get anymore."

He whimper-moans, grabbing my cock fast. A startled sound escapes me as he tugs on my dick, returning to sucking Kang's almost viciously between his lips. Kang is breathing harshly, chest fluttering, his fingers slipping up into Ren's wet hair.

The sensation of what's happening feels too good… And it's too much. I slap Ren's hand away from my dick, and he glares at me with his mouth full of cock.

His lips pull off, a line of saliva coming with them. "And *I'm* the liar. This is what you *want*, Lexington."

"No, it's fucking not," I hiss. "I told you I was done with you. It's been *years*, don't you get it by now??"

He stands up slowly, and I gulp, our fiery, mutually stubborn gazes melded. He eases closer and my back hits the wall, our chests bumping, dicks touching. It feels insane, but I'm not letting it. I *refuse* to feel good with him.

He doesn't deserve it.

Ren's eyes fall to my mouth. My heart is thumping so hard I'm shaking.

"Fuck me, baby," he whispers over my lips.

I'm frozen. Just shivering between his scorching hot body and the freezing cold concrete.

His eyes flit to Kang. Mine move to him too.

Kang is visibly tense; angry, pent-up, and unsure. His jaw strains, and he blinks heavily for a split second before grabbing Ren by the hips. Whipping Ren off of me, Kang shoves him up against the wall. Ren's chest connects with the concrete right beside me, and he whines, resting his head on it with our eyes locked. Kang moves behind him, pumping soap into his hand, stroking it onto his erection.

My gaze stays with Ren's, and his with mine. I can't even blink for fear of missing it...

The way his lips part and tremble, the way his dark lashes flutter... The way he forces his eyes open even though I know they want to shut as he's filled from behind.

"Mmmfff," escapes him when Kang's pelvis crashes against his cheeks. His eyes roll back, and he gasps, "Ohhh*fuuck*."

Kang is growling, working his cock in Ren's ass with fierce thrusts that are smashing Ren into the wall *right* in front of me. We're standing so close, my dick is almost touching him. So I back up, just an inch.

"Fuck me," he whispers. To *me*. "*Harder*, Lex."

Gnawing on my lower lip, I shake my head subtly.

"Lex..." He says my name again, and my chest tightens. "Please..."

No. No, it's not me.

I want to scream it in his fucking face. *I'm not fucking you! It's* not me, *goddammit!*

Ren's hand reaches out, fingers almost brushing my hip. Like he wants to pull me closer. Like he wants me to be *with* him while he's getting railed in the ass by another dude. It's fucking ridiculous, and moronic, and so goddamn manipulative. But I just can't stop my stupid hand from extending to his.

Our fingers touch and we both hum. His eyes close. Like he's *happy*.

I'm here... I'm with you. I'm—

No. I snap myself out of it, shaking my head and yanking my hand away.

"I'm not yours to ruin anymore," I whisper.

Ren's look of sadness, longing, and regret is being swallowed up by the arousal he can't help feeling while bent over and panting like an animal in heat. Unfortunately, it's a look I know all too well. Glaring at him, I turn and snatch up my clothes. All I can hear are grunts and wet slapping echoing around me as I storm away, dressing quickly, not even caring that I haven't dried off yet.

Fuck this. Get me away from him.

I leave the showers in a huff of rage, years' worth of frustration and need so thick it's like a fog I can't see through. I swing around the doorway fast, paying no attention, crashing right into Joy.

"Whoa. Easy there, loverboy." She grabs me by the shoulders. "Where the hell you think you're going?"

"I'm sorry, I just…" I'm out of breath for literally no reason. "I needed to get out of there."

Joy squints at me, then peers around my body at the obvious sounds of Ren being turned out ringing through the showers. Her gaze comes back to mine, softening a bit.

"Can you just bring me back?" I plead softly, not even trying to hide the desperation in my tone. "*Please*, Jamesy? I can't… be here anymore."

"I can't leave," she tells me firmly.

"Where's Velle?"

I can hear his voice rumbling from inside the showers. But then I hear Dash.

Shit, where's Dash??

Joy and I look back into the room, but all I can see is Ren having his ass split open by my *friend*.

Fuck this fucking place right now.

"Hang on, you sad sack," Joy huffs at me. "Let me just make sure Velle's got this and I'll bring you back. Jesus, what is it with you two—"

"*Argh!* You little fuck!" Velle roars from around the corner.

We both turn as Dash skids from inside the showers, jumping into his pants.

"What the hell?" I gasp.

"What just happened??" Joy barely has the words out before Velle comes charging after Dash, grabbing him literally by the throat.

"Bad move, 101," Velle snarls, then hurls his fist at Dash's face so hard, *I* feel it. "*Very* bad fucking move!"

"Can someone explain to me what the hell is going on here?!" Joy barks as Velle aggressively cuffs Dash's hands, huffing and puffing like he just ran a mile.

"This little shit is going to the hole," Velle hisses. "*Now.*"

Dash looks dazed, his eye already a little swollen as he peeks at me nervously. I just shake my head.

You fool. You've been here one day!

"Alright," Joy mutters. "You gonna take him?"

"No," Velle grunts, shifting on his feet and wincing. "My nuts hurt. Call Peters."

Joy smirks, cocking her head as she pulls her walkie off her waist, eyeing Dash like she's a little impressed.

Dash spits blood onto the floor, seething in Velle's direction.

"Petey Pablo... get up to the showers ASAP," Joy says into the walkie.

Velle snatches it, pressing the button with his fingers over hers. "Bring a stretcher. Can't guarantee this bitch will be able to walk in a minute."

I'm worried about Dash... I know he wouldn't have just attacked Velle for no reason, and it's safe to assume Velle was probably pulling that *preying on the new meat* bullshit, as he does. But all I can hear are the lingering soft groans coming from inside the showers, and my brain is aching too much to focus on anything else.

Joy peeks at me, then turns and shouts into the room, "Get dressed, assholes! Everyone out of there right now!"

"Joy," I whine, silently begging her to take me first so I don't have to walk back with Kang and Ren in a bubble of awkward tension.

She glances at Velle. "You good?"

"Oh, yea," Velle sneers at Dash, tilting his head. "Fuckin peachy."

"Alright, 35," Joy sighs, grabbing me by the arm. "Let's go."

I cast one last look at Dash, who clearly doesn't want to be left alone with Velle. Velle cracks his knuckles.

"Wait..." I hesitate. But Joy just keeps pulling me along, around the corner, as Officer Peters storms past us.

Well, Dash is fucked.

And he's not the only one.

CHAPTER SIX

Ren

Days later…

THE MOOD IN THIS ROOM IS GLOOMY AS SHIT, AND IT'S BUMMING ME OUT.

I don't necessarily care that Kieran's been gone for over a week, and none of us know whether he's dead or alive. It doesn't bother me that Dash is rotting in solitary because of his own pride and newbie stubbornness.

The only reason I'm even noticing the tension is because Lex is upset.

I've always been able to sense his moods. I can feel his sadness, and yes, most of the time it's directly related to something I did. But that doesn't mean I'm impervious to it.

In fact, he's the only person I've ever felt direct empathy for, and for the life of me, I still don't truly understand it. From the moment we met, it was like my soul reached out and grabbed onto him, clutching with desperate, greedy fingers, trying frantically to smoosh him in and make him a part of me.

I used to think the reason I was so drawn to Lexington Deon was because of how uninterested he was in fucking me. At first, it was refreshing. He was the only man who looked at me and saw something more than an object to devour for his own amusement. Instead, he saw me for what I am…

A damaged, destructive mess of emotional issues, not worth the time or effort.

And you know how it goes with us spoiled, brats... Pay us no attention and we'll go feral trying to get it.

He's just so aloof, and the real kicker is that he's not even trying to be. He isn't playing some game, like a cocky asshole who knows he'll eventually get what he wants, in the form of me begging on hands and knees. Lexington *sincerely* has never made an active attempt to fuck me.

I know he wants it. Probably more now than he did back then, though he'd never admit it. But he's just not that type of guy. *You know, the sex-crazed kind.*

He's a four-leaf clover. A one-in-a-million, *let's wait until we're married* type of delicious virgin. Sweet, decadent innocence you just wanna lick. And he'll never let me close enough to try again.

Not after he ran away from yet another of my shameless attempts to lure him in.

Glancing to my right, I watch the friend who fucked me raw in Lex's place as he picks apart a sandwich, visibly lost in his thoughts. Byron is a quiet one. It's just the way he is. I've known him for years, and I still barely ever know what's going on in his head.

Right now, I'm sure he's worried about Kieran. It was hard on all of us when Parker got sick and disappeared, and he's probably concerned that the same thing could be happening to Kieran. *Except that Kieran would totally deserve it.*

The Warden's had his eye on Kieran O'Malley for a while, because he's an obvious sociopath with a lot of issues. He's been here a year, still going buck wild on a regular basis, which is the perfect way to get your ass sent to the place where prisoners become test subjects, and the already fleeting notion of *humanity* in this shithole goes completely out the windows we don't have...

The East Wing.

A memory flickers in my mind... *of being strapped to an exam chair and cooked like a Toaster Strudel.*

It gives me chills, and I rub the goosebumps off my arms.

Choosing to end the moping, I turn to Byron. "Have you thought any more about the piece on your shoulder?"

His eyes slide to mine, and he raises a dark brow, but says nothing.

"I got a bunch of new ink and stuff," I keep going. "If you wanted me to work on it some more, I could..."

"I'm good," he grunts, going back to his sandwich.

Shifting, I steeple my fingers on the table.

Okay… I guess he's mad at me too. Great.

My chin lifts. "What about you?" I reach across the table, grazing a finger along Lex's wrist. "Is it finally ink time?"

He jerks his arm away. "Fuck off, Ren. We're not in the mood."

"So we're just gonna sit in silence, then?" I slump in my seat. "This place is boring enough as it is without everyone going all emo on me."

Lex glares. "I know this is hard for you to comprehend, since you don't care about anything, but I'm worried about Dash."

My jaw tightens. "Alright… him worrying about Kieran I get." I nod in Kang's direction. "They're close, and Kieran's been here a while. But you barely know Dash."

"He's my *friend*," Lex hisses. "You know what that is, right?? A person you care about without needing anything in return…"

A dull stab happens in my chest, but I ignore it. "You *just* fucking met the kid. And he's already proving himself to be as moronic as your last cellmate. Grow up."

Lex grips the edge of the table, shooting me with the sparkling light green in his irises. It's my favorite color, even when it's laced with hatred. "He's new, and he's scared. We all remember what that's like. What the fuck is your problem with him, anyway? Worried you might not get the opportunity to screw him over like you do the rest of us?"

Frustration is sizzling in my veins. I shove my tray out of the way and bang my hands down on the table. "Would you be this upset if it was *me* down in the hole??"

Lex tilts his head, holding my gaze. He's so good at this… fighting my fire with ice. "So you're jealous?"

"Stop," I growl under my breath.

He folds his arms over his chest. "That's rich coming from you."

My brow lines, mouth hanging open with sudden speechlessness. I know any and all possessiveness I have when it comes to him is irrational. But rationality has never been my strong suit, and where Lexington is concerned, it's downright impossible.

I'm all mussed-up emotion for the kid with the sea-green eyes.

"Lex, I just want you to—"

"I don't *care* what you want, Ren!" he barks. "Jesus, you're like a tornado! Destroying everything in your path without an ounce of regard for who you mow down. It's exhausting!"

"Hey!" Velle snaps, stomping over to us. "Cut the shit over here, inmates, or you can continue this piss party in the hole."

He pins us with one of his *I mean it, don't fuck with me* glares, before turning and stalking off.

I watch him until he's far enough away, then lean in on the table, whispering, "You can keep blaming me for anything and everything, but you know damn well you're at fault too. Stop acting so innocent."

"You're full of shit," Lex grumbles. "I never asked you for anything."

"You didn't have to."

"For the love of God, stop with the bickering!" Byron whisper-shouts at us. "You're both driving me nuts." He picks up his tray and stands. "Do whatever the fuck you want to each other, but leave me out of it from now on."

He's about to leave, but I stop him. "Don't bother. *I'll* go." Snatching up my tray, I shoot one last look at Lex. "Sit here and be butthurt about the new guy. He deserves your fucking attention, right?"

I storm off in a huff, my heart crawling up into my throat as Lex's words echo in my head. I'm fucking pissed, and I know it's stupid. To be jealous of his concern for Dash…

But it's the fact of the matter. They've only spent like *a day* together, and already Lex is attached to him, missing him when he's gone like Siamese twins split down the middle. It's obnoxious.

I never got that. I had to work for every single drop of attention he's ever given me. I've had to dig and dig at his layers to unearth even the *tiniest* of affections, but Dash just gets it, right away, just by being him.

Fuck 'em both. They can be two aloof dickheads together forever, sailing off into the oblivious sunset.

Plopping down in an empty seat at a different table, I squeeze my eyes shut tight and try to breathe. This is all so annoying. I hate this. I hate that I'm still groveling *years* later, when in truth, it's not my fault. What happened between Lex and me was inevitable, and I told him that.

At least, I think I did. I can't really remember now… It was all such a haze.

"Hey, sweetheart," a voice rumbles at my right, and my eyes peel open. "What's got you down?"

My face slants, and I lock eyes with Percy Gage, this big asshole I don't really like, though I've found myself underneath on more than one occasion, when I'm bored, or restless, or… frustrated by certain other inmates.

"I'm just… upset," I hum, blinking at his face while his eyes linger on my mouth. "I think it's the anniversary of my little brother's death. He was killed in a car accident when he was only two."

"Sad story," Percy murmurs, either not believing my words or not giving a shit. Probably a little of both. "Why don't you find a way to get me into your cell tonight..." He scoots closer, sliding a large hand onto my lower back. "I've got something to help you forget."

Oh, do you? I sigh sarcastically in my mind.

My gaze drifts back over to my usual table. Lex is tearing bread off his sandwich, stuffing it into his mouth. We make eye contact for a split second before he looks away.

Twisting my fingers in my lap, I pick at some skin around my fingernail. "Sounds fun," I mumble to Percy with his fingertips gliding into my pants, teasing down to the crack of my ass.

"Good boy." He pulls his hand away, but not without first grabbing a fistful of my hair and yanking it until I wince.

It's all part of the burn.

Just another fresh plunge into my skin.

Thank God for Joy.

I can barely walk this morning after Gage practically split me open last night, so she brought me an ice pack to hold between my legs. And she did it without expecting a damn thing in return.

Not that I would be able to give her anything, anyway. I have nothing to trade, and as cool a chick as she is, I find the idea of lady parts rather off-putting. Granted, I don't usually put my dick in men either. I'm a power bottom, through and through. But even if by some twist of fate I were to find myself fucking a woman, I just *know* I'd spend the entire time reaching for a dick that isn't there.

I officially came out when I was a teenager, but I've always known I was gay. My first crush was on Superman when I was nine. *The cartoon, not Henry Cavill. Though, let's be real... I'd let Henry into literally anywhere in my body he could think to put it.* Girls have kissed me before, in junior high and high school, at parties and whatnot. I guess back then I didn't *seem gay*—whatever that means.

Regardless, it did nothing for me. *I need the aggression and inherent thoughtlessness that only men can provide.*

All that said, I'm kind of lamenting my sexual preference right now...

I just don't see a scenario in which a woman could debilitate me the way Percy fucking Gage did last night.

The soreness in my lower half matches the ache in my chest. And all the obsessing over my fight with Lex has topped off this miserable morning with a throbbing migraine attacking my temples. So I opt to skip breakfast, staying in my cell and drowning my sorrows in chocolate chip mini muffins while watching movies on the iPad.

I'll keep trying to convince myself the body pains have me holed up in here, not the fact that I'm avoiding Lex and Byron. I don't want to admit it, but the thought of facing them is bumming me out way more than my swollen undercarriage.

The stuff with Lex is complicated, and it never won't be, but I'm used to Byron being on my side. We have a good relationship. Or at least, we *did*. Now it seems like he's starting to hate me as much as Lex does.

The whole thing makes me want to hurt myself so damn bad, but all I have is—

Hobbling off my bed, I grab a piece of drawing paper, swiping it hard and fast along my wrist. The papercut stings, but it's nowhere *near* as satisfying as it would be if I could draw actual blood.

It's just so frustrating. I want the pain… I *need* the release.

Slashing again and again with the paper, I mark myself up with little bullshit cuts, whimpering as I go.

You deserve this.

Just like Gage holding you down and raw fucking you to pieces…

Because you deserve *to hurt. To be degraded, ripped apart, and left for dead.*

It's all you have to offer.

With my wrists throbbing and an ice pack in my pants, I crawl back into bed. My entire body feels like a festering wound as I curl up and wince at the hopelessness in my gut. All night long, I'm stuck in this hole of internal torment. For hours after the lights go off in the row, I'm just… obsessing. Neurotic and jealous, and so very *fucked up*.

When I'm alone, I disappear. And in prison, you're alone a *lot*. Which is why I've spent pretty much my entire time here trying not to be. That's the part Lex doesn't understand. He thinks I *choose* to hurt him on purpose, but it's more of a burden than anything.

My urges drive me, not the other way around. Betraying him was just a different version of opening a vein in a room full of my mother's friends.

The next morning, my body seems to have recovered, but my head is more jumbled than ever. I'm sure if I were a normal person, I'd join my friends for breakfast. Play nice with Dash, apologize to Lex and Byron for involving them in my mess, and work on regaining their trust.

But I think we all know that's not how I function.

Instead, I wait until Rook is inside my cell, delivering me the new charger for my iPad, and I punch my manipulative slut timecard.

"I'm gonna need another favor, Harley," I croon, stepping in front of him so he can't leave.

His mossy green gaze narrows on my face. "You seem to forget that of the two of us, *you're* the prisoner here, 48."

"Oh, trust me, I'm well aware of that fact." I reach out to brush my fingers through his sandy-blonde hair, and he jerks away from me. "I'm also pretty damn certain Velle would tear your ass to shreds if he found out how much you enjoy sneaking in here when you're *supposed* to be working. And not in the good way."

His jaw ticks visibly. "What the fuck do you want, Ren?"

I smirk triumphantly. "I need you to get me alone with Dash."

"Why?" His brow arches.

"Why do you think?"

He pauses for a moment, staring at me like I'm a creature from another planet, before conceding with a huff. "*Fine.* Where would you like to go, your highness?"

"That empty room between the caf and the showers," I tell him. "The one that used to be an infirmary or some shit."

He runs his fingers through his hair, breathing out slowly. "Sure. Whatever. But this squares us. No more bullshit favors. I'm done making deals with the devil."

I purse my lips, leaning in close to his ear. "It's sweet that you think that."

Rook growls, quickly cuffing my wrists and yanking me out of my cell. We walk the long corridors without a word until we reach the empty room. Inside, Rook removes my cuffs, but when I notice he isn't leaving, I peek up at him.

"So… Luthor is straight?" he asks, and my spine stiffens.

"Where'd you hear that?" I glare at him.

"Nowhere." He shrugs. "I'm just wondering…"

"If you're thinking of trying to get him on his knees, you might as well just chop your dick off now and save me the hassle," I hiss with sudden rage pumping in my veins.

Rook's brow arches, his lips curving into a rather dimply snide smirk as he tilts his head. "I was *wondering* why you can't seem to seal the deal. Is it because he doesn't want dick?"

My anger retreats just a tad, though the frustration of his words is still very much alive. "He doesn't know what he wants… And as *you* now know from personal experience, there's no such thing as *straight* in here."

His grin fades, and he blinks at me. "You don't know shit about my situation, 48."

"I know that you nut like someone who probably *thought* he was straight once…" I smirk.

He grumbles, "So hopping on Dash's dick will… what? Have Luthor falling in love with you?? Make it make sense."

He's really starting to annoy me. "First off, I'm not going to have *sex* with Dash. I'm just gonna throat his cock until he comes in my mouth and pretend he's Lex while it's happening. Just like I do with all of you assholes. It's called a proxy job."

"A *proxy job*?" Amusement dances in his eyes.

I fold my arms over my chest. "Yea… *TM*. I invented it, and it works. But more importantly, I don't need to justify any of my actions to you. You're the *rookie*."

Rook gawks at me, his Midwestern innocence really shining through. He's too new here. Just like Dash. Despite getting their hands a little dirty, they still have no *clue* what it's like to survive in a place like this for so long.

"Does it… get his attention?" he asks, suddenly sounding much more curious than judgmental. "Luthor's, I mean?"

I nod slowly, glancing down at my fingers as I pick at my cuticles. "Yes. It's our thing."

I'm becoming more and more fidgety with every passing second, standing here while he grills me for information like it's somehow his business.

"But then why hide it?" He keeps prodding, and I'm biting down on the inside of my cheek so hard I taste blood. "You wanted to come in here so Luthor wouldn't see you with Dash… Right?"

"Harley, please…" I whine, rubbing my eyes. "Stop being such a cop. This isn't a case that needs cracking. Just go get Dash and bring him here. Let me worry about my relationship with Lex. I'm pretty good at it."

He continues to stare at me for a few more moments while I'm squirming inside my skin with tension swallowing me whole.

Finally, Rook sighs, running his fingers through his sandy-colored hair. Then he grunts, "Don't move," stalking off with a slam of the door behind him.

Releasing a jittery breath, I pace around the exam chair in the middle of the room, pushing that frustrating conversation out of my mind and contemplating the many ways Dash could react to this little outing. Hooking up with someone to get to someone else *is* a game I'm more than familiar with. Even before I got here, before I started using it as a way to sate my cravings for Lex that he refuses to fulfill, I developed a knack for playing on the one weakness I know just about everyone shares. *Jealousy.*

It's an effective method in most cases. It can be a gamble, though. Because if the person you're trying to reach doesn't fall into the trap, then you fucked around with a rando for no reason. Fortunately for me, I already do that anyway, so it's not much of a loss.

With Lex, however, it's a little different. I'm not necessarily trying to make him *jealous* by using someone else as his proxy. If I do, it's an added bonus. This is more about getting him to think… making him understand that I can still *have* him, even if it's not him.

I want Lexington constantly and painfully aware that as far as I'm concerned, *everyone* is him at this point.

Sounds of shuffling grow nearer, and I lean up against the wall by the door, awaiting the arrival of today's version of Lexington Deon. The door swings open to reveal Rook clutching Dash by the arm while his face pivots all around. When he spots me, he looks immediately nervous.

"What the fuck is this?" Dash grunts, and I nod at Rook.

"I'm good. Thanks."

"You have ten minutes." Rook shoves Dash into the room, and he stumbles. Dash gawks as the door closes in his face. Then he slowly turns to me.

"Why am I here?" he asks, checking out the dingy room. "What the hell is this place?"

I shrug. "It's a random empty room." His brow is lined with confusion. "I just needed somewhere private to talk to you for a second."

"Talk to me about what?" He inches backward, away from me.

I step closer. "About your cellmate."

"Right…" Dash murmurs. "You and Luthor. You guys have something going on, hm? It's pretty hard to miss…"

His words and the genuine look on his pretty face make a lot of different things happen inside me. I both hate and love that it's readily apparent, even to people who just got here, that Lex and I have *something going on*. I love it because it means Lex is still affected by me, no matter how hard he tries not to be.

And yet I hate it. Because it can *seem* as obvious as it wants to, but the fact remains… nothing between us has ever actually worked, and it most likely never will.

Gripping the back of my neck, my eyes fall to the floor. "See, that's the thing. We *almost* had something going on. But then I sorta fucked it up… It's a long story, but that's why I need a favor from you."

He folds sculpted arms over his chest defiantly. "Well, I don't think I owe you anything. I already got a toothbrush on my own. No thanks to you."

I chuckle. *The kid is too cute.* And his toothbrush obsession borders on psychotic, which just makes me like him more. "Dude, you disappeared. I wasn't sure if you were still with us."

He narrows his gaze at me. "There's nothing I can do to help you, Ren. If you fucked up with Luthor, you'll have to figure out how to fix it yourself."

Despite how much of a pain in the ass he's being, I can't deny that I'm starting to see the appeal. He's a rational person, a little weird, but also sort of sweet. I understand why Lex likes him, and although I'm still jealous of their instant connection, I honestly don't think he's interested in Lex the way I am.

Okay, I'm sure no one *is interested in Lex the way* I *am.*

"Dascha," I sigh his name, stepping in closer. "Luthor is very… complex. He's not like the rest of us. Definitely not like me. And I *love* that. But it's hard for me to be myself and try to keep him. He's…" My voice trails for a moment before I breathe, "He's *mine*. He just doesn't know it yet." Dash stares at me, hazel eyes wide, save for the occasional flutter of long lashes. "All I want is to get close to him, but he won't let me. He doesn't work that way. So instead, I have to get close to him through someone else."

I push into his space, and he lurches away, crashing down into the exam chair in the middle of the room. "What the fuck are you talking about?"

He tries to stand up, but I lean over him, caging him in. "I need you to be like a proxy," I tell him my game, and he appears as perplexed as he is nervous.

"I'm not into guys," he grunts, attempting to stand again.

Placing a hand on his chest, I shove him back down. "I know, I know. But everyone has needs, Dascha." My mouth hovers over his, our eyes locked. "I can suck your dick so good, you'll go cross-eyed for minutes afterward." I make a slow display of tugging my bottom lip between my teeth, which catches his attention. "I'll pretend you're Lex, and you can pretend I'm some girl from back home. Have you ever had your cock throated by a dude?"

The way he's gaping at me, you'd think I asked *him* to suck *my* dick.

"I haven't been in here long enough to be that desperate," he rumbles, holding on to his defenses like a child grips their blankie.

Still, it's there… that twinkle of curiosity in his beautiful eyes. *Some guys break quicker than others.*

"It's not about desperation, sweetheart," I hum, easing my body over his. "You're never getting out of here. Might as well take a little entertainment out of death row."

His breathing is picking up already as he stares up at me, gaze doing a quick sweep down my frame. "I don't understand how sucking my dick will help you with Luthor…"

Dropping a hand onto his thigh, I trail my finger up toward his crotch. He snatches it before I can get there.

"I told you, I have to pretend," I persist. "You can go back to your cell and tell Lex what happened. He might be mad… but deep down, he'll like it."

"I'm not gonna fucking tell him shit," Dash mutters.

I shrug. "Then don't. He'll find out regardless." *I'll make sure of it.*

"This sounds like a stupid fucking plan," he scoffs. "I think you're just gay as fuck and desperate to swallow cock."

Well… yea. If the shoe fits.

"So? How is that a problem for you?" I point out casually. "You get to come down my throat, and I get what I want, too. Win-win."

The stiffness in his muscles is still there, but I can tell he's sincerely considering it. Either way, I'm not giving him any more leeway to protest. Reaching for the drawstring on his pants, I tug it until it unties. He's glaring at me something fierce, but I really don't care. I just keep yanking his pants down, enough to get his dick out. Then I fist the shaft, giving it a few slow tugs.

I'm immediately all warm and stiff between my legs. As bizarre as it sounds, Dash's dick is shockingly similar to Lexington's. Long—*even when it's not all the way hard*—pink and velvety soft. It looks like candy. And growing so fast in my hand.

Just like Lex's did…

He was always so unsure, and it drove me fucking *wild* with the most intoxicating desire to prove myself.

My fingers glide down to his balls as I whisper, "You have a really nice dick."

"Don't fucking talk," Dash growls, peeking down at me with flushed cheeks, reminding me of who I'm actually touching.

Lex would've liked that. He used to love when I fawned over him a little.

"Sorry," I hum, sloping my face down in his lap and sucking his fat crown into my mouth.

He releases a jagged gust that draws up my balls like elastic. *Mmm... Just like Lex's shivery little breaths.* I suck slow, moving him deeper into my mouth with my tongue cradling his warm, thick cock, remembering the way Lex used to lie back and let me take him how I wanted. The way he'd melt into the bed and become *mine* in an instant.

It's not long before the hips start moving, flicking against my hungry mouth, fucking deeper and deeper into my throat. I play with his balls, teasing them, tugging them until he moans, and then I swallow his plump, juicy head, earning me a raspy, "Jesus *fuck*..." accompanied by a little pulse of precum.

And only moments later, his hands are holding my skull down, and he's *pleading*, "Suck my fucking dick."

I groan on his cock, because even though he doesn't sound like Lex, in my mind it's still him. His long, masculine fingers threading through my hair, his legs spreading for me to work in between them... His big, delicious, purely *perfect* cock throbbing in my mouth, aching while my tongue praises him.

God, I'm sucking Lexington *so hard*, slurping with saliva spilling, wet sounds slicing through the gasps and pants in the air. There are words being growled from somewhere far off, but I barely hear them. My heart is pumping fast in my chest, blood rushing in my ears while I groan and suck, and *chase*, desperate to make Lex *come* so sweet in my mouth.

Because he deserves to be pampered. He needs to know how good I can always make him feel, even if it sometimes hurts afterward.

The pleasure is more than worth the pain, I know it is.

I can make it better, baby...

I promise, I can soothe the ache I cause, if you just give me the chance.

My hips are grinding, my dick twinging against the material of my pants, *dying* for him to reach down and touch it.

Lex... Lexington. Spill for me, baby. Burst into a million glowing embers and rain it all over me.

I fucking love the way it feels to make you mine.

His fingers lace at the nape of my neck and he holds me still, choking me with his cock as it bursts, shooting thick, tasty spurts that I suck out ravenously. I suck every last drop of him, whimpering as I pull my mouth off and writhe against his legs. My balls are *humming*, dick leaking all over the inside of my pants.

"Fuck, *Lex*..." I purr and whine, dazed and trembling.

I just want to climb on top of him. Kiss him hard and dizzy. I want our tongues to tangle while he mewls out satisfied sounds and touches me in that shaky post-orgasm stupor that makes him almost as needy as I am.

It's been years, but I *remember* it like it was yesterday... the feeling of him clinging to me, because I'm the only one who gets him.

I'm the only person in the world who can make him feel this way.

But when I peel my eyes open, I slowly cool off into reality.

Dash is the one seated in the chair, flushed and breathing heavily, glaring at the door to the room... as if someone's there.

Turning over my shoulder, I see no one. But Dash is still looking, a nervous sort of delight etching his eyes... Like maybe he's seeing someone else, too.

Someone he *wants* to see.

CHAPTER SEVEN

Luthor

Later that night…

WONDERING GETS YOU IN TROUBLE… AND I'VE BEEN HERE FOR TOO MANY years to get swept up in imagining life outside these walls. It's a dead-end.

No sense in dreaming when you'll always wake up in Hell, right?

That said, this place just sucking isn't enough to fully stomp out my curiosity of spirit. So I make sure to only wonder about what goes on *inside* the prison, not out. Which, believe it or not, is much more than you'd expect from a rock in the middle of nowhere.

It's a goddamn drama factory in here sometimes.

For example, right now, I'm wondering if Dash's silence means he's thinking about what happened with Ren…

It annoys me to no end that Ren's actions still surprise me. I shouldn't be taken aback by anything he does anymore, no matter how haphazard and destructive. I've known him too long to find his behavior *shocking*.

But for some reason, when Dash got back to our cell a little while ago—after Rook hauled him off in another direction from the rest of us leaving the cafeteria—the last thing I expected was to see him dripping with guilt and shame. Eyes wide and cheeks flushed, wearing that post-coital stupor only *Ren* can cause.

I knew something was up before he even said it, but Dash was quick to confess that he'd been cornered in an empty room for some of that patented Warren Xavier seductive manipulation he pulls off so well he could teach it at the college level.

Honestly, I feel bad for Dash. He clearly doesn't know how to handle being trapped in a place like this with someone like Ren. That, and I think he was worried I'd be upset with him… Which I never would be. After all, it's the furthest thing from his fault, and despite how he likes to make it seem, Ren and I *aren't* a thing. At least, not the kind of *thing* Ren wants us to be…

It's just what Ren does. He uses people to get what he wants. Ironic, considering what I know about his life before he got here…

The last thing I'd want is for Dash to feel uncomfortable, being caught in the middle of the ongoing *Luthor and Ren nonsense-fest*, like Kang clearly does. So I made sure to quickly change the subject to something less *gay love triangley,* and we moved on.

Unfortunately, the more seconds tick by in silence, the more my mind refuses to quit boomeranging back to my ex-whatever he almost was, the fire-starter.

What exactly did he do with Dash in that room, anyway? Did Dash like it?

I know Dash is straight, but he must be realizing I was right about how fucking blurry the lines can get in here. And since Ren is habitually bored and in need of constant human contact, he likes to be the one to make those lines nice and fuzzy.

I haven't even seen Ren in days at this point, since our argument in the caf. I guess he's avoiding me. *And I should be glad about that, right? It's what I wanted…*

But naturally, even when he keeps his distance, he has to do it in his *Ren* way, never really letting go. Planning and scheming…

Confusing my new friend just to make me jealous…

"Dash…" I squeak his name when the silence gets to be too much.

"Yea?" he answers quietly.

"How did it feel… with Ren?"

I hate the way I sound right now. I sound like I *care*, when I really, *really* shouldn't.

"Dude, I don't—" Dash starts to protest my question, but I interrupt.

"I just mean, like… did it feel like he was really into it?"

God. What is the fucking point of asking him that? Why on earth are you still *torturing yourself??*

"Yea." Dash sighs the word hesitantly. "But not for me."

My forehead lines, face swinging left, though I obviously can't see him from up here on my bunk. "What do you mean?"

He goes silent for a few more seconds before he murmurs, "He said your name."

Stupid.

It's so painfully *stupid* how my heart reacts to those four words.

Swallowing a lump in my throat while ignoring the flutter of dumbassery in my chest, I release a long exhale. "He usually does..."

It's the truth. Ren has been pulling this *proxy* shit for a while. It's just a game he's perfected to get a rise out of me. And I'm playing right into his hand. Because here I am... *reacting* to it. Prying Dash for all the dirty details, just like the liar wants me to.

Damn him.

"I don't know what's going on with you guys, but can you let him know I don't want to get in the middle?" Dash mumbles. "I'm just trying to get by here."

And now I feel awful. And *I* didn't even do anything.

Standard. Thanks a lot, Ren.

"I know, bro," I hum, remorsefully. "I'm sorry."

"Don't be," he says, not exactly sounding pissed or anything. Just... confused. "Just don't expect it to happen again."

I feel him flopping around down there, and I sigh, scrubbing a palm over my scalp. I'm supposed to be showing Dash the ropes, helping him get through this as best he can while simultaneously making sure he doesn't follow in the footsteps of my past cellmates.

And I'm sort of failing miserably.

"I guess trying to keep Ren out of your head is easier said than done..." I fold my hands behind my head as I stare up at the ceiling. "I would know."

"He's pretty intense," Dash murmurs.

I chuckle. "You can say that again. Probably one of the most complicated people on the face of the earth. Add to that the fact that you can never really tell whether he's lying or not."

"Does he lie a lot?"

"Uh, yea. That's putting it mildly." I twist over the edge of my bunk to look at him. "Dash, Ren's a pathological liar. You can't believe anything he says."

He gapes up at me, mouth hanging open as realization dawns on his face. I roll back up into my bed, nestling into the starchy fabric of my blanket.

"They've done polygraph tests on him before," I go on, lips quirking nostalgically. "He almost broke the machine. And then there was another time… a few years back, when the Warden ordered Velle to use this device on Ren…"

"Device?" His tone grows audibly curious.

"Like a… male chastity… thing," I mutter, shaking my head. "It's a cock cage. Basically, that's what it is. A cage… for your cock."

I feel Dash spring up in bed. "A cock *cage??* What is that, like a cock ring?"

"No." I chuckle. "It's literally a cage. It goes around your dick when it's soft and keeps you from getting hard. There's even a little padlock on it…"

"Are you fucking serious??" He gasps. "What would be the point of that?"

"Control," I answer with a shrug. "Sometimes humiliation, I guess… degradation. But mostly control. The one they put on Ren could even shock him with the push of a button, like a shock collar… but for your dick."

"Jesus…" Dash's voice goes breathy and contemplative. It's clear he's never heard of something like this before. To be fair, I hadn't either until they did it to Ren. "How long did he have to wear it?"

"Not long. Maybe a week?"

"A *week?!*"

I can't help but laugh at how outraged he sounds. "Yea, until they realized it didn't work on him, just like most other forms of research, or experimentation, or torture. The dude's completely impervious to all of it… He can't be tamed."

Suddenly, a wave of melancholy crashes over me, and I'm instantly tired. Joking about Ren's lunacy is all fun and games… until I'm reminded of how eager I'd been to skip through his minefield picking fucking daisies.

And how much it hurt like hell when I was blown up into a million pieces.

"I wonder how it feels…" Dash whispers, cutting into my inner torment. "To be controlled like that…"

"Not really sure," I rumble, then yawn. "But it's probably better when you actually *want* it."

Sleep is stealing me quickly now that Dash has stopped talking. And within only a couple of minutes, my lids flutter and I drift off.

But I'm yanked back by whining noises.

At first, I think I'm dreaming, my unconscious mind filling my head with panting whimpers. But the more I wake up, the more I realize I'm actually *hearing* these sounds. Accompanied by shuffling beneath me.

Flopping over the edge of the bunk, I peer down at Dash's bed to find him rocking in the fetal position, gripping the blankets with his fists. His eyes are still closed, so I have to assume he's having a nightmare. And I feel bad because he seems really upset.

Should I wake him up? Aren't you not supposed to do that...?

No, that's sleepwalking. You can totally wake people from nightmares.

Climbing down from the top, I stand at the edge of the bed, watching Dash squirm. I step closer, my heart thumping and stomach wringing at his ragged breathing and quiet sobs. Reaching out, I'm all ready to shake him awake. But then I pause.

Because it looks like his hips are rocking. And his breathy little noises are starting to sound more like... moans.

Oh God... Is he having a sex dream??

If he is, it's a pretty hectic one. It's like he's half enjoying himself, half absolutely miserable.

He begins muttering something in his sleep, but I can't tell what he's saying, jaw straining as if he's grinding his teeth.

I shouldn't be watching this. I thought I could help him out by waking him up, but now I feel creepy, standing here while he has some bizarre, painful sex dream.

I move away as slowly as possible, because I really don't want him to wake up with me lurking by his bed like a weirdo. Going for the bars, I start to climb back up to my bunk so I can pretend this never happened. But his voice stops me, words catching my ear.

Through the mumbles, I make out him rasping, "Feels so good..." Followed by a shivering, "Suck harder."

My gut clenches like a fist. *He's... dreaming about someone sucking him off.*

Is he dreaming about Ren??

For whatever reason, the thought is making me sick. Earlier, he seemed like he just wanted to forget what Ren did to him in that empty room... Now, he's dreaming about it?

Maybe he liked it more than he let on.

The nauseated jealousy climbing up my esophagus is just plain foolish. Dash can't help what happens in his dreams… None of us can. It's not his fault if his unconscious mind is messing with his confusion from earlier.

Quickly, I grab the bars and climb back to my bunk, curling up in bed. I close my eyes, ignoring the sounds of Dash getting sleep-head.

None of my business.

He makes a choking sound down there, and I cover my ears.

Not listening.

But I can still hear him. And when he murmurs, "*Dash,*" my eyes snap open again.

Why is he saying his own name?

"I'm gonna come down your tight throat, baby…"

"What in the holy hell…?" I whisper, snatching my pillow.

His muffled groans cut off when I smash the pillow over my head, humming a song to distract myself from whatever my cellmate is doing down there. I know he's still speaking, but I'm not listening. I can't…

Because if it's anything to do with Ren, then this just got a buttload more complicated.

A few days have passed, and things have seemingly gone back to normal. Well, as normal as they can be in here.

Kang is still a bit mopey, but now I can't tell if it's because he's worried about O'Malley, or if he's letting Ren get to him. He *claims* he only ever messes around with Ren when Ren begs him to be the proxy, but part of me thinks he enjoys it more than he wants to, and that twists him up.

Dash has been jumpier than usual. I didn't mention the whole overhearing his sex dream thing, because where would that get me?

Avoidance is the best bet when it comes to stuff like this. Plus, I don't want him to feel awkward or ashamed. I care about him. He's my friend, and I love having him around, regardless of his odd behaviors, sex dreams, or him talking to himself at night. I've always felt better with a cellmate.

Being alone sucks ass.

I can relate to both of their struggles with understanding your sexuality in prison. It's a complex topic. We're trapped forever in a building full of dudes with rampant sexual appetites. Frankly, it's unavoidable. But we all deal with it in different ways.

Ren is probably one of the only people in here who's never questioned his sexuality, not even for a second. That's why it's hard for him to comprehend the confusion he causes with his careless sex games.

That and he also just doesn't give a fuck, because he's a dick.

We still haven't spoken more than a few words to each other since our last argument, and I don't think it's any coincidence he's been going to the showers and cafeteria at different times. I know I'm supposed to be relieved that he's drifting away a little, but it's just frustrating me more.

He's the one who agreed to try… After we stopped doing whatever stupid shit we were doing together—*a mistake I'm still trying hard to regret*—I asked him if we could stay friends, and he said yes.

But I guess it was just another line of bullshit he fed me to get what he wanted.

Shaking off the memory, I focus on my steps as we leave our cell with Joy, who's bringing us down to the basement for some rec time. She stops outside of Kang's cell, and when he trots out, cuffed and ready to go, she continues on up the row to Ren's.

I never would have known this before I got here, but trying to stay friends with someone you've fooled around with is sort of difficult. At least, it is for me. Maybe it's because I'm not a very suave person, and when it comes to sexual relationships, I'm a total noob without a clue. But it's weird for me to constantly be puttering around a person who's seen me in a *lot* of compromising positions.

Sex, or any variation of hooking up, is vulnerable for me. Because I don't do it often, or *ever*, really.

Another concept that's completely foreign to Ren.

For him, hooking up is detached, meaningless. Strictly physical. He claims it wasn't like that with us, but I believe that like I believe the Earth is flat.

Regardless of how long it's been since it happened, every time I see him now, I'm reminded of how it felt when he wrestled me into submission, literally and figuratively. Not only that, I also can't look at his face without remembering how goddamn *stupid* he made me feel for trusting him even when I knew it was only going to fuck me up.

Out of his cell, Ren pauses to shoot me a wide-eyed flash of blue, and in the interest of being friendly, I give him a quick nod. Then I skirt around him, catching up to Joy and Kang while ignoring the gaze I can feel on my back like a warm body standing directly behind me.

The five of us walk the long corridors, through doors that bring us lower and lower in the building. The clomps of our footsteps and clinking of our cuffs are joined by Ren and Dash mumbling to each other behind me. I'm trying hard to ignore it, but that whisper of jealousy is like a loud, nagging voice in my ears.

What the hell are they so chatty for? Reminiscing about their little rendezvous in the dark room?

Clenching my jaw, I decide to overpower the sound of them whispering sweet nothings to one another by talking to Joy.

We finally reach the rec room, and I scamper inside the giant space, making a beeline for the one shoddy old basketball. Ren follows me while Joy and Kang go to the other side of the room and begin taping up their knuckles. The two of them have their own prerogative down here, which is to spar and practice Tae Kwon Do, a shared hobby of theirs. They're both really good, and sometimes I like to watch them kick and punch each other.

But today, I'm in the mood to blow off some steam with one of the only other activities offered in this dreary gymnasium. Basketball.

I'm not very good... *Okay, I suck.* I'm a gamer and computer wizard, so the fact that I'm terrible at sports is a fully justified stereotype. Still, it's the only opportunity for exercise in this place, shy of push-ups and sit-ups, or maybe jogging around the room. I could punch the bag a few times... That might get out some of my buried aggression.

For now, I'll just stick to basketball.

I dribble the ball a few times, passing it to Ren, who does the same. He's much better than me. Actually, he's damn good. He loves to play, and the only reason I can even attempt the game is thanks to him teaching me a thing or two.

Because we're *friends*. It's what friends do.

Ren passes the ball back to me, and I dart up the court toward the hoop, dribbling until I'm close enough to shoot. But Ren is fast, and really good at defense. He crowds me, getting all up in my space, then snatches the ball away, jumping to dunk.

He's grinning up a storm, all proud of himself, while I roll my eyes.

"Get over yourself," I mutter, and he chuckles, passing the ball to me.

My eyes scan the room for Dash as I bounce the ball. He's standing over by the entrance awkwardly, like he doesn't know what to do with himself.

"Dash! Come on!" I call out to him while Ren tries to steal the ball again. "Cover this asshole for me."

"In your dreams, bitches," Ren laughs.

Dash still looks hesitant, and pretty exhausted, which reminds me of how little he's been sleeping since he got back from solitary. In general, he doesn't sleep much, but right now, you can tell he's out of it.

Nonetheless, he jogs over to us, and I pass him the ball. He starts dribbling, weaving around Ren, and bounding toward the hoop, juking out of Ren's cover just in time to shoot. The ball sinks through the hoop, sans net.

"Nice shot!" I cheer him on. "Wow, I'm glad we brought you. I'm not great, and Ren always beats me."

Ren gives me a snide look. "Two against one isn't exactly fair, though."

He tugs his shirt over his head, and I do the same, to avoid getting it sweaty. "Shut up. Don't be a baby." I purse my lips at him to contain my grin, and he beams.

I don't want to admit it, because where would that get me? But I missed spending time with him. I miss having *fun* with him… As friends. Despite all the nonsense of the past, I've always liked hanging out with Ren, playing around and being *normal*. We get so few of these moments. When they present themselves, I can't help wanting to take full advantage.

The three of us dribble around and shoot for a while, running and passing, jumping and dunking. Well, *Ren's* dunking. He's the only one who knows how, though Dash comes close a few times. It's fun, and I'm having a blast. We're all laughing and talking trash, pausing once in a while to watch Joy and Kang kick the shit out of each other—*in a nice way.*

We're beating Ren, but not by much, because Dash is carrying the team. Our collective huffing breaths and sneakers clapping on the concrete floor echo as I get the ball and dart toward the hoop. I dodge Ren a few times, but he's really all over me. More than before. His defense is slipping from casually rambunctious to downright stifling, and I'm getting too hot.

He's touching me too much… pressing his body into mine.

My head is fogging. *I can't fucking concentrate with his crotch on my ass.*

"Come on, babe," he breathes a warm taunt at the nape of my neck that sends a shiver up my spine. "You got this."

"Fuck off, Ren," I growl, frustration vibrating my limbs. The mood is quickly shifting from fun and light-hearted to a simmering fury that unfortunately seems to follow Ren and me around like a shadow.

"Since when do you let people push you around?" I can hear his smirk as he grinds into my ass. And I'm *fuming* when his hand drops onto my hip. "Come at me, Lexington."

That's it.

Straightening, I toss the ball, immediately getting up in his face. "Is this what you want, Ren?" I hiss, so close to him, the tips of our noses are almost touching. "A fucking reaction, you goddamn attention whore?? Well, here it is!" My volume has risen pretty significantly, to the point that I'm basically shouting over his lips.

"I just want you to care," he sneers.

I'm fucking enraged. *Again with this bullshit?!*

"Well, guess what, *Warren*?" I seethe, leaning in even closer, "I don't."

In a flash, all of the amusement falls from Ren's face, and he roars, shoving me hard in the chest. I stumble, but catch myself, instantly diving on top of him, tackling him to the floor.

We're rolling around, limbs flailing, rage and testosterone clouding the air with sizzling heat. Ren gets on top of me quick, arm slightly cocked back like he might just want to hit me in the face. I'm not sure he would, but I'm *begging* for it.

"Go ahead, *bro*," I croak from beneath him. "Fucking do it. *Hit me!*"

Before anything else can happen, Dash lunges at us, knocking Ren off of me.

Now *they're* wrestling around on the floor as I sit up, dazed and not really sure what's going on or what I'm supposed to do. It's all a blur.

The next thing I know, Dash is on top of Ren and he's swinging at his face.

Over, and over… and over.

Staggering to my feet, I watch with wide eyes as Dash's manic fists pummel Ren in the face and Ren just lies there… *taking* it. He's not even trying to fight back.

Joy and Kang rush over, hauling Dash off of Ren, each of them holding his flailing arms. He must be in some sort of rage blackout. But then, in a snap, he goes still. He blinks down at Ren, who's lying on his back on the floor with blood pouring from his nose.

I gulp, stepping forward. My chest is on fire, regret crawling up my throat. Almost like an instinct, I find myself drawn to Ren, seconds from dropping to my knees to make sure he's okay.

I'm stopped when a bubbling laugh bursts from his lips, holding me in place.

The rumbling chuckles quickly turn hysterical. And now he's straight up *cackling*, loud and maniacal, with blood running into his mouth and all over his teeth. He's gone full lunatic, practically choking out psychotic fits of bloody laughter.

I don't like this...

My eyes dart to Joy when I hear her growl, "You're going back to solitary, 101."

She's visibly irate as she slaps cuffs beneath Dash's bloody hands.

"No! Wait, please," Dash cries, face going ashen.

"Joy, come on," I jump in. "It was a mistake. He was just—"

"Shut the fuck up, inmate," she hisses at me, whipping her walkie off of her holster. "Velle, get down here. Bring backup."

Dash's eyes are wide and glassy with fear. It's a stark contrast to the dead eyes and unkempt wrath he was unleashing on Ren mere moments ago. I have no idea what came over him, but I highly doubt it had anything to do with Ren, or him messing with me.

That was all Dash stuff.

"Joy, please!" he gasps, chest heaving like he's about to lose it again, only this time he might fall into some kind of panic attack.

But Joy's not having any of it. She barely even seems like she's listening, clutching his arm while she watches Ren rolling on the floor, cackling like a crazy person.

Dash grows visibly twitchy. He's blinking an awful lot, shaking his head over and over and mumbling to himself.

"Dash?" I murmur, stepping closer to him with chills of unease buzzing across my skin.

He doesn't look good... I'm fucking worried about him. *He looks like he might pass out.*

Joy flips her hand up and barks, "Stay where you are, inmate, or you'll go to the hole with him."

Mouth hanging open, I stand helpless, with one friend about to collapse and the other losing what's left of his mind. My eyes flit to Kang, who's staring at Ren with concern lining his face. He glances at me, and we share a telepathic *what the fuck??*

Dash crumbles to his knees and stares at the floor, eyes as wide as saucers.

Joy arches a brow at him and mutters, "Oh, boy…" under her breath.

Stomping footsteps come from the distance, and moments later, Velle and Rook burst into the room, pausing to take in the scene. Velle storms over to Ren, dropping to his knees next to him. He grabs Ren by the arms, pinning him to the floor in an attempt to maybe rein in his episode. Ren squirms beneath him, laughter echoing as he gasps for air, coughing spatters of blood.

"Jesus…" Rook grunts. "What the hell happened to him?"

"This one happened." Joy nods down at a trembling Dash.

"I didn't… I… didn't…" Dash stutters.

My nervous gaze bounces between Dash and Ren, but I'm weighted to the floor. I want to do something, *anything,* to help either of them, but I can't move. If I do, Joy and Velle will stop me, throw me in the hole, or worse.

I hate this feeling… I *hate* being forced not to react.

I'm *suffocating*.

Velle barks over his shoulder at Rook to get Dash out of here, smacking Ren on the cheek. "Focus, 48. Snap the fuck out of it."

Rook hauls Dash to his feet and tugs him, stumbling and barely walking upright, out of the room.

Joy stomps over to Kang and me, cuffing our wrists. "Come on, inmates. Back upstairs." She grabs her and Kang's things, already walking toward the door when she turns to snap at us over her shoulder, "Let's go."

Kang follows after her, but I'm hesitating, eyes still stuck on Ren. "Is he gonna be okay…?"

"What the fuck did I say, 35??" Her voice bellows at me, but I'm too busy watching Velle fasten cuffs around Ren's wrists and hoist him up over his shoulder.

Ren's not small by any means, but Velle's just lugging him like a sack of wacky potatoes.

"Move your fucking ass, inmate," Velle snarls at me, eerily calm as he carries Ren past me. He glares at Kang on his way out the door. "Don't think I forgot that shit you pulled with the cell phone down here."

"This has nothing to do with that," Kang mutters, but Velle's already gone.

Scuttling along, I'm trying to catch up to him and find out where he's bringing Ren. Hopefully, he's just going back to his cell. It's not like there's an infirmary or anything... But my main concern is that he'll dump Ren in the East Wing.

I really hope not. I can't deal with that again...

By the time we get through the end of the long corridor, Velle is already gone, and I can't tell which direction he went. This place is like a maze, with some hallways leading to the same place, others going somewhere completely different. It's a fucking mess. I've been here forever, and I still barely understand the layout.

There are distinguishing marks in certain places, and we try to memorize them so we can remember where we are. It helps to have a good sense of direction, though it's essentially a labyrinth of leaking concrete.

Joy and Kang are whispering about something while we walk, but I can't even be bothered to pay attention. I'm too busy obsessing over what just went down.

I hope Dash is okay...

And Ren. Jesus. He just lost it.

I mean, I've seen Ren behave in a lot of troubling ways. I've seen him get into fights on purpose... I've seen him hurt himself. It's part of the reason why even just having him as a *friend* drives me mental. Being in his presence is like being on a rollercoaster that never stops.

I swear to God, I need to keep my distance for my own sanity. This friendship is gonna give me ulcers.

Joy gets us back to the row, and much to my dismay, Ren's not in his cell. Once I'm stuffed back into mine, alone, I really start to panic. Dash is gone... back in solitary. Ren is off, God knows where.

And I'm here. In my same cell, by myself.

It's like I'm doomed to always end up this way. No matter what happens in this place, I'll always be right fucking here, *alone.*

I'm sick of it. The revolving door of cellmates who always disappear. Unreliable friends constantly being dragged out of my life. And I just have to sit here and watch it happen.

Exhausted and mentally drained, I crawl into Dash's bed and curl up in a ball. It's times like these when the thoughts start to creep in... the ones I never allow myself to have. The ones I keep on the other side of a force-field in my mind, because it's just going to make things worse.

But right now, I just can't help it.

I miss my parents. I miss my friends.

I miss school, and my computer, and the beach.

Sushi, and In-N-Out...

Fireworks over the ocean.

Rolling onto my stomach, I bury my face in the pillow. It smells like Dash.

I fall asleep to memories of all the things I'll never see again, for the rest of my life.

I dreamt about designing a computer, and when I wake up, I have the strongest urge to make it happen.

Doing it in here is nothing shy of impossible. I know that. Even if I were to find spare parts somehow, they'd never let me keep them. And even if they did, the Warden would shut that shit down, and maybe even kill me.

After all, a computer in my hands is like a gun or a knife in someone else's.

Still, I can't stop thinking about it over the course of the day, which ends up dragging more than most others. I guess because of what happened yesterday, Velle decided to keep us in our cells longer than usual. I get no shower or meal until dinner time, and when I do, I'm brought in without my friends.

It reminds me of my early days, when I used to sit alone, looking over my shoulder every few seconds for fear someone would start shit or try to attack me. It didn't happen much, but it would on occasion. Luckily for me, I always became friends with my cellmates, and they were pretty protective. It should come as no surprise that I'm not really a fighter. I learned to scrap a little because I *had* to, but I would always much rather use my words, which isn't the preferred method of conflict resolution for guys in here.

Not too long after that, Ren showed up. And even though I never asked him to, he made it his personal business to look out for me.

It's different now. When I come into the caf alone, a few of the guys call me over to sit with them. But I don't. It feels like high school again... I'm the young one, opting to eat by myself, rather than deal with trying to socialize or fit in.

On my way back to the row for the night, I pass Ren's cell and stop short when I see him in there. He's lying on his bunk holding an iPad. The glow of whatever he's watching illuminates his face, and the visible black and blue around his right eye.

I wander over to the bars, and he looks up, immediately lowering the device and hopping out of bed when he sees me.

"Hey," Jasper grunts at my back. "No bullshit shit, 35. Back to your cell."

"Jake," Ren murmurs to him, tilting his head.

Jasper sighs out of annoyance. "Make it quick." Then he saunters off, bringing the other inmates to their cells.

Stepping up to the bars, I clutch them in my fists as Ren walks up, his eyes set on mine. As soon as he's close, I can see a nasty cut on his bottom lip to accompany the black eye.

Wanting nothing more than to keep this casual, the way it needs to be, I mutter, "iPad, huh? Nice..."

His split lip twitches. "Movie night sleepover?" I scoff and shake my head. "I'm glad to see you..."

"Are you alright?" I ask quietly, riddled with complex stuff I don't want to be feeling.

Ren's vibrant blue eyes shimmer at me. "Yea," he says softly. "Never better."

I cock a brow at him, and he grins. "You look like shit."

"You're looking at me," he hums. "I call that a win."

Rolling my eyes, I shove down the way my mouth wants to smile. "What happened to you yesterday? What the hell was that with Dash?"

"He was defending you." His head slants. "It was cute. I think he likes you."

"He's my *friend*," I tell him for the tenth time. "Are you saying you let him kick the shit out of you because he was *defending* me?"

"I deserved it," he sighs and shrugs. "I'd do the same thing... if someone was fucking with you. I've done it before."

"That makes no sense," I grumble. "*You* were the one fucking with me. You could just act normal and not do that."

"I don't do normal..." he whispers. "You know that."

"Yea, no shit."

"And I wasn't *really* fucking with you, Lex." He eases in closer to the bars between us. "I think you know that, too."

There's honesty in his words... At least, I think there is. *It's so hard to tell.*

"You're a head case and a half," I breathe, exhausted already from a two-second conversation with him. But for some reason, it just feels… necessary. I don't know where this bullshit draw comes from, keeping me attached to his crazy. But it seems way too strong to sever. "That nutjob laughing like a madman on the floor… That was the real you, Ren. And it's fucking terrifying."

He rests his head on one of the bars, eyes falling to my mouth. "You don't like it?"

My stomach twists, and I swallow hard. "Why would I…?"

"Dunno…" he breathes, lifting his fingers to trace mine. "*I* like stuff that hurts."

"Yea, well… I *don't*." My voice comes out raspier than I want it to, making my words unconvincing.

"Are you lying to me, Lexington?" His gaze is heavy, smothering me while his finger grazes mine slowly.

And I barely even notice how close we are to each other, with only some steel bars keeping us apart. Ren's hand covers mine where I'm holding the metal, and I want to pull away. I *want* to, I know I do…

But I can't. My body won't move.

"I'm not the liar, Ren," I whisper, heat rushing up my neck at his proximity and the intensity in his eyes, bluer than the sky on a perfect California day.

He makes me *nervous*. He always has, and I've never been able to understand why.

"You lie all the time." He smirks, tugging his lower lip with his teeth. Then he winces, clearly having forgot about the cut.

Before I can even stop myself, my fingers lift, sneaking between the bars to gently brush the cut on his mouth. As soon as it happens, his lashes flutter, and he hums out a pleading sound. It hits me hard in the junk.

He's so *needy* for touch.

Mine?

No… Everyone's. It's not specific to me.

"It hurts…" I shiver out the words, meant to be a question, though it doesn't come out that way.

His head does a little shake. "You were worried about me…"

Same thing. Not a question. A statement. A soft, eager one, but still. He's not asking.

My hand lingers between the bars, my lips parted without the slightest clue of what to say. I can't tell him I missed him today, because, I mean, as *friends*—I think—and he'll just take it the wrong way. I can't tell him I hope I get to see him tomorrow, because I'm not even sure if I do.

It's a seesaw with us. We're never just… even.

"35!" Jasper barks, and I flinch. "Let's go."

Before I can pull my hand back, Ren places a quick kiss on my fingers. "I want more of this, baby."

"Ren…" I sigh, shaking my head. "No."

"If getting my ass kicked means you'll worry about me, then I'll take a beating every fucking day." His mouth curves into one of his wicked smirks, dimples on display.

I huff at his ridiculousness, moving back. "You're a dumbass."

"Mm… Don't be mean." He pouts. "I'm injured. You should be kissing it better."

"Okay, now I'm really leaving," I grunt, releasing the bars, though he holds onto my hand for an extra couple of seconds. "Goodnight, Warren."

"Goodnight, Lex," he croons. "And don't worry… I'm sure you'll get me out of your head eventually."

Ugh… Annoying, gorgeous idiot.

Glaring at him, I step back as Jasper grabs me and shoves me up the row. And Ren watches me go… I can feel it.

CHAPTER EIGHT

Luthor

5 years ago…

USUALLY, DATA AND SOFTWARE PROGRAMMING CAN HOLD MY ATTENTION better than most things.

It's my favorite part of attending Berkeley, because it's what I came here to do. To follow in the footsteps of the great tech geniuses of our time, and more importantly, to have fun doing it.

I'm still not exactly sure what my goal is for after I graduate, but honestly, Silicon Valley is a viable option.

Maybe a startup. Join a team developing apps. Worst-case scenario, I'll start out running code somewhere and work my way up. But even that sounds like fun to me.

All the different ways to use my powers for good, and make an honest living doing it.

But my side-hustles… *those* are what earned me my nickname.

See, when you're as good as I am at weaving the worldwide web, you begin to feel sort of limitless. For me, a firewall isn't so much a *wall*, as it is a door to be opened. And rather effortlessly, I might add.

In high school, I developed a foolproof system for creating fake IDs. It made me pretty popular with my classmates, even if deep down I knew they were only using me. Still, the money was good, not that I necessarily needed it. We were never struggling or anything, but it was helpful in getting ahold of all the parts needed for my machine…

LOIS.

That's her name. *Her* being the computer I designed in my garage… Lex's Optimal Intelligence System, aka LOIS. Superman's girlfriend.

I know, right? I just nerd leveled up, big time.

Needless to say, once I had LOIS on my side, there was no possible *way* I could stop.

Junior year, I accessed the national database to change a bunch of my friends' SAT scores. After that, I hacked into the UCLA admission's office to get my friend Jessie in.

That one I did as a sort of romantic gesture. I'd always kind of liked her, but I guess she didn't see me that way. Even after hacking her into her dream school, all I got was the same ambiguous response I so often got from the opposite sex…

Things like, *"You're such a great* friend, *Lex."*

"I really love having you as a friend.*"*

"I would never want to do anything to ruin our friendship.*"*

Hearing it however many times, I began to realize these girls were actually being pretty blunt, but in a nice way, as females tend to.

Believe it or not, when a girl says the word *friend* to you over and over, she's not speaking in some sort of riddle for you to decode. She *literally* means that she sees you only as a friend, and will never be attracted to you sexually.

It's fine, though. I wasn't Jessie's type, and I'm okay with that.

Most of the girls I'm drawn to are like that… Out of my league. Not *physically*, but they always seem to be interested in the jocks and the frat bros. They tell me I'm *so smart,* like it's a bad thing, and really, I think it comes down to confidence. I've just never been good at making the moves necessary to attract the girls I like. My idea of flirting is to have *conversations*, to share common interests and debate differences of opinion.

Basically, I should be looking for a hot bookworm or a cosplayer or something. Not Malibu Barbie.

Anyway, when I realized that none of the kids I knew in real life would ever get me the way people on the internet did, I just stayed in my lane. I made friends online, built up my social media relationships, and stopped caring about trying to fit into the mold of who I'd thought I needed to be. I've spent all my free time over the last few years perfecting LOIS, while simultaneously becoming a god of the internet.

Using my powers for evil, in true Lex Luthor fashion.

Okay, that's a bit of an exaggeration. I don't hack into people's banks or their Amazon accounts or anything like that. In fact, I feel stealing is beneath me. *Give me a challenge, at least.*

Origin story aside, the normally titillating Berkeley curriculum is taking a backseat in my mind at the moment. Because I can't stop thinking about my friends. My *real* friends… The ones I've never actually met.

I haven't spoken to Leah in two months. None of us have. After she hung up on me that night, she ghosted. All of my texts have gone unread, no social media posts, no gaming… She hasn't been online at all. Complete radio silence.

She's disappeared on us before, but never for this long. And I can't get that last conversation out of my head… How scared she sounded. Those men's voices.

I'm really worried about her. I just want to know that she's okay.

To top it all off, last week a news story broke involving my friend Cyrus. **Cyclops180**.

It's been big drama, all over the internet. Apparently, his twin brother wound up in the hospital… Both of his parents are now in jail. There were rumors swirling about their stepfather having some kind of sexual relationship with Cy's brother, but most people are discrediting it as bullshit, made up by their mother to pull focus from her crimes.

It's hard to know what's true and what isn't when all online reporting is like one long game of telephone.

Real or not, the story is wild. Cy's stepdad is a legend in the tech world, especially on the West Coast. Cyrus never had anything but great things to say about him… So I'm sure there's no way he'd hurt Cy, or his twin brother, Colson.

But then, the video…

A couple of weeks ago, Cyrus messaged me, begging for my help to hack into his mom's iCloud and delete some video. Which I did, because he's my friend. And naturally, because I'm a trustworthy motherfucker, I didn't watch it. But now that all this crazy shit has come to light, I can't help but wonder what was on it…

Shaking my head, I focus on the screen of my laptop, and the research I'm supposed to be doing for class. I've been staring at the same page for ten minutes, lost in my thoughts. Between Cyrus and Leah, I'm distracted as shit. I can't concentrate on anything, especially since every time I check Twitter, all I see are tweets about the *Solana Beach twins* and their billionaire stepdad, Tauren Vance.

All of Cy's social media accounts have been deactivated. His Twitch, his Discord, everything. It sucks. Not being able to check on the people I care about when they're going through stuff makes me feel helpless.

It makes me feel like maybe we're not really as close as I thought we were.

Class ends, and I pack up my stuff, heading home. *TGIF, man.* I just want to veg out in the garage, fuck around with my homegirl LOIS, and lose myself in some virtual reality.

It's not my job to worry about what's happening to other people. I'm sure they're fine. They can take care of themselves.

I'm no superhero, after all.

At home, I kick off my shoes and settle into my chair. I power her up and crack my knuckles, watching my baby come to life. Lines of green run through the black, neon colors flashing with code *I* created. I feel like Dr. Frankenstein, minus the shame surrounding my monster, of course. Honestly, I couldn't be prouder of this thing.

With her, I'm unstoppable.

I mess around for a bit, sliding effortlessly between all my various workings; profile to profile, hopping, skipping and jumping from one account to another, like it's a complex game of chess I'm playing against everyone else in the world. And I'm definitely winning.

My clicking and clacking is cut short, however, when I notice that Leah is online... The little green dot is telling me she's *active*.

Without a thought, I pull up a DM, writing out yet another message, similar to the others I've been tossing at her for weeks.

Me: Leah... what's up?

Me: I can see you're online ok...

Me: I just wanna talk

Of course, she doesn't respond. Doesn't even read them, and my insecurities are starting to creep in.

Maybe she's fine, and she just doesn't care enough about me to write back. Maybe I've been fooling myself into thinking these people are my friends, when really my parents were right. They're just strangers.

Maybe I am all *alone*.

Deciding to give it one last shot, I type some more.

Me: I'd rather you tell me to fuck off than just ghost...

Me: I thought we were friends.

Another minute or so passes. Only this time, the messages are being read. My knee is bouncing while I chew on my lower lip, eyes widening when a new message *finally* comes in.

Leah: 10 mins

Leah: Call me from your computer.

Relief washes over me, though I'm still beyond confused, and growing increasingly paranoid.

From my computer…?

Why… Because it's encrypted?

I have so many questions, but I force myself to sit still and wait for ten whole minutes. It feels like ten *hours*. Then I use one of my encrypted text-app numbers to place a call to Leah's phone.

It rings a few times before she picks up. But I don't hear anything right away.

"Leah?"

"Okay, stalker. You got me," she teases through a sigh, and I laugh.

I'm just so damn *happy* to hear her voice, despite how cagey she's being. And the fact that she's whispering.

"All you had to do was respond to one of my eight million texts asking if you're okay…" I tell her, melting back into my chair.

Until she says, "Well… if I said that, I'd be lying."

My spine stiffens, and I sit up straight. "What does that mean?"

She breathes into the receiver. "I'm not *okay*, Luthor. I haven't been okay in longer than I can remember."

Without even realizing it, I'm up and pacing around the room. "What's wrong? Are you, like… sick or something?"

"No…" she mumbles, clamming up, as usual.

"Leah… if you don't wanna talk to me anymore, it's fine." I swallow down my insecurities. "I'd rather you just be honest."

"Are you kidding?" She scoffs. "You're like… the best thing in my life."

My stomach is suddenly flopping around, fluttery nerves attacking my chest. "Okay… then why are you always disappearing?"

"It's not like I *want* to…" she hums. "I don't have a choice."

Stowing my anxiety, that goddamn nervous uncertainty that always keeps me from expressing myself to girls, I force out the words, "I think you should tell me the truth. If… if you care about me, you'll tell me what's going on with you."

Damn… That was tough to get out.

Leah goes quiet for a moment before she whispers, "You really wanna know?"

Duh. "Yes. I really wanna know."

She lets out another long breath over my computer speakers. "Fine… I'll tell you."

And I brace myself. Because honestly, who the hell knows what she's about to say.

She's married, in an abusive relationship. She's a criminal, or a con artist.

Seriously, what could it be that has her so closed-off??

"When I was twelve, I was at the mall in Omaha—that's where I'm from—with my aunt..." she starts, tone serious. Slightly reminiscent, but not in a good way.

And I'm already fascinated, because I never even knew where she was from.

"We were in the food court. I still remember it like it was yesterday..." she goes on, breathy with audible emotion. "I was having an Orange Julius, and one of those cinnamon sugar pretzels. My Aunt Becky ran to the bathroom... She'd taken me out because things weren't great at home. My parents were fighting a lot, and I didn't want to think about it, but I knew they were probably going to get divorced. So that day, in the mall, I was just glad to be out of the house. It was a good distraction, ya know?"

I'm nodding, though she obviously can't see me. I barely even notice that I'm sitting on the floor.

"Anyway, I guess I was *too* distracted," she mumbles. "I got up to throw away my trash, and two strangers came up to me. A man and a woman. They looked normal... Clean, well-dressed. They told me they were looking for a birthday gift for their daughter, who was my age, and asked if I could point out a store where they could get something nice. They just seemed like regular parents who loved their daughter... No red flags, none that I could see, at least. So I walked away with them to help.

"I was barely even out of the food court when the man slapped a hand over my mouth and dragged me through a doorway. It happened so fast, I doubt anyone saw anything. Last thing I remember, I was in a stairwell with them, kicking and screaming as the man held me still and the woman stuck a needle in my neck."

What... the... fuck??

Leah releases a heavy breath, and my head is spinning. I can't even believe what I'm hearing right now. My mouth opens, but I can't speak. Only listen.

"I woke up in a hotel room," she says, voice devoid of emotion. "I wasn't tied up or anything, but there were men guarding the outside, and there was no phone. Turns out, I was in D.C."

"Washington?" I finally murmur, like a stunned idiot.

"Yea," she sighs. "A guy came into my room a little while later and brought me dinner. He was kind... asked if I needed anything. Naturally,

I was terrified. But he told me if I tried anything… Like, to scream or escape, they would kill me, then my family. He explained the situation to me… totally forthcoming about it all. But I didn't understand any of it until a few days later, when I met the rest…"

My gut is churning, pulse racing as I croak, "The rest of what? Of who…?"

She pauses. "Luthor, the people who took me all those years ago, they're called The Finders. Kids who disappear aren't lost… we're *found*, by them. And I've belonged to them ever since that day…"

Terror and confused rage coil through my insides, and I think I'm going to be sick. This is all so crazy… *Too* crazy. I can barely process it.

I suck in a breath. "What did they… want? Why… What h-happened to you?" Tightness clutches my chest as I await the answer I already know.

Barely audibly, she murmurs, "You know, Luthor… You *know* what they make us do. What our purpose is…"

"Leah…" I shoot up and start pacing again. "You're telling me you were kidnapped when you were twelve and turned into a child sex slave? Is that what you're telling me right now??"

She stays silent while I walk in circles, hands clenched into fists, overwhelmed by the *awful* I'm feeling.

As much as I'd love to believe this is all bullshit, I know in my gut that it's true. The whisper of doubt, the idea that maybe she's just a severely troubled person, making all of this up for attention, is snuffed out right away.

I know this girl… In person or not, I don't give a damn. I *know* her, and she's my friend. She wouldn't lie about something like this.

All those hours we spent chatting on PlayStation with our crew, laughing at each other and arguing about nerd stuff… All the late-night phone calls, the FaceTiming and daily text conversations…

They happened through a lens. And on the other side, one of my best friends in the world was actually living in a nightmare.

Leah just breathes for a moment, working up to the words, as if this might be the first time she's ever said them. "It was worse when I was younger. When they first took me, it was… fucking terrible. *Torture*. Think of the worst things you can imagine happening to anyone and multiply it by a hundred. For a long time, I wished I was dead… I wished so badly that they would just *kill* me and put an end to it."

Her voice cracks, my heart splintering in my chest. "As I got older, they started phasing me into different… things. That's why I was able to go online and meet you guys, even though I know they still monitor everything I do. When I turned eighteen, they moved me to a new place. It's better, I guess… in theory. But I'm still under their thumb because I have no education, no life of my own. I'm just… *stuck*. A twelve-year-old girl, frozen in time. As far as the rest of the world is concerned, Alleah Tilsen doesn't exist anymore. I've been missing for so long, they all just assume I'm dead. I might as well be…"

My head starts shaking back and forth, bile lurching up into my throat. "*No*. Don't say that. You're not dead, Leah. You're *alive*, and you're a witness. We need to do something… We need to stop them! They can't be getting away with this… I'll help—"

"You don't get it," she sighs, audibly exhausted. "This isn't the movies… They'll never be caught, or stopped. I'm not supposed to be talking about this…"

My muscles are straining as my feet give up and stare at the wall, gulping again and again. "Okay, but there has to be *something* we can do. Where are you now?? I'll come find you and—"

"No, you won't," she huffs. "And even if they let me go, it wouldn't matter. Look at the Franklin cover-up… That's just one small part of it. It goes *so* much deeper. I'm really not supposed to be telling you any of this. If they find out, they'll kill me…"

Slamming my eyes shut, I rub them hard, trembling down to my core. I can't fucking *believe* what I'm hearing. Never in a million years could I have anticipated this…

"This can't be true," I rumble, digging my fingers into my eyes until I'm seeing spots. "This is like… the shit you read about in fucking conspiracy theory subreddits. This isn't *real*…"

"Mhm. That's good, Luth," she rasps. "Keep thinking that. It's definitely for the best, trust me."

"This is fucked!" I growl, and I can picture her wincing. "Fucking *Jesus*…"

"Luthor, please calm down," she replies, way too casually for my jacked-up emotions to handle. "I don't want you to freak out, okay? The only reason I'm even telling you this now is because I know they can't break through your encryption."

Despite how much I'm freaking out inside, I can't help the momentary spot of pride, because she's right. It's a smart move, and obviously she's confident in my skills, which soothes the pain and rage I'm feeling for a moment, just a dab.

It also makes me think…

Staggering over to my chair, I sink down into it. "I can't…" I breathe unsteadily as pressure builds behind my eyes. "I can't let this happen, Leah. I need to help you. We have to stop this..."

"Luth, *please*," she sniffles. It sounds like she's crying, and I *hate* it, like a knife of sadness plunging into my heart. "I didn't tell you this to upset you, or for you to try to save me or some bullshit. There's nothing you can do. There's nothing *anyone* can do. I'm only telling you because I care about you... I care about you *so* much, and I just didn't want you to think I was vanishing because I don't like you. I do." She pauses for a moment, then whispers, "You were right... We *should* love each other. I mean, I wish we could..."

Tears are pushing painfully, creating a throb inside my skull. "We can. We totally can... I love you, Leah."

"I love you, Lex."

As a friend, I expect her to say. But she doesn't.

She *doesn't* say it, and I feel like I'm falling apart.

I'm not sure if the love I feel for Leah is romantic... Honestly, I've never been able to tell. Becoming friends with someone is my default setting; it happens a million times easier for me than the relationship stuff.

But it doesn't matter, because I care deeply for this person, and despite the lack of details she's giving me, I know what's happening to her... what's probably been happening since she was a child and way too young to be put into such situations. It's making me sick to my stomach with furious despair.

The logical side of my brain has always been just as loud and persistent as the emotional side, and it's *screaming* at me right now.

"I have to... do something." I choke on the words, gripping the edge of my desk. "I'll call someone... The police, or the FBI, or..."

"Come on, man," she almost chuckles. "You're smarter than that. These are the most powerful people in the country, even the *world*. The only thing you'll accomplish by pressing this is getting yourself into trouble. They're like Houdini... They can make anything disappear."

"Okay, well, what do you expect me to do, then??" I snap. "*Accept* this?? You really expect me to sit here and play Fallout with you like nothing is wrong?! Leah, you're a *human being*, not someone's property, to be paraded around for their sick amusement!"

A tiny sob escapes her, and I feel just awful for making it happen. But I can't help it... She's being way too casual about this. It must be some kind of Stockholm Syndrome or something, a symptom of living the way she has for so long.

You never how terrifying your reality looks through the fresh eyes of an outsider.

"You think I'm an idiot, don't you?" Leah croaks. "You think I should have been fighting tooth and nail to escape them?? Well, guess what, Lex? You don't know shit!"

"No, Leah, that's not—"

"I *saw* what happened to the kids who tried to escape… I've seen more disgusting, depraved, devastating shit than you can even imagine, okay?? Yea, I used to fight back. But it only made things *worse*, and so I made a choice. I chose to keep my head down, and to survive as best I could, no matter how much I *hate* it. No matter how much I want to fucking *murder* the shit out of these assholes for ruining my life… and the lives of so many poor children. Believing you can fight back is naïve."

Her voice trails off for a moment, and we both just breathe in silence.

"The thing about evil," she whispers, "is that it masquerades as good. True *evil* doesn't look like a monster with horns and a forked tongue. It's beautiful, charming, and powerful… An exceptional liar, and a *master* at manipulating its camouflage."

She falls quiet once more. And I sit, helpless, with my mind aching in emotional logic.

"There are no *heroes* in this world, Lex. Just villains with a better disguise."

I feel like my sanity is wearing thin, and that's something that worries me deeply.

I've always prided myself on being a very grounded person. Social hang-ups aside, I keep it real. I understand who I am, my strengths and my weaknesses. I choose not to let emotions get the best of me, because acting *rationally* is the best way to keep from floating away in a cloud of the unknown.

No, sir. Not me.

Lex Luthor Deon will stay right here on solid ground, thank you very much.

But ever since that conversation with Leah a couple of weeks ago, when the grand illusion was shattered like a plate of glass being brought down over my super smart noggin, I've been cruising up the delusion highway, watching my grip on reality disappear in the rearview mirror.

Leah and I left things the only way we could… With her promising to keep in touch, and me promising not to do anything crazy, like tell someone what she'd confessed to me.

Obviously, I'm not stupid. Any attempt I could make at getting her to safety and exposing the truth would just put us both in danger.

But that hasn't stopped me from spending every waking minute thinking about it.

I'm not much of a conspiracy guy, because I like my information based in *fact*. That said, I'm also not a sheep. Blind following just because someone *tells you to* directly contradicts our ability to think cognitively.

We're *supposed* to question things. Our minds are made to do it.

Human trafficking exists. Child sex slavery is real. But the majority of us view it as objective tragedies we occasionally read about in the news; horrors we assume would *never* affect *us*.

Because if it were a real, active threat, they'd be doing something to stop it… *Right?*

For me, this is no longer just a *story*. It happened—*is* happening—to someone I know. Someone I love.

And so, the more I thought about it, the more I've continued to think about it. And *obsess* over it.

I can't sleep, I've barely eaten… I've lost all focus on schoolwork. This thing has woven its way around all the logic and rationality I possess, because who are *they*, anyway? What do we really know about *them*? Enough to put all of our blind faith and trust in them doing the *right thing*…?

Leah's words play over and over in my brain, like a song on repeat that you've listened to so many times, you start hearing things you didn't notice before.

Evil masquerades as good.

Heroes are just villains with a better disguise.

And while I've never given any stock to the internet's brand of *Pizzagate, New World Order, 9/11 was an inside job* bullshit, I seem to have slowly but very surely fallen into an insomnia-ridden caffeine-fueled hole of doubt and endless questions.

Because if the people at the top were *involved in something so nefarious… wouldn't they do everything in their power to keep it quiet?*

In 1990, state and federal grand juries dismissed allegations of a child prostitution ring organized by a well-known Nebraska politician. Despite a shit-ton of evidence, they still called it a "carefully crafted hoax," and shut down all further investigations.

But then the victims received money from a civil settlement…

The CIA, the FBI, everyone was fully aware of what was happening, and yet *nothing* was done to stop it. Which would lead one to believe these organizations had a vested interest in keeping it going.

I mean, are we to believe that Epstein was working alone??

Yea... I'm saying things like that now.

Don't forget to like and subscribe.

The thing is, I know I'm chasing a white rabbit. I know I probably sound crazy and look crazy... Empty cans of Mountain Dew and pizza crusts scattered all around my desk. Bloodshot eyes from a lack of sleep and staring at screens for way too long.

I don't feel good, and I'm fading, and I *know* I promised Leah I would leave it alone, but it's not that simple.

Once the veil is lifted, it doesn't go back down. *You can't just un-learn things like this...*

I love Leah. I do. She's my friend, and it kills me inside to think about what she's been through. But the more time I spend digging, the more blogs I read, the more subreddits turn to sub-subreddits turn to sub-sub-subreddits, the less it's even really about *her*.

Sure, it's about her, and them—the children who are ripped from their lives and tortured in ways I'm sure I could never even begin to understand. But it's also about the men who've made it happen, and the people who have *allowed* it to happen. It's about the people who act like they have the citizens of this country's best interests at heart, when in actuality, they're using us as pawns in their fucked-up games. When they're not actively chewing us up and spitting us out, that is.

Leah was right. There are no heroes. My eyes are fully opened to that fact now more than ever, as I work up recursive algorithms, coding and decoding and recoding, creeping around the dark web and into secure servers like a spy, completely unseen...

The way I see it, if you're going to be a villain, you might as well be the smartest one.

I'm so deep in the weeds of what I'm doing, I barely even notice the chat notification popping up on my other monitor. LOIS has three monitors. Three is usually enough for what I do, but now that I'm hacking my damn brains out, I might need to look into getting a fourth.

Sighing, I rub my eyes and click on the flashing icon, pulling up a private message on Discord. It's from Tony. He and Reno have been trying to reach me for days. I guess they're worried about me, and I feel kind of bad.

First Leah disappears, then Cyrus, now me... It's fucked up. I should at least *try* to pop in and let them know I'm alright, but it's really easy to lose track of time when you're digging for skeletons in government files like some sort of online grave robber.

Jumping into our private server real quick, I type out a message.

BerkeleysLexLuthor: Hey guys. Sorry I've been kinda MIA. I'm deep in this really important project that's kicking my ass.

I run my fingers through my hair, noting how long it's getting. The fact that I can even sift them through the pale blonde locks means it's longer than I usually keep it.

DamnDatTony: oh you're still here??? We were starting to wonder if you'd been abducted by aliens...

LuckyShot: he still could have been...

LuckyShot: Luthor. were you probed? Does your rectum feel wider than usual??

I huff and shake my head, eyes flinging up to the code running on my top monitor. I just found some encrypted files I'm trying to break into and it's taking a while.

Hacking can be very tedious at times, like playing with a Russian doll. One door leads to another, then another, and so on and so forth. At this point, I've burrowed through so many layers of this shit, I barely even know where I am.

DamnDatTony: lol bro sounds like you have experience

LuckyShot: fuck off

BerkeleysLexLuthor: I told you before, homie, that wasn't an alien. It was your creepy uncle Todd. Ya know, the one who isn't really an uncle and always wants to tickle fight

DamnDatTony: LOL!!!

LuckyShot: oh yea I missed you tons

LuckyShot: get back to your schoolwork dick

I chuckle, reaching into my fridge for another soda. But it's empty. *Dammit.*

DamnDatTony: so can we expect to see you in the Vault anytime soon?? It's super weird to play without you

Even typing out a response takes longer than it should because I can't stop watching my malware chiseling its way through the Fort Knox security of whatever I'm trying to access right now.

BerkeleysLexLuthor: I'd love to but I really gotta get this project done

LuckyShot: Luth, have you heard from Leah at all?

At mention of Leah, the reason for all of this comes rushing back to the surface, and I check my progress once more. *I'm almost in...*

BerkeleysLexLuthor: guys I gotta get back to my work. We'll talk later.

Closing the screen, I hop out of my chair, reacquainting myself with the sensation of standing on two feet as I rush into the house. I need to stock up on sugary beverages because I think I'm about to make a breakthrough. I'm so close I can smell it...

What *it* is, I'm not exactly sure. But I'm positive it'll yield some fascinating new information.

Not that I even know what I'll *do* with said information when I find it. But the obsession is driving me. I feel like a hunter, seeking out the biggest, baddest game possible just to *know* that it's out there. Maybe tag it and move on.

I'm in this thing. I can't just *stop.*

Not when I've come this far.

Dashing over to the pantry, I grab a six-pack of Mountain Dew and a bag of Doritos. I'm just about to slink back to the garage, when my father's voice stops me.

"Lexington..."

Damn. So close.

I turn and blink at him, trying to appear casual when, really, I'm sure I currently resemble a slightly hotter version of Gollum. "Hey, Dad. What's up?"

"What's *up*?" he grumbles, looking me over. "We haven't seen you for more than five seconds in days. You look like shit. What are you doing in there??"

"I have an important project due," I lie.

"Bullshit," he retorts. "Your mother says your car hasn't moved all week."

"I don't always need to *physically* be in class," I mutter. "I can do all my assignments from home if I need to. It's less distracting..."

"Lex, you look sick." He shakes his head. "Whatever you're doing isn't healthy... You should really..."

His lecture continues, but I've tuned out his voice. I can see his mouth moving, but all I can hear is static, like a ringing in my ears.

I need to get back to my work... Back to LOIS.

I need to see what's on the other side of that wall. I need answers.

The truth. *They'll see. When I find it, they'll all understand why this was so important.*

"Dad, I just... I have to go," I cut him off, mid-scold. "I'm fine, I promise."

Stalking back into the garage, I drop everything on the floor, returning to my chair like I'm magnetized to it. My eyes are instantly glued to the screen once more while I crack open another Mountain Dew.

I click and type, and click some more, stomach twisting in thrill, and nerves.

I think I'm in…

The walls are down. I'm through the final door…

On the back-end, it reads *United States Department of Homeland Security: Pentagon database clearance granted.*

I gulp down the fizzy sweetness on my tongue with a whole fuckload of startled disbelief.

The… Pentagon?

That's where the server brought me??

"Oh fuck, oh Jesus…" I whisper to myself, scrolling through the confidential files. "I'm in the fucking *Pentagon. Oh God oh God.*"

I don't even know what I'm doing. I barely know what I'm looking for. The FBI information was locked up tight. I figured I could use my malware to get into it, but somehow it brought me… here.

To the goddamn motherfucking Pentagon.

Files are just opening up with a touch and it's beyond wild. My eyes are dry as hell, but I can't even blink. I'm just scouring them for anything I can understand. And honestly, it's an overload of information. Literally, *everything* is in here…

It's heavy. More than heavy… It's *detrimental.*

I feel like I'm staring at the arc of the covenant. *This shit is about to melt my face off.*

Reality hits me like a palm upside the head, and I start to panic.

I gotta get the fuck out of here.

This is national security… I'm a domestic fucking terrorist right now!

The sheer volume of crazy shit I'm seeing is making me want to puke, so I scuttle my way out, dropping a bomb of recursive algorithm that erases any sign I was ever there. Like a virtual DNA sweep.

Everything is coming back clean. I take a breath, rubbing my face with my hands.

That was insane. I can't believe I just did that.

A laugh bubbles in my throat, and I shake my head. Sipping from my drink, I get up and stretch, still reeling from what I just saw.

It was a lot… Like, *a lot,* a lot. *Too* much.

It's not like I meant to see it… I didn't take pictures to send to foreign enemies or anything.

I just wanted to find out about government-funded human sex trafficking...

Not launch codes for biochemical warfare, nuclear missile targets, a dossier on JFK's assassination, and what looked like some kind of intergalactic trade agreement...

Jesus fucking Christ.

It's all in my head now. That means I'm a threat...

I'm public enemy number one. Me... *an eighteen-year-old virgin, who's clearly too smart for his own good.*

My paranoia spikes quickly into the red, and I power LOIS down completely. I'm shaking as I pick up my phone, wondering if I should smash it. *Would that even do anything??*

No, dumbass, you know it won't. You're in your house. They can obviously find you.

Maybe I should leave...?

Slinking over to the window, I peek between the blinds. Everything looks normal.

No drones... No helicopters. No suspicious looking guys in sunglasses speaking into their wrists.

Okay, you've seen way too many movies. Get a grip, man.

Your algorithm worked. If you'd been traced, it would have alerted you.

My internal placations aren't really working, though. I'm jacked up to the max and on the verge of a giant freak-out.

Opening a text to Leah, I type a message with trembling fingers.

> **Me: I just want you to know that I love you. You're my best friend.**

I stare out the window for so long, I end up dozing off, startling awake with my face pressed into the blinds. Breathing becomes a little easier when more time passes and I realize that nothing is happening. *I was all worked up for no reason.*

Yawning, I head into the house, dragging myself upstairs to my bedroom. My phone buzzes in my hand as I'm crashing into bed.

> **Leah: I love you too Luth... But don't text me shit like this. It sounds like a goodbye.**

My lips quirk, eyelids so heavy I can't even keep them open enough to text her back. I pass out clutching my phone to my chest while it buzzes and buzzes.

Sounds wake me abruptly. Loud ones.

Tires screeching. Pounding on the front door.

Booming voices.

Footsteps.

I jump up in bed with my heart immediately lodged in my throat. Stumbling to the window, I peer through the curtains, only to find four black SUVs… in our driveway and on the lawn.

Oh. Fuck.

I gulp and bite my trembling lip, backing away slowly.

My mother is screaming, my dad is yelling.

Am I dreaming?

The footsteps are coming upstairs.

Is this real??

Blowing out a breath, I stand up straight, facing the door.

It's not a dream. This is really happening.

I'm officially dead.

The steps clunk up the hall, then my bedroom door smashes open as my entire life flashes before my eyes. I just stand still, quaking in place as two huge men in black suits aim guns at my head.

I'm fully prepared for them to shoot me in the face. I'm *waiting* for it…

I wonder if dying hurts…?

But instead, one of the men grumbles, "Lexington Deon?"

I stare at him for a moment, lashes fluttering as I force out a shivery, "Y-yes…"

They lower their weapons, giving each other a quick look while my brows furrow. *Maybe they're not going to kill me?*

Relief eases in for a moment… It's probably pretty foolish.

Because they quickly step forward, grabbing me by the arms. The guy on my right squeezes my bicep, and I feel a small pinch.

"Ow!" I gasp, gaping up at him as the world instantly blurs.

My legs give out, and I try to speak, but I can't move my mouth. Darkness swallows me up…

Great work, genius.

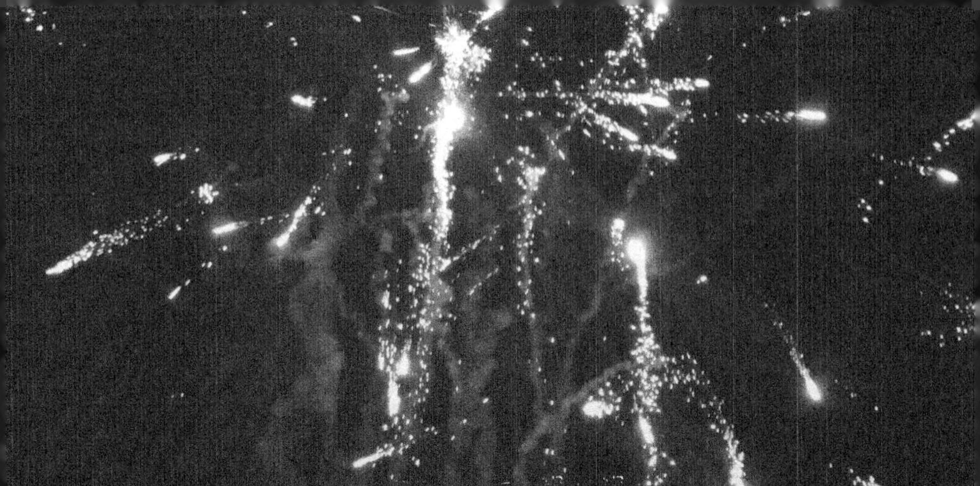

CHAPTER NINE

Ren

Roughly one year after that...

THEY SAY IF YOU LOVE WHAT YOU DO, YOU'LL NEVER WORK A DAY IN YOUR LIFE.

I've really put that theory to good use at Club Edge.

Honestly, I think I've found my calling. Maybe that should worry me, considering what my profession entails… But it doesn't.

Why would I worry? Because *society* tells us it's *wrong*?

Who the fuck is society, anyway? What do they know??

Sex workers as a whole get a bad rep. It's just a fact. As enlightened as humanity is pretending to be in this leg of the twenty-first century, they're still pretty much the same people who burned women at the stake for being *different*.

And yes, I know they never *actually* burned people in Salem. They hung them. But *burned at the stake* has a much better ring to it.

I can understand why the misnomer took off.

Man, I'd love to be burned at the stake. I even know what I'd shout while it was happening!

Back to the point, regardless of how *woke* society claims to be, they still put a stigma on people who love sex. The notion that all sex workers are diseased, toothless drug addicts living in the bathrooms at Port Authority is still very much alive, and it's extremely offensive. In general, if you love sex and want to have it with lots of people, you're looked upon as a damaged creature.

"Oh, man... What happened to them? Their parents must have really fucked them up." Things like that.

Of course, casual and frequent sex is more widely accepted in the gay community than it is for women, which just hurts my heart for all the ladies out there who love a big dick—real or fake—and want to have their hair pulled and their insides jabbed at on the regs by whoever the hell they please. *Go figure the one time us gays get the upper hand on something, and it's also the thing angry old Bible thumpers use to condemn us.*

Nevertheless, if you're someone who enjoys casual sex after a certain age, people assume you either have an STD, or are some kind of weird pervert. Or both.

That's one reason I've really taken to working at Club Edge. It's a place where I can just be myself. And *myself* is someone who thoroughly enjoys being a big ol' slut.

And an expensive one, at that.

I'm definitely not saying The Edge is a haven that celebrates sex publicly. It's still very much in the shadows, keeping business on the low to ensure the privacy of our clients. And unfortunately, I don't think everyone who works there is as *enthusiastic* about their line of work as I am. Some of them are in the exact situation I pretended to be in to get this job—broke and out of options. *But that's really none of my business.*

Dom finds the talent and offers us up to his list of wealthy, high-profile clients based on what they're looking for. Confidentiality is key, especially since so many of our regulars are elites; well-known and often very important people who sure as shit don't want their kinks on blast.

Like my father's various business associates... Hence the reason for my current quagmire.

Screaming echoes in my mind, and I stiffen, pressing my fingers to the spot where my father smacked me in the face earlier. It doesn't hurt anymore, but I can still feel it.

On the inside, I feel every lash he's ever inflicted on me. No one else can see them... But *I* can.

My emotional scar tissue nearly covers my entire body.

John Doe's friend bent *himself* out of shape when he saw me outside of The Edge, because I reminded him in the daylight of the secret stuff he does at night. It's a tale as old as time. He's ashamed of who he is, therefore lashing out at me. It's just sad.

My asshole father losing business is a nice silver-lining, though.

What bothers me just a tad is how all these high-powered men act like *I'm* somehow responsible for their problems, just like my idiot parents. They treat me like I'm some queer spider, luring them into my web of gayness. As if they weren't *fully* aware that they liked to fuck men before I came along.

If it weren't for me, they would never even dream *of dunking their balls in cocaine and tea-bagging me with them, or spitting whiskey into my ass just to suck it back out.*

Yea, all that stuff is my fault. I'm definitely the problem.

John Doe's friend, like so many others—usually only *after* they've been caught—paints me as the villain, because it's easier than just accepting the truth.

And they say *I'm* the liar.

I do lie a lot, but at least I'm honest about it. Ha!

My mind is in a fog, but my body is determined as I head back downtown to Club Edge. I'm ready to work, because frankly, I could really use the distraction. Some *real* pain for my flesh, to pull focus from the internal wretched ache. That's what this job does for me. *That's* why I love it.

Truth be told, Club Edge isn't all sunshine and rainbows. In fact, it's the opposite. It's all darkness; illicit hedonism brought to you by some nameless man of mystery none of us have ever met. Dom knows him, of course, because he runs the place for this silent owner, hiding behind all his money. But nobody else has seen his face, or even heard his name.

He's only referred to as *El Jefe*.

Whatever. Doesn't matter to me. I don't need the specifics. I just show up each night ready to get torn to shreds, then collect an envelope full of cash at the end of the week. This job fulfills me, sates my need to for release in the form of decent orgasms, and the spectacular pain that *I deserve*.

Striding in through the back, I'm immediately hit with the booming bass of music from the main club. I make my way through the corridors toward the changing rooms, nodding at bouncers and elaborate security guards, of which we have many. You'd think it would be comforting, but it's really not. They're not here to protect *us*. They're here to handle things if they get out of control, which has happened on more than one occasion.

This isn't an upscale sex club, where safety is usually a top priority. It's *upscale* because of the clients we serve and how much money we make. And yea, it's got some nice opulent decor. But Club Edge is designed to serve the *client* above all else, and they're rarely penalized for anything, shy of killing one of us.

And even then, it's not handled the way you'd hope.

I get changed and leave my stuff in my locker, doing a quick bump of molly off my knuckle before heading in the direction of the stairs. I'm almost there when I stop in my tracks.

He's here. Go figure.

I'm suddenly very twitchy and far too warm, which is probably mostly the drugs. But every time I see Mr. Kade, I'm simultaneously filled with rage and sorrow.

He's almost fifty, but he's aging very well. It really grinds my gears...

The least he could do is be balding and wrinkly, for fuck's sake.

But *no*. Instead, he's all tall and broad and gorgeous, still always in his expensive suits. The salt and pepper in his hair turning a little more salt over the years. But he looks *damn good...*

My chest aches with memories.

I'm watching him from afar as he heads for one of his usual reserved rooms. But my forehead lines when I notice him holding the door for someone. A young man wanders up beside him, and Mr. Kade takes his hand, pulling him along.

So that's who he has for the night...? I've never even seen that kid before.

And frankly, using the term *young man* to describe this person seems generous. He looks like he's barely seventeen.

I bite down hard on the inside of my cheek. *Of course. That's his type, after all.*

"What the hell are you doing just standing around??" Dom barks, startling me. "You're supposed to be upstairs. Your client is waiting."

Despite Dom's scolding, I can't take my eyes off the kid with his hand clasped by that of my dad's former colleague. The man who took my virginity.

"Who the hell is that?" I seethe in their direction as Mr. Kade brings his new toy into a private room.

"That is none of your fucking concern," Dom replies, grumpy asshole he is. "We've been over this a hundred times. *He* is not your business. He's not your client, and he never will be. *Your* client is waiting upstairs. Now, get your shit together and go take care of him."

Now that Mr. Kade and his little friend are out of sight, I slant my face to glare at Dom. He's a real self-righteous prick. Always has been, though he was certainly a lot nicer to me a year ago, when I first started. When it was *him* I was taking care of.

Call it his version of *employment training*, I guess.

I started at Club Edge as a bartender, quickly moving onto the role of dancer and *hospitality specialist*, which is Dom's way of saying someone pretty to flit around the club, flirting with guys and making them feel special. Basically, I was a human hors d'oeuvre, charming current clients and enticing potential new ones. The *main course*, however, is served in private rooms and the upstairs VIP section, which is where I work now.

I climbed the ranks fast, rising to entrée within barely three months. Mostly because Dom *loved* fucking me, but also because I'm hot, charming, and down for anything. It was the whole reason I started working here in the first place.

It's the perfect job for me. *Getting paid to fuck, while pissing off my parents as an added bonus.*

I will say, though, I *loved* being a dancer. Having all eyes on me, the captivated gazes of men shimmering ravenous desire. They were *desperate* for me, and Dom was definitely one of them. He used to shove me into his office or a dark corner somewhere in between my sets, yank my tiny leather shorts down and pump me full of cock with his hand over my mouth.

Good times.

Now, he spends our every interaction scolding me about bullshit, and it's not surprising. Men get bored pretty quickly. *I know I do.*

Plus, as fun as it was to be a dancer, what I really wanted was to be added to the *menu*. Specifically, to get into one of those private rooms with Mr. Kade. To be alone with him again, like when I was fifteen and he'd sneak into my bedroom when no one was home. Or when he'd send me to the penthouse suite he has on reserve at The Plaza, and we'd spend all night giving each other stupefying orgasms.

I know it probably seems super cliché to fall for the person who takes your virginity, but it was out of my control. My obsession with Mr. Kade started as a flicker and grew to a roaring wildfire over the few months we spent meeting up in secret.

Until he dropped me, like an ocean's worth of water, putting out the inferno we'd become.

At the time, I was highly distraught. The pain of heartbreak wasn't something I'd ever felt before, and it was insufferable. *Excruciating*. But naturally, my sadness morphed quickly into anger, and I did what every young, jilted ex-lover tries to do...

Blackmail him back into a relationship with me.

I threatened to tell his family or report him to the police. But he just laughed it off, smug fucking prick he is, and said, "Who would believe you, Warren? You're a *liar.*"

And he was right. I fucking *hated* him for it, but he was.

My entire life, I've been getting in trouble for lying, and despite how good I've gotten at it, once people find out you've lied about one thing, they assume you're lying about *everything.*

Trust is nearly impossible to regrow once you've chopped it off.

When my blackmail plan failed, I went berserk. That's also when I discovered how much I loved fucking, *and* that it was just as good with other people. So I allowed myself to get over Mr. Kade by getting under lots, and lots, and *lots* of other guys.

But I never forgot about him. *How could I?* He was the one who showed me who I am.

He was the first man to ever push himself inside me, grab me by the throat, and call me his *wicked little slut*. He gave me my awakening. And no matter how many other men I used to fill the void, I could never truly let go of that emotionally distant talisman.

Mr. Kade is what brought me into The Edge that day, over a year ago. He's the reason I'm doing this right now. And yet, I've still never been able to get him back.

Releasing a breath, I blink at Dom's dissatisfied expression, mumbling sarcastically, "Yes, Sir Dominic. Your wish is my command."

He purses his lips, jaw ticking visibly. "Don't get cute with me, Ren."

"Too late." I show him a cheeky smirk, and the set line of his mouth twitches.

"You know, that new client from last night complained about you," he rumbles. "He said you were breaking confidentiality."

"He's a whiny little bitch," I mutter, picking at my fingernails. "You know he followed me to my house??"

Dom sighs. "Well, regardless, I can't have it. Just lock it the fuck up."

"Anyone ever tell you you're a spitting image of Mussolini?" I hold in my chuckles.

He's clearly not amused.

"Enough." He glowers. "Get to work. I texted you the assignment for tonight."

I roll my eyes. "Yea, I saw it."

"Good." He smacks me hard on the ass. "Then get the fuck up there before I dock your pay." Sighing, I wander in the direction of the stairs, stopping when his voice assaults my back. "And Ren… If I catch you lurking around Kade again, we're going to have a problem. Got it?"

My jaw strains, the rage I've been suppressing since the fight with my father earlier heating my blood to a rolling boil. Ignoring his little threat, I storm up the stairs to room seven, where my client is waiting for me.

The room is dark, muffled beats traveling through the floor as I glide inside and close the door. I spot him immediately, sitting on the couch across the room, sipping a drink. He's wearing a rubber devil mask, which is sufficiently terrifying, but I ignore it, padding over, barefoot and wearing only fishnet stockings, per his request.

I don't believe I've worked with him before, unless he's a regular who's choosing to shake things up by being a total weirdo. But the text from Dom specifically noted that he asked for me by name. I can't help feeling flattered.

The table by the couch is covered in supplies; a sugar bowl of coke, candy dish filled with pills, bottles of booze, feathers, nipple clamps, a few vials of GHB and ketamine, a nine-inch dildo, and what looks to be a plate of exotic fruit.

Alright, then. Looks like we're gettin' freaky.

"Hi, Daddy," I whisper—*also, per his request*—sidling up to him and sinking onto the couch. "I've been waiting for you to come home from work."

A deep noise rumbles from within his chest, giving me tingles.

Things progress slowly, rather than the fast shoving of my head down into the lap that I'm used to. The mystery man rarely speaks, save for a curt, growly command here and there. I think it's obvious he's wearing the mask to hide his identity, meaning he's probably a politician or something.

He's sort of slim, and obviously very tall, apparent even when he's sitting. The mask covers his entire head, so I can't tell anything else about him. But it really doesn't matter.

He feeds me pieces of fruit, dark eyes set on my mouth while I suck his fingers. Then I sit on his lap and whisper, "I missed you, Daddy," while he touches my body all over.

The atmosphere in the room is hot and sticky with fevered lust, and by the time he's shedding his very expensive jacket, my cock is visibly aching through the fishnets. He's wearing a three-piece suit, only removing the jacket, vest and tie, unbuttoning his shirt and pants slowly, but keeping them on while I writhe around on his lap, holding my waist so I can grind my leaking erection on his abs.

I'm lost in my thoughts, the fire in my head burning memories with crackling orange. It's not exactly the same, but all of these older, dominant men only remind me of one person...

The guy who's downstairs right now with yet another cheap knockoff of fifteen-year-old Ren.

I know he knows that's what he's doing. Desperately clinging to the memories of us, just like I've been.

The man in the mask tears open my stockings and sits me down on his long cock, my eyes rolling to the heavens in stardust sensation.

And I bounce on him with greedy chase, whining, "Fuck me, *Daddy*. You're the only one who fucks my little pussy so good."

I see him lusting after my cock the whole time, and when he lifts the mask enough to free his mouth, leaning down to swipe my crown with his tongue, I'm fucking *flying*.

He comes in my ass, then makes me suck him until he's hard again while he plays with my wet hole. With his dress shirt hanging open, I can help but note one distinguishing mark; a tattoo on his chest...

The sexual game has my body coiled more than usual. I'm swimming in this lush, heady sex, not nearly as painful as I usually need, but still driving me higher and higher. In fact, I think this might be giving me *more* pleasure than I feel from the pain. And it's confusing...

Because I deserve *hurt*, not bliss.

I *need* to be beaten and choked and ruined. But this is different...

This is the agony of *passion*.

The masked stranger moves between my legs, fucking me slow, and deep. He puts his hands around my throat, not to punish me, but to *own* me. He rasps that he wants the dildo, and though I'm not a top at all, I find the notion of fucking him while he fucks me very exciting.

I slide it inside him slowly while he purrs and groans from beneath that stupid rubber mask. The rhythmic rocking of his hips, back on the slick object, then forward, thrusting his bare cock deep in my ass, pushes me over the edge before I'm even ready.

Clenching on him, I come, unexpected and so fucking bright. And he comes with me.

We're both just coming and crying, and this is so unlike anything I've experienced with any other client before, but it's *euphoric*. It's a moment that sets me ablaze...

I'm being held and caressed by the pleasure. A warm embrace. Like it's cradling me in a way I haven't felt since the first man who lit me up...

Callum Kade.

Riding the high of such illustrious sex goes on for much longer than I can process.

My body feels weightless. My head is in the clouds.

But I'm *awake*.

At a time like this, the last thing I want to do is go home. But I have to. It's calling me... That Upper East Side prison housing terrible memories like inmates.

I'm cleaned up and ready to leave the club earlier than usual, thanks to my mysterious client, who shall henceforth be referred to as *Mask Daddy*.

I wander outside, flipping off the black Town Car parked along the curb; the driver my parents hired to follow me around everywhere, claiming it's for my *convenience* and *safety*, though no one believes that. They're spying on me, and I find it funny.

God only knows how much money they've spent paying this ding dong to sit outside the same place for a year. What idiots.

The entire subway ride back uptown, I'm thinking about the sex tonight, with Mask Daddy. I have to squeeze my thighs together to trap my erection from growing visible at the memories.

Tonight was so much better than it's been with any of my regulars over the last year. For once, I'm swollen and achy, not from pain... from *pleasure*. And I'm buzzing on the notion that maybe the hurt in sex doesn't always need to be from physical abuse.

It can hurt just as good when your body throbs greedily for a deep, satisfying climax.

Maybe that's just how it feels when you connect... When your bodies click together, like fated stars in a constellation.

I believed I was in love with Callum Kade... *And what's love if not complete and total obsession, right?* But he only wanted me for what he could take from me, like all of the men I've been with since him—until tonight.

Hell, even my *parents*. That's why they've hated me my entire life... Because I'm not benefiting them.

Callum Kade reached into my brain and began twisting wires together like he was hot-wiring a car. It wasn't love, I know that now. It was the one thing that drives us even more than love, or sex ever could.

Power.

That's what I want right now, that's what I need to prove to them all that I have over them. I shouldn't be chasing Callum Kade…

I should be setting him free.

Strolling up our block, I pause in front of the house, remembering my father's words earlier, before I left.

Burn you to the ground…

I pull a pack of cigarettes out of my bag, sticking one between my lips and striking the match. Yellowish orange flickers, dancing before my eyes. Hypnotizing me.

I watch it burn, the flame inching toward my fingers.

Burned at the stake, huh?

The match goes out. So I strike another, lighting my cigarette. I stand on the curb, smoking and staring.

Burn…

I should set them free, too.

Fire has a way of wiping things clean. It's like a fresh start… And my parents are in need of some freshening for the stale world in which they live.

Boring rich assholes… What do they know about life, and love… Sex and pain. They exist in a mirage.

Watch it burn…

Just like him, they'll never want me, no matter what I do. I could slice my wrists open and bleed out in front of them, and they'd just stare down at me like, *"Who's going to clean up this mess??"*

Give in, Warren.

Watch it burn.

In my mind, an image of flames flicker… *A giant, scorching inferno.*

The thought tickles the pit of my stomach, like the way it feels to be on my knees with a strange man's skin slapping against mine. Like the way it feels when I watch droplets of my blood trickling out.

Release it…

Set it free.

Burn it down.

I'm in a trance, my mind buzzing in a hypnotic state as I drop my cigarette and wander slowly up the walkway, around to the back. On the patio, I find two cans of kerosene in the storage shed.

Mhm… This'll work.

The house is dark and silent inside. The staff has gone home for the day, and my parents are likely deep in their liquor and Ambien comas.

Tiptoeing through each room, I leave a trail of pungent fumes in my wake, soaking kerosene into our expensive carpets and curtains, on the furniture. Upstairs, I peek into my bedroom. And though it's been a long time, I can still see that first night, like billows of smoke in a clear sky...

In my bed, lying on my side, staring at the wall. The marks from my father's belt were nearly healed. But each lash was still fresh in my mind.

Was he trying to beat the gay out of me? Or was it just an excuse?

The knock at my door... I remember being so confused when it opened and he peered inside. My father's business associate was at our house without my father... It was odd.

At first, he was just talking to me, making up some excuse about why he was there, which I now realize made no sense. And then he told me he thought I was brave for standing up to my parents and coming out to them.

I'd actually forgotten he'd been there until he mentioned it.

I guess I was more focused on my father whipping the shit out of me with his belt.

But suddenly he had my attention. Because he seemed highly invested in my newfound sexuality.

I can still hear his words in my mind, feel the way my stomach flipped...

"Have you kissed a boy yet, Warren?"

I told him I hadn't, but that was a lie. I'd already made out with three boys from school over thay past year. But I didn't want Mr. Kade to know that. I didn't want him to judge me... *Or* I wanted him to offer to kiss me himself. And that's exactly what he did.

Because I can lie to ease things in my favor, and I can lie to correct the truth.

I can lie to give people what they want.

Callum Kade was a man in his forties, bigger than me, stronger and more experienced. *Dominant*. And the haze of hormones and unrivaled arousal blurred everything else together; all the consequences, the *wrong* and the *bad*, until we were nothing but forbidden sensation.

It feels good, you know it does...

Give in to the fire, Warren...

This is who you are.

I'm *staring* at the bed where that man kissed me and touched me and fucked me, remembering how salacious it felt *back then*.

Now, I see it for what it actually was... an illicit affair.

I know it was wrong as fuck. Does that mean I regret it? *Hell no.* It felt fucking *great.*

Most kids my age had awful, embarrassing stories about losing their virginity. *Not me. Mine was hot as fuck.*

But Callum Kade didn't love me. And I didn't love him. Because how can you love someone who sees you as an object?

You're only good at being bad.

This is who you are...

Burn it all down.

I dump kerosene all over my bedroom, then go to my parents'. As expected, they're out cold. So I empty the rest on them and leave the room, using a tie to triple-knot the door handles together on the outside.

Downstairs, in the foyer, I take one last look around, woozy from the fumes. My vision is wavy, but I don't mind. Actually, I like it.

I think this is what I was made to do. This is the control I was always meant to have.

It's the most comforting truth of all... I'm not *afraid* of being bad. In fact, I prefer it.

You think I'm evil, Dad? Well, guess what? You ain't seen nothing yet.

I'll show you a fucking villain.

Striking a match, I light myself another cigarette, holding the flame up to one of the curtains. The orange spreads, and crawls, advancing fast. *Much* faster than I thought it would.

My eyes widen as I watch the glow grow bigger, spreading *faster,* from curtain set to curtain set. A piece breaks off and falls to the floor, igniting the carpet.

Whoosh! That one goes up fast, too.

Wow... It's so bright. So beautiful.

Standing inside, I'm surrounded by dazzling fire for far too long, until the entire inside of the downstairs is engulfed in flames, the heat kissing my face and hands. Walking backwards, toward the front door, I don't want to take my eyes off the roaring glow, but I have to. I step outside just in time to see a curtain rod fall, the fire spreading up through the ceiling.

Fuck. Shit.

Get the fuck out...

I leave the house running, the frantic beeping of the fire alarm ringing in my head and synching with my heartbeat. It might wake my parents...

Regardless, I know I should get far away. But I want to watch this.

This is my creation. My art... It's gorgeous.

I decide to duck between two parked cars across the street, just to see how long it takes the fire department to arrive. The house is *filled* with rippling orange now, smoke coming from a few open windows. I still don't see my parents...

The thing is, I've never thought of murdering them before. I didn't dream of stabbing, poisoning, or choking them to death.

But *this* is fate.

If I'm meant to take their lives, it'll be in a blazing spectacle of the part of me they've always hated most... my fire.

The flames of my soul, a wild, unkempt roar.

Sirens blare from off in the distance, but I hear crashing inside the house. They're far too late.

A sinister smile passes over my lips.

Goodbye, Mr. and Mrs. Xavier.

Enjoy the burn.

"I told you, I was at *work*," I grumble, rubbing my tired eyes.

The NYPD Detective nods, jotting down everything I say. "Which is... where again?"

"Club Edge," I sigh. "On 51st and 9th."

"And you left there at what time?"

I'm sure he's asking me the same questions over and over in an attempt to trip me up, but it's not working. I have an alibi. For now... unless they're able to tell when the fire started down to the minute. I'm not sure if that's possible. *I guess we'll see.*

They're probably going to find signs of accelerant, anyway... And when they do, I'm sure I'll be the prime suspect.

"One-thirty," I tell him again. "I stopped and got a hot dog, ate it by the park. Then I went home. That's when I saw all the commotion."

Letting out a breath, I put on my most shocked and devastated face. My parents are dead, after all. The house I've lived in my whole life burned down.

I'm *sad*.

The detective peers up at me from his notepad. "Alright, Mr. Xavier, you're free to go. We'll be in touch."

In touch... Bite me.

I leave the police department feeling like the cloud of black smoke is surrounding me. Following me everywhere I go.

I killed my parents last night. I fucking *burned* them *alive.*

I'm probably going to jail.

Should I run? Get a fake passport, leave the country before they can stop me?

It's one idea… But where would I go? I *love* New York. Nowhere else is as good as here.

Maybe there won't be enough evidence. Maybe I won't get arrested…

Maybe if I do, it won't really matter.

The emptiness I normally feel is buzzing as I walk the streets, heading back toward my hotel. But I decide to stop off at Edge first to grab some drugs from my stash, since everything else I had burned up with the rest of my house.

Inside the club, I rush straight to the back. It's still kind of early, but there are people around. The faces I do recognize are all blurring together.

I go to my locker and fill my nostrils with bitter-tasting powder, doing way too much, too fast. Then I park my ass at the bar and rip a few shots, twitching while more people show up and the dancefloor fills with bodies.

My knee is bouncing rapidly while I sip my cocktail, flames flickering behind my eyes.

It looked so good… Purely stunning. The way they swallowed everything up like that…

A familiar face enters my vision, and it takes my fuzzy mind a moment to verify that he's actually there.

Callum. The *real* Callum, not a memory.

This time, I don't care about Dom's warnings. I don't really care about *anything* right now as I stand up and stalk over to my former lover; stealer of virginities.

When he sees me, his face shifts from casual to irritated in one pass over his gorgeous features.

Is that any way to look at the minor you had sex with for months?

"Hi, Cal." I smirk, fidgety and strung from all the drugs in my system.

"I can't believe you're here," he scoffs, skipping the pleasantries. "I heard about the fire on the news… I'm—"

"Don't even fucking say it," I growl.

We stare at each other for a moment in silence before his eyes soften. "You don't look so good… Maybe you should go get some rest."

"Fuck you, I always look good," I grumble.

For a split second, I think he might grin. But instead, he kills his drink, looking past me. "Well, great catching up, Warren. I must be going."

My face shifts to see what he's looking at. Surprising no one, I see a new kid—*again, probably, like, seventeen, max*—heading into his private room.

I shake my head. *This dude is unbelievable.*

Callum Kade shoots me a wink, then saunters away, taking some of my delusions with him.

I won't say it doesn't still hurt, because I think on some level it always will. But he's just a man, nothing special or worth fawning over. He's made of flesh and blood and bone, and he can be burned up just as easily as anything else.

Burn.

I swallow hard, watching him disappear into the room.

Watch it burn, Warren.

Give in to your evil nature, and set him free.

Burn it all, because this… is… Who. You. Are.

Shaking my head, I stomp toward the back exit, ready to leave. But as I turn the corner, I bump right into Dom.

Perfect.

He grasps my shoulders, steadying me with his brows zipped together and anger in his eyes. "What the hell are you doing here?? You're not even working tonight…"

"Yea, no shit," I mutter. "I just came to—"

"*Jesus*, Ren! You look like shit," he rambles over me. "I can't believe you'd come here after what happened to your house last night! Do you have any idea what kind of attention that draws??"

"*What?*" I grunt.

"Just… get outta here, okay??" He stalks past me, bumping my shoulder. "Stay away until your drama cools off."

Cools off…?

My drama*…?*

Is he fucking firing me??

My head is woozy, a giggle slipping from my lips.

Nothing is cooling off.

My eyes flick right…

Burn.

I bite my lip, fingers twitching with need.

Without a second thought, I rush to the nearest supply closet and grab a bunch of chemicals. Anything that says *flammable* on the bottle.

And I head straight for that private fucking room.

I press my ear to the door, listening as Callum loudly fucks the kid inside. I can hear them, and it reminds me so vividly of him in between my legs, jamming his cock into my virgin ass, I'm growing increasingly dizzy.

I need to burn it all, all the memories.

Who fucking cares where I end up. This has to be done.

The *power* is *mine.*

Minutes flick by like seconds while I dump chemicals everywhere, then light a match.

"You created a monster, Callum," I whisper. "In a way, you birthed me as much as my parents did. So it seems only fitting that you kiss the flames with them."

The fire in The Edge is only supposed to trap Callum inside that room. But it turns much bigger than I expected, just like last night. Before I can even process what I've done, I'm in a circle of flames, and this time I'm not sure if I'll get out.

I'm not sure if I even *care.*

Black smoke surrounds me, filling my lungs, and I cough.

I'm burning myself at the stake!

Grinning, I yell out my clever *burning at the stake* line, "I've had pee that burns worse than this!" Choking and coughing, I'm *laughing*, struggling to breathe.

This might be it… I'm probably gonna die.

I cackle even harder.

This is who you are…

Firestarter.

People are screaming, alarms sounding. And I'm *giggling.*

It's all over. I always knew it would end this way.

Just another whore burned at the stake.

My eyes flutter shut, and I fall to the floor. The vague sounds of shouting come from off in the distance.

Someone, a large man in a thick suit, dives into the room. He grabs me, hauling me over his shoulder as I pass out.

Welcome to Hell, Warren.

Satan will see you now.

CHAPTER TEN

Luthor

Today…

"I never even got to say goodbye to my parents…"

Heaviness lines my tone, the truth of this permanent reality weighing like wet cement.

"I just wish they could have had a normal son," I go on. "One who liked playing baseball and going to the movies. Instead, I'm… their biggest disappointment."

"Aren't we all?" Dash hums in response. "That's why we're all here, man. We're fucking disappointments. You're not alone. And look, your parents should feel lucky to have a kid like you, because you're smart and driven."

He pauses while my lips twist, his words of consolation easing the burden just a bit.

I can't believe how much I really like this guy already. I know he hasn't been here all that long, but somehow our personalities just click.

Then again, I'm familiar with bonding in *friendship*. It's the other part that still ties me up.

"I spent my entire childhood chasing my father's approval," Dash rasps, some clear, painful contemplation in his voice. "Trying to be just like him… And then he ended up leaving me, anyway. Leaving me with *her*…"

I'm not sure who *her* is, but if I were to guess, I'd say it's most likely his mother. He hasn't mentioned her yet over the course of our few conversations, but Dash just strikes me as a dude with no shortage of parental issues.

"I guess we're all fucked in here, huh?" I huff a chuckle, and I hear him breathe out a rumbly one in response.

"You've got that right."

We both go quiet for a bit, just thinking. Individual thoughts in a shared space.

After the basketball incident last week, Dash was in solitary for a few more days. He got out and showed back up in our cell, malnourished and dirty, but a little more refreshed than the previous time he was down there. As weird as it is for him to come back from the hole looking like he just got off a spa weekend, I'm just glad he's okay.

We didn't talk much about what happened in the rec room. He asked if Ren was alright, and if we'd talked. And I told him Ren was fine, because he always is. *It'll take a lot more than a black eye and split lip to throw him off his game.* But I left it at that, because I don't really know what to say about Ren and me. It's all too confusing.

I'd rather think about the computer I'm almost certain I'm going to find a way to make.

Despite him learning to live with his bouts in solitary, Dash is still acting sort of strange, and I'm beginning to see that it's the way he always is. For the most part, he's just Dash… My new friend, who stays up talking to me, sings about crimson and clovers, and puts me to sleep with his incessant counting out push-ups.

But every once in a while, he changes. He turns into a jittering, mumbly, panicked version of himself that makes me seriously wonder what the hell is going on in his head.

Tonight, we just got back from the showers and settled in for the night, launching into some more comforting conversation I've really grown to enjoy. But Dash seems fidgety and nervous. He keeps looking around, like he's waiting for someone.

Rather than focus on it—because it's none of my business—I decided to regale him with the story of why I'm here. I'd hoped being forthcoming might allow him to open up about his own stuff. Not that I'm *dying* to know exactly what happened with that bank robbery gone wrong. I'm just interested in everyone's super villain origin stories.

The sounds of his unsteady breaths and his squirming around rock me to sleep, as they tend to, and I begin to drift off. Floating into an easy slumber, my mind picks apart the fragments of my subconscious; memories that are distorted into strange new storylines. *Dreams…*

And suddenly, I'm in the bed with Ren. The bunk is moving around, but I can't tell if it's from us, if it's part of the dream, or if it's really happening.

Ren's wide chest of curved muscle is fluttering up and down as he shoves his pants down below his ass. *"Put your fingers in me, Lex…"*

My lips trail all over his neck and throat, soft kisses turning to ravenous sucks and bites. This feels like a memory; a distant view of the past I'm somehow seeing and feeling like it's real.

God, I wish it was real…

My balls are tight and throbbing. The bunk is moving even more now. A hushed voice that might not be us breaks through, but I'm too busy burning to pay it any attention.

I want to feel this… I've never felt it before with anyone.

Breathing heavily, my finger pushes inside a warm, tight place, all silky slick with wetness. Stretching the lace fabric aside and watching it move in and out.

"Yesss… Finger fuck me, baby…"

We shouldn't be doing this. I remember thinking that.

But I also remember my fucks slowly fading away when I felt him inside… All hot and tight and *so* soft.

My body likes being inside him…

Could we have sex? What would that be like…?

Ren wants to, I know he does. He loves sex… He has it all the time. With everyone.

But he wants to have it with me…

More than them.

My balls have their own pulse, and my dick is leaking everywhere.

He moans, but it doesn't sound like him.

"Mmm…" a voice rumbles, inserting itself into my dream. "Sweet candy Luscious… Tell me what you want."

I grind my hips into the mattress, into Ren's muscular thigh while I pump my finger, adding a second.

"God, you're tight, Dash…"

Huh…?

The bunks are rocking, and I'm on the edge… hearing and feeling different things. Sweating through my clothes while my dick jams into the plump cheek of an ass in black panties.

Gasping and muffled groans mingle in the air. It sounds like more than just me and Ren.

It sounds like Dash… But also not.

"Your ass is so snug, baby… I can barely move my fingers."

Was that me? Did I say that…?

My cock is pulsing, and I'm winding up tighter and tighter, working my hand faster and harder.

"Are you gonna come?" my echoing voice asks the body beneath me.

It's Ren, I know it is. But he's pretending he's someone else.

"Yes," he whispers, pushing back desperately against my hand. *"Make me come, Lex."*

"I wanna fuck you…" someone else groans, deep hunger in his tone. "God, Dash, let me fuck you."

Why is Dash's name slipping into my dreams??

"Feels so good," I hum, nipping his shoulder as my orgasm rushes to the surface. *"Come on my fingers, sweet flame."*

"I'm gonna…"

My body coils and I erupt quick, stomach clenching, balls contracting with every pulse that shoots out of me, all over him. Soft cries are bouncing off the walls, moans and whimpers from Ren, and me, and Dash? *I think?*

As it fades off, I feel more movement below me, and I breathe out a long exhale, consciousness still fluttering just beyond my reach. My eyes creep open, and I cringe at the puddle of cum I just left on the bed. *Dammit…*

Shifting, I nestle up in bed, saying fuck it. Because I'd rather just feel this… the warmth of being back with him, even if it isn't real.

"What's your name?" I hear him ask.

It's Dash… He's speaking to someone else. Someone who isn't me.

Maybe he's dreaming too…

As I drift deeper into my now sated slumber, I remember Ren kissing my neck and whispering that he'd *try not to hurt me.* And as good as it felt to believe him, I think I always knew it was a lie.

I wonder who Dash is seeing in his dreams…

And if they're as complicated as the person I can't get out of mine.

I wake up with the lights turning on in the row.

To this day, I'm still not sure exactly what time they go on, but my best guess is about six-thirty. Still, I wouldn't put it past them to do it at different times every day just to fuck with us. They could be on some sort of timer…

Who knows in this tomb.

Regardless of the time, with the flicker on of fluorescent lights comes a Lex Luthor lightbulb.

I damn near shoot up in bed and yell, *Eureka!*

It just came to me… the *perfect* design for a computer I might actually be able to build in this place.

Flipping around to the bottom of my mattress, I begin sifting through my secret stash of hidden goodies. I'll need a specific tool for this. I don't have the time or patience to wait until later so I can borrow a pencil and paper from Ren. This needs to happen now, while the idea is still fresh.

Hmm… what can I use?

I rifle through the contents of my mattress hole, plucking out items as I go.

Toothbrush? *No. Too dull. And if we're being honest, too valuable.*

Flashlight? *Also no. It needs to be at least relatively sharp.*

Soap, mouthwash, bottle of Tylenol, old pack of peanut butter M&M's I'm saving for a special occasion…

Landon's copy of *Catcher tn the Rye* I'm saving in case we ever need to start a fire. *Fucking hate that book.*

No no no, none of this will work.

My fingers brush a piece of paper, and I pull it out, unfolding it. It's actually two sheets. I blink at the first, tugging my lip between my teeth.

It's the drawing Ren did for me years ago… It started out as a sketch of a tattoo he wanted to give me, of fireworks. But he kept adding to it, making it more and more elaborate, until there was no way he'd be able to make it happen correctly with his shoddy tattoo gun. He's good, *really* good, but he can only do so much without the proper equipment. At least that's what he says.

This picture is fantastic, though. The fireworks are bursting into little shapes, shooting stars and bleeding hearts, with all kinds of detail woven into their embers. And at the bottom of the page, he drew two people sitting on the ground, watching them. They're holding hands.

"You make me feel like fireworks over the ocean…"

Closing my eyes, I shake my head, folding the paper back up. The one behind it is a letter Ren wrote me… An apology letter.

Breathing out slowly, I fold them both back up and stuff them away.

Can't go there. Not now.

With my arm plunged into my mattress, I finally feel something I know will work, and I tug it out quick.

My shiv!

It's essentially just a piece of cement that's been sharpened into a point made for stabbing someone. Brutal, I know, but I didn't make it, nor do I plan to use it on anyone, unless I absolutely have to. My first cellmate, O'Bannon, gave it to me way back when, and I've kept it hidden well enough that it's never been confiscated during checks.

Good thing too, because I believe this to be the perfect tool to help me carve some schematics into the wall. Having them on the wall will ensure they can't be taken away. *I mean, what are they gonna do? Paint over it?*

Fat chance.

That would require actual work to be done to this place, which is something I've never once witnessed in all my years here. Hence the reason why AP shivs are a common form of weaponry. There's no shortage of cement chunks falling from the ceilings as the building slowly erodes from lack of upkeep. Inmates scoop them up and grind them down. They're a staple in this place.

That said, they're about as sturdy as a piece of chalk, so I'll have to go easy on this thing while scraping my plans into the wall. Hopefully, it doesn't crumble to bits before I can finish.

And I'll need to be careful. If Velle finds the shiv, I'm sure he won't hesitate to shank me with it.

Putting the rest of my stuff away, I settle on my bed, facing the wall. And I get to work.

I draw a quick mockup, then label out each individual piece I need, making sure to abbreviate and detail instructions so only I can understand them.

To anyone else, it probably looks like a portrait of a washing machine or something. But to me, it's a beauty. Obviously, a mere *fraction* of the technological goddess that was LOIS, but still a worthwhile device. Like an old-school Linux; a back-alley version of what Wozniak probably used to build in his garage. Archaic, but complex in its own right.

Some of these parts will be easier to track down than others. Honestly, I'm not sure how I'm going to get this stuff, but it's something to do. And if I could actually make this, in *prison*... Well, wouldn't that just be the ultimate test to my abilities?

I'm frantically scribbling math into my wall when the bunk shifts, and

I hear the familiar sound of Dash yawning. I can feel him standing up, quietly hovering on the floor behind me, so I peek at him over my shoulder.

"Morning, roomie."

"Hey," he croaks in his sleepy voice, only a little raspier than his usual velvety brogue. *The dude has a great voice.* "Whatcha doin'?"

"Making a computer," I answer him, rounding off remainders in my head and factoring processor capacity for a standard CPU.

Dash is quiet until he murmurs, "Elaborate, please."

Chuckling, I launch into an explanation of what I'm looking to do, and we end up chatting about it for a bit. Eventually, I climb down from my bunk, preparing for my morning routine by pulling out my stashed toothpaste and toothbrush, stuffing my shiv-pencil back in there nice and deep.

I can't help but notice that Dash is extra fidgety, giving me an expectant look, like he's waiting for me to address an elephant in the room that I just don't see.

And a piece of last night ripples in my memory... *The dream I had, about me and Ren. And the unprecedented addition of Dash.*

I do remember him speaking to someone. Like someone else was in here, when I'm positive we were all alone. I thought it was part of my dream, but now he's acting like something *actually* happened last night. Something he feels like I was present for.

Oh my God... Did he hear me getting off??

Was I the one talking in my sleep?

He starts messing with his baggy jumpsuit pants, and my eyes fall to his waist, a distinct band of Calvin Klein boxer briefs peeking out. He tugs his pants up to hide it, but something is definitely going on. He didn't have jack shit a week ago. Now, he's got fancy boxers, and what looks to be a travel kit of toiletries resting on his bed.

Come to think of it, there was a bag left on his bed when we came back from dinner last night... I was so distracted, I forgot to ask him about it.

We stare at each other in silence for a beat. He looks like he wants to tell me something, but he just can't find the words.

It can't be from Ren... Can it?

No way. Dash wouldn't do that to me.

Not that Ren is *mine* or anything... He can do whatever the hell he wants, which is exactly what he does do, all day and night, with pretty much everyone in this building *other* than me.

But still, Dash is different. He's supposed to be *my* friend, above all else.

My wayward thoughts are interrupted when Joy bursts into our cell for checks, followed by Rook and Velle. Dash and I stand side by side against the wall as the two of them ransack the place for specific contraband—mainly drugs and weapons—throwing shit everywhere while Joy leans up on the bars, watching us.

Rook and Velle have this palpable sexual tension drawing them together, and it's definitely not the first time I've noticed it. But I can't even pay attention to their vibrating chemistry right now. I'm too busy peeking at my friend, wondering if he really has it in him to hide something as sneaky as fooling around with my ex in exchange for boxers and toothpaste.

My ex? Really??

Ren is *not* my *ex*.

We were never dating. Whatever the hell we were doing was over before it started, and I don't qualify to whine internally like a jealous moron just because he happens to be the only person I've ever fooled around with.

It was all a huge mistake anyway, and he's spent every day since getting railed enough to make him the official sponsor for prison sex.

Either way, my mood has officially gone lemon sour as Rook brings us to the showers. And much to my confusing dismay, Ren isn't there.

I don't get it. He's *always* around.

For years, it's been the two of us, despite how things changed for a while after he fucked me over, then spent that time in the East Wing. The point is that he came back.

He's the only one who *always* comes back.

He's my constant, no matter how crazy he makes me, and how much it sometimes *kills* to be around him, like his proximity is laced with toxic fumes.

But for the last few weeks, he's been showing up less and less, disappearing on me just like everyone else does, and I don't understand *why* the fuck I even care, but it's playing on my neuroses real bad.

Did he give up on trying to be friends? Or… is this him actually following through?

I'm quietly glum as we head back to our cell, but the moment we set foot inside, Velle pops in without a word, slapping cuffs on my wrists and shackles on my ankles.

"Where are we going?" I ask nervously, glancing at Dash and the uneasy look on his face as Velle hauls me back out into the row.

He doesn't answer me at first, and I just shuffle to keep up with his long, chain-free strides. Passing Ren's cell, I peek through the bars. It's empty.

My jaw clenches. "Velle…"

Sauntering through the doorway, he glances over his shoulder. "Your assistance is required in the East."

My pulse speeds up exponentially while we walk through doorway after doorway, hallway after hallway. The lower we get, the colder it gets, and the more pungent the scent of the ocean. In solitary row, the air feels damp, walls streaked with white from the salt.

Cracks adorn the floors and ceilings. Dead roaches decorate the corners.

God, this place sucks ass. It's a miracle anything in here actually works.

Out of solitary, we reach the East, and as we're ambling through their row of cells, my eyes catch sight of someone familiar. My gut seizes in panic I don't want Velle to see, my steps slowing in front of an exam room.

O'Malley is in there. He's strapped to a chair with electrodes on his temples.

Jesus Christ…

My brows knit in concern, but Velle barks, "Keep moving, inmate."

Scuttling along, I'm trying to stay hopeful, but I've seen this happen too many times… Inmates scooped up out of nowhere and dropped in the East Wing, whenever it tickles the Warden's fancy. It happened to Landon, and now he's gone.

Darcey, O'Malley… *Am I next?*

The reality of what's likely about to happen to me settles in my limbs, and I wrap my head around it as best I can. But rather than stuffing me inside a padded cell or an exam room, Velle opens a different door.

Peering inside, I see desks adorned with computer monitors.

I glance at Velle while he holds the door open impatiently, gesturing for me to go inside. "Let's go, 35. We don't have all day."

Swallowing my unease, I step into the room, which I can tell right away is one of the control rooms, gazing around at the setup. The monitors are displaying various parts of the East Wing, a large wall of servers opposite the desks. It's pretty dark in here, the glow from the screens providing most of the light.

Everyone in the room is *staring* at me. Two younger-looking guys sit in chairs by the desks, and a tall man whose face is vaguely familiar stands beside them. Joy is propped up on an empty desk with her arms folded over her chest… And in the middle of it all, the man of the hour.

Manuel Blanco.

The Warden of Alabaster Penitentiary isn't around all that often, and believe me, we're not upset about it. He's like a ghost who haunts these weathered halls. You don't see him, but you just know he's there.

Frankly, the man has always scared the shit out of me, and I'm not ashamed to admit it. He's creepy, with his affluent attire, pale skin, charcoal eyes, and bone-white hair. It doesn't even matter that he's technically attractive. His presence oozes evil.

I bet dogs bark at him for no reason.

Ren told me he goes by *The Ivory*, a nickname given to him from his days as a hitman for the Colombian cartel. None of us know the true origin of this island, but it's said that Alabaster Isle was a gift given to Manuel Blanco by the US Government—some sort of bargaining chip—with the stipulation that they could build a giant prison on it to house the country's worst criminals; people they wouldn't trust in the hands of federal prisons on U.S. soil.

You know, ones that actually have to adhere to constitutional law.

The Ivory wanted it to be more of an institution, where the morally bankrupt could be studied and experimented on, which is how the East Wing came to be. I'm guessing they compromised.

And like a real narcissistic sociopath, he also had a lavish mansion built on the other side of the island for himself and his minions… the guards.

I've never seen it. None of us have, but apparently, it's quite the gaudy, sumptuous monstrosity. For all the stories passed around in the Pen, there's still a great deal of mystery surrounding the Warden and his island kingdom. It's all prisoner folklore. Who knows what's true and what isn't, but the fact remains…

Manuel Blanco, *The Ivory*, reigns over this rock in the middle of the ocean… And everyone on it.

The Warden watches me for a moment in silence, his lips quirking ever so slightly before he takes a step closer. I can't even help it. I back up, bumping into Velle with a start. Velle shoves me forward, farther into the room, and my chains rustle with my anxious squirming.

"Lexington Deon," the Warden sighs, moving up to the front of me. He's got a solid few inches on me in height, but it feels like a few *feet* as I tip my chin upward to make eye contact. "My favorite of all my special little monsters. Wonderful to see you again. It's been too long."

I'm just gawking at him, fully speechless. I wouldn't know what to say right now if I was given a year to prepare.

He looks over my head, nodding behind me. And Velle immediately unchains my wrists and ankles. "I trust that you're faring well?" His black eyes freeze me solid. All I can do is blink. "You've been with us quite some time, haven't you, #35? I can only hope you're finding adequate ways to pass the time."

My heart is jackhammering in my chest. *What the hell does that mean? Does he already know about my computer blueprint?? Honestly, I wouldn't be surprised.*

"Nonetheless, this isn't a social call," he hums, pursing his lips. "Shame, too. You're quite the conversationalist." He grins, a smug display of power to frame his dickhead remark. "I require your expertise on something of the utmost importance."

I finally manage a reaction, though it's nothing more than a slow bob of my head.

"There's a glitch in one of the servers." He nods behind him. "Damn thing's been on the fritz, I'm afraid. And there's a big storm rapidly swooping up the East Coast, due to reach us in about a week's time. I need to be assured that the servers will hold up, despite the weather conditions."

My eyes glide around the room, to all the faces staring back at me blankly. My gaze lingers on Joy, since she's the only person in this room I even remotely trust. As usual, she has no reaction.

Peeking back up at the Warden, I force my voice to scrape out the words, "Sure. No problem."

He rubs his hands together. "Splendid. I knew I could count on you, Lexington."

Stepping aside, he motions toward the servers. I barely make it an inch before he stops me, holding me in place by my shirt plucked between his long fingers.

"I know this goes without saying, 35… but if you screw this up, in any way, I will personally see to it that you're hogtied and dropped into Shark Bay."

My lashes flutter at his face.

At nothing more than a slight nod of his head, both Joy and Velle remove their Glocks from their holsters, holding them at their sides. I gulp.

"Accident or not," he goes on, "if you fail to fix this issue… if you try anything, and I mean *anything*…" His subtle smirk goes wide, into a cryptic gleam. "It's a slow, painful death for you, young man. Torn to shreds by razor-sharp teeth."

He stares at me with his brows raised until I nod. But he's not satisfied.

"Speak, 35," he growls.

"Yes, sir," I mumble. "I understand. I… I'll fix it. No issues."

The Warden shoots me a pleased expression that's probably fake, dropping a cold, bony hand on my shoulder. "Perfect. Get to work, my boy genius."

He gives me a gentle shove in the direction of the server wall, and I stow my unhinged breathing and twitchy movements enough to wander over. I'm checking out the setup as I hear him tell the tall man, "Get him whatever he needs."

Then he stalks out of the room, casting a look at Velle on his way out that's hard to miss.

I'm confident enough in what I do to fix this. Which is good, because as it would appear, my life *literally* depends on it.

It's this notion that has me working extra slow, and careful, to make sure I get it right. I can't overlook anything or make a careless mistake. Every move is important.

Hours go by while I work diligently. The Warden returns to check up on me, but he's pulled away once more when his phone rings. Velle leaves to go handle something too, and I'm just reprogramming, reinforcing, rebooting and short testing. Everyone is silent for the most part, except Joy's occasional chatter with the guys, who, it turns out, are control room guards. I can't help but eavesdrop when they mention some fancy world-renowned doctor they're sending in specifically for Felix Darcey.

I'm not surprised. Manuel Blanco hit the jackpot when he scored The Carver.

Nerves fade off fast, especially once I get in my zone. This is what I do, and I find it interesting that I'm the only person on this island who knows how to do it.

No wonder the servers are in such poor condition. No one maintains them. No diagnostics are run, updates to the software or hardware… It's a free-for-all.

You'd think because of how important the system is, they'd be more inclined to take care of it. But apparently, a twenty-three-year-old *prisoner* is the only one who understands how they operate.

It gives me an immense sense of power. I mean, I could fuck shit up right now if I wanted to. If I had a *death wish*, that is. Because I don't doubt that the Warden fully intends to murder me if anything goes wrong down here, whether it's my fault or not.

With great power comes great responsibility.

By the time I'm finished, my stomach is growling, and my back is aching from standing, bending and crouching for so long. Joy brings me back up to gen-pop, straight to the caf for dinner. They even set aside a tray for me.

How sweet... I guess handling their shit for them doesn't warrant any kind of special dinner.

Ungrateful pricks.

Carrying my tray, my eyes swoop to my usual table, relief washing over me when I see my friends. Dash, Kang... Ren. They're all here, alive and well. Not rotting in solitary or having their brains cooked into scrambled eggs. I've never been happier to see them. Even Ren.

Okay, I might be really *happy to see him right now, but I'll deny it if anyone asks.*

When I sit down, Ren is visibly distraught, looking like he's about to lunge over the table to get to me. It sets off serious tingles in my gut that I'm trying like hell to push away.

I explain to them what I was doing down there, and they're all super interested. I don't want to feel like such a cornball, but I'm warm over it. Their obvious concern for me. Especially Ren's...

The group of us eat together, joking and laughing like usual. It's all I could ask for when I have nothing more than *them*.

My friends are all I've got.

After dinner, we're being walked back to the row with no cuffs, and my wrists are grateful. Ren is striding beside me, close, like he usually does. And for the first time in a while, I'm not trying to inch away.

I know it's ridiculous, but I can't help feeling like things are better when he's around... annoying me the way he does so well.

We're friends. I missed him as a friend, *that's it.*

"Can I tell you something true?" he whispers, and my face tilts in his direction. "I *was* worried."

My lips quirk. "You don't say..."

"I couldn't stand the idea of something happening to you," he murmurs as we all herd through the doorway to the row.

Joy opens his cell, and we stop in front of it, giving her the puppy dog eyes. She glares at us, but gives up quickly and proceeds to walk everyone else to their cells, leaving us alone for a second.

Hesitantly, my gaze returns to Ren's face as he growls, "If anyone even tries to hurt you, Lexington, I'll burn this fucking place to the ground."

My brow arches slowly. "That's… hypocritical."

The blue in his eyes shimmers, falling to my lips, making me instantly uncomfortable. His hand reaches for mine, slowly threading our fingers. I try to yank it away, but he only squeezes tighter.

"Let go," I grunt.

"You *do* like when it hurts." He tugs me until I stumble into him. "I know you… You hate to admit it, but having me around hurts *so good* for you."

Our chests press together, my heart jumping wildly into his muscle.

"Fuck off," I hiss, backing up. But his left hand slides onto my lower back and he pulls me closer, holding us together, hips and abs sealed. "Ren… stop." Breathless, I struggle against his grip. "You're being crazy."

"Tell me I'm wrong," he urges, using his strength to keep our bodies pressed. His fingers untangle from mine, gliding up my arm. And I don't feel like I'm trying to get away anymore… Not as hard as I should be. "You've missed me, haven't you? I can see it in your eyes… You don't *want* me to stay away."

God-fucking-damnit, this insufferable asshole. He always knows…

I can't stop picturing my dream last night; that salacious mixture of needy sensation and nostalgic shit I could've sworn I left behind.

Swallowing a lump in my throat, I gaze at him with little bits of fight slipping away. "But you have… You disappear so easily, Ren. Where did you go?"

My voice is barely audible, because I can't *believe* I'm falling back into this…

I can't believe how easy it is to forget the pain he's caused.

His fingertips move up my shoulder, grazing my neck until I shiver. "I've been trying to keep my promise, Lex… But it's far from easy. It's really *hard*."

The way his deep voice almost moans out the word *hard* has me sweating inside my clothes. Standing still with him touching me, I know I should move. I should *stop* this, the way I should've stopped it back then.

But he's right… I hate it so fucking much, but he is.

I'm a goddamn moron, but I think I really like it when he hurts me…

His hands are possessive, just like they always were… One resting just above my ass, the other brushing my jawline.

And the words rise up in my throat like bile…

"H-have you been hooking up with Dash?" I stammer, easing my stiff muscles. Leaning on him, because surrendering to the way he holds me always feels *so* fucking good.

Ren smiles; straight white teeth, dimples… *Beautiful.* Always looking like a fucking model, even in *prison*.

A little chuckle rumbles within his chest, and he hums, "*God*, baby, I want you so bad."

"That's not an answer," I croak, and he purrs teasingly.

He's seconds away from kissing me, I can feel it. Just like that first time, his lips a mere breath from mine. I hadn't even noticed my eyes closing…

Stop this… You have to stop it.

You're too smart for this.

"Keep being jealous," he whines as I fist his shirt at his sides. "It's so fucking sexy."

"Ren," I whisper, firmly.

"*Luthor…*"

"Answer me," I demand, though it quakes like a plea.

"I'm not hooking up with Dash," he says, swallowing my nervous breaths.

My head is spinning, but I manage to hold him back just enough. "Don't lie."

"I'm not. It was just that one time… when I pretended he was you."

My grip on his shirt loosens, fingers timidly touching his waist. *Did his body get harder…?*

Fuck, maybe I should just… let him kiss me. A little… just for a second.

I held out for a long time. I think I deserve a reward…

Just a quick one… for old time's sake.

While I'm persuading myself, he whimpers softly, "Will you come into my cell?" He's already walking backwards, not waiting for an answer, as he pulls me inside with him. "Let me have just a *little* taste? I've been so good, baby, I *promise…*"

I scoff over his lips, and he grins. "Fuck you, Ren… You're never *good.*"

He mewls, rumbly and desperate, greedy fingertips teasing that spot behind my ear where he used to kiss me *oh so good*. "I'll be good for you, sweet boy."

"God, you make me so fucking stupid…" I breathe, brain completely switched off as he moves us closer to his bed.

"Maybe," he croons, brushing my mouth with his. "But only I can make you come just by kissing these sweet, soft, *stupid* lips…"

Fuck me.

My dick is *throbbing*, and all I can think about is letting him have whatever he wants because I already know it'll feel *so* mind-numbingly fantastic.

Fuck it. I'm gonna do it... Let him push me down and crawl on top of me for just a few minutes of deep kisses and greedy friction, and...

A loud bang startles me out of my trance and my eyes spring open. We both turn to the entrance of his cell, looking hella guilty, flushed, and panting with our cocks pressed together.

Joy is standing there, hip popped out, billy club in hand. "You can't be serious." She shakes her head admonishingly.

"Piss off, bonerkiller," Ren grunts, running his fingers through his hair.

"Nice try," she sneers. "But I'm not fucking you, so that shit doesn't work on me. Back to your cell, 35. I thought you were better than this."

Gulping down my humility, I dip out of Ren's hold, stalking toward her with my head down.

She's totally right. *I'm such a dumbass.*

How can I be so easily hypnotized by him?? It makes no sense.

I don't like his hurt... He's just manipulating me all over again.

As soon as I'm out of Ren's cell, Joy slams the door with a loud clang. I peer back one last time, shooting him a look that's both apologetic *and* accusatory.

"Face it, Lex," Ren hisses venomously through the bars. "You will *never* get over me." I'm shaking, following Joy up the row while his voice echoes off the walls. "I'll bend over for *every* motherfucker in this place until you fucking *come back to me!!*"

Cringing, I'm practically running as the pressure pounds behind my eyes.

"Ignore him," Joy says softly, placing a gentle hand on my back as she deposits me back in my cell.

Once inside, I crash down onto Dash's bed by his legs, covering my ears with my hands while Ren screams from up the hall.

Yea, right. If only it were that easy.

CHAPTER ELEVEN

Luthor

4 years ago…

ONE OF THE MANY, *MANY* SYMPTOMS OF BEING LOCKED AWAY IN ALABASTER Penitentiary is that you start to forget details about life outside of here. What you used to do, places you used to go.

Familiarity fades. Everything before prison begins to blur, and the one thing that stays clear is *this place*.

Such could be true of any prison, but I'm sure it's worse here. Because *here,* there are absolutely no ties to the outside world. You exist in a bubble of despair; nothing but agonizing boredom as far as the eye can see, which is not very far, I might add.

At least regular prisons allow television, phone calls, visitation… Hell, *internet.* We don't even get to go outside.

I'm not kidding. I haven't seen the sun in almost a year.

So much for my glorious California tan.

This concrete tomb, located on an island conveniently outside of U.S. jurisdiction, is more like a post-apocalyptic wasteland than a prison. Life here is all about survival, the most primal of instincts. We've been reduced from human beings to numbered animals.

I'm not a person anymore. I'm inmate #35. And I've had to learn to live with that.

I won't say it comes easily, because it definitely doesn't. I've been here for almost a year, and I still wake up on occasion, expecting to be back in my bedroom.

When I first got here, it was understandably worse. I was just a petrified eighteen-year-old college student, plopped in the middle of a sea of rapists and murderers. My default setting, loner that I am, was to retreat into myself, which is a surefire way to tumble deep into a hole of depression. After all, you have nothing but time to sit around and think. And for me, it was all about how much I took for granted.

My friends, my family, school… my entire *life*. I let the good things slip through the cracks when I had them, and now the cracks have all been plastered over.

It's too late to tell my parents I love them one last time. To watch movies with them, and have dinner… I should have done it when I had the chance, instead of spending all my time online. They'll never know just how grateful I am for everything they gave me.

Sure, they didn't get me, and they never really tried. But I also didn't make an effort to bring them into my world. It's a two-way street, but we were driving in opposite directions. But despite all that, they always *loved* me, and that's the most important thing. Not everybody gets good parents, and knowing I'll never see mine again had me overflowing with gut-wrenching regret. If we're being honest, it still does.

I've made a few friends here, because talking to the crazies and weirdos is better than talking to yourself—*we steer clear of the guys who do that*. But still, I miss *my* friends every day. Tony and Reno. Cyrus. Leah… It kills me to think that they won't know why I logged off and never came back. At night, I stare at the blackened concrete ceiling and *ache* inside, imagining that they'll assume I never really cared about them.

I'm trapped alone with nothing but criminals and my thoughts. A constant haze of *what ifs*.

I hate *what ifs*. I'm a man of ones and zeros. *Uncertainty makes me itch.*

But still, human beings are adaptable. We're designed to keep ourselves alive, no matter what, which is really *all* I've been doing since I got here. *The present dominates the past.*

This is my life now, and I have no choice but to accept it. Scrape up what little joy is available to me and use it to get by. Otherwise, I'll go completely nuts.

It happens exactly as often as you'd think.

I spent three days in solitary a few months back for slapping Nieves is the face with a ham sandwich, and man, is it *quiet* down there.

In my defense, he totally had it coming. He kept trying to steal my juice box. That's a personal foul even outside *of prison.*

Solitary definitely sucks. But even worse than that experience were the few days I spent in the East Wing shortly after I arrived. That place is the kind of quiet that feels intentional.

I'm sure every bit of torture that happens down there is on purpose.

The visit consisted of being strapped to a chair and shot up with sodium pentothal—*the truth serum*—while dudes in white lab coats asked me all kinds of questions about my hacking. I assumed once they got what they wanted out of me, they'd just kill me.

That was when the Warden showed up, and told me I was *too valuable to destroy.*

Trust me, there's very little comfort in those words.

Today is your typical Whateversday in AP. Lester McDermott, aka *Dirt*, bit some guy's balls in the showers this morning and got tased by two different guards while he was ass naked. We had watery Egg Beaters for breakfast, and Toby found a toenail in his. Joy broke Parson's hand with her billy club for flipping her off, and I borrowed a book about birds from Freeman that I read two pages of before it put me to sleep.

Just another day in the Pen.

I was already tired, and the bird book didn't help. I think my body can tell it's probably nice outside, and not being able to experience it is like forced seasonal depression. I might have a Vitamin D deficiency.

Speaking of D...

A familiar booming voice and heavy footsteps wake me from my cat nap. Sitting up, I'm rubbing my eyes as Officer Chevelle blows into our cell like a tornado, followed by one of the newer guards. I think his name is Hancock.

"Checks!" Velle purposely hollers as loud as possible, even though we obviously know what he's doing.

I climb down from my bunk, joining my cellmate, Toby Turner, on the wall with an annoyed sigh while the guards toss our shit everywhere.

I used to bunk with this older guy named O'Bannon, but for some reason, they moved me to a new cell, in a completely different row. I had it to myself until Toby got here a few months ago. He's a nice guy, polite. A good conversationalist. The only problem is that he hasn't figured out the golden rule of prison: *never talk about what's happening outside of prison.*

Constantly yammering about what your friends are probably doing, obsessing about your ex, complaining about shows you're missing and ranting about food you wish you could eat is only, like, the *most* obnoxious thing you can do in here. It's the best way to drive yourself and everyone around you completely batshit.

Toby doesn't seem to follow this concept, and sometimes it makes me want to throat-punch him. But I won't, because I guess he's a friend. *A really annoying one.* He and Parker Freeman are the only guys I associate with. And between Freeman's Eeyore personality and Toby's nonstop blathering, I sincerely miss the ability to mute people.

Prison's tough for a young millennial.

"Boss," Hancock calls to Velle, and I peer over to find him holding up the bird book. "What about this?"

Velle pauses his search of Toby's mattress, squinting at the book in Hancock's hand. Then he glances at me, arching a brow. "Where'd you get that, 35?"

"I borrowed it." I give him a pointed look paired with a condescending tone I can't help using when I speak to him.

He's not amused. "From…?"

"Who cares?" I grunt. "It's a book about birds. What's the big deal?"

Velle purses his lips. Hancock is flipping through every page of the book, shaking it around as if he expects something to be hidden inside. But he finds nothing and sighs, "It's clean."

"You lucked out, Birdman," Velle sneers at me, and I roll my eyes. Cocking his head, he glowers at me. "Cool it with the attitude, inmate. I'm just looking out for the safety and wellbeing of my prisoners." His mouth curves in a patronizing smirk.

"Protecting us against ornithology?" I smirk back, fighting his attitude with my own.

"Cute," he grunts, then snaps at Hancock. "All clear."

Velle stomps toward the bars, slapping me hard on the back. "Be careful what you bring in here, inmate. Wouldn't want you to take the fall for someone else's mistake."

I'm just shaking my head in annoyance as the two of them leave, slamming the cell door on their way out.

"He's the worst," Toby sighs.

"Pretty close," I rumble while we walk around cleaning up the mess they left, keeping my thoughts on Velle to myself.

Another thing that makes Alabaster Pen sufficiently worse than other prisons is its *commissary*, if you will. In lieu of money, we pay for goods in sexual favors, either with other inmates—*a dick-trade of sorts*—or with the guards directly.

So, yea. That was a fun realization. I've never even had a girlfriend, and I suddenly had to wrap my head around servicing strange men in exchange for toothpaste.

It was the most out of my element I could ever be. With sex, yes. But with *gay sex*?

I might as well have been watching the alien Olympics.

Thankfully, I've been able to narrowly avoid becoming someone's *bitch*. That's not to say I haven't done things… It *is* about survival, after all. But apparently, I'm one of the only people in here with a skill that doesn't revolve around polishing the knob.

I know tech.

Officer Chevelle has a tendency to look out for me now because I've fixed his laptop three times since I've been here. *It's usually always malware from sketchy porn sites.* And his partner in crime, Joy Jameson, doesn't believe in paying for movies, so she has me download them for free onto her tablet.

So, there you have it. I've made it almost a year without succumbing to the sexual pressures of Alabaster Pen by being the resident IT guy. There was one time I let Dirt watch me showering in exchange for a giant bottle of Old Spice body wash and a six-pack of Orange Crush…

But that's all. I've yet to compromise myself, or my integrity, and I'm proud of that fact.

Sure, I know I could get more stuff, *better* stuff, if I were willing to give up my morals. But it's just not me. I can survive just fine on my own.

I don't need to whore myself out.

A little while later, I'm back in my bunk, leafing through the bird book when I hear the door opening at the other end of the row. Catcalls immediately echo from the other cells, and my forehead lines. *That's more noise than usual…*

Listening closely, I recognize the shouts and yelps as taunts; the kinds that are indicative of a new body on the roster.

"Fresh meat!" someone wails, followed by barking scolds from the guards.

"God help him," Toby grumbles from the bottom bunk.

Lying back, I try to ignore it, focusing on my book. But now my mind is tied up.

A new inmate, huh? I wonder who he is… If he realizes what it means to be here.

Another hour or so passes, and it's time for dinner. We mull about with our wrists cuffed as Joy and Jasper pluck inmates in our row from their respective cells. But when we reach Parker's, an unfamiliar guy wanders out before him, face tilting all around as he takes in the drab scenery.

"That must be the new guy," Toby whispers to me. "He looks young. Well, not as young as you, but still..."

Parker trots out of the cell behind the guy, and they stick close to one another while the guards herd us through the doorway. My eyes are following the new person, taking in his appearance and demeanor. He *is* young, maybe only a few years older than me, which would still make us the youngest inmates here. He's tall, maybe has a couple of inches on me, and visibly in shape, despite the baggy gray jumpsuit. Dark hair, though it's been shaved; standard practice for newcomers.

I might be the only person who likes it.

As a kid, I kept my hair longer and shaggy, rocking the surfer look. But at fourteen, I chose to shave it all off rather than getting a haircut, and I ended up liking it. The look helped cement the *Lex Luthor* nickname. Although back then, people kept calling me *Slim Shady*. But I didn't mind.

There are worse things to be called, after all.

I even went as Eminem to a Halloween party one year, and no word of a lie, had my first kiss with a girl dressed as Mariah Carey. Naturally, she was way out of my league, and like the alleged relationship between the two musicians, I suspect she only did it to throw me a bone.

Anyway, where I pull off the buzzed style, I think this new guy might look better with a full head of black hair. He's very striking. Sharp jawline, full lips, high cheekbones.

Maybe he's a model, or an actor or something.

I'm curious about the guy, and what he did to wind up here. I suppose I'm always curious about new inmates, but something about this person is intriguing me more than usual. Not just his appearance, but the way he's striding up the dingy hallway with an uninhibited air about him—*a hard thing to pull off in chains.*

He doesn't seem shocked or devastated... almost as if he *expected* to wind up in a terrible prison.

My muddled thoughts are cut short when someone bumps into me from behind, and I stumble, crashing right into the backside of the guy I've been internally scrutinizing.

"Shit, fuck," I grunt, straightening as he peers over his shoulder, brows zipped in annoyance. "I'm sorry… Someone just…" But my stuttering fades when his forehead smooths out and his eyes widen.

He slows down, turning his body toward me as he *stares*, a vibrant blue gaze gliding over my face, down my neck, torso… The rest of me, before it pops back up and his long, dark lashes flutter.

Why is he looking at me like that?

The way his bright eyes are *burning* on my flesh is unsettling. Confused and oddly jittery, I whip my face around to see who bumped into me, and what they have to say for themselves.

It's just Simmons. This scrawny idiot who's known for being notoriously clumsy.

"My bad, Luth," he grumbles, eyes on his feet. "These damn pants are too long—"

"Move it along, fuckheads!" Jasper barks at us, shoving Simmons to get him walking again. "It's just walking, not rocket science."

The new guy blinks himself back to planet Earth, pausing his gawking just long enough to resume shuffling. Although now, he keeps peeking at me over his shoulder. His lips part, like he might want to say something, but he's more wide blue doe-eyes than words, apparently.

"Like he knows anything about rocket science," I joke to Toby at my right, my gaze flicking to the pretty boy with the staring problem.

At least *I* have an excuse. He's walking in front of me. I have no choice but to look at him. But he's actively slanting his head every two seconds to glance back at me in between paying attention to where he's going.

Finally, I give up on playing coy and call him out. "Are you alright?"

You're fucking staring, *bro.*

He tugs his lower lip between his teeth, slowing his pace to fall in step at my left.

Okay, that wasn't an invitation to walk next to me…

"What's your name?" He finally speaks, voice deep and softly inquisitive.

"I'm Luthor," I answer quietly, opting for the nickname.

In prison, it's either nicknames or last names, and I definitely prefer *Luthor* to *Deon.*

The guy blinks at me as we approach the doors to the caf. "Is that your actual name? Your first name…?"

Why do you care*??*

The guy is really strange already. But there is no shortage of weirdos in here, so I guess he'll fit right in.

"It's a nickname," I grumble, following the line of inmates as we file into the cafeteria and up to the *food station*, aka the pre-made slop already arranged on trays for us to take.

The chow line moves along while guys pick up their trays and wander off, but not fast enough to get some space between me and this oddball, who's standing a bit too close for my comfort. He's *all* up in my business.

Ever heard of personal space, homie?

"What's your first name?" he asks me, sounding way more interested in a damn *name* than one should be.

"What's *yours*?" I snap, frustrated by this bizarre conversation with the nosy stranger.

We both pause in front of the next available tray. My eyes drop to it, then come back to his, and I gesture as if to say, *By all means.*

His lips curve into a delighted smile, and he picks up the tray, moving out of the way only slightly so I can grab the next one.

"Warren," he hums, right by my face, startling me with how damn close he is. His breath actually brushes my cheek. Thankfully, it's not bad. *It's actually minty.* My brow cocks, and he grins again. "That's my name. But if we're using nicknames, I go by Ren."

I stare at him for a second. *Ren... I like that. It's a nice name.*

Shaking it off, I walk toward my usual table in the back, assuming *Ren* is following me, which he is. He's dropped the awkward gawking, and is now scampering after me like an excited puppy.

I don't get why he's so fascinated by me—*if that's even what this is*—but I guess it could be worse. *He could be trying to kill me.*

So, in the interest of being polite and kind to someone who just got dumped into a shithole prison, I murmur, "My first name is Lexington. Lex."

"*Lex...*" he sighs dreamily, and I shoot him a befuddled side-eye, sloping into a seat at the table. He plops down right the hell next to me, scooting in close. "Lex Luthor!" His face whips in my direction, alit with glee. "Like from *Superman*?"

My lips quirk, and I nod. "Very good."

Either he doesn't pick up on my sarcasm, or he doesn't care. He just wiggles triumphantly in his seat. "That's clever. You kinda look like him. I mean, from the comic books. Not the Jesse Eisenberg version."

A cackle bursts out of me. It's so foreign, I cover my mouth quick, like I just burped loudly in public. *Wow. I can't believe how long it's been since I've laughed...*

Ren appears positively thrilled by it. He's pursing his lips, biting on the inside of his cheek to keep his elated smile in check.

Maybe it's been a while since he's made someone laugh?

Clearing my throat in an attempt to regain some control over this weird situation, I glance across the table at Toby and Parker, who are just eating quietly, staring at the two of us with interests piqued.

"This is Toby." I introduce my cellmate, nodding in his direction.

Ren's eyes linger on me before finally peeling them off to look at Toby. His smile fades from overjoyed to indifferent as he says, "Nice to meet you. Warren Xavier. You can call me Ren." His gaze flicks to me once more, and he winks.

Why is he winking at me??

"Toby Turner," Toby mumbles, clearly excited to join the conversation. "It's short for Tobias, but I don't like to be called that."

Ren's brows furrow. "Why not? It's a cool name."

Toby shifts. "It's my father's name... *Was*," he corrects. "I hated him..." Forking a bite of tasteless food into his mouth, he chews for a moment before adding, "That's why I killed him."

My eyes slide to my right, watching Ren's expression. His eyes are *so* blue... It's almost unnatural. They're the actual color of the sky when it's nice out. I know people always say that... *Sky-blue eyes*, and whatnot. But for him, it's accurate.

I suppose we have that in common. My eyes are really bright too, only they're light green, sorta like jasper. Everyone always comments on them. It was the one compliment I'd always get from girls...

You have the most beautiful eyes.

Ren's sunny-day eyes glisten at Toby's words, and he smirks. "I killed my dad, too."

Ohh-kay... I guess that's why he's here, then.

Toby nods, but Ren goes on. "And my mom."

"Aren't parents the worst?" Parker chimes in, chuckling. And the three of them laugh together in agreement, bonding over their shithead parents.

"What about you, Lex?" Ren pins me in place with a much more intense line of eye contact than he was giving the other two. "Do your parents suck?"

I shake my head hesitantly. "Uh, no... Actually, my parents were really great. They *are*, I mean... 'Cause they're still... alive..."

My voice trails because of how severely he's looking at me. It's really throwing me off, and I'm not sure why. He's not technically doing anything weird, just giving me his full attention. But still, it's making me uneasy.

Something about him gives off a vibe, like he's different from the rest of us. It could just be his looks, I guess, because now that I'm seeing him up-close, he really is a stunningly attractive man. Like, unfairly so. It's the sort of physical beauty that doesn't even seem real. The kind you see on TV, in movies or magazines, that makes you feel hideously inferior.

I don't consider myself unattractive at all, but sitting next to him is like sitting next to a prince.

Seriously, if he's not a model or actor, then he missed a calling.

Needing a quick distraction, I force myself to take a bite of my food. I can feel Ren watching me in my peripheral before he faces forward, picking up his fork.

"You're lucky. All I ever wanted was for my parents to love me..." His index finger begins tapping on it methodically. "I was adopted when I was two. My real parents were drug addicts. They died of an overdose..."

"Both of them?" Parker asks, wearing concern on his face. "Like, *together*?"

Ren's eyes jump to his, only for a split-second before they drop back to his food. His jaw clenches. I see it happening, but it's very subtle.

It must just be painful to talk about this...

He nods slowly. "Yea. I belonged to the state from pretty much the moment I was born. Then I was adopted by even worse people." The rapid *tap tap tap* of his finger against his fork is drawing my attention from his face. "We were dirt poor, and what little money we had, they spent on themselves, not me. I did everything I could think of to make them proud, but they just despised me. And then came the abuse..."

Toby and Parker are nodding along, as if they can relate to his story. I can't, not even a little, but I do feel bad. And yet, there's still something about this conversation that seems off...

Is it normal for prisoners to share their life stories with strangers on their first day? I've literally never met anyone who's done that.

Yea, we talk; open up about our lives outside of here, and whatnot. Some of us more than others—*cough, Toby.* But it usually takes a little going. I've never known anyone to spill their guts to random people they just met willingly.

"How'd you kill 'em?" Toby asks Ren, clearly invested.

Ren's chin lifts, eyes aimed right at Toby as he responds blithely, "I burned them alive in their bed."

Chills zip up my spine, and I shiver.

Ren must have noticed my movement, because his gaze darts away from Toby, landing on me again. He cocks his head. "What did you do? To end up here…" I swallow, feeling like I'm on trial, being cross-examined. My lips part, ready to give him the most basic version of why I'm here. But he keeps talking. "No, wait! Don't tell me. I wanna guess."

He bites his lip, eyes drifting around like he's thinking.

"Don't try to guess…" I shake my head. "It's not—"

"Lexington," he sings my name admonishingly. "You'll spoil the fun." I give him a look like he's crazy, but he's entirely unaffected by it. "If I get it right, will you tell me?"

This guy is by far the most unusual person I've ever encountered. And we're in an Alcatraz-style prison filled with nothing but cagey characters.

"You're never going to get it…" I huff.

Ren glances at Parker and Toby, both of whom know why I'm here—*the abridged version*—their amused faces corroborating my words. Ren drops his fork, shifting to face me in his seat. His knees bump mine under the table, because of how close he still is to me, but he doesn't scoot away like a normal person would. He leaves them pressed against mine, and when I try to inch back subtly, he moves in closer.

Jesus. Where did this guy even come from?? He's so… intense.

"Hmm…" Ren hums, rubbing his lower lip with his fingers while he squints like he's trying to read me. I gulp down the feeling that he might somehow be able to. "How many guesses do I get?"

"I don't know…" I mutter, uninterested. But he pouts until I sigh. "Three?"

"Psshh," he scoffs. "That's a cakewalk."

I just chuckle and shake my head. *Whatever, man.*

His eyes run a slow dip over me that makes me want to cover myself up. Then he says, "You… blew up a school with a homemade bomb?"

My forehead creases, and I gape at him, stupefied. "*What??* No."

He purses his lips. "You went on a raping spree at the old folks' home…?"

An outraged laugh gusts from my lips, and I hear Parker and Toby snorting. I glare at them, scowling away my grin. "Not even close, sicko." He beams while I eye him speculatively. "You're down to your last guess. Better make it—"

"You went after someone for revenge and bit off more than you could chew." The words come out casual, cocky and blasé, like a metaphorical mic drop.

How did he...?

My entire body freezes while I gawk at him like he's nuts, but also maybe a genius. I expected another joke answer... Instead, he just hit me in the face with pretty much the exact reason I'm in here, lacking details, of course. *But after knowing me for ten minutes.*

I'm still staring, flabbergasted, as leans in and hums, "You have to tell me if I'm right, Lex."

My lashes flutter at his face. Shaking my head, I choke out the words, "Well, yea. *Yes*. But that's... There was more to it than that."

Ren smiles, showing off pearly white, perfectly straight teeth. The smile you'd expect from someone who looks like him. "I would assume so. There's definitely more to my *burning parents alive* story."

I don't like this. I feel like I'm on display, but not even just because he's prying into my life and somehow nailing it without knowing more than my first name.

I'm gonna need to pause The Luthor and Ren Show... Put something else on for a bit. The pilot's already overwhelming the lineup.

"Did Parker tell you his story?" I ask, forking another gross bite.

Please get the attention off of me.

Parker's lips curl. "Oh yea. He dragged it out of me pretty much right away."

My gaze flings to Ren, who's grinning at Parker fondly, like they're already good friends. But there's also a wisp of cunning conviction. I'm starting to think it's a personality trait.

"Oh, I see." I glance at him between bites. "So this is, like, your thing?"

His forehead lines. "What *thing*?"

"You emotionally dissect people. Probably store up the juicy bits for gossip, or to use as leverage..." He's close enough that I can almost feel him stiffen. "I'd ask if you're a shrink, but clearly none of us are paying you for this super fun dining experience."

Ren is quietly staring at me, but I'm still just eating, forcing myself not to face him fully. I'm pretty proud of how witty I'm being right now.

But then he huffs. "You're just mad I'm figuring you out after only knowing you for a few minutes. You fancy yourself a pretty little enigma, don't you, *Lexington*?"

Pausing mid-chew, I drop my fork and turn slowly to face him. "Okay, who the hell are you?? Where did you even come from?"

He blinds me with another one of those smiles; annoyingly shiny and flawless. "Oooh, I've got him on the hook." I blink, and he bites his lip. "Time to reel him in…"

No, but seriously… what's up with this dude??

These aren't the games I like to play, man.

I'm exhausted. Talking to him for five minutes is more mentally taxing than the entire previous year in prison. I don't think it's good for me to associate with this person, regardless of how interesting and funny he is, in an unhinged basket case kind of way.

"I'm not on any hook," I mutter firmly. "I'm just identifying how much of a frickin' weirdo you are."

Glancing across the table, I look to the guys for confirmation, but they're both just watching the two of us interact like it's highly entertaining. Toby is smirking at me, and I don't like what I think that look is saying.

"Yea, well, I'm sure the same could be said about everyone in this place," Ren rasps, picking at his food, though it's clear he's not going to eat it. "We're on the island of misfit toys."

My mouth wants to slope into a grin, but I won't let it.

"You should eat." I nod at his tray. "They might not feed us again until midday tomorrow, and the sedatives in your system could make you sick."

His face slants, blue eyes sparkling at my face. "You're very thoughtful, Lexington."

"Can you please just call me *Luthor*??" I grumble in annoyance.

He shakes his head, declining to acknowledge my request. "Plus, from what I understand, there's a way to get better stuff in here… And it's probably something I'd excel at."

My gaze narrows. "You mean, like… through the guards?" Ren purses his lips and shrugs, playing it coy, but it's obvious that's what he means. I peer at Parker. "Man, you really told him everything, huh? In a matter of hours??"

"I just figured I'd let him know what to expect…" Parker shrugs.

"I have no confusion about where I am," Ren says with full sincerity. "I'm not one of these guys pounding my fists on the bars, and you won't catch me whining or complaining about the things I can't change. If I want something, I get it. But make no mistake… I fully *deserve* to be here."

We're staring at each other for a few heavy seconds that feel like minutes on end before I clear my throat and murmur, "So you're cool with selling your body in exchange for goods?"

"I'm used to it." He lifts a shoulder. I show him a puzzled look, to which he expands, "I'm a sex worker."

Alright… didn't expect that.

"Oh…" I mutter, my blinking going sort of rapid. "Really…? That's, um… cool."

He flashes me an extremely charming smile, leaning in a bit closer. "Even more interested now, huh?"

Um… Why does it feel like he's flirting with me?

My gut is churning, but I ignore it, going back to my food once more. "No, I'm just… I just think you should be careful. It might be different in here… from what you're used to, I mean."

"Do you have experience with male escorts?" he asks through a sly grin.

"No," I scoff, too defensively. "Not that there's anything wrong with it, I just…" I clear my throat again. "I'm straight, so…"

When he doesn't say anything for a moment, I peek at him, and go figure, he's still watching me. But a bit of the amusement is gone, and his blue eyes are getting this stormy look to them.

"So how have you managed to procure items in here?" His brows lift.

I'm shifting in my seat. "Um, I haven't, really," I lie, feeling like he can totally tell. *I'm a terrible liar.* Our eyes meet for a moment, but I look away fast. "I have a different skillset…"

"Like what?"

"He's a tech wizard," Parker butts in, and I seethe in his direction. *Stop telling him everything, Parker! Dammit.* "He can do anything with computers."

Ren blinks at me like he's mesmerized. "Really?" I nod reticently. "*Wow*… A hot nerd. I like it."

He bites his lip, and I'm becoming very warm inside my clothes.

Okay… He's definitely flirting.

I mean, it's fine. I don't care if he's gay. It doesn't affect me.

"Yea, well… it works for me as much as it needs to." I push past the vexing compliment that's flushing my cheeks. "Honestly, I don't need much, anyway."

Ren lets out a quiet breath. "I'll get things for you. Whatever you want."

My brows zip. "No, that's not necessary. Thanks, though."

"I want to," he presses.

I shake my head slowly, gaping at him. "Why…?"

"Because I…" His voice drifts, and for the first time since we started this strange meet-n-greet, he seems a little flustered. Staring down at his hands, he begins fiddling nervously with his fingers. "I like you. I don't want anyone to use you. You don't deserve that."

His eyes flit to mine, shining raw. Very different from the way he's been looking at me, and I can't tell if this is better or worse.

"Okay," I mumble awkwardly. "That's nice of you to say, but you don't *know* me. We just met…"

"That doesn't matter," he says with confidence. "I'm good at reading energy. And I can tell already that we're going to be *very* close, Lexington."

"I don't know… You can't seem to read the fact that I don't like being called *Lexington*," I mutter petulantly, stiffening with tension.

He cracks a smirk. "You like when I do it." His hand slides onto my leg, and I jump from the surprise of it.

"Alright, that's enough," I grumble, moving his hand off of me. "You sound like the obsessive girl who mentions getting married on a first date. Take it down a few notches, crazy pants."

He chuckles, clearly not offended by my words. *Because they're probably true.*

"You're cute," he sighs. "I don't think I've ever met anyone like you… I definitely didn't expect to in prison."

Man, this guy just isn't getting it. He seems content to keep hitting on me, no matter how hard I try to brush him off.

There's a new wave of frustration bubbling inside me, and it's definitely his doing.

"Well, you don't know everything about me from this one encounter. I deserve to be here too."

"Hmm… I don't know." He purses his lips. "You didn't kill anyone, that much is clear."

I squint at him. "How do you…" I stop and shake my head. "Shut up."

The rumble of his little chuckle is jacking my annoyance up into simmering anger.

"I'm just saying, I can tell you're here because you're loyal and selfless, and that must have gotten you into trouble." He keeps going with this bullshit, like a finger poking me over and over in the chest. "You're the hero, not Lex Luthor. You should be called *Kal-El*."

My jaw ticks, hands squeezing into fists. That's it.

"Oh yea?" I snap, whipping in his direction. He's so damn *close* to me, our faces are inches apart. "How the fuck would you know?? You're obviously insane, off your meds or something. Don't assume you know me, *Warren*, because you don't know shit. Just back the fuck off before I waste you."

Ren pulls his lip between his teeth, not intimidated by my threats in the slightest, which only pisses me off more. Because I'm *not* a fighter, and he probably thinks he knows that too. Even at my most wrathful moments, I've never been driven toward violence. But this dude shows up, and within minutes of knowing each other, I want to bash his pretty fucking face in.

Conceding, he holds his hands up, though his stupid mouth is still quirked at its corner. "Okay, Lex…" I'm seething as he corrects himself. "*Luthor*. I'm very sorry. You're right, I don't know anything about you."

I feel like he's totally patronizing me, but I'm losing all my energy to argue.

"Whatever," I grunt. "Let's just not talk anymore. You're way too new to be stressing me out so much."

I can feel him staring at the side of my face, but I refuse to look at him and keep this going. I won't play into his hand anymore.

The rest of the meal goes on in silence, for the most part. Once Ren is no longer torturing me with craziness and I'm no longer letting him, Toby and Parker break the tension with their own chitchat, much less dramatic than what this new dude brought to the table. Ren is just sitting there, poking at his food, and I don't know *why* I'm watching him, but I can't seem to stop. Honestly, I hate myself a little for being such a simpleton.

Thank God Joy shouts that it's our two-minute warning, effectively ending what will go down in history as the most fucked up dinner I've ever had. We get up to throw our trash away, and unfortunately, my reprieve is cut short when someone jabs a finger into my side.

I don't even need to turn. I already know who it is.

Jesus, he's not gonna leave me alone, is he?

"Luthor." He speaks my nickname slowly, like he's spitting out something yucky. He obviously doesn't want to call me that, and for whatever reason, I'm finding it highly amusing. I have to bite away the potential smile because I don't want to give him the satisfaction. "I hope you know I'm sorry for upsetting you. I really didn't mean to. I shouldn't have stuck my nose into your business."

He seems sincere, and I guess that's all I could ask for. I still don't know how much of him I'll be able to handle, but I'm also not one to hold grudges. It's too much effort.

"No harm done," I sigh, walking back to the table with him prancing beside me. "It's your first day. I don't blame you for wanting to feel us out."

"And when I say you're *different*, I definitely don't mean it in a bad way," he goes on. "It sucks when people are all the same, right?"

I nod. *Yea, I guess... Fair point.*

We stop next to the table, and he sways in front of me, coming across much less cocky and overconfident than before. I don't want to keep judging him by his appearance, but it's odd to see someone who looks like that fumbling.

Ren reaches out and plucks the material of my shirt between his fingers. "Do you forgive me?"

I'm a little jittery with him touching my clothes like this... Because it feels like he's trying to pull me closer to him, and I can't seem to make my feet move me away.

"Yea, totally." My palms are sweating. "Water under the bridge."

His lips curve, and he straightens, breathing out slowly. "Good. That's good... I was worried for a second there." He chuckles, a nervous breath leaving my lips in response. "Can't have you hating me now, can we?" His dark eyebrow cocks, and I nod robotically.

"Mhm..."

He finally releases his grip on my shirt, allowing me to pull away. But he's still watching me, and he doesn't stop. I can feel it happening while the guards stomp around the room, cuffing everyone and corralling us back in the direction of our cells.

It's unsettling that out of all the dangerous psychos here, this GQ model is the one to put me on edge.

"Well..." Toby sighs next to me. "Looks like someone's got a new boyfriend."

My face springs, and I scowl at him while he chuckles. "Uh, more like *stalker*." I keep my voice down, glancing over my shoulder to make sure Ren's far enough away. "Is it just me, or is he nuts??"

"Aw, come on." Toby grins. "He's harmless. Smitten... Maybe a little instantly infatuated." He laughs again at my misfortune. "But harmless."

"Let's hope so," I grumble.

"I think it's cute. *And* he's a sex worker who came from nothing?? You could be his Richard Gere!"

I balk at him like he's insane, and he cackles. Not that I even have a response to that, but it's cut short when Ren wanders up to my left side, showing me a small grin. I peek at Toby, and he winks, smirking as he slows down to walk with Parker.

Leaving me alone with my *Julia Roberts*, apparently.

Fuckin' jerk.

Ren nudges my arm, and I glance up at his shimmering blue irises.

"Will you tell me the rest of the story?" He asks, right back to the curiously seductive tone from when we walked the halls earlier. "Of what you did to end up here?"

"You pretty much guessed it," I tell him stiffly. "In a nutshell."

"I don't want bare bones, Luthor." He grins. "I want the meat."

I chuckle, unable to help it. It just comes out, and I shake my head. "The *meat* might take a while."

He laughs out loud, and something happens to my insides... Something I don't understand because I'm not sure I've felt it before. And I don't know *why* I'd be feeling it now...

It's like the warmth I used to get when I'd make Leah laugh, only more confusing. Because this time, it's deeper than just the joy of making someone else happy. It's like an appreciation for the way his laugh sounds, and how good he looks doing it.

Not in a lusting way or anything... It's just that he still looks and seems so much like the popular kids I used to go out of my way to do things for in high school, so they'd like me. Those girls who were way out of my league.

Except this time, I think the feeling might be mutual.

"Fine," Ren sighs, pursing his lips at me. "Story for another time, I guess. The tale of how you wound up here without ever killing anyone."

Another chuckle rumbles from my chest. "You don't gotta kill someone to get in here, man. You just need the right sales pitch."

Ren's smile goes wide, and he hums, "You're funny, Lexington."

"Right," I mutter.

"Smart and funny... and gorgeous," he murmurs, and my breathing shallows as I glance at him. "The whole package."

We're shuffling through the doorway to our row of cells while my stomach twists like a pretzel.

Alright, so... This might be bad.

The new guy has a crush on me.

I swallow. *It's no big deal. I'm flattered.*

And objectively, he is very good-looking. I mean, almost too good-looking, which I didn't know was possible.

But I'm not interested in guys, so it doesn't matter.

He'll have to stick with just friends.

Ren stops at his cell, and I pause too, hovering in front of him. I probably have thirty-seconds max before Joy yells at me to keep it moving. Ren is gazing at me expectantly while I fidget, wondering *why* I'm even standing here, like we just got back from a blind date and I'm walking him to his door.

God, what the hell is going on today??

"Well, I guess I'll see you… around," I mumble like an idiot, and he grins.

"Mm… maybe. I might be going out of town tomorrow." He smirks, and I chuckle.

He's funny… Why is he funny?? It makes no sense.

Guys like him don't have a sense of humor.

I guess… maybe we could be friends. Just because he's gay, he won't stop flirting with me and he makes me a little nervous, doesn't mean we can't just platonically hang out.

My lips part to say something along those lines, but before I can, Jasper stomps over, pushing open the bars to the cell.

"Alright, Richie Rich," he rumbles, shoving Ren inside with Parker and removing their cuffs. He smirks at Ren. "Survived your first day without caviar and Dom P. Wasn't so bad, right?"

Wait… What?

Ren rolls his eyes at Jasper, but I'm just standing here—when I *should* be leaving—laser-focused on what he just said.

"Hold on…" I step up to the bars as Jasper leaves the cell, slamming them shut between me and Ren. "I thought you said you grew up poor…" Ren stares at me through them, blue eyes glistening as his head tilts like a curious animal. "With your adopted… parents."

My voice goes quiet, and I blink, waiting for him to voice an obvious explanation for why Jasper would comment on him being rich.

But he just keeps staring, chewing on his lower lip, until finally he whispers, "Lex…"

His patronizing tone says it all…

He was lying.

He lied through his teeth… Maybe about everything.

My chest feels all tight, like I'm suffocating, but I don't know why.

I can't… I don't…

"35!" Jasper shouts, and I flinch back to reality. "Get back to your cell, or I'll hang you up by your pubes!"

Ren chuckles. "I think I like him."

I'm still stuttering in place, baffled down to my core.

I can't be friends with someone who lies like that. He's a sociopath.

Jasper grabs me and hauls me off, grunting, "Okay, say goodnight."

"Goodnight, Lex!" Ren calls after me, waving while I'm dragged down the row with my head spinning. "I'll be thinking about you."

Lex... Not Luthor.

My real name spoken from the pretty boy with the flaming pants.

CHAPTER TWELVE

Ren

About a year later...

"DUDE..."

"Hm?"

"Are you... Are you *jerking off?*"

Pressing my lips together, I breathe out through my nose, eyes creeping open. Now, I only see the weathered underside of Parker's bunk, rather than the beautiful images I was swimming in behind my eyelids. It's a huge bummer.

Releasing my stiff cock from my grip, I sigh. "Listen, darling, I thought we went over this when I got here... The safe assumption is that I'm *always* jerking off. So unless you're going to whisper sexy things to help move me along, keep your lips zipped, 'kay?"

Parker shifts above me, and I grin. "Sorry. It's just... you're a loud masturbator."

A cackle leaves my lips. "Really? Loud how??"

"The whole shebang, man," he grumbles. "You're whining and breathing heavy... I mean, I can *hear* you jerking your dick off. I know the expression is *beat your meat*, but damn. Take it easy on the thing!"

Now I'm laughing so hard, I'm crying. Shifting, I drape my head and shoulders off the bed. "Parker, come look at me."

"I don't want to..." he mumbles while I chuckle.

"My dick isn't visible, I promise."

He sighs, and a moment later, his head pokes out from over the edge of his bunk.

"You mean to tell me you don't like it rough?" I ask him, fully serious.

"Maybe sometimes." He shrugs. "But not *that* hard. It sounds like you're trying to rip it off."

"My guy's tough." I wink at him. "He can handle it."

"Not that I even want to know, but what's got you so wound up?" He cocks a brow.

Like I need a reason to jerk off.

But there is something… an image I've been consistently seeing in my brain, every day, for the last year, since my arrival here in Alabaster Penitentiary.

His name is Lex Luthor Deon.

And he is oh-so foine.

Even imagining him now, just regular, not necessarily naked and dripping wet from the showers earlier, has me wiggling in bed.

Lexington is *sexy as hell*, and sweet, *and* smart. Funny, loyal, very introspective. He's shy and kind-hearted and three years *younger* than me, meaning he is exactly the opposite of every guy I've ever hooked up with in my life.

And I'm fucking *obsessed*.

Coming to this prison was an adjustment, as I'm sure it is for everybody. But I'd already thought I was going to die, so I guess being shipped off to a hunk of rock in the middle of the ocean wasn't as bad. I mean, Alabaster Penitentiary *is* worse than death for a lot of people, but to me, it's not. Because on my first day here, I met some cool people, who have been my friends ever since.

And one of them is a drop-dead gorgeous hacker with the sweetest looking pink lips I've ever seen.

Fuck, just *thinking* about them gets me rock hard. Hence the need to rub out the tension frequently.

If we're swapping thoughts, Lex kind of looks like a pretty skinhead. He's *not*, of course. In fact, he doesn't have a mean bone in his body. Sure, he can be a little grumpy at times, but I blame that one where we are. He had options for the rest of his life. I didn't.

It was either die in that fire I started at Club Edge, or go to prison. And if I *had* died, I never would have met Lex, so… I'd say I hit the jackpot.

I know, right? I told you, I'm obsessed. It's not even normal.

As it happens, that mysterious owner of the Edge? It was actually the same man who runs this prison-centric island. Manuel Blanco, *The Ivory*.

Or in here, *The Warden*.

Needless to say, he was pretty pissed off about me burning down his club. Didn't seem to care that four people died... One of whom was Callum Kade. He was more angry about me ruining his thriving sex business.

On my first day here, The Ivory sat me down in a dark room, with a wall of massive, foreboding officers to my right. He bent at the waist, placing his face right before mine, dark eyes scanning over me in a way that brought up some nerves I don't usually feel when being assessed.

He's a very intimidating man, with a look that *screams* anime villain. Tall, slim, sharp angles. Older, but definitely no more than fifty, which makes his snow-white hair seem out of place. But it more than explains the nickname.

He's very attractive; cold and scary, with an air of dominance around him like the crack of a riding crop against your skin, meaning he's everything I'm usually drawn to in a man.

Except that he wanted to murder me. Maybe he still does.

Minor hurdle.

"You cost me a lot of money, Warren," he whispered over my lips, and I licked them to see if I could taste him. The black diamonds in his eyes fell to my mouth. "What do you have to say for yourself?"

"I... I'm sorry." I shivered. *Not sorry in the slightest.*

He cocked a light brow. "Are you?"

I nodded fast. "So, *so* sorry. I was just upset... The manager, Dom, had been abusing me for a year, since I got the job! Then my father's friend, who also raped me when I was fifteen, showed up and I just—"

The Warden grabbed my face in his slender fingers, squeezing so hard I was effectively shut up. "You are a fascinating creature, #48. I look forward to exposing the mold beneath this sweet candy coating."

So, that was my first meeting with the Warden... *Lovely guy.*

Then I was brought to my cell where I met my good pal Parker Freeman, the new roomie. He's a total sweetheart. A little depressed, but who could blame him?

After that... I met Lexington.

And everything went from dull gray, to magnificent technicolor. Like in *The Wizard of Oz*.

I hope I'm not dreaming...

"I can tell by the way you're gazing at nothing, you must be thinking about Luthor," Parker says, and I blink myself back to reality.

"I have no idea what you mean." I roll away in bed, slipping my hand back into my pants. "Now, if you'll excuse me, there's a completely *different* hot-bodied nerd with piercing green eyes I'm dating in my mind. And I'm *so* ready to put out..."

My eyes flutter shut as my hand tugs slowly, imagining Lex's soft lips trailing down my neck, and my chest... Maybe stopping at a nipple.

Mmm... good, baby. Bite it while you suck.

"Fuck my life..." Parker grumbles, flopping around enough to jiggle the bunk bed.

"Remind me to get you some noise-cancelling headphones," I grunt, fighting to stay in my fantasy because it's too damn good.

Lex slithers his tongue between my abs, peeking up at me while he moves lower, sliding his warm mouth over the head of my cock.

Jesus... Fuck, Lexington, you're so good at that for someone who's never, ever been with anyone else ever because that thought would literally destroy me...

Writhing up to my hand, I'm trying to be as quiet as a can, but it's difficult when this is *all* I want.

Honestly, I barely understand how my attraction to Luthor is as strong as it is. Sure, he's fuckhot and adorable, and when he smiles at me it feels like my heart is spontaneously combusting. But, like... *How??*

I've never felt this strongly attached to someone before. Especially someone I've only fucked in my dreams.

My toes are curling when a loud thunk followed by another loud clang breaks into my imaginary blowjob. *Fuck everyone who won't let me get my nut off right now.*

"Get up, you sorry sluts," the unmistakable voice of Officer Jameson has me rolling my eyes even harder.

Living on an island stocked with men is pretty much a fantasy of mine, and Joy throws a vagina into that fantasy, where one isn't exactly wanted. That said, I don't hate her presence here, because she's a total baddie. *She's like this hot, ass-kicking ninja Barbie.*

Stuffing my dick away, I slide petulantly out of bed, standing still while Joy cuffs Parker and me. Then she brings us into the long row of cells where Officer Peters is gathering up the rest of the inmates for dinner. My eyes are immediately springing around in search of Lex, and when I spot him towards the end of the pack, I nearly burst out of my skin.

Oh my God, play it cool, psycho! When have you ever acted like this??

Lex's face swings in my direction. Our eyes meet and his lips twitch as he gives me a subtle nod. Like a *sup, bro?* kind of thing.

Ugh, he's so straight.

Pursing my lips, I give him a little wave in return, immediately scolding myself inside.

Why are you waving? You're being entirely too gay right now. Get it together.

Joy and Peters march us along, and as much as I want to slow down and go talk to Lex, I don't think I should. I need to be at least five percent more aloof. I'd love to go ten, but when it comes to this kid, I just don't think I can pull it off.

For nearly twelve months, I've been crushing on him in secret, and it's *killing* me more and more each day. Granted, I think he probably knows... I'm sure everyone does. I'm clearly very bad at hiding it, which is nuts, because I'm not usually this guy. Outside of prison, I was always super chill with men I liked. Or rather, men I wanted to bone.

Okay, maybe I used to get a little whacky around Callum at times, but that was just because he was blatantly using me.

Lex is my *friend*. We've been friends since the first day we met, and I won't say I hate it, because he's a great guy and I just love being around him. But if I ever want him to see me as *more*, I'll need to play it way cooler than I am.

I mean, honestly... The first day we met, I basically declared my love for him. Not in so many words, but it was an epic disaster. And since then, I've been actively trying not to scare him, while also spending as much time around him as is possible in prison, which is nowhere near as much as I'd like. It's already a mild form of torture only being able to see him a few times a day, for meals and showers.

Don't get me started on the showers...

But hanging out alone? *Forget about it. Completely out of the question.*

My options in getting him to notice me as maybe more than a friend are seriously limited. But I refuse to give up.

I ain't no quittin bitch. I've turned many a straight boy in my day, and the thing about prison is... nothing but time.

I feel like someone's watching me, and my face springs up, hoping it's Lex. Instead, I find Officer Peters giving me a shifty side-eye. I have to roll mine.

We fucked last night. *I know, big shocker. Ren's getting laid in prison. Alert the media.*

I would have been fucking in prison regardless, because I love to do it; it's my coping mechanism, and word on the street is that the one thing prison allows, in abundance, is sex. But when I found out the only way to get stuff in Alabaster Pen is to fuck people?

Well, ya girl rolled up her sleeves, cracked her knuckles and said, Step aside, boys. I got this.

There's a new sheriff in town.

"Can I help you, muffin?" I murmur to Officer Peters, whose first name is *Josh*, by the way. He likes football, Italian food, long walks on the beach… *Oh, and his dick is fuckin* huge.

He shoots me a surly glare—an expression that must be a stipulation of the job because they all pull it off quite well—only for a moment before he grumbles, "Just keep walking, inmate."

"I *am* walking." I grin.

He peeks at Joy, then leans in a little closer to whisper, "I have some things for you."

"Appreciated," I respond, feigning professionalism. "All deliveries are to be made between the hours of nine a.m. and five p.m. within forty-eight hours of the transaction. Late fees may apply."

I snicker to myself, but Josh clearly isn't as fond of my sterling sense of humor as he is my dick-taking abilities. He narrows his gaze at me. "Stop running your mouth, 48."

I press my lips together. *Jeez… What a grump.* "Apologies, Officer. Sheesh, here I am trying to bring some light into this dark and dreary hellhole…" My rambling trails off when I glance right, catching his gaze zeroed on my mouth.

Ah, I see. He wants more.

Not the first time my services have been requested back-to-back. This place is so much better than the Edge. I've never felt more powerful.

"Tell you what?" I keep my tone hushed. "Come by after lights out and you can make two deliveries."

I lift my brows to make sure he's following my innuendo, which he definitely is. He doesn't respond, simply gives me a curt nod, straightening and shifting away from me to yell at some inmates straggling. He seems like a good guy; quiet and stoic. He was a lot less aggressive last night than some of the others, which makes me think maybe it was his first time with a guy. I never see him messing with inmates.

Not like Velle. That dude slings dick on this island like he's handing out candy on Halloween. But he's by far my favorite guard to do business with.

I'm telling you, the way that piercing lights up my prostate…

My head is swirling with sex as we enter the cafeteria, meandering up to the line for food. Lex is a few dudes down from me, so I snatch up a tray before the guy behind me can take it, shooting him a warning glare.

"Move," I growl, and he does, despite looking confused and put-out. Lex is watching me, and I nod him over, handing him the tray. "For you."

He grins, accepting it. "Thank you, kind sir."

Simmons tries to grab the next tray, but I smack his hand, picking it up myself. Lex chuckles while we walk over to our usual table side-by-side.

"So, how was your day?" I ask him as we sit down, fully invested in watching his beautiful face.

I just love looking at him. I don't even understand why, but the subtlest shifts in his facial expressions are captivating to me. I love the way his brows knit together when he's confused, the way his mouth slopes down when he's upset or worried. Even better is his smile, pillowy lips curving, the slightest indents on each side, like parenthesis for his mouth. And his eyes? *Lord have mercy.* They're just the brightest, most beautiful color green I've ever seen. Like the sea glass from the Caribbean, or mint ice cream.

Fucking stunning.

"Eh." He shrugs, picking up a dry chicken nugget. "Same shit, different day, right?"

I frown. "So, you're not having fun?"

He laughs, and I'm *swooning*. "Honestly, I don't think I've had fun once since I've been here."

Hearing those words is like a knife to the chest. "Really?" I gulp. "Not even once…?"

He peeks at me, his forehead lining. "Oh… I didn't mean… Of course I have fun with you." I blink at him, and he clears his throat. "You, Toby, Freeman… I love talking to you guys. I just meant, like, even the most fun thing we can do in here is pretty lame, ya know?"

My stomach is churning, between the despondence of knowing he's right, the incessant need to make him happy and the frustration of this platonic fucking bubble we seem to be trapped in.

I'm all torn up over this kid, from every angle.

"Lex, I…" My voice begins quiet, but I force myself to remember the confidence I have with literally *everyone else* in the world. "I want you to have fun." His eyes widen a bit. "I don't like the idea of you wasting away. You're my… You're very special to me. I'm gonna get you something cool. Don't you worry."

I place my hand on his back, rubbing gently. I feel like it's totally friendly, but he stiffens, so I pull it away, even though I so badly want to keep touching him.

"Ren, don't take this the wrong way..." he murmurs. "But I don't like accepting gifts from you."

My brow furrows. "Why not?"

"Because... we all know what you do to get that stuff." His eyes flick to mine for a second. I can't tell if he's shaming me, or if he's beating around the bush, trying to tell me he's jealous without actually saying it.

That might be wishful thinking, but what's the alternative? *He's calling me a slut??*

"You mean, the same thing everyone does to get stuff in here?" I mutter, only slightly accusatory.

"You know what I mean," he grumbles, picking at his food.

"No, I'm not sure I do..."

He sighs. "Yes, everyone does it, but you do it like... *way* more." A gasp of outrage leaves my lips, mouth hanging agape. "Look, I'm not judging..."

"It sure as shit sounds like you are," I hiss.

"No, I'm not. I'm just saying, I don't want you to feel like you have to do that stuff to get me things." He turns his face, and I catch some emotions glistening in his jasper eyes.

I don't know what they mean. *He just confounds me so much, this kid.*

"I know I don't have to," I tell him sincerely. "I *want* to. I mean, I want to give you things. I like giving you things."

I'm fumbling. I can't seem to get my point across right now. He's got me all flustered.

I want to take care of you, Lexington.

The words are on the tip of my tongue, but I feel like saying them will scare him. *I don't think friends say stuff like that to each other...*

"What if I want something so ridiculous, there's no way you'd ever be able to get it?" He smirks, turning the heavy into light, the way only *he* can.

It's one of the things I love most about him.

"Don't test my abilities, *Luthor,*" I sneer, leaning in closer. "What is this ridiculous thing you want, anyway?"

An easy smile rests on his lips while he pokes at his food. "Remember when we were talking about watching the fireworks?"

"Of course," I murmur, pulse steadily increasing.

We've spent a lot of time talking over the past few months, getting to know each other, becoming *friends*. And it should come as no surprise to learn that we're very different people. We like different music—he likes classic rock and hairband stuff from the eighties, while I like pop you can dance to, and mopey emo music... *The two wildly different sides of my fucked-up personality.* Different movies—he likes Tarantino and I like *Twilight*. He's an introverted computer nerd, and I'm a drug-sniffing club kid.

I mean, shit, we're the quintessential pieces of our opposite coasts; his Cali boy, who loves the sun and smiling, to my New Yorker, who hates everyone and everything.

But the *one thing* we have in common is a shared favorite memory of watching fireworks as kids. We bonded over it, in fact, and it lifted my heart to think that every July fourth—which also happens to be his birthday—we'd both watch fireworks over the ocean.

Three-thousand miles apart, but still... *together.*

Lex peeks at me, a sweet curve to his pink mouth and twinkle of dare in his eyes. "That's what I want."

My brows lift. "You want fireworks...?"

He nods, casually popping a nugget into his mouth.

I purse my lips. *Challenge accepted.*

Our little moment, however, is interrupted when Toby plops down aggressively at the table. He looks stressed, exhausted, rubbing his eyes and mumbling nonsense.

"Toby...?" Lex calls to him. "You alright, buddy?"

"I can't do it." Toby shakes his head over and over. "I just can't do it anymore, man. I gotta get out."

Lex sighs, and I roll my eyes.

Toby has been blathering about wanting to get out of here for the last couple of months, and it's driving us all nuts. *Yea, sure.* We *all* want to get out of here. But it's not an option, so the way I see it, just shut the hell up and serve your time.

Lex agrees with me on this.

We've seen guys try to escape before. Well, I've only seen it once, but I've heard rumors of inmates trying and failing miserably. Best-case scenario, you wind up in a padded cell down in the torture chamber known as the East Wing. Worst case, you die, shot by one of the guards.

Say by some miracle, you actually make it *outside*—which no inmate has ever successfully done before—this island is ten miles off the coast of New York. That's ten miles of ice cold, raging sea, which also happens to be infested with sharks.

The West coast of the island has been aptly named *Shark Bay.*

And yet, for some reason, despite all this information, idiots like Toby still think they're the exception. *Some people are so dumb it hurts my brain.*

"Dude, we've been over this." Lex palms his scalp. "It's never gonna happen. You'll just get yourself killed."

"No, I'm being serious," Toby whispers with his eyes bulging. "I overheard something about a sewer channel last time I was in solitary. You can get to it through the East Wing. Hamlin gave me directions." He holds up his palm to show us some writing on it.

It just says *left, right, left* a bunch of times.

My gaze lifts slowly to his, portraying my skepticism. "Homie, I say this with love... You sound cray cray."

Toby huffs, frowning down at the table.

"Yea, man... Hamlin is a wackjob," Lex adds. "He was in the East for a reason, and when he was down there, they basically turned his brain into popcorn. I wouldn't trust him with directions to his own asshole, let alone some magical sewer in the East that probably doesn't even exist."

"It does exist! I know it does," Toby whimpers.

I'm starting to feel bad for the dude. He's clearly not doing great.

"Okay." Lex folds his arms. "Let's say it does. You get to the East Wing... then what? I mean, how would you even get out of the cell?"

"I have a plan," he mutters, standing up. "I suggest you guys come with me. But if not, I guess I'll see you around, boys."

Lex and I share a look. "No, you *won't* see us around," I hiss quietly.

"Yea, if you do this, you're just gonna get yourself killed." Lex's worried eyes dart around the room for any sign of the guards.

Toby just shrugs, totally disregarding our warnings as he stands up and wanders over to the table next to ours, where the new guy, Matthews, is sitting. He climbs up onto the table.

And he takes his dick out.

"What the fuck?!" Matthews barks.

"What the fuck...?" Lex and I whisper in unison.

Before anyone realizes what's happening, Toby starts pissing. He's actually fucking *pissing* all over the table, and Matthews's food.

"You sick little bitch!" Matthews roars, jumping up and out of the spray-zone.

Then he tackles Toby to the ground.

The two of them are rolling around, throwing punches while inmates cheer and chant. Three guards rush over with their Glocks out, breaking up the fight.

"You fucking worthless maggots…" Joy pulls a Taser off her holster and sticks it up to Toby's neck, zapping the shit out of him quick.

"Fuck," Lex grumbles quietly as we watch Toby twitching on the floor.

Joy cuffs and shackles him, huffing out of exertion. "Take this prick to the hole."

Officer Peters and Linetti hoist Toby up and carry him out of the room. I don't really feel bad for him… It's his own damn fault. We told him it was stupid, but I guess this is what he was hoping for.

The dumbass really thinks he's going to somehow escape once he's down there? Poppycock.

More than anything, I'm aching for Lex right now. Toby is his friend, his cellmate. And Lex is a very empathetic person. He wears his heart on his sleeve, darling that he is. I'm sure this is highly upsetting to him.

Joy kicks Matthews on the floor, and he groans while she yells at the room, "Finish your shit, fuckfaces. Señor Piss over there just cut your dinner short. Now we gotta clear the room to clean this place up…"

Everyone whines out loud, mumbling their displeasure.

"Damn." I peek at Lex, who's chewing on his bottom lip. The sight has my nuts throbbing, but I force myself to focus, touching his arm gently. "Hey… you okay?"

"I'm just worried about him," he sighs.

Nodding, I run my fingers up and down the slope of his bicep. And he's not telling me to stop, or giving me a weird look. He doesn't feel tense, like he wants to pull away, and I'm *elated*. Eagerness thrums in my veins while I keep touching him in calming strokes of my fingertips.

God, I want to hold his hand so bad… I wonder if he'd let me. Would he freak out?

Do friends ever hold hands? I'm sure straight guys don't hold hands with their gay friends…

Parker strolls over, and I glance up at him. "You get your meds?"

He nods, eyes falling to where my hand is resting on Luthor's arm. Then he shoots me a knowing look, to which I purse my lips.

The guards gather us all up, bringing everyone back through the halls to the row in general population. I'm walking next to Luthor the whole time, casually checking on him, racking my brain for how to behave.

Back home, I had fake people I used to party with, and then I had guys I slept with. That's about it. Even the *straight* guys I used to hang out with just wanted to fuck on the DL. This stark-raving crush on Lexington is as foreign a concept as me stumbling through trying to be *platonic*.

"Ren..." He says my name quietly, disrupting my thoughts while we walk side by side, only a few inches between us. "I just wanted you to know that you don't have to... give me stuff. For me to like you." His eyes are on his shoes, and mine are on him. And I'm not breathing. "I like you anyway." My heart is leaping up into my ribcage, fingers reaching for his, until he adds, "You've become one of my best friends."

My hand retreats, and I exhale slowly to mask the ache in my chest.

I don't want to be just friends.

"You *are* my best friend," I hum.

He nods, showing me a small smile, like there's more he wants to say, but he doesn't know where to start.

I know the feeling.

We get to the row, and Lex wanders off toward his cell at the opposite end, mumbling, "Later."

Then he waves. The same small, corny wave I gave him earlier.

I can't... I can't even do this anymore.

Joy is distracted with getting the rest of inmates into their cells, so I make my move. I stroll casually past her, walking behind Peters as he brings Lex inside his cell, unlocking his cuffs. I slink inside with them, and they both gape at me.

"What the hell are you doing, inmate?" Peters growls, hand falling to his Taser.

"Just give me five minutes," I beg, desperation in my eyes. "Please?"

Peters glances to Lex, who appears sufficiently baffled. Then he returns to me, shaking his head on a frustrated exhale. "Five minutes. That's it."

He turns to leave, but I grab his shirt, holding up my cuffed hands. He rolls his eyes before unlocking them, striding out of the cell and slamming the bars behind him.

Turning to Lex, I have this overwhelming buzz of a thrill moving through me. I'm actually in his cell with him. *This has never happened before...*

We're only ever able to talk and hang out around other people, in rooms filled with criminals, psychos and the noise they bring with them. This is totally different. We're *alone*.

"Why are you in here?" he rasps, a grin breaking out on his lips at the ridiculousness of it.

"I... wasn't ready to say goodnight," I whisper, taking a step closer to him.

His eyes widen, and he backs up. "Okay..."

"I wish we had more time." I keep going, easing myself into his space while he keeps moving away. "It's so crazy to be alone with you, ya know? Good crazy, I mean."

"Ren, what are you..."

"Imagine if we weren't in prison? We could hang out alone like this all the time." I push in closer.

He seems really nervous, taking a quick seat on his bed. I plop down next to him.

"I d-don't know if we... would," he stutters, bright green eyes all round and shimmery, driving me mad. "You think we'd be friends on the outside?"

I shrug. "Maybe we wouldn't run in the same circles. But if I saw you, I'd need to meet you."

His lashes flutter, shoulders a bit bunched. "Really?"

I nod, focusing all my attention on the sudden pinkness in his cheeks... and the way it matches those pillow-soft lips. "Without a doubt."

He fidgets next to me, rubbing his palms on his thighs. "Why? I mean, what's so interesting about me?"

Oh, sweet, shy boy... fucking everything.

"I can think of a few things..." My voice travels on another whisper, eyes zeroing in on his mouth when his face slants in my direction.

Those lips are just too damn pink... I can't even fucking stop myself anymore.

Leaning in quick, I press a soft kiss on his mouth. One *second*, and it's already the best thing I've ever felt in my life.

Mouth still hovering over his, I open my eyes to find him gawking at me in pure shock.

"Ren..." he tremors. "What are you doing??"

"I'm sorry," I hum without an ounce of remorse in my tone. "I've just... wanted to do that for a while."

"Okay, but we're not..." He leans away from me. "I'm not gay."

I nod, still staring at his mouth while I suck my bottom lip. "I know."

"So you can't just *kiss* me," he grunts, sounding like he wants to be pissed, but his voice isn't cooperating. "Is this why you came in here??"

"Yea..." I sigh, reaching for his jaw.

Despite his protesting words, I pull him back for more, melting my lips onto his, a deeply blissful noise rumbling out of me from this magic sensation. He's stiff, resisting because he's scared, and confused, and I get it. I *understand*, but I also know he's not repulsed by me, or the feeling of my mouth. I know it for a fact, or he'd be fighting way harder to get me off him.

Still, when I give his bottom lip a tender suck, he yanks himself away.

"Ren!" he gasps, his hand on my chest holding me back. I can only imagine how lust drunk I must look right now. "You've gotta stop."

I exhale steadily, frustration and need clawing at my insides. "I don't want to make things weird, or confuse you. But I just think if you *tried* it… If you let me show you how good it can feel—"

"That's not gonna work," he grumbles. "I can't just pretend…" His voice trails, and something flashes over his face.

I wish I knew what he was thinking right now.

He looks anxious, confused and vulnerable, and I don't want to be the one to do that to him. I want him to *want* to kiss me… I don't want to be forcing myself on him like some kind of predator.

So as much as it fucking *kills* me, I move back, giving him some space.

"I'm so sorry, Lex." I comb fingers through my short hair. "That was fucked up. I shouldn't have done it."

His lashes flutter as he stares at me, cheeks flushed. He looks so *motherfucking good*; I swear I could devour him like the sweet, timid little cupcake he is.

But I have to restrain myself. I *have* to.

"Are you lying, Ren?" he whispers, watching me studiously.

In this moment, I hate that I'm so fucked up, and that he knows it. I hate that he sees me as a liar—*rightfully so*—and I hate that I *do* lie to him, even though I don't want to.

I can't help myself. It just happens.

My head wobbles. "I mean, it felt good kissing you just now. *Really* fucking good for me…" He shifts, clearing his throat. "But I am sorry that I lunged at you." A little chuckle slips through, and he cracks a shy smile.

"You're gonna fuck up our friendship, bro." He purses his lips to keep it in check.

"It's a risk I'm totally willing to take," I growl, blinking hard. *Down, boy.* "Sorry. Again."

"It's okay, I guess," he murmurs, and I'm just so floored.

Most straight guys would be punching me in the face right now, or at least trying to. But Lexington Deon isn't most straight guys. He's not even most *guys*. He's his own mesmerizing entity.

And in that spirit, I decide to be honest.

I know, shocking. Of course I'm still me, *so there are ulterior motives.*

"Lex," I croon his name, going for broke and touching his hand where it rests between us on the bed. "I just need to tell you that I've wanted to kiss you since the moment I saw you." I witness him swallow while he gives me a total deer-in-headlights look. "But I know you're not into guys, and I don't want you to hate me."

He glances down at my hand covering his. "I… I mean, it wouldn't exactly be fair to hate you for wanting to… kiss me."

Pulling the thread a little more, I lace my fingers through his. And he doesn't pull away.

"Did it feel good…?" I ask him, my voice barely there. "When I kissed you?"

The pinkish hue in his cheeks darkens, his gaze purposely avoiding mine.

There's my answer.

Unfortunately, Josh fucking Peters chooses this moment to whip open the bars and growl, "Alright, 48. You had your fun. Let's go."

Lex peeks up at me, our eyes melting together. I lean in a bit, and he gulps again. But he *still* doesn't move away.

"Sleep tight, beautiful," I whisper, pausing. "Can I have just one more?"

To my surprise and immense satisfaction, he nods quickly. I can feel him shaking as I drop one last kiss on his perfect mouth. Slower this time, lips barely parted, but still so warm and sweet. The fucking innocence of it has my dick aching in my pants.

God, kissing him feels like a first. A timid, trembling, greedy first kiss.

A hum leaves me as I pull back, using every ounce of strength I have to release his hand and stand up. My cock is sorta full. I'm sure he can see it, but I don't even care. I want him to see.

I want him to know this is what he does to me.

Wandering away, I feel him watching me go. And I stop at the bars, turning to him one last time. "I'll dream about you, baby… like fireworks over the ocean."

I'm in a fucking cloud of cotton candy and rainbows as Peters walks me back to my cell. He puts me inside and rumbles, "I'll be back in a few hours," before stomping off.

Oh, right. I'm supposed to suck his dick later.

But my thoughts are stuck on Lexington, sitting alone in that cell at the end of the row. What I wouldn't give to go back there and just lay with him. We wouldn't even need to hook up. I just want to touch him, and smell him, feel his warmth coiling around me.

I can't believe I got to kiss him. I can't believe he *let* me. Even just those little ones were the best kisses of my *life*. And I know he liked it… I *know* he did.

His head is tripping him up, but that might not be the hardest thing to overcome.

I wonder what he might let me do to him next time…

Sighing, I wander over to my bed, slumping onto it while Parker peers at me over the side. "How'd it go?"

I grin, brushing my thumb over my lips where they touched his. "I think we're more than just friends…"

Parker doesn't say anything, but a few moments of silence later, I hear a sniffle. My forehead creases and I sit up. "Hey, you alright up there?"

"Yea… I'm fine," he whimpers, not sounding fine at all.

"That's it. I'm coming up." I get up and climb onto the top bunk, crashing in at his feet. "What's wrong, babe?"

He doesn't look well, the dark circles under his eyes getting worse, redness around his nose from constant sinus issues.

His fingers twist in his lap as he mumbles, "I'm happy for you and Luthor. That you guys might be able to have something. I swear, I am, but… and I hate myself for feeling like this, but I'm also… kinda jealous."

I nod along, fully understanding what he's saying without him needing to elaborate.

"I'll never get that chance again," he croaks. "I'll never get to fall in love and be with someone…"

"Yes, you can," I tell him, taking his hand. "Anyone would be lucky to have you. Not that there are many great choices in here…" He snorts a tiny laugh, and I feel great for making it happen. "You're a ten, so you need to hold out for at least a seven."

"I hate you." He chuckles, but it fades fast. "Ren, I'm serious. Even outside of here, it was damn near impossible."

"The stigma's a bitch," I grumble, angry on his behalf. "But people are just idiots, and it doesn't matter. I love you, and Luthor loves you. You *are* loved, Parker. You're not defined by your condition."

His bottom lip trembles, and he bites it. I hate seeing him so upset. The kid has become like the brother I've always wanted. "I haven't been feeling well…"

"You'll be fine…"

"It's a miracle I'm even getting meds in here, but they're bullshit. It's not even all the stuff I need."

"I'll get you better meds," I tell him firmly. "Whatever you need, I'll get it for you."

He scoffs. "Ren, I'm not going to have you fucking guards to get me HIV medicine, okay?? You need to be focusing on Luthor..."

"It's not the same," I mumble.

"It is, though," he snaps at me. "You know if you want him, you're gonna have to want *only* him, right?"

He stares at me for a moment, and the weight of what he's saying sits heavy on my chest.

Would Lex want me to be... exclusive?

I don't know why that thought never even occurred to me.

I'm desperate to be more with him. Not even just for sex, but like... the boyfriendy stuff I've never done before. I would love to try it with him. But I guess that also includes me not hooking up with other people... and that definitely isn't something I've ever attempted.

I'm a free bird. Even when I'm trapped in a cage with other birds, I'm flitting around, getting my freak on. *Could I actually stop doing that? Is it even possible?*

If anyone could make it happen, it would be Lex. He's more than worth it, I know that.

But still... I'm scared. I'm nervous that I'll fuck it all up and hurt him.

He brought me back to life. I feel like a real human just from *knowing* him.

Pushing aside these hectic thoughts for now, I scoot up to Parker, wrapping my arms around his waist and just hugging him for a bit, until he eventually calms down and falls asleep.

Then I slink out of his bed and back down to my bunk. When Peters shows up, there's a brief flicker of a moment when I consider telling him to leave.

But in the end, I have to do it... What I do best.

I'll tell myself I'm doing this for Lex, and for Parker. That I'm getting them things, stuff we all need, and so it's okay. But I know it's not true.

I'm doing it for me.

Outside or inside, I'm still the same person.

The man with too much fire for his own good.

CHAPTER THIRTEEN

Luther

Weeks later…

I'VE ALWAYS BEEN A BIT OF AN OVER-THINKER. BUT IN HERE, I'M STRAIGHT-UP *neurotic.*

Maybe it's because we have time in abundance. There's so much extra time, I'm about to put it out on the street with a sign that says *Free! Please take.*

Lately, my excessive self-reflection has been dedicated to a certain prisoner friend of mine, who's done nothing but play hopscotch on my limbic system for the last eighteen months.

I'm referring, of course, to Warren Xavier—*or should I say, Miley Cyrus… Since he came in like a wrecking ball.*

Let's face it, I stood very little chance of resisting Ren's friendship. Even if I'd wanted to, he probably wouldn't have let me. And it probably seems foolish to associate with him, being that he lies as easily as breathing and manipulates without realizing he's doing it. But from the start, I just couldn't help being sort of dazzled by him.

He's not like any of my other friends. *For starters, he's actually cool.*

Ren is charming as hell, smart and generous. Easy to talk to, with the jaded witticisms you'd expect from a New Yorker who's been around the block a few times.

He's also next-level obsessive, and totally fucking crazy.

But despite staggering through this friendship like I'm drunk in a cornfield maze, the most complicated aspect of hanging out with Ren is the fact that he apparently has a *diesel* crush on me.

At first, I assumed he was just a flirtatious guy, which he is. But lately, it seems to have upgraded, from casual remarks and lingering looks, to a constant, possessive fawning.

A few weeks ago, he punched Gomez in the face for bumping me in the showers. I mean, I'm not saying it wasn't hilarious, but it was also totally unnecessary. It's like if anyone even comes *near* me for anything, Ren steps in. Like he's my bodyguard.

Or worse... My hothead boyfriend.

He's always giving me gifts, and finding little excuses to touch me. *And then there's the matter of him kissing me in my cell that time...*

Yes, it was awkward, and it made my stomach feel strange, but I'd prefer to just act like it never happened and move on. Unfortunately, denial doesn't work when the person who kissed you is Warren Xavier.

Just the other day, for example, we were the last ones out of the showers, and he came up behind me, and whispered in my ear, "I think about your lips all the time..."

I think about your lips all the time?? I mean, who even says that??

What would there be to think about, anyway? They're just *lips*. Everyone has them. But he acts like mine are some rare delicacy he had to travel far and wide to find, and now he's just *desperate* to spend long amounts of time savoring them.

It's a confusing thing to know your friend is thinking when he's looking at you.

I've stressed to him countless times that I'm not gay, and I'm *not* going to reciprocate whatever it is he's trying to do. But he doesn't seem worried about it. For someone so apparently smitten, he sure as shit takes rejection well. Almost too well... Like he doesn't believe me when I say it's never gonna happen.

The whole thing has thrown me all outta whack. I'm constantly wondering if today's the day he's going to shove me into a corner and assault with me that soft, lying mouth again.

He won't do it... I'm sure he won't.

If he wanted to kiss me again, he would've done it already.

After all, it's been weeks...

My thoughts are jumbled and hectic as we're brought out of our cells for the rare late shower group. It's strange having no cellmate again.

While everyone else is walking out as a pair, I'm all alone. I guess I should be used to it, but it just feels weird.

The night Ren kissed me, Toby tried to escape. He was sent down to solitary after he made a scene in the caf, and he never came back. We asked and asked if he was okay, but no one would tell us anything. Finally, Officer Porter—this affable dimwit known for having loose lips—caved and told us the truth.

Toby managed to get out of the prison. I guess that plan of his worked because he actually made it *outside*. Porter wouldn't tell us how, but apparently, Toby was cornered by guards on the West coast of the island, where this huge, jagged cliff overlooks the water. Rather than facing the repercussions of coming back, Toby dove into the ocean and was eaten by sharks.

Not kidding. That's what we were told... Fucking Jaws ate my cellmate alive.

It was likely the fall that killed him—he would have impaled himself on the rocks for sure. But either way, the sharks got a nice meal, my friend gone, and I have a cell to myself once more.

I was pretty upset when it happened, but moving on is the only option. Grieving does nothing to help you get by. People die everywhere. In here, it serves as a warning to the rest of us.

We're trapped for life, even if the *life* part isn't guaranteed.

Sauntering to the end of the row, I sidle up next to Ren. He notices me right away, as usual, but his greeting tonight is a little less enthusiastic than usual.

I can always expect him to offer me a smile with extra eye contact that warms my face. Sometimes, he'll brush his fingers on my back and whisper a corny pick-up line, like, *"Did it hurt... when you fell from heaven, angel?"*

It makes me squirm uncomfortably when he does it... But when he *doesn't* do it, I'm even more tense. So who the hell knows what's going on.

Today, however, his smile seems a bit strained, as is his voice when he murmurs, "Hey, Lex."

Why doesn't he seem excited to see me? Is he mad at me or something??

The neediness I'm feeling from not getting his full attention is beyond fucking moronic, and I stuff it down inside myself, focusing on being a *friend*, rather than a codependent weirdo.

"What's up...?" I ask nervously, noting that Ren's hand is on Parker's back... Not mine.

But when I peer around him, I notice that Parker is sorta slumped, and Ren is helping him walk. Parker's skin is too pale, almost a grayish hue taking over him, and it's clear he's lost more weight than normal in this place. He was already a slim guy, but now he's almost skeletal.

"Is he alright?" I watch him cough into his arm while Ren rubs his back tenderly.

Ren peeks at me and shakes his head. The worry in his blue eyes sends my heart crawling up my throat.

Parker is Chronic HIV positive. Against all odds, he's managed to get some medication in here, though I'm still not even sure from *where*. Sometimes Joy brings him down to the East for a few hours, or a few days, when he isn't feeling well. But lately, he's been not feeling well more and more, and it's fucking dreadful because there's nothing any of us can do to help. His body is turning on him, and I hate to sit here and watch it happen.

Ren and I help Parker to the showers, then we get him cleaned up. I can tell he doesn't want to let us, but Ren is very insistent. Seeing it warms me inside. He's a good friend, and he really has his moments that make you forget about all the fucked-up shit he's done.

The murders, and the lying and the nonstop meaningless sex… It's just one part of who he is.

Parker gets dressed and leans against the wall, wrapping his arms around himself to calm his rampant quivering. I don't want to leave him alone, but Ren and I have to shower ourselves and we're running out of time. I get undressed and quickly hop under the water, closing my eyes and biting my lip at how fucking freezing it is at first.

"You're insane." Ren chuckles, and I peek at him.

"It wakes me up." I shiver. "Can I borrow some of that?" I nod at his bottle of expensive body wash.

Grinning, he hands it over. I squirt some out, the scent that fills my nostrils reminding me of *outside*. Somewhere nice, maybe a fancy hotel with a marble shower and a window overlooking a beautiful view. *Really, anywhere but here.*

"This stuff rocks," I hum, lathering myself while Ren does the same to my right.

"Want me to get you some?" he asks, and my eyes fling in his direction.

"Uh, no. It's okay," I mumble. "I still have some of my Old Spice, I just forgot it."

Ren gives me a look, like he knows I'm lying. He can always tell, I guess because he's such a good liar himself. *He sniffs out lies like a drug dog sniffs out kilos.*

"It's my treat," he says.

I'm about to argue, but he holds his hand up to stop me, and I just roll my eyes, a small grin tugging at my mouth.

Turning away, I'm trying to focus on washing myself, but I find my gaze slinking over to him against my will. He's so tall, and despite being in a place with the worst food ever, his body is still immaculate.

I've never seen a body like his in real life. So sculpted… *everywhere*, like someone carved him out of stone. The shoulder traps and the pecs and the abs, and that *V*… I have them too, but his look photoshopped, occasional splatters of ink decorating his muscles.

My eyes move up to his face, and I flinch when I find him smirking at me.

Shit… He saw me looking at his body. That's totally gonna send the wrong message.

But why was I looking…? Why do I look at it so often??

"It's okay to look, curious boy," Ren murmurs, lifting his arms to sift fingers through his dark, wet hair. "I won't tell anyone."

He winks at me, and I scowl. I'm about to quip back when a noise pulls our attention to Parker.

He just collapsed.

"Jesus Christ." Ren rushes over.

I grab us both towels, handing one to him while he lifts Parker off the floor.

"Yo! We need help in here!" I shout.

Velle and Joy come stomping into the room, faces falling when they see us holding up an unconscious Parker.

"Fuck…" Velle hums, taking Parker's limp body from Ren. "Shit shit shit." He looks and sounds… worried.

I never thought I'd see the day.

"Can you tell if he's breathing??" Joy examines Parker's face, lifting his eyelids.

"How would I know?" Velle puts his hand up to Parker's throat. "I think so? It's hard to tell…"

"You assholes really have no EMT training at all?!" Ren barks.

Velle glares at him. "Do *you*??"

Ren's forehead lines, and he bites his lip. "I do, actually. I… I was a trainee. Hold on, let me see him…" He steps over, but Velle shoves him back.

"I don't have time for your bullshit," he snaps, then growls at Joy. "Call Johansson."

"We're so not equipped for this..." she mutters, pulling her walkie off her belt and stepping off.

My pulse is hammering while I wring my hands.

Parker needs to be okay. I can't deal with losing another friend.

"Hancock!" Velle shouts, and Officer Hancock, who's been guarding the exit to the showers, perks up. "Get everyone back to their cells."

The rest of us get dressed while Velle and Joy haul Parker away, most likely bringing him down to the East, since it's the only place that's even remotely like an infirmary.

"He'll be alright," I tell Ren.

He's visibly distraught, and it hurts my heart.

We're uncuffed as we walk back to the row, I assume because Hancock didn't have time to cuff us all. When we get to Ren's cell, he takes my hand, the sudden contact startling me. Before I can process what's happening, he pulls me inside with him. And to my utter shock and disbelief, Hancock just closes the bars. *Leaving* me in here.

He must be too distracted to notice... What the fuck?!

I stare at Ren for a second with wide eyes, and he stares back at me, his mouth sweeping into a tiny, elated smile. But he crushes it and clears his throat, wandering over to his bunk to sit down.

"Sorry, I just... I can't be alone right now," he says. "With him gone... I'm so worried, Lex."

"I know." I take a seat next to him. "Me too."

"I'm glad you're here," he says softly. "You're all I have."

His hand slinks over and scoops mine up, threading our fingers. My skin is buzzing, despite the chill in the air. I'm tense, because he's holding my hand, and now, we're sitting in his bed, *alone*, and this is the same thing that happened the last time... When he kissed me.

I peek at him, biting my lip.

He's not gonna kiss me again...

Ren pulls his legs up onto the bed, then rests his head on my shoulder. My stomach is flipping and flopping like a fish out of water.

We're just friends...

He's upset about Parker and needs to be comforted... by a friend. That's it.

"Can we talk about something?" he hums.

"Like what...?" My thumb grazes his.

"Anything. I need a distraction. My thoughts are running crazy right now."

"Yea," I mumble. "What do you wanna talk about?"

He's quiet for a moment before he asks, "Remember when you told me about your friend? And how you were digging for all this information to maybe help her..."

I nod. "Yea. Leah..."

Ren stiffens. I feel it happening before he shifts his face off of my shoulder to look at me. "Was she your girlfriend?"

I don't know why the obvious jealousy in his tone warms my chest, but it does, and I can't help choking back a grin. "No. She wasn't my girlfriend." He breathes out slowly. "I mean, I did love her. I *do*. But I'm not sure if it's that kind of love."

"Shouldn't it be easy to tell?" He blinks, looking very curious.

"I have really no idea," I mutter. "I was starting to think maybe relationships... weren't for me. Like, I never got that feeling, ya know? I was waiting for it to come, but it didn't..."

"Maybe you just hadn't met the right person." He tilts his head, vibrant blue eyes calling me out.

A chuckle puffs from my lips. "Really? *You*, of all people, are saying that? You're monogamy-repellant. Would you even know *how* to have a relationship?"

His gaze narrows. "Well, Bridget Jones, not all relationships have to be *monogamous*. Some people believe in freedom of love and sex, outside of the archaic social constructs that have been drilled into our heads for a millennia."

"Jesus..." I cackle, and he grins. "Tell us how you really feel."

"I'm just saying. People act like loving sex makes you an evil harlot, but the human body is designed to enjoy sex. It's not just for making babies."

"I guess you're the expert on that," I tease.

"Pretty much," he sneers. "Not that you'd know this, breeder, but sex still feels *really* fucking good without a vagina involved."

A gulp follows my forced laugh. The sex topic tends to make me a little jittery.

"Yea, well... I wouldn't know either way." I chew on my lower lip.

My hand is getting kind of sweaty, but he refuses to let go of it.

Ren straightens, turning his body to face me. "What do you mean?"

My eyes dart to his, then down to my lap, awkwardness coiling my muscles.

God, this is humiliating. We don't talk about sex much, so the fact that I've never had it hasn't come up yet. I mean, *Ren* talks about sex all the time, but I usually just listen and nod along. I have no contribution to the sex conversation, outside of a few measly makeout sessions, a couple boob-grabs, and some phone sex with random internet girls, which is pretty much the same as masturbation, in theory.

Am I really going to tell the most sexually active person I've ever met that I'm a virgin?? He'll probably never speak to me again.

"I… It doesn't matter." I yank my hand out of his.

"If it doesn't matter, then just tell me." He scoots closer, and I back up.

"No."

"Come on… *please*?" He pouts. "I wanna know what's got you all clammed up." He grins, walking his fingers up my leg. "It's pretty adorable."

I smack his hand away. "Cut it out."

"Lex…" He flutters his lashes, and I shake my head. "*Luthor…*"

"Ugh." I roll my eyes. "Just drop it, please."

"Not a chance." He grabs me by the thighs and yanks me fast until I crash onto my back. Then he quickly climbs on top of me, straddling my hips.

My eyes are wide, chest pumping frantic breaths. "Ren! Get off me! What are you—"

"Tell me what you're hiding." He leans over, trapping me beneath him on the bed. I try to fight him off, but he snatches my wrists and pins them down. "Or I'll have to kiss it out of you…"

What??

"Dude… stop," I whimper, my blood rushing like a waterfall in my ears. "I thought we said no more kissing…"

"That was your rule," he says pointedly. "I never agreed to it."

"Fine," I huff, glaring up at him. "I'll tell you. Will you please just… let me up?"

He shakes his head, smirking like the annoying idiot he is. "Not until you spill the beans."

"*Ren,*" I whine. "It's embarrassing."

His face lights up. "Ooh! I love embarrassing sex stories. Go."

I purse my lips, working up to this. *Fuck my life… Here goes nothing.*

"I don't have any embarrassing sex stories…" I mumble. "I don't have any sex stories at all…" I blink up at him, raising my brows while I wait for him to catch onto what I'm saying. But he's just staring blankly at me. "Because I've never… had it." His brows zip. "*Sex.* I've never…"

"You've *never* had sex?" he murmurs, like he's repeating a phrase I'm trying to teach him in another language. I shake my head. "You're a... *virgin??*"

I'm sure my face is Hawaiian Punch red right now. There's fire burning from my neck up, humiliation and discomfort causing me to wriggle beneath him. "Yes, I'm a fucking virgin, okay?? Now, can you *please* get off me? I can't breathe..."

Ren eases up a little, releasing my arms and sitting back on his knees. He looks sufficiently shocked. I might be the first virgin he's ever met in his life, which makes me feel like an even bigger loser.

The hot, popular kid knows I'm a virgin. Great.

And why did you need to add hot *to that statement?? We could've done without it.*

"Lex... Wow," Ren gasps, head shaking in disbelief. I roll my eyes, propping up on my elbows. "I had no idea."

"Really?? 'Cause I wear my *I'm a virgin* sandwich-board everywhere I go, so really, that's on you," I growl, grinding my teeth.

He grins and bites his lip. "You've never had sex with *anyone...?*"

"Not that I'm aware of," I mutter sarcastically. "Can we please change the subject? This is super awkward."

He blinks. "I'm sorry. I didn't mean to make you feel weird."

"Yea, well... I get it. Being a virgin is pretty much the opposite of sleeping with literally *everyone*, so I guess you wouldn't be the person to understand, would you?"

His jaw tightens visibly. "Are you saying I'm a slut?"

"Are you saying you *aren't* a slut?"

Our heated glares are stuck together, tension palpable in the air.

"I'm not ashamed of who I am," he hisses, deadly quiet.

"I never said you should be," I tell him, trying to get across that I'm not shaming him for being himself. "I'm just pointing out that we're two very different people. It's not a bad thing, it's just... a fact."

The fury on his face fades, Adam's apple bobbing in his throat. "Are you ashamed... of being a virgin?"

"No, I'm not *ashamed*, I just... I don't know, it's embarrassing," I grumble.

"Why is it embarrassing?" He lies down on top of me, propping his chin up on his hands, resting on my chest.

Okay, so I guess we're staying like this.

"Trying to get laid was never a top priority for me," I explain. "Plus, I was always younger than everyone in my classes. I went to college when

I was sixteen. Most girls want to hook up with older guys, not younger ones."

His lips twitch. "Girls are stupid."

I laugh, rolling my eyes. "Yea, like you're not exactly the same way. You forget how much you've told me, *Warren*. The professor, your boss… your dad's friend? All the guys you went for were older than you."

He purses his lips, like he's annoyed that I'm right. It's kind of adorable.

"Yea, well… maybe I'm done with older guys," he says quietly.

My chest tightens, and I can't help fidgeting. We're both quiet for a moment, but it's not comfortable. It feels like all the air is being sucked out of the room by a giant vacuum.

Breaking the silence, I ask, "Are you judging me? For being a nineteen-year-old virgin…"

Ren's lips slope into one of his blinding smiles, dimpling to the max. "No. Virgins are cool."

I have to laugh at how much of a fool he is. "Right."

"I'm serious," he says firmly. "You know that whole thing where guys fantasize about popping a girl's cherry…? Well, it's not just a straight dude fantasy…"

I clear my throat. "Yea, but… I'm not…"

"I know you're not gay, Lex," he sighs, finally rolling off of me.

But he doesn't exactly let me free either. He nestles up to my side, slinging a heavy arm around my waist.

"What are we doing…?" I breathe, unsure of what the hell is happening here. We're supposed to be *friends*.

Straight guys don't cuddle with their gay friends… I'm not positive about this, but I'm pretty sure.

"You're cold," he hums, pulling my body into his. "I can feel you shivering."

It might not be from that…

Relaxing just a little, I allow myself to melt into him. I know it's weird, but honestly, when does this happen? You don't get this kind of human contact in prison. Even if you opt to have sex with someone, it's not *this*.

This is comfort. The warmth of being held, inside and out.

So what if we're two guys? Boys should be able to cuddle with their friends if they want to.

"I can't believe this is happening…" Ren sighs, fingers trailing my back.

"W-what?" I quiver. "What's happening?"

"You're actually in my cell." His chest rumbles. "Hancock is an idiot."

"Oh," I breathe, chuckling. "Yea. I hope we don't get in trouble."

"Worth it," he murmurs.

I go quiet for a moment, peering at him. His eyes are closed, a comfortable smile resting on his lips.

"Just so you know, sleepovers are usually where friends experiment," he croons, that teasing flirtation he spouts easier than breathing.

I laugh softly, scolding him with a look, though his eyes are closed. "Nice try, pervert."

I'm drifting off, liquifying into his big body. I can feel myself easing deeper and deeper, giving up my incessant neuroses as the serenity of this moment puts me to sleep, the lights eventually flickering off in the row.

I can't remember the last time I was so calm. *I definitely haven't felt like this while in here.*

We're out for a while, I think. What feels like hours later, consciousness tickles my mind, waking me from my slumber. I'm confused at first, but then I recall where I am.

It's not a dream. I fell asleep in bed with Ren.

Lying with my head on his chest, the cadence of his heart thumping against my cheek distracts me from the overactive thoughts that immediately want to creep in.

It feels odd to be in bed with a guy. To be… cuddling. With a *man*.

But then I've never actually cuddled with a woman either, so what the hell would I know?

Ren's legs are tangled with mine and his fingers are dancing up and down my back like maybe he's half-awake too.

I'm sure it's innocent, though, so it's okay for now. We're not doing anything bad…

We were just lying together, and we fell asleep. Who says two guys can't platonically nestle up in bed? It's so cold in this fucking cell, and Ren is warm. Plus, he always smells good, and he seemed so happy when I gave in and let him hold me for a while.

I'm sure it's fine. We're not *doing* anything.

We're just friends. *Guys like to cuddle sometimes too, right?*

My mind is drifting, like Ren's fingers, up and down my back. Up, and down… *Up*… and *down*.

So, Ren is gay. It's just a fact, one he's never cared to hide from the world, especially not in here. Ren is gay, and I'm straight. But it doesn't *matter*. Sexuality doesn't define you, and I care about people for who they are, not who they're attracted to.

Just because I don't personally date the same sex, that doesn't mean I'd judge anyone who does. I haven't exactly dated the opposite sex either, so I have no frame of reference for any of this.

All I know is that I'm smooshed up against the hard body of my friend, who just so happens to be a guy, and it feels good.

It feels *so good*, in fact, that I might want to be even *closer* to him. I don't know why, but in this moment, I want to be as close to him as two men can get. Without crossing any sort of line, of course.

Because we're just friends.

Just... friends.

My hips shift, arm sloped around his waist, with my head tucked into that sweet spot between his neck and his chest. His throat is right in front of my face, and when my eyes crack open, I see his Adam's apple dip.

Is he awake?

He's such a man... There would be no disguising it. Not that I should want to...

I don't know what I'm thinking.

One of my hands trails along his side as I subtly push myself into him some more, melding our bodies together like a fusion of two very different metals. Ren hums, and the sound tickles the pit of my stomach.

He's definitely awake. And he likes it... how close we are. It makes him happy.

I make Ren happy.

My mind drifts to his teasing before we fell asleep... about friends experimenting.

Maybe that's what we should do... Because I have no experience with anything, and Ren's here, and he feels really good... *Warm...*

Maybe I could see how it feels to just... try.

The air around us grows a hundred degrees warmer in a split second. My hips are moving. They haven't stopped. It's just happening, so slowly it's barely noticeable. But the more it happens, the more the gentle rocking turns into an intoxicating *writhe*. A gentle, sensual grind that he's meeting with his own.

God, this is awkward. What am I doing? I should stop...

I should... not stop. I don't want to. Not yet.

Just a little more...

We're moving together now, an ebb and flow of our hips, taut, heated bodies crashing together like easy ocean waves. A ragged breath leaves my lips on its own, and I feel my face flush in humility at my eagerness to chase this new sensation.

Fire is spreading below my waist, an unfamiliar ache building between my legs that's embarrassing me because I don't know where it came from or why I'm suddenly so needy for more.

We're supposed to be *just friends*, innocently cuddling… and now we're humping through our clothes.

I'm such a weirdo… Why am I doing this to him? He probably thinks I'm a freak.

I bury my face in the crook of Ren's neck, my entire body shivering with confused want that I just *don't understand*.

"W-we should… s-stop." My lips tremble against his warm flesh. But I'm *not* stopping.

"Don't stop," he purrs, clutching me to him. "This feels too good."

He's right. It feels *so fucking good. Way too good to stop.*

I have an erection. My dick is actually *hard*, harder than it's ever been before. And I can feel his too… Big and solid.

He's a man with a big, hard cock, just like mine.

God, my friend's dick is so big… and hard…

My hips seek it out, dragging mine along the length of his. The *throbbing* between my legs with our cocks rubbing together is almost painful. But I like it.

I didn't know I liked it… I didn't know I could feel this with a guy.

"I… I'm confused," I whisper. "You make me nervous, Ren…"

My face is like a furnace, but now I've shifted on top of him, and I'm *thrusting*.

Ren spreads his legs to make room for me. "Just do what feels good." His voice is rich and smooth, like melted caramel. "Don't overthink it."

My face is still smashed in his neck because I'm too afraid to look at him. But I refuse to stop working my hips between his legs. It's some kind of primal instinct to move this way… To fuck into him for some friction to soothe this desperate ache.

"You're so hard…" I whimper, timidly slipping my tongue between my lips to lick his neck.

He tastes salty and sweet.

My heart is racing faster than ever.

"Want me to move it?" he breathes. "I can roll over, or…"

"No. I *like* it." My voice cracks.

I'm fucking humiliated, but it feels way too good to care.

"Just use me to get off, baby," he whispers. "Use me to see what you like."

I'm fucking spinning, gripping his shirt in my fist while I pump my cock against his. It's euphoric, grinding into him like this, my dick pulsing sticky stuff all over the inside of my pants. I'm lost in a haze, sexual desire and lust clouding everything around us. I'm gasping and Ren is groaning, and I'm trying to be as quiet as possible, but it's hard when I've never felt anything so intoxicating.

"Ren..." I mewl his name, my balls drawing up tight like I might come.

No, not yet... I don't want to embarrass myself.

But then I remember what he said about wanting a virgin...

Does he think it's hot? Me being so needy and inexperienced I'm about to come in my pants just from rubbing myself on him?

This is a guy who has sex *all* the time. I try not to think about what he actually does, but I get the idea that he likes to be the one who *receives*. How can someone who knows about that kind of pleasure be turned on by a virgin dry humping him?

This is the problem... I know it is. It's not about me not be able to feel this with a guy. Clearly, I can.

It's about me feeling like I couldn't possibly be enough for *this* guy.

"Mmm... Lex," he hums, gliding his hands down to my butt. He cups my ass and shoves me down harder into him.

I groan, loins coiling up. *He likes it. He likes it too.*

"Could you... come," I choke out the words. "Could you c-come like this?"

His broad chest lifts as he arches up to me. "Baby, *anything* you do with me will make me come."

I swallow hard, kissing his throat. "Really?"

"Mhm..."

"Are you sure?"

"Yes, Lex, baby, I'm *so* sure..."

Baby...

"Are you l-lying?"

He shakes his head. "No. Not this time, I promise." He pushes his hips up. "Feel this, beautiful?" I nod slowly, trembling, my knees shaking as our cocks rut together. "This doesn't lie."

"It's really big," I purr, grinding into him so hard I'm getting rug-burn on my dick. But I don't even care. *God, it feels so good.*

"Yours is too," he croons, squeezing my ass in two fistfuls.

"I know," I murmur, sucking on his neck just a little.

He chuckles, such a deep, sexy sound. "Mm… *Cocky Lex.* I like it."

"What if I come?" I rasp. "It'll get everywhere…"

"You can use my mouth."

A thump of nervous arousal hits me in the nuts, and I shudder. "I… I don't know…"

That might be too much. We're going too far.

Friends don't come in their friends' mouths…

"Whatever you wanna do, baby," he moans. "I'll give you anything, you know that."

I'm suddenly overcome by intense, gnawing emotions. I have no clue where they came from, but they're blazing inside me like huge, ravenous flames.

"Ren," I whimper, lifting my face and grabbing his jaw.

And before I can even process it, I'm kissing him.

I'm kissing *him.*

Hard and soft at the same time, whining into his mouth, from the way the burn of his stubble is registering a deep pulse between my legs. He gives up to me easier than I think anyone's ever done anything; just offering me his mouth to kiss and suck as much as I want to. My tongue slips inside and he meets it with his, and I know I'm going to come any second, I can feel it.

So I reluctantly pull off him, our eyes locking for only a split second, wherein he reads my mind. I sit up, grabbing the bars of the top bunk while Ren tugs my pants down, my big, erect cock springing out, beads of precum spilling from the tip.

Ren's eyes meet mine as he glides his mouth over it, sucking just enough to have my eyes rolling back in my skull.

"Ohh… ohhfuuck." My hips flex, eyes drooping while I watch him sucking on me slowly, pulling out my orgasm like a sweet, thick vanilla milkshake. "God, *fuck fuck fuck*, Ren, I'm *coming.*"

The words spill from my lips while my seed spills into his mouth, pulse after pulse of aching throbs. My balls are thumping, emptying every drop onto his silky, eagerly waiting tongue. I just can't take it…

This is the most intense thing I've ever felt. I might be dying.

My head is floating off my body as I come down, watching Ren's hollowed cheeks, eyes closed, his chest fluttering while he breathes through his nose. He looks *beautiful*… like he loves what he's doing, and I can only hope it's because of *me*. Not just that he loves sucking dick.

My fingers graze his jawline while I catch my breath and drift back down to earth. He eventually releases my cock and trails his plush lips all over it, affectionately peppering it with kisses, teasing my head and my slowly softening shaft.

"I love this dick…" he mumbles, dazed. "Your dick is perfect, Lex. I never want another dick as long as I live…"

My heart expands in my chest at his words. *Please don't be lying…*

Crumbling down onto him, I hold his face. Our eyes lock, all manners of friendship going out the window. *I just don't see how…*

I kiss him fast, distracting myself from the ardent thoughts. This feels so good. And he's a *guy*.

But I don't think it's because I'm in prison. I'm sure that has nothing to do with it…

Unfortunately, I'll never know. There are no girls in here. Sure, I'd like to know the truth of my sexuality, but for now I'm just really loving the way kissing him feels.

"Baby, can I come?" Ren whimpers into my mouth, his jagged voice sounding so sexy when he's falling apart.

I feel like a bomb was dropped on my brain, and now I'm playing in the rubble. This is all so confusing. But in a good way. It's scary, but I *like* it.

"Um… I don't th-think I'm ready to…" I shiver nervously at the idea of putting my mouth on his dick.

But he grins on my lips. "No, I just mean… could I come… on you?"

My sleeping cock twitches at the idea. I suck off his lips, brushing them with mine. "Where?"

"Maybe on your abs…" he whispers, slipping his hand up into my shirt. "Or your chest."

I nod, still nervous, but eager to watch him get off. Ren pulls me down, rolling on top of me and sweeping his cock out of his pants. My eyes widen.

It definitely looks bigger than it felt.

His hand wraps around the shaft, working up to a thorough stroke, his breathing echoing all around us. He uses his free hand to drag my shirt up my chest, our eyes sticking together.

He bites his lip, and I bite mine.

"You're a dream come true, baby," he whispers. "All I want is this..." His lashes flutter, head tips back. "Just you... Baby, oh fuck, *Lex*..."

I'm tight and anxious, awaiting the burst. I don't know what it's going to be like.

This is so intense. Is it just gonna shoot out? What if it hits me in the eye?

Ren's rapidly pumping fist starts to slow. He shivers. Then he groans.

And cum sprays from his cock, hitting my chest and abs in warm splatters.

Wow... That was the sexiest thing I've ever seen.

Swallowing hard, I suck on my bottom lip with my eyes locked on his hand milking it all out. Just lying here, with my friend's cum all over me.

Glancing down, I swipe my fingers through it. *Silky.*

I wonder how it...

"Fuck yea, baby." Ren collapses on top of me, grabbing my hand and sucking his cum off my fingers. "God, you are *so hot*."

"I barely did anything." I grin lazily, and he chuckles. I snort, both of us laughing like idiots with our softening dicks resting together.

"Did you have fun?" Ren beams, taking off his shirt to wipe my chest.

I nod slowly, face burning up. *This is weird... I can't believe we just did that.*

I can't believe how *awesome* it was.

"Sleepover was a success," I mumble, and he hums, pressing a kiss on my lips.

I don't know why I'm feeling suddenly reticent. Call it the post-orgasm reality smack, I guess, but I just feel like maybe it's not smart for friends to hook up. Especially when one of them is Ren. *He's very intense.*

But I *do* like him. It's not that I don't. I'm just worried about what all this means.

"Wow, look at you," he sighs, and my brows furrow. "Already overthinking everything. At least give it a few minutes."

I chuckle. "I liked it, Warren," I feign annoyance, to which he laughs some more, settling into the bed next to me. "I really liked it."

He lies on his side, facing me. So I do the same. "You know you don't have to freak out about it... You can just do what you want and be happy. No label required."

"Yea, I guess," I gulp.

What he doesn't seem to be picking up on is that this unease is less about him being a guy and more about him being *Ren*.

I like him... Maybe it's just the orgasm-high talking, but I liked him before that too. He just happens to be the most complicated person ever invented.

"How would you feel about… more experiments?" he asks, and my heart skips in my chest.

"You mean more of this?" I touch his chest gently, tracing the curves of his muscles. "I don't think Hancock is going to keep accidentally putting me in the wrong cell."

He laughs. "We can find a way. I have magic powers, after all."

My hand slows, right over his heart.

Yea, he does. He sure loves magic.

My lips part, but I can't bring myself to say what I want to. *Don't hook up with anyone else, please…*

Even thinking it makes me feel like a pathetic virgin. I'm already clinging to him, and we just hooked up. It's crazy to be thinking this so soon… And Ren doesn't believe in monogamy, so there's just no way.

"I'm not sure…" I rumble, the rest of it getting lodged in my throat.

"Don't take this away from me…" Ren sighs, curling his big arms around my waist and pulling me into him. "Not yet. Just let me savor it, okay?"

My mind has a million more questions. But none of them matter enough to keep me out of his magnetic field.

"You still make me nervous…" I whisper.

With my head on his chest, and his beautiful, black heart rocking me to sleep…

He hums, "You should be."

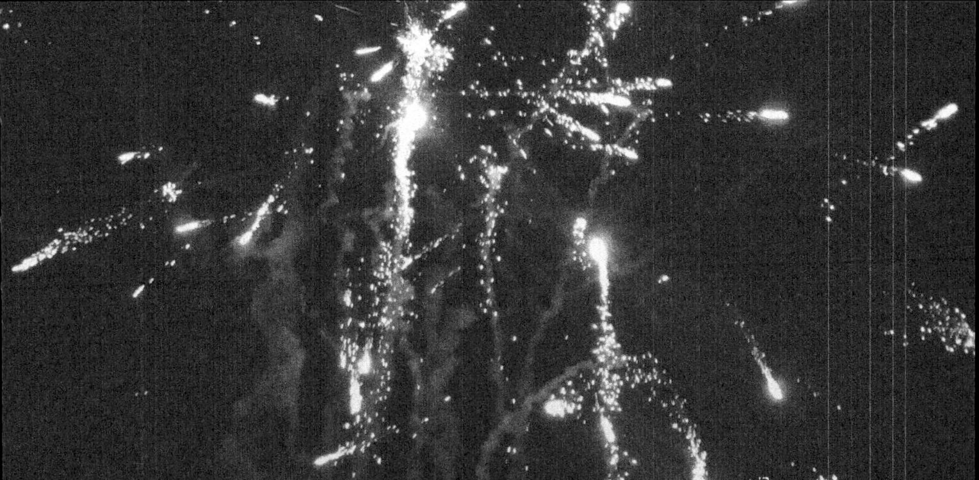

CHAPTER FOURTEEN

Ren

A few days later...

A VIRGIN. *HONESTLY, I'M SHOOK.*

I don't surprise easily. It takes a lot to pull the wool over ol' Ren's eyes, but Lex Luthor Deon managed it. He kept this little secret locked up tight. And when he revealed it, like a magician's final trick, I was stunned. Flabbergasted. Bamboozled.

More fucking *awestruck* than I've ever been by anyone or anything.

The man I've been crushing on for over a year is actually a *virgin*, and it just makes me like him a million times more. Because now, more than ever, I can see how infinitely *different* we are.

He's never had sex. Ever. Not once.

And I've had enough sex that if orgasms were electricity, I could power all of New York City Proper for years.

The next morning, after that revelation of a sleepover, Velle showed up to bring us for breakfast. And naturally, he was enraged when he found Lex in my cell instead of his own. I had to lay on some real thick charm to get us out of that hot water.

Definitely gonna owe him a deep one.

The whole time we were eating our flavorless eggs, Lex was being all shy and fidgety, and it was everything I could do not curling around him to feel his every sexy shiver of timid boy energy.

It all makes sense now… He's not just a straight guy venturing into kinda gay territory.

He's a virgin who's nervous about fooling around in general.

God, it's just the hottest fucking thing on earth. Honestly… Dominant older dudes are all well and good, but I never knew how sensational it could be to watch someone falling to bits for the first time, because of me.

Not that I want to sympathize with Callum, but the idea of stealing Lex's virginity has turned me into a walking hard-on. I had to rub one out the second I got back to my cell before my balls exploded from sheer excitement alone.

I just don't see how I'm expected to keep my cool with him now. Now that I know his secret, *and* we actually fooled around…

I just feel like he's *mine*, and there's no going back.

I *need* to be Lexington Deon's first, more than I need to breathe.

It's been a few days since our sleepover and nothing more has happened between us. But my mood is still positively stellar. Parker came back from the East yesterday, and he looks a little better. He's not one hundred percent, but he's well enough to be in gen-pop and he seems to be in high spirits, which is all I could ask for.

Also, I've spent all my free time cashing in favors from guards to arrange something special for Lex.

I know I'm putting myself out there right now, and for all I know, he could totally brush me off and decide he's fully straight. But I think what I have planned might help him. I won't pretend my intentions are selfless here, because they're obviously not. But if assisting him in his sexual journey gets me more alone time with my sweet virgin, then I'll gladly be a man of many salacious disguises.

It's just after dinner. We're supposed to be in for the night, but I bribed Officer Porter with a world-class blowjob earlier, so I'm expecting him any minute. Lifting my mattress, I go for my personal stash of goodies, stuffing everything into my pants. I'm freaking *giddy*, pacing around the cell while I count the seconds.

"You're making me dizzy," Parker whines.

I grin up at him. "Sorry. I'm just so excited. I feel like I'm going on a date."

"I didn't know dates start with you sucking off another guy," he grumbles.

"You've clearly never dated me." I smirk, winking at him.

He chuckles, but is still shaking his head down at me from his bunk, like an admonishing older brother. "Ren, I'm telling you… Be careful with Luthor. He's obviously not like you. Chances are, this stuff you're doing together might mean something different for him than it does for you."

"He means the world to me," I tell him sincerely. "I don't want to hurt him… I want him to be happy. And I think I could make that happen."

"Just make sure you're both speaking the same language," he goes on. "For you, sex is just sex, and feelings are something completely different. That's not the case with everyone."

My brow furrows, stomach twisting into a yucky knot. I know he has a point… I guess that's the risk you run being someone's first. There will always be some attachment. I know I had it for Callum…

But the difference is that I *want* Lex to have that attachment to me. I'm desperate for him to see me as more than just his slutty friend. I want him to be *mine*.

I want that handholding, googly eyes, kissing and touching and smiling at each other like you've lost your minds stuff. The *relationship* stuff I've never had before, because I never deserved it. I'm still not sure if I do, but if Lex wants to give me those things, then who am I to tell him he's wrong?

After all, he's a million times smarter than me.

I could change myself for him, I'm sure of it.

My anxious thoughts are interrupted when the door to the row opens and Officer Porter clomps in, peering through the bars. He doesn't look anywhere near as excited as I am, but I don't care. He agreed to the deal.

No refunds.

He nods me over as he opens the bars. "Let's go, 48. Hands where I can see them."

I show him my hands, and he keeps his on his Glock while he brings me out into the row, closing the door behind me. I give Parker one last look, biting my lip.

"You kids have fun," Parker says with a grin, and I have to contain my bouncing zeal. His eyes shift to the guard, and he rolls them, to which I chuckle.

Porter brings me down the row, to the very end, and I'm so excited I'm shivering. *I hope I'm not interrupting anything…*

I wanted this to be a surprise, so I didn't tell Lex I was coming over. It's not like I could shoot him a quick text…

I really hope he's not, like, taking a shit or something. I guess it's the risk you run for the prison pop-in.

We reach Lex's cell, and relief washes over me, my heart thudding when I see him lying on his bunk, reading a book. He hears us right away, his face popping out from behind the book, face immediately swept up in surprise and confusion.

Ugh. He's so fucking cute, I can't stand it. I just wanna kiss his cheeks and squeeze his butt.

Porter opens the cell and shoves me inside. "I'll be back before my shift ends. I expect you up and ready to go at oh-five-hundred."

"I don't speak solider," I murmur to him, though my eyes are stuck on Lex, sitting up in his bed with wide eyes.

Porter scoffs and leaves, slamming the door, muttering on his way out, "Pain in my fuckin ass..."

"What are you doing here?" Lex asks, climbing down from his bunk.

My brow furrows while I watch him. "Why don't you sleep on the bottom? Toby's gone..."

He stands in front of me, staring. "I like the top."

My mouth swoops into a wicked grin. "Mm... promising."

He looks even more confused, and I step over to the bottom bunk, taking a seat and patting the mattress. It takes him a second, but eventually he putters over and sits down next to me.

"I missed you, baby," I whisper, turning to face him. His eyes get all blinky, and he clears his throat, gaze stuck on his lap. "I wanted to surprise you, so I bribed Porter into letting me stay over."

His face snaps. "You're staying the night?"

I can't tell if he's excited, or nervous, or both. But he's definitely not angry, so that's a good sign. Just a little hesitant, but I'd expect nothing less from my sweet virgin daiquiri.

Nodding, I inch closer to him, removing my supplies from my pants and setting them down by the pillow. His eyes flick. "What's that?"

"Just some stuff I brought over," I croon, fingers running along his shoulder while I lust over the sweet spot on his neck, behind his ear. I want to kiss it *so* bad, leave a few hickeys and bite marks on him like he did to me, unintentionally, I'm sure. "I've been thinking about you nonstop since the other night. You were so *hot*, Lex... You drive me fucking wild."

"Ren, look..." he rumbles, breathy and hoarse already. "I'm worried about all this. I mean, you're my friend. I don't want to mess anything up..."

"We won't." I can't take it anymore. Leaning in, I nuzzle the crook of his neck with my lips, toying with his earlobe. He shivers, a raspy whine escaping him. "It can just be casual... If that's what you want."

"I know, but I'm not sure…" His voice trails, and he pulls away from my merciless lips. "I still don't really understand what happened that night. It was all kinda like a… blur."

Locking my eyes on his, I observe the concern in them. I don't want him to be confused anymore, which is why I devised this plan in the first place.

"I said I wanted to help you experiment," I mumble. "And I do. You're so young, and it's not fair that you got locked away in here before you could even figure yourself out. I'd like to help. Will you let me…? Help you?"

Staring at him with raised brows, I await his inevitable questions. His throat dips before he asks, "How would you help me? What are you going to do?"

I nod at the items I brought over. "I'm going to be whatever you need, Lexington."

His forehead lines as he reaches over, sifting through my stuff. His face is immediately flushing deep crimson, eyes bugging. He's clearly stupefied, and I have to chuckle at how adorable he is.

"You're going to… wear this?" he stammers, plucking some lace fabric between his fingers. "Why??"

"I told you, I'm going to be whatever you need. To help you figure out what you want." I tilt my head at his look of horror. "You've never had sex with a girl… I'll pretend to be one so you can see what it's like."

He's gaping at me like I'm insane for several seconds in silence before he bursts out laughing. "Ren… I'm sorry, but that's fucking *nuts*."

"Why is it nuts??"

"Because you're not a girl!" He cackles. "I didn't think I needed to specify that."

I sigh. "True, we're only working with what we have. But I can pretend. I don't mind. I used to do all kinds of things like this for my clients at Edge…"

"This is fucked." He rubs his eyes. "I *know* you're not a girl…"

I tap on his forehead with my fingertip. "Use your imagination, smartypants."

He squints at me. "Doesn't it feel… different?"

I purse my lips. "Honestly… I'm not sure." He scoffs, and I gasp, "But neither are you! So it won't matter. You can just pretend, and it'll help. I promise."

He's just chuckling, shaking his head, cheeks blushed from the nature of this conversation. But then his amusement slips away, and he swallows. "I'm not… I don't know if…"

Shifting beside him, I take his hands in mine and pull him into me until he's forced to sit on my lap. He looks beyond nervous, but I hold his taut body in place, all long limbs and sharp cuts of muscle beneath my cherishing touch.

"What's wrong, baby?" I whisper in his ear. "Tell me and I'll fix it."

"I'm just… This is all moving really fast," he shivers. "I don't think I can have… sex with you, Ren. You're my friend. It's gonna get weird."

"It won't be weird," I murmur, gently nipping the sweet, warm flesh of his neck.

"You don't know that…" he hums. "What if something happens, and we end up hating each other? I can't… lose you. I have no one else in here."

My heart is chipping and cracking in my chest, the trembling fear in his words reaching inside me, to a place I thought was hollowed out empty before. I can't believe I've actually found this… Someone who truly *cares* about me. Someone who wants *me*, for who I am.

He's saying no to sex because he wants to keep *me?? That doesn't even make sense…*

No one has *ever* wanted Ren the person before. It's so overwhelming, that for a second of pure terror, I feel like I'm falling. Out of the sky, plummeting down through the clouds, into a dark, scary abyss of the unknown.

This guy is so stupendously different from anyone I've ever been with before, and I know he's right. I know I *should* hang onto this, and try my hardest not to screw it up like I always do.

Don't destroy the good with your bad.

Don't burn this down.

But I'm also selfish, and evil, and I want him *so* badly. I want to be his everything, not just his friend. And if that means taking this chance, then I can't stop myself from grabbing it and squeezing with all my might to hold on.

We're already in Hell. Whether it's wrong or not, I will keep Lex Luthor Deon here so he can burn with me forever.

"You're never going to lose me, Lex," I tell him with certainty. "Whatever happens, I'll always be right here with you. That part won't change." He nods, reluctantly, but still. I'm getting through to him. "I just want you to be happy. I don't want you always wondering, you know?"

I want you to see that I can be what you want, no matter what.

He's stiff for only a few more seconds, before his fingers twitch, gradually grazing my shoulder. "Can we try something else...? Not sex..." His voice trails, but my heart and dick simultaneously jump when he adds a breathy, "Yet."

"We can do whatever you want to do, gorgeous," I hum, kissing a slow line up his throat.

I'm trying so hard to calm myself down, but it's difficult when he's just the sweetest, sexiest shy boy with a hot, hard body I've ever come across in my twenty-two years of life. Grasping his jaw, I pull his mouth to mine, kissing him hungrily. He falls into it so easily, like he missed me too, our mouths working up sensual sucks, panting breaths over one another's lips. His tongue pushes between mine first and I growl, licking him, tasting him, his excitement and his fear, so delicious it's like the most decadent dessert ever created.

Before I know it, I'm horizontal, and he's grinding into me while we makeout like horny teenagers. It's occurring to me that maybe this is all he's ever done, because he seems to like the kissing, and the touching, his hands sliding up into my shirt to curiously caress the lines and curves of my muscles.

His cock is already like stone. I'm fucking *obsessed* with everything about it. Sure, I've snuck my fair share of peeks in the showers, but seeing and feeling it, up close and so *hard*, is a revelation. His dick is just so big and beautiful. Pale enough to accentuate those lickable veins and that blushed pink head.

It's always the slim, cut guys who have the biggest cocks, I'm telling you.

Lex writhes into me, squirming when my hand slips between us to touch him over his pants. "*Mmff*... I don't wanna come too soon," he gasps, and I'm seriously going to die from maximum arousal.

"Then slow down, baby," I whisper. "When the lights go off, we can play."

"I still think this is crazy," he murmurs, and I grin.

"Who doesn't love a little crazy?"

We kiss for a few more minutes, until the lights switch off in the row. Then Lex pulls his mouth off of mine, gazing down at me with his lips all swollen and his gem green eyes glistening.

Pushing him off, I nod. "Sit over there and close your eyes." He gives me a puzzled look, but does as I say, scooting over to the edge of the bed, facing the wall. "No peeking."

I spot a ghost of an eager smirk as he covers his eyes with his hands, and I pick up my stuff, getting to work. This is certainly not my first time wearing women's lingerie. It was a requirement for a lot of my clients at Club Edge. This also isn't my first time pretending to be a girl, though with all of those guys, it was more about their shame regarding their sexuality, whereas with Lex, I'm *choosing* to do this for him, and a little for me.

Honestly, I don't think he would care if we just kept messing around as two guys. But I also don't want to fall any deeper into this with him, only to wake up in however long with him wondering if he'd rather be with a woman. Not like it really matters in here, because there are no females available to him, unless against all odds, Joy suddenly decides she wants a piece. But honestly... it's not outside of the realm of possibility, and it would completely *destroy* me.

This won't be like it was with the guys at The Edge. No degrading, or pain, or purposeful humiliation to get them off. With Lex, it's more like the last client I ever had... The man in the mask.

Passion and pleasure, and crumbling *together.*

This is *Lex.* I want him to be happy, above all else.

He won't hurt me... Because he likes me.

Stripping out of my clothes, I peek at Lex to make sure he isn't looking before I squirt out a generous helping of lube onto my fingers. I have to make my asshole feel wet, like a pussy. So I stuff lots of lube in there. I even stick the tube up and squeeze to fill myself with it, clenching as best I can to hold on to it, so I'll be nice and gushy for him.

Then I pull on the black lace panties I got from Jasper. They're a snug fit, but still... I like the way they make my ass look. Around the front, it's all wrong. My cock is semi-hard, so it barely fits inside, and I have to flip it up, pushing my balls up too so that when I lie on my front, all he'll see is an ass in panties. I have a lacy little top thing I slip over my head, and the ensemble is finished.

Ready to be a lady.

Crawling into the bed, I get beneath the covers, positioning myself just right. Then I grab the pillow to cover most of my head, and mumble, "Okay, you can look."

I feel him shifting on the bed, and already my excitement is through the roof. It's super hot to be lying here like his ready-made sex toy, especially with my face hidden. It feels like some naughty game we're playing. I'm already shivering with anticipation.

Lex crawls closer, easing himself up to me. I hear him breathing out steadily, and I can only imagine the look on his face.

"Wow..." he hums, and I shudder when his hand drops onto my ass, cupping it gently. "You look so pretty."

"Play with me," I whisper, as quietly as possible, keeping my voice smooth.

He makes a noise, fingers tracing the crack of my ass over the lace, innocently exploring at a gradual pace. The air in the cell is already stifling hot, my cock aching where it's trapped beneath my body as he squeezes and kneads my cheeks. Knelt behind me, I feel him whip his shirt off, then he lowers himself over my back, dropping sweet kisses all over my shoulders.

"Your skin is so soft," he rumbles, pushing his hips forward to shove his erection against my ass.

I whimper, eyes closed, head clouded with lust. I wish he would just rip my panties open and stuff that big dick inside me. But this is Lex we're talking about... He's not going to do that. And believe it or not, the temptation, the tease, and the build is a million times better.

He kisses down my shoulder blades and my back, soft lips driving me fucking crazy. He even trails his tongue down my spine until he reaches the panty line, breathing heavily with his hands gripping my cheeks. I wish like hell I could see what he's doing, but all I have is sensation, turning up the heat beneath my skin.

I feel his warm breath on me through the lace while he observes my ass like this. Then his lips ghost over the crack, and my eyes roll back in my skull.

Fuck, I want him to eat me. God, I hadn't even thought of that. I wonder if he wants to eat me out... I will come so motherfucking hard if he does.

"What should I do with you?" he rumbles, almost like he's talking to himself while he touches my butt, all draped in lace panties for him. He grips the material, tugging at it like he might want to rip it off.

"Put your fingers in me, Lex," I plead softly, pushing my hips up for him, displaying my plump booty, ready and waiting.

He makes a shaky sound as he shoves the material aside, stretching it so much that it might rip, but obviously neither of us cares. Then he pushes his long fingers between my cheeks, swiping them over my hot hole.

"*Fuck*," he grunts, swirling fingertips around and around on my rim. "You're slippery wet."

"Make me wetter, baby," I purr.

"Like this?" he asks, and now I know for sure he's never done this before.

I'm certain he's only ever kissed a girl. *Maybe some under the shirt action.* But this is a first, and I'm *flying*.

I get all his first moments. If I could have had his first kiss too, my life would be complete.

But I have his first gay kiss, so it still counts.

"Mhm..." I hum. "Rub my little pussy, Lex."

"Jesus fucking Christ..." He rubs me faster, holding my cheeks open with his other hand.

I can feel more of the lube seeping out of me, coating his fingers and running down my taint.

"You're gushing all over my hand, baby," he croaks.

My heart is fucking bursting, jumping up into my throat at hearing him call me that.

He called me baby... Lexington just called me baby...

I've never swooned so hard in my life.

"Mmm... *fuck*..." I moan into the pillow. "My pussy's dripping for you."

"It is," he croons, a fingertip pushing up to my hole. "I could slide right in."

"You can," I breathe. "It's so hot and tight and *aching* to be filled..."

I can feel him trembling, but he obviously likes what we're doing. I can't tell if it's because he wants to be doing this with a girl, or if he's just turned on by the game like I am. Either way, it doesn't matter. This is *fantastic*.

Lex slowly eases one finger inside me, groaning as he does. My whimpers are just rolling out, abs clenching with need. The burn is minimal because of all the lube, and the fact that it's only one finger. It just feels amazing, and I can't help pushing my hips back, to get him as deep as possible.

"It's... very tight," he croaks, moving that curious finger in and out of my ass. "So, *so* tight..."

"You feel so good, baby."

"Do I?" he murmurs, and I hum.

"Yea..."

He melts over my back again, lying on top of me, but resting to the side, with his erection smashed into my hip. Then he whispers, right by my ear, "This feels good in your tight little pussy?"

Oh God. Mini orgasm.

My balls throb, ass squeezing on his finger as some precum spurts from my cock.

Lex moans softly. "You can get tighter?" There's fascination in his tone.

"Mhm… my body is holding on to you, baby."

"Mmm… What if I stuff you more?" He slips another finger in to join the first, my hole quivering around them. "You like that?"

"Fffuck yea…"

I'm *writhing*, desperately humping back against his hand while he fills me with his fingers, licking and biting my neck and shoulder. The burn in my loins is building, the heat between our bodies making us sheen with sweat.

"Tell me how to find your spot," he pants greedily with his fingers sliding in and out of my hole. They're just so long and masculine. I never knew *fingers* could feel this fucking good. "I wanna touch it. Fuck, *baby*, I wanna make you shake…"

"Mmmfuck… *Lex*," I squirm into the bed to get some friction on my aching cock. "Push your fingers in deep, then twist… A little curve… Like th-that… *fffuck*, my *God*…"

"Did I get it?" he rasps eagerly, doing it again. His fingers brush my prostate, lighting me right the fuck up.

"Yes… *yes yes yes* that's so good," I whine. "*Mmmyea*… Finger-fuck me, baby."

Lex gasps, then shifts, pulling his dick out of his pants. He pushes his hips forward, rubbing his hard cock on me while his fingers pump in and out of my ass, harder and *harder*. Just having his erection so close to my ass has me quaking. I want him to shove it in me so bad, but the tease of knowing he won't is coiling me into a throbbing ball of desire.

"Are you gonna come for me?" he purrs, and I feel the wetness his cock is leaving on my skin.

I nod fast, face buried in the pillow. "Fuck yea… You feel so fucking good in me. Make me *come*, Lex."

"I wanna make you come," he groans, humping against my thigh to match the tempo of his fingers, driving in and pulling out, such a delectable taunt of frustrating pleasure. "You burning up for me, baby?"

"Yes… *ohhyes*, I love how you finger-fuck my ass, Lexington…"

I have no idea what I'm even saying. I'm in a lust-spiral, wound up so tight I can't remember where or who I am. All I know is that I want him. More than anything, I just want *him*. In any way he wants to give himself to me.

I've been fucked hundreds of times over, by some of the biggest dicks, attached to the most confident men who know how to use them. And yet *this*, Lexington Deon fingering me while he kisses my neck and humps my leg, is a pleasure so insurmountable, it's about to have me erupting harder than any of those dime-store fuckboys ever could.

God, these fucking fingers… I love these fingers. I love the boy attached to these fingers, with his mischievous innocence, poking at my prostate over and over and ohhh-ver, holy balls, I'm gonna come so hard…

The elastic of the panties is digging into my flesh, my fists gripping the sheets, hips moving furiously against his hand to chase my orgasm. Lex moves on top of me, pinning me with his body weight as he straddles my legs. Then he stuffs his dick between my thighs, just beneath where his hand is. His big, thick shaft is rutting against my balls in sensual agony, driving me up to the edge.

Can't… hold… on…

"So good… you're so, so *fucking good*," he growls while fucking my thighs. Gripping the fabric of my top in his fist, he yanks until it's constricting my chest, all the while teasing my prostate with his wicked fingers. "You're so *hot*. Hot fucking body, hot little hole… *God*, you're burning me alive. Nothing feels as good as you do…"

My heart is soaring, stomach clenching, balls tightening.

"L-lex… *Lexington…*"

"Feels so good," he hums, biting down on my shoulder while his whole body tenses. "Come on my fingers, sweet flame."

That does it. Sets me right off.

"Ohhh, I'm gonna fffucking come… I'm *c-coming, baby…*"

My cock throbs, shooting my orgasm all over my abs and the bed almost viciously while I whine and whimper muddled up versions of his name. Lex pushes his fingers into me as deep as possible, leaving them there while my hole squeezes on them tight.

This climax is *insane*. I'm whirling around and around like a feather caught in a cyclone.

Buzzing, I can barely breathe as he gently tugs his fingers out of me, pushing my legs apart to reach between. His palm covers my dick and my balls from behind, and he groans, playing with me while I'm still quaking and leaking. Thrusting hard, he holds his cock firmly against my balls as his hips smack into my ass from behind, like he's fucking me without fucking me.

"I love this," he whimpers. "This feels… uhh, *Ren*… Baby, *fuck yesss.*"

Writhing into me, he starts to come, pouring warm pulses onto the bed while he fucks between his hand and my nuts, *squeezing* our dicks together.

"*Lex…*" I cry, the oversensitivity in my balls causing wild shivers with his stiff, wet, throbbing erection moving against mine.

"Ren," he sighs in a sated purr, releasing his cock to massage my ass with both hands. "That was… *amazing*."

Mmmff… Wow…

He's saying my name. His orgasm came from rubbing his cock on *mine*, touching *me* and kissing *my* skin. While saying *my* name.

He wasn't imagining a girl… That was just a fun, stupid game we were playing. But he likes *me*, and *my* body.

Only I make him come this way.

This is such a revelation, I have tears seeping from my eyes. I can't even understand this, these emotions attached to getting off. I've never felt this way in my entire life…

I've never been so glad to be *me*.

Lex collapses onto his side, lips still trailing along my flesh, anywhere they can reach. I exhale, higher from *him* than any drug could ever make me.

I expect him to pull my back against his front for cuddles. But instead, he rolls me over… So we're face to face.

"Hi…" I whisper like an idiot, frozen to stone by the vibrant sea green in his eyes.

"Hi." He grins, then bites his lip, pulling me closer by my hip.

I clear my throat. "So… that was fun."

He laughs, the sight and sound of which cracks my chest wide open. "Mm… it *was* fun." His fingers trail up my side, then onto my chest, brushing along the lace covering my chest. "You do look good in this…"

I swallow, blinking at his face. "You like it?"

"I think you would look good in just about anything," he murmurs. Confidently.

He's nowhere near as nervous and squirmy as he was earlier. I think he's… comfortable with me.

He might want to be more than friends…

Out of nowhere, a giant, ice-cold tidal wave of fear crashes over me.

Parker's words, all of those terrifying thoughts are ringing in my skull like alarm bells.

You're going to hurt him...

He's too good for you.

Too sweet, and kind and beautiful a person for someone as rotten and awful as you.

If he falls in love with you, you'll break his heart.

What the fuck are you thinking, you monster?!

"Lex..." I whisper his name, while he's ogling my dick in these panties.

"Hm?" He peeks up at me.

We should stop this.

I'm going to hurt you.

I don't think I can be... what you need from me.

Pressure is building in my skull, nausea rolling up my throat. I chew on the inside of my cheek, gasping for words I can use to make this better.

Any words I can say so this doesn't end.

"I think we should be more than friends." I shove them out into the open air, focusing my twitchy fingers on his shoulders and his arms. "I know you're worried, but you shouldn't be. We should be *more*, Lexington. I know you feel it..."

His lashes flutter, hand resting over my heart. "I feel it." He nods. "I do... but I..." His voice fades as he chews on his lip.

He has every right to be nervous...

"Tell me what you need, and I'll be it," I whisper.

You're lying.

"I don't know if you can," he sighs, like he knows, and I try to keep my gulping subtle. "Ren, I do like you. *A lot.* And seeing you with all these other people is just... I mean, it's *you*, and that's fine. I just... can't be with you like that."

My stomach is rolling in disgust with myself. I *hate* myself right now more than I ever have.

"I would never ask you to be someone you're not," he goes on. "But we'll just have to stay friends..."

"I can't just be your friend." I shake my head. "I'm f—"

I stop myself quick before the words can slip out and scare the shit out of both of us. But I think he knows what I was going to say. His eyes have never been wider, more shimmery, and less sure.

"What's the alternative then?" He rests his head on my shoulder to kiss my neck. "I won't share you. I know myself; I wouldn't be able to stand it."

"You don't have to," I croak, jaw straining to keep myself in check. "I'll stop."

Liar.

He shakes his head. "No, you won't, Ren… I *know* you. You won't."

"I will," I tell him with as much sincerity as I can muster. "For you, I will."

Liar, liar, pants on fucking FIRE.

Lex lifts his head, peeking up at me. "You will?"

I nod, touching his jaw and his cheek and his lips.

Jesus, you're the worst.

No, I'm being serious. *How could I not for this guy?? He's perfect.*

How could I ever say no to being with only him?? I'd have to be the biggest, dumbest fuckboy on the planet to want to keep sleeping with randoms instead of being his, making him mine.

My heart is rapping fast, stomach churning as that goddamn voice of reason keeps badgering me.

Whatever, idiot. You won't be able to do it. You know you can't.

You're just going to hurt him…

And when you do, he'll hate you forever.

"I want to be with only you, Lex," I whisper, shockingly convincing, even for me. "I'll do anything to make that happen. Baby, I will try *so hard* not to hurt you. I'll be what you need… *Anything* for you."

He looks skeptical, and he's more than right to. But he wants to believe me, and it's dropping his guard, exposing him. So soft and vulnerable, without the scars of past pain… He's too innocent. Beautiful, naïve… *Perfect.*

His pink lips sweep into a tiny, beautiful smile of elation. "Promise?"

Leaning in, I swipe his mouth with my finger, breathing the lie over that sweet spot.

"Promise."

CHAPTER FIFTEEN

Ren

Present day...

Storms on Alabaster Isle are a production.

Thunder rumbles the building, lights flicker, pipes creak. The far-off sounds of waves crashing and wind whipping outside the walls…

This place isn't equipped for big ones. And the ones we've been getting over the past two weeks have been enough to knock the power out a few times. There are back-up generators, but still. It's an even more ominous in here when the lights go out.

Fitting, really. My emotions feel like a storm, raging inside me. Calming at times, then gusting back with a vengeance. Darkness brings with it thoughts you can't escape from.

I combat it the only way I know how. The way I've been fighting depression my entire adult life.

With lots of depraved sex.

And it's fine. Better than fine. It's fucking *great.*

I love having sex with people I don't care about in the slightest…

Puffing out a breath, I wipe the water from my eyes. I've been standing beneath this shower head, just staring at the wall for minutes. Thinking, remembering… *Feeling* while pretending I'm not.

I really don't know how much longer I can do this…

How much more of this constant pining can I take?

It's been weeks since the night I had Lex in my grasp again; when he pulled away from me, *again*, for the billionth time. And every time it happens, every time I lure him closer, only for him to wake up, shake it off and remember that he hates me, I fall deeper into this internal pit of despair.

I drove this goddamn wedge between us. *I* did it, on *purpose*, and I have no one to blame but myself. So what do you do when you just can't get over someone who wants nothing to do with you? What do you do when there's no hope, any and all specks of optimism you were holding on to are swept away, and you realize you're chasing a ghost?

Getting fucked up seems like it would be a viable option. A way to numb myself more than the meaningless sex, which I don't want to admit is starting to feel like a chore rather than a recreation. I have drugs, and some booze I've been hoarding over the years, but I usually save that stuff for trades. Drugs are worth more than gold in this place. More than sex, even.

Still, I won't say the temptation isn't strong at times like this. I used to do a lot of drugs before I was arrested. But the thought of sitting in my cell getting blasted by myself is even more depressing than how I spent last night...

Letting Matthews fuck my face, then lying on the floor and scraping my wrists with concrete.

Flipping my arms over, I watch the water pour over my jagged scars. All the tattoos I've done on my wrists are warped and messy, since I never let them heal right.

I guess it doesn't matter. I'll just keep ruining them and covering it up, because I'm incapable of ever moving from this purgatory.

Some people are a lost cause...

Clangs and shuffles have me looking up, watching as Dash is shoved into the room. He looks around, and I can tell he's probably searching for Luthor, or Kang. Not necessarily me...

I guess we got off on the wrong foot, which is another thing that's strictly my fault. But Dash is a sweet kid. Definitely misunderstood, but he genuinely cares for Lex, and that should make me happy. He's a part of our group now, maybe even a better part than me.

They're always trying to phase me out, I'm sure of it.

Dash notices me as he slinks over to the showers where I'm standing. He picks the one by the wall, so there's space between us, eyes going shifty as he quickly strips out of his clothes. He's wearing nicer boxers than mine. Brand-new Calvins.

Interesting...

He seems very jumpy, peering over his shoulder while he washes up fast, covering his dick with his hands pretty much the whole time. His gaze meets mine, and he nods.

Grabbing a towel, I dry myself off while sauntering closer to him. "Hey. You okay?"

He blinks his wide hazel eyes at me, showing off his enlarged pupils. "Yea… Yea, I just got back from the East so I'm just kinda…" His voice trails, and he gusts out a breath, blinking hard.

"They had you in the East??" I ask, surprised.

When I didn't see him for a few days, I just assumed he was in solitary, since he's there a lot.

"Sorta… I mean, not like *officially*," he rambles. Then he rubs his eyes. "This place is so fucked up. I don't know what's happening to me. I feel like I'm… losing myself."

I nod, picking up my boxers and stepping into them. "You wouldn't be the first inmate to lose his shit in here. Especially spending so much time in solitary. It takes a mental toll, for sure."

"It's more than that," he goes on. "I haven't been here long at all, but I'm doing things I never thought I'd… do."

I watch him for a moment, a visible flush rising in his pale complexion. The water's not hot. That's not it. He's blushing. And biting on that pouty bottom lip.

My gaze narrows. "And you're enjoying it, which confuses you…"

His face snaps in my direction, and he scowls. "*No*… I don't…" His throat bobs. "I don't know…"

"You do, though," I state firmly. "You *know*, Dash."

He keeps shaking his head. "It's this place… This place and the fucking people in it."

His lips are shivering, and I can see goosebumps all over his wet skin.

Sighing, I reach over and turn off his water. "Dash, let me tell you a story."

I hand him a towel, and he pauses before taking it. "Is it true?"

My lips twitch and his do the same as he dries off.

"I lost my virginity when I was fifteen to a man named Callum… Callum Kade. He was a business associate of my father's. Much older than me, obviously. Quiet, gorgeous, *married*… a real emotional terrorist. Anyway, he was actually at my house the day I came out to my parents. It was a whole thing… My first gay *scene*, if you will."

Dash chuckles, and I grin. But the amusement slips away when I add,

"My father beat the fucking shit out of me when I told him I was gay. I was so covered in bruises and welts, I couldn't go to school for a week."

Dash's eyes go wide. He looks horrified as he gasps, "That's fucked. I'm sorry, Ren."

I shrug, swallowing down the misery of this story, and the shining image of my loving parents.

May they fucking rest.

"Didn't much matter, I guess. About school…" I go on. "A few weeks later, they pulled me out for good, and I was homeschooled for the last two years of high school. My parents really thought keeping me away from other kids, or other *boys*, would somehow delay the gay."

I pause to scoff. "But the thing is, it wasn't the boys at school they needed to worry about. Because the same man who sat in my living room with my parents that day, watching them berate me for coming out, listening while my father beat me for telling them my truth… He came into my house, into my *bedroom* a few days later, and took my virginity. He fed me all these lines, about how brave I was, and how *special* and *sweet* and *blah blah blah*…"

My words fade into a tired growl. "Whatever, he fucked me. He fucked me again and again, on repeat, for *months* at a time, until he was done. And then he just dipped out. Basically, he preyed on my vulnerability to get what he wanted, and yea, at the time, I fucking *loved* it. But I also didn't know any better. It was like he dropped a bomb on me and ran. I never truly recovered from that hit…"

My gaze is stuck on my wrists for a moment, staring intently at the scars and black ink.

Dash shakes his head. "Why are you telling me this?"

My eyes lift to his. "Because I think you should know that pain usually leads to *clarity*. Obviously, I'm the last person who should give anyone advice. I'm not exactly *emotionally stable*. But if there's one thing I *know*, it's that who you are is always going to be *who you are*… No matter what happens, where you start out or where you end up. You're *you*, Dash. And sometimes chaotic beginnings can lead to a beautiful end."

He bites his lip, lashes fluttering at my face. I can tell he's piecing it all together, taking my words and my experience, laying them down over his own situation.

I'm not sure if what he's struggling with is thinking he might be gay, or bi… Or if he's just realizing that sexuality can be fluid, and enjoying something new doesn't have to be scary. But I've seen it enough times in my life to know that the circumstance is only that.

Prison doesn't turn you gay. *Nothing does.*

Your sexuality is a part of you that's always been there, something you discover and develop over time. I hope he's starting to see that.

Dash takes in a breath, letting it out slowly before he squints at me. "You're sorta wise, Warren. Did you know that?"

My head falls back in a laugh. "Story of my life, boo. My hotness gets in the way of people realizing how smart I am."

He grins, running his fingers through his short hair. "So what happened to this Callum Kade guy, anyway?"

"Oh, I killed him."

He gawks at me, and I wink.

"I can't with you..." he mutters while I chuckle. "Now, if only you could point some of that Confucius-style shit at yourself."

"What's that supposed to mean?" I frown.

"You know damn well what it means," he huffs, his eyes flinging across the room, in the direction of Gage and his crew, who are hooting and hollering like dumb jocks in a locker room. "You're *not* stupid, Ren. And despite what you might think about yourself, you're not evil either. You say you just want to get close to Luthor, but even when you're in the same room, you act like you're on different planets."

My lips part, but I can't speak. I'm just staring at him, dumbfounded.

"I'm just saying, he's never not reaching for you," he goes on. "Even when it hurts."

My forehead creases, my pulse speeding up while I contemplate his words.

Do I really disregard Lex... Even when he's right here?

I didn't think I did... Sure, sometimes I flirt with guys in front of him, but honestly, I flirt with everyone all the time. It's my thing. I like making Lex jealous with the proxy jobs, and yes, I acknowledge that it's sorta messed up, and definitely immature. But isn't that the nature of this whole dance we've been doing?

It's just sex. He knows he's the one I'm thinking about... Right?

Now that I'm actually considering all of this, my chest is caving just a tad. If the shoe was on the other foot, I'd be murderous. And I guess I must be a real narcissistic sociopath, because this is honestly the first time I'm thinking about how I would feel if Lex did that stuff to me.

Jesus... No wonder he hates me so much. I'm a fucking terror.

Before I can pry Dash for more details on what Lex might have told him, the group of big dickheads in question come trudging over. I'm praying they'll just walk by, since I'm really not in the mood to deal with them right now.

Unfortunately, no such luck.

Gage sidles up to me, smirking as he gives my ass a hearty slap. "You over here waiting for me, cumdump?"

My jaw grinds, and apparently, I'm not the only one.

Dash steps between us, squaring up in Gage's face. "What the fuck did you just call him?"

"Dash..." I mumble, gently moving him away while he visibly seethes on my behalf. It's really sweet, actually. Glaring at Gage, I mutter, "Guess you can suck yourself off tonight, Percy."

He won't like that. Hates his first name... Which he should, because it's fucking stupid.

"I told you not to call me that," he growls.

I shrug and mouth, *Oops*.

"Ren, your mouth is better at taking things in," Benson sneers, and I roll my eyes.

"That's very original."

Matthews is whining, he and Gage bickering while I peek at Dash. I've never seen him so pissed.

Thawing my ice-cold heart.

"I want Ren and his friend to apologize for being inconsiderate little bitches," Gage hisses at me.

"Man, you really didn't learn last time, did you... *Percy*?" I teem, fists clenched, rage and adrenaline jacked to the max right now.

I'm so sick of this asshole. I'm sick of his dick and how he thinks good sex involves mimicking a jackhammer. I'm sick of his dumb, oaf face and cocky attitude, and I'm *so* motherfucking *sick* of him always forgetting that me loving to get fucked doesn't negate the fact that I can fully kick his ass.

I put the power in power bottom, bitch.

Dash is still posted up by my side, his jaw visibly ticking. "Take another step, Percy. I dare you."

"Dash, go. I can handle this." I tell him while Gage is still talking shit. I'm so beyond ready to waste him. "Dash," I snap once more. "*Go*."

"I'm not leaving you alone with him," he grumbles.

Warmth blooms in my chest, and despite how pissed I am, I almost grin.

I guess we are friends...

We're friends because of Lex. He's like the glue that holds everything together. He doesn't deserve to feel like this dumpy moron has any sort of advantage over him. He's just one of many placeholders; people I force myself to tolerate because it's better than being alone—*is it?*—when I can't have the one person I really want.

But it doesn't matter, because I'll take him over anyone else in the world, any day of the week and twice on Sundays. I know I'm at fault in this too, not just Gage. But I beat his ass before for insulting Lex, and there's no reason I shouldn't do the same thing on behalf of myself.

"That's so sweet," Gage taunts. "You two boyfriend and girlfriend now? How do you decide which one bends over when you're both bottoms?"

I don't even have time to react before Dash throws a swift fist at Gage's face.

Whoa... My eyes widen as Gage stumbles backward. But then he lunges at us, and I block Dash with my body.

The crazed shouts of other inmates immediately come from all sides, distracting me enough for Gage to nail me in the gut. It only pisses me off more and I straighten, shooting three jabs right at his nose in rapid succession. He's disoriented, which is my opportunity to hit him with a left hook.

Dash is wailing on Benson in my peripheral, and it has me grinning. Until Rook, Velle, and Joy storm into the room, weapons in hand and immense displeasure on their faces.

Velle roars at everyone, and I flinch, peeking at Dash. Of course, he's the first to be cuffed, since apparently he just can't stay out of trouble. But he doesn't look worried in the slightest about going back to solitary.

He nods at me, and I nod back while Rook cuffs me, and Velle cuffs Gage and Benson.

"Gonna be a packed house in the hole tonight, shit for brains!" Velle barks at us as Joy helps me put my pants on.

"Deja vù, huh?" she mumbles, and I shake my head while they drag us all out of the showers.

"Your dick comes near me again," I whisper to Gage on our way out, "and I'll bite it off. That's a motherfucking promise."

Nothing like two days in solitary to clear your mind and give you some fresh perspective.

Don't get me wrong, when Jasper comes to take me out, I'm so hungry he looks like a walking slice of pizza, and my teeth are in desperate need of a thorough brushing. But other than that, I spent the entire time in the hole thinking, and now, I'm uncharacteristically determined.

The reason I act on impulse so much is because, if I stop and think, I'm bombarded with insecurities that usually send me into a depression spiral. But for the first time in a long time, I couldn't avoid them. I had no distractions, no way out. I was *trapped* in a small, dark room with nothing but my thoughts, and once I got past the initial torment of it, I came to some really solid conclusions.

The main one being that I need to see Lex. *Right away.*

I need to apologize to him. I know my apologies don't really mean shit to anyone, especially him, but this one is a little different. I'm not doing it because I feel like it's what he wants to hear.

I'm doing it for the sake of our friendship, and for myself. Whether he believes me or not, I'm going to *apologize* for making him uncomfortable and playing head games, and I'm going to mean it.

I know I can do this.

On my way out of solitary row, I try peeking into the tiny windows of the other cells to see if Dash is still down here. I assume he might be, since I didn't hear anyone else leave yet. But I'm also a little worried, because based on the noises I heard last night, someone got fucked in one of these cells. Someone got fucked *real good*.

It was too far off to tell if it was Dash, but it kinda sounded like it might have been… And it also sounded like he might've enjoyed it.

Hey, none of my business. I just hope he's alright, and he's taking my advice, learning to find his truth in all this darkness.

I guess I should be taking my own advice on that one, too.

Jasper lets me stop off to brush my teeth before bringing me to the cafeteria for lunch. I get there feeling somehow tired and wired at the same time. And even though I'm fucking *starving* and my stomach is eating itself alive, I forgo grabbing my food and make a beeline right to our table.

Right to Lexington.

"Hey." I crash into the seat next to him, nodding at Kang real quick.

"Holy shit, are you alright?" Lex asks, eyes wide. "We heard you and Dash were in a fight in the showers…"

"Yea… We sorta took on Gage together." I chuckle at the memory of me and Dash fighting side-by-side. "Dash is… He's a really cool guy." Lex's lips quirk, but it falls away when I face him fully, getting all serious.

"Look, there's something I need to talk to you about. And I know you might not want to hear it, but I just need to get this off my chest..."

He looks a bit startled, but he nods hesitantly. "Okay..."

"Lex," I start, pulling in a breath and letting it out slowly, "I'm *sorry*." *Whoa... It feels crazy when I actually mean it.* "The truth is, I *haven't* been taking our friendship seriously. I thought I was, but really, I was just saying the words because I didn't want to lose you completely. For the first time, I thought about what it would be like if it was the other way around... Like, if *you* were flirting or hooking up with people in front of me. And, Lex, I would absolutely lose my shit. I mean, I would probably, *definitely* kill, like, a bunch of people."

He huffs, shaking his head at my craziness. He's not even fazed by it anymore, which is endearing. *For me, anyway.*

"Maybe that means you don't have the same kinds of feelings that I have for you..." I gulp over these potential truths. "But whatever. The point is that I *am* sorry, and I want you to know I'm always thinking of you. You're... so much more important than you realize."

Lex is quiet for a moment, just staring at me, eyes all wide and sparkly pale green. It's the best color ever invented, even when it's reflecting my vulnerability back at me.

"So..." I clear my throat. "You have the floor. If there's anything you'd like to, um, contribute to this, uh... dialogue."

Fuck. How do people do this honest communication shit?? It's exhausting.

He blinks, then peeks at Kang, who's just sitting there with his hands folded on the table like a mediator.

"I guess I appreciate your apology," Lex murmurs. "If it's true..."

"It is."

"I like that you're finally acknowledging how batshit psycho you'd be if I did even a *fraction* of the stuff you do." He tilts his head, giving me a pointed look.

"I was never very good at math, baby," I whisper, reaching for his hands.

He rolls his eyes, yanking them away. "Stop. I'm always the one who has to sit back and watch you doing fucked up shit. I just wish you knew how that felt, for once."

I swallow hard, my muscles tensing. "Do you... really?"

He bites his lip. "I'm not saying it would fix anything between us, but... yea. I mean, karma's a bitch, right?" He smirks.

I don't like where this is going, but I just barged in here, hoping to prove myself to him in some way. I have to at least hear him out.

"Look at you and Kang, for example." He gestures to Kang, who straightens. "You guys have sex, in the showers, right in front of me..."

"I'm pretending it's *you*," I whine, but Lex lifts a hand to shut me up.

"That's irrelevant," he snaps. "It's *not* me, okay. Everyone knows it isn't. I mean, shit, what if *I* hooked up with Kang in front of *you*? You think me just saying, *'But, baby, I'm thinking of you the whole time,'* would really make you feel any less murdery about it??"

I know we're fighting right now, but I can't help the smile that snatches my mouth when he imitates my voice. *So fucking cute.*

Shifting in my seat, I channel every ounce of chill I have, fending off the jealous rage from even discussing this, to keep myself stiff and composed.

My jaw might snap from grinding so tight, though.

"*Fine*," I croak, softly. *I can't believe what I'm about to say...* "You can... hook up with Byron." I gulp over the words like a gag. "In front of me. And I won't... interfere."

God, even just speaking the words is making me want to drink bleach.

Both of their faces immediately shift in bewilderment.

"Um, wait..." Lex stammers. "I don't think that's really what I—"

"Come again?" Byron coughs. "We're doing *what*, now??"

I breathe out slowly. "You two fool around, and I'll just sit there and take it. So I'll finally know how it feels..."

"Ren, that's kinda crazy." Lex sighs an awkward chuckle. "I mean, it might literally be the *craziest* thing you've ever said."

I shake my head. "No, it's not." *Yes, it is.* "In case you haven't noticed, I'm highly self-involved. Maybe this will bring me down a touch. And then I can relate to you better, and maybe—"

"This just sounds like another one of your games," he cuts me off, squinting accusingly.

"It's not, I swear!" I gasp, pleading with my tone for him to hear my honest to God sincerity. "Do you really think I *want* to watch you with someone else?? It's not exactly my dream scenario..." Lex's face softens. "But I'll do it, for you. I'll do *anything* for you, you know that by now. Or at least, I'll try..."

He's staring at me for a few heavy seconds before he mumbles, "I'm nervous..."

"Excuse me!" Kang barks, glaring only at me. "Do I have a say in this?? Now you're pimping me out to other people, too? Unbelievable..."

Turning to face him, I give a calming look. "No one's forcing you to do anything, Byron. I'm just saying, I think it might be helpful."

"Well, shucks, how romantic. For *you guys.*" He rolls his eyes. "I'm glad I can be of service, just offering up dick to whoever needs it for dumbass fucking experiments."

"Dude, it's okay," Lex huffs. "This whole conversation is stupid. We're obviously not doing it, so don't worry—"

"I'm not worried," Kang seethes. "What, you think I'm *afraid* to hook up with you??"

Lex's eyes go round, and he looks fully baffled. "Uh, no... I don't think you're afraid. I just know that you're not—"

"Not *what*?" Kang grunts. *"Gay??"*

I lean in on the table and whisper, "Are you?"

"No!" he snaps. "But I'm not afraid of touching some dick. I'm not afraid of shit." He stands up aggressively. "In fact, let's go. We're doing it. Right now."

Lex and I are gaping at each other like we haven't the slightest clue what's happening. My buddy Byron is *way* too defensive right now, which just confirms my suspicions I've had since I met him... He's a little bi-curious, but doesn't want to admit it.

Seems to be a common theme around here.

"Wait, now??" Lex gasps.

"Yes, *now*," Kang says firmly. "I don't care. I'll save your stupid relationship. My dick is like the fucking Red Cross at this point."

It takes a lot to shock me, but ya girl is straight thrown right now.

"Okay, but we can't just *leave*." Lex is getting all blinky. *Maybe this won't be so bad... I really love when he's nervous.* "It's the middle of lunch. And where would we even go?"

Kang gestures to me. "Work your *Ren magic*, bro. Have Jasper take us to your cell." He picks up his tray, wandering away to throw out his trash while barking at us over his shoulder. "Come on, chop chop. We doing this, or what??"

We're both staring at him while I whisper, "He wants some, baby..."

"This is way too weird," Lex hums, gnawing on his lower lip. "I was being hypothetical!"

"Are you attracted to him?" I ask hesitantly, then add, "Feel free to be very concise and unenthusiastic with your answer."

He rumbles a tiny laugh. "I… I'm… I can't get into this with you right now, okay?? Apparently, I need to wrap my head around hooking up with one of my best friends."

"So we're really doing this??" I whine, rubbing my eyes.

"No…" Lex mutters, standing up then tilting his head down at me. "*Byron and I* are doing this. You're watching."

He scampers off after our friend, and I'm just sitting here, stewing in what a fucking *great* plan this was. *Good job, genius. You really nailed it this time.*

I didn't expect either of them to go for it! Honestly!

But now Kang wants it. And I guess Lex wants it… The only one who doesn't want it is me, and it was my fucking idea.

What if they realize they enjoy hooking up with each other?? They do it some more, start dating, fall in love, run away together… I mean, this is all too fucking much!

Can't we just go back to me being the slut of the group??

I wanna go back.

Kang whistles, nodding me over to the doorway where Jasper is standing, eyes flicking between the two of them like they're mental.

Tip of the iceberg, my friend.

Standing up with a tired breath, I wander over and force myself into charm mode, pleading with him to bring us to my cell.

Come on, Jake… Just say no. Let that grumpy bitch side shine!

The universe clearly hates me, though, because Jasper *doesn't even argue*. He just asks Hancock to *hold down the fort*, leading us out into the hallway.

He's not even cuffing us!

What the hell is going on in this place?! The one time I could use the rigid rules and regulations of prison, *and everyone's acting like we're guests on a Carnival Cruise!*

When we get to my cell, I'm stewing. Jasper pushes on the bars a few times, but they won't budge. He turns and flips off the camera at the ceiling, pressing once more to finally open the door.

"I'll be back in a half-hour," he mutters. "Forty minutes, tops."

Then he leaves, slamming the door behind him. I watch him go until he's fully out of sight, spinning slowly to face my friends, already dreading this with every fiber of my being.

Lex and Byron are just shifting awkwardly, peeking at each other in between looking around my cell. It's pretty nice for a prison cell, because of all the stuff I've accumulated over the years. I have pictures I drew hanging up on the walls, a Styrofoam cooler full of drinks and snacks, toiletries and products lining my sink, clothes hanging from the top bunk.

It's a prison bachelor pad, for sure. The perfect place for a theoretical cuckhold.

"Would anyone like a… drink?" I offer, wringing my hands.

Byron shakes his head as he takes a seat on my bed, kicking off his shoes. Lex is too busy staring at my drawings, I assume the one I did of him from memory catching his attention.

He peeks at me. "I just want to be clear… Doing this doesn't mean you and I are getting back together, or whatever. It's just something to… even the score a little."

"Fine," I sigh. "Where should I, um… sit?"

"Wherever you want." Kang smirks, reclining on his elbows. "It's your cell." His gaze flings to Lex, who grins like they're already in on some secret joke, and it's making me want to gouge my eyes out.

"Alright, listen up," I bark, plopping on my knees on the bed next to him. "Ground rules… No fucking, no sucking."

Kang sneers at me, "Sorta limiting, no?"

I shrug. "Don't care. *I* get his firsts." My eyes are on Lex, who's all squirmy and flushed.

But he forces a scowl and mutters, "Not that anything of mine *belongs* to you… But I guess I agree." He looks to Kang. "I don't want it to get weird."

"Why would it get weird?" Byron breathes, whipping his shirt over his head. "Just two homies messing around, right?" His face turns to glare at me. "All in good fun."

I lean over him quickly, grabbing his throat. "You got something you wanna say to me??"

"Yea," he croaks, lifting his foot to run it up my leg. "I'm gonna fuck your boyfriend."

I'm *seething*, two seconds from head-butting that smug look off his face, when Lex pushes me off.

"Alright, you guys. Jesus…" he grumbles, eyeing Kang. "He's right. No fucking."

"Your loss." Kang shrugs, taking Lex's hand and pulling him onto the bed. "We could've hooked up without him, ya know? That night in the hallway, when Velle jerked Rook off into Dash's mouth…"

Say WHAT?!

"Wait, hang on a sec..." I grumble.

Lex peeks at me, then goes back to Byron. "Voyeurism at its finest. I came just fine watching that little show."

Byron chuckles. "So you didn't want me to touch you...?"

"You can touch me now..."

"Good." Byron plays with Lex's fingers. "But I probably would've come way harder if you gave me a hand in that dark hallway." His eyes slide to me, and he winks. "Just sayin'."

I'm fucking livid, fuming so hard, steam is practically coming out of my ears.

Okay, what the fuck is up with him right now?? My normally quiet friend is acting like a gay nutball all of a sudden.

Is it because he's always secretly wanted to hook up with Lex? Is he messing with me because he's upset about something?

"Um, what's this little memory you guys are sharing right now??" I huff. "And where the hell was I when all this was going on?"

"I'll tell you later," Lex says. "But you were off being Percy Gage's personal fleshlight."

Fuck me. So that's what happened the night of the blackout??

You mean to tell me I wasted my time on Gage when I could've been with Lex and our friends, catching a live performance of the John and Harley Power Hour??

I've never felt FOMO so deep.

I'm obsessing over it, but my concerns fade into the background when Lex lies down at Byron's side and Byron runs his fingers up Lex's abs, dragging his shirt up with them.

God, I feel sick. I hate this so much already.

Before I can even psych myself up to it, they're fucking *kissing*.

"Okay, you guys..." I whimper, fisting the blankets while my heart screams bloody murder. "Message received. I already know how it feels... It *sucks*. Can we be done now??"

"Ren, back off," Byron mumbles on Lex's lips.

"Stop kissing him," I snarl, leaning over them, ready to rip them apart.

"Go over there." Lex kicks me away, and I slump petulantly against the wall, swallowing repeatedly as bile tries to rise in my throat. He glances at me. "Sit down and shut up, okay?"

Ohh, you sweet, infuriating boy... You are so lucky I'm obsessed with you.

Byron pulls Lex's shirt off and now they're kissing *more*, touching each other slowly. They both look a little stiff, but it's obvious they're just easing into it, the panting and suction echoing inside my skull.

Because I'm a man who's turned on by other men, the sight of these two hot as fuck guys making out is definitely buzzing my balls a little. But any arousal I could feel is being chased by a persistent ache in my chest from watching someone who's not me kissing *my* Lexington.

Fuck this. I was the only guy he'd ever kissed before… Now it's ruined.

My fingers squeeze into a fist. *So this is only like one-one hundredth of how Lex feels, then… knowing how many people I've been with who aren't him.*

I guess I'm seeing the point of this experiment. But it doesn't mean I have to like it!

"Do you wanna be on top?" Byron whispers, both of their eyes closed, lips brushing and hands… exploring.

"It's up to you," Lex hums.

"I don't mind either way…"

"Jesus, are you two fooling around or picking seats at the movies??" I sullenly fold my arms over my chest.

Lex grins, opening his eyes to peek at me. "He's getting upset."

Byron chuckles. "I bet he'd *hate* this, huh…?" His hand slithers below Lex's waist, cupping his cock.

Lex groans quietly and I whimper, chewing my lip bloody.

"Yea, he really doesn't like that," Lex croons. "He'd probably hate it even more if I did this…"

He pushes his hand inside Byron's pants. My eyes bulge, stomach rolling with intense nausea. I can't really tell, but I think Lex has his hand around Byron's dick, and is… stroking.

Kill me. Kill me right the fuck now.

"I like it," Byron purrs, eyes closed, head tipped back.

Lex is watching me, lips dropping to Byron's neck. "He's *so mad…*"

"I hate you both," I whine hoarsely.

"Doesn't feel good, does it?" Lex glares at me with hooded eyes, his hand working up and down on Byron's cock inside his pants.

"*Fffuck* yea, it does." Byron's lips shiver.

Lex peels his eyes off of me to look at him. "Oh, no, I meant… Never mind." He crawls on top of Byron and straddles his hips, licking and sucking his earlobe, heated gaze back on me while he whispers, "I like your big, hard dick, bro…"

"Dude, you should totally rub your long, thick cock on mine, fam," Byron's voice grates, lips twisted in amusement, though he's definitely into this, writhing around beneath Lex, humping up into his hand.

Dear God, I hate them both. These two fucking idiots are sending me!

Lex bites his lip, still watching my reaction while shoving his pants down. His dick flops out, and I guess I can delight very slightly in the fact that it doesn't look as painfully hard as it used to get with me. But it's still hard, and now he's bringing Byron's pants down, their two erections resting together.

"Ooh... my first uncut," Lex chirps.

Impotent fury seizes my muscles. "I think you've made your fucking point," I snap, vibrating in place. "I never did anything like this in front of you..."

Lex's amusement falls fast. "Are you kidding me?? What about the time you gave Velle a handjob in the middle of the cafeteria? Or the time you let Simmons suck on your nipples in the showers for like twenty minutes... *Or* the time Jasper was fucking you against the bars with a literal *crowd* of inmates watching—"

"Hey, I did that for your birthday cake!" I pout.

Lex rolls his eyes, then grabs his and Byron's dicks, stroking them slowly together. "The point is that I don't hate you for any of it, but you *definitely* deserve this."

I despise what he's saying so damn hard. Because it's true, and he's totally right.

I never knew until *right now* how much I've taken his virginity for granted.

The fact that he's a good, sweet little hot boy genius who doesn't spread himself around everywhere like I do is now officially the best gift I've ever received. I have to appreciate it, because watching this is like being torn apart, limb from limb.

"*Fuck* yea," Byron groans, gazing down as Lex jerks them off together. "Rub your balls on mine."

He moves their pants out of the way and Lex presses his hips down. "Like this?"

"*Mmm so good...*"

Quaking, my hand runs between my thighs, massaging my aching erection. It feels good, despite how angry I am. They fall back into kissing, slow and deep, and as much as it's killing me inside, it's *Lex*. Just seeing him like this is fucking *fire*, and I hate that it's not happening with me.

His eyes keep casually flicking open to look at me, and I cannot just *sit* here anymore. Pulling my dick out, I prop against the wall right next to them and curl my fist around it, building to a gradual stroke.

Byron's hands cup Lex's ass, gripping and squeezing him as their hard dicks grind together.

"You're leaking," I whisper, subtly inching closer to them.

"It feels… *uhhfuck*… really good." His tongue swipes Lex's lip. "I wanna feel his mouth…"

"Absolutely not," I growl.

"Wrap these sweet lips around my cock, homie," he purrs to Lex.

"I… can't," Lex shivers. "I've never done it before."

And he won't be doing it, for anyone but me.

"Neither have I…" Byron croaks, and the way his voice trails makes it sound like he kinda wants to.

"Lex," I whisper, and he aims his foggy gaze at me. "He wants to suck something…" I reach out, running my fingers over his nipple.

"H-huh?" he stammers, all flushed as he rocks his hips into Byron again and again, frotting them together desperately.

"Trust me," I hum.

Lex lifts himself up, and Byron doesn't hesitate. His tongue feathers over Lex's chest, lapping at his nipple, sucking it between his lips.

"*Fuck*, that feels good," Lex whines. "*Harder.*"

Byron goes on assaulting Lex's flesh, sucking and pulling it between his teeth until Lex is crying jagged moans. Then he moves over to the other, licking it sloppy, leaving the sweet, pink little point dripping in his saliva.

"This is so fucking hot," Byron grunts, kissing all over Lex's chest, holding him by the ass and helping him move. "You like this sucking, bro?"

"*Ffuck*, I think I might come," Lex whines, spitting into his hand to get their cocks slippery.

He keeps jerking them together, though his eyes are stuck on *my* hand and *my* dick, and the way just watching him is pulsing precum from the tip.

The jealousy has somehow swirled its way into a furious lust, clouding the air around the three of us. I know I'm not supposed to be involved in this, but I can't help it. The lesson has been learned, and now I just want to play with them because it's been *way* too long since I've been close to Lex like this.

"R-Ren…" Byron whispers through quivering lips. "What does his cum taste like…?"

My eyes slide to Lex. "He's the sweetest thing I've ever swallowed in my life."

Lex bites his lip.

"Can I try some…?" Byron is blissed out right now, a subtle flush in his complexion, muscles all tight and glistening, chest heaving.

"Jesus, I think I'm… gonna…" Lex pants, rocking his hips, fucking against Byron's cock as his lashes flutter.

"Come in your hand, Lexington," I command softly, making sure my gaze is locked on my sweet, shy boy.

I can't miss this… It's been *forever* since I've watched him come, and he's just so beautiful when he falls apart.

A broken sob leaves his lips, eyes squeezed shut as his dick shoots, and he milks each pulse into his left hand. "Fuck fuck *fuck…*"

Byron is chewing on his bottom lip, staring down in fascination.

"You come *so good*, gorgeous," I rush out, hoarsely. "Hold on to it. Don't spill any of that sweet stuff, baby."

He nods fast, blowing out a steady breath as he slowly returns to earth. His eyes creep open, that beautiful post-orgasm sparkle aimed right at me. Our gazes stay melted together, galaxies of desire and sexual tension between us. I have to use all of my strength to keep from lunging at him, grabbing his face and kissing those perfectly soft lips until he's crying into my mouth.

My eyes fall to my cock in silent instruction. And without a word, Lex reaches, fisting my erection with his cum-soaked hand, stroking it up and down to coat every inch in slickness.

"Oh God… *fuck me*, baby, it's been way too long since you've played with my dick," I whimper, crumbling from one touch. "It missed you *so bad…*"

"Easy," he scolds me in a hushed tone, releasing my erection when it's all wet with his cum. Then he grasps Byron's jaw. "You know you wanna suck on that juicy cock, my dude."

Lex bites his lip to contain his grin as Byron eyes my dick, lips parted and ready. But he's trembling, clearly never having done this before.

He's fucked me, jerked me off a little, sometimes we makeout, and I've *definitely* sucked his dick. But to my knowledge, Byron has never had a cock in his mouth.

Because he's *straight… Quote, unquote.*

"I'm not gay," he whispers while Lex pushes his face closer.

"Definitely not," Lex murmurs. "But I mean, look how pretty it is… all covered in my cum."

"Just a little taste…" Byron mumbles to himself, slipping his mouth gently over the head of my cock. His eyes immediately roll back in his skull.

"Mm… suck this dick, straight boy," I hum, watching him fall easily into slurping me deeper and deeper between his greedy lips.

In seconds, he's hungrily devouring my cock, sucking all of Lex's cum off while bobbing on my inches like a fiend. My gaze moves up to Lex's face, and he stares back at me, chest shuddering.

Reaching for his jaw, I run my thumb along his lower lip, and he whimpers, eyes falling shut. I stuff it into his mouth, and he sucks, the sensation curling my goddamn toes.

"You're gonna make me come," I whisper to Lex, because it's always *him*. But my fingers comb through Byron's hair. "Wanna swallow it?"

He nods frantically, sucking me harder and messier. The occasional scrape of his teeth sets me off, because I just *love* the bite of inexperience from hungry straight dudes. I shiver as cum spills from my cock, filling my friend's mouth. And I watch his throat adjusting to swallow it down while he moans on my dick.

His own orgasm sneaks up quick, pulses of cum jetting from his cock all over his abs with literally nothing touching it.

"That is so fucking sexy…" I rumble, caressing his jaw and neck, tracing from his dragon tattoo to the one I did for him on his chest.

Tugging my cock out of his mouth, I hold the back of his head, stuffing his face onto my nuts. He's all over them, licking, kissing, sucking, heaving for breath while I pull my fingers from Lex's mouth. Swiping them through Byron's cum, I stuff them into his mouth so he can taste himself too.

"Who has the best tasting cum?" Lex giggles.

"Me, duh," Byron rasps when I take my fingers out.

Lex gives me a look, curiously biting his lip. I can read his mind right now.

He wants to know how it tastes…

"You'll put that sweet mouth on my dick one of these days, baby," I whisper to him. "It's just a matter of time."

Lex whines petulantly, then slopes down and grasps Byron's face to kiss him, sliding his tongue into Byron's mouth. I still hate watching it, even after that wild little threesome we just had unexpectedly.

I don't want him with anyone else again… Ever.

But just as I'm about to rage, Lex slurps off of Byron's lips, reaching for my jaw and pulling my mouth to his.

Fireworks.

That's all I see behind my eyes. *Fireworks* are all I *feel* popping off in my chest.

He's actually kissing me... I'm not dreaming, right?

God, it feels amazing. I could cry.

"Baby, I missed this so much," I whimper into his mouth, because I can't help it, gripping his face and feeding him my tongue.

He groans, sucking and biting my lips like he fucking missed it too, just as bad.

But then he pulls away, ending it way too soon. "Sorry..." He brushes his swollen mouth over mine. "Got swept up in the moment."

"Please keep getting swept." I clutch his neck. "Never stop sweeping..."

He presses one more soft one on me before backing away, curling up next to Byron. Byron's eyes peek open, shifting to Lex. And they bump fists.

I can't help the laugh that rumbles out of me as I lie down next to them.

Fuckin straight guys.

"I don't want to get in the middle of you two..." Byron sighs, even though that's literally exactly where he is.

I reach over his chest, taking Lex's hand in mine. "You're not a wedge, love. You've been keeping us together."

"Good," he yawns sleepily. "'Cause I'd rather kill myself than date either of you." Lex snorts. "Plus... I'm totally straight." I cackle, and Byron grins. "What?"

CHAPTER SIXTEEN

Luthor

Weeks later…

NOT THAT I'M A PESSIMIST OR ANYTHING, BUT SOMETIMES IT'S HARD TO admit when things are going well. I always feel like acknowledging when life is good is just asking for it to all suddenly blow up in your face.

Do me a favor, if you see me floating away, just grab my ankle and pull me back down to earth. Please and thank you.

Since that ridiculous, hot, sexy, foolhardy romp I had with Kang and Ren, the vibes around here have been surprisingly good. Things actually didn't get weird, at least it doesn't feel like they did. We've all been hanging out like we used to, and believe it or not, Ren has been great.

Of course, he's still insufferably flirtatious. It's just the way he is, but he seems to be directing it more at us than anyone else, which is good and bad.

Either way, I'm not getting my hopes up for anything, and like I told him that day, we are *not* starting back up again. We're still just friends, even if it's admittedly nice to spend time with him the way we used to, before he fucked everything up and made me hate him.

And maybe the platonic nature gets fuzzy sometimes when I remember how kissing him the other day set fire to my insides. But that's true of most things that are bad for you. I just need to remember the steps of my sobriety and stay strong.

I will not relapse on my fuckboy best friend.

After all, Ren doesn't change. We know this.

Him apologizing and getting a taste of his own medicine was all well and good, but he's still *him*. So, I give it a week. He'll fall back into his usual ways, and when he does, I refuse to be upset about it. There's only so much back and forth, toxic bullshit I can partake in before I become just as complicit as he is.

Ya know... fool me once, et cetera...

Outside of all that, it's good to feel settled for a change. I was able to get my hands on some spare computer parts to build my machine, and the craziest thing is that no one had to suck anyone off to get them.

I know, right? What dimension am I in??

Joy actually agreed to sneak me some old junk from the control rooms in exchange for a tattoo from Ren, and a promise that I wouldn't do anything stupid with this device.

Her exact words were, *"If you get caught or fuck anything up, you don't know me, and I don't know you."*

I laughed at her, though she wasn't even cracking a smile. *"But we* do *know each other... No one would believe that."*

She just rubbed her eyes and sighed, *"Lord, beer me strength."*

I like her. She's one of the best people on this rock, by a Stevie Nicks Landslide.

So with that, I've got a decent mock-up going on my janky alpha LOIS, and Ren keeps teasing that he's going to tattoo *Twat Waffle* on Joy in Korean, but Kang won't tell him how to write it, which causes some pretty hilarious bickering between them.

Good times.

Still, it wouldn't be Alabaster Pen without distress festering beneath the surface. We're all still wondering about the state of O'Malley, especially after Dash said he saw him in the East Wing getting old Mister Shocky.

He also told us he saw Darcey down there too, who didn't look any better. None of us really know Darcey that well, but Dash never hesitates to vouch for him. I guess they formed some kind of bond in solitary. Now Dash is worried about this fancy shrink they're sending in to study his pal, The Carver.

Honestly, I don't blame him. If the East Wing doctors are as sadistic as we all know they are, then I can only *imagine* what kinds of fucked-up shit this mysterious Psych Superstar hand-picked by Manuel Blanco will be like.

It's not looking good for anyone in the padded cells. Prisoners rarely come back from the East. Landon, my last cellmate, is a perfect example. He started to lose his shit, talking all crazy about wanting to break out, just like Toby did. It was that behavior that got him sent to the East, and the official story is that he's *still down there.*

But off the record, just like with Parker, we all know it isn't true.

Summer is upon us, a bittersweet time here that's much more bitter than sweet. On the plus side, it's less freezing during the summer months, and when it gets hot outside, this building still manages to stay cool, like it has built-in AC thanks to all the concrete and lack of windows. But the downside is we never get to actually *enjoy* the nice weather. Over the years, we've begged and pleaded with Joy to take us outside, even just for a few minutes. We told her she could chain us to a tree if she wanted to. But her answer is always the same…

"It's the one thing I can't give you."

Being here for so long, you overhear a lot of conversations you're not supposed to be hearing. Things about the layout of the island, the forest-like smattering of trees between the prison and the mansion… The fact that there's a small dock with a boat stashed somewhere out there.

After Toby tried his escape, we learned that the guard tower actually isn't *guarded…* by anyone. *Can you believe that shit??*

Because of all that, I guess it's the Correctional Officers' ultimate mission to make sure none of us ever get to see it for ourselves. It's one thing to hear stories, but it's an entirely different brand of hope to witness it with your own eyes.

But none of that matters to me. I've already lost two cellmates—two *friends*—to the obsession of thinking they can escape not only the Pen, but the Isle itself. That won't be me.

I'm here, and I'm never leaving. I have to be okay with that.

So this lovely evening is spent delighting in the simple joys of prison life. Dash and I are chatting casually while I tinker with my machine. But I must be really tired because I wind up falling asleep on top of it before the lights even turn off in the row.

Noises and movements startle me awake, and I groan quietly from the pain of the motherboard digging into my arm. Blinking the grogginess from my eyes, I look around, a whimper drawing my attention to my cellmate, who's up and pacing in the dark, mumbling to himself.

"Dash?" I whisper, but he doesn't acknowledge me.

He just keeps walking in a circle, rubbing his eyes. "Where is he?? Is he coming back…?"

My brow furrows, unease pinging like alarm bells in my head. *Something isn't right...*

Dash has easily become one of my best friends, but you'd have to be completely oblivious not to notice his issues. There's been no shortage of worrying behavior on his part since the moment he set foot in this cell. But I don't judge him. I just care about him, and I want him to be okay.

No, I need *him to be. I refuse to let* another *friend slip through my fingers.*

"Dash..." I call to him again, quietly, my pulse picking up.

He still hasn't heard me, or even looked up. He's too busy pacing and muttering. I can barely make out what he's saying, but I hear something like, "I am what you are," and a name...

"*Callum*... Where are you, Callum?"

Who the hell is Callum?

Wasn't that the name of Ren's ex...?

Peering fully over the side of the bunk, I whisper-shout at him. "Dash!"

Finally, his face springs up. "Luthor... You're awake." He glances at the door. "He'll... He'll probably be here soon... I'm sorry, I thought you were sleeping."

My brow cocks. "Who will be here soon?"

Dash chuckles, shaking his head. "Ehh... *God.*" He runs his fingers through his hair, mouth twisted in some knowing amusement that's really baffling me. "I guess you had to find out eventually... Honestly, I'm surprised it's taken this long." He peeks up at me. "You could sleep through an earthquake, bro."

Okay, I have literally no fucking clue what he's talking about.

"Dash... are you alright?" I blink, watching him closely.

He lets out a breath, rubbing his eyes. "No... I don't know." Stepping over to his bed, he plops down like he's suddenly exhausted.

I have to figure out what's up with him. He's acting way weirder than usual right now.

Climbing down from my bunk, I stare at him where he's sitting with his face in his hands, knee bouncing rapidly.

"Hey..." I take a seat next to him on the bed, placing my hand gently on his shoulder. "What's wrong?" He shakes his head, face still buried in his palms. "You can talk to me. We tell each other everything, remember?"

"You're such a good friend, Luthor," he mumbles into his hands before finally lifting his face to look at me. His eyes are glistening in the low light, pupils noticeably large. "That's why I feel so bad for keeping this from you..."

My heart crawls up into my throat, and I gulp. "Just tell me, man. No matter what, I'm here for you."

He goes quiet for a moment, muttering something under his breath, then blinking hard. I've seen him do it before, when he gets all twitchy. It's like he's trying to ctrl-alt-delete something out of his head.

"He might show up..." he says quietly. "I mean... I hope he does. Because I miss him... God, why the fuck do I *miss* him??"

His tone is softly distraught, and I feel bad, but I still have no idea what the hell he's talking about. It's like he's speaking in riddles. He's obviously torn up about something, or *someone*, and I just don't know who.

Yesterday in the showers, Ren was grilling Dash about where he's been getting all his stuff, and Dash claims it's not from anyone specific, but that makes even less sense.

No one just gets things *in here. He has to have been seeing someone...*

Someone *has been sneaking in here, leaving his gifts.*

Could it be Rook?

He said no, but the two of them seem to have a little back and forth. They've been known to flirt... *And then there was the whole Dash swallowing Rook's cum extravaganza.*

Man, if Rook shows up in our cell, it's gonna totally blow my mind.

"Dash... *who* are you talking about?" I ask carefully.

He closes his eyes, head bowed as he whispers, "I never wanted a guy before, but I feel like you were... *made... for... me.*"

I swallow, growing more confused by the second. "Hey, it's okay to like it. You're definitely not the only one who's gotten swept up in—"

"The lines get blurry in here," he interrupts, peeking up at me. "You told me that. The lines are very... *very* blurry now." His gaze flings to the bars and he gets this faraway stare thing going on.

I stick my face in front of his, but he doesn't seem to even *see* me. I snap my fingers.

Nothing.

"Dash...?"

Suddenly, he shoots up off the bed and stalks over to the door, peering through the bars. "He's coming. I can hear him..."

I listen for any sound that would indicate someone in the row, but I don't hear shit. There's *no one* out there... Nothing but snores coming from the other cells.

Standing up, I stare at him, watching him fidget and touch his face. He says something in Russian, repeating it over and over, like a soft chant.

This is really freaking me out.

Summoning my courage to buck up and help my friend, I step over to him slowly and take his hand. "Dash, let's just go sit down, okay? Just take a breath…"

His eyes are stuck on the floor. And when his chin gradually lifts, they set on mine, and they're *dark*; somehow much darker than usual. It must be the overwhelming size of his pupils.

His fidgeting has stopped completely. In fact, he's standing straighter, breathing slower. In the blink of an eye, his entire demeanor has completely changed, and there's this air of bored dominance suddenly oozing from him while he eyes me like I'm something he's been looking for.

"I missed you," he rumbles. He doesn't even *sound* like him.

He sounds… deeper. Scarier.

It reminds me of that night, when I was dreaming about me and Ren, and I kept hearing Dash, like he was speaking to himself as somebody else…

This person, who's looking at me right now.

He steps forward, and I step back, dropping his hand. But as soon as I do, he reaches out slowly, placing his finger under my chin.

My heart is pounding in my skull. I have no idea what's going on, but I'm low-key terrified.

Why is he looking at me like that?

He keeps stepping toward me, and I keep backing up, gulping down my nerves. "Dash…"

"Did you miss me… *Luscious*?" He cocks his head.

"Okay… um…" I stammer for words, head wobbling back and forth. "Hang on, can we just… talk for a sec?"

He shakes his head. "No more talking, Dascha."

"Wait… *I'm* Dascha?" My blinking speeds up in perplexity as he pushes into my space.

I try to get some space between us, but my legs hit the bed and I crash onto it. And he immediately crawls over me, trapping me beneath him.

Oh God, oh fuck… What's happening??

"The only words I want to hear from you are about how fucking good I'm making you feel," he growls over my lips, his breath hitting my face. It's minty, like those Wintergreen candies I sometimes see him sucking on, though I haven't the slightest clue where he gets them from. "Do you understand?"

Placing my hands on his chest, I push to keep him at a distance, so I can think for a second. I need to wrap my head around this and not get distracted by the fact that I'm very warm right now.

Seriously, I feel like my clothes are going to melt off my body.

Swiftly, he grabs my hands and pins them over my head.

My lashes flutter at his face. "W-wait… stop…"

"Don't get up in your head, Dascha…" he whispers, holding my wrists with one hand while the other lowers, traveling up my side. "Just let me do bad things to you."

"But you're my friend," I huff. "We shouldn't be doing this…"

His head cocks.

And I just don't get it… It makes very little sense.

But I can *see* it now, plain as day.

"You're not… Dash…" I whisper nervously. "Are you?"

He doesn't respond, just regards me curiously, fingers brushing along my navel, a ticklish spot that makes me flinch.

Okay, uh… this is crazy. This is fucking insane… *Who am I dealing with right now??*

Taking on a new tactic, I ask, "What's your name…?"

"Call me what I am to you, inmate," his voice rumbles into my chest from his.

Inmate… holy fuck. He thinks I'm him. I'm *Dash.*

So then who is he??

I just stare up at him blankly, observing how his eyes are almost squinted, like he's in a trance.

"Who are you?" I ask again.

His hand slides up to my throat, fear lancing my stomach. "*Officer*, inmate 101." His hips press down into mine, and I don't want it to happen, but my dick begins to fill at the friction.

"Officer…" The word slips from my shivering lips.

I want to keep him talking, to find out more while also verifying that he's not going to hurt me. But I'm way out of my comfort zone.

I don't know how to deal with this… Whatever it is. Split personality?

"You know I wanted you from the moment I saw you," he whispers, easing in closer until his lips brush mine.

And before I can even try to wiggle my way out of this, or think of what to say… he's kissing me.

Dash is fucking *kissing* me.

But this isn't Dash… I mean, it *is*, but not really. *God, I'm lost.*

And his lips are really soft.

I gasp a jagged moan into his mouth, instantly subdued by the way he's taking over my mouth. I don't know that this is how Dash would kiss… It's much more dominant; almost aggressive, but also tender and cherishing.

Not that I've thought about kissing Dash before. He's my friend and this is… odd. I won't say he isn't attractive, because he *is* the kind of beautiful that takes your breath away, whether you want it to or not. But still, we're supposed to be friends…

Why am I hooking up with all my friends now?? Jesus, I'm on a rampage!

I know for a *fact* I should be stopping this, but there's something about it that has me falling… panting and squirming and sweating like I'm in a fever dream.

I'm not Luthor… I'm Dash.

And he's the officer who wants me.

One of my hands slips free from his hold, gliding down shakily to cup his jaw. Our mouths are moving in tandem, sucking and nipping, tongues pushing together to feather and flick. It feels good… It feels *really* fucking good, actually. As is confirmed when he grinds his crotch between my legs, his hard dick grazing mine through our clothes.

"*Fuck…*" I whimper into his mouth.

"My sweet Dascha Luscious." He groans praises that make me weak, sucking and biting my mouth numb while my pulse pounds like a bass drum in my skull.

I need to stop this… He doesn't know what he's doing. It's not right.

Just a few more seconds… and we'll stop.

"Fuck, this is so good," he growls into my mouth.

My head is spinning. This is the strangest makeout session ever, but it's blowing my mind right now.

Dash releases my hand, gripping my chest while he writhes into me. Without even noticing, my hands slide down to cup his ass.

And then something changes. He mewls, this sexy raspy little noise, instantly shivering against my body. In the blink of an eye, he's suddenly much softer, *needier*.

"Mmmff," he groans. "Fuck me, Officer."

Now, I'm Officer?? What on earth??

"Dash…?" I mumble, pulling our lips apart.

We're both panting like crazy, and he's looking down at me, resembling himself again. But I still don't think it's *me* he's seeing.

He lets out a sated purr and nestles up on top of me, his head tucking into the crook of my neck. "You're always so *warm*..."

My fingers absentmindedly trail down his back. *Who does he think I am right now?*

Whoever it is, he clearly has strong feelings for this person. And the other version of him has strong feelings in return.

As batshit loco as this whole experience is, I can't help feeling a pang of jealousy... I'm actually *jealous* of this strange relationship Dash is having with himself.

I do miss the feeling of being held and cherished like the most valuable treasure in the world. Being pinned down and comforted and cared for, while also being needed, above all else.

A few minutes of calming breaths later, Dash is passed out on my chest, leaving a puddle of drool on me. Smiling fondly, I carefully move him and slip out of his bed. I cover him with a blanket, admiring the perfect lines of his face. He looks so *peaceful* right now. Much more than he was before that bizarre interaction started.

And I guess that's because *he* showed up, just like Dash was hoping.

Crawling back to my own bed, I curl up and let my eyelids droop. But something rustling beneath my pillow has me reaching underneath.

It's one of the wrappers from the mints he likes.

That's weird... How did that get up here?

Shrugging it off, I close my eyes and drift off to sleep.

We'll just keep the making out to ourselves for now.

It'll be our little secret... *Me, and Dash's Officer.*

See? I knew it.

I just *knew* the good vibes would erode in this fucking place. And here I was going on and on about how *happy* I was, like some prison noob.

I've been here too long to fall for that shit. Good things never last in Alabaster Penitentiary.

Ren and Kang are arguing about something, playfully shoving each other back and forth like very muscular children, but I can't even focus on how cute it is. I'm too busy watching Dash.

He looks exhausted as he fidgets in his seat, tearing tiny chunks off of a piece of bread to make a pile of discarded food he's not even eating. He seems more anxiously despondent than usual, and I feel purely awful… Because I think it's all my fault.

I kinda lost my cool with him last night.

And I'm not talking about the inadvertent makeout session with his split personality.

After that whole thing happened, it was painfully clear to me that Dash's mind is quite sick. But even knowing that, I—one of his *only* friends—yelled at him when he was just trying to talk about his feelings.

Yea, I know. I'm a total dick.

Last night, I was in a mood, I guess. Not to shift responsibility or anything, but it was sort of Ren's fault. *We'll just blame him for everything, it's fine. He's used to it.*

At dinner, Kang was voicing some more concern about the fact that we haven't seen O'Malley in two months, and Ren, the emotional kamikaze pilot he is, decided to bring up Landon and Freeman in the same goddamn breath. He bummed us all out, and to top it off, I came back to our cell to work on the computer only for it to start giving me grief.

Certain pieces weren't fitting, the power supply box was weak, and the CPU was proving to be a giant turd. I was frustrated… Probably more with Ren than anything else. So when Dash started talking shit about how we shouldn't be stuck in here forever, sounding *way* too much like Landon, I just snapped.

It wasn't a huge fight or anything. I just bitched at him for a second, and we didn't talk for the rest of the night, falling asleep in tense, awkward silence. I apologized to him first thing this morning, and he seemed totally cool about it. He claimed it was fine, almost like he'd forgotten about our argument altogether. But all day since, he's been acting weird.

Maybe it's not my fault… It might have something to do with his disorder, but I still feel bad. I can't shake this feeling that he's mad at me. And after I knowingly made out with him while he was in the midst of a major psychological episode, I'm wallowing in some serious guilt.

I mean, who the hell makes out with their best friend while he's suffering like that? Sure, he started it, but still. I'm the level-headed one. *I* should've stopped it. And I definitely shouldn't have barked at him when he was just trying to talk, taking out my frustrations on someone in need of my help.

I'm a shitty friend, and a terrible human being.

Ren stands up, distracting me from Dash-watch. "I'm heading back early to set up," he sighs, poking Dash on the jaw. "See you in a few, peaches."

Dash shows him a tiny smile, though it definitely looks strained.

Ren winks at me before wandering off, my eyes following him until he's out of sight. Then I'm back on Dash.

"That's right… You're getting inked today," I murmur to him, casually supportive. "Are you excited?"

His eyes finally slink up to mine, a genuine smile sloping on his mouth. "Yea… Actually, I am. It's been a while."

"Ren's good," Kang says with his mouth full. "The gun isn't great with fine lines, but his script work is excellent. You know what you're getting?"

Dash's lips part to answer, but then he pauses for a second. "I have an idea… I don't know, it might be stupid."

"I'm sure it's not," I tell him. "I think any tattoo is cool because it's, like, self-expression, ya know?"

"Says the virgin," Kang teases through his chewing. I'm glaring at him as he swallows, containing his evil smirk. "Sorry… *tattoo* virgin."

I roll my eyes. "I'm seriously regretting telling you that…"

"Hey, I think it's cute," he goes on with the obvious ragging. "There are *so many* things little Luthy's never done."

"You sure you wanna pull that thread, Hoover?" I taunt him with my own wicked grin. "I'm calling you *Hoover* now, since you really like to suck—"

"*Okay*, fine," Kang grunts. "You made your point, shithead. I'll never mention your cherry ever again." He draws an X over his chest with his finger.

"Much obliged." I smirk at him, and he makes a face feigning amusement.

"For real, though," Kang says. "Are you ever gonna get one?"

"I've been thinking about it for a while." I nod, my mind mulling over tattoos.

"You know Ren would die." He chuckles. "Putting something permanent on you must be like his dream come true." Heat rises in my cheeks as I purse my lips. "Just make sure you get it where you can see it. Otherwise, you'll end up with *Property of Warren Xavier* on your lower back."

He cackles while I shake my head. Still, he's not wrong about the tattoo thing. Ren has been not-so-subtly hinting that he wants to tattoo me for years, and it's not that I'm opposed to it. I'm just very indecisive about what I'd like to get. Ren has drawn me a few ideas since he got his gun, but for some reason, it's still dragging my feet.

I have no qualms about it being permanent. Plus, it's something exciting to do in a place where excitement is in short supply.

Maybe it's just the idea of my first tattoo...

Kang might be right. I seem to have a *virgin mentality*. Always dwelling on the first time needing to be *special*.

I'm distracted from these thoughts when Velle shouts about the two-minute warning. We gather ourselves up and head back, at which point Rook grabs Dash and brings him to Ren's cell. On my way past, I peek inside at Ren, sitting on his bed fiddling with his tray of tattoo supplies.

Man, this mood is a tough one to shake.

I still feel guilty about what I said to Dash, and now, on top of it, I can't stop thinking about Ren. In my defense, I have a tendency to think about Ren, and it always irks me when I can't make myself stop.

In my cell, I try to shake it off, climbing up to my bunk to work on my machine a little.

Everything is fine. Dash is good, Ren and I are better as friends, and I'm just having a bad day. No reason to get all Edgar Allan Poe about it.

Focusing my energy on the computer gives me a renewed sense of determination. Twenty-minutes later, I've had a mini breakthrough, which is unfortunately cut short by voices out in the row. I think Rook is bringing Dash back, but when I hear Velle grumbling, I can tell right away he isn't happy.

I mean, when is that dude ever happy?

Still, I can decipher his moods and his tones pretty well, and the one I'm hearing now usually means, *Ultimate Bitch Mode: Activated.*

Jeez, I guess everyone's having a bad day. It must be a full moon... Mercury in retrograde or some shit.

Easing toward the edge of my bed, I try to listen to what Velle's saying. He's obviously talking to Dash, but they're a little too far away for me to make it out. Dash's voice raises in volume, and it sounds like they're definitely arguing.

Then I hear Velle say something about *murder*, and the name *Karly Clayton*.

Oh shit. He's talking to Dash about his crimes... about killing the governor's niece.

My stomach is churning. *Dash really did suppress memories of what got him sent here. My poor, broken friend...*

Velle snarls, "Fucking high-profile goddamn bullshit…" And the next thing I know, he's dragging Dash up to our cell and shoving him inside.

Dash crashes to the floor with the echo of Velle slamming the bars and storming off.

Quickly, I rush down from my bunk to get my friend, who's literally curled up in the fetal position on the floor, trembling and rocking himself, muttering under his breath.

"No… *no no no*… I don't… I didn't… *mean to*…"

It's exactly like the panic attack he had in the rec room that day, after he beat the shit out of Ren. And I'd say this sort of PTSD-like unearthing of trauma has the potential to stir up more symptoms of whatever disorder he has.

I can't have that. I need to help him.

"Dash, are you alright, man?" I lift him up off the floor, carefully helping him to his bed. "What happened?"

He's sputtering for air, face ashen, sweat breaking out on his forehead. "I can't… breathe…"

"Here." Gently grasping him by the shoulders, I lean him forward. "Put your head between your knees. Like this."

I have some experience with panic attacks, due to my mild social anxiety, so I'm familiar enough with how to get your heart rate under control when it feels like your lungs are shriveled to the size of a deflated balloon.

"Breathe in through your nose, and out through your mouth." I demonstrate. "Do it, Dash."

He nods uneasily, sucking in air through his nose, blowing it out slowly through his mouth while I do it along with him, rubbing his back in calming circles. He's shaking so badly, he's practically vibrating next to me. But I just keep breathing with him and rubbing his back until *finally* he starts to relax a little.

My eyes shift to some visibly new ink on his wrists… *My* on one, and *Officer* on the other.

Holy… whoa.

I try to focus as his bunched-up muscles ease, breathing beginning to regulate. It takes minutes, but eventually, he sits up straight, blinking as he looks around the room.

"Dude, what the hell happened to you?"

Dash peers at me, forehead lined in some very intense emotions. He's looking at me fondly, but also with some guilt and worry shimmering in the hazel of his irises.

"Luthor." He says my name on a ragged breath. "If I told you to come with me to solitary tomorrow night… If I told you we could get out of here, and all you have to do is follow me… would you?"

Oh, no.

No no no… Not this again.

My spine stiffens. "Dash… I think you need to get some rest. You're not making any sense."

"No, I'm serious." He rubs his face. "I'm getting out of here tomorrow, Luthor, and if you want, you can come with me. I think you should. This place is…" His voice trails as he blinks desperation at me. "I don't want you to waste away in here. You're my friend."

The strongest wave of déjà vu washes over me while I stare at him, mouth hanging agape. It's like I'm right back to last year, sitting in this *exact same spot*, gaping at a frantic Henry Landon who swore to me he was *getting out of here*.

My heart clenches inside my chest. "What are you even talking about?" I gasp, pretty much the same words. "How could you be getting out? It makes no sense…"

"I have a plan. We do… One of the guards is…" Dash stops abruptly, staring at me for a moment before he says, "It's going to work. Tomorrow night, through solitary… You have to come with me, Luthor. You can be free and *live*. Live the rest of your life, outside of this shithole. *Please*… Come."

He's begging me, *pleading* with his eyes and a tone dripping affection. And I'm falling apart inside. This feels *just like* with Landon, only worse. Because Dash seems like he needs me to believe in this with him, and I just *can't*.

Not again… I've seen it too many fucking times.

Jumping up from the bed, I begin pacing around the room. "No. You're fucking nuts. There's no way that would ever work, and I can't…" I exhale roughly, shaking my head over and over to expel the angst crawling up my chest. "You don't know what you're talking about. No one gets out."

I mean, seriously. Is the cell fucking cursed or something? Am I cursed??

Why does this keep happening to me? How come every time I get a new cellmate, they wind up desperate to leave? Is it me?? Am I driving these people away?

Why would everyone rather risk death than just stay with me in my cold, quiet little cell…?

I must be a real fucking loser…

My insecurities are raging like a storm as Dash shoots up and grabs my shoulders, forcing me to look at him. "*I* am. I'm getting out, Luth. And you need to come."

"I can't," I whimper, pressure in my head building to a swift migraine.

"Why not??" he hisses. "Why the fuck can't you at least *try*?"

My lips tremble, fighting to hold in the words.

I don't think you're crazy… Wanting to escape isn't the crazy thing.

The crazy thing is wanting to stay.

"Because…" I whisper, sorrowfully. "I *can't* leave…"

Because there's more than just fear of the unknown holding me here…

There's a piece of me in this prison… *sitting in the cell at the end of the row.*

I think Dash realizes what I'm saying without words, the frustration on his face fading as his hands slip away from my shoulders.

The Luthor from five years ago would have gone with him in a heartbeat. Back then, I wouldn't have cared about risking death. Getting out of here, *freedom*, would be well worth the gamble of my life.

But it's not just me anymore…

No matter how toxic it is, how codependent and confusing and downright fucking stupid, I could never leave Ren. *Ever.*

I'll be right here in this prison for as long as he's here. I'll fucking die here in this concrete tomb, with him. *Because I know he would do the exact same thing for me.*

Dash stares at me, and I stare back, both of us just silently breathing. Living in the truth of all this…

Prison, inside and out.

He nods in understanding, pulling me into a tight embrace. My friend hugs me hard, arms around my shoulders while mine slink around his waist to hold him back.

I don't want to lose him…

I don't want to lose another friend, but I especially don't want to lose *Dash*.

Sometimes souls find each other on purpose. The universe is not random. Things happen the way they're supposed to, based on chemical reactions, the buzz of electric alchemy in this giant cosmic experience.

Dash came into my life only two months ago, and I can say with full certainty that I love him, deeply, as a friend. As *family*. Just like Toby, Parker, and Landon, may they rest…

Like Byron.

And Ren.

They're not perfect, but they're *my* friends, and I love them.

I don't know what makes Dash feel so confident that he can pull off what no inmate has ever successfully done, but for *him*, I'll hold out hope. I'll fight the skepticism, the cynicism, and be optimistic for him. Because I don't want him to die.

If I have to lose him, let it be to chance, not this fucking island.

"You're my best friend, Luthor," he whispers in my ear.

I nod with my face in his neck, holding back the tears as best I can. *Stay positive for him.*

Pulling from his embrace, I lock our eyes. "Regardless of how fucked up it is, I'm glad you came here. I'm glad I got to meet you."

He shows me a small smile, and I smile back.

I'm selfish. I don't want this to be goodbye...

But I also know that Dash has been the least contained prisoner I've met in my five years of being here. He seems almost... too big for this place.

If anyone could break out and soar free, it would be him.

Pursing my lips over my grin, I ruffle his hair that's been slowly growing back. He chuckles and finally lets me go.

This isn't the end, I tell myself, desperate to believe it.

Maybe it's just the beginning.

CHAPTER SEVENTEEN

Ren

The next day…

WALKING THE HALLS TO THE CAFETERIA, MY GAZE, UNSURPRISINGLY, IS on Lex. The familiar slope of his neck, and all those spots I've loved kissing whenever he's ever allowed me the opportunity. It might be my favorite part of him.

I mean, he has no shortage of amazing body parts. Masculine hands, a torso of cut lines that appear effortlessly panted on. The gemlike eyes, those puffy pink lips… His dick.

Lord, help me, that beautiful, big dick. It deserves to have statues of it erected…

LoLz.

But his neck, I find to be purely *wondrous* terrain. The bridge between his broad, sculpted shoulders and the sharp jawline that blazes the trail to his brainy noggin. The *neck*—mainly his throat and that sensitive spot behind his ear—is a sexy little erogenous zone my lips are constantly pining to explore. Maybe leave some purple marks in their wake.

I gave him a hickey once. It was when we first started hooking up way back when, and naturally he wasn't amused. He felt like I was doing it on purpose, to *brand* him.

He was totally right.

The way I see it, he's always been mine, whether he realizes it or not… *Agree to disagree, I guess.*

Right now, though, my appreciation for Lexington's creamy, unmarked flesh is being sullied by the frown tugging at his mouth, and the worry in his eyes as he watches the person walking in front of us... Dash.

He's so invested in watching Dash that he didn't even hear me speaking to him. So I graze my fingers on his lower back and try again, "You okay?"

Lex flinches at my touch, face flinging in my direction to *finally* acknowledge me. "Huh?" My brow arches, and he sighs. "I'm sorry, I'm just..." His eyes dart to Dash once more before he whispers, "I'm worried about Dash. He seems really off today..."

"Yea, you know what? I did notice that myself." I nod animatedly.

"Really??"

"*No*, babe," I huff, and he rolls his eyes. "Dash is *always* off. Not a day has gone by in the two months we've known him when he didn't seem like the voices in his head were reciting every line from *Full Metal Jacket*."

"Ren, be serious," Lex grunts. "He's our friend. We should be supporting him, not making fun of him behind his back."

My gaze narrows and I give him a studious look. I won't pretend it still doesn't irk me just the tiniest bit that he's so damn attentive to Dash's feelings.

You might not have realized this because I hide it *so well*, but I'm a jealous fuck. And I just don't *understand* their relationship.

Yes, they're cellmates, and they spend pretty much every minute of the day together—*when Dash isn't in solitary, that is*. But still, I can't fathom the protectiveness, to an almost overbearing degree, that Lex has for Dash.

Maybe Lex knows something he isn't letting on... Some intimate details about the complexities of our pretty, Russian friend. I'd really like to press him about it, but now's not the time. Not when Dash is right in front of us, twitching and glancing all around like a motel room crackhead.

We file into the caf, and as soon as his cuffs are off, Dash is booking it across the room. In the wrong direction.

"Where is he going?" Kang mutters, clearly just as confused as the rest of us.

"I should go check on him," Lex says, ready to static cling to his bestie. But I grab him by the shirt, redirecting him over to our table.

"Leave him be. Sheesh, you're like a mother hen," I grumble. "Go sit down with Byron, and I'll get your food. Dash will be right over, I'm sure."

He doesn't seem confident in the plan, but he does it anyway, following Byron to our table while I scurry up to the line and grab our food.

Sliding into the seat next to Lex, I nudge his arm, nodding at the food in front of him. "Eat."

He exhales, forfeiting the nervous staring long enough to take a bite of spaghetti.

An Alabaster Pen delicacy… Pasta with red sauce.

It's literally just mushy Costco brand spaghetti and jar sauce that's obviously been made in bulk and frozen, but still. It's one of the better things we get. A stark contrast to the *mystery meat casserole*, which you should only eat if you're in need of a colon cleanse, or have accidentally ingested poison.

"So… what's new?" I ask the boys, in an effort to act normal and distract Lex.

I need to keep him eating and talking so he doesn't notice that Dash *is* actually behaving very strangely. He's over in a corner, pacing and talking to himself. I don't want to freak Lex out more than he already is, but even I'm starting to worry about the kid. He seems totally unhinged.

"Nothing…" Lex sniffs, pushing his pasta around with his fork. "Have you, um… watched any new movies on your iPad?"

"Well, it only has four movies, so I've already watched each one about five times." I chuckle. "But it also has season six of *The Big Bang Theory*, so… I definitely have that sombitch memorized by now. I swear to God, that show makes you smarter. Go ahead, ask me anything about String Theory."

My rambling fades into awkward chuckles, brows furrowing at Dash, who's across the room having a heated argument… with himself.

I tap my fingers on the table. "Let's see, what else… It has the soundtrack to *Hedwig on Broadway*, the Neil Patrick Harris version, so that's pretty cool. Some eBooks I'm assuming are smut based on the shirtless dudes on the covers… Ooh! There's an audiobook on there that's gay as fuck! I skipped to the middle to try to find a sex scene, and let me tell you… *Boner-approved.*"

Dash shouts something at the wall, and I bite the inside of my cheek. *God dammit…*

Peters and Brenner rush over, all eyes in the room now on Dash, who's deep in a psychotic episode, yanking at his hair and yelling at no one. Around the room, inmates call out taunts, a few jumping up from their seats.

"Sit the fuck down!" Rook barks at the guys, and they slink back into place.

He and Joy are lingering by our table, watching on with the rest of us as Brenner and Peters try to subdue Dash. I know I was trying to downplay it, but Lex was totally right. Dash is not doing well *at all*, and now I'm kind of scared for him.

My chest constricts at the sight of Brenner and Peters grabbing our friend, lifting him by his arms and legs, attempting to cuff him while he struggles against their hold.

"Shit shit shit..." Joy mumbles, stepping forward like she wants to intervene, but can't.

She actually looks *nervous*. That alone is worrying, since I can count on one hand the number of times I've seen an emotion on her face other than annoyance.

Dash is wriggling in Brenner's arms while Peters tries to secure the cuffs. A whimper comes from Lex at my side, and I reach over quick, grabbing his hand.

"What's going on?" Lex cries quietly. "What are they doing to him??"

"Calm down," Rook mumbles, but even he looks concerned.

Heavy footsteps charge up from behind us.

And here comes Daddy to get the kids in line...

"What the fuck is going on over here?" Velle barks, storming up to his men and our panicked, sobbing friend.

I can't hear what Dash is saying, but the fear in his eyes and the tears streaming down his cheeks are breaking my fucking heart. Lex is squeezing my hand so hard, it's going numb. Kang is anxiously gnawing on his bottom lip.

We're all just frozen, staring on helplessly as Velle pulls a syringe from his holster and sticks a needle into Dash's neck. In an instant, Dash goes limp.

Jesus...

Lex releases a hoarse whimper, burying his face in my chest. Folding him up in my arms, I press my lips to his head, kissing his soft, short hair. I can feel him shaking; he's so torn up over this, and I get it. Dash looks like a broken doll...

This is terrible.

It reminds me of when Parker came down with pneumonia... When they told us he was being air-lifted to a medical center for treatment, and even though we wanted to believe he'd be okay, I could feel in my chest that something was seriously wrong. Despite how strained things were between Lex and me at the time, he didn't even hesitate.

He launched himself at me, hugging me *so* tight, stroking my hair and whispering calming words into my ear… Just like I am right now.

"It'll be okay, baby," I shush him, rocking his trembling body while keeping his face in my neck so he doesn't have to see them carrying Dash away.

No surprise that Velle instructs Brenner and Peters to bring Dash to the East. Still, it sinks my heart like a fucking stone in the sea.

"Fuck, man…" Kang rasps, dropping his face into his hands and rubbing his eyes hard.

Velle storms off, shouting at everyone on his way out, "Alright, fuckers. Show's over. Eat your food and shut the fuck up."

The rest of the inmates go back to their regularly scheduled programming, though the room is much quieter than before, a cloud of gloom covering us all.

"Hey, maybe he'll be okay," Kang says hopefully, like he's trying to convince himself. "Maybe he'll just cool down a little and they'll let him come back…"

I nod, but even that movement is a lie. After an outburst like that, there's no way Dash will be coming back to gen-pop.

Kieran used to pull shit like that, and look at him now.

Lex straightens a little, though he's still leaning into my side. I know he needs touch right now… Even if it's just friendly consolation. So I keep my arm around his waist, drawing circles on his hip with my thumb.

"That wasn't what he wanted." Lex shakes his head, scraping a palm over his face. "It wasn't supposed to go down like that."

"What do you mean?" Kang asks.

Lex looks around, biting his lip as if he's contemplating telling us something. But then he leans in, and Kang does the same from across the table.

"Last night, Dash told me he's trying to escape," he whispers. Kang and I share a look. "I guess he had some plan… I don't know, something about a guard in solitary." He shakes his head. "He didn't give me specifics, all he said was that he's trying to get out."

"So that was all an act?" Kang looks baffled.

"No," Lex hums. "He was only supposed to go to *solitary*, not the East. That was definitely… unscripted."

"Goddamn, man," I breathe, my head spinning through his words. "This is Toby all over again…" Lex swallows visibly. "You really think he has some connection to a guard downstairs? I mean… who would it even be?"

I can't help the curiosity overshadowing my thoughts. Dash has some kind of connection, that's for sure. You don't just inherit all the fancy shit he has out of nowhere...

Nor do you get My Officer *tattooed on your wrists unless you have an officer worth doing it for.*

"Honestly..." Lex stares at the table, blinking. "I doubt it."

There's more he isn't saying, but again, I don't want to pry right now. I just want to make him feel better. He needs a distraction.

A few minutes later, I get up to throw away my trash, playing it coy while I inch over to Rook, who's guarding the doorway with stress lining his features.

"Hey, Harley," I hum, extending my leg to tap him in the shin with my foot. "Whatcha doin?"

"What do you want, Ren?" He sighs. "In case you haven't noticed, today's not the day."

"Yea, exactly why I'm over here," I reply. "Dash is our friend. What just happened was pretty fucked up to witness..."

"I can't get him out of the East," Rook says definitively.

"Yea, I wouldn't think so. All I'm concerned with right now is making Lex feel better." I lean in a little closer. "You weren't here for it, but his last cellmate also ended up in the East, and well... we never saw him again after that." I give him a pointed look, and he visibly gulps. "We're missing O'Malley... now Dash." I shake my head. "It's taking a toll. I'm sure you can understand."

Rook glances behind me, at the table where Lex and Byron are still seated, staring despondently at their food. "Well, what do you expect me to do about it? Like I told you, I have no control over anything..."

I can't help but notice an anxious air about him that I'm guessing has to do with Velle. Harley's a good guy. And I've had my ups and downs with Velle, but I also know he's dealing with his own shit. Being The Ivory's lapdog can't possibly be fun.

I think Rook and Velle would be cute together. But who knows if it's even a possibility, given the circumstances of this island...

"All I'm asking is for you to let Lex come into my cell for a little bit." I give him my most pleading eyes. "He shouldn't be alone in his right now..."

Rook stares at me for a moment in contemplation. "I brought an inmate to your cell last night and Velle yelled at me." He raises a brow.

"Yea, that was Dash," I mutter. "Velle clearly isn't a fan of Dash. Plus, don't act like getting yelled at by Velle doesn't make your pussy wet."

I smirk teasingly while Rook rolls his eyes. But then he exhales slowly. "Just the two of you?" I nod eagerly. "Alright. I'll give you an hour. But no bullshit, okay? I can't deal with any more inmate drama..."

I bounce around in excitement. "You have my word, Officer Samuels."

I didn't tell Lex my plan, but it's obvious he really needs to get his mind off the whole Dash thing as we walk back to the cells. He's wearing the blank face of someone whose mind is running so fast on a treadmill of emotions that it's completely shut down.

I *hate* seeing him like this. It really just crushes my soul.

Once back in the row, Jasper herds the rest of the inmates into their individual cells, while Rook hangs back with Lex and me. Kang nods at us, one of his *see ya* expressions, and Lex begins to wander off too, but I grab him by the shirt.

He gives me a bemused look. "What are you doing?"

I don't answer him. I just drag him inside my cell with me, where Rook removes our cuffs and leaves without a word.

"I thought you could use a distraction," I tell him softly. He blinks over wide eyes. "We can do whatever you want... Watch a movie, play a game, or even just talk. But the point is, I don't want you stressing, okay?"

He bites his lip. "What makes you think I would...?"

I offer him a pointed look. "I know you, Lex. If you go back to that cell alone, you'll spend the whole night obsessing. Let me be your distraction." His brow arches suspiciously, and I grin. "As a *friend*, I mean. Strictly platonic, of course."

His mouth quirks as he murmurs sarcastically, "Of course."

I assume he's going to accuse me of being too clingy, or presumptuous. What I don't expect is the soft hum he lets out before pushing into my space, draping his arms around my shoulders and melting his body to mine.

Wow... I get a hug. So he's not mad...?

My hands sink onto his lower back like an instinct, pulling him in for the closest embrace physics will allow. He rests his chin on my shoulder, that sweet neck spot *right* in front of my face...

It's calling to me... I *have* to press a tiny kiss there.

Goddamn, his skin is so fucking soft, I'm in agony. And he smells delicious, like sandalwood and warm, clean flesh. I want to bottle it up and spray it all over everything I own.

Seriously, who even smells like that?? Those Lexington pheromones float a direct path to my brain.

"Thank you," he mumbles, toying with my hair at the nape of my neck.

I think I might *die* from not kissing him right now. I just want to hold his jaw and sink my tongue between those pink lips. I want to shove him backwards onto my bed and just kiss the living daylights out of him until he forgets why we ever stopped doing it in the first place.

But I hold myself together, croaking, "You're welcome." I clear my throat, pulling back to look in his eyes, though my hands refuse to leave his hips. "What do you wanna to do? Anything at all. Name it and it's yours."

He gazes at me, a teasing look I love seeing on his face. "I'm still waiting on those fireworks…"

I grin, eyes trained on his mouth. "You want some bang bang, beautiful?"

He quickly pinches my lips together with his fingers. "No more talking. You're ruining the moment."

I'm chuckling as he slides out of my hold, meandering around my cell, poking at things. I know he was just in here a couple of weeks ago, but it's still amazing to have him back. I miss the way he looks when we're all alone.

Plopping down on my bed, he picks up my iPad. I take a seat next to him, nodding at the screen. "We've got *Gone Girl* and three of the five *Twilights*."

"Whose iPad is this??" He scoffs. "It sounds like it belonged to an eighteen-year-old girl."

"I got it from Rook," I chuckle. "So either he has a sister, or his personality is very bizarre."

Lex laughs. But then it fades, and he sets the device down, shaking his head. "I don't think I can do a movie right now… I'm way too worried about Dash to concentrate."

"Then we'll do something else. Something more distracting…" He glares at me, and I smirk. "I swear, that's really not what I mean. But I like where your mind is going."

He rolls his eyes, staying quiet for a moment before an idea visibly dawns. "I think I want you to give me a tattoo."

I can feel my face light up in shock. "Are you serious??"

He nods. "Yea. I think that would be a great distraction, don't you?"

"Well… *yea*. I just… You never seemed to want one before."

"I have," he says. "But I wanted to be sure, ya know?"

I'm radiating instant excitement. I *love* tattooing. Honestly, I love it more than any other random hobby I've ever picked up, and I've been dying to give Lex some ink since I started doing them. He's finally ready to let me mark him up, and I'm *vibrating*.

"Alright, then. You're the boss," I murmur. "Get comfy. Do you know where you want it?"

He shifts in place for a second before answering. "I want it on my side… A line of code that runs vertically down my ribcage." He shows me with his finger, drawing a line from below his armpit to just above his hip. "Remember the code I drew for you that time? The ones and zeros?"

I have to bite the inside of my cheek, because *fuck me,* I already know that's going to look *so* damn sexy on him.

Nodding casually, I wander over to get my tattoo supplies, before unearthing the piece of paper, which naturally I saved. "You mean this one?"

His eyes sparkle, and he nods, apparently quite pleased that I still have it, cheeks flushing a little at the notion that I've clearly wanted to do this for quite some time.

Hands folded in his lap, sitting on my bed, he looks like the tastiest, most innocent little snack ever. So *sweet*… Pure and unsullied in so many ways.

Maybe some people would want to preserve that. But not me. I want to be all manners of *bad* with him, for him… *on* him. Shit, I probably sound so toxic, but I want to *ruin* everything about this boy so he's mine forever.

Beginning with marking up this blank canvas.

Grabbing my things, I sit down next to him on the bed with my tray. "Shirt off, please."

"Oh. Right." He lifts his shirt over his head while I try to be subtle about the fact that I'm blatantly drooling.

I've been seeing the kid naked for *years* at this point in the showers, and yet I'm still heavily affected any time he removes any article of clothing near me. It's fucking bonkers. I've probably seen hundreds of guys naked; touched them naked, rolled around in all sorts of elaborate positions. Pretty much everything you can do with a naked man, I've done.

But sweet virgin boy simply pops that top off and I'm *squirming*.

"Why are you staring at me like that?" Lex mutters.

I shake myself out of my obsessing. "Sorry. I'm just… trying to visualize it."

Yea, visualize a way to get through this without sucking on those little pink nipples… Jesus.

I remember Kang doing it to him last time he was in here, and my teeth clench.

That should've been me. Mine mine mine.

"Okay." I clear my throat. "There are a few ways we could do this. You can lie down on your side… But honestly, it might be easier if you kind of drape… your body over my lap."

He swallows visibly, pulling another accusatory glare. "You want me to lay on top of you? Is that how the professionals do it?"

"Well, *professionals* have chairs and special furniture." I cock my head. "This isn't *Ink Masters*. I have to work with what I've got." I pat my lap and grin, to which he shakes his head, biting back a smile.

"You're already being creepy," he huffs. But he's inching closer.

"I have no idea what you're talking about. This is strictly business." *No, it isn't.*

"Right."

He's correct to be questioning me. My intentions are entirely lascivious right now. If anything, him lying on me will be *less* convenient. But this is the level I'm at…

Shamelessly talking him into crawling on top of me… for the logistics.

Lex doesn't argue any further, though. He just shifts onto his hands and knees, then lies down on his side, over my lap. He's facing me so I have access to his left ribcage, knees bent as he nestles up, getting comfortable with his head resting on my pillow.

I peek down at him, my eyes meeting that effervescent green gaze, like the ocean in Miami Beach. I'm so fucking warm already just from feeling his body weight on me. I might combust by the time this is over, so I'd better make it quick. It's bad enough he's resting right on top of my dick.

Just control yourself… I know you get hard when he looks *at you, but now's really not the time.*

"Arm up." I take his wrist and lift it above his head.

He repositions to get more comfortable, leaving him cuddling around my seated body, his hips curved and our stomachs together.

Opening up an alcohol pad, I swipe it along his skin to clean the area.

He flinches. "Cold…"

"Sorry." I shift. "*So,* ribcage tattoos can be a little painful. Not the worst spot, but let me know if you want me to stop for a second. Also, I know it sounds crazy, but you have to try not to breathe..."

His brows jump. "You want me to not breathe??" I have to chuckle at how offended he is by this request. "You do know breathing keeps us alive, right?"

Grinning, I run my fingers up his back. "Sweet boy, I just mean try not to breathe *heavily* while the needle is down."

"Whatever you say," he sighs. "And stop calling me that. Don't be weird."

I purse my lips, feigning remorse. "So sorry, precious."

"Ugh." He rolls his eyes.

I have no stenciling tools available, so I just prop the scrap piece of notebook paper with the code on it next to my stuff, prepping some Aquaphor and the portable gun with black ink. Taking a deep breath, I try to prepare myself mentally for this, all the while lusting after the feel of him on my lap, and the way he looks stretched out before me... Pale skin waiting to become my artwork.

"Ready?" I ask.

He nods, but doesn't speak words, and I think he's nervous. My dick likes it. A lot.

Dipping the needle into the ink, I press it up to his skin, switching on the gun for my first touch. The buzz has him tensing, but he doesn't flinch when I go in.

He *does*, however, release a tiny hum of a noise that has me chewing aggressively on my bottom lip already.

The tattoo is easy. It's just a line of numbers, but I'm taking my time with it, savoring every second I get to have him splayed out, *trusting me*. He's literally in my hands, and I'm so obsessed, I'm purposely going as slow as possible just to make this experience last.

Watching his face in between carving ink into his skin, I admire the calm in his features. He's not cringing or whining about the pain. If I didn't know any better, I'd say he likes it... The soothing ache that pulls focus from everything else.

Tattoos are magic that way.

A few minutes in, I ask, "Doing okay?"

Lex nods, waiting until I pull the needle back to respond. *Such an obedient boy.* "Yea... it's not as bad as I thought it'd be."

I wipe some excess ink away with a cloth. "You like it?"

"Am I weird if I say yes?" He licks his lip.

I'm deceased.

"No," I rumble, as casually as I can pull off right now. "Lots of people like the feeling of getting tattooed. In some weird way, the pain is relaxing."

He blinks at me. And this time when I start back up again, I feel his fingers brushing my side… moving around to my lower back.

Swallowing a mouthful of saliva, I'm trying to push past it and focus. But the more I grind my inky needle into his perfectly creamy skin, the more his fingertips press into me. I think the sensation of it is getting to him… but not in a bad way.

If anything, he's enjoying this a lot. As evident when he starts subtly *writhing* on me.

A breath escapes me when his hipbone shifts over my cock.

"Are you…" I lose my grungy words for a moment to the throb in my pants. "Uncomfortable?" Lex peels his eyes open to stare up at me, the green shimmering as he slowly shakes his head. "Do you want to move?"

"Um…" His voice shivers, and now I'm really sweating. My left hand slides from where I'm holding him in place, down to gently cup his pectoral. I stifle a groan at how fucking hard his nipple is. "Ren…"

"Mm…?" I murmur, lost in tattooing him while rubbing his nipple tenderly beneath my palm.

God, that's good… Feel it, baby…

"I… *mmff…*" A needy hum slips out, and his lashes flutter.

"Tell me, love," I whisper, being swept out to sea by this feeling. I know this isn't supposed to be about fooling around, but he's burning up on my lap… Hips flicking. Not enough movement to mess me up, but he's definitely squirming like he just can't help himself. "I told you, it's okay to like it…"

I hear a small whimper as my hand leaves his chest long enough to slide up his sternum, fingers grazing the base of his throat.

"Ren…" he whines my name, raspy and unfettered. "I'm… *aching.*"

I suck in a breath. *Fuck me sideways.*

I can tell he doesn't understand why he's feeling this way, but he wants more. It's classic Lex behavior, just like that first time we hooked up, right here in this exact spot.

His rational mind hates not being able to identify these lustful cravings.

"Does it hurt?" I ask softly, dragging the cloth over his ribcage in a slow caress, smearing away black ink.

"It's n-not that…" he stutters, a pink blush rising up in his face.

Rolling my lip between my teeth, my eyes fall below his waist, quaking at the sight of his big, beautiful cock, all hard and tenting his pants. My gaze moves back to his face, where he's burying it in the pillow to avoid looking at me. To hide that flush of embarrassment I love *oh-so much*.

"Lexington…" I hum, touching his pulse as it jumps in his neck. "Look at me, gorgeous." He shakes his head. "Please?" He shakes it again. *Goddamnit, stubborn boy…* "Fine. You can keep your eyes closed."

Tugging his jaw, I free his face from the pillow just enough to tease his lips. The second my fingertips brush them, they part. And his tongue peeks out, licking them slowly.

"Jesus…" I rasp, pausing the tattooing to gently stuff two fingers inside his mouth.

He takes them willingly, a satisfied mewl vibrating around my index and middle fingers as he sucks on them, moving his mouth to get them deeper while his tongue slides and my cock *fills*.

"You wanna suck on my dick like this, don't you?" I breathe, proceeding to carve him with ink while he groans and throats my fucking fingers like the naughtiest virgin I've ever had the immense pleasure of being teased to death by. Of course he doesn't answer me with words, but his own fingers slink under my shirt. "Don't play games with me, Lexington. I know you can feel how hard this is making me…"

He breathes through his nose, shifting his hips again to rub himself on me. I can't even take it anymore.

I'm going to explode.

Tugging my fingers from his mouth, I drag them down to his chest, making a wet circle around his left nipple. I flick over it gently, massaging it, pulling, squeezing and toying until he's whining out the purest *need*.

"Take my cock out," he croaks as soon as I lift the needle. "*Please*, Ren, I'm so fucking hard too…"

"God, baby, you're ruining me," I rush out, shoving his pants down so his giant erection can poke out, head all swollen pink and dripping. "Look at you…"

"Keep going," he pleads, pushing his bare cock into my waist. "Give me more ink, please…"

"Anything you want, gorgeous," I breathe, readying the gun. "I wanna make you feel—"

My words dissolve when he grinds on my lap once more, drawing out an aching pulse of slick arousal that wets my pants.

Fuck, I could come like this… He could actually make me come *just writhing around on my lap. Sweet, flushed little virgin, holy fuck…*

I can barely think, but I somehow manage to dunk the needle into the ink and carve into him, as steadily as my hand can manage when all I want to do is roll him over and slide my ass down on that big dick.

"You have such a pretty cock, sweet love," I swoon, etching his skin while teasing his nipple with my free hand, watching his dick leak all over me. "It feels good, doesn't it? The hurt while I touch you like this…"

He nods fast. "Your mouth… Ren, I want it so bad…" As soon as I lift the needle up again, he curls around me, lifting my shirt more to press kisses all along my side. *I fucking losing it here…* "Will you kiss me… on my cock?"

"Baby, you're being so fresh." The hoarseness in my voice betrays my admonishing words. "What about the tattoo?"

"You can suck and ink at the same time," he purrs. "If anyone can…"

There's zero rhyme or reason for me to protest.

Lex wants my mouth… Lex gets my mouth.

I quickly tug my shirt off because I'm burning alive, then shift him a bit, scooting down to lay by his side. I'm sure I'm spilling ink all over the bed, but I don't even care. Holding his waist in my hands, I brush my lips over his nipples first, those needy little points waiting to be sucked as much as his cock.

The second I have one in my mouth, he's sighing and rubbing his erection desperately on my abs, yanking my hair in his fists.

"Uhhh… *fuck,* why does that feel so… *good*?" He gasps, legs spreading, toes curling.

Humming with his nipple between my lips, I suck *harder*, feathering and flicking his peaked flesh, biting and pulling it almost viciously with my teeth. I don't know what it is about his chest, but I could spend hours playing with him like this. I'm so turned on, my boxers are soaked with precum.

Finally leaving his nipples wet and sore, I slide down his abs to his cock, curling my tongue around the tip. I lap up his flavor hungrily, his moaning above my head nearly doing me in.

I pull my mouth off just long enough to scrape a few more symbols into his side. Then it's back onto his dick, gliding him between my lips, giving him my best slow suction. Deeper, *rougher*. I want this head to feel so good it hurts.

"R-Ren... *God*, that's so fucking good, baby..." He threads his fingers in my hair, pushing himself into my throat. "*More.*"

I let him fuck my mouth before slurping off his sweet dick with a pop. "You like this, wicked boy? I'm making you feel good, huh..."

Dipping the needle, I decorate him with more ink. Keeping still long enough for me to work must be driving him nuts. Because the second I lift the needle, he groans, grabbing my head and shoving me back onto his dick.

"I missed your fucking mouth..." he growls shakily, and I'm fucking *flying*. "So, *so* bad. I missed how warm and wet it is, and how your tongue slithers around like... *uhhmff* like that."

Fuck yea... Goddamn, I love sucking him.

It's been *so* fucking long since I've sucked his cock. Too many other meaningless cocks pumping between my lips when all I've wanted is *this cock*. This long, thick, solid hunk of velvet-wrapped stone that just fits so perfectly in my mouth.

I missed the way he shudders and holds my hair. The way his knees shake and his abs clench. All of it and then some.

I could lick, suck, kiss, *worship* this cock every day for the rest of my life and still never get enough.

Letting him go, I drag my teeth gently underneath his head until he's trembling, moving down to kiss his nuts. I'm barely done sucking one between my lips as I'm digging the needle into his side again, keeping my hand from shaking as best I can.

"Baby, I'm gonna come so soon..." he whines. "You're gonna make me come like this. It's too... fucking... *much.*"

"I know, naughty boy," I croon, holding him still for some of his last ink. "You can't help spilling all over me, can you?"

"*No*... I c-can't. *Uhh,* babe... b-baby, come with me." He gazes down at me, all flushed and desperate for his orgasm. "I wanna w-watch you... come."

"Yea?" I groan.

"Mhm..."

"You want me to come all over your pretty cock?"

"Fuck yea," he whimpers.

"Can you wrap your fist around me, baby?"

He nods, shaky fingers slipping inside my pants to grasp my dick. He starts pulling on it, slow and hard, just like he used to when he didn't know how to touch a dick that wasn't his own. Like he's not sure how it'll work, but he's too impatient and greedy to care.

Thrusting into his hand, I put the finishing touches on his tattoo, biting my lip raw to keep my hand from trembling. Lex moans, lying still for me until I'm done.

But as soon as I am, I lunge at him, whipping everything out of the way as ink spills on my fingers. I grab him by the jaw, smearing black marks on his face.

"You're so fucking sexy." I growl, sucking his bottom lip into my mouth while fucking his fist hard. "Such a needy thing… trying to distract me. Make me fuck up your ink…"

"You… d-didn't tell me it would feel so… *good*," he shivers.

"I always knew you liked my hurt, baby boy," I rumble in between kissing him deep, our tongues lashing and tasting while he pushes his cock against mine.

"You… it's just *you*, sweet flame," he mewls, grabbing my hands and dragging them down to his chest, leaving smudges of black ink on his pale skin, like the sexiest mess ever. "You make me crazy."

"I missed you so bad…" I breathe, feeling like I could cry, this is so damn good.

Everything with him is incredible. Just kissing Lexington, being touched by him, will get me off better than being fucked by a million aggressive men who aren't him.

He's all I want. He's always been… *All* of it.

"Come on me," he pleads on a growly whisper.

"Where?"

"My dick…"

"You want me to soak your big dick, sweet love?"

He cries out loud. "Yes, *please*, *Ren*… fucking *bust* for me, baby."

"You want me to lick it all off, then suck the cum out of your cock?"

"Mmffuck*yesss*…"

"Make me come, baby boy. Show me how you get me off…"

He sounds like he might get there first, and it pushes me over the edge. I hump up to his hand once, twice, three more times, and then I erupt.

His tight fist slowly milks my orgasm all over his throbbing cock, drenching it in hot spurts while he pants and purrs, watching with stars in his eyes. My brain is swirling and twirling, an electric buzz flowing in my veins as ragged moans fill the room.

My balls are officially empty.

Fucking damn, that was a lotta cum...

Dropping below his waist in a daze, I lick it all up, stuffing his cock into my mouth and sucking my flavor off of him like a fiend.

"Keep it in your mouth," he whispers, and my drunken gaze lifts. His cheeks are pink as fuck, smattered with black smudges, eyelids drooping. *A fucking masterpiece, this kid.* "Leave your cum in your mouth and suck my dick with it."

God, he's so deliciously dirty. I love when his innocence flips to filthy lust for me.

"Baby, *fffuck*, suck my cock," he groans, fisting my hair. "Suck it with all that slippery cum in your mouth..."

He's so very unleashed right now, it has me thrusting my tired dick against his leg because I just can't get enough. I feel him stiffen, swelling up between my lips while I'm bobbing on him furiously, chasing my reward.

Then he sobs, and shudders, shooting off all inside my mouth, feeding me his decadent flavor I've missed *so* fucking much.

"Ren... Ren, Ren... *God, Ren*, my sweet, perfect flame, you fuck me so good with that mouth." His hand glides down around my throat and he holds it while I swallow, my Adam's apple sliding in his palm.

I'm *destroyed*, rocked to rubble like ten goddamn points on the Richter scale by this boy.

He seems so into this... Into me.

He fucking wants me again... I know he does.

Eventually, everything evens out, and while I'd love to keep his dick in my mouth forever, I pull off of him with a satisfied hum. Squirming up to lie in front of him, I hold his neck and press a super soft kiss on his lips; only one. But when I go to pull away, he grabs my jaw and kisses me *more*, deeper, like he's not done.

"This doesn't mean anything..." Lex whispers hoarsely. I think he's losing his voice, and it's so fucking hot. "We're not getting back together, okay?"

I grin on his lips, grazing his face with my black fingertips. "Whatever you say, my sexy little mess."

"Shut up," he growls, though he's not stopping with the kisses, totally undermining his words. "I just... wanted this. I wanted you to make me... come. That's all."

"So you're using me for orgasms now?" My hands slide down to rest on his chest, thumbs circling his nipples. "Do friends do that?"

"I don't... Who knows," he breathes, then whines. "Stop touching me there. It feels too intense."

"Sorry, baby." I pout.

Not sorry. Not even a little.

"Ren, don't fuck with me, okay?" he breathes over my mouth. "I'm confused right now... I don't know what I'm doing with you."

"Please," I huff. "You've been confused about us since we met, because you're always running from what you want. Just keep doing what feels good, and we'll both be happy."

Lex blinks at me. "*I* won't..." I bite the inside of my cheek. *I don't like where this is going.* "When it feels too good to be true, it's because it *is*, Warren."

I don't know what to say, so I just stare at him with a desperate itch beneath my skin to somehow keep us together. He's totally justified in not wanting to give me another chance... I get that. But it still feels shitty. Because if I wasn't such a fuck-up, we could do it all... Hook up *and* be together, like he wants.

At least, he *used to* want it...

Lex pulls away from me, reacquainting himself with reality. And rather than continuing down this dark path of our tumultuous relationship, he checks the fresh tattoo on his ribcage.

Biting his lip, he peeks at me. "It came out good."

I stifle my smile. "You like it?" He nods. "I did a pretty great job considering you were sexually harassing me the whole time..."

I show him a teasing smirk, and he scowls. "Not my fault at all. You like... hypnotized me or something. You gave me the tattoo in a spot you knew would feel really good..."

I chuckle, touching his jaw. "You're so cute, I wanna kiss the life out of you."

Yanking his pants up, he rubs his eyes. "Enough, Ren." He crawls off the bed, glaring down at me. "I'm serious. This can't keep happening."

"You sure about that?" I raise my brow.

And although I know he wants to stay fighting it, all he's doing is blinking at me, staring at my mouth. He clears his throat and shakes his head. "What do I do with the tattoo? To take care of it...?"

"Just put some of this stuff on it for the first week," I tell him, pointing at the Aquaphor.

He nods, then goes quiet for a moment. "Ren...?" I tilt my head.

"Did you plan this? I mean, is this why you brought me in here… to fool around?"

I grab his hand in mine, placing his palm flat over my heart. "I didn't plan it, Lex. Because I *am* trying to be your friend. But I'm also trying not to lie to you… Being able to kiss you and touch you and do all the amazing, dirty things we *should* be doing together makes me insanely happy. I'm not manipulating you, and I'm not trying to coerce you into something. I just really miss the fuck out of you, every minute of every day. That's it, love. That's the *truth*. Do with that information what you will. But just know, every moment I'm with you… is fireworks over the ocean."

He blinks at me, eyes boring into mine with that beautiful shade of green that's stolen my breath since the first time I saw it…

The boy with stormy seas in his eyes… Vibrant beauty in a dark, gray wasteland.

And then he does something I probably never would have predicted… *Always surprising me.* He eases himself back down onto my lap, curling up on my body and burying his face in my neck.

I don't know what it means. I don't think he does either…

But there is absolutely *no way* I can let him go without more neck kisses and unspoken words of truth.

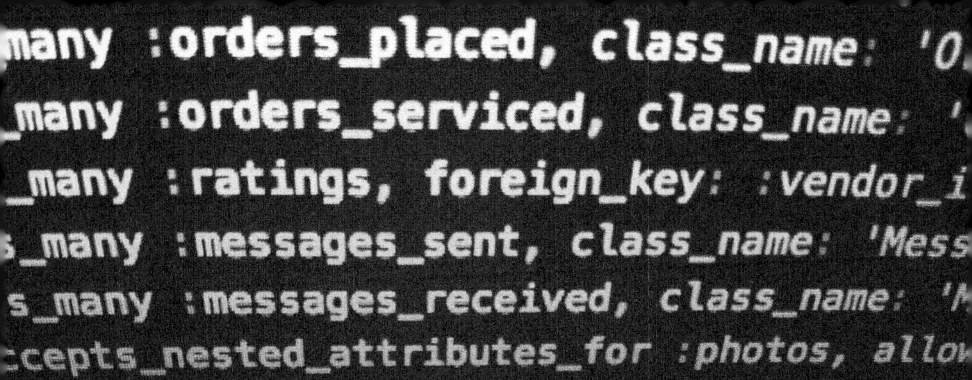

CHAPTER EIGHTEEN

Luther

3 years ago…

I used to think the reason I was so slow-moving with girls was because I'm shy as hell, and I overthink everything to death. But as it turns out, maybe it's because none of those girls were… boys.

Or maybe it's because none of them were *Ren*.

Officially, Ren and I are still just friends. But we're also hooking up, and I can't lie… *I'm Mickey D's lovin' it.*

At the same time, I'm wary of letting this thing go any further, because Ren is complicated as shit, like a jigsaw puzzle that's missing a bunch of pieces. I'm not sure he's someone I should be interested in…

Not because he's a guy. That fact really isn't throwing me as much as you'd think, although I do find myself staring at the ceiling an awful lot at night wondering how the hell I ended up liking dick.

Have I always been interested in guys, and I just didn't know it? Or did Ren literally badger me into becoming bisexual?

If anyone could do it…

The thing is, despite his many issues, I *am* very much attracted to him. Not just physically, though I've certainly fallen into the spell of just how beautiful he is. From his silky dark hair that, thankfully, he's somehow convinced Joy to let him keep for a while, to his striking topaz eyes. That perfect dreamboat smile, and his *body*… It's the kind of body even straight guys can't resist.

Warren Xavier is a bi-curious dude's wet dream.

But more than his blinding hotness, I'm attracted to who he is. Who he *really* is, not the hot mess everyone else sees. Because if you're brave enough to wade through the murky waters of all his problems, you'll find someone truly wonderful.

And now he might be my… boyfriend?

Maybe. Not yet… We'll see.

Dating in prison is like being in a long-distance relationship when you're right next to each other. While we got away with hanging out alone those few times, this place isn't a college dorm. You can't just come and go as you please, sneaking into each other's cells for late night makeout sessions and slow blowies. And with Ren no longer servicing the guards, they're much less inclined to put their asses on the line for him.

Still, we've managed some workarounds. The other day, after lunch, he pushed me into a dark corner and kissed me so dizzy, I had to grip onto his waist for fear I'd fall down from the vertigo.

He draws me pictures—*some sweet, some dirty*—and sneaks them to me in the hall. We hold hands under the table at lunch, and when no one's looking, he kisses my neck, letting those brazen fingers slide a little too close to my crotch. All in secret, of course, keeping the affection away from prying eyes as much as we can.

Plus, sneaking around is supremely hot.

Whatever we're doing, we've agreed to take it slow. But then there are instances when we just can't help ourselves.

Like right now, in the showers…

I mean, come on. We shower next to each other *every day*. I don't know of any new couple, official or not, who'd be able to resist that kind of play time, no matter how many people might be around. Plus, inmates are always fucking in the showers. It's not exactly *news*. They're just a lot less *affectionate* when they do it.

Let's be clear, though. Ren and I are *not* fucking. *Yet…*

That's not to say I don't want to, but it's a big move for me, and I'm still afraid it'll change things. Every step we take is nerve-racking. I live in constant fear that Ren will get bored with me and go back to his default setting of hooking up with everyone. He hasn't given me any reason to think it'll happen, but that doesn't stop me from overanalyzing his every movement.

Times like this put my mind at ease, though. We're in the showers, washing up while peeking at each other, being about as subtle as two Mack trucks headed for a collision.

Ren is biting his lip like he's in pain, watching my hands move over my own flesh. Never one to deny himself, he quickly gives up the coquette, glancing left, then right to make sure no one's paying attention before he pushes his way under my shower head.

"I think we should conserve water," he growls in my ear while taking over my washing to do it himself. "It's more environmentally conscious."

"Mmm… You're so green, baby," I tease, grinning with my eyes shut, basking in the feeling of his fingers gliding along my wet skin.

"That's me," he murmurs, sucking on my neck with his hand around my cock. "Captain Planet."

I chuckle, cupping and squeezing his ass. I swear to God, he has the nicest butt ever. It's so firm and round, plump and juicy, like a peach. *Total hot guy butt.*

"Look at you…" I whimper, casting one last gaze at his huge dick before we fall into kissing.

We kiss a lot. Every chance we get, we're making out, because he's a phenomenal kisser. So good, he could add it to his resume. Once, he actually made me come just from kissing me.

Needless to say, he's quite proud of that fact.

Right now, though, in this shower turned naughty, the kissing is interrupted when he pushes me into a corner and drops to his knees. I'm expecting one of his killer blowjobs… Another Warren Xavier superpower.

Able to drain balls with a single suck.

But when he spins me around and starts kissing my butt cheeks, I'm overcome with fast nerves.

"What are you doing back there…?" I hum, peering at him over my shoulder.

"You know what, gorgeous? Your man is still hungry," he croons. "Breakfast really didn't satisfy my raging *appetite*."

He grabs my dick, aiming it downward to suck between my thighs. I'm instantly leaking into his waiting mouth.

"*God*… Suck me, sweet flame," I groan, biting my lip to keep quiet.

He slurps at my cock for a bit, then licks his way up my balls, over my taint, and… farther up.

"Mmff," I grunt at the foreign feeling of his tongue playing with my ass, forehead falling forward to rest on the cool concrete.

Nothing has ever breached my ass before, nor has anything ever fluttered around on it the way Ren's tongue is at the moment. I'm not *opposed* to letting him in there… But he sincerely loves to be penetrated.

And yet here he is, kissing and sucking on my hole like it's a Hostess cupcake and he's licking out all the cream filling.

"Imagine if Superman caught Lex Luthor," Ren rambles with his face buried in my ass, "and instead of turning him in, he tied him up and ate his ass out? Now *that's* a storyline I could get behind."

I can't help bubbles of laughter erupting from my lips, but they turn quickly into mewling moans when his tongue starts probing me ever so slightly.

"*Ffuck… Warren…* I don't think I could love you more," I mumble with my eyes rolling back in my head.

But when I realize what I just said, they snap open.

Glancing over my shoulder, I find him gazing up at me with wide eyes, his mouth still tucked between my cheeks. His movements have slowed to a halt and we're just staring at each other.

Did I really just drop the L bomb while he's eating my ass??

Classic virgin behavior.

"Baby…" Ren whispers, blue eyes shining vulnerability up at me while he presses slow, sweet kisses on my ass.

I clear my throat, chewing the inside of my cheek. "Move past it?"

He nods quick, breathing, "Conversation for another time," then picks back up with the punishing licks.

Sixty-seconds later, and I'm coming all over the shower floor. Then Ren stands up, and I jerk him off until he's coming all over *me.*

Filthiest shower ever. Prison perfection

We're brought back to our cells after that, and I kiss him goodbye before he's shoved into his, smiling at me through the bars. He seems so *happy*, but I'm up in my head for the rest of the day.

I can't believe I said I loved him… Isn't it too soon for that?

We've only been hooking up for a couple of months, and I was the one who said I wanted to take it slow.

Do I love him?? I know I said it, but sometimes things just slip out in the heat of the moment… Like when a drop-dead gorgeous guy is talking about comic books while tonguing your ass.

Something burns in my gut, spreading up to my chest. It feels like my stomach and heart are having a race to see which one can climb up my throat first.

Is this love? Am I in love with Warren Xavier?

The feelings I get when I'm with him, even when I'm sitting alone in my cell thinking about him, are similar to how I felt for Leah, only much more intense. The same affection, but turned up a hundred degrees. It's friendship boiling over.

I might love him... Would that be bad?

It's scary, that's for sure. I have so many insecurities when it comes to Ren. He might be okay giving up other dicks for now, but how long will it last? We're in here *forever*. Forever is a long fucking time.

God, what have I gotten myself into?? I'm such an idiot.

You can't fall in love in prison. Death row is no place for a relationship.

A few hours later, Joy and Velle scoop us all up for dinner. I'm uneasy, lurking off to the side like a wallflower as Ren and Parker traipse out into the hall, chatting and laughing. The loser feels are coming on strong until Ren scoots in next to me and grabs my hand.

"Fancy meeting you here." He grins at me, leaning in to kiss my neck as he whispers, "You must be exhausted..."

My brow furrows as I slope my face in his direction.

"'Cause you've been running through my mind *all day*," he hums, shooting me a sly wink.

A chuckle rumbles out of me, and I bite my lip to tame the smile trying to hijack my lips like a Somali pirate.

"Dumbass," I grunt, while he laughs at my forced scowl.

All of my doubts have vanished in seconds. It's truly fascinating. I squeeze his hand tighter, downplaying the obvious flush in my cheeks.

Maybe he loves me too...

In the cafeteria, we all sit down for a dinner of stale chicken nuggets and fruit punch. Parker is telling us about this book he's been reading, and Ren's hand is dancing up my inner thigh, distracting the crap out of me.

"Oh! I almost forgot," Ren chimes suddenly, reaching into his pocket. "I brought you a gift."

He smiles excitedly at me while holding out his closed fist.

"What is it?" I ask, and his head cocks.

"What are the magic words?"

I roll my eyes and sigh. "Ren has the best dick on earth..."

"You're so good at that." He beams.

I laugh as he opens his hand, revealing a ketchup packet. My eyes widen, mouth falling agape.

"For me?!" I gasp, snatching it up quick, wiggling around in pure zeal.

"For *my* man," he croons, decorating my neck with kisses. "Who also has the best dick on earth."

"Thank you, sweet flame." I give him a look of adoration. "I feel bad, though. I can't be the only one with ketchup." My eyes fling to Parker. "You want some?"

"No, no. Please, use it." Parker grins. "These meds make it so I can't taste shit, anyway."

"I hope you can't taste *shit*," Ren jeers. "It probably tastes pretty bad."

I snort while Parker shakes his head. "Luthor, your boyfriend is annoying."

"He's not my boyfriend," I murmur, tearing open my packet and squeezing out a dot of ketchup onto each nugget while Ren chuckles.

Taking a bite, I'm in fucking heaven. These things really need sauce. They're so dry and boring. To be honest, anything they serve us would be better with ketchup, but naturally it's hard to get.

He must have saved this one packet just for me.

My thoughts spin while I'm enjoying my food, watching Ren in my peripheral.

"Where'd you get it?" I ask him, trying to sound as casual and non-accusatory as possible. "The ketchup..."

"I found it in one of my old bags of snacks," he answers calmly. No twitching or fidgets. *It's a good sign.* "I've been making the stuff last, but I just got to the bottom of the one from Monroe and there it was." He smirks at me. "For my sexy little tomato."

My gaze narrows. "Why am I a tomato?"

He leans in, poking my chin with his fingertip. "Because you're a fruit and no one knows it."

I'm trying so hard to crush the amusement on my face, but when he bursts into a loud cackle, I can't help letting the laughter slip.

"I really hate you." I bite petulantly into my nugget.

"Now, we know that's just not true, *Lex Luthor*." His fingers slide up into my shirt.

This guy... I can't.

I think I believe him, about the ketchup. Usually, when Ren's lying, his body language shifts, his subtle movements in his fingers or his jaw giving him away. At the same time, he's so damn charming that a lot of times it's difficult to tell.

I remember last year, he went on this whole tangent about how he slept with Lance Bass at a party in The Hamptons. We all believed him until he slipped up a few days later and revealed that he didn't know the difference between 'NSYNC and The Backstreet Boys.

He can be very convincing sometimes.

"So, baby, I was thinking..." he murmurs, gripping my thigh under the table. "I'm gonna ask Velle to let us hang out for a little bit this weekend."

My forehead lines. "And how exactly do you expect to pull that off?"

"You let me worry about the details," he chirps. "Just get that hot body ready to be worshipped."

As much as I'm loving the idea of spending alone time with him, and the way it sounds when he calls me *hot* in that illustrious tone of his, the icky feeling is returning to my chest.

"Babe, I don't—"

"If it isn't Peter Pan and Twinkerbell..." A rumbling voice comes from my left, and our heads spring up to find Percy Gage—this giant asshole who's been here less than a year and already somehow thinks he owns the place—standing with his arms folded over his chest. "You boys are pretty cute together."

Ren's fingers tighten on my thigh.

"Seniority, Gage," I mutter. "You're forgetting your manners."

"I'm being polite," he keeps pressing. "Extending an invitation." His smug gaze lingers on Ren. "Bring your boyfriend with you next time, princess. I'd like to try him out."

Ren jumps up from his seat, and I'm instantly nervous. "Ren... don't."

"Who the fuck do you think you are?" He ignores me, getting in Gage's face.

"I think I'm one of many who have ridden your sweet ass raw," Gage hisses, leaning in closer. "And I'm ready for more. So are my friends over there." He nods at the next table over, where a bunch of other meathead assholes are looking on, grinning.

My stomach is churning, from his words, and the wrath in Ren's eyes. I knew it wouldn't be easy dating someone who's made his rounds in this place. But usually, it's an *out of sight, out of mind* situation. As long as it doesn't come stomping over announcing itself, you can pretend it never happened.

Unfortunately, Gage isn't the type to keep his mouth shut.

I really fucking hate this guy.

"I'm gonna need you to apologize to Lexington." Ren squints at Gage's face. "For interrupting our dinner with your overcompensating bullshit."

"Adorable," Gage sighs, not backing down.

"I'm serious, two pump," Ren hums, eyes falling down Gage's front for a moment. "Say you're sorry for acting like a little dick prick."

"Ren…" I mumble, placing a hand on his back. I need to stop this before something bad happens. "Please, just leave it—"

"You're right." Gage's eyes flick to me. "I'm sorry, Luthor." Then he sneers at Ren once more. "Sorry I stretched your boyfriend out so bad, you'll barely even feel it when you f—"

The words are cut off when Ren's fist hammers into Gage's face.

Oh shit…

Gage bends at the waist from the hit, and Ren proceeds to elbow him, grabbing him by the shoulders and tossing him onto the floor.

It's pandemonium in a flash. Ren's on top of Gage on the floor, swinging over and over at his face while inmates are scrambling, crowding around and screaming *fight!*

And I'm just sitting here, rubbing my eyes because I already know how this is going to go.

"Fucking animals!" Velle roars, storming over to pull Ren off of Gage and cuff him quick. "You kidding me, 48??"

"No regrets," Ren breathes, hair all tousled in his face as he winks at me.

"Really?" I shake my head admonishingly.

"Get these morons down to the hole," Velle growls at Joy and Peters. "Both of them."

"Fuck you, Ren." Gage spits blood on the floor. "You'll pay for this."

"You take Discover?" Ren smirks.

I can't help but chuckle, frowning over it because I really shouldn't be encouraging him. Joy grabs Ren by the arm while Peters drags a snarling Gage toward the door.

"Ren, what the fuck…" I sigh, shuffling out of my seat to follow after Joy dragging him away from me.

"I'm sorry, baby," he whispers, pouting. "Raincheck on our date night?"

My chin wobbles, worry eating away at my insides. He's going to solitary… It's fucking awful down there. And who knows how long he'll be gone.

I'm still following him, until Velle grabs me by the waist.

"Stay put," he grumbles behind me. "This isn't a fucking rom-com."

"Hey, Lex..." Ren shouts my name as he's being hauled off. Then he mouths the words, *I love you.*

I'm smacked upside the head with radiant emotion, my lips sweeping into a delighted, purely terrified grin.

Okay, so... He said it.

He really does love me.

I'm so stunned and baffled and happy, all I can do is wave as he's pulled out of the room by Joy, who's shaking her head like we're total idiots.

"I don't know what I just witnessed, but it seems beyond dysfunctional," Velle mutters, shoving me back to the table.

He's probably right, but I'm too blinded to care.

All I can see are bright blue eyes, and a killer smile mouthing, *I love you.*

Ren is in solitary for five torturous days.

When he gets back, he's exhausted and dirty and it looks like lost ten pounds. He also came back with a little stubble-beard that looked *crazy* sexy on him, but of course, Joy shaved it off before I could even try kissing him to see how it felt.

Either way, I'm just so damn happy to see him. I can't wait to talk to him, sit with him at lunch, watch him watch me showering; our only allotted moments of intimacy.

Unfortunately, I don't think prison dating is on the menu right now.

A week passes with Ren back in gen-pop, and the only time I get to see him is when we pass each other in the hall on occasion. For whatever reason, it seems like they've split us up out of nowhere, taking us for showers and meals in different groups.

I just don't get it. Ren and I have always been in the same group, because we're in the same row. It doesn't make any sense to bring him at different times.

What's worse, Parker is going with Ren now, because they're cellmates, meaning I'm all alone. No friends, no one to talk to. It feels like when I first got here all over again, and it's the fucking worst.

Ten days, and I can't take it anymore. I decide to approach Joy after showers.

"Hey... Why are Ren and Parker in a different group now?" I ask her, attempting to stow my intense vulnerability. "We've always been together, and now they're just… gone."

Joy gives me a look. "It's not my call, Luth. Schedules are random."

She's probably one of the hardest people on this island to read. But I've known her for years, and I can tell there's something she's not saying. Or something she *can't* say.

"That's bullshit," I grumble. "The schedules, sure, but the groups usually stay together."

Her jaw ticks. "What can I say, inmate? Warden's deciding to switch things up."

I blink at her, listening to the words between her words.

The Warden… Is he responsible for this?

Is he trying to separate me and Ren? Why would he do that? Who cares if we eat and shower together? Who is it affecting??

"Wait, but—"

"No more questions, 35," she barks. "Get your shit together and let's go."

I'm all twisted up while we walk back. My stomach is rolling with unease, the rampant obsessing giving me a migraine.

Things with Ren just started… They were *just* getting good and now we're being separated like kids in a timeout? *It's pure horseshit.*

How are we going to make a relationship work when we can't even see or speak to one another??

When we reach the row, my eyes slide frantically into Ren's cell, and he's there. Doing push-ups.

Glancing at Joy, I make a quick, probably very stupid decision, to scurry over to his cell. He notices me right away and stands, stepping up to the bars.

"Hey," I breathe, gripping the steel in my fists.

"God, I fucking miss you so bad," he whispers.

My forehead drops, and his does the same, our heads resting together between the bars.

"Goddamnit, 35," Joy grunts.

I flick my face in her direction, giving her my most desperate look. "Joy, *please.*"

She peeks up at the camera in the corner, then back at me, sighing. "Fine. Make it quick."

"This is so fucked up," I mutter to Ren, taking in the vibrant skies in his irises. "I can't believe they're keeping us apart. It's so stupid…"

"Yea..." he sighs, nervously biting on his bottom lip.

"Yea?" I scoff. "I only have minutes to talk to you for the first time in weeks and all you have to say is *yea*??"

"I'm sorry, baby. I just feel awful." He pauses to shake his head, sadness and longing coming off him in waves. "It's all my fault. I was acting too cocky about our relationship. I got sent to solitary for defending you..."

"So what?? I hardly think that matters," I point out. "Look at all the fucked-up shit that happens here every day. Why is me and you getting close such a problem?"

"I don't know..." he says quietly. "Don't you feel like... this might be a sign?"

"A *sign*??" My hands are shaking, and that somber blue gaze is ripping me in half.

"You're too good for me, Lex. I mean, we've always known it, but this proves it even more. I'm fucking shit up for you. What happens if next time they send *you* to solitary? Or the East! I wouldn't be able to handle it, baby..."

"Where is this all coming from...?" I gasp, my heart sinking deeper and deeper into the pit of torment in my gut.

"I don't know." He shakes his head, like there are too many thoughts bunching up in there. "I'm so lost right now... It doesn't feel right when I can't hold you and be with you all the time."

I gulp, hating the way this stupid conversation is progressing. *Despising* how obviously fragile this thing between us is, if all it takes is a few days of separation for the bubble to burst. I feel like an idiot all of a sudden for being so happy before...

Nothing good here ever lasts.

"Okay, well... we'll just hold out," I tell him softly, and his eyes spring to mine. "They can't keep us apart forever, right? I'm sure it will all blow over, and they'll put us back into the same group again."

"Yea, maybe..." he mumbles, chewing on his lip some more.

I'm losing him...

Brushing his fingers with mine, I seal myself to the bars, wishing like hell they'd just disappear. "Do you... not want this anymore?"

His face sweeps up in startled, panicked confusion. "*What??* Of course I do. Lex, you're the *only* thing I want. You make everything so good, baby."

Relief washes over me, and I take in a deep breath.

"Maybe... I mean, there *is* another way we could see each other again," he whispers. My muscles tense as his fingers sweep along mine. "I know it's not ideal… and it might make you sad, but if I could just bribe the guards again…"

"Ren," I whimper, shaking my head. "*No*. You said you were gonna try…"

"I know, but if it's the only way—"

"It's not!" I bark. He swallows. "It's not."

He's just staring at me, and I'm glaring at him, trying to get him to focus on what I'm saying. He doesn't need to sell himself for us to be together. I *refuse* to let that be the way this happens.

"Tell me you understand what I'm saying, Ren…" I plead with him through my eyes.

Eventually, he puffs out a tired breath and nods. "Yea, I understand. I'm sorry, baby… I just miss you, ya know?"

"I know."

"35! Get a move on," Joy calls for me, and I kiss Ren's knuckles through the bars.

"We'll figure this out," I tell him, as confidently as I can manage.

He nods while I wander off, our eyes holding one another until they absolutely have to let go, speaking words without words.

I know I should tell him… I should *say it,* right now.

That I love him, because I think I really do.

But I don't say it. I'm scared, and I hate that I am.

He didn't say it either…

And as I walk away, back to my cell, I'm praying his silence wasn't the truth.

You never notice how much time there truly is until it's all you have.

When things are good, it goes by too fast. When they're not, you feel every aching second.

I still haven't seen Ren for more than a few minutes here and there. And of course, those minutes flew by in an eye-blink. The rest of it is all just prison life, killing me slowly with boredom.

But I'm trying to stay positive. I'm trying desperately to keep up hope that this will pass. That this stupid freeze-out will eventually thaw, and they'll realize that keeping me and Ren apart is unnecessary.

A new inmate came in yesterday. His name is Byron. Byron Kang. He seems cool.

He sat with me at lunch, most likely because he saw an empty table and a non-threatening depressed dude sitting alone, with zero visible interest in fucking with him. We chatted for a few minutes, and it felt good to talk to someone again.

Living alone, being back to no friends and no would-be relationship, has been the most isolating time of my life. I don't even have technology to keep me company, like when I was younger. It's just me, myself and I, the lonely loser trifecta.

It's time for showers, but a fight in the row holds everyone up. Nieves is scrapping with Simmons over God knows what, and it takes three guards and a lot of tasing to subdue the idiots. By the time they're finally bringing us to the showers, over an hour has passed. I'm frazzled and tired and I just want to wash my damn balls.

Sauntering inside, I grab a towel and head to the cluster of showers I usually use. I hear moans, paired with the distinct skin-slapping that almost always means fucking, and I roll my eyes to myself, hoping some assholes aren't taking up my area with their rapey shenanigans.

But when I step around the corner, my feet skid to a halt. My stomach binds up tight and it kills, like a cramp so profound, all the air squeezes right out of my lungs.

No...

My eyes widen. They stare, unable to look away.

No... Ren.

He's here. Ren is *here*, in the showers. With some guys. And he's...

No... Why...?

They're doing exactly what you'd expect, and my first instinct is to feel so achingly fucking *stupid* for reacting the way I am.

No, Ren... Stop...

The way my heart is lurching up into my throat, making me gag, and the tears trying to push out of my eyes like idiotic, worthless dribbles of water.

"Fuck yea..."

No no no... No.

All I want to do is fucking *leave*. Just turn and *run* away as fast as possible, but my damn body is frozen solid. Like I'm in some form of purgatory, witnessing the guy I thought I might... *Oh, God, I can't breathe...* being filled with random cock from way too many angles.

No, but… No. Why??

The groans and pants and sounds of wet fucking seem to go on for hours with me just *standing* there, being forced to watch it because my goddamn legs are broken. Really, it's no more than a few seconds, but it feels like an eternity… Until Ren notices me.

And then time speeds back up to ultrafast.

Stupid fucking idiot… Why are you so upset?? You knew this would happen. Just turn around and LEAVE.

The thing is, Ren doesn't react the way a guy normally would when getting caught cheating. He just stops what he's doing and kind of stares at me. And yea, he does look upset. In fact, he looks devastated. Shame and guilt, anguish and remorse practically seeping from his pores.

But he doesn't *do* anything about it. He doesn't call out to me and scream that he's sorry. He doesn't even move from where he's still getting fucked in half by Percy fucking Gage and his dipshit asshole bitch bastard fucking friends.

He just keeps giving me that look… the one that says, *I'm sorry, but you knew this would happen.*

Like it's *my* fault.

Like *I'm* the idiot for even thinking he could change, or be someone other than a lying fucking whore, because that's *who he is.*

And honestly, he's probably right.

I really must be that *fucking* stupid.

Choking back uncontrollable sobs and this morning's breakfast, I *finally* get my legs to work, and I spin out of the room, jogging as *fast* and as *far* away as I can before someone stops me. But even though I've left the scene, it's still all I can see.

It's been burned permanently into my brain…

Ren's body… belonging to *everyone* but me.

The sounds of it are drowned out, though. By my heart pounding in my skull. It's so loud that I don't actually hear the guards yelling at me as I run right past them. I barely even notice them until their arms wrap around my waist and they lift me off the ground while I kick and fight against their hold.

"Let me go!" I wail, pressure clawing to burst from my eyes.

I don't want to cry in front of these assholes. I don't want to cry *at all*, but I feel like it's about to happen and I just need to get back to my cell.

I refuse to cry over him… I will not break down in public like someone who just caught their boyfriend cheating, because he's not my boyfriend, he's just a beautiful, lying fucking slut I believed in when I shouldn't have.

I'm too rational for this... I don't need to feel this way.

Let me go so I can... prove how... little this... hurts.

"Calm down, 35," someone—maybe Peters—growls. "Or you're gonna end up in the East."

"P-please..." I beg, holding it in with all my might. "Just t-take me b-back..."

"Let's just throw him in the hole to cool off," the new guy, Linetti, grumbles.

"Hang on a minute." Joy pops up out of nowhere. I didn't even see her before. I can barely see her now; everything is so blurry. "Put him down."

"But he just tried to run—"

"Was that a request??" she barks. "No. It was an order. Put him the fuck down, *now*."

The other guards reluctantly set me down, and I'm wheezing, out of breath from struggling against my emotions more than the giant dudes who were just holding me in the air.

"Come on," Joy murmurs, grabbing my arm. I flinch, aiming a devastated glare at her.

She doesn't say anything else. Just wanders away. But after a few seconds, I follow her, because I just need to get away from the goddamn showers before I lose my shit even more.

Joy walks for a while, and at first, I think she's bringing me back to my cell. But then we arrive at the cafeteria, and I give her a confused look.

"What are we doing here?" I mumble, already grateful as hell for the distraction, though it's not working to erase the images in my head as much as I wish it were.

I can't believe he did that to me...

I rub my eyes painfully hard.

I mean, I can believe *it. But fuck, it still hurts.*

It hurts so damn bad, and I hate myself for it.

"Over here." Joy nods, waltzing to the chow line.

I follow her as she goes around back, through the doors and into an actual kitchen I never knew was here.

"This place has a kitchen?" I gasp, looking around in mild shock. "Why the fuck do we eat the nastiest shit ever??"

"Do Velle and I look like Martha Stewart and fuckin Emeril to you?"

She huffs, and against all odds, I crack a smile. "This place is a dump, look around."

I sniffle. "So why am I here?"

She stares at me for a moment before murmuring, "I thought you could use some rage-therapy."

I have no earthly clue what she's talking about, and she must see that, because she picks up a rusty old frying pan, turning the handle in her hand a few times before raising her arm and swinging it down on a pile of dishes.

Everything scatters to the floor with a loud crash, and I jump.

"Jesus..." I mutter.

Joy grins, handing the pan to me. "Your turn."

I gape at it, stomach all twisted up, pain radiating throughout my extremities like I've suffered third-degree burns on the inside. I'm fucking *destroyed*...

The only thing worse than coming to prison is having your heartbroken in prison.

That dude fucked me up... My first relationship, my first almost *boyfriend*. My first... so *many* things. And he just doused me in kerosene and lit a fucking match.

I don't know if I'm angry enough to break shit right now...I'm just *so* damn *sad*.

"Go for it, Luthor," Joy says. "Bash your troubles away. It'll feel better, I promise."

I promise...

Those words. From his lips.

His sweet, soft, lying whore lips.

A guttural roar escapes me, and I swing the pan as hard as possible, slamming it into a bunch of trash. The stuff goes flying, empty glass bottles smashing all over the floor.

"Whoa..." I breathe a chuckle, peeking at Joy. "That felt good."

"More!" she growls, grinning wider than I've ever seen her before.

So I swing it again, smashing more dishes, and pans, and boxes. I run all around the room, smashing and bashing everything I can find. And when the pan isn't doing the trick anymore, I smash a bottle in half and use it to stab a big sack of flour.

"Fuck you," I choke, stabbing over and over. "Fuck you with your blue eyes and your perfect smile... Your whole fucking *lying, betraying* whore *face*! *Fuck you!!*"

By the time I come up for air, I'm panting and covered in flour. I peek at Joy, and she bursts out laughing.

"I'm sorry, but you look so cute," she sighs.

I grin, puffing flour off my lips. A chuckle slips out and I whip the bottle against the wall, where it crashes into shards.

Joy cheers out loud, and we both laugh.

But mine fades fast, the anger going with it. Giving way to the pain I was really hoping to avoid.

Slumping down onto the floor in a pile of flour and stale oats, my head falls into my hands.

And I fucking *cry*.

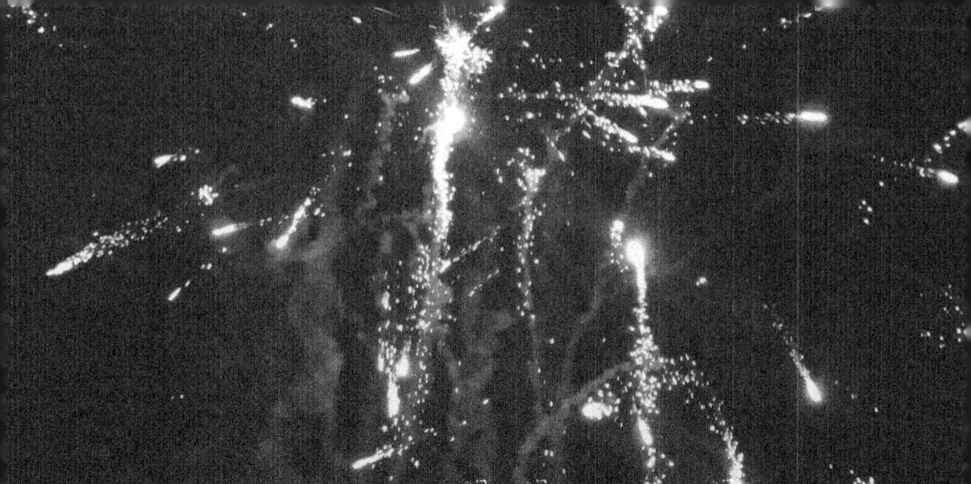

CHAPTER NINETEEN

Ren

Weeks later…

I know, I know.

You must fucking hate me right now.

I'm probably the last person you want to hear from, and believe me, I get it.

I'm not going to ask you to understand, or to see it from my point of view. My point of view sucks, and it'll just make you hate me more. I'm also not going to beg for your forgiveness and tell you how sorry I am.

You know me… You know how sorry I am. And you know I'm not lying when I tell you I hate myself for what I did.

If you are looking for an explanation… a reason that might just give you a light dusting of solace amidst the pain and hurt I've caused, then what I'll say is this…

It's fully possible to become so good at lying that you yourself don't even know what's the truth anymore.

Sometimes I think back on the night I killed my parents. I think about how things progressed, what led me from the fight with my father to burning down our home with him and my mother in it. The client I saw that night… the way the truth presented itself to me in blazing embers.

I don't need the pain. It doesn't actually sustain me. But I tell myself it does, because without it I'm responsible for all of my heinous actions. Self-sabotage is the name of my game. It has been ever since I was a child, and my nanny had to sit me down and explain to me that she wasn't my mother.

She was lying to me when she said the words... Your mommy loves you very much. She's just quite busy sometimes and needs help caring for you, Warren.

I was young, but still. I read between the lines.

Your mother is too busy to love you.

And too busy doing what, by the way? Busy being a whore??

Anyway, the point is that it became clear to me in that moment that if my own parents didn't love me, what chance was there that anyone else ever would? There was a reason they couldn't stand being around me... Something that made them despise me, and whatever it was, it would sure as shit make other people hate me too.

And so that was it. The lying, cheating and stealing, the shrinks diagnosing me with everything under the sun, stuffing me with medications that only fed my need to inflict physical pain on myself and emotional pain on others... It became who I am. It is *who I am.*

Because when people treat you like a villain your whole life, eventually you become one.

But enough about me. We know I'm fucked up, and we know it's never going to change.

This is about you, Lex. It's always been about you.

Since the moment I saw you, I knew you were that perfect antidote to the poison in my soul, and I knew I would end up burning you down, reducing you to nothing but ash.

It's what I do to the people I love.

And it's a real shame too, because being with you felt so good. You're all I think about, even now. The way your lips taste, the way they shiver when we kiss because you're nervous, and you have every right to be. The way your heart races and your breathing shallows. The way you used to smile at me, like you wanted so badly to believe that I might not hurt you.

I do hate myself, Lexington. I just need you to know that.

I hate myself for not being what you need, even though I told you I could be. I wish I could say I just want you to be happy, even if it's without me, but that would be a lie.

I guess all I can say now is that seeing your face every day after what I did to you will be the most horrendous, withering, soul-crushing pain of my life.

You're welcome. Hopefully, it helps just a little bit.

Scribbling out the last words, I let out a sharp exhale. Inside, my chest stings, like I have a punctured lung.

It's been hard to breathe recently.

Folding up the piece of paper, I stuff it into my pocket for safekeeping. Then I get ready for the day, brushing my teeth, washing my face, giving Parker his meds. I was able to secure some stuff for him, better than the generic nonsense they'd been giving him, and he seems to be doing better.

It's good. It's the one good thing I have right now, except that I constantly have to deal with him berating me and giving me disapproving looks every time Velle sneaks into our cell at night for some head, or I come back all rumpled from a bang-sesh with one of the many guards, all of whom have since blended together in my mind.

He thinks I am idiot, and an asshole, for what I did to Lexington, and I get it. He's not wrong.

But what else can I say? I fucked up, just like I knew I would. I hurt him, just like we all knew I would.

And there's nothing I can do about it. Nothing but live with myself and my mile-high pile of mistakes; its own form of torture within these walls.

The door opens, and Velle clomps in, ready to bring us to lunch. But he has a bag in his hand, which he shoves at me.

"You remembered my birthday?" I grin, snatching it up and peeking inside. "Aw, Jonathan. You shouldn't have."

"Shut up, Ren," he sighs, tired and grumpy, which is his personality eighty percent of the time. "No time for dillydallying. Let's go."

I pout, giving one last look to my special bag of tattooing supplies before setting it down on the bed and following him out into the row. I'll have to check everything out later. I've been dying to get my hands on the necessary tools to start tattooing in here. After a lot of convincing, Velle finally caved and got it for me, and I'm super excited. I've never actually tattooed before, but I can draw so I figure, how hard could it be? I'll learn as I go; I just need to find some willing participants who will let me practice on them.

I'm so busy thinking about all this that I barely even notice Joy is also out here, gathering the rest of the inmates… From *this* row. Which includes the new guy, Byron…

And his pal Luthor.

My gut flops in nerves and excitement, joy and pain. But when he sees me, I'm getting nothing but negative stuff from Lex. Hatred, betrayal, disgust. *You know… The regulars.*

I haven't seen Lex much since that day in the showers. It's been a few weeks, but that look on his face still remains forever up in my mind, like a poster on your bedroom wall.

I did try speaking to him once… Jasper let me stand outside his cell for a few minutes. Needless to say, Lex wanted no part of my apology, and I don't blame him one bit. I mean, I willingly hurt him.

In a way, I feel like it was beyond my control… But still, that doesn't make me any less of a raging scumbag.

So it would appear we've moved on from those blissful months, during which I honest to God thought the whole thing might work out. And yes, I'm miserable without him. But like any addict, I fill every second of silence with my drug of choice, in order to avoid ever having to think about what a fucking monster I am.

It works well enough. When it doesn't, I write him letters. *Like the one I have in my pocket.*

I doubt he's read any of them, but I still bribe inmates to pass them to him like we're kids in detention. I imagine him doing lots of things with them, and reading is pretty low on the list.

Lex purposely ignores me while the group of us trudges through the halls. It's weird to be around him again… I guess they're done keeping us apart, now that we're no longer an almost-item. At first, it seemed kind of baffling that the Warden had actually instructed the guards to keep us from seeing each other. But the more time has gone on, the more I think it makes perfect sense.

Manuel Blanco isn't just running a prison. This entire place is like one big game to him, and I wouldn't put it past him to pull a power move and separate two of the key players.

I'm lingering behind Byron and Lex, holding Parker's hand to keep him close to me. But my eyes are glued to the back of Lexington's head. *God*, I used to love kissing his neck. His skin is baby soft, and it smells so damn good… Like the sexy, sweet innocence of a boy who should have run far in the opposite direction.

"Ren, slow down," Parker whines at my side, stumbling to keep up with me.

"Sorry…" I mutter, not wanting him to fall or anything, but also just needing to be as close to Lex as humanly possible without actually touching him.

I'm still staring when I see his eyes shift.

"Stop looking at me, Ren," he growls, and my heart nearly bursts when he says my name.

"It's a free country," I mumble, knowing full well he'll hate that response.

And sure enough, he slows, face flinging so he can glare at me. He looks like he's about to chew me out, but then Byron clears his throat. Lex's shoulders drop a bit, and he just rolls his eyes, facing forward once more.

I narrow my gaze at Byron from behind. I don't know the guy too well, but we've talked a few times. He's very quiet, but in his limited words, he expressed his loyalty to Luthor, while also adding that he has no desire to be a middleman in our *gay prison drama*.

If you're looking to avoid gay drama, you came to the wrong prison, Byron Kang.

In the caf, I grab trays for Parker and myself, and when I go to sit down, I find him seated at our usual table with Lex and Byron.

Looks like the gang's back together again. Except that Byron has taken Toby's place, and honestly, I'm okay with it. Byron is way hotter.

Slithering into a seat next to our sexy new friend, I slide Parker his tray, my eyes naturally fixed on Lex, who's diagonally across from me making extreme efforts not to glance in my direction. I peek at Parker, and he shrugs, a look I assume means Lex begged him to sit there so I couldn't.

Sighing out a strained breath, I peer down at my lunch. "This sandwich actually doesn't look half ba—"

"Why are you sitting here?" Lex barks, and I glance up to find him shooting flames of fury at me through his pretty, green eyes. "Wouldn't you be more comfortable over there?" He nods at the next table over, where Percy Gage and his band of dunces are sitting.

"No…" I murmur, trying to contain my delight that he's actually looking at me and talking to me, regardless of how much he clearly wants me to choke on my sandwich. "I would always rather be near y—"

"Ugh!" He cuts me off again with a frustrated snarl. "You know, the one good thing that came out of that whole debacle was knowing I wouldn't have to see your fucking face every day. And now here you are! Popping back up like goddamn herpes."

I know he's pissed, but I can't help rumbling a little chuckle at his joke. "Cute."

"You just can't help yourself, can you?" he seethes. "If ruining lives was a sport, you'd take the fucking gold."

Swallowing hard, I'm shivering from the intentional hurt he's doling out right now.

Mhm... This is it. This is what I deserve.

"Guys, come on..." Parker sighs. "Can't we all just get along?"

My head shakes sorrowfully. "I really don't see how—"

"No, we can't," Lex snaps, refusing to let me get out a damn sentence. "Well, I mean, *we* can." He gestures to the three of them. Then he motions between the two of us. "But we can't."

The table goes silent for almost a full minute, tension buzzing in the air.

I know I should probably just shut up and eat my food, or move to another table. But I can't do that. Not with him *right here*, in front of me. It doesn't matter that I hurt him... I mean, it *does*, but in the grand scheme, it doesn't. I'd sit here and let him throw rocks at my head for all eternity if it meant that I get to be in the same room as him.

"This might not be the best time to bring it up, but I wrote you another letter," I whisper to him, pulling it out of my pocket and placing it on the table.

He stares at me for what feels like an hour, his rage morphing into baffled disbelief. Eventually, he shakes his head and huffs, "You're completely psychotic."

"Lexington, you know I still love—"

"I'm gonna throw up," he mumbles, rubbing his face.

"Sweet Jesus, what did I walk into...?" Byron whispers.

"Ren, for the love of God, stop," Parker grunts, scolding me with his eyes.

"*What?!*" I gasp, anxiety filling me fast. "I'm an addict! I have an *addiction*. If I relapsed on heroin, would you all be coming at me like this?!"

My head is all cloudy with emotions, my limbs racked with shivers as I pick incessantly at the skin around my nails.

You worthless fuck-up. Everyone hates you. See what you do??

You ruin everything.

"I'm sorry, okay??" I gasp as my breathing becomes labored. My head drops onto the table, and I cover it with my arms. "Stupid worthless whore..."

All I can hear are my parents' voices, *screaming* it at me over and over. The doctors, teachers, clients... Callum.

Liar.

Whore.

Disgusting.

Worthless.

You. Are. Worthless.

Before I even know what's happening, I'm smacking myself in the head over and over. Banging my skull repeatedly on the table, *hard*.

But I don't feel it. I actually laugh because it's *funny*.

I don't feel the pain anymore.

It's just a part of me.

Ren the gorgeous disease, infecting everyone around him.

Voices are echoing. Hands are touching me.

I think I feel Lex… I *hear* him…

But it can't be him. He doesn't care what happens to me. I hurt him, and he'll never forgive me.

He'll *never* be mine, no matter how badly I want him.

Suddenly, I'm hoisted up out of my seat by large arms. Cuffs and shackles are fastened on my wrists and ankles.

I pry my eyes open, vision blurred with tears. Velle is holding me up, and I can barely make out what he's saying over the mess in my head, the ragged sobs of laughter I'm choking out. But when I catch the word *East*, my lips tremble with fear.

Velle is hauling me away as my frantic gaze lands on the table, where my friends are staring. And Lex is sitting right where I was, chewing on his bottom lip while vibrant green worry glistens up at me.

"I'm *sorry*," I whimper to him one last time before a needle is stuck into my neck, and everything goes black.

I always assumed I'd end up here eventually.

The East Wing is where they bring the most fucked up inmates in Alabaster Pen, and I'm nothing if not a complete and total mess. *I'm their prime target.*

I actually have no idea how long I've been down here. It feels like months, but is probably no more than a couple of weeks. Still, it's exactly as awful as I knew it'd be.

I spend most of my days laced up in a straitjacket, in a padded cell with no furniture, just wandering around in circles, waiting for the guys in white lab coats to show up and fuck with me some more.

They've done it all, from electroshock therapy, to miscellaneous bloodwork, to dosing me with hallucinogens. I've lost count of how many polygraph tests they've given me, and how much sodium pentathol they've injected me with. The last time they did it, the Warden himself showed up to watch. I don't know if they got what they wanted, but I think the needle snapped off the machine and it broke because they haven't given me another one since.

The worst part of being down here is that I don't have access to any of my stuff, nor have I been able to seduce any of the doctors or orderlies into giving me things. But I did get to come a few times, during their bizarre sexual stimulation tests. It was like a brief field trip from the torture. Not that any of the doctors are good-looking. They're all trolls, especially the red-headed fuck who stuffed a twelve-inch long, three-inch thick dildo inside me and put clamps on my nipples.

Naturally, I got off, but still. *He was gross and a little too into the whole thing, if you ask me.*

Anyway, when I saw Velle outside my cell window, I foolishly thought it meant I would be getting out of here. But then he brought me into one of the exam rooms and cuffed me to a chair. So I really have no idea what's going on.

"What's going on?" I ask him, exhausted and partially hallucinating from all the torture and experiments and lingering drugs in my system. "When can I leave?"

"Soon," he grumbles, rifling through a drawer.

"Hey… Jonathan," I put on my sexiest voice, hoping to lure him in. "If you get me outta here, I'll let you come inside me. Hm? You can just lie back if you want, and I'll do all the work. Please?"

His face slants slightly in my direction, dark, pierced eyebrow quirking in that cocky asshole way he always does.

I swear, I love to hate the guy. He's just so *hot*, it almost makes up for how treacherous he is.

"Keep that offer on deck, inmate." He smirks, holding something in his hand. "You're getting out right now."

Relief washes over me, and I breathe out steadily. "Oh, thank God…"

"But I've been instructed to put this on you first." He steps over to me, holding up what looks like a cock cage; steel casing, with a little lock and everything.

"Fuck me…" My eyes widen. "Why?? Haven't you done enough?!"

"Your beef isn't with me, darling," he sighs, tugging my pants and boxers down to reveal my flaccid dick.

I'm just so damn tired. They've killed my ability to even get shame or rage-hard. And if they haven't all the way yet, something tells me wearing that contraption will do the trick.

Velle slips my cock into the cage, snaps it shut and locks it, his fingers trailing down my balls when he's done. It gives me a little rush of blood to my dick, and I can already feel the frustrating ache of not being able to get wood.

This is going to be just unbearable.

"Who has the key?" I ask breathlessly, and he grins again, holding it up in his hand. "Fuck my life."

"Yea, pretty much." He slips the key into his pocket, then pulls out a small remote. "And you're gonna want to behave, 48. Unless you like electricity."

I whimper and shake my head. *No*, I *hate* electricity now. I don't care if it powers everything. After being tased and having my brain sizzled like a piece of bacon, I'm officially over electricity.

"What is really the point of all this??" I grunt. "I mean, honestly. What is he expecting to gain here?"

"Well, I'm not privy to the specifics, but I'm guessing it's because when you behave like an animal, you get treated like an animal." He gives me a pointed look.

My jaw clenches. "Why is everyone always slut-shaming me?? What's the big deal? So I like sex, it's not like I'm… hurting… anyone…"

My words trail off, and I see Lex in my mind; his devastated face when he walked around the corner and saw me overflowing with cock, when I was supposed to be *trying* for him.

Professor Kensington, the dude who lost his job and his family because I was bored.

The kid who died in the fire at The Edge… because he was with Callum.

Velle simply shakes his head, pulling up my pants and releasing me from the chair. He then fastens new cuffs and shackles on me and brings me out of the room, walking us out of the East Wing and back up to gen-pop. The whole time, my mind is swirling through all these thoughts, my dick feeling suffocated in this stupid cage, weighted between my legs.

He brings me to my cell and puts me inside, where I lie down in my bed, drifting off into a cold, lonely sleep. I wake up to banging on my cell door, groggy and confused.

Where am I??

Oh, right. Prison.

Sweet.

I don't see Velle anywhere, which is promising in the not-having-my-dick-shocked department. But also, I would like to know how long I'm expected to wear this thing. I'm sure no one plans on telling me.

Joy brings me to shower alone, then immediately to the caf, and when I get there, some asshole is in my seat. Not even giving a fuck about food, I stomp over to the table, glaring at the stranger sitting next to Lex.

"Who the hell are you??" I grunt, eyes narrowed at him. But then I remember myself and peek at Lex, who looks positively *beautiful*, as always.

"Ren," Lex gasps, appearing shocked at my return, and not totally pissed off, so I guess that's good. "You're... back."

"Yes, I'm back," I rumble. "Now, who... *the hell*... is this?" I point in the guy's face.

"I'm, uh... Landon," he answers, glancing at Byron and Lex briefly. "Henry Landon. 75. You're..."

"Warren Xavier," I tell him. "The *Ren* you've probably already heard about."

His face shifts in realization. "Oh, yea! I have heard of you." He smiles, a dopey-looking thing. He seems kind of sweet and innocent, like a puppy. But still, I don't trust him, just sitting next to Lex while I'm gone like he's trying to replace me. *Psshh, what do you know about being a life-ruiner, pal??* "These guys talk about you all the time..."

Both Lex and Byron start clearing their throats, making faces at Landon as if to shut him up. But he just gives them an airhead look.

"All bad things, I'm sure," I grunt, slumping down next to him, forcing him to scoot over. "So, where the hell did you come from, anyway?"

"Um... Baltimore," he answers like he's asking me, and I'm already confused. My lashes flutter. "I'm Luthor's cellmate." Landon grins, but my stomach is grinding like gears that need lubrication.

My eyes flick to Lex, who's chewing on his lower lip. "He's your new cellmate?"

Lex nods. "He's been here for, like, a week."

"Oh, congratulations," I gulp, eyes falling to the table. I start picking at my fingernail. "I'm sure you two will be very happy together..."

"Oh, I'm not—" Landon starts, but I jump back in.

"That was obviously not sincere," I hiss. "I don't want you anywhere near him, do you understand??"

Landon's brow furrows. "That might be sorta tough since we sleep in the same cell…"

My jaw ticks, and I growl, "I will light your face on fire…"

"Alright, *enough*," Lex huffs, grabbing me by the arm. "Jesus. Can I talk to you alone for a second…"

He drags me up and pulls me over to a free table in the back, shoving me down into a seat.

Then he plops down in front of me with a tired sigh. "Ren… You're being crazy."

"Yea, no shit," I grumble, rubbing my eyes. "You've known me for years. This shouldn't surprise you…"

"Okay, but you need to stop," he barks, in his soft Lexington way, that doesn't sound mean at all. *Like the way a Smurf would yell at you.* "You're making everyone else crazy with your nonstop craziness. It's too much."

"What do you want from me, Lex??" I snap. "I just got back from the East, I'm all jacked up. I've got a cage on my cock, and now you're sitting here with this new cute little cellmate, phasing me out." I stop to breathe.

I'm still just so tired. *It's exhausting being me sometimes.*

Lex blinks at me like he doesn't even know where to start. But because he's Lex, he starts in the way that smashes my heart up into my throat.

"Are you okay?" His lower lip even juts out in this tiny pout, and I just want to lunge at him and kiss all the air out of his sexy lungs.

I dig my fingers into my thighs to keep my composure. "Been better, but I'll manage… As long as you're not hooking up with him."

He laughs, and I'm instantly a few degrees warmer. "You are such a hypocritical nutbag, I swear to God…" I grin while he shakes his head. "*No*, I'm not hooking up with him, okay? He's my *cellmate*. And I'm glad he's here because I was getting really lonely."

A frown tugs at my lips. "I'm sorry, Lexington… I'm sorry I haven't been here for you."

"Please," he scoffs. "Even when you're here, you're not here."

Ouch.

"They zapped me up pretty good in the East…" I mumble. "Maybe they cooked out my addiction. We could give it another shot…"

He rolls his eyes. But then his head slants, forehead lining. "I'm sorry, did you say you have a *cage* on your cock??"

"Oh, yea." I peel my pants open and show it to him.

His face flushes in an instant as he slaps his hands over his eyes.

"Dumbass! I don't wanna see it!" He peeks through his fingers. "Why are you wearing that??"

I shrug. "The Warden had Velle put it on me. Apparently, it shocks too. Velle has the remote. Luckily, he's not around right now..."

Lex looks flabbergasted. "Well, I'm guessing your addiction wasn't *cured*." He huffs. "Regular people don't have cock cages put on them."

I feather my hand at him. "Get off your high horse, Princess Di." He chuckles, scowling it away fast. "Forget the cock cage for now, though. We really need to talk about this..."

"No, we don't..." His head wobbles vehemently.

But I ignore him and go on. "Lex, *please*. I know I fucked up big time, but it didn't mean I don't want you in my life." Reaching forward, I slide my fingers onto his leg. "You're the only person I want—"

"Fuck, Ren!" He smacks my hand away. "It's *over*, okay? You *have* to get that. You were in alpha testing, and you showed too many system errors. That's it. Game over."

"I love when you talk nerdy to me." I grin.

"I'm not gonna forget what happened, Warren." He shrugs, wearing a sad expression that melts the amusement off my face. I hate myself *epically* for that look alone. "It's too bad, really. But this is the harsh reality. You're incapable of loving anyone but yourself."

My head shakes. "That's not true. I love *you*."

"You don't," he grunts. "You love the *idea* of me."

"Sorry, I didn't realize we were in a Nancy Meyers movie..." I roll my eyes. He goes quiet for a moment while I chew the inside of my cheek, staring down at my hands. "I just don't want you to hate me..."

I'm afraid to look at him, but he's not saying anything. So I slowly bring my eyes to his. They're round and full of a lot of heavy stuff. Stuff that might not even be all about me.

"I don't think I'm capable of hating you," he whispers. "Which is really unfortunate for me..."

I nod, feeling marginally better. Which also makes me feel worse, because it just goes to show how good he is for me, and how fucking tragic it is that I'll probably never get to have him.

"Let's just stay friends," he breathes. "Can we be *friends* at least, without you torturing me all the time?"

I purse my lips. "I'll try, baby..."

"No more *baby*, Ren," he mutters. "We have to be friends *only*. That's it. Otherwise, we can't talk anymore."

I know for a fact I'm incapable of just being his friend. But I'm also incapable of being what he needs in a partner. *It's the Hoe-bag Catch 22.*

So I just exhale, keeping myself as calm as possible while I nod. "Whatever you want, Lex. I'll be your friend, then."

He blinks over wide, hopeful eyes. "Promise?"

There's so much riding on that one-worded question, it's beyond overwhelming. But again, there's no alternative. This is the only way I get to stay around him. And *I* need that.

Swallowing down my uncertainties, I mumble, "If I have to… then I'll do it."

"Well, you don't *have* to…" His gaze falls to the space between us.

"No. I *do*. I told you I'd be whatever you want me to be. And if that means friends, then I guess we're… friends."

He doesn't appear convinced in the slightest, but he definitely looks happier than he was a moment ago. *So that's something.* "Okay, then…" He exhales slowly.

I lean in a little, running my fingers gently up his arm. "Friends who touch…?"

He squints at me. But he doesn't move away. "No. Just regular friends."

It's going in one ear and out the other. Because if there's one thing I know about Lexington, it's that when it comes to me, sometimes his words are as meaningless as mine.

I think he knows damn well I'm never going to stop trying. I'm way too stubborn and obsessive. And he'd never admit it, but I think he likes being chased.

Scooting in even closer on the bench seat, until his body is between my legs, I brush my lips along that yummy spot on his neck; the one that's about as soft as a marshmallow and just as sweet.

"Friends who kiss… here?"

Before I can kiss, he pulls back. "You obviously don't know how friends act…"

"No, I guess I don't." I shrug, showing him a wicked grin.

He scowls at me. "Friends don't kiss, Warren."

God, he's just so fucking cute.

"They can… if they want to," I rumble, touching him some more, though he keeps backing away from it.

"Well, I *don't* want to," he protests, standing firm, working me up even more.

My dick is straining against the cage between my legs, the steel cutting off circulation. I'm about to go in for one last shot, when a buzz of electric fire tingles across my dick, spreading all over my loins.

"*Fuck*," I choke, coughing because it literally knocked the air out of me.

My head flings around the room, and sure as shit, there's Velle standing in the doorway, holding up the remote and smirking like Satan in a cop uniform. He winks past me, and when I turn back to Lex, he's grinning up a storm.

"Maybe we found something that could make our relationship work," he sneers.

I grumble in pain, flipping my legs over the side of the bench and squeezing them together.

This sucks. Goddamn cock prison.

Lex and I go back to the table to finish our meal, and the whole time I'm flinching, expecting a shock out of nowhere. It doesn't happen, but the fear of waiting for it to happen is almost worse.

Afterward, we're all filing through the hallway, but before I'm shoved back into my cell, I sidle up to the new guy and murmur a threat that I'm sure will be the first of many.

"If you touch him, *ever*, in *any* way… I'll kill you slow, and painful."

A week of wearing this stupid electrocuting male chastity thing has just reaffirmed what I already knew about myself.

Cage or no cage, nothing's gonna hold Warren Xavier's libido down.

I've learned to live without the use of my dick, though the shocks are really no picnic. Yesterday, Velle caught me outside of the showers, eating Hancock's ass, and he shocked me for so long I thought my pubes were going to start sizzling.

Yea, it hurt. So what? It's just pain, and *pain* is what I deserve.

It really doesn't matter. Nothing matters.

I'm completely unhinged in this place. Which again, just goes to show that prison or not, I'm still just a hopeless, raging sex fiend, and without that, I have no fucking *clue* who I am.

Lex and I are trying to be *just friends*. I guess for him, it's working well enough, though it's noticeably different. We don't talk anywhere near as often as we used to, and I can tell being around me is hard for him. Part of me wishes I wasn't like this... That I wasn't such an epic disaster of a person, and could *really* be what he needs.

But that's just a lie... *Isn't it?*

We're in the showers, and I'm trying to wash around my cock cage, even though Velle told me it's water resistant. Not sure how that's possible when it contains electricity...

Lex probably knows. He's so smart.

Byron is between us, which usually happens now. Lex tries to put as much physical distance between him and me as possible, like some sort of self-imposed restraining order. Of course, I'm stealing glances when I can, trying to be subtle because if he catches me, he might leave. But I can't *not* look at him...Remembering the way we used to be.

When I could touch him whenever I wanted, and even though he'd act chagrined, he would shiver and hum and lean into it.

When he kinda, sorta let it slip that he *loved me*, right over there, in that corner.

Unfortunately, that's only one thing that's happened in these showers. And the *other* is what's written on his face every time we come in here.

Frustrated, my eyes slide off of Lex's hot body, creamy flesh covering definition of slim, perfectly taut muscle, and they land on our new buffer, Byron. Byron is also cut, but his skin is a slightly deeper complexion than Lex's, due to his Korean heritage. He also has some tattoos, whereas Lex currently has none.

Byron is another one who claims he's *straight*. I'm sure he *was*, outside of this place. But that doesn't mean he's going to stay that way, a notion that becomes especially apparent when his gaze sneaks over to mine. He catches me looking at him, but doesn't say anything. Just licks a droplet of water off his lip, letting his eyes travel briefly over my naked back and ass.

It'll probably happen. He'll fuck me at some point, and I'm sure we'll both get off, because that's the point. I'll do what my body needs, even if my mind isn't totally there...

And that rotten lump in my chest is somewhere else altogether.

I'm contemplating this as we get dressed and head out, back to the row. But Velle grabs me before we can get there, hauling me off in another direction. Toward the East Wing.

I'm instantly tense. "I don't wanna go back..." I shiver, the farther down we get in the building. It's so fucking cold in here right now, the dead of winter hitting the island hard. "P-please, Velle."

"You want that thing off, don't you?" he grumbles, pulling me along.

"Yea, but can't you just take it off now?" I slam on the brakes, skidding and holding with all my weight so he's forced to stop.

He glares at me, one of his impatient, grouchy looks. "Why are you such a fucking pain in the ass??"

While I'm sure the question is rhetorical, I still open my mouth to deliver some form of smartass response.

But before I can, he stomps up to me, features hardened in clear frustration. "Honestly, it's like a disorder with you. Everything has to be a twisted fucking game. Well, guess what, inmate?? Life isn't a game!" His chest is heaving, and he's fuming out of nowhere while I just stare at him, dumbfounded. "You can't just play people, and push their buttons… Push and push and fucking *push* until they have no choice but to *snap*!"

Over the course of his tirade, he's gotten closer and closer, and now he's up in my face. I'm backed against the wall, and he's trapping me there with his size and his blatant anger. I'm nervous, because he looks like he might beat me into the ground, but even more so, I'm confused as shit. I have no idea where this sudden wrath is coming from.

Is he talking about me and Lex? Why would he care what happens between us?

He's never alluded to caring about Lex enough to want to protect him.

I squint up at his face, watching his jaw tick, muscles all stiff and bunched.

No, this isn't about me… This is about someone else.

And just like that, an idea flickers in my mind.

Velle is raging right now, clearly torn up over someone, or something they've done. How I imagine Lex is feeling about me…

Maybe we can help each other.

Maybe he can be like a… proxy.

Raising my arms, I slip my cuffed wrists over Velle's head, draping my forearms on his shoulders to keep him close. He blinks at me, a bemused flash in his deep blue eyes.

"What are you doing, inmate?" he growls, not trying to back up or restrain me in any way. In fact, he's actually easing closer.

"Take it out on me, Officer," I hum, writhing into him.

My cock is still stuck in its cage, but it wants to be hard. In my mind, it is, and I think Velle likes the feeling of the metal rubbing against his junk.

He shakes his head slowly, eyes set on my mouth.

Moving my lips up to his, I brush them gently and he rumbles like an animal contemplating the pounce. "It's not right that I've been toying with you… *Punish me*, Jonathan."

He snarls, slamming me hard into the wall, practically crushing me with his weight against the concrete. His hands grip my waist, slowly falling onto my ass. I can feel how hard he is already; how wound up he is from whatever the hell is stressing him out. A tremor runs through my loins at the idea that he might make this rough.

Come on, Lex... Give in to me.

Hurt me the way I hurt you.

Velle's eyes flick away from my face, his chin slanting up and left. I follow his vision, to the camera in the corner of the ceiling, aimed right at us.

A small smirk tugs at my lips. *Okay... now we're getting somewhere.*

This definitely isn't about me and Lex. *It's about who's on the other side of that lens.*

Honestly, I don't care who it is. Am I intrigued? *Fuck yea.* But I'm more interested in getting a steady dicking from this notoriously well-hung man so I can fantasize about it being who I really wish was about to nail me to this wall...

Lex Luthor Deon.

"You're evil, you know that?" Velle's words vibrate into me through his wide chest.

Nodding, I close my eyes and tip my head back against the wall. "I know... I'm sor—"

He grabs my face, cutting off my words with a gasp. "No more bullshit. You made me into this..." His lips trail over my throat, and I'm fully certain he's talking to someone else, just like I am. *Damn, he really fell right into this plan...* "Someone needs to fuck you right off that throne, your *highness.*"

My brain whirls with immediate theories. *I mean, there's only one king of this island...*

But I won't go there right now. Not when he's unbuckling his belt and opening his pants, basically ripping mine to shreds to get access to my ass.

We're in a twister of furious desire as he scoops me up in his arms, curling my legs around his waist and pinning me to the wall. He pulls his long cock out of his pants, and my eyes roll back as he opens my cheeks and grinds it in between.

His dick isn't like Lex's, but it doesn't matter. It's all about what I'm seeing in my head; my sweet, sad boy, overcome with fueling anger.

God, Lex... Baby, give it to me.

Fuck me like I'm yours and you hate it so, so much...

I'm sweating and squirming with need, clinging to him as spits on his hand, massaging as much wetness as possible onto my hole. Only a moment later, he's pushing into me, setting my whole body on fire.

"Ungghhfuuuck," I groan, and he shudders.

The piercing... Holy fuck, it gets me every time.

"That's it. Open for me." His voice is deep and hoarse, but his tone has gone soft, as if he's talking someone through this raw fucking. Someone who is definitely *not* me. "Is this how you want it in you? Deep and hard, tight hole stretching wide for this cock..." He gives me a diesel thrust, driving up until his pelvis is on my cheeks.

"*Fffuck...*" I choke, body jostling in his arms as he pulls back, then pumps me full again, developing a steady pace. "Oh God, *Lex...*"

"Mmm... You're such a slut right now, aren't you...?" His voice echoes, and it sounds like Lex. Because I want it to be him. *So it is him.* "Anyone could walk in here and see you full of cock..."

I'm whimpering, whining, *leaking* inside the cage. My dick is numb from the steel trapping it in place, but I'm still pulsing out throb after throb while he pounds me good, hips rippling, feeding me. Nourishing me.

"Baby, I l-love y-you..." The words spill from my lips on broken sobs. "I'll... n-never... hurt you... again."

"No, you won't," he growls, holding my ass in one hand while the other grasps my jaw. "'Cause now you kneel for *me*."

His lips capture mine, kissing me deep and possessive, purring and panting, his tongue dominating my mouth. I imagine Lex kissing me this way... It's been too long since I've tasted his frantic need, felt his greedy lips sucking, teeth hungrily biting me, subduing me like only he can.

My body is quaking, rushing closer and closer to an orgasm I shouldn't be able to reach every time his dick stabs at my prostate.

A large hand falls to my caged cock, and he moans softly, "Does it hurt?"

I nod fast and whine, "Yea..."

"You aching in here, Daddy?"

Fuck... What?? My nuts throb. "*Yea...*"

"You think you're gonna come like this?" His fingers massage my balls, pulling my orgasm right up to the surface.

"*Ohhfuck*yeaa..."

"Mmm, that's good, Daddy... Squeeze my dick in that ass."

The pure filth filling my ears mixes up with the fantasies in my brain, my hole clenching on Lex's perfect cock. "Lex, *baby*, I'm gonna come..."

"Come with my dick in you." He rushes the words out, fucking and fucking, every muscle in both our bodies tight and ready. "*Fuck*, I'm gonna breed you so deep you'll never get rid of me."

Holy oh my God...

Suddenly, I feel movement. Hear a clinking of metal.

And a wave of euphoria crashes over me at the sensation of my dick being freed from the cage.

"Oh, fuck oh fuck ohhh*fuuuck*..." I'm crying. *Literally.* Tears are streaming down my face as my dick blows up and sprays everywhere in an instant, so fast it hurts. It actually fucking *kills*, but it feels *so fucking good*. "Fuck the c-cum out... Fuck, Lex, fuck the fucking cum out of... m-my..."

A hoarse groan leaves his lips as he kisses me hard, swallowing all my rambling words while cum shoots from my cock in such aggressive pulses, it hits us both in the jaw.

"Take this hot load," he pants, dick swelling and bursting inside me. "*Fffuck, Daddy*, take it good..."

The spinning goes on for a while. Longer than I knew it could. I can't feel anything for minutes on end. I'm just breathing Lex in, our lips brushing together, chests heaving in tandem.

By the time I'm back on solid ground again, I'm swollen and sore.

Sated. *Perplexed.*

And when reality dawns, and my eyes creep open to find Velle gazing up at the camera again, biting his lip, my satisfaction is lined with sadness.

He's not Lex.

He's a dude I don't love, dealing with his own issues.

We somehow wound up on the floor, Velle on his knees, holding me on his lap. He blinks at me, brushing a strand of hair away from his face before pulling out and standing us both up on wobbly knees. We're both silent as he brings me to a locker room so I can get cleaned up. But rather than taking me down to the East, he brings me back up to gen-pop.

Outside the door to the row, Velle pauses, shooting me a look. "Never a word about that. To anyone."

I nod slowly. I don't plan on telling anyone the details of what just went down. But I do find myself wondering how Lex would react, knowing I used someone else's body to be with him...

If I can't have him, I'll have to settle for the next best thing.

Velle pulls me into the row, opening the bars to my cell.

And both of our faces drop when we find Parker Freeman lying on the floor, lips blue and shivering.

CHAPTER TWENTY

Luthor

Today…

DON'T DO IT.

Don't… do… it.

My fingers are twitching with need, but I'm trying *so* hard to ignore it. I know I shouldn't do it, but stopping myself is becoming increasingly difficult. It's been gnawing at me for two days, and I know it's only going to get worse.

Don't. Stop it.

Do not touch.

It's one of those things you *know* is bad, but *man*, it would feel *so damn good* to give in and… *Scratch that itch.*

"*God*, say something to distract me from this hell, please," I whine, wiggling in discomfort.

"Don't scratch your tattoo, Luthor," Kang sighs, a knowing smirk on his lips as he rinses off next to me.

"But it's just so *itchy!*" I pout, scratching all around it.

Not satisfying. I wanna scratch it, damn you!

My first tattoo came out really good—*especially considering my slutty and ultimately foolish behavior while I was getting it*—and it's healing fast. I just never anticipated how itchy a healing tattoo could be, and Ren told me under *no circumstances* am I to scratch.

I'm desperate for some relief, and I can't get it. *Highly frustrating.*

On the plus side, the itchiness is serving as its own distraction from the overthinking I feel inclined to avoid, regarding the *other stuff* Ren did to me that night in his cell…

Getting tattooed was supposed to be a distraction on its own. Now I need a distraction from the distraction.

My head is a very messy place right now.

I don't know what to think about any of it. The situation with Ren has taken a turn for the crazy again, and it's making me hate myself more than a little.

The thing is, when we're deep in the thick haze of a lust so strong it can only be described as *chemical*, it feels like the greatest thing ever. I know I don't have much frame of reference, but fooling around with Ren is satisfying on a molecular level. Like we're *supposed* to be doing it; tangling together to make vital elements.

But then the literal *second* it's over, I get the cold, hard bitch-smack of reality, right upside my head. With Ren, it's *never* as easy as just fooling around, or even exploring our feelings for each other. We tried that shit, and guess what? My heart got curb stomped.

Objectively, I think I've forgiven him for hurting me way back when. But I'll never be able to *forget* what happened, despite how much my dick conveniently gets amnesia when we're alone.

How could I forget when I come back to the scene of the crime every day??

Right over there is where it happened…

The startling, gut-wrenching sight of the guy who was supposed to be mine, with hands that weren't mine touching him, body parts that weren't mine inside his body… Proving once and for all that he wasn't mine.

And he never would be.

I can still hear the sounds… I can see him, hair hanging in his eyes, the flush on his face while his body moved with forceful thrusts. Visible guilt and remorse framed by the dazed arousal of secret sex…

It's all still there. Nestled like a permanent back-up, never to be erased, no matter how badly I want it to disappear from my brain's Cloud.

So even though Ren somehow casts these magical orgasm spells on me, doling them out like a sex wizard waving around the Elder Wand in his pants, I just *know* if I keep this up, I'll always come away from it feeling stupid and sad.

Because he hurt me back then, he's liable to hurt me again if I give him the chance, and I care about him too much to run the risk of fully torpedoing the friendship this time.

It's too much. A place this boring shouldn't be this stressful.

Thankfully though, right now I'm enjoying a few quiet, tension-free minutes to shower in peace, since for whatever reason, Ren is nowhere to be found. It's a good thing too, because I think I'm going to give in and scratch this itchy fucking tattoo…

Just a little. One quick scratch. No one needs to know…

"Oh my God!" The familiar voice assaults my ears right as my fingers touch down on my ribcage and I jump, whipping my hand away fast.

"I wasn't doing anything!" I spin to face Ren sheepishly.

He's fully dressed, clearly not here for a shower as he scurries over to us with wide eyes. "You are *never* going to guess what I just heard…"

I let out a silent breath of relief that he's not here to yell at me for scratching. "What happened now?"

Ren's eyes slide down me briefly, lingering on my new ink in a way that sends a flush over my entire body. I can barely process what we did while he was tattooing me. My nipples are hard and achy just thinking about it… which means I have mere seconds before my dick decides to get involved. So I grab a towel, quickly cinching it around my waist.

Ren tilts his head like he wants to say and do so many things right now, and I'm just standing here, cursing these goddamn chills I get whenever he looks at me.

But I'm saved from the awkwardness when his eyes fling to Kang, expression turning grim.

"Uh, Byron, you might want to get dressed for this," Ren says, and the mere fact that he's telling someone to put clothes *on* is beyond worrying.

"That sounds serious…" Kang mutters nervously, grabbing his towel.

"Yea, I have some news." Ren's eyes shift around the room, making sure no one's close enough to overhear. Kang and I share a look, dressing quickly as Ren takes a breath. "It's about Kieran…"

Oh God… Not again.

Kang swallows visibly. "What about him…?"

"He's dead," Ren replies, phoning in the mourning a bit, if we're being honest. "They found him dead in his cell… Yesterday, I think."

Inside, my chest grows instantly heavy as I glance at Kang, my forehead lining. He's obviously distraught, though he's not one to show many emotions. But I can see it in his eyes, the sparkle of confusion and sadness; the rigidity in his posture and the way his fingers are squeezing into s fist at his side.

He blinks at Ren. "Was it… like…"

"Suicide? No." Ren shakes his head. "He was stabbed. Like a bunch of times."

A shivery breath escapes Kang, and he clears his throat to cover it up.

I feel *sick* right now, sorrow rolling in my gut. I'm all mixed up from so many different things, overpowering emotions flooding me with nowhere to go.

A breakdown is coming on, I can feel it... *But a ragey one, not a sad one.*

The bullshit of life in this prison is stirring up sudden irrational anger inside me, and I'm really just *dying* to take out on someone...

My eyes narrow at Ren. *Might as well be the Disney Prince with no soul.*

"Where are you getting this from??" I snap at him. "I swear to *God*, Ren, if you're lying..."

"I heard it from Linetti," he chirps, tone and expression still *too* casual. It probably means he's not lying, but it also seems like he's not even mildly affected by the fact that our friend was *murdered*.

I glower at his damn sexy sociopathic face. "So he just walked up and told you O'Malley was stabbed to death?"

"Not exactly. I overheard him and Brenner talking. I guess Joy called a meeting with all the guards..." He pauses for a second, in something that looks like fascination. "Kieran's death actually isn't even the biggest news..."

"Ren, are you fucking kidding me right now??" I interrupt his blasé shit-talking with a frustrated bark. "You are being entirely too flippant about this. O'Malley was our *friend* and he's fucking dead. Don't you care??"

Kang mumbles a curse under his breath, scrubbing his palms over his face while he turns away from us for a moment. O'Malley wasn't just his cellmate, and they were close. I mean, none of us really had the best relationship with the dude, because he was an irrational, unpredictable wacko. But still, he was one of *us*, especially where Kang is concerned.

"Yes, I care." Ren blinks at me. *Fucking liar.* "I liked him just fine." He lowers his voice, watching Kang as he speaks so only I can hear him. "You and I both know he was nuts..."

"Takes one to know one," I hiss.

He bites his lip like he's trying to smother a grin, and I can't stand it. I *hate* how much he loves when I lash out at him. He thinks my insults and my frustrations are *cute*, and it's infuriating.

Seriously, there's nothing worse than raging at someone while they just grin at you like you're a toddler throwing a temper tantrum.

"Lex, listen to me," he hums, stepping closer while I inch back.

"Kieran was a sweet guy, but he was seriously damaged. After what he did… You have to admit, he sorta deserved to be stabbed a bunch of times in the face."

I groan and rub my eyes. *This dude is testing me right now.*

He has a bit of a point, though I hate to admit it. Kieran O'Malley wasn't just an angry Irish terror within these walls. He was *actually* fucking crazy. He drowned his baby brother in a bathtub and hid the body for four days. *So yea…* I liked him as much as you can like any of the lovable lunatics in this place, but his crime was like a neon sign flashing above his head every time you saw him.

I just can't fathom harming a child…

"Okay, well, even so…" I mutter. "Byron is obviously upset, so could you at least *pretend* to have human emotions for a second? For him??"

Ren is nodding, pulling an obviously fake face of concern as a visibly edgy Kang stomps back up to us.

"Did they say who did it??"

Ren stares at him for a second, like he's trying to gauge how much more what he's about to say might upset him. "Well, no. But something else did happen around the same time." He stops again to glance at me, and I'm about to slap him.

"Ren, for the love of God, just spit it the fuck out!" I huff. "Jesus, you're driving me *insane,* and you've only been standing here for three goddamn minutes."

Why am I so annoyed by him right now?? It's like just being in his presence is making me all hot and itchy and fucking pissed off. I'm gonna scratch this fucking tattoo…

"Lexington," he says my full name in his calm, patronizing way that drives me up the wall. "Do we need to talk in private?" His lips twitch, eyebrow cocking. "You seem really wound up, like you might need me to—"

"I am going to rip your tongue out of your head if you don't stop fucking with me and just *say* what you need to say," I growl, pushing into his space.

And he lets me, of course, blue eyes twinkling as he rumbles, "Dash is gone."

Wait… What?

It actually *hurts* how fast my stomach drops. Like it just fell out of my body.

All of my unnecessary rage retreats fast, evaporating into nervous fear. "W-what do you mean *gone…?*"

"I don't have details, but from what I heard, he's not in the East or in solitary." Ren takes my hand, lacing our fingers, and I'm too numb to pretend to hate it right now.

"But then where... where would he be??" I'm spinning out, shivering through impending doom.

Dash can't be dead... He just can't be.

My lip is quivering as Ren holds me by my waist, pulling me closer. "I'm gonna try to get some more information, okay, baby?"

He lifts our joined hands, placing mine over his heart. Then he swipes his thumb gently over my trembling lips. And I'm just too fucking *shaken* to pull away.

It always feels really good to be close to him when I'm freaking out, something he's well aware of and uses to his full advantage. He knows that taking care of me when I'm upset is a way to weasel his way back in. And as calming as it is, I hate how he treats me like I'm some fragile doll made out of glass. It's insulting.

I'm no bitch. I can take care of myself.

At the same time, his fawning attention has a way of settling some bizarre part of my makeup I just don't understand. His hands on me are like a sedative...

"Wait, so then who killed O'Malley?" Kang jumps back in, snapping me out of it a little. I step back, Ren's hands sweeping off me slowly as I go. Kang shoots me a quick, disapproving look that makes me feel stupid all over again. "Do you think Dash did it??"

"No way!" I gasp. "Why the hell would he do that? It makes no sense..."

"I don't know, maybe because he's fucking *crazy*?" Kang grunts.

"O'Malley is way crazier than Dash," I argue.

"Okay, whatever. They're both fucking nutjobs," Ren intervenes. "The point is that they said Kieran was *dead* specifically, but they only said Dash was *gone*."

"Yea, well... who knows what the hell that means," Kang scoffs. "They're probably both dead. Because that's what they do in this place; they kill our fucking friends." He hucks his towel at the bin. "You two need to get your shit together, and remember what's really important here."

Then he stomps away, leaving me standing here like the statue of a confused idiot who knows nothing. So many thoughts, all jumbling around like a big, fat mess in my head. All of this confusion and anxiety is making me sick.

"I need to lie down," I breathe, shoulders slumping in defeat.

But Ren grabs them, holding me upright in front of him. "You wanna know what I think?" I just stare at him, letting his complete lack of concern fill me with an odd sense of comfort. "I think Dash got out."

My lashes flutter. "What would make you think that?"

"Well, you told me he was going to try, right? He goes down to the East and disappears... O'Malley turns up dead. It has to be connected."

"Dash wouldn't kill O'Malley..." I mutter again, although I'm not exactly confident in this statement.

The truth is, I don't *think* Dash would kill O'Malley... Definitely not the Dash who used to stay up talking with me until lights out, discussing our favorite movies, TV shows and music, the types of cars he'd love to restore, and why al pastor tacos are superior. The Dash who wanted to get me out of here because he cares about me, who hugged me just the other day and told me I was his friend... *That* Dash wouldn't viciously kill someone, especially not one of us.

But the Dash who freaked out in the cafeteria... The one who blacked out and punched Ren's face bloody... The one who kissed me thinking I was someone else.

The *officer*...

He might.

"Maybe it was Dash," Ren says, pulling my attention back to him, and the way he bites the corner of his lip sometimes when he's deep in thought. "Maybe it wasn't..."

"Who else could it be?" I ask him quietly. "I mean, who else would stab O'Malley repeatedly..."

My words trail as Ren and I share a knowing look.

Darcey.

"The Carver *is* down there..." Ren smirks, lifting a casual shoulder.

It's obvious he's thrilled at the idea of playing detective. This whole thing is really combining his mutual loves of scheming and gossip. *No wonder he flew in here all excited.*

"Just don't be making shit up without any actual facts." I shoot him a pointed look as I go to leave.

He grabs my arm. "I'm gonna find out what really happened. Don't worry, baby. I'm sure Dash is okay."

I don't even have the energy to scold him for being too affectionate when we're *not* a goddamn couple. Sometimes I think he doesn't really hear what I'm saying, anyway.

I have to give it to him… *He's one persistent motherfucker.*

"Okay, Ren. You do that," I puff the words on a tired breath. But of course, he doesn't let me go, reminding me not to confuse persistence with psycho-level obsessiveness.

"I still have the movies, if you wanna come by and watch." He runs his finger gently along my side, where the line of ink he gave me is hidden by my shirt. It feels *so good* because of how goddamn itchy the thing is. "We don't have to fool around… We can just cuddle."

His lips twist, and I shake my head. "I'm not watching *Twilight* with you, Ren."

"Fine, you can sleep while I watch it." His grin widens. I chuckle, shaking my head at his foolishness, and he leans in, whispering, "Just let me make you feel good, sweet boy. You know you want it…"

My insides buzz, but I push it down fast. "Yea, you do make me feel good, Ren. *Until* you make me feel really fucking bad. And do you know why you do it?" I pause, watching his brows knit and his grin fall away. "Because you're selfish. All you care about is *Ren*, and that's never gonna work for me. So just… leave it alone, okay?"

Yanking out of his hold, I stagger away while he calls out, "But what about the fireworks?"

Turning back one last time, I mutter, "There are no more fireworks for us. Not in here."

He actually fucking did it.

Dash escaped.

He fucking *escaped* Alabaster Penitentiary.

Gone. Flew the coup.

Ren has spent the last few days working all his connections for information, but really it was confirmed when we spoke to Rook. We were pestering him for verification of Dash's mortality status, and while he didn't exactly say the words, his confirmation that Dash was *not* killed and is *not* even on Alabaster Isle anymore felt like the craziest wave of relief, fascination, and simultaneous nausea I've ever experienced.

This island is pretty far away from the rest of civilization. Ten miles of raging sea that's said to be riddled with sharks…

Just because Dash didn't die *here*, it doesn't mean he didn't die trying to get back to the mainland in that little fucking boat I'm sure Velle is strongly regretting keeping out there now.

But I can't think like that. He actually made it out, undetected, which is something no one has ever done, *ever*. If he could pull that off, then I need to hold out hope that he made it back to the shores of New York safely and got himself the fuck outta dodge.

To top it all off, Ren heard from an anonymous source—he won't even tell *me* who it is—that Felix Darcey *was* actually the one who killed O'Malley. Ren claims he doesn't know how The Carver managed it—how he got the keys to the cells and the knife he used to slice up our Irish friend—but to be honest, I'm not so sure I believe that. He might be protecting his source, or maybe he's protecting me by not giving me all the details, to keep me out of trouble or something.

Who knows.

But either way, yesterday at breakfast, he told Kang and me that little Felix Darcey, the scariest, most normal-looking dude on the planet, somehow got into O'Malley's cell, stabbed him a fuckload of times, carved up his face, then wandered the halls of the East Wing covered in blood and opened Dash's cell to let him out.

And he's *still here.*

That might be the wildest part of this whole thing. Dash bounced, like I'm sure any of us would if given the chance, but Darcey didn't. He stayed in this god-awful shithole, *on purpose.*

Why?? Who the hell would even do that…?

Oh, right. Me. I did that.

Maybe Darcey also has something holding him to this island. Or someone.

Regardless of his reasoning, staying here might not have been the smartest play for the world's cutest serial killer. As soon as Kang heard who was responsible for slaughtering his friend in such grandiose fashion, he kinda flipped his lid. Joy was able to calm him down a little, but when we ran into Darcey in the showers up here, Kang was out for blood. Ren had to actually break them up, and ever since, Kang's been acting a little butthurt.

Listen, I get why he's upset. But at the end of the day, if a goldfish is dropped into the tank with a piranha, you don't blame the piranha.

Blame the twisted fuck who put them in the same shared space, unsupervised.

After Kang stormed out of the showers, Ren and I spoke to Darcey for a few. He honestly doesn't seem like a bad guy, though on paper, we know that just isn't true. But this place is full of psychos, some more experienced than others.

I appreciate him looking out for Dash. That's all I've got for right now.

I've been walking around in a jittery fog for days. It's been, by far, the most chaotic week in Alabaster Pen since I've been here, and unfortunately, I think it's only getting worse.

Word is that the prison is now on lockdown. This isn't something they would tell us officially, but with traveling word comes passed information.

The Warden is fucking pissed. *Makes sense*... He lost an inmate, and another was killed in the span of one day.

Lockdown in a place like Alabaster Pen doesn't even seem possible. In *theory*, we don't have shit. But apparently, it can always get worse, which is evident from the sounds of Velle storming around the row. It's been going on for hours, inmates shouting and cursing his name while he fucks with their things.

Up at the bars, I try to peer through, listening to the rampant complaints coming from other cells as Velle confiscates their hard-earned stuff, a sudden wave of panic sweeping through me.

My computer. Fuck...

Rushing over to Dash's bed—*aka* my new workstation since he left—I frantically shove all my spare parts into a pillowcase, lifting my mattress and stuffing them underneath, alongside my computer. The thing isn't much bigger than a regular tablet, except that it's obviously thicker to fit the homemade motherboard.

It's still a work in progress, but it's *mine*. It's all I have to pass the time, other than fooling around and fighting with Ren, and working on it helps me overcome the stress of that, along with all the other traumatic things that exhaust me on a daily basis.

This machine is the only thing tying me to my old life. Without it, I fear I'll lose myself completely.

I'm adjusting the blankets, hiding it as best I can when Velle's clomping footsteps approach my cell. Taking a deep breath, I try to act normal as he strides inside and barks, "Against the wall, 35. You know the drill."

I do as he says, peeking in his direction while he flings things everywhere. My stomach is all twisty, anxiety kicking up dust as my mind runs like the fucking Roadrunner. If Velle takes my computer, I'll be devastated. But what if it's even worse than that? What if he tells the Warden about it and they send me to solitary... or the East?

For all they know, the thing could be a bomb or some elaborate device that could wipe out the servers...

I gulp down a mouthful of dread like sand, my eyes locked on Velle's fingers gliding along my mattress. He pushes it up, revealing a hidden stash of items much more elaborate than deodorant and stale candy.

His dark gaze slinks to mine. I'm gnawing on my bottom lip, giving him a sort of pleading look, attempting to wordlessly appeal to his human side. He wasn't always a rabid animal. There's a man with empathy buried beneath all the hardened layers he's had to build up over the years, being the Warden's henchman.

That guy is still in there. He has to be.

Just as I'm about to start begging, Velle drops my mattress and steps up close to me. "I'm leaving this stuff here." I gawk up at him, unblinking. "Because your stalker made a promise. But if he doesn't deliver, I'll be back."

My head spins as he storms off, slamming my cell shut behind him.

What in the hell was that??

He barely took anything from my cell... A few pairs of old socks, my flashlight, and some batteries. He left most of it, but more shocking is that he saw my computer and willingly just ignored it.

Your stalker made a promise...

I spin around and lean up against the wall, staring through the bars out into the row.

Ren? Did Ren talk Velle into letting me keep my stuff??

How would he even manage something like that?

My stomach clenches so tight, I think I might puke. There's only one kind of deal Ren makes... And if that's what he's offering Velle for me to keep my stuff, then I don't fucking want it. I'll gladly throw it all away right now.

Nothing is worth that much. *Not to me.*

Pacing around in my cell, I feel myself spiraling. From what I can tell, Velle and Rook have something going on, and he hasn't been hooking up with anyone else. At the same time, Velle and Ren have a history...

Maybe he's looking for some relief from the stress of his treacherous life at The Ivory's helm, and decided to get it between Ren's legs.

The thought makes me so dizzy I feel like I might fall down.

I can't even fucking do this anymore, man. I'm losing it.

Friends don't obsess this much about who their friends are fucking.

It's totally unhealthy. And I can act like I'm ignoring it all I want, but I think we all know I'm not.

I need to talk to Ren right away, and tell him I don't want him fucking Velle just so I can have a toy to play with when I'm bored.

This shit is toxic as fuck. I'm over it.

Unfortunately, it's getting late. We're in for the night, and shy of screaming this conversation up the row to his cell, I have no other option but to wait until I see him tomorrow.

Unless...

Striding up to the bars without a second thought, I start kicking them over and over, gripping them in my fists and rattling the door to make as much noise as possible. "Hey! Help! I need medical attention! I'm injured!" I holler out into the row, banging the door around in hopes either someone will hear me, or the control room guys will send someone.

And it works. Footsteps come marching, and as soon as the guard is in my view, I release an exhale of relief.

It's Rook. *Perfect.*

"What's wrong?" He staggers inside with concern on his face. "Are you alright??"

I can't help the bloom in my chest at how sweet he is. Like a chivalrous Midwestern cowboy with dimples and golden hair. I swear, he's the *only* guard in this place who isn't completely devoid of emotion.

I fidget in front of him, offering a weak smile. "Um... yea. Yea, I'm good. How are you?"

I know I sound like an idiot, but I'm a little out of my wheelhouse right now. I *never* bribe guards.

Rook stares at me like I'm crazy. "You said you were injured..." His eyes trail over me for some sign of damage.

"Oh... yea, not necessarily," I mutter, feeling guilty for luring him in here under false pretenses. "I just needed to get your attention."

He squints at me, lips forming an unamused line. "48 is rubbing off on you. I don't like it."

I huff, shaking my head. "That's why I need your help. I need to see Ren... Like, right now."

He pops off a derisive chuckle. "Yea, sorry... Not this time."

"Rook, please..."

"You must be fucking kidding!" he barks, shocking me with uncharacteristic hostility. "Do you have any idea what's going on in this place??"

"I know, but I—"

"Luthor, that fucking psycho's out here slitting dudes' throats right in front of us..." He rubs his eyes. "We're all fucked... Us too, not just you guys. No more favors, no more deals. It's all over."

My spine stiffens. "Wait, who slit whose throat?"

Rook purses his lips. "Never mind. Just forget it. The point is, I can't help you. End of discussion. I won't give that prick any more leverage against him..."

I have no idea what he's talking about, but he's *leaving,* and I can't let him.

I grab his arm. "Rook, wait. *Please.*"

He spins to face me, stepping in closer. "The Warden killed one of the control room guards, okay?? Slit his fucking throat right in front of us. And we just had to stand there, watching him bleed out. His name was Steve Islo. He worked in the East, and now he's just *gone.*"

My blood runs cold. I can feel the color drain from my face.

Jesus, I had no idea it was that bad.

"I'm sorry..." I mumble, not knowing what else to say.

"And who do you think is taking all the brunt of this shit?" His jaw strains visibly, a mix of wrath and torment lighting up the mossy green in his eyes.

Velle.

"Rook, listen. I understand the risks, but this *is* very important. Velle and Ren made some kind of deal so I could keep my stuff, and I need to talk to Ren about it before anything... happens."

Raising my brows, I'm hoping to get my point across without having to say the words. *You probably don't want Velle hooking up with Ren either.*

Rook's forehead lines. His lips part like he wants to ask a bunch of questions. But instead, he just grabs me by the arm, quickly dragging me out into the row. His eyes fling to the camera while we walk, but he doesn't stop until we're at the end of the corridor in front of Ren's cell.

I can see him through the bars, picking up the remains of his stuff that Velle tossed everywhere. He glances up as Rook is opening the door and pushing me inside, his eyes round with obvious surprise.

"Work this shit out. I'll be back," Rook mutters, leaving with the clunk of metal.

"Hey," I address Ren on a tired breath, rubbing my eyes. "Sorry to just burst in here like this..."

He's gawking at me, like he never expected this in a million years. Historically, he's the one who comes to me.

"Velle just came by," I go on, watching his face. "He let me keep my stuff..."

Ren nods, Adam's apple dipping in his throat. "Good."

"Is it??" I hiss, stepping closer. "What did you have to do to make that happen, Ren? And *don't* fucking lie to me. If you lie about this, I swear on my life, our friendship is *over*—"

"Nothing," he answers fast, head shaking back and forth. "I haven't done anything... yet." My jaw ticks and I scoff. But Ren grabs my shoulders. "I'm not going to do anything, Lex. Velle doesn't want that, and neither do I..."

"Then *how*?" I snap. "He said you made a promise, and we all know what that means from you..."

"I swear, it's not that," he insists, forehead lined and blue eyes sparkling sincerity I *so* badly want to believe. "I'm trading him information. I found out some things I'm sure Velle doesn't know, and I figured if it could help you keep your stuff, then..."

I stare at him for a moment, my heart thumping rapidly in my chest from the adrenaline of all this. Everything that's happened over the last few weeks has filled me to the brim with *too many* emotions. I feel like I could explode.

"So you decided to swoop in and save the day? *Ren to the rescue*, like I can't take care of anything for myself..." I scrub a palm over my scalp. "You don't always need to *save* me. We're not *boyfriends*, Ren. I'm not your fucking responsibility!"

His brows furrow. "I know you're not. You've never needed me... But I fucking *want* you to." His fingers slide up my neck, and my eyes fall shut because it still feels too *good*. I'm so confused and wound so tight, I'm seconds from snapping. "I just want you to see this again, Lexington... Me and you. We're the only thing in this place that's ever been good."

Frustration weaves into my muscles and I grab his hand hard, cutting off his treasuring touch. "That's just it, though... We're *not* good. It feels good, yes, but together we're like ammonia and bleach. We're fucking *toxic*. Why can't you just let me fucking go?!"

"I can't..." he whispers.

"Why not??" I growl.

"Because I fucking love you!" he shouts in my face, and I falter. "I've loved you since the second I saw you, and I don't *understand* it! I don't want to feel this shit... This twisted up ball of need in my chest like fucking *disease*. I don't even know if it really *is* love, that's how fucked up I am. I never knew what this felt like… until you."

He stops to breathe while my mind races.

I didn't know either…

Is this it??

I thought love was supposed to be all shiny and vibrant, warm and freeing and *good*. Not painful and full of anguish, second-guessing and insecurity.

If this is really love, then love sucks balls.

Ren eases our chests together. My eyes are holding his steady, but the rest of me is shaking.

"H-how do you know?" I ask him on a frightened whisper. "What makes you think that this is… that?"

He licks his lip slowly, lacing our fingers where I've been unwittingly squeezing his hand. "Because I want to do *everything* in my power to make you happy… even when you hate me and refuse to look at me. I want to be next to you all the time… Just breathing the same air as you. I want to hold your hand and kiss your neck, and I want you to *want* me to… more than I've ever wanted *anything*. I feel like I could slaughter anyone who causes you pain, *including* myself. It's so unbearably fucked up, but I would open a vein and bleed just to make you smile… That has to mean I'm in love with you… *Right?*"

I can't do any more than blink while he shakes his head. "It doesn't matter if I've never felt it before. In my *soul*, I *know* what this is… I'm *desperately* in love with you, Lexington, and I never won't be. Believe me, I've tried. Even if it tears us both to shreds… I'm so sorry, baby, but I *can't* stop. As long as I'm breathing, I won't *ever* stop feeling the way I feel about you. In crazy, fierce, burning fucking *love*."

My lips are parted, hanging open while I stare at his beautiful face.

I think he's fucking nuts. He might just be the craziest person I've ever known… and he hides it *so* well. He's got a goddamn Encyclopedia Britannica of issues underneath that glowing skin and perfect body and immaculate smile. It's the best camouflage…

A villain with the face of a hero.

But despite all the red flags, and the hurt he's caused me over the years, here I am. Still standing right the fuck here, in his cell, *drowning* in him.

I chose not to go with Dash, but to stay. For *this*.

I'm clearly just as fucked up as he is…

Because I think I love him too.

"You're insane," I whisper, blinking baffled, awestruck eyes at him. He nods. "No, like, I think you might be *certifiable*, Ren. You're so fucking needy, and obsessive, and *manipulative*..."

"I know," he hums, gently touching my collarbone. And that unstoppable force moves my face closer to his. "I am all those things, and probably way more bad stuff we haven't even scratched the surface of yet..."

"You're goddamn chaos, Warren..." My forehead drops to his. "But I was wrong before. You're not selfish. Not all the time..."

"It's just *you*, Lex." His words warm my lips. "Any good I attempt is only for you."

"I hate myself," I breathe, pulse pounding inside my skull as the flames melt us together. "I hate that I can't break this..."

His fingertips glide up to grasp my jaw and hold me still. "Stop acting like you don't know *exactly* what you want, baby."

The resistance I've been clutching for so long is my battle shield, and it's slowly slipping from my grip. I'm struggling to hold on to it, but I don't know if I can...

I just don't think I'm strong enough to fight him off anymore.

Maybe I was never really fighting him at all.

"I know what I want." I nod, shivering. "It's s-so... bad..."

Both of our chests heave while we flutter in this cold, dark prison cell, keeping each other breathing; surviving on the electricity that flows between us.

He's the negative to my positive, and here we are... Together.

Fully charged.

"You came in here for a reason..." Ren touches my throat.

"I didn't... I don't want you to fuck Velle just so I can keep my stuff."

"No?" His smooth voice slips in through my ears, curling around my brain. "You don't want that...?"

I shake my head. "No... I don't want that."

"Who should be fucking me then, Lex?" His lips brush mine before he runs them down my jaw.

"I... I don't know," I stammer, hesitantly touching his chest. It's always meant to push him away... But it never seems to go down like that.

"I think you do." His lips dance over the mound in my throat as it bobs.

I'm burning in his sea of fire, but shaking as if I'm freezing. My logic has switched off, the way it always does when we're close like this.

My beautiful villain… He thinks he loves me.

I think he does too.

So… shouldn't it be me then…?

"*Who*… should be fucking me?" he asks again, pressing kiss after kiss on my neck until I'm so dizzy, I'm falling into him.

"M-me," I tremble out the word, barely audibly.

"Hm? Sorry, I couldn't hear you over how fast your heart is beating." He grins on my flesh while playing with my fingers.

Grabbing his face fast, I rip him off my neck so I can see the skies in his eyes. "*Me*, Warren," I growl, and he bites his lip. "I think it should be only me."

He whimpers. "You know I've been waiting for you, baby…"

A ragged breath flees my lips, slipping between his. "I guess I was waiting for me, too."

My fingers slide into his hair. My eyes close…

And I fucking kiss him, slow but hungry. Because I'm *starved,* and I need to be fed.

There's no other explanation, no excuse for this asinine behavior. I'll never understand it… But maybe I'm not meant to.

All I know is that his bottom lip fits *perfectly* between mine. His hands feel like bliss touching me everywhere. His moans sound like my favorite songs, and his tongue tastes like the sweetest thing I could never have imagined before I tasted it.

In an instant, I've lost all semblance of reality and I'm kissing him as *hard* as I can. Deep, my tongue is pushing into his and he's biting me and whining.

We're moving… I guess we are, because we wind up in his bed, and he's underneath me with his legs spreading and I'm panting because my cock is already so hard it's almost painful.

It's happening on its own—desire with a heartbeat. Frantic movements from greedy fingers. I'm sucking and biting on his mouth, trying to remember to breathe, but it's difficult when I don't want to stop for one-second. Ren's body is scorching to the touch as I pull his shirt over his head, and he does the same to mine. Our chests bump together while we writhe and squirm, his nipples brushing mine.

God, it's *euphoric*… Like the feeling of his big cock beneath mine.

"I want…" My broken thought fades off when I shove his pants and boxers down.

"Take it," he purrs, kicking them off the rest of the way. "It's yours. Everything I have is all *yours*, Lexington."

My hands are shaking, face burning a deep flush from what we're tumbling into. But I have to pull my face back for a moment, because he's naked. He's actually fully *naked* under me, with his dick, perfectly *long* and hard, leaving a sticky mess on his abs.

Taking a breath to calm myself down, I push my pants off too.

Out of them, everything feels swimmy. I know we've been naked together before, but it's never been like this. This is *real*… This is him opening for me and my cock throbbing at the knowledge of where it wants to go.

Ren grabs my face and kisses my quivering lips. "You can be nervous… I like it."

"I don't want you to expect…" My voice trails and I gulp. "I just mean, it probably won't be…"

"Baby, I'm gonna come if you keep acting all hot-boy virgin like this," he says on a hoarse whimper. "You're my *weakness*, Lex. You, just the way you are… my goddamn kryptonite."

Shuddering, my dick aches as I reach between our bodies, curling my fist around us both. "I've wanted to do this for so long…"

"Mmm, I'm sure," he groans, pushing his hips up to mine. "Losing your virginity is exciting…"

"No, I mean *this*, specifically. With you," I rumble, and he opens his eyes. "I wanna fuck you, Ren. I've wanted to fuck you for years, and I've never felt like that for anyone else before."

He blinks his hooded gaze up at me, our chests moving in synchronized panting. "Are you being serious?"

My lips twist into a tiny grin that I drop onto his mouth. "Yea, I'm serious."

"You wanna fuck me, Lex?" he hums, his deep, sexy voice lulling me into a trance, just like the feeling of his hard cock in my hand, rubbing on mine. It's all just so heady.

I can't believe this is happening.

"I wanna fuck you…" I whisper into his mouth while our hips move together.

"Fuck me," he croaks, then moans, head tipping back as he arches up to me. "God, *fuck me*, Lex. Right now. Put your cock inside and fuck me how you want me…"

"Jesus," I gasp, wound up and suddenly frantic.

I'm actually going to lose my virginity. To a guy.

Never imagined this before I got here, that's for sure.

But I literally don't care at all. I'm not sure if I'm gay or bi or what... But what I *am* is way beyond just *attracted* to Warren Xavier. I'm just as obsessed as he is, and the idea of putting my dick in his ass throbs my balls until precum is dripping all over my hand.

Wedging between his open legs, I run my fingers along his nuts, up his shaft, feeling his erection and how hard it is for me. I kiss his lips more, sucking and nipping at their swollen soft shivers, pushing my tongue into his mouth while his hands drift down to cup my ass.

"How can I..." Kissing down his sharp jaw, I tremble at the roughness of his stubble, "get you wet?"

"*Mmff*, sweet boy, you're making me *crazy*," he rasps, that sick body of sculpted muscle writhing all around beneath me. "I have lube, I think... It's under the mattress, if Velle didn't take it all."

"'Kay," I sigh while sucking on his earlobe, kneading his firm thighs in my hands. "Want me to get it?"

"Seems like you're busy," he purrs with a dazed smirk. "I'll get it."

He shifts, rummaging under his mattress while I get lost in giving him hickeys I'm pretending are accidental, tracing the immaculate lines of his abs with my fingers, teasing his cock and his balls, then gliding them between his legs. I just want to touch every spot on his body. I want to explore it all, because I'm fascinated. Every inch of him is mesmerizing to me.

"Only this one left." He hands me a tube.

I hold it up, reading the label. "Is this not a good kind?"

"It's fine." He shrugs. "It'll work for now. But not in, like, the shower, or a pool or anything."

I blink at him. *Sex in a pool? That sounds fun...*

"I wanna fuck you in a pool," I tell him, opening the tube and squirting some onto my fingers.

"Yea?" He grins, taking my wrist and guiding my own hand down to my cock. "Where else do you wanna fuck me?"

"Um... in a car," I ramble, stroking the slick stuff onto my erection. "At the beach..."

"Mmm... hot," he croons. "Where else?"

"In the library at Berkeley," I hum, and he bites his lip. "There's this private spot in the back where we could go. But you'd have to be really quiet. 'Cause, ya know... it's a library."

He chuckles. "Lexington, I would *love* to ride your dick in your college library."

Crushing my smile to his lips, I suck his mouth while squeezing out more lube. "I was thinking more like… bending you over. Making you grip the shelf while I… slide my cock into you. From behind."

"Baby… I'm gonna need you in me right the fuck now," he groans, this time guiding my hand between his legs. "Here. Put the lube inside."

Following his instruction, I push my fingers between his cheeks, grazing them over his tiny hole. I keep kissing him while I slide a finger in slowly. It sucks me right in, just like last time, and I *love* it.

"*Ren…*" I croak, fingers wet and shaking. "Is this good?"

"*So* good," he whines, grinding against my hand. I give him another finger, and he growls as I work them in and out. "That's enough fingering. I want your big cock, wicked boy."

"Okay," I whisper, pulling my hand back.

I thought he might want me to get him ready… but this is Ren we're talking about. He knows what he likes. I'm just the virgin without a clue.

And now my insecurities are ballooning.

What if it's bad? What if he hates it…

Oh God, what if I can't make him come?? I'll literally throw myself into the ocean.

"I fucking love how nervous you are," he purrs. "Give me your virginity, sweet boy. I *want* it."

Swallowing down my nerves, I focus on Ren… because he wants *me*. He's not lying… It's obvious, in the blush on his skin, and the dazed sparkle in his light blue eyes. The way his dark, Disney Prince hair is all tousled around, and his full lips quivering eager breaths.

This is one thing he's never done… Had sex with me.

It'll be good, I'm sure it will. It's us.

Our chemistry is too strong for it to be anything but fireworks.

"Hey…" I guide my dick between his cheeks. "You know where I really wanna fuck you?"

"Mmm… Where?" His thumbs circle my nipples.

"In a bed," I whisper, with my cock anxiously waiting to push inside. "In prison."

He gazes at me, lips sloping into a grin. "Sounds like the best place for me to pop that cherry, gorgeous."

Chuckling, I capture his mouth in more hungry kisses while I move my hips, pressing the slick tip of my cock up to his hole. It seems almost too tight, but I feel him relaxing enough to let me in.

Time slows to a stop. His lips are melting with mine, trapping their trembles in lush sucking, tongues lashing, teeth biting. I'm *shaking*, nudging at the entrance with euphoria on just the other.

And the moment the curve of my crown slips into his ass, I'm seeing fucking *stars*.

"Uhh*ffuck*... Holy fuck," I hiss, letting go of my erection with just the tip in him, inching my hips forward to slide in a little more. "*Oohh* my *God*..."

"Lex," he whines, both of us shuddering together. "*Lexington*... baby, fuck, you're finally in me... God, *yesss*."

I groan, fingertips digging into his thigh. "*Mmm*... I c-can't believe my dick is... in your ass." I sink in even deeper, and my lashes flutter. "Fuck, *Rennn*... Sweet flame, you f-feel *incredible*."

"I can't handle how good you feel," he gasps, lifting his legs to wrap them around my waist, swallowing up even more of my cock with a new magical position.

Ohhh-kayyy... Holy motherwow...

I guess I'm not a virgin anymore.

Time to fuck him the way I've always dreamed of fucking him.

Tugging my hips back, I thrust in once more, then again, reveling in this marvelous sensation while getting so deep my balls press up to his hole. Drawing back and driving in, I stroke my cock in him, slow at first, building a salacious rhythm within the clenching fire of his perfect body.

My lips are blazing a trail from his mouth, down his neck, on his throat. Grabbing his hands in mine, I lace our fingers and pin them by his shoulders, losing myself in fucking every solid inch of my cock into this hot, tight space that feels like it was *made* for me.

"You're so warm, baby," I croak, biting his Adam's apple while he groans and tightens. "Your hole is *perfect*... The way it sucks on my cock."

"*Ummfff*, Lex... *Fuck me*. Your dick is so *big*, baby, *fuck* me," he rambles, body rocking with the bed from my increasingly ravaging thrusts. "You're... *fuck*... hitting my spot."

"Yea?" My chest expands in thrill at the idea that I'm making him feel so good my first time doing this. "Is my dick touching it?" I push my hips between his legs, and his eyes roll back.

"*Yesss*... Yes yes, God, how are you...? I can't even... *Jesus*." He's not making any sense, and I love it way too much.

I was afraid he might feel inclined to fake it or something, but his pleasure is palpable. His entire body is quaking, delicious cords of muscle straining. Thighs squeezing tight around my hips, holding me close while he paws at my chest. Big cock trapped between our abs, stretched past his navel and leaking.

Oh, that's good. Fall apart for me, Warren.

"Baby..." I hum, pumping in him deeper and harder. "Ren...?"

"Uhhh... *yess.*"

God, I love how pink his cheeks are. "Will you look at me?"

"Hm...?"

"I wanna see your eyes while I'm fucking your sweet ass, baby flame."

For me, he forces them open, the incandescent blue twinkling up at my face. My hips keep rocking sturdy thrusts, and the more I drive, the more the bunk bed creaks, metal banging against the wall.

"*Ohhh Goddd,* you fuck so good." Ren's back arches when I reach as deep in him as possible.

Mmm... feeling his balls on my pelvis is life-affirming.

"This is the best thing I've ever felt..." I breathe ragged. "Baby, I'm so fucking glad I never did this before you..."

"Fuck, I love being your first," he whimpers like he's all fucking *mine.*

Sex with Ren is next-level bliss. He's just so *beautiful*, and sexy, and his body fits mine like a glove. A scorching hot fist, squeezing and stroking me...

Jesus, he's gonna suck the cum right out.

"L-Lex... *Lex*, fuck me. Fuck my... *ass*," he groans.

"You love me, baby?" I purr onto his mouth, thrusting harder and harder, stuffing him so full of my cock he can't seem to breathe.

"I *love you*," he rushes the words out, his hole suddenly clenching so tight I can barely move. "*Fuck*, Lexington, I *love* you, and I love your *cock*... and I... I can't—*oh God oh God oh... God!*"

Holy fuck, that's his orgasm face...

Suddenly, I feel warm pulses between us, and I look down to find his cock shooting.

He's coming already?? Hot damn, that's amazing.

This is my first time fucking, ever. I thought I'd have to work for it a little more.

"Baby, that is so hot." I kiss his mouth while he cries and sobs nonsense, toes curling up by my shoulder blades. "You come *so* beautifully, Warren... I love making you come for me."

"I... I'm... *Mmmm.*"

I chuckle a growly one, pounding into him hard, riding him out and following my own orgasm he's leading me to. "I love how uncool you are right now."

"Ffuck y-you," he grunts, rasping out once last long moaning sigh as his dick finally stops its spraying. We're both covered in cum, and it's the sexiest thing ever. "*Mmm*... I'm dead."

"But what about me...?" I faux pout, biting his lip. "I wanna come too... inside you."

"*Please*, come in my ass, Lex," he gasps. "I wanna feel you pulsing in me as deep as you can."

"Fuck." My forehead falls to his, hips rocking faster and faster. "*Fuck*, Ren, I'm so close..."

"Mmm, hold on. I know what you want," he hums, leaning down.

I release his hands and he holds me just under my ribcage, bringing his mouth to my chest. Feathering my nipple with his tongue, he sucks and bites, sending those crazy pleasure shocks through my loins.

"Ohh... *fuck me*, I'm gonna fucking come," I choke, movements slowing as the climax descends. "Baby, I'm... *coming* in you."

Hard and fast, it hits me, racking my body with chills. My cock bursts inside his tight channel, balls thrumming as I fill him with every drop, working it into him deep.

"Fuck yea, gorgeous," Ren whimpers. "Fuck *yess*, that's it. Come inside me, Lex... uhh, it feels *amazing*."

"Yea?" I pant, gripping his hair and biting him... I think.

I can barely even feel anything, my whole body is numb.

He nods fast. "You breed me *so good*, baby..."

"Baby, I'm dizzy," I rasp, head full of fuzz. "You are... a *revelation*."

We're clinging to each other, collective breaths echoing in the cell. Bodies all hot and sweaty, slipping together as my hips finally come to a gradual halt.

I'm weightless, floating in space, past stars and between galaxies.

So that was sex...

"How soon can we do it again?" I cup his jaw, laying kiss after kiss on his puffy lips. Ren laughs, clenching on my softening cock. "Oh my... that feels *good*."

"Stop it, fresh boy," he scolds through raspy giggles. "I think there's cum leaking everywhere."

"So?" I grin, nuzzling his neck. "I wanna make all the sexy messes with you."

"I can't even deal with how adorable you are," he rumbles, playing with the inch of hair on my head.

"*I* can't believe you came first!" I lift to beam down at him. "The virgin beat the nympho."

He bites his lip. "You just slayed my ass, Lex Luthor. Bravo." I can't help snorting a laugh into his neck. "No, but seriously… it's all you, baby. I always knew it would feel like this with you."

"Like what?" I kiss his jawline.

"Fireworks," he sighs, and I grin.

"Over the ocean?"

He chuckles. "Mmm… the best kind."

We're quiet for a moment, just breathing together, touching, kissing and swooning in sweet blissful static. Eventually, I pull out of him slowly, but we stay cuddled up, despite the mess. I rest my head on his chest, tracing his lines while my mind swirls around the fact that I'm not a virgin anymore… And I might be falling for the most complicated man I've ever known.

I think he finally caught me.

"Ren?"

"Yea, baby?"

"What happens now?" I peer up at him, and he tips his chin.

"Happily ever after?" he teases, and I roll my eyes. "I'm not sure, love. I just can't give you the same empty promises as before…"

In an instant, pain lances my chest like I'm being stabbed. "Oh… Okay…"

"But only because I don't want to feed you bullshit words," he adds quickly, and I can breathe again. I blink as he slides his thumb along my lower lip. "I have to *show* you, baby. Words are meaningless sometimes. I think you need action."

I nod. "Yea… that would be nice."

"I'm still not sure what will happen." He swallows. "I'm terrified of hurting you again."

"I'm terrified of you hurting me again…"

He gives me a wounded look, eyes glistening the prettiest blue there is. "I'm terrified you'll realize you're too good for me."

I take his hand in mine, toying with his fingers. "That's not true. You're just making excuses for yourself, so when you fuck up, you can blame it on that."

He exhales slowly. "Lex, do you really want to be with me? I mean, *really?*"

"I want to be with *you*, Ren," I tell him honestly. "The real you. Not the person you think you are."

I can tell from the look on his face it's getting heavy and he's worried. So I kiss his fingertips, pulling a soft smile out of him.

"The real me wants to get you hard again so we can do virginity theft round two."

I laugh, tugging him on top of me.

Giving in to the inevitable.

The Luthor and Ren Show... Back by popular demand.

CHAPTER TWENTY-ONE

Luthor

A few weeks later…

Alabaster Penitentiary is on full lockdown.

Most of everyone's stuff has been confiscated. The guards' leashes have been shortened immensely. Nothing is coming in or out of this place. Which means the guards aren't *coming* either.

I know… Yuck. But it's true.

From what I've heard, the parties they used to have in the mansion, the lavish bouts of techno and hedonism, with booze flowing from ice sculptures and people dressed like pixies blowing sparkly coke in your face—*at least, that's how I always pictured it*—have been shut the fuck down. The wells of drugs and sex have all but dried up, meaning we are now in a building full of men in withdrawal who aren't getting laid.

The mood is tense, to say the least.

But as awful as things are in theory, I'm walking on *goddamn sunshine.*

I finally lost my virginity.

That's right! Ya boy finally punched his V-card!

Internally raises the roof.

Not only that, but I lost it to the hottest dude on the planet. The rich, popular boy with the perfect hair, and the killer smile, and the Instagram model body…

Yea, that guy. I fucked him.

In reality, Warren Xavier stole my virginity like an art thief who'd been casing the joint for four years. And I've gotta say… I'm not mad at it. All confusing sexual awakenings aside, if I knew fucking him would ease all the pain he's caused me, I would've done it years ago.

I'm working toward a progressive view of my sexuality. For now, I'm just calling myself *queer*, because I think that's what I am. Maybe bi, maybe pan, maybe omni.

Who even knows, really… I'm still figuring it out, but isn't that the point?

Sexuality isn't necessarily something you're going to pin down from age whatever to the end of your life. It's likely to change as *you* change and grow as a person. I never used to think I'd be attracted to guys, but when I met Ren, his hotness really smacked me in the face. My sexual attraction to him is the easy part. Everything else with us is a shitshow, but that part is very straightforward. I think he's gorgeous, his body is bangin', and I like his dick… *a lot.*

The point is that I'm very gay for him. But I don't think that means I'm *gay* in general, because I still find girls attractive, too. I'd like to just ride this out and see where it takes me before getting too hung up on what it all means. Plus, it's not like I have to worry about coming out to my parents, or my friends.

Maybe I'm fortunate in that regard. Dealing with acceptance doesn't matter much in here. I suppose prison has a way of simplifying certain things.

My main point of contention right now is that I lost my virginity, and it was amazing, and it felt *divine*… And then it just *stopped*. I was tossed back into my cell alone when all I wanted was to have more sex. *Buttloads* more. *Hehe.*

Okay, ew, Luthor. Don't be gross.

But because I'm in stupid *prison*, I don't have the luxury of seeing my fuck-buddy—*the only label I'm comfortable with right now*—whenever I want. And I'm pouting about it just a little.

I'm not even a big masturbator, but I've been jerking it left and right to nothing but the memories in my head. The way Ren's tight body squeezed mine, that first push that felt like breaking through the pearly gates of heaven. Sinking as deep as possible and just swimming in the passion and pleasure and raw sexual appetite.

God, it was fantastic.

And now I'm basically a boner with legs.

It's a little embarrassing, because I feel like it's more socially acceptable to be this way in your teens. At twenty-three, you're supposed to have reined it in a little. But not me. I have sex on the brain, which is making me just as squirmy and petulant as the rest of the dudes in here.

This entire prison is one big pair of blue balls.

Glancing around the caf, I can see it in everyone. At least I'm not alone… The whole place is on edge, prisoners and guards alike. There have already been three fights today alone.

The only difference is that Ren and I can't stop making googly eyes at one another, whereas everyone else is looking like they actively want to gouge each other's eyes *out*.

I know, it's pretty stupid of me to be falling back into Ren's web, like a fly who narrowly escaped being eaten then decided to flutter right back in the deadly spider's direction. But I can't help it. I just want to bask in this a little while longer, before it inevitably turns to yet another emotional castration.

I don't think that's too much to ask, right? Can't I just have a few more weeks of boning my friend before we have to start rehashing all our old trauma??

Speaking of, the friend in question is sitting across from me at our table, his foot casually running up and down my leg. And even *that* is winding me up like a matchbox car.

I mean, it's a *foot*. On my *leg*.

Not exactly scandalous.

But my balls are aching, and my dick is screaming, and *holy fucking shit*, I'm using all my strength not to lunge over this table and hump his sexy brains out.

I can only distract myself with stale bread and bland chicken noodle soup for so long until I'm biting the inside of my cheek so hard, I'm sure I'm bleeding.

"Goddammit, Ren!" I bark, kicking him in the shin.

"Ow." He pouts, reaching under the table to rub his leg. "Jeez, what crawled up your butt??"

"Nothing," I grumble, acting like a stubborn, horny brat. "Nothing is up my butt. Or *anyone's* butt, for that matter. All butts are just sitting there, looking all pretty and sweet… And freshly showered so they probably smell really nice…" My voice trails, eyes set on his plump lips while I release a shivering breath. "Never mind. Just stop… stop *touching* me."

He tugs his bottom one between his teeth, and my dick *throbs*. "The butt misses you too, baby. Real bad."

I hear a scoff from my right, and I glance at Kang, who's rolling his eyes.

Leaning in, Ren whispers to me, "How much trouble do you think I'd get in if I slid under this table right now and gave your perfect cock a few kisses?"

I whimper, rubbing my eyes. "A lot."

"Might be worth it to ease some of the burn my gorgeous former virgin is feeling, hm?" he purrs, tracing my fingers from across the table.

"Will you come sit next to me?" I plead quietly, free hand running up and down my thigh because I'm *literally* about to combust, and now I'm wondering if there's any possibility I could sit him on my lap real quick for an inconspicuous public display of *affection.*

Ren looks positively elated by the thought of coming closer to me, which takes away some of the discomfort. *At least he's happy.*

He's about to stand when Joy stomps over to us.

"Everybody, fuck off. Luth, I need to borrow you for a sec," she grunts, grabbing me by the arm.

"Wait, what??" I mumble, staring helplessly at Ren and Kang as Joy literally pulls me up out of my seat and drags me across the room.

My first assumption is that they need me in one of the control rooms again, which has me on high alert. But instead, she just brings me into the corner of the caf and shoves me up against the wall.

"What the hell, man?!" I grumble. "I swear, I wasn't really gonna do it—"

"Just shut up," she sighs, pulling her phone out of her pocket and handing it to me. "Make it fucking quick, okay?? If someone sees this, we're even more fucked than we already are."

I'm gaping at her like she's insane, but when I glance down at her phone in my hand, the screen shows a call connected to an unknown number. I peek at Joy, then back down at the phone, hesitantly lifting it to my ear.

"Hello?"

"Luthor…" A familiar raspy voice sighs, and my chest tightens. "It's Dash."

Ummmm… WHAT?!

"Holy fuck…" The words puff out on an exhale of disbelief, and I peer around the room, then back at Joy, wondering how the hell this is even happening right now.

First, he escapes from prison, and then he calls me?! The dude is like a Bond villain! He's literally Hannibal Lecter in Silence of the Lambs. And I'm Clarice, just trying to enjoy her celebratory FBI welcome party…

"Are you fucking serious right now?" I scold Dash on a whisper. "How are you even… Why the fuck are you calling me?? How stupid are you?!"

"Not enough time in the day, Luth." I can hear the grin in his voice, and it's throwing me for such a loop.

I'm so *glad* that he's alive, I feel like I could fall down and cry on the floor. He's alive and well enough to be calling me… it's amazing.

But at the same time, he's an idiot. *Who calls the prison they just escaped from?!*

You're killin' me, Smalls.

"Bro, I can't believe you escaped! You're a fucking madman." I turn away from the noise of dinner in the caf, resting my head on the wall. "And now you're calling Joy to get to me? Are you nuts?? They're gonna think I was in on it with you!"

I don't mean to be admonishing him like this, but he's kind of fucking me over a little. That, and I'm in a horny rage, being cockblocked by this stupid prison and everyone in it, so I can't exactly be held accountable for my grouchiness.

"Come on, man," Dash says calmly. "You know the Warden won't tell anyone I escaped."

My brows furrow, eyes jumping to Joy. She's just standing there, posted up with her body blocking the view of me. She could have told Dash to fuck off when he called, and reported it to The Ivory instead of entertaining whatever this is. But based on what Rook told me the other day, and now this… I'm starting to think the relationship between the guards and the Warden is more strained than ever.

I'm sure Manuel Blanco has people looking for Dash. But he's right… No one will *publicly* be aware of his escape because, as far as the rest of the world knows, he's dead. We all are.

That's the gimmick.

The Ivory doesn't need my help to track Dash down, and if he was going to interrogate inmates, he would've done it by now. Chances are he already knows exactly how Dash got out. It's just a matter of what he'll do with that information.

"Okay…" I mumble, clinging to my frustrations because there are just so many of them at the moment. "Well then, how can I help you? Did you just miss me and want to chat? Because Joy could still tell someone…"

"She won't," he cuts me off. "Look, Luthor, as much as I do miss you and really would love to talk forever, I called for a reason. I need to ask you about Kemp—Officer Kemper."

Huh? My face scrunches in confusion. "Officer Kemper? Who the hell...?" I don't even know who he's talking about for a second, until my brain fog clears, and I remember the quiet, growly guard from solitary who quit a few months back. "*Oh*, you mean that dude who quit?"

I think I said like two words to the guy in my entire life... Why is Dash asking me about him?? Of all the things he could call to talk about...

"So he did quit... When?" he asks, sounding really invested in this.

"A while ago," I tell him. "I didn't think you even knew him."

Dash is quiet for a moment, and I can feel our shared confusion stretching from both ends of the line. "Why wouldn't I... *Huh??*"

"Because his last day was the day you got here," I speak into the palpable awkwardness.

The day Kemper quit was the day Dash arrived in Alabaster Pen. I remember it now because the guards were all complaining about being a man down in solitary. That was why Rook had to bring Darcey up to the cafeteria during Dash's first dinner.

Right. It's all coming back to me.

Unfortunately, Dash isn't sharing my sudden clarity. He's breathing heavily into the phone like he has no idea what's going on, and the feeling is sort of mutual because as much as I'm remembering these details, it still doesn't explain *why* he's even asking me about this in the first place.

"What the fuck are you talking about??" Dash croaks in my ear.

"Dash... what are *you* talking about?" I ask, my tone taking on a more sympathetic edge. I have a feeling this is somehow very important to him, and it's not making a lick of freaking sense. "Officer Kemper hasn't worked at Alabaster in months."

I hear a swift breath leave my friend, and then a thunk, like maybe he dropped the phone. I check the screen to see if the call is still connected. It is.

"Dash??"

He doesn't respond. But I hear him grumbling *no* over and over in the background, shuffling and rustling.

"Dash, are you okay, man?" I ask again, though it's obvious he's not focused on the call anymore.

I feel awful. Confused as fuck, yes, but I still feel bad.

Dash has so many issues, and now he's out there, alone, on the run. Off in hiding by himself, dealing with the twisted mess in his brain. I don't know what Officer Kemper has to do with any of this, but right now I wish more than anything that I could comfort my friend.

I'm so glad he's alive, but something about that call tells me just *breathing* might not be enough.

Handing the phone to Joy, I rub the back of my neck. "He's uh… done? I guess?"

Her forehead lines as she checks the screen, which still shows the call as connected. She lifts it to her ear, blinking at what must be more sounds of Dash panicking. So she just ends the call, stuffing the phone back into her pocket.

I'm about to walk back to the table, but Joy grabs me. "Did he mention Officer Kemper to you?"

I stare at her for a moment before nodding slowly. "Yea."

"What did he say?" She seems to have a vested interest in this herself, though I'm not sure why.

"He didn't really say much…" I mutter. "He asked when Kemper quit, and when I told him it was the day he got here, he seemed really… confused. And upset."

Joy rubs her face. "Jesus, this is all just… *wonderful.*"

"What's going on?" I ask nervously.

I'm even more worried for my friend now than when I thought he was dead.

"I barely understand it myself, kid," Joy sighs. We start walking back, but she turns to me again. "Dash has some issues, huh?"

"Yea," I huff, remembering the night we made out. "That's putting it mildly."

She brings me to the table, whispering, "I'll let you know if he calls again," then she stomps back over to the doorway, where Rook is standing, looking exhausted and stressed.

It's par for the course right now, I suppose. As happy as I am that Dash got out, his escape set off a chain of events. And something tells me it's only just getting started.

I don't always love being right.

Sure, it's satisfying to say *I told ya so*, but when the thing you predicted is a whole bunch of mayhem and uncertainty, well… Sometimes I'd rather be wrong.

Things are getting even weirder in this prison. I haven't seen Velle since the day he was running around, tear-assing through everyone's belongings, and now, as it would appear, Rook and Joy have also vanished.

It's been four days since that call from Dash. That was the last time I saw Joy, and Rook also hasn't shown up anywhere. It's honestly a bit troubling.

The guards in this place aren't *good* people, we know that. But they're our only links to the outside world, and after seeing them day in and day out for years, you start to rely on them for stability. It's not that I adore Velle's cocky asshole-ish ways, Joy's no-nonsense attitude, or Rook's undying sheep-like following of the both of them, but they're also the only ones who truly keep this place running. Velle and Joy in particular, but Rook is clearly the new, sweet and understanding addition to their brain trust.

Love him or hate him, when Velle isn't around, Alabaster Pen begins to crumble from the inside out.

I noticed it first the other day, when no one came by to bring us for food or showers until more than half the day had passed. I know things can get a little unorganized when the guards do their monthly trips off-island, but still, it was odd.

The day after that, still no sign of the power trio. A flustered Peters was ordering everyone around, and we ended up sitting in the cafeteria for three hours because there was no one to bring us back. They've also been taking larger groups at a time for meals and showers, amplifying the fighting and general loudness.

We were all pretty confused by the sudden change, but figured it was just temporary. *Maybe Velle was sick or something, and Joy and Rook stayed home to take care of him?*

But now it's been two more days of the same thing. They're just *gone*, and I'm beginning to worry that something might have happened to them. It's a stressful thought, because the guards we're left with are clearly in way over their heads.

We're on our way back from the showers, uncuffed, and in a much bigger herd of inmates than I'm sure Velle would ever allow. Jasper and Hancock are bickering about something personal, while Peters is just trying to hold it all together.

Suddenly, someone swings at someone. I can't tell who started it, but the next thing I know, there's a pig pile of inmates on the ground, bodies flying everywhere. Roaring and snarling fills the air, punches being thrown left and right. It's a huge mess, like a mosh pit without the music.

I'm trying to stay out of the way, but now guards are tackling people, guns and tasers everywhere. I'm afraid I might get shot by accident.

"Lex!" Ren calls my name, but I can't see him. There are too many people rushing around this small space, bumping me from every direction.

While my face is whipping around in search of Ren, I catch an elbow to the temple.

"Fuck!" I growl, kicking the asshole next to me.

I don't even know if it was him who hit me, but I'm pissed.

"Lex! Jesus, *move*, you fucking oaf!" I hear Ren, then I see him, weaving through the wall of idiots, shoving people to get to me. I'm holding my face as he rushes up, cupping my jaw. "You okay?"

"Yea, I'm fine," I breathe, flinching when another arm flies near us. "This is fucked."

"Let's get out of here," Ren grunts, grabbing my hand.

He pulls me to the other end of the hallway, peeking up at the camera before he tries the door.

It *opens*.

We share a wide-eyed look of shock, stumbling through and slamming the door behind us.

"Where are we?" I look around the drab corridor.

"Oh, shit," Ren mumbles. "This is near that old infirmary..." He brings me up the hall to another door that looks like it might be a closet or something.

"How can you tell?"

"I've used it more than once." He smirks.

He opens it, revealing a dark room with an exam chair in the middle. Ren pulls me inside, and my pulse is rapping faster than usual.

"We shouldn't be in here..." I mutter. "We're gonna get in trouble."

"Please, they won't even notice we're gone," Ren says while poking around the room. "Peters is like a deer in headlights, the poor thing."

"Yea..." I sigh. "I guess no one really understands what Velle goes through until they stomp a mile in his combat boots."

Ren chuckles, leaning up against a counter. "Do you recognize this room?"

I tilt my head. "Is it a place where you've had your organs rearranged? Because honestly, that could describe more than half this building."

He fakes a laugh, and I grin. "No... Well, *yes*, but that's not what I meant." I roll my eyes. "Do you remember you and me being in here together...?"

I purse my lips, allowing him to tug me closer by my hand, though I'm still pretending to stand my ground and act mad at him. I'm realizing it's kind of my thing.

I like playing hard to get with him, because he's so used to getting whatever he wants from men.

But don't tell him that. It makes me seem like a willful cocktease.

"I do remember you forcing Hancock to bring me in here with you..." I murmur, easing up to his front. "When I was still *really* mad."

"Mhm..." he hums, petting my jawline. "You should've let me kiss you that day."

"I think I handled it well." I smirk, and he chuckles.

The memory is fresh in my mind now. *We ended up fighting, and I punched him in the stomach.*

"What about now?" he purrs over my lips. "Have I earned a little sweetness, beautiful boy?"

A growl leaves my lips as I press myself into him, brushing my fingers through his silky hair while our mouths hover. I know I should resist him, try to cool things off again for my own sanity and the wellbeing of my heart, which only *just* started beating normally again after the last time.

But ever since we had sex, I've been in a daze, desperate to explore this side of the fuck-buddy relationship we never reached years ago because he messed it all up.

"I don't know, Ren..." I whisper, pinching his chin between my fingers. "Have you?"

He nods, peeking up at me with sparkly topaz eyes. It's so dark in here, save for the light streaming in from the hallway through the cracked-open door. We probably should have closed it, but I want to be able to see him, and I don't know where the light is.

Also... it's hotter this way. Being in here when we're not supposed to, knowing someone could find us at any moment. My dick is rock hard already from the thrill of it. And from *him*...

The way he smells, and his strong hands on my ass, pulling my hips so we can rub our cocks together.

Fuck, I just love this... I love the way it feels to be bad with him, knowing with almost absolute certainty it's going to thrash me. *I must be a real masochist...*

"I want you," I whimper, kissing his mouth softly while he mewls. "I want to erase all the others who came before me... Pun intended."

He grins. "I also sucked Dash's dick in here..."

"Ren," I whine his name in a frustrated, snarling way, grabbing his throat while he chuckles. "It's not funny. I *hate it*, and you know that."

"I know, baby." He pouts. "I'm only teasing you because I feel like shit, you *know* that. But I want only you, Lexington… So bad. No one else matters."

I'm still humming out my displeasure, but I nod… Because I do *want* to believe him.

I want to be the only one who gets him.

I sound like every pathetic loser who chains themselves to a bucket of red flags and says, *I can change him*. But the problem is that they're red flags for a reason. If they were dumpy idiots, then we wouldn't be so drawn to them.

Instead, they're hot as fuck and have amazing dicks, and they're the best kissers in the world because it's their superpower.

Wouldn't it just be so satisfying to tame one? I'm sure it's happened before…

I could be the exception… Maybe? The one in a million who domesticates a toxic fuckboy.

Ren's breaths pick up when I kiss him slowly, sucking his bottom lip and toying with it between my teeth. Our tongues flutter and our hands explore; mine are in his hair and on his chest, while his are feeling up my ass and cupping my cock. It's *sublime*, just making out with him, feeling his heart fly into me. The way his jaw strains with our ravenous kissing, his mouth overpowering mine because he's infinitely hungrier.

Having him writhing against me is hypnotic, all those hard curves and slopes of muscle… his big dick, always stiff and ready for me. He's the most confident, sexually experienced person I've ever met, and yet when we're together, he's shivering and needy for *me*. It has me soaring with thrill…

That nerdy little Lex Luthor could get someone like Bizarro World Superman.

"How much time do you think we have?" I pant into his mouth, thrusting into his hands while he pulls my dick out to stroke it slowly.

"Maybe not much…" he whispers, kissing his way down my neck. "But definitely enough for me to make you purr like a kitten."

God, I fucking need this. Having sex only that one night, with *him*, of all people, was absolutely not enough. I need to get him on my dick again. *Right now.*

"Let me inside this gorgeous ass, sweet flame," I hum, sliding my fingers into the waist of his pants to cup his perfectly plump cheeks. "I need it."

"Mmm..." He licks a circle around my pulse, our hips grinding together as his warm mouth moves up to my ear. "I actually have something I want you to do for me, baby. And this might be the perfect time..."

Eyes closed, head tipped back, I breathe out jittery arousal. "And what would that be, you filthy pervert?"

He chuckles, nipping my earlobe. "I want you to fuck me... *rough.*"

My dick twinges hard in his hand, but I'm also a bit stiff as I peek down at him. "Like... how rough?"

"Very." He bites his lip, blinking innocently up at me. "I want you to pretend you're taking it... against my will."

My lashes flutter. *That's a tall order for someone who just lost his virginity, am I wrong?*

Holding his face, I kiss his lips softly. "Are you sure?" He nods fast. "Why...?"

"You wanna know why I did the proxies so much?" he asks with his fingers grazing my dick.

It makes it hard to think straight, but I still manage to frown at him. "Not really..."

His lips quirk, and he huffs. "It was because I could pretend you were punishing me. I wanted it to be you every time, but I also wanted you to be... hurting me. Fucking me up, because that's what I deserve. For... fucking you up so much."

With our eyes melting together, I can see how sincere he is right now. The shimmer in his gaze tells me he's being serious, and I wish I understood it. The problems he has surrounding sex are a goddamn mystery to me, but after everything he's been through in his past, all the ways he's been used and thrown away, it sort of kills me to think that he doesn't know how special he is.

The difference between me and his proxies is that I would never hurt him.

I won't say the thought never crossed my mind... I mean, he did fuck me up. Badly. And he did it as easy as striking a match...

"Do you hate me?" Ren whispers, dark brows swooping together. "You think I'm a dirty, broken whore, don't you?"

"What?? No," I gasp, shaking my head. "I'm just... wondering if that's something I could even do. You know me, I'm not exactly *dominant...*"

He bites his lip with blue flames in his eyes. "Baby, you're a lot more demanding than you think you are..."

"Am I?" I pluck the lip from between his teeth, pressing a kiss on it. He hums and nods. "So you want me to pretend...?"

"I want you to dig up the anger I know you have for me." He taps his finger on my chest. "Mix it up with your pent-up aggression, and *unleash*."

This idea sounds crazy to me. But the more I'm considering it, the more I'm thinking it could be a positive thing... Like therapy. Not to mention I desperately need to fuck him again, and the thought of doing it in this room, when we're not supposed to...

Yea, he can get it. Any way his black little heart desires.

I push my cock into his hand, mouth falling to graze his throat. "You can't tell me you didn't like the way we did it last time... You came so hard you could barely breathe."

A chuckle rumbles from his chest. "I'm *definitely* not saying I didn't like it. You get me off better than anyone, just by being you." His thumb grazes the underside of my crown, causing my dick to flinch. "As does this monster cock that seems *way* too big for your body, by the way..."

I grin while sucking on his neck, shoving him hard against the counter. "So what should I... do?" I gulp nervously. "Do we need, like, a safeword or something?"

I peer up to find him beaming at me. "How about if I call you *Lex,* then you'll know it's getting to be too much."

"But you always call me Lex..."

"I know. But right now, you're *Luthor*." He releases my dick, fingers grazing my abs. "The prisoner who's gonna ravage me for being an awful, thoughtless slut."

I can't help the way my mouth suddenly goes dry. "Ren..."

"Yes, dear?"

"There's a tiny problem with your storyline," I rasp, and he blinks at me. "You *always* want it." He gasps in faux-outrage, and I chuckle. "I'm serious. You're gonna have to pretend to be someone else."

He purses his lips. "Fine. I'll be a random, unsuspecting inmate who wants nothing to do with you. Is that better?"

"I guess," I sigh, straightening and backing away from him.

"You're the best." He smirks while I rub my face and take a deep breath.

It's worth a shot, I guess. And I do *really* need to get laid.

How hard can it be to harness my angry side? I might have some aggression I need to get out, who knows.

Ren runs his fingers through his hair, leaning against the counter and bending at the waist. "Oh, how I *love* being an unsuspecting prisoner in this dark room by myself..." He peeks at me over his shoulder, stifling a grin. "I sure hope no one comes in here, because I'm busy thinking about my *girlfriend* back home and how *awesome* her boobs are."

My head falls back in a laugh. "Wait, hold on... you're *straight* in this scenario?? That's the least believable part of the whole thing."

He scowls at me. "Don't ruin it." Then he shifts his face back to the nervous act he's putting on. "Oh, no! Who are you? I wasn't expecting anyone to come in here..."

"You're a terrible actor," I jeer, stepping closer.

"What do you want, *Luthor*?" He glares at me, cocking his head.

The use of my nickname shifts the vibe a little. He never calls me that, so when he does, it's kind of sexy. Like I'm someone else in his eyes.

"Just admiring the view," I hum, gaze sliding down to his ass and the way it somehow looks taut and delicious even in these shapeless jumpsuit pants.

"Don't look at me, creeper," he snarls, committing a little more to the character.

"Don't have such a mouthwatering ass." I lift a brow, moving in quick to trap him against the counter.

My hands fall to his waist while he tries to wriggle away.

"Don't touch me, faggot," he growls, and I back up, shooting him a look.

"Whoa... babe. *Really*?"

"It's part of the act, it's fine," he huffs. "Come on, stay in character. You're doing so well."

He continues struggling against me, so I press into him harder, grabbing his wrists and pinning them to the counter.

"Hold still," I grunt, partially serious because he's moving around too much, and I can't get a good grip on him.

"Get off me," he hisses, laying it on thick.

I hate to admit it, but there is frustration winding in my muscles. I'm telling myself it's part of the act, but I think it's due to a lot of different things...

The fact that I don't understand why he wants this and the worrying confusion is making me feel inadequate. The way he's squirming in my grip like he really wants to get away from me, which is an honest to God fear of mine... that this will happen someday in real life.

Not the corny show he's putting on about being straight, obviously.

But I *am* afraid that if I give him my heart again, somewhere down the line, he'll decide he doesn't want it anymore.

On top of it all, I'm fucking horny as *fuck*, and his ass is pressing against my rapidly growing erection while he shivers and grunts, winding me up into a thick frenzy of need.

The words pour from my lips, without a thought. "Keep fighting me, and I'll fucking kill you."

Ren's brows shoot up, and he gives me a look of surprise, like he's impressed. I swallow and shrug, heat rushing to my face.

I don't know, man. It just came out... Does that make me weird?

No time to overanalyze it. I just keep going because we're already in this, placing a hand between his shoulder blades to bend him over forcefully, splaying him on the countertop. Then I rip his pants down quick with shaky fingers.

"One way or another, I'm shoving my cock in your ass," I snarl. "So just hold still and take it, little bitch."

Jesus, I can't believe I just said that...

"*Fuck. Off.*" Ren is committed. He keeps fighting back, bucking against me while I drop kisses on the nape of his neck.

Shit, what am I supposed to use for lube??

Thinking for a moment, I lift his shirt up around his shoulders, biting my lip when an idea pops into my head. And I quickly drop to my knees behind him.

"Um, holy fuck." Ren trembles, peering down at me. "What...?"

"Shh..." I rumble, spreading his cheeks open with my hands. "Gotta get you wet."

This part isn't an act. I'm *really* dying to lick his ass. That time he did it to me, I felt like I was going to collapse. Plus, I've never eaten anything out before, and I'd like to try it. *Seems fun.*

"G-get the fuck out of m-my..."

His words dissolve when I sink my mouth between his cheeks, opening him up wide enough to press a kiss on his hole.

His body shudders. "*Jesus* fuck..."

I bite his ass cheek hard, and he yelps. "You don't *like* this, do you, princess?"

He clears his throat. "Fffuck no. Leave me... *uhh fuck*... alone... you s-sick... *fuuuck*."

Grinning in triumph, I kiss his rim over and over, slipping my tongue between my lips to swipe it over his quivering little hole. Remembering himself, Ren struggles again, trying to squirm out of my grip. It only makes me squeeze his ass harder.

"*Fuck*, what are you doing to me...?"

"Making your tight cunt wet so I can fuck you," I growl the filthiest thing I can think to say.

Honestly, I'm turning myself on with it. My dick is heavy between my legs, balls buzzing while I lick him again, and again, slowly lapping at his hole, feeling it clench under my tongue. I really love this... Licking him here. It feels so naughty, especially with the door open. Someone could peek inside and find me on my knees with my face buried in his ass.

Fuck, I'm leaking... I want more.

Spearing my tongue as best I can, I force it into his ass.

"S-stop," Ren groans, gripping the counter, using it to support his body weight while I slide my tongue in and out to get him nice and slippery, ignoring his futile protests.

It's *so* fucking hot. I never knew I'd enjoy what's essentially making out with someone's butt so much, but this is incredible. I could do it for hours.

But I'm sure we don't have that kind of time, so when I feel like he's sufficiently soaked, I force myself out of his ass with a sigh, wiping my mouth. Standing up, I cup his ass in my hands, kneading it while brushing my lips along his neck.

"You want a big cock in your ass?" I hum, hypnotized by the sticky warm lust in the air.

"N-no," he shivers, replacing the words, but the need I feel in his muscles is there. "No, *please*..."

"You're such a fucking liar." I push my pants down enough to get my dick out, spitting in my palm and giving it a few strokes. "I'm gonna fuck you hard, little slut. And you're gonna *love* it."

Ren starts struggling again, fighting me with probably only fifteen percent of his strength. But still, it's enough to make it seem like he kind of doesn't want it, and I have to keep reminding myself that he does.

I won't say the idea of punishing him just a little isn't making my cock pulse, though... because it definitely is.

I wonder how rough I could fuck him without losing myself...

Fisting my dick, I aim it between his cheeks, whimpering when my head presses up to his hole.

"Please don't fuck me, Luthor," he gasps, resting his top half on the counter, eyes squeezed shut. "It's gonna hurt..."

My balls are throbbing. *I need to get in here now before I come all over him and totally embarrass myself.*

"You've never been fucked in this tiny hole before?" He shakes his head. "Good… I can't wait to pop your cherry nice and hard, baby."

"Stop… No, no, wait…" he sobs softly, and I lean over his back, fingers combing through his hair.

"You're gonna scream my name," I whisper, kissing behind his ear.

"I promise I fucking won't," he grits out the words that give me a surge of confidence.

He wants this.

Holding my dick in one hand and his ass in the other, I give a hard shove, watching with hooded lids as I break into him roughly. He cries, then bites down on his lower lip, and I really can't tell if it's an act anymore. But I don't care, because my dick is in his ass again and it feels every bit as euphoric as it did last time.

Driving in deeper, and *deeper*, I fill him with every swollen inch until my hips are smashed into his cheeks and I'm pinning him against the counter. I fist his hair and yank, maybe a little too hard, pulling back and fiercely thrusting back in.

"God, your ass is so tight," I hum, working my cock in him, getting high on the sensation.

I missed this so much… I've been dreaming of stretching his hole with my cock again.

"*No*," he whines, squirming beneath my weight. "Ah, *please*… It hurts."

Biting my lip, I ignore his words and aggrieved tone, focusing on the way his body is gripping mine. This is *Ren*, and he *loves* me…

Pound pound pound.

He needs this.

Slam slam slam.

He likes it this way.

Before I even realize it, I'm fucking him so hard his ass cheeks are red from all the skin slapping and he has tears pouring from his eyes. Kicking his legs open wider, I hold him up by his hips, forehead dropping onto his shoulder blade. My cock is thick, engorged and throbbing as I pump him full, balls drawing up with the need to come.

The way his body is stroking me so tight, just barely wet enough for me to move in him, is getting me there fast. He has a physical hold on me, just like the one he's always had on my heart. And yea, maybe in the dark corners of my mind, I like the idea of hurting him a little. Because he *destroyed* me… Ripped my heart out of my body and threw it into an incinerator.

For *this*.

For rough, meaningless sex. His body's insatiable need combined with his mind's reluctance to believe he deserves anything more.

I don't want him to feel this way. I don't want him thinking he needs to be beaten up and fucked to pieces, because it's not true. He deserves so much more than that… No one *deserves* to be hurt.

Reaching around his body, I grab his cock, and he hisses. "You're so hard…"

"I don't… want to… be," he chokes out the words unevenly with my powerful thrusts.

"Is it because my dick is jamming at that sweet spot up in your ass?" I hum, pushing and pushing in him, driving viciously at his prostate.

"Uhhmmff, *Luthor*…" he sobs. "You're ripping me apart."

Melting over his back, I hold him by his hair, brushing his lips with mine. "It's so sore, isn't it?"

"Fffuck," he mewls helplessly.

"Begging to be touched… 'cause you're a slut for cock, and everyone knows it."

"L-luthor… Oh *God*…"

"It'll be our little secret, cockslut. Your shame can stay in this dark room… ass wide open and full of my big dick."

He gasps as I capture his mouth, kissing him, hungry and possessive, completely lost to this now. Shoving my tongue into his mouth while he cries out hoarse moans, my thrusts shallow, dick stuffed all the way up in his body. His hips wiggle while I play his with his cock, squeezing his balls hard enough that he whines into my mouth.

"I'm gonna come in you," I pant, abs clenching.

"*Don't* come in my ass…" he pleads nervously.

"I'm gonna pour every drop in you because you're *mine*." I release his hair, hand running down his back.

He's shoved so far up on the counter at this point, his feet are barely touching the ground. Gripping his waist, I hum, "Work your hole on me." He shakes his head, so I smack him on the ass. "Do it. Suck the cum out, or this doesn't stop… I'll stay in you all night if I have to."

His ass tightens, squeezing on me as precum flows from his cock all over my hand. Writhing against me, he rocks his hips as best he can with only the leverage of my body holding him up.

"That's it, baby." I bite his lip, stroking his dick in my fist. "Such a good little slut..."

Ren gasps, his movements becoming frantic. *I think he likes when I call him that.*

"Do you hate me?" I mumble onto his mouth, and he nods. "Do you *hate* having my dick up in your guts?"

"Yesss, *fuck*, I hate it..." he croaks. "I hate you fucking me so hard, like a greedy animal."

"Mmm... more."

"I hate how I can feel every inch... how your fat head keeps touching that spot, making my dick hard when I don't want it to be..."

His hips grind on me harder and faster, and I meet his hips with my own thrusts, our skin slapping together to make the illicit sounds of rough fucking.

"You hate that you're my little slut now, don't you?" I growl, a shivering climax approaching quickly.

"Yes..."

"Feel how big my cock is in you, baby...? It's about to burst."

"Mmmfuuck *yess*," he whimpers.

"Come with me," I rasp in between kissing his lips raw. "Let me show you how good it feels when I spill deep inside you..."

"N-no... *yess*... stop jerking me. Stop, stop, it feels so *fucking good*..."

His body begins to shudder just as my balls are contracting.

"Baby, I'm coming in you." My words are barely out before I'm shooting off deep inside his body. "*Fuck*, take my cum..."

"Oh God, *fuck fuck*..." He tenses, his dick spraying pulse after pulse all over the place.

"S-such a g-good... ohhhfuck, *Ren*, suck it out."

"I'm sucking it, baby... Soak my insides."

My hips are still thrusting, his tightness milking it out of me until I can't even feel my legs. Knees wobbling, spine tingling, I'm fucking *full*.

Ren is mewling, bouncing his ass on me slower and slower while my hand lazily caresses his cock, rubbing it with his silky orgasm.

"N-no more," I quiver. "I want you back."

The high has settled over me like stardust. My chest is wide open right now, and all I want is to be done with this stupid fucking game. Yea, it was hot, but it's not *us*.

I want us back.

Brushing his hair away from his face, I gaze into his blue eyes.

"I'm here, Lex," he whispers, and my heart jumps. "I'm here… I'm *sorry.*"

"I don't want you like that," I breathe, kissing his soft lips, then his cheeks, tasting the salt from his tears. "I want *Warren*, and I want him to want *Lex*. No fucking games…"

"I do, baby," he breathes. "I promise, I do."

Straightening enough to set him down on his feet, I rub his ass and his back, kissing his neck over and over. But I don't pull out. I keep my dick in him because I'm not just rough-fucking him full of cum, then running off. I want to *stay* with him.

If I could live inside him forever, I would.

"I didn't mean to upset you." His eyes are hooded from the orgasm, but still shining blue remorse at me over his shoulder.

"You didn't," I sigh. "I just don't want you to feel like that's what you deserve. It's not. You don't *deserve* pain, Ren…"

His face is all flushed, hair messy and hanging in his face as he trembles. "I just thought you might want to… I thought maybe it would make you feel better if you hurt me. But I don't *need* it, Lex. I only need you…"

I hear what he's saying, but all of my vulnerabilities are back with a vengeance. That angry guy, the *act* I just played… it wasn't me. Not at all.

I couldn't hurt him even if I wanted to, which I have before. But it doesn't matter.

I'm not trying to get back at him. I'm trying to get him *back*.

Ren peers at me over his shoulder, and I don't feel as close to him as I want to be. My dick is inside him, but it's like there's still a wall between us.

I like it better when we're face to face.

I think he senses it and moves like he's going to pull off my dick so he can turn around. But I hold his hips to stop him.

He raises a brow and my face heats. "I wanna stay inside you…"

He chuckles, biting his lip. "It still feels good… *You* feel amazing, Lexington."

I rest my head against his. "I was angry with you… Of course I was. I was hurt and sad, Ren. But it never occurred to me to make you feel pain in return. Because that doesn't accomplish anything. Then we're just two idiots hurting."

He huffs, and I can feel his smile, even without seeing it. "You shouldn't be afraid to want to change me, Lex… I'm overdue for a few updates."

I snort a laugh into his hair. "You're using nerd terms. I'm so proud."

"I try," he hums.

Letting out a breath, I circle his waist with my arms, hugging onto him tight. I kiss my way up his neck, and he turns his face to get my lips.

"You're so confusing," I mumble.

He grins. "I know…"

"You're a hot mess, Warren."

He nods. "The messiest."

"And the hottest." My mouth sweeps into a smile while we kiss slowly. "Are you *my* mess?"

"All yours," he murmurs. "You're like my housekeeper."

I laugh, and he beams with pride. We stay nuzzling together, kissing and touching for minutes on end, avoiding the rest of it and just focusing on being *us*.

And as it always does, it ripples from sweet and cherishing to fire before our eyes.

"Fuck me again," he breathes hoarsely. "As Lexington… I missed you, baby."

Grinning, I finally pull out of him, only to spin him around and lift him up.

"Hang on," I grunt, carrying him over to the chair.

I'm proud of myself for being able to do it, because he's not exactly *light* with all those muscles.

"Jesus fuck, that was hot." He smirks, grasping my jaw as he gets settled on my lap, finally facing me again.

"It's so much better this way," I whisper into his mouth while we paw at each other, sucking and nipping one another's lips like fiends. "I love seeing your face, sweet flame."

"Sit back and let me love you," he purrs.

And within seconds, he's riding my cock. It's not rough, or angry, or mean, but it's hot as fuck, passionate and sensual and exactly what we *both* need.

We might be way too different, but maybe it doesn't matter when we have one thing in common… Each other.

Ragged breaths, soft groans, and his body cradling mine, we fuck each other like we were made to do it. And right as he's moaning that he's about to come, and I'm clutching his shirt in my fist preparing to unleash another ball-bursting orgasm inside him, footsteps stomp and voices boom from up the hall.

"Uh oh…" I whisper, and he giggles, leaning back while I fist his cock to pull him over the edge.

Ren comes all over me, and I come inside him, all doors wide open…

Consequences waiting outside.

CHAPTER TWENTY-TWO

Ren

More weeks later…

We're on our way to the cafeteria for lunch when Velle pops out of nowhere and grabs me.

I actually jump, my hand slapping over my heart. "Jesus! You scared the shit out of me. You're too huge to be creeping around corners like that…"

"Not interested in your witticisms right now, 48," he grumbles, pulling me in the opposite direction. "Private convo time."

"But, but…" I reach out for Lex and Byron, but they just stare at me, watching Velle drag me off.

It's okay, guys. I'm fine. Just being hauled away by John Cena's evil twin.

Velle has us walking for a bit, and it doesn't take me long to realize where we're going.

"Oh, come on, man," I whine, pumping on the brakes. "I didn't do anything! This is fucked up… Where's my lawyer?!"

"God, do you *ever* shut up?" he mutters.

It may be summer, but my teeth are chattering. I don't want to go in the hole… I just *can't* do it. Not now, with all this drama everywhere and stuff happening with Lex.

I'll drive myself nuts in there without my new favorite toy, otherwise known as Lexington Deon's big, pink cock.

Velle gets us to solitary row, and even though it would completely derail all my hard work, I'm seriously considering offering to blow him real quick to get him to reconsider.

I really shouldn't... I don't want *to.*

But I might have to. Maybe just a quick swallow?

I'm still arguing with myself when Velle stops us in the middle of the row, his face slanting all around, much shiftier than I've ever seen him behave. Then he folds his arms over his wide chest, gazing down at me with a pierced brow raised.

He's not opening any cells... We're just standing here.

Okay...

"Alright, here's the deal," he starts. "We don't have long. I need to know what you know."

I blink at him, surprised and not hiding it. "Wait, so you're *not* putting me in the hole?"

His gaze narrows. "*Should I* be putting you in the hole?"

"No, no." I shake my head vehemently. "Not at all."

Either Peters chose not to divulge the details of Lex and me giving them the slip, or Velle knows, and he just doesn't care enough to do anything about it. Regardless of which, I'm grateful I'm not being punished for sneaking off to have some of the best secret sex of my life. Although, let's be real... The punishment would be more than worth it.

"48, I'm gonna need you to harness all of your extremely limited attention right now and focus, okay?" He gives me a very serious *Daddy* look that makes my nipples hard. "You made a promise. And if you'll recall, the bargaining chip was me allowing your crush to keep his Gameboy or whatever the hell. So, give me something worthwhile, and keep in mind that I've known you a long time, and I'm more than capable of sniffing out your bullshit."

Biting my lip, I stare at him, unable to help noticing that while he's still as much of a hardass as ever, he looks infinitely less exhausted and marginally less stressed than usual. Whatever vacation he disappeared on with Joy and Rook for almost a week must have been refreshing.

And now he's back, and he means business.

I can't help the smirk that spreads over my mouth as I mimic his stance. "Ah, how the tables have turned. I've been waiting for this moment for years! The Big Bad Wolf needs help from the sheep..."

"Ren," he growls admonishingly. "*No one* believes that you're a sheep. Now, fucking spill it."

As a default, my brain wants to make something up. It's not that I *want* to lie to him, but it feels almost like a reflex. It's a sickness, one of many I'm currently trying to overcome, and I just wish there was a way to stop it at the source. But my mind is a treasure trove of issues, and sometimes I think it'll take years to even scratch the surface of all that's wrong with me.

Gulping, I swallow down the lies that want to rise up on my tongue and tell him, "That new shrink... Dr. *Love*... he's the one who gave Darcey the keys to the cells."

Velle's gaze lingers on me for a moment. He looks a little skeptical, but not enough to outright scoff in my face.

"How do you know this?" His head tilts.

"I can't give up my source," I tell him firmly. "But just know that it comes from someone who sees a lot." My brows lift, and he nods.

"Got it. Well, I'll be honest with you... I had my suspicions about that." He purses his lips. "It's not exactly shocking, and it's not enough to get me what I need."

"What do you need...?" I ask curiously.

"That's none of your business."

"Velle, if you don't tell me what you're trying to do, I can't help you." I lean up against the wall.

"You can and you will, because it's what you agreed to," he grunts, being, as usual, a *massive* pain in the ass. "I'd have to be the biggest dope on the planet to share any details with you. Your lips are so loose, you have to tie them up like a ponytail."

"That's beyond rude," I gasp, more offended by the visual than anything. He just shrugs, and I sigh. "Alright... *hypothetically*, if you were to tell me you were interested in something deep... Like *rock the foundation* type shit, then I could give it to you."

His dark blue eyes sparkle like he just hit the jackpot. "That's what I want."

"Well then, I need guaranteed immunity." I grin. "I need to know for a fact that you won't turn around and use this shit against me... When Daddy whistles for you to come running."

I witness his jaw tense and tic, hard, like he might snap his teeth. "That's not going to happen."

I shrug. "How do I know that? It's been a long time, darling. What... ten, eleven years?" His gaze is simmering, but it doesn't scare me. "If I give you this personal little anecdote, I need to know without a shred of doubt that it won't come back to bite me."

He leans in. "You have my word."

"And Lex too. I want his safety assured at all costs... Even above my own." Velle huffs, shaking his head. "I'm serious. Promise me you and Joy will watch out for him... no matter what."

My tone is softly pleading, as is the look I'm giving him, and I think he can see that.

His chin dips in a little nod. "I promise you nothing bad will happen to Luthor. Not on my watch. He's too important."

Warmth floods my chest at his words. "Good. And on that note, before we seal this deal, I'll need one more thing from you..."

Velle brings me back up to gen-pop after our little talk, and there's a renewed sense of determination filling my limbs. It's odd to be feeling such contentment in a place like this, but I guess it all works subjectively.

I've never actively *despised* being here, at least not all the time, because I know what I need to get by. And whether I get that by hopping around from dick to dick, from spending time with my friends, or from badgering the dude I've been in love with for years into finally accepting a reluctant relationship with me, it's still always better than being *out there*.

It would seem that Alabaster Pen has allowed me to embrace who I am. Or at the very least, it strongly enables me.

Peeking at Velle while we stomp through the long corridors, I feel questions bubbling up. And due to my lack of filter, there's nothing to stop them.

"So where did you go?"

He gives me the side-eye, but doesn't speak.

"I mean, you've never left in all the time I've been here," I keep going. "This place kinda fell apart without you..."

"Yea, I heard," he grumbles, lips twitching in mild amusement.

"Well?" My brow cocks. "Finally got around to using those vacation days?"

He huffs, shaking his head. But the little grin falls away fast, and he gets this somber air about him. I even notice his throat dip.

At first, I'm pretty sure he's not going to answer me, but after a few more steps of silence, he mumbles, "My mom died."

My feet stop working for a second. Gaping at him as he keeps walking,

I experience something I'm not all that familiar with. I think I actually feel *bad*…

It doesn't usually happen to me, especially when it comes to other people's loss. *I don't even feel bad about my own loss, so why would I care about someone else's?*

But Velle is just the epitome of a giant chunk of stone… He's always been an emotionless, rabid animal. You tend to forget that he's actually *not* that. He had a life before Alabaster Pen, and granted, I know next to nothing about it, but just like the rest of us, he's become hardened by this place.

Sharing this little sliver of vulnerability is really humanizing him right now.

"I'm… sorry," I mumble, scampering to keep up with him. "That sucks, Velle."

He grunts an apathetic noise by way of response.

"So you went to… be with family or something?"

His face slants, and he sucks in a breath like he probably wants to tell me to *shut up* or *fuck off*. But instead, he says, "I brought my family *with* me. To say goodbye."

My stomach coils at his words, immediately registering what he means.

Rook and Joy are his family… That's why they all left.

His mom died, and they went to be with him… to support him.

It's such a fascinating concept to me. I've never been close like that with anyone. I've never had a friend, or a boyfriend, who would care enough about my life to leave theirs behind just to stand by my side during difficult times. And I've definitely never been that for anyone else; a shoulder to cry on, or a peaceful presence.

Sure, I love to console Lex when he's upset or stressed, but I think I wreak more havoc on his life than anything else. Is it really a benefit if I'm the one causing the hurt I'm trying to comfort?

Back at the cafeteria, Velle delivers me when lunch is nearly over, and I go to sit down at our table, settling in with the knowledge that I guess I won't be eating today.

But as soon as my ass is down, Lex slides a tray over to me.

"I saved you some food," he says quietly.

I glance up at him, then down at the sandwich.

God, I just love him… How could I not? He's fucking perfect.

"Thank you, baby," I whisper, trying my best to disguise how goddamn smitten I am as I pick off pieces of bread.

"So what happened?" he asks.

I blink at him while chewing. His face has some tension to it, and I can't really decipher what it means. "Velle and I talked."

"About what?" His mouth is set in an unamused line. If I didn't know any better, I'd say he was... *jealous*.

"Stuff," I grumble, peeking at Kang. He too is giving me a suspicious look.

I feel like I'm being ganged up on just a tad.

"What kinds of *stuff*, Ren?" Lex sits back in his chair, head slanting as he awaits my response.

"I can't tell you that," I mumble.

"Why not?" he hisses, gaze narrowed.

"Because."

"Because *why*?"

"Because it's... personal." I chuckle to ease the tension, but they're both looking so serious. "What's the problem? Am I in trouble?"

"You tell me, Ren," Lex grunts. "You disappear for almost an hour with Velle... The two of you walk in here looking all chummy..."

My forehead lines. "We weren't looking *chummy*..."

"Where did you go? What did you *do*?" he breathes angrily. "I mean, if you can't even answer these simple fucking questions, then—"

"What do you think happened??" I bark quietly. "We fucked real quick? I sucked him off in the hallway for no reason?? Seriously, what would be the point—"

"There is no *point* with you, that's the problem!" he seethes. "There's no fucking rhyme or reason to it; you just do these things, and I need to know if that's happening now. I think I deserve to know, Ren. So I can... So I don't..." His stammering dissolves into a tired growl, and he rubs his eyes. "I just need to *know*. No bullshit..."

All of the delight I was feeling a moment ago is completely gone. I feel sick to my stomach, like I drank rotten milk.

This is always going to be the problem, isn't it? He's never going to trust me, even when I'm not doing anything. And I don't blame him one bit, because if I was in his position, I'd be freaking out too. Probably a lot worse, since we all know I'm a fucking drama queen with a short fuse.

But Lex isn't like that. He's calm and collected, and sweet... *Forgiving*. But he's not made of metal, and obviously he doesn't know how to deal with these feelings either.

We fucked. That line has officially been crossed. And because of that,

I've been doing my absolute best to stuff down my irrational impulses, fighting to be what I know he needs.

But he doesn't *know* that. And I'm afraid that if I tell him, *then* fail, it'll ultimately gob-smack him in the heart again, even worse than last time.

Here's the thing not many people know… When everyone projects their negative images of you all the time, it makes it damn near impossible to see yourself as anything else.

Lexington expects me to fuck up again. They all do…

So maybe I should just save them the trouble and be the bad guy…

Whether I want to be or not.

"Lex," I rumble, shoving down my every urge to lash out and scream. The desire to inflict pain on myself right now is so strong I'm shaking a little. "I didn't fuck Velle. I *didn't*… you can ask him."

He blinks at me. "Like he would admit it…"

"You know he would. He doesn't give a fuck," I tell him with certainty, and his eyes soften a bit. "He's with Rook and Joy now. It's serious… He told me that."

"He actually said *it's serious*?" Byron cuts in, disbelief all up in his tone.

"Not in so many words." I glare at him. "But he told me about how they all left together… They're a thing. The three of them. Like a throuple."

Lex nods, chewing on his lip for a moment in silence. "Okay."

"Do you believe me?" I ask, overflowing with hopefulness.

"I want to," he whispers.

I nod. I guess that has to be enough… *It's all I'm going to get right now.*

We're quiet for a bit, just sitting, picking at our food until Velle, Rook and Joy start gathering us up to head back. I totally see it now… The three of them. It makes sense.

The connection turned into more than just physical. They make each other better.

I wish I knew what that was like…

"So… a *throuple*, huh?" Lex sighs by my side as we leave the cafeteria.

"Yea…"

A throuple of badass motherfuckers.

My body is rejecting this. Like withdrawals from years of hard drug use.

I've been antsier than ever these past couple of months. Sometimes I wake up in a cold sweat—if I'm even able to fall asleep at all. I've chewed all my fingernails down to the skin, and my balls have been aching for so long, I've almost gotten used to the dull throb that now lives in my lower stomach.

This shit is real, man. Why doesn't anyone ever talk about detoxing from casual sex?? We need to spread awareness! Work on a cure or something...

All in all, I think I'm doing well. But it doesn't *feel* like it. Every minute of every day, I feel like I'm on the verge of making a terrible mistake. And when your default is to give in effortlessly to temptation, that little voice in the back of your head starts to sound like it's screaming.

Burn...

You don't need this stress.

They just don't understand you.

They're jealous of your lifestyle, because they want what you have.

Burn...

This is who you are.

You're the bad guy, Warren...

Burn it all to the fucking *ground.*

"Fuck," I grunt, ripping my hair in my fists.

I swear to God, I'd love a cigarette right now. If I had more than that one goddamn match that I'm saving.

Ugh.

Today feels like it's been happening for days. I haven't left my cell since dinner last night, and not that I know what time it is, but my body can tell it's well into the afternoon. I'm anxious as fuck, with *nothing* available to distract me. Velle promised he would get me some stuff back, now that he's apparently running the show around here. But he has to do it discreetly, I guess, since he's trying to tread lightly with the Warden.

I still don't really understand what happened. No one has seen Manuel Blanco in weeks, and Velle has a noticeable bounce in his step. He, Joy and Rook are leading the pack, and even though we're technically still on *lockdown*, it feels like they're rebuilding a little, after the drama the double Ds caused.

Darcey and Dash.

You'd think that would mean I could get a damn notebook and pencil, or my freaking tattoo gun back. But I suppose my needs aren't as important to the guards now that I've stopped bending over for them.

I'm trying to get myself Zen by bending over in a *different* capacity—*doing yoga in my cell*—when I hear a door open. I ignore it at first, expecting the sounds of more guards gathering inmates to finally go somewhere. But instead, my bars open.

"Lookin' good." A rumbly voice I know well comes from behind me, and I peer through my legs.

It's Jasper. He's inside my cell, leaning up against the door with his arms folded over his wide chest.

Namaste, asshole.

Straightening, I turn and lift a brow. "About time. I'm starving."

I wander over with my wrists out, waiting for him to cuff me. But he doesn't.

Instead, he steps forward, creeping into my space. I back up slowly, but he keeps coming.

"*Hungry*, inmate?" He grabs my jaw, easing his lips over mine. "Been a while since you've been fed, huh?"

My head shakes back and forth as if to say *no*, but the words get lost when he presses his mouth to mine. I try to step out of it, but now his hands are on my waist and he's pulling me flush against him.

He's already rock hard. I can feel it through his uniform as he grinds into me, sucking on my mouth while I stand there completely still. *Frozen*, like I'm back in eighth grade history, fumbling through an oral presentation on the Civil. War.

Uh… Robert E… Lord, what am I doing??

No… No no no, I'm not supposed to be doing this. Tell him to stop!

It feels good, Warren. You know it does.

But I'm trying—

Don't. Stop *trying. It's not you.*

I whimper a helpless noise into Jasper's mouth while he unbuckles his belt and opens his pants. My blood is rushing so loudly in my head, it's all I can hear. The waterfall drowning out everything but that goddam idiotic fucking *voice*.

It's so familiar…

This is you, you dirty little slut. You're only good at being bad.

No. No, please. This isn't right… I'm trying. For Lex…

"Let me come in you, and I'll give you whatever you want," Jasper growls, grabbing my hand and shoving it onto his cock.

"*No…*" I gasp, remembering the dark room, with Lex.

How I begged him to act like he was forcing me…

Something like this. Aggressive, greedy, *rough*… Detached.

With Lex, it's different. He's just so *good*, and I know I want that. I want *him,* just the way he is.

Not this. This doesn't make me feel happy... Not like he does.

He said I don't deserve to hurt... I wanted to believe him.

"Lex..." I whine, with my heart screaming at me to pull away.

But my body betrays me, like the fucking slut it is, cupping his cock and squeezing.

A ripple of thrill rushes through my loins. I hate it. It makes me fucking *sick* to my stomach, but I can't stop.

I... just... can't.

Jasper shoves me toward my bed, spinning me and pushing me down onto my stomach. My head is foggy, clouded up so thick I can't see.

I don't think this is me... Is it?

It must be someone else; the desperate, panting whore who wants to get fucked so bad, he's lifting his hips while his pants are yanked down.

Maybe this is me. The real *me.*

Jasper spits into his hand, and suddenly, a cock is pressing up to my hole.

"Lex..." I whimper into the bed, tears seeping from my eyes.

I'm... sorry...

"You're resisting," the voice rasps from behind me. "Let my cock in, little slut, so I can fuck this hole like it was made to be fucked."

H-huh...?

No... wait.

All of my muscles clench below my waist. I wriggle and squirm beneath him.

No... Don't do this.

"Stop," I huff, pushing up onto my arms.

But he's still trying to get his dick in me, and now I'm freaking the fuck out, shivering all over like I'm about to make a *huge, terrible* mistake.

"N-no," I stammer, managing to roll out from under him, shoving him back. "I don't want to. Back the f-fuck off."

Jasper blinks at me, sufficiently shocked. "Are you *serious*?"

"Yes, I'm serious." I mimic him, sniffling and rolling my eyes as I whip my pants up, staggering to my feet. "The sex bank is closed for business." My fingers rake through my hair as I breathe out shakily, putting as much space between us as possible. "Just scram, okay? Make like a tree and get the fuck out of my face."

Jasper's head tilts. "Did I slip through a wormhole or something?"

"Jake… *Go.*"

He stands up, stuffing his cock away while shaking his head like he still can't believe what's happening. Hell must have frozen over, because *Warren Xavier* doesn't want to get fucked.

But at least he's registering my rejection. And he slowly spins around to leave.

A chill rushes over me, and I'm fucking *high*.

Heart hammering in my chest, heat rising up my neck into my face. My hands are shaking… My knees are wobbling so much I'm about to fall down, but I did it. It was a *really* fucking close call, but I did.

I actually rebuffed someone. Me! The slutbag!

Up until this point, I've just been avoiding it. Running and hiding like a coward, pretty much getting by on sheer luck and a solid resting bitch face. But this right here was an active sexual advance. A dick I've had before—one I actually happen to think feels *really* good inside me—and I *declined it!* I *stopped* because it wasn't what I wanted.

I want Lex. Only his dick gets to go inside me.

I can do this… I can be more than just a hole for everyone to fuck.

I can be his. *And maybe Lex will love me back if I keep proving to him that he's the only one I want.*

I'm really proud of myself for stopping it.

I wish I hadn't let it come as close as I did, but hey. Baby steps.

Unfortunately, all of my inner glee vanishes when I look up to see Lex standing outside of my cell, eyes wide and stuck on Jasper, zipping up his pants while I wipe my mouth with the back of my hand.

Oh… crap.

"Shit… Hang on." I shove Jasper out of the way, stumbling out of my cell. "Lex…"

"You've gotta be fucking kidding me," he hisses, green eyes wide and glistening with unkempt rage.

I guess all the adrenaline rushing around inside me blocked out the sounds of Hancock in the row, rounding up the rest of the inmates. Because now I see them all out there. And none of them appear shocked that Jasper is coming out of my cell, looking disheveled.

I mean, why would they? It's a regular occurrence.

Byron is out there too, shaking his head. Hancock is sort of glaring at Jasper like he's pissed off about something, but I can't even worry about any of that.

All I care about is Lexington, and the purely devastated look on his beautiful face.

"Wait. It's not what it looks like." My pulse is popping even more rapidly now, ribcage crushing my lungs as I struggle to breathe. I rush to Lex, grabbing him by the arm, but he yanks it away angrily.

"*No??* 'Cause it looks pretty fucking straightforward to me, Ren," he snaps while I flutter nervously before him.

Yea, mhm. He's not wrong. It looks real bad.

Here's me, all flushed and flustered, and shirtless, with the big guard I've been known to spread my legs for, in my cell with his pants open. It looks like *exactly* what's been going on in here for years at this point, and that's the problem.

My fucking reputation proceeds me… How can I expect him to ever believe me when this is all he's known of me since pretty much the moment we met?

How could he ever believe the truths of a liar?

"We weren't doing anything, Lex, I *swear!*" I gasp, stumbling after him as he tries to get away from me. "Jake, tell him nothing happened!"

Jasper's not even paying attention. He's too busy watching Hancock silently seethe at him. I never noticed it before, but I'm sensing some tension there. And my chest caves in even deeper.

Okay, not only am I ruining Lex's life, but now I'm also coming between these two. This just gets better and better.

I know it wasn't all my fault. Jasper came on to *me*, and for the first time ever, I actually did the right thing and turned him down.

But it doesn't matter. Because no one's going to believe me.

You should've just let him fuck you.

You're fighting a battle that's already been lost.

"Lexington, *wait.*" I jump in front of him one last time, cupping his face in my hands, not ready to give up. "Just listen to me, okay?? I said *no*. I stopped it. We didn't *do* anything, you've gotta believe me."

My palms are sweaty, fingers shaking, lips trembling. I can see it in his eyes…

He thinks I'm lying. Because I *look* like I'm fucking lying….

But I'm not! I swear to God, I'm not!

"You're a disease, Ren." Lex shakes his head, the rage slipping away into hopeless disappointment.

It's so much worse than the anger.

At least when he's pissed, it means he still cares. But now, he's gone despondent on me. He's numb, and I can feel it; crushing me down like a hundred pounds on my shoulders.

"It's my fault," he whispers. "Seriously, there's no one here to blame but me." He covers my hands with his, pushing them off his face. "This is who you are."

My black, shriveled up heart, the one that's been slowly fighting to pump back to life, sinks; plummets, like a hunk of cement in deep water. Pressure builds behind my eyes, bringing a diesel throb to my temples so fast and harsh, I suddenly can't see.

My vision blurs, shivers of anguish racking my limbs as Lex brushes past me, following the rest of the group out of the row.

Byron stomps after them, scoffing on his way out. "You're about as good a liar as you are a friend…"

My feet are weighted to the floor, that pain I've caused filling every crevice of my insides.

They just left me here, *alone*, surrounded by crumbling concrete. The cracked gray walls are closing in on me as I struggle to breathe, the sudden silence in these halls growing louder and louder until I have to cover my head with my arms to get it to stop.

This is who you are…

It is. They're right, all of them.

Why am I even trying?

In a daze of misery, I pad slowly up the hall, bending to pick up a piece of stone that's fallen from the ceiling.

Worthless, lying little slut…

That voice… I know who it is now.

You were good for only one thing, and you can't even do that anymore.

My feet shuffle, bringing the hollow husk of my body back into my cell where I collapse onto the floor.

Give up, Warren. You can't fight it anymore…

With Callum Kade's words ringing in my skull, I flip my wrist over and hold the jagged object up to my waiting flesh.

Give in to who you are.

Your fire will set you free.

The slice is a delicious agony; a rough, burning cut that releases all my pain with pulses of blood bubbling from the open wound. My lashes flutter and I topple onto my side.

Behind my eyes, I see flames engulfing me. I hear the crackling, feel the heat kissing my sticky skin.

Laughter erupts from my lips, manic giggles flowing as the blood trickles down my arm. I'm cackling, coughing, and choking for air… *surrounded by smoke.*

Burning alive, just like I should have that night.

I should've died with Callum in that blaze of wickedness I made… But instead, I wound up here, causing even more destruction.

It's all over. I'm done infecting the only good thing I've ever known.

I have to save him from me.

In a dizzying haze… I give up the fight.

I let myself bleed. Because I *deserve* it.

Luthor

I don't even know how to process this…

Just because you knew something awful was coming, it doesn't negate the reaction. If anything, it's *more* painful the second time around, because the hurt is framed by self-loathing.

Always a fun combo.

I'm so torn to shreds, I can't even eat. I'm just sitting and staring for the entirety of the meal, and what's worse, I can feel Kang radiating hostility from across the table. He doesn't need to say anything. I know he thinks I'm a dumbass for letting Ren in again, getting my hopes up only to be hacked apart when I *swore* up and down we were just casually fucking in the first place.

The naïvety is probably the worst part. My lack of relationship experience makes me the perfect target for someone like Ren. Because I don't know any better, so I just keep falling for his sugar-coated words every time.

I lost my virginity to the dude, for fuck's sake. Apparently, that was all it took for me to drop the guard I'd worked so damn hard at building back up after last time. All the *never gonna happen* in the world was no match for the love spell he cast the second my dick made its way inside him.

After that, *bang*. I literally just tossed my shield down and offered him my wide-open chest to stab.

Did I seriously think I was capable of just sleeping with him a few times and moving on? Or continuing some nonchalant, friends-who-fuck-on-occasion agreement after he told me he fucking loves me, *while simultaneously banging all kinds of other dudes??*

Yea, right. Sounds plausible.

Tell me more about that plan, you gullible twat.

I was so blinded by the sex, I completely forgot that the person I was having it with is a beautiful, blue-eyed spawn of fucking Satan. I might need to have my head examined, because I'm supposed to be a genius, and I'm acting like total buffoon.

Isn't that the definition of insanity? Doing the same thing again and again, expecting different results...

My brain is in a shame spiral, and everything inside me hurts so damn bad that I'm just zombie-shuffling along as they herd us all out of the cafeteria. I don't even want to look at Jasper. I've never had anything against the guy, but he's consistently been one of Ren's top *sponsors*. I wish I could just ignore him, but the whole walk back, I can't stop my eyes from slinking over his way.

This feeling is just plain gross, rising up my esophagus like heartburn while I watch him stomping up the hall, awfully tense for someone who just blew his load in a gorgeous, tall, puffy-lipped hunk of pure evil.

Whatever. It doesn't make a lick of sense to hold a grudge against Jasper.

For what? Fooling around with someone who isn't mine? Getting his dick wet with a single guy who doesn't do monogamy, and who's made that abundantly clear to me since day one??

I wasn't being passive aggressive before. This *is* totally my fault. Ren's brain doesn't light up for things like love or companionship. He thinks it does, but it's all just lust and desire and overly sensitive pleasure receptors. I can't blame him for how he was made...

But I also can't keep running after him, hoping he'll change, or grow out of it. He *won't*. And as much as I've tried over the years, I'll never stop hating the way this jealousy feels.

He's gonna have to let me go... and I have to let him.

Hancock smashes open the door to the row, and Jasper stomps in after him, paying much more attention to what he's doing than the rest of us. I'm all prepared to just breeze past Ren's cell, in a totally chill, *I couldn't possibly care less* kind of way, but of course my eyes don't get the memo. They slink traitorously in his direction for just a quick peek.

I stop short when I notice that his cell is open.

And he's lying on the floor... with a pool of blood next to him.

"Jesus fucking Christ," I grunt, darting inside so fast I almost trip over my own feet.

Falling to my knees next to him, I grab his face with trembling hands.

He's unconscious and pale.

"Holy fuck, oh my God." In an instant, I'm sweating and shaking, and my heart is in my fucking throat. "Ren? *Ren?!* Jesus, Ren, wake up!" I start shaking him around, freaking the fuck out at the sight of the nasty gash on his wrist.

I'm panicking. All of my previous thoughts have vanished, along with all my rational thinking. My brain is immediately clouded by a thick haze of fear and worry, guilt and terror.

No no no… Oh my God, no, this isn't happening.

I'm gonna lose him.

I can't. I fucking can't…

Blinking hard, I pull myself together as best I can, checking his pulse. It's there. *Thank God…*

He hasn't lost all that much blood, but it's still coming, and I need to stop it.

Jumping to my feet, I find a t-shirt. I stumble back to him, clutching his bloody wrist, my hands already coated in sticky red. Shakily, I wrap the shirt around his wrist tight, keeping it elevated.

"Ren… baby? Wake up." I give his face a little tap. "*Please* wake up for me…"

Scooping his lifeless body into my arms, I hold him against my chest and carry him to the bed, laying him down. My pulse is racing. I'm *terrified*, not only because of Ren's state, but also because if Jasper or Hancock notice any of what's happening, this could earn him a one-way ticket to the East Wing.

I mean, a suicide attempt?? Jesus, I just can't…

Focus. Stop freaking out and help him.

Quickly, I find another shirt, using it to wipe up the blood on the floor as fast as possible. Then I jump into the bed next to Ren, whipping the blanket over both of us, keeping myself hidden so hopefully they'll assume Ren is asleep and just walk by. Sure, they might notice that I'm not in my cell, but they both seemed pretty preoccupied with their own bullshit before. Maybe they'll just forget about me… It's definitely happened before.

Lying as still as possible, I hold my breath and wait. And sure enough, I hear the door to Ren's cell clank shut, followed by the door to the row,

Jasper and Hancock's voices booming from the other side, like they're arguing.

These motherfuckers and their drama…

Says the guy whose fuckbuddy just slit his wrist open.

Peeling the blanket back with a ragged sigh, my eyes set on Ren. He looks like he's sleeping, breathing a bit labored, but at least he's *alive*. I hold his hand up in mine, resting my head next to his on the pillow with my heart splintered like glass in my chest.

"What the fuck, Ren…" I brush his sweaty hair away from his temple. "*Why* would you want to hurt yourself like this? Don't you know how special you are?"

My voice trails and I shake my head. "No, I guess you wouldn't." I press a kiss on his forehead. "I hate that you think you need this… I hate that you feel like you fucking *deserve* this. I told you, you *don't*."

Memories shimmer while I watch his beautiful face, dark lashes fanned over his cheeks. He told me once before that he used to self-harm when he was younger. Honestly, I don't think it ever stopped. He's always finding ways to hurt himself, in any form he can get. It's just so fucked up because I don't *understand* it, and therefore I don't know how to help him.

I shouldn't enable this kind of behavior, but I also don't want to worry that every time we fight, or something goes wrong between us, he's going to hurt himself.

Minutes turn to hours with me just lying next to him, keeping my head on his chest to make sure his heart is still beating. I can't keep from dozing, especially after the lights turn off in the row. But I startle awake when he begins mumbling and tossing.

"Sweet, broken flame," I whisper in the dark.

I hadn't even noticed that our fingers laced together.

Ren's eyelids flutter, gradually creeping open to pin me with vibrant blue, crystalline enough that it almost glows.

"I'm dead…" he croaks, blinking at me. "Aren't I? I died and somehow went *up* instead of down…"

I can't stop the grin that sweeps over my lips, a breathy chuckle of relief gusting out. "It worries me that you think Heaven is a moldy prison cell."

"Well, you're here," he sighs. "I must have done something right. Either that or I finally succeeded in corrupting you."

I roll my eyes, and he shows me a tired smile. Bringing his hand to my lips, I kiss his knuckles, his gaze falling to the bloody t-shirt wrapped around his wrist.

"You should've just let me go…" he mumbles petulantly.

"Jesus, Ren… Why would you even say that??" I glare at him. "I mean, what the fuck is this shit? Were you really trying to…" My words dry up, and he purses his lips, chin dropping defensively. But I grab it and force him to look at me. "I'm being fucking serious. Just because we can't be together, doesn't mean I want to lose you, okay??"

"You don't get it…" he rumbles. "I'm so fucked up that even when I'm doing my best, it doesn't matter. *No one* believes in me. Not you… Definitely not *me*." My forehead lines and I shake my head, but he goes on. "And I don't blame you at all. I didn't do this to get your attention, or to punish you. I did it because I just can't… fucking *do this* anymore."

"Do what…?" My voice crawls from my throat.

"Be the anchor that pulls you under," he murmurs with a profound sadness in his eyes. "Whether I keep fighting or give up, it makes no difference. Lex, there're no second chances when it comes to you and me. One was enough, and now you'll always be waiting for the other shoe to drop…"

My mouth hangs open for a moment while I stare at him. "But that's… It's no reason to…"

"Lexington… come on," he breathes. "Were you surprised today when you saw what you saw? Or were you expecting it?"

A coiling tightness winds up in my chest, making it hard to breathe. "I don't know…"

"Yes, you do. Look at me." He moves my hand down to his chest, resting it over his heart. "I am telling you right now… *I didn't* hook up with Jasper. He tried, yes… He kissed me, and… it kinda came close. But I stopped it. I didn't suck his dick, and he didn't fuck me… None of it. And whether you believe me or not, I need to tell you this… I haven't been with anyone but you in months. That's the *truth*, Lex. As real as it gets…"

Our eyes stay locked, holding strong while his pulse rocks easily beneath my hand. No shifting gaze, no twitching facial expressions or sweaty hands.

I know he's the most skilled liar I've ever met in my life, but right now… He's telling the truth. I can *feel* it, and it brings on a wave of remorse unlike anything I've ever felt before. I have to keep swallowing out of fear that I might hurl.

"I'm… I just…" I can't even speak. I have no available words right now.

He nestles up next to me, squeezing my hand. "But the thing is, you were always going to think the worst of me, because that's what I've shown you since the moment we met… The *worst* possible version of Warren Xavier. And I hate myself for still being able to hurt you without even hurting you."

I can't breathe. I feel like I'm falling apart.

Fuck fucking me, he's telling the truth. He actually is.

"Wait, so you *really* didn't do anything with Jasper…?" I'm sinking *deep* in this guilt. Drowning in it.

Ren shakes his head. "He did kiss me for a few heavy seconds… And he pushed me into my bed, and I was about to… let him." He gulps visibly. "He was just doing what he's used to doing… what I've always let him do, or encouraged even. But no, nothing actually happened. I stopped it before it could."

I stare at him. "And you said you… haven't been with anyone else… in *months??*"

He huffs out a strained chuckle. "Yea… Not since this talk I had with Dash before he broke out."

"Hold on, since *Dash* was still here??" I gasp.

His head wobbles as he smiles wistfully. "That fucker really got in my head…"

"Goddamnit, Ren!" I bark, and he flinches. "Why didn't you say anything?!"

"Because I didn't want to jinx it or put too much pressure on myself." He chews on his bottom lip. "It hasn't been easy… And I know you probably don't get it at all, but for me, it's like kicking a serious habit. I didn't want you to get all excited, only for me to let you down." He blinks heavily. "I came really close to letting Jasper fuck me. It's like a reflex or something, I don't know. But I didn't want it. I *don't*, and I think… Hopefully, today was like the first step. The hardest one. And I still beat it, even if everyone expects me to fail. At least I did it for me."

Wow… I have never wanted to rip my own balls off more than I do right now.

"*Fuck*, Ren…" I hum, dropping my forehead to his. "I'm so fucking sorry… Jesus, I can't even tell you how horrible I feel right now."

"Well, good, because that's exactly what I was hoping for," he grunts sarcastically, and I snort.

"No, I mean it. I should've let you explain…"

"I lost the right…"

"No. That's not true." I can feel that he wants to protest, but I don't let him. "Just because you fucked up in the past, that doesn't give me the right to project future fuck-ups onto you." I grab his face in my hands, dizzy as my breaths brush and he whimpers. "I'm *so* sorry I didn't listen… I'm sorry I didn't see that you're trying. You've been *trying*, Ren, and it all makes sense now… I should've tried harder to understand what you're going through."

He blinks. "I don't want you to apologize."

"Well, I'm going to. Over and over. I feel like shit."

"Then I'm sorry too… for scaring you."

My lungs are tight, stomach flipping and flopping. "I *can't* lose you… No matter what, I don't want to lose you, sweet flame."

His throat bobs. "Really?"

"Yea." I nod, our foreheads pressed together. "Don't do that again… Please?"

"Okay…" he whispers. "I won't."

"Thank you." I press a soft kiss on his lips, and when he kisses back, it lifts me up out of the atmosphere. "Are you okay? Tell me what you're feeling…"

"I still hate myself," he mumbles, chewing on his lip.

"That's to be expected." I smirk, hoping to lighten the mood by teasing him, and it works, because he smiles.

But it falls away quick. "I'll keep trying…" He shivers out the words, nervously, in that deep voice that rumbles from his chest, melting me into a puddle. "I *want* to keep trying for you, Lexington. You still need action, not words."

"I believe in you… I do." I kiss him again because I can't not. My lips part over his, sucking gently while my fingers comb through his silky hair. "I'm still afraid. I won't tell you I'm not, but that's never mattered before."

"I swear to God, you should be running so fast in the opposite direction," he croons into my mouth, fisting my shirt as our kisses grow hungrier.

"I know… Apparently, I'm not very smart."

Chuckling, he rolls on top of me, the heat around us nearly stifling while we kiss and pant and tongue each other like two inseparable idiots.

A broken soul and the foolish man who won't stop trying to hold him together.

Brushing my fingers up his arm, I hum, "Do you have a first-aid kit? We should really try to take care of that cut…"

"We will…" His mouth goes for my neck, kissing and nipping while our hips move together. "I just need you right now, beautiful boy."

It doesn't take long before he's lowering himself with my pants.

When his lips wrap around my cock, I become weightless. Every moment I'm with him is hectic as fuck. It's been this way since the day we met. He's an unpredictable storm, this man. Constantly tossing me back and forth, knocking the air out of me while I keep scrambling up, just trying to hang on.

But I want to see this through to the break. No matter how dangerous, or scary, or downright stupid, I can't help how starved I am for his rainbow when the clouds part.

Even if it destroys me in the process, from such a sweet, beautiful scorching flame… I can't help but crave his *burn*.

CHAPTER TWENTY-THREE

Ren

Days pass...

"MORNING, BEAUTIFUL..."

My face slopes right. And I smile. "Hi."

Lex frowns. "That's it...? Just *hi*? That's all I get??"

I purse my lips, playing coy for all of two-seconds before it starts to drive me crazy and I murmur, "Are you a parking ticket?"

He's already cracking up while I hold in my own giggles as best I can. "Wha—"

"'Cause you've got *FINE* written all over you," I gasp, immediately dying.

"I really cannot with you." He sighs out his laughter, shaking his head.

"You love it." I peek at him while we leave the row, following the rest of the group along to dinner.

"Mmm... maybe a little," Lex hums, slipping his fingers over the bandage on my wrist before threading them through mine.

Things feel... good, for the moment.

The gash on my wrist is healing nicely.

From what I hear, the summer heat is cooling off outside, and the leaves between the mansion and the prison are changing colors. *It sounds lovely.*

Joy's been letting me, Lex, and Byron walk around uncuffed, for the most part. It was supposed to be just me, while my wrist healed. But I threatened to make a scene if she didn't allow my friends free use of their hands too, and she conceded. I mean, she called me an *obnoxious bitch*, but that's to be expected. *Plus, it's true.*

And to top it all off, things with Lex are… *Sigh.*

That's how they are. *A dreamy sigh from the lips of a former skank.*

He still refuses to call himself my *boyfriend*, which irks me to no end. But I get it. We're taking things slow… Fucking whenever we have the chance, but keeping our affections toned down in public, so as not to trip the Warden's radar again.

But I don't think we need to worry much about being kept apart. Because this time, I have the head honchos on my side.

Velle is in charge of this island right now, with Joy and Rook as his partners, both inside these dank halls, and out. And thanks to the deal I made with him, I can breathe slightly easier. The fact that I'm no longer offering up my services to guards in exchange for supplies and extra privileges doesn't matter as much when I have Alabaster Isle's own power throuple watching out for me—and Lex, by association.

I'm still not sure what happened between the Velle and the Warden, but I assume it was some kind of big blow-out, from which Velle emerged victorious. Joy even told us they got to take the Warden's yacht out for a prison guard boat party over the summer—*wasn't jealous of that at all.* And according to my sources, Rook's family came to visit him at the mansion, after the three of them went to Boston for a long weekend to visit Joy's parents.

It's beyond crazy. I used to think the guards were chained up just as much as we are, and sure, at one time, they probably were. But whatever went down between Velle and The Ivory has apparently changed up the game quite a bit. Manuel Blanco's guard dog is officially off his leash… *I have to assume he isn't pleased about that.*

But who knows. Maybe it was an amicable agreement they came to. The Ivory doesn't seem like the type to let things slide… Though if there *was* one person I think he'd potentially bend to, it'd be Velle.

Not getting involved. But I'm sure my little birdies will tweet tweet soon enough.

Lex's warm hand envelopes mine as he tugs me along. My eyes have very little interest in leaving his stunning features for more than a second, but they manage to extract themselves long enough to glide over to Byron, who's scowling at nothing.

He's been doing that a lot lately.

"Psst... Hey, B," I whisper. He ignores me. "Um, hello... Earth to Byron!" I start snapping my fingers at him, and he pauses his grumpy, cold-shoulder routine to peek at me. "Velle's getting me my gun back this weekend. Wanna celebrate? I'm thinking, a nice big butterfly tramp-stamp on your lower back. Ooh! Or, how about the Hamburglar on your pelvis?"

Byron's lips twitch, but he forces it away, clenching his jaw tight on purpose to avoid showing any amusement.

"Ren." Lex jabs me with his elbow. "Enough."

"I'm just saying, it'd be cute!" I keep going, watching Byron's face for any sign that I'm getting through to him. But he's still actively pretending he doesn't hear me. "Or are you more of a Grimace man?"

"I'm not in the mood," he growls, speeding up to walk ahead of us.

My gaze narrows at his back. "What the fuck is up with him?"

"I don't know..." Lex sighs, uneasily. "He's been this way since O'Malley. You think he's still pissed you stood up for Darcey that day in the showers?"

"Excuse me, we *both* stood up for Darcey," I mutter, and he rolls his eyes. "I don't fucking know, he still talks to you. Why don't you find out what his deal is?? He's been acting all whiny goth-kid around me for months."

"I feel bad," Lex murmurs.

Sloping my chin in his direction, I pout at how goddamn adorable and sweet and just overflowing with loving empathy he is. "Of course you do, beautiful boy."

"Ren, I'm serious," he grumbles, though his cheeks are flushed. "Try thinking about someone other than you and me for a change. He's probably feeling like a third wheel. You and I are... whatever we are, his best friend is dead... He's all alone."

"So you're saying he's... jealous?" My stomach flips. "Of us??"

Lips twisting into an elated smile, I gaze off into space while my chest opens like a bloom. I've never had a relationship that someone was *jealous* of before... *Okay, I've never had a relationship at all.* But the idea that Byron might actually be envying what I've got going on?

It's basically the eighth world wonder.

All those years ago, watching guys holding hands, coveting what they had... And now *I* have it.

I never thought something like this was possible for someone like me. But it is... It's happening, now. In real time.

I'm in love with Lexington Deon, and I think he just might love me back.

Sure, he hasn't said it yet. He says he *loves* my ass, and my mouth, and how beautiful I look when I'm riding him. But he won't say the words, *I love you, Ren* out loud, in an effort to protect himself.

Because as good as things are going between us, we're still just wandering through the rubbled remains of the devastating hurricane of our past, attempting to slowly rebuild.

I'm sure he'll say it, eventually. *Maybe when I manage to get him those fireworks...*

Lex is still talking about Byron, and of course I'm listening to him, but I'm still reeling from the idea that someone might be jealous of *my* relationship. I'm on cloud nine while we enter the cafeteria, heading up to the chow line while Lex goes to sit down.

I like to get my man's food for him. *I'm chivalrous like that.*

Grabbing two trays, I turn to saunter toward our table. I barely get a full step before almost crashing into Officer Brenner.

"Shit..." I grumble. "My bad."

My spine stiffens when he steadies us both with his hands... on my hips. Dangerously close to my ass.

"No harm, 48." He winks at me, fingertips subtly slinking down to my butt before he lets me go. But not without first tapping my chin with his knuckles.

Bleh... Look at this idiot.

My stomach is rolling as I spin away from him quick, muttering, "Fuck off."

I make a beeline to the table and plop down next to Lex with a frustrated breath, shoving the tray in his direction.

"You okay?" he asks me quietly.

I'm afraid to make eye contact, because I know he saw what just happened.

"Mhm..." I mumble, picking at my cuticles.

"Are you sure?" he presses, firm tone giving away his displeasure. "'Cause he was touching you, Ren..."

"Yea, I know," I huff. "Everyone's always fucking touching me. I've got a building full of dudes slapping my ass and making bullshit excuses to rub their dicks on me. Linetti showed up at my cell last night while I was dead asleep."

"Wow..." Lex's fists clench on the table. "I really fucking hate what I'm hearing right now..."

"Fuck, I fucking *know*, baby." I rub my eyes, exhausted by this whole thing. "Me too. I promise nothing happened… You know that, right?"

Peering at him, I observe the strain in his jaw and his rigid posture. He nods, though it doesn't even look like he's breathing and he hasn't blinked in a while.

"I do," he answers me, stiffly. "I believe you. I know this isn't your fault…"

"What the fuck are you talking about?? Of *course* it's my fucking fault," I hiss. "I brought this on myself. What did I think would happen… I'd give up whoring around and everyone would just get the memo??" Slouching over, I drop my forehead onto the table. "It's too hard. I quit."

"You're being such a bitch right now," Lex growls.

I turn my face to look at him through the hair in my eyes. "That's not very supportive…"

"*Supportive??*" He scoffs. "Don't give me that bullshit, Ren. I'm the one who has to fucking watch all these assholes touching you and hitting on you… And I can't even fucking react because I'll get sent to solitary and I'm terrified of leaving you alone up here!"

My head lifts slowly. "You wanna react…?"

"Are you kidding me??" His voice has taken on this snarling rumble that awakens my dick. "I want to chop their hands off so they can't touch you, pluck their eyes out so they can't look at you… Rip their goddamn tongues out so they can never speak another word to you again."

I pull my lower lip between my teeth, breathing shallowed, as I shift in my seat. My balls are aching, dick filling up fast from how sexy and possessive and downright *murderous* he's acting right now. For *me*.

Scooting closer to him, I reach for one of his balled fists, uncurling his fingers so I can play with them. "I thought I was the jealous one…"

"That's different," he grumbles. "No one hits on me. Not the way they do to you…"

"Want me to kill the next person who tries to touch what's yours?" I whisper, subtly moving his hand down between my legs.

I push his fingers onto my erection, and he whimpers, lashes fluttering. "Ren…"

Easing myself closer, my lips brush his ear and I purr, "Oh, *Luthor*…"

"You're such a dick," he groans quietly, cupping my cock, trying to be subtle while I chuckle wickedly. "You actually like this, don't you, you horrible, sexy nuisance? Having me acting all jealous, like some caveman…"

"Mmhmm… Show them all who I belong to, baby boy." I lick his earlobe, and he shudders.

But he reluctantly pulls away and breathes, "Not now, sweet flame." I pout, and he grasps my chin. "But you will *not* be quitting, do you understand me? If I don't get to quit, you don't get to quit." My lashes flutter, and I nod slowly. "You're doing a great job, baby. You're so strong."

He presses a small kiss on my lips, and I think I'm actually defying gravity, like my heart is full of helium.

Lexington believes in me… He knows I can do this.

"Thank you," I whisper.

He winks at me, and I'm swooning. "You love me?"

"More than anything," I hum, leaning in for more kisses.

But Lex backs away and gives me a knowing look, eyes flinging briefly to Byron, who's sitting a few seats down at the table, staring at his fingers.

I do feel kind of bad. Either Byron is jealous, or lonely, or pissed, or some combination. And I just wish I knew how to fix it…

I mean, shit, he won't even sit near us.

"Yo, Kang," Lex calls to him, and his sullen gaze lifts. "You never told me how that book was."

Byron stares at him for a moment, losing a lot of the hardness around his eyes. "It sucked."

Lex laughs, and Byron cracks a smile. And now *I'm* the jealous one—*back to normal.* Because I just don't understand why Byron will give up his hostility for Lex, but with me, it's like he suddenly hates my fucking guts.

Maybe he has feelings for Lex… and he's mad because I'm taking Lex away from him.

The thought sours my stomach until it's rolling.

The two of them are chatting about some book, then Byron asks Lex about the computer, which he's happy to talk about in great detail. And as much as I wish I could join the conversation, I'm just sitting quietly, letting them have their moment. I guess it's all I can do… Hopefully, Byron just misses having time with Lex as a friend.

Lex's hand stays on mine the whole time, his fingers absentmindedly trailing from my palm up to the bandage on my wrist and back down. Glancing over at the door, I see Joy and Rook teasing each other. And I remember the morning after I cut my wrist open, when Joy gave me stitches.

Admittedly, she's not great at it, but she managed. Eight of them, to be exact.

I still feel a little foolish for doing that to myself, especially after seeing how much it upset Lex. The need to self-harm is something I've been struggling with since I was a kid, but I think I'm getting better. At least, I'm trying to... Just like I'm trying to overcome my lustful afflictions.

It's been difficult, not just because the guys in this prison aren't registering that I'm done letting them plow me like a cornfield. The issue with my sex addiction is that it has nothing to do with my feelings for Lex. It doesn't mean I don't love him, because I do. More than *anything*. It doesn't even mean I *want* to have sex with people who aren't him, because I don't.

Sex for me has always been a way to escape from myself. To feel something raw and rough that fills the empty void in my chest. It's the pleasure and pain I'm addicted to, the burn of them both singeing inside me.

But now that I have Lexington Deon, now that I'm giving it a *real* shot with him, I know I don't need either of those things to feel alive anymore. Because he gives me everything I've been missing all my life. He gives me affection, and purpose, hope... He gives me *love*.

It probably sounds corny as fuck, but I feel like his love cures me.

Alright, that's enough before I break into song.

Joy steps away to take a phone call just as Velle is slinking into the room, he and Rook giving each other the hungry eyes. I don't even think they're saying anything, but I guess they don't need to. It's all in the heated gazes, the lip-biting, and the subtle slip of Rook's finger through one of Velle's belt loops to pull him closer.

Shifting my face back in Lex's direction, I bite the inside of my cheek. He makes me so much better... but I'm not sure he could say the same about me. And the thought bums me out a little.

I don't want to be the liability in the relationship.

My burdened thoughts are interrupted when Joy strides up to our table, falling into the seat next to Byron. His eyes are immediately on her, and it reminds me that they've hooked up before—a few times, from what I understand.

That could be another thing weighing on him... He lost both of his fuck-buddies—me and Joy. I can see that being a drag.

"Listen up, chiclets," Joy says to the three of us, her voice hushed. "There's something I'm going to allow you to do, but you need to keep it discreet. It has to *stay* between you three. Any of you flaps your lips, and you'll be answering to me." Her accusatory glare finds me specifically. "Got it?"

"Why are you singling me out?" I frown.

"Yea, we got it," Lex answers for us, ignoring me. "What's this... *thing* we're allowed to do?"

She stands up and nods. "Come with me."

She starts walking away, and the three of us share a confused look before quickly scrambling up to follow her. Joy brings us out into the hallway, casting a quick grin at Rook and Velle pawing at each other as we pass them.

Once we're around the corner, she stops us. "Stay right in this spot, okay? Out of sight of the cameras." We nod in agreement, and she pulls her cell phone out of her pocket, holding it up to her ear. "You still there?"

I glance at Lex, his wide eyes meeting mine as he shakes his head nervously. I'm intrigued as hell right now. *Who the balls is she talking to??*

"Yea, yea," Joy rasps over the line, smirking. "You definitely owe me more than one at this point. Your man owes me about a hundred himself. Okay, here's Luth."

She hands the phone to Lex, and he snatches it up quickly, some kind of hopeful excitement on his face.

"Hello?" he speaks quietly into the phone, and immediately his eyes widen, mouth sloping into a massive smile. "Oh my *God*, I'm so fucking happy to hear your voice again!"

Lex falls back against the wall, his free hand resting on his chest.

"Who is it??" I whisper to him, but he's paying me zero attention, fully immersed in whoever is speaking to him on the phone. I look at Joy, but she just grins, spinning away to give us some space.

He said again... *Whose voice would he be excited to hear—*

"Holy fuck, Dash," I gasp, tugging Lex's shirt over and over. "It's *Dash*, isn't it? Dash, is that you?!"

Lex laughs out loud, nodding. "Yea, totally. Hang on." He switches to speakerphone, lowering the volume. "Okay, you're good."

"Hi, guys!" the familiar voice croons through the phone, and I can't even help it.

I'm freaking out.

Obviously, we don't get phone calls in here. *Ever.* The one time I managed to score a cell phone, Byron's dumb ass got it taken away. So the fact that we're talking to *anyone* on the phone is fucking awesome. But it being Dash just makes it even sweeter.

I'll admit it. I miss the kid. He's cool as shit, and we really started to bond towards the end there.

After he escaped, he called Lex to ask him frantic, confusing questions.

But understandably, we didn't expect to hear from him again. And now he's calling from wherever he is to catch up, I guess.

The dude is fucking nuts, and I'm here for it.

"This is amazing," Byron chuckles. "Miss you, buddy!"

"I miss you too, chingu," Dash chirps some word in Korean. "Did I get it right?"

Byron cackles. "Close enough."

"Dascha, how are you calling us right now??" I ask him, gripping Lex's wrist as he holds the phone, beaming. "Are you alright? Have you grown your hair back?? Talk to me, Goose."

Dash laughs. "Yea, I'm alright. I'm more than alright, actually. I'm on top of the motherfuckin' world. And yes, my hair is grown out, and it's pink. It looks hot."

He sighs, and a quick pang hits my chest. Because I *do* miss him, but also, he sounds great and I'm a little jealous. For the first time since I've been locked up in this damn prison… I kinda wish I wasn't here.

I wish I was wherever Dash is right now. All of us, together.

"Homie, you have no freaking idea how glad I am that you're okay," Lex hums. "I've been worried about you since the last time we talked…"

"I get it," Dash says softly. "I wasn't in the best place when I called you. But I need to tell you something…"

"Okay…" Lex mumbles. "I'm nervous. Go on."

"I'm seeing someone," Dash whispers. "I, um… I have a boyfriend. And he used to work there…"

We're all quiet for a second before I mutter, "I'm living for this right now."

"I don't get it," Byron croaks.

"Oh my *God*, Kemper!" Lex gasps.

"Mhm. Yea," Dash murmurs, an audible grin in his voice. "It's Kemper… *Kellan* Kemper."

"How the…" Lex shakes his head. *"How?!"*

Dash chuckles. "We met up here. Where I am… It's a long, complicated, confusing fucking story, but against all odds, we made it. And now we're… together. And he loves me."

I feel like such a loser right now, but I can't stop smiling. "Do you love him?"

"Oh, fuck yea," Dash rasps, and I cackle.

"Hold on… *Kellan Kemper*? The dude who used to work in solitary??" Byron sounds as shocked as we're all feeling.

It's pretty fucking insane. How Dash ever would have escaped and then somehow met up with a guard who used to work in the prison he just escaped from is like something out of a movie.

But more than anything, I'm happy for him. He was so anxious about discovering his sexuality when he was in here. Now, he's out in the real world, and he's in love with a beautiful fucking man.

Honestly, that dude Kemper... Yowza.

"The very same," Dash says with swoon in his tone.

"He's so fucking hot," I rumble, and Lex elbows me. "What?? Kemper is a *smokeshow*. Nice work, queen. Fuckin' slay."

Dash snorts. "He's the best thing that's ever happened to me... And I never would have found him if it weren't for Alabaster fucking Pen. So really, I just wanted to call and thank you guys... For being my friends, even when I know it probably wasn't easy. Luthor... you especially." He pauses to sigh. "You're my best friend in the world, and I miss you so much. But I need you to know how grateful I am for you sticking by me when I was... spinning out."

Lex's eyes are glistening, emotion etching his features as he smiles wistfully, clearing his throat to cover it up. "Have you been... feeling okay?"

"Yea, for sure." I can picture Dash nodding. "It's been tough... But also eye-opening." He clears his throat. "I'm, um... I found out I'm Schizophrenic."

Wow. My eyes spring to my friends. Byron also appears surprised by this, but Lex doesn't. He's nodding like it's something he might have already been suspecting.

"I mean, I just found out, like officially," Dash goes on. "And Kemper's been amazing. He's so supportive and sweet, and I just can't believe I actually have him now. The real him..."

My forehead lines. I don't quite get what he means by that, but Lex has some serious realization dawning on his face right now.

"He's the officer..." Lex whispers to himself, eyes wide.

"What was that?" Dash asks, and Lex shakes his head.

"Nothing. Listen, man, I'm really fucking proud of you for figuring your shit out. Seriously. I just hope wherever you guys are that you're safe..."

"I think we are," Dash says. "Kemper's been talking to Joy a lot... I know it isn't exactly smart, but I'd love to call you guys again, if I can."

"That would be awesome." Lex grins.

"Gives us something to look forward to," Byron murmurs.

"If you could just put your phone on speaker while you and Kemper get busy, it'd mean a lot to me," I tease, and Dash laughs.

"You're such a pervert." Lex rolls his eyes at me.

Leaning into his side, I whisper, "A pervert who licked your ass for twenty minutes yesterday..." I press a slow kiss on his neck, and he shivers.

"Warren!" Dash snaps over the line, and I jump.

"Huh?? What did I do?"

"How are you guys doing?" Dash asks, sounding much more stern all of a sudden. "Have you been thinking about that talk we had before I left...?"

My lips twitch. "Yes, Dascha. I'm practically a Boy Scout at this point, thanks for your concern."

"I don't remember Boy Scouts sixty-nineing each other for badges," Byron scoffs.

"You and I clearly had different experiences, then," I sneer at him, and he fakes a laugh.

Hey, at least he's talking to me.

"I expect an update on this next time I call," Dash says, obviously to me.

"You're giving me homework?" I whine. "You've changed, man. "Coming out turned you into a party-pooper."

Dash chuckles some more, and I just know he's shaking his head.

Joy stomps over to us, snapping her fingers and making the wrap it up motion in the air.

"Alright, well, we have to go," Lex sighs, frowning like he doesn't want to end the call yet. "But we love you, Dashy-poo! Stay safe, enjoy wherever you are. Watch your back, ya know?"

"Definitely," Dash replies. "Eyes open, mouth shut. My dad used to say that..."

"Really?? Where's the fun in leaving your mouth shut?" I mumble, and Lex elbows me again, even harder this time. "Ouch! Dammit... Dash, your friend is *abusing* me!"

"I'm sure you deserve it. Okay, bye, guys!" he chirps. "Miss you tons! I'll call again soon."

"Bye, Dash!" Byron leans over the phone.

"Later, 'bater," I hum, making kissing noises.

"Tell Kemper we said hi!" Lex cheers while Joy grabs her phone out of his hand.

She switches it off speaker and wanders away again, still talking to

Dash while the rest of us stand around, dazed from the high of speaking to our friend, the only prisoner in Alabaster Pen history to break the fuck out and actually *make it*.

"I can't believe it…" Byron sighs, sifting fingers through his short hair.

"I know," Lex says. "He's just out there… living. He's got a boyfriend, he's… managing his mental illness and stuff."

"I guess flipping out in the caf that day was the right move," Byron huffs.

My mind is wading through all of this, the conversation with Dash, how much healthier and happier he sounded, and the longing I can feel coming from Lex as Joy brings us back into the caf and we finish dinner.

Noticing the subtlest shifts in his moods is a skill of mine, and with how much quieter he's being right now, I can't help wondering if Lex wishes he'd gotten out too.

Ever since I met him, he's been very realistic about his situation. The rational voice to all of his past cellmates when they whine about trying to break out of prison. But now that Dash made it, and he's calling us, regaling us with his tales of finding love and acceptance for himself, I'm seeing the first ever flash of doubtful contemplation on the face of my sort-of-boyfriend.

Walking back from dinner, I squeeze Lex's hand. "So, Dash and Kemper… crazy, huh?"

"Yea…" he sighs introspectively.

"I remember the day I overheard Kemper talking about Dash coming in," I tell him. "He definitely seemed personally invested. I have no idea how they found each other, but it almost seems like…"

"Fate," Lex finishes my thought, peeking at me.

I pull my lip between my teeth.

When we get to the row, Joy wanders off, giving me and Lex a few minutes to say goodbye, something she's been doing more and more lately.

Not wishing to waste a single second of it, I wrap him up in my arms, kissing a line up his throat. "Should I try to badger her into letting you stay over? It might work…" My head is all fogged with lust as I rub my crotch on his.

"I need to tell you something…" he mumbles, his thumbs drawing circles on my hips.

"Is it about how badly you want my ankles in the air right now?" I nip his jawline.

"No…" He starts to fidget. "I mean, I *do*, but that's not what I have to tell you. It's something that might upset you... But in the interest of being open and honest with each other, I think you should know."

My muscles stiffen in sudden nerves. "Okay." I pull my face back to lock our eyes. "What is it, baby?"

Lex takes in a breath like he's preparing to drop a bomb, and now I'm freaking out a little. "It's just that you've been so good to me lately... With the honesty and everything. You deserve it in return, ya know?"

"Lex, please," I whine hoarsely. "You're freaking me out. Just fucking say it—"

"I kissed Dash," he blurts out, immediately chomping down on his bottom lip.

I can feel my eyes bulging out of my skull. "You... what??"

"W-well, *he* kissed *me*," Lex stammers. "I didn't initiate it. I never would have... But he was having some kind of episode... At first, I thought maybe it was, like, a split-personality type thing. But now that we know he's Schizophrenic, I guess that explains it better..."

"Hold on... wait," I let go of him, rubbing my eyes. "Go back to the kissing, please."

"Right, right." He shakes his head. "He was acting like someone else. He said he was this *officer*... And he thought *I* was him. I was Dash... And the officer started kissing me—*Dash*, I mean."

"Am I in a K-hole right now??" I blink.

"Babe, be serious." He gives me a look, and I scoff.

"Oh, I'm sorry! Am *I* being crazy?? You're telling me your friend kissed you while acting out some role-play fantasy!"

"You're not listening to me," he grumbles. "I'm telling you, it happened in a fit of his psychosis. He thought he was the *officer*... Officer Kemper, I assume. And I was Dash, and it kind of just... started happening."

My chest is caving in so hard it hurts, ribs cracking and puncturing my lungs.

The jealousy is rising in my throat like bile, and I hate it. But I have to just keep reminding myself not to be a hypocrite.

This is what he feels when I hook up with other people...

God, no wonder he hated me for so long. This is awful.

"Please tell me it was just a kiss..." I whimper while my face falls into my hands.

"I swear, it didn't go any further," he says sincerely, and some minute relief soothes the ache. But then he adds, "I mean, it was a solid few minutes of making out..."

"Ugh!" I bark, and he flinches. "And he has the nerve to give *me* attitude about cheating, that prissy little shit! *Well*, I've got some words I'd like to share with Dascha next time he calls from convict paradise!"

Lex grabs my face. "Babe, please. You *can't* say anything to him."

"Why the hell not?!"

"Because! He doesn't even know he did it!" He pins me with those round, sparkly green eyes. "He's sick, Ren. The poor thing… I can't even fathom what he must experience. What he must see in his head that isn't really there…" He pauses while I gulp. "I'm sure he's still trying to wrap his head around everything that happened while he was in here, and I don't want to embarrass him, or make him feel awkward around me."

My lashes flutter. "So you're just never gonna tell him?"

"Maybe someday," he sighs. "But not yet. Not now, when he's only just getting some clarity."

"You're too fucking sweet for real life," I huff while he brushes my hair back gently with his fingers, calming me, almost like he's hypnotizing me with his affectionate touch. "Sometimes it makes me nuts."

"It only seems that way because you don't care about anyone else's feelings." He smirks, fingertips dancing down my jaw.

"Not true," I grumble, and he kisses it. Over and over. He's kissing the stubborn frown right off my lips. I grab a fistful of his shirt, and he hums. "So you've literally made out with *everyone* in our group of friends…" He smirks, nipping my lip. "Unless you wanna count Darcey, I guess."

"Give it time," he teases, his beautiful grin all wide and wicked. "I could cross kissing a serial killer off my list…"

I growl as Joy barks behind us. "Dammit, you horny squirrels! Say goodnight already! Jesus…"

"Joyful, may we please be excused to my cell for a few minutes?" I plead with her, though I'm still glaring at Lex. "For once, my boyfriend needs to do the groveling."

He brushes his smile over my mouth. "I'm not your boyfriend…"

"I will eat you alive," I snarl.

"No bullshit right now!" Joy snaps, shoving my cell open. "Luth, get over there before I spray you with the hose."

"Gotta go, jealous flame." Lex presses one last peck on my lips before Joy rips us apart.

Shoving me into my cell, she slams the bars in my face, and I grab them, watching Lex leave.

"I'm not forgetting about this!" I call after him. But he's just smirking as he wanders away, like the sweetest, sexiest little devil around. "I could easily withhold sex, ya know! Lexington?! Are you listening to me??"

I can hear him chuckling.

"Goddamnit," I huff, pacing and rubbing my eyes while I mutter to myself, "Like he'd ever believe *you* could withhold sex…"

Realistically, this little makeout session with Dash isn't a big deal. I had to accept what happened between him and Byron, and that was much more intense than a few minutes of kissing while Dash didn't even know who he was.

Lex deserves understanding from me, especially after everything I've put him through. In fact, he deserves a whole lot more than that.

Mulling this over, I plop down on my bed, grabbing my tattoo gun. I take out some ink and dunk the needle, carving lines onto a spot on my chest, right above my heart.

It'll have to do for now… *Until I can get him the real thing.*

There's a secret spot where I stash my shower products. Makes things easier than always having to locate stuff when they show up to bring us for showers, especially since a lot of times they're really rushing us along.

Sure, someone else could find it and use it. Maybe they have… *Because this bottle of body wash is feeling pretty damn light.*

I'm frowning as I squirt some into my hands, then pass it to Lex.

"Why do you look pissed?" he asks. "Are you suddenly opposed to sharing?"

"No, it's just… I don't know when I'll be able to get more," I mumble, lathering up under the stream of water. "This stupid lockdown, ya know?"

I used to be able to get things much easier… *When I was actively fucking everyone and their fathers.*

Lex is watching me, I can feel it. My gaze slides over to meet his, and he looks away.

"I don't know… you've been managing well enough begging Velle and Joy for stuff," he says quietly, hands gliding over his scalp, through the inch-or-so of light blonde hair on his head.

The water sends suds running down his muscles. My eyes follow them, a jolt hitting me in the dick. I love seeing the ink I put on his skin… The scars I've made on him.

He's still perfect, but this place has definitely changed him, in both ways that are visible, and those that aren't. A lot of it is my fault, I know that. But the rest has to do with being caged for so long.

I wonder if he'd even remember how to run free...

Would I?

Would we even know what to do with ourselves outside of here?

Such thoughts have been plaguing me more and more recently, since Dash got out and started calling us. I never used to wonder what it would be like to be back in the real world. But lately, it's all I can think about.

I show Lex a small smile while my hands run over my chest, down my abs. "You're right. I'm sure I can sweet-talk them into getting me some products." My fingers continue down, his eyes creeping over to watch as they crawl over my semi-hard cock, onto my balls. "Gotta keep it nice and fresh, right? My sexy little green-eyed tease."

I wink at him, and he rolls his eyes, though he's visibly flushing, and as hard as he tries, he can't keep his eyes off what I'm doing.

Washing the dick, washing the balls, washing the ass... Washing washing washing.

In theory, cleaning your undercarriage isn't supposed to be *hot*. It's hygiene. But when you're doing it next to the guy you love, the guy you've been hopelessly infatuated with for years, and the *only* person you're allowing yourself to sleep with, the act of massaging soap onto your nuts and between your ass cheeks can quickly becoming arousing as fuck.

Because of this, we're taking much longer to shower than usual. Everyone else is already getting dressed while we're still standing side by side, with water flowing over our bodies. Chests heaving breaths of desire, eyes locked to convey all manners of pent-up need.

It's been a few weeks since the last time we were able to sneak off and bang out this tension real quick. Despite being on Velle's good side, it doesn't mean he's going to let us do whatever we want. Sometimes Joy will look the other way when I pull Lex into my cell to makeout a little. Last week, I begged Rook to bring us back from dinner five minutes early, and we jerked each other off in the row, with the clock ticking.

Not exactly *romantic*, but it's all we have...

Stealing little moments in a place that isn't built for budding relationships.

I can't complain, because even *one second* with Lexington touching me or smiling at me is more than enough. But when I think about doing this *forever*, and never really getting to explore how it *could* be between us, I'm filled with frustration. Not only sexual—though that's a big part of it now that I'm learning to live without constant orgasms from miscellaneous people—but also just a sudden resentment for where we are, with all its limitations.

What could our lives be like together if we weren't separated by steel bars?

I'm so lost in my thoughts, and the way my heart is racing faster and faster, I don't even notice how close Lex is inching toward me, until he's joining me beneath my shower.

He blinks at me, droplets falling from his lashes, tumbling down his lips. I'm instantly several degrees warmer, even with cool water rushing over me.

His hand reaches out, fingers gently tracing the recent tattoo I gave myself, right over my heart.

"So you can see fireworks whenever you want," I explained when I first showed it to him.

He kissed me so hard, I can still feel it.

"Ren, I was thinking..." Lex whispers, allowing his touch to drift slowly, over the curve of my pectoral, down the lines of my abs. "I know this has been an adjustment for you, not being able to get whatever you want whenever you want... I know it isn't easy to change, and you trying so hard is probably one of the most incredible things anyone's ever done for me."

"I don't mind," I tell him with confidence, though I can't deny that what he's saying is true.

It really *hasn't* been easy, what with constant temptation around every corner, and prison getting in the way of me having the one dick I truly want.

"I just need you to know how much I appreciate what you're doing for me," he breathes, hands now gripping my waist.

Our bodies are so close together that the slightest movement has our dicks touching. Hums leave us both in unison at the sensation.

Lex leans in, kissing the corner of my mouth. "You deserve something special..." More kisses, peppering my jaw and my throat. "For your efforts."

He's bending a bit at the waist to kiss lower, over my collarbone, down to my chest. I swallow hard and he peeks up at me with green, glittering mischief in his eyes, kissing the tattoo, dragging his lips over my nipple for a quick, luscious *suck*.

The desire rippling around us has me dizzy, my cock filling rapidly with every throb of pleasure from him kissing and tonguing my peaked flesh. It feels incredible, the warmth of his breath and his little pants. I can't help releasing a soft moan when he nips it gently.

And despite the eagerness flowing through my veins, I still expect him to straighten back up. To maybe move to my other nipple, or return to my mouth so we can kiss the way we always do when we don't have time to explore everything we want.

But he doesn't.

Lex leaves my nipple swollen and aching to kiss even lower, gliding his tongue between my abs.

"Don't tease me," I whimper on jagged breaths, fingers caressing his nape.

I'm losing my fucking *mind* right now, because it really seems like he might…

Shooting me one last innocent gleam, he drops to his knees.

Wait, am I hallucinating?

Lex's eyes are wide and stuck on my cock, where it's resting hard and heavy right in front of his beautiful face. "Just tell me… if I'm doing it right." He peeks up at me from the ground, and a shivering exhale gusts between my lips. "If I'm sucking how you wanna be sucked…"

"Jesus fucking Christ…" I breathe, precum beading at the tip of my cock.

Lex stares at it. And when he parts his lips, it's like time rolls to a stop.

I watch in slow motion as his pink tongue slips out to gradually swipe the curve of flesh. The sensation it brings has my head falling forward, my entire body shuddering almost violently.

"Like this…?" Lex mumbles softly. I can barely hear him over the blood rushing in my ears.

But his voice is silky soft and draped in curious desire, the best sound, especially when it's coming from him… on his knees.

Licking my fucking cock for the first time ever.

I manage to nod, eyes set on his, while he goes in for more, licking a long, warm line up my shaft. "Fuck me… *Lex…*"

I'm falling apart already, watching this sweet, sexy boy drag his tongue up and down my inches, feathering over the veins like he's lapping at a melty popsicle on a summer day. I can't even believe this is happening… My heart is exploding in my chest.

I get his firsts.

Only me. Mine mine, all mine.

"Tell me if it feels good, Ren," he whines, licking me all over, from balls to tip. It's so clear he has no idea what he's doing, and it's the fucking hottest thing I've ever experienced in all my life.

"Baby… *yes*," I pant, petting his jaw. I could probably come just from him licking me up and down like this. "It feels incredible. I can't believe you're… doing this."

I know I sound like an idiot, but I can't help it. I've been dreaming of this moment for *years*.

"I always wondered what it would be like…" His warm breaths tickle my erection. "Putting my mouth on your dick."

"You look like my fantasy come true down there," I rasp.

Lex trails his lips underneath my head. Then he parts them and slowly sucks me in. Just the tip… barely anything at all, and my balls twinge, pulsing out a hearty gush of precum.

"*Mmff*," he grunts, sucking it out and swallowing.

"Uhh, *God*," I croak. "Sweet fucking boy…"

Hooded gaze lifting to mine, he hums on my cock, sucking a little deeper, sliding another inch into his warm, wet virgin mouth.

"Fuck… *fffuck*, Lex." I hold his face gently in my hands. "Suck a little more, baby."

He immediately does as I say, sucking on me while gliding his mouth down farther, until half my cock is in there and the head is lurching toward the back of his throat.

"Mm… Mmmmm," Lex rumbles, looking like an orgasm for my eyes, on his knees, lips stretched wide with his mouth all full of my big cock. Flushed and fucking *loving* it.

He sucks more, taking me deeper with fevered determination.

"Easy, gorgeous," I breathe. "Take it slow, or you'll—"

He gags, pulling off quickly as he sputters a little, eyes watering, a trail of saliva from his mouth to my dick.

"Shit… my bad. I wasn't ready." He wipes his mouth with the back of his hand before bracing himself against my hips. "Let me try again."

"Baby, you don't have to…" My voice dissolves when he slurps back onto my cock. "Holy mother*fuck*…"

Sucking up and down on my length, he slowly eases me deeper and deeper once more, teeth scraping just a little as he bobs. My legs are shaking, fingers trembling on his jaw, feeling the strain of it, wide open to fit me. He's puffing through his nose, trying to breathe, pushing himself to get me down as far as he can.

This time, my crown slides back farther into his throat, and I hiss a garbled noise at how goddamn *tight* it is, how warm and untouched by any other cock ever. He gags again, just a little, but keeps going, moaning as if he likes it.

He *likes* the chase, the illicit discomfort. He seems driven, desperate to get me past his tonsils.

"*Oh*… ohh, baby, suck my fucking cock," I groan, as quietly as possible.

I don't even know where I am right now. I have no concept of *anything* happening outside this bubble where Lexington Deon is on his knees, gripping my waist while he gives me the best, most uncoordinated head of my life.

Saliva is spilling from his mouth, and he tries to swallow, throat tightening on my dick. He whines while I mewl helplessly, at the brink of an orgasm already.

Pulling off, he hauls in a long gasp of air. "Your dick is… too b-big."

"Use your hand."

He blinks up at me with glassy eyes, and my head tilts, as if to say, *trust me.*

Lifting his hand, he curls it around my shaft. Then I cover it with my own, helping him stroke me slowly.

"Now suck," I whisper, tugging his face back onto me gently. "*Slow*, beautiful boy. Jerk me into your mouth…"

Lex shivers, but takes my advice, pumping his fist up and down while he sucks timidly on my head. It feels *fantastic* just like that, but still, it doesn't take long before he's sucking me deeper once more. He seems to have found his rhythm now that he's not so focused on trying to swallow me whole.

"Mmm…" His lashes fan over his cheeks.

He likes it this way.

God, he's such an innocent, sweet piece of fucking sex candy, this kid.

"You like it, baby?" I grip his jaw, giving him a few gentle flicks of my hips to feed my cock gradually into his waiting mouth. "Sucking my big dick…"

He nods frantically, huffing through his nose as he bobs with my thrusts between his soft pink lips.

"You understand now why I love doing this to you?"

He nods again.

"*Uhh*… God, Lexington… *Wicked boy*, your mouth is the best thing my dick has ever been in." My fingers dig into his jaw, holding him harder. "You suck me better than *anyone*, baby. Fuck my cock with those plush lips..."

His groans are becoming uneven as he sucks on me furiously, cradling my shaft with his tongue. Sliding his lips up to my head, he assaults it with sloppy suction, then glides back down. My crown slips past that barrier, but this time he doesn't gag. He's zoned-in, too busy going to fucking town on me to notice that I'm fucking so deep in his tight throat, I might wind up in his stomach.

My vision is swimming, balls aching, as I glance down between his legs. His cock is standing up straight, all swollen, bobbing and flinching like it could use some love itself. And I just wish like hell I could suck him while he sucks me, because honestly, nothing would make me happier.

"Look at you, baby," I growl. "Your dick is so hard..." He nods fast, fingers massaging my nuts. "You really love sucking on my cock, don't you?" He nods again, whimpering vibrations into me. "You gonna come with me in your mouth?"

"Mmm *mmm*." His head bobs, eyelids growing heavy.

He must be exhausted. They don't call them blow*jobs* for nothing, and this is his first time. But he's already going at it with more gumption than anyone I've ever met. *Except maybe me.*

"Touch yourself, Lex," I grunt a hoarse command. "Stroke that pretty cock for me so we can come together."

Lex finally pulls his mouth free again, breathing in deep. But he doesn't stop pumping my cock in his fist, using the other hand to jerk himself while his mouth glides down to my balls.

"Ren... I want you to come in my mouth," he purrs, deep voice all jagged. He leaves soft kisses all over my nuts, lapping at them with his tongue. "I wanna swallow for you, sweet flame."

"Mmm, then you should probably get back on my dick," I hum, head dropping back at the fire he's breeding in my loins. "'Cause I'm *so* fucking close, baby..."

"You taste so good," he whispers, running his lips back up my swollen shaft. "Those little pulses weren't enough. I need more of your flavor... Pour it into me, baby."

I have to chomp down on my lip to keep the groans in. "Jesus, you fucking ruin me." Brushing through his hair and down his cheeks, I hold him steady again as he greedily sucks me into his mouth. And I help him, pushing in deep, feeding him inches. "Baby boy, you are so fucking *mine*."

He whines, eating me alive while stroking himself harder, and faster. I'm a slave to the way his dick looks right now. So fucking *big* and blushed, standing up nice and tall for me.

God, I wanna watch him come. Shoot it out of that long cock, all the fuck over me.

My orgasm is fast approaching, balls drawing up tight. And when he cups them in his hand and gives them a rough squeeze, my eyes roll back, chills washing over me.

"I'm gonna come for you, baby," the words rush through my quivering lips. "Lex, I'm gonna… *fucking bust* hard in your sweet mouth."

He keeps groaning, and sucking, and beating his dick, practically falling forward into my body.

"*Ohhfuck*, you ready, gorgeous…?" He nods fast. "Suck me… suck suck *suck* it all out, baby, *fuuck*…"

Shivers sweep through my loins as the climax descends, and I erupt…

Coming in Lexington Deon's *perfect* fucking mouth.

Balls quaking, shuddering and aching, I pour my cum all over his tongue, throbbing down his throat while he sucks it out hungrily. Not an ounce of surprise, or a single gag. The kid was prepared, just gulping it back, swallowing and swallowing every last thick pulse.

My fingers caress the mound of his Adam's apple, feeling it bob. So goddamn sexy, I think I might collapse.

Son of a motherfucking bitch, holy shit fuck, what a fucking orgasm…

And my legs are giving out.

Yup, there they go.

I'm falling…

Barely even finished coming, I pull out of Lex's mouth, crashing onto my knees before him. He's more startled by that than anything else, though he can barely keep his eyes open.

"Come for me, baby." I grab his face and kiss his lips in a flourish of passion, my greedy tongue slipping inside his mouth to taste my cum. "Come all over me. *God*, fucking soak me in it…"

"I'm gonna come," he grunts, fist working furiously on his cock.

"You're gonna come, love?"

"Yea…"

"For me?"

"Fuck yea…"

"Who owns your orgasms, sweet boy?"

"Y-you... *fffuck*, Ren, they're all yours. Only..." His words cut off into a groan when he starts coming, spraying me down with warm splatters.

Our breathing is labored, echoing off the walls. I clutch him to me, kissing him hard and swallowing his whimpers. And as soon as he's finished, he falls forward, licking it all up. Messily lapping at my chest, sucking and biting my nipples while he eats his own cum off my body, grabbing me by the jaw and feeding it into my mouth from his tongue.

"You're so dirty," I breathe, biting him, coiling around him like a vine. "So sexy, filthy, fucking *perfect*..."

"Yea?" he gasps, hands running all over my body. "You love me?"

"I love you so hard, Lexington. You're *everything* to me..."

"I... I love... you too," he stammers, and my movements slow. "I *really* fucking love you, Warren."

Foreheads resting together, chests fluttering, I'm splitting down the middle. "Don't toy with me..."

He huffs a breathy chuckle, fingers sliding into my wet hair. "But you're my toy."

"Shut up. Don't change the subject."

He laughs even harder. "You've stolen all of my virginities, Warren..." he hums. "I think you know that I'm yours, and I think I believe that you'll be mine..."

"I already *am*." I crumble into him. "I've been yours the whole time, baby. I've *always* been yours, there's no one else I could ever even—"

He kisses me to shut me up. "Shh... I get it. But I'm in love with you, regardless. No matter what happens, Ren, I don't think I'll ever stop."

"I'll be good for you, baby," I whimper, pressure building up behind my eyes. "I *promise*, I'll be exactly what you need. I'm done fucking up with you, Lexington. Let me be yours... Please?"

He nods, touching his lips to mine. "No one's ever belonged to anyone harder than you belong to me."

I'm fucking shaking, down to my rotten soul. That this incredible man, this smart, sweet, angel of fucking perfection could actually want me, *love* me, is like the biggest wave of bliss I've ever felt.

Stronger than any meaningless sex could give. Better than any burn.

Lexington Deon is *finally* mine.

He's the balm to smooth my every scar.

"Alright, you two, let's—" Rook's voice cuts out while we slowly tear our enamored gazes off of one another, peeking up at him from the floor. "Oh, balls. You're in love, aren't you?"

CHAPTER TWENTY-FOUR

Luthor

Weeks later…

"SAY IT."

"No."

"Come on…"

"Uh-uh."

"*Please*, say it?"

I roll my eyes. "If you don't shut up, I'm never kissing you again."

Ren pouts almost aggressively. It's really hard not laughing at how dumb and adorable his face looks.

"Way to go straight for the jugular." He whips his shirt over his head, stepping out of his pants while I do the same. "You really think you could just *stop* kissing me?"

I shrug. "Might not be that tough…" The smirk on my lips is obviously teasing, but Ren is gawking at me, horrified. "Anything to get you to stop badgering me."

"Oh, darling…" He shakes his head, doing that *tsk tsk* thing. "*Badger* is my middle name."

I cackle out loud. "Really? Your name is Warren *Badger* Xavier??"

He nods, fully serious. "Mhm. Yep. My parents were big fans of anything in the weasel family."

The chuckles are just pouring out of me at this point, and he's grinning like it's giving him life.

"Is it weird that I don't know your middle name?" I ask him once I pull myself together. "You know mine…"

"Yea, because I badgered that out of you too." He grins triumphantly. "Admit it. I can wear you down, Lexington *Shiloh* Deon."

Frowning, I press the button for my shower, stepping under the freezing water. "It's such a weird name." Ren chuckles, shivering while he waits for his to warm up. "My parents were obviously huge stoners. Plus, my initials are LSD. Red flag, right there."

"Better than being named after your piece of shit father," he sighs, finally dunking his head under.

My mind instantly clicks over all of our past conversations. "Kenneth? Warren *Kenneth* Xavier… That's cute."

His lips twitch, but he scowls it away quick. "Nope. Kenneth was a fuckhead. I'll stick with Badger, thank you very much."

Cool water runs over me while I laugh scoffingly. "It certainly fits…"

He goes quiet for a moment while we wash up side by side. I know he's watching me. I mean, he *always* is. And the thing is, my eyes can't help sneaking back over to him either.

I guess he's right. I've never been able to resist him. Whether it's looking at him, talking to him, touching, kissing, even fucking him… Whatever it is, I just can't *not* do it. My feeble attempts at staying away were just that. Wishful thinking.

And now, the tables have turned, and I'm just as obsessed as he's been since the moment I bumped into him in the hall all those years ago. Frustrating because he totally knows it, too. He's well aware that I love him detrimentally, and that I think I'd like to be with him for as long as we can make it happen…

And yet, I'm *still* hesitating to say the words he wants to hear… Give him that label he keeps pestering me for.

Jeez, you'd think I *was the one allergic to monogamy.*

"You have to say it eventually, Shiloh." Ren grins. I give him the side-eye. "Otherwise, what we're doing won't make any sense. And you're way too logical to let that slide."

"Is that right?"

"Mhm."

Sighing stubbornly at his assessment of me, I hold my hand out for the soap bar.

Last week, he did some tattoos for Jasper and Hancock in exchange for a bunch of toiletries. I was nervous about it at first, being that he used to get busy with both of them, *often*. Then there was that whole *almost fucking* thing with Jasper…

But he says nothing like that has happened since, and the kicker is, I actually believe him. Plus, from what I understand, Jasper and Hancock have something going on. Not that any of us have witnessed it firsthand, but you can sense the tension when they're close.

Doesn't surprise me. This prison makes more love connections than e-fuckin-Harmony.

Ren steps forward with the soap. But when I go to take it, he yanks it back. "Tell you what, I'll make you a deal."

I purse my lips to cover up my grin. "Listening…"

"If you say it… even just once, only to *me*… I'll give you my last can of Mountain Dew."

My eyes widen with excitement. "You still have one??"

"I was saving it for our anniversary," he sneers. "But apparently, we'll never have one of those because you won't even call me your damn *boyfriend*."

Warmth sweeps through me, and I start to fidget. I'll be honest, just the thought of a can of Mountain Dew has my mouth watering almost as much as his wet, naked body.

I shouldn't be opposed to giving him what he wants. After all, if he's not my boyfriend, then what the hell is he?

But at this point, teasing him about it is much more fun. He's been playing games with me for years. *It's only fair I get my licks in too, right?*

I'm weighing my options as Kang trots over, snatching the bar of soap from Ren's hand.

"Mind if I use this?" he asks, though he's already wandering off with it, running it over his chest as he ducks under his shower.

"Hmm… I see how it is." Ren squints at him. "You're still my friend when I have something you want."

"It's a concept you're familiar with." Kang fakes a smile.

Gulp. Oh boy.

Kang's been distant lately, but definitely with Ren more than me. He won't tell me what's wrong, but he's a lot quieter than usual, and when he does talk to Ren, there's this underlying simmer of irritation I just can't pin down.

"Fine, you can use my soap," Ren mutters. "But we need it too, so we'll all have to get under the same shower head and wash each other." He stomps up to Kang, pushing into his space.

"Dude, back off," Kang growls.

"Why? You don't like playing with me anymore?" Ren pouts, then peers over his shoulder at me. "Come on, Lex. We're showering with Byron today. Prison-style."

Ren starts trying to touch Kang while Kang jerks away from him.

I pad over quickly. "Ren, just let him use the damn soap."

"I *am*." Ren grabs my hand, pulling me in closer. "Go ahead, Byron. Wash Lex's balls for him. That's what you want, right?"

"You're such a dick," Kang huffs, shoving him back. "Luthor, get your boyfriend under control..."

"He's *not* my boyfriend," I mumble.

"Yea, see? He's single and ready to mingle," Ren hisses, leaning closer to Kang once more. "Make your move, sweetheart."

"I'm gonna kick you in the dick if you don't get the hell out of my face."

Kang and Ren are shoving each other back and forth, so I decide to step out of the way, lest *I* accidentally get kicked in the dick myself.

"Step off, bitch!"

"Not until you admit that you're *jealous*."

I rub my eyes in annoyance. *Fucking children, I swear to God. And they're both older than me!*

"I'm *not*," Kang seethes. "Here, take your fucking soap."

He whips the bar of soap at Ren, and it bounces off his arm, falling onto the floor and sliding a few feet. We all stop and stare at it.

Uh oh...

He dropped the soap.

"Go pick it up," Ren rumbles.

"No way," Kang scoffs. "You do it. You're the one who loves bending over... Especially in the showers."

"Really? Slut-shaming, from *you*, of all people??" Ren gripes. "You were pretty desperate for both of our dicks that time in my cell."

I'm about to just go pick it up myself because they're being such immature jackasses. But suddenly, a tall form emerges from around the corner, heading straight for the soap.

He has a towel around his waist, jet black hair, wet and hanging in his eyes. I can't help the way I'm gawking, because I've never seen this person before in my life.

But he's in here, so... he must be a new inmate?

They haven't taken in a new inmate since Dash.

The guy bends to pick up the soap, then saunters directly up to us. He's very tall, with at least three inches on Ren, who's the tallest of the three of us. His pale complexion is a stark contrast to his dark hair, like a *Snow White* kind of vibe. More than anything, I'm fixated on him even having hair in the first place.

New inmates always have their heads shaved...

Peering down, his eyes travel over each of us individually. They're a very interesting shade. At first glance, they just look blue. But upon further inspection, they're actually a deep purple, almost like violet. *I've never seen eyes that color before...*

Remembering myself, I quickly cover my junk with my hands, because it seems weird to be standing here naked while this stranger assesses us with his oddly colored eyes.

From me to Ren, they jump, but when they land on Kang, they kind of stick there for a few generous seconds. Then he holds out his hand, offering Kang the bar of soap.

"I believe this is yours," the guy says, voice deep and soft, with a British accent that gives it some casual elegance.

Kang simply blinks up at him, mouth hanging open. Dumbfounded. Speechless.

But as usual, Ren is none of those things.

"Who the hell are you?" he snaps at the guy.

The dude doesn't answer him. He doesn't even spare Ren a glance, just keeps staring at Kang, head slanted curiously.

"Are you alright?" He speaks to Kang only again, and this time, Kang looks like he might respond.

But Ren grabs Kang by the shoulders and hustles him away. "He's fine. Don't worry about him." Ren snatches the soap out of the guy's hand. "I asked you a question, asshole. Who *the hell* are you?"

British dude's eyes finally slide off of Kang, shifting to Ren. His facial expression doesn't change much, but it seems obvious that he's not that interested in getting to know Ren, which is surprising, to say the least.

Everyone's always interested in Ren, even when he's acting like a dick.

"My name is Trevel," the guy finally answers, blithely. "And who, might I ask, are you?"

Ren ignores his question, glaring at him. "You new here or something? Why have I never seen you before?"

The guy—*Trevel*—glances at Kang once more, and I witness Kang swallow.

My brow arches.

"Well, if you've never seen me before, it would only make sense that I'm *new*... yes?" He blinks at Ren.

Ren is not amused. "Watch the attitude, Mary Poppins, or I'll slap the shit out of—"

"*Hi*, I'm Luthor," I interrupt Ren's threat before things escalate. "Don't mind Ren. He's a little overprotective."

Trevel offers me a kind smile, though his attention is still mostly on Kang, who isn't saying a damn word, *or* moving, for that matter.

"This is Kang," I offer the introduction for my friend on mute.

"Hello..." Trevel says quietly.

"Hi..." A single word finally crawls out of Kang's throat. It's noticeably hoarse.

Okay, what is up with these two?? This Trevel guy is staring harder than Ren when we first met. And apparently the cat's got Kang's tongue. Sheesh...

Ren inserts himself in front of us. "Okay, Trevor. Run along back to your beanstalk. We need to get dressed."

"It's *Trevel*," he corrects, eyes gliding over us again, as if Ren's words reminded him that we're all naked.

"Don't care," Ren grunts, spinning Kang around and shoving him toward his clothes. "This is *our* side of the showers. Do yourself a favor and remember that for next time. Come here, baby," he says to me, wrapping his arms around my body, using his to shield my nakedness from view of the stranger. "Let's get you a towel, hm? I don't want this weirdo looking at you anymore."

"You're being so rude," I whisper, though I'll admit, I feel a lot more comfortable with him draped around me like a blanket.

"I know, I'm awful." Ren kisses my neck, giving me a little tap on the ass.

I'm scowling, but that possessiveness, the way he coddles me like a bodyguard protecting a prince... It flips my stomach and casts a chill over my flesh.

I used to think I hated it, but as it turns out... I guess I like the way he fawns over me.

Just a little, okay? I don't need him feeding me grapes and fanning me with giant leaves or anything.

Although...

Ren grabs us towels, his watchful glare darting over to Trevel once more.

Trevel backs away, fiddling with the towel around his waist. "Maybe I'll see you around…"

He doesn't specify who he's talking to, but if I were to place a bet, I'd say it's our dear friend Byron Kang, the bullseye his violet gaze lingers on until he's out of sight.

As soon as he's gone, I hear Kang letting out a long breath, like he'd been holding it in.

"Wow… new inmate," I sigh, shaking my head. "It's been a while."

"I don't like him," Ren grunts, and I chuckle.

"Yea, I think we got that."

Joy shouts into the room that it's time to go, and we hustle back into our clothes.

"I got a weird vibe from him," Ren says. "He's like the Grim Reaper."

"What's with his eyes…?" Kang finally mumbles an actual sentence, fingers racing over his scalp.

I smirk at him. "You mean the way they were melting over you like Velveeta?"

He shoots me a withering glare. "Shut up. You have no idea what you're talking about."

Laughing softly, I hold my hands up in defense. "Alright, simmer down."

Kang huffs, shaking his head. "Whatever. I'm still pissed at you." He peers at Ren.

"Yea, yea. You'll be begging me to protect you next time Sid Vicious's creepy cousin comes skulking around." He pokes Kang in the side, and he flinches, smacking Ren's hand away. "We're *friends*, Byron. No matter what. Don't forget that."

Kang peeks at him. And something softens in his features. I can tell he doesn't want to be mad at Ren. But he's stubborn, and whatever his beef is, he seems to be hanging onto it pretty tight.

"I haven't forgotten shit," he sighs, then storms out of the room.

My gaze follows him out and I sigh tiredly, slipping my fingers through Ren's as we slowly shuffle after him. In the hall, I notice Trevel toward the front of the pack, walking with his head down.

"Jamesy," I whisper to Joy, and she glances at me. "What's up with the new guy? I didn't even know anyone new had come in…"

Her eyes follow Trevel for a moment, the visible unease on her face directly contradicting her typically aloof gaze. "Yea, 102. He came in rather… abruptly."

"What does that mean?" Ren asks.

"Just be careful around him," she grumbles. "I think there's more to his arrival than meets the eye."

Joy's ominous words cause a stiffening of my spine. I peek at Ren, and we share a look before slowly glancing back to Trevel. Kang, who's marching a few feet ahead of us, seems to be looking at Trevel too...

But with a little more curiosity, and a little less concern than the rest of us.

"So I come back from my run, and I open the door to find Kemper chasing Sobaka around the house. Turns out, the damn mutt had one of my jocks in his mouth and was playing with it like a toy."

A cackle flies from my lips while Dash laughs in my ear. "Oh God, please tell me it wasn't dirty."

"Of course it was!" He chuckles. "He picked it up off the bedroom floor, giving Kemper even more ammunition to bitch at me about leaving my clothes everywhere."

"The dog was sniffing your dirty panties??" Ren leans in closer, basically resting his head against mine so we can both listen at the same time.

My eyes flick across the table, where Darcey and Kang are both giving us disturbed looks. I can't help but laugh harder at their faces.

"Excuse you, I keep my shit fresh," Dash chirps. "You'd be lucky to bury your face in my used jockstrap."

"Sounds like a fun Tuesday afternoon," Ren teases, and I elbow him.

Dash sighs out his laughter. "Anyway, Kemper clearly isn't familiar with how dogs operate. I was like, 'The more you chase him, the more he thinks it's a game.'"

"We're pretty familiar with that concept," Ren says, winking at me.

"Poor Kemper." I giggle. "Dealing with you *and* Dog? The dude deserves a spa weekend or something. Plus, you've got him remodeling your house to your exact bougie specifications, like a spoiled, purple-haired princess."

I smirk while Dash chokes in my ear. "Trust me, he's very well compensated."

"You two would make great porn," Ren speaks into the phone.

"Hell yea," I add. "Big hulking Kemper, and Dash in his hot pink jock."

I chuckle, but Ren aims a fiery glare at me. Swallowing hard, I bite my lip, a flush rising into my cheeks. I already know what he's thinking. I can read it in his sky-blue eyes.

He's still jealous about Dash and me making out.

But so far, he's kept his promise. He hasn't said anything to Dash about it. Honestly, I couldn't handle making things weird between me and Dash. He's my best friend in the whole world, and I love hearing him sound so happy, considering how purely miserable he was the last time I saw him.

These weekly phone calls have become a highlight, for all of us. Even Darcey started coming upstairs to talk to Dash, and it's been fun getting to know him a little better too. Although, Kang still isn't happy about it.

Truth be told, Kang doesn't seem happy about *anything* lately.

"Alright, you filthy perverts," Dash sighs. "I gotta get going. I'm almost out of pesos for this payphone. And I promised Kemper I'd stop at the fruit stand to get him some mangos. He's been making these smoothies every morning, they're fucking bomb."

"I love that your life is all sex, fast cars, and tropical fruit," I say with a grin, and he giggles a raspy thing in my ear.

"I miss you guys…" he hums, sounding suddenly a little less joyous. "Like, *so* much. More than words."

"Uh oh…" Ren grumbles.

But it's too late. I'm off.

"Sayin' I *loveee youuu* is not the words I want to hear from you…" I sing, chuckling at the wide grin on Darcey's face.

"Oh, here we go," Dash chirps, joining in. "It's not that I *want you* not to say, but *if you only knew…*"

Ren rolls his eyes. "How easy it would be to show me *how you feel!*"

And now we're all singing it. "*More than words…* is all you have to do to make it real…"

Even Darcey is swaying across the table. "Then you wouldn't have to say…"

Ren and I are motioning for Kang to join in, and he's scowling, obviously trying hard not to break. But when we start pouting, he concedes. Maybe just mouthing along, but still. It's awesome.

"That you *love me…* 'Cause I'd all-reaaadyy knowww!"

"Yeaaa!" Dash cheers.

I'm leaning into Ren's side, laughing hysterically. Darcey is clapping.

Even Kang is finally breaking a smile.

"Prison sing-along!" I cackle.

Ren's hand grips my thigh under the table as he kisses my neck. "You're fucking adorable."

I'm blushing as I exhale slowly. "Okay, now we really have to go. Everyone in the caf is staring at us like we're mental. Definitely drawing attention."

Kang's face shifts subtly over his shoulder to where the new guy is sitting by himself.

Trevel is already looking this way, and when their eyes meet, Kang whips his face back, fiddling with his fingers on the table.

I still don't know how to feel about this *Trevel Fenwick* character… Or the fact that he and Kang seem to *really* love staring at each other.

It's been a few weeks since we met Trevel in the showers, and because Ren insists there's something *off* about him, we don't interact with the mysterious, strikingly attractive newbie. But according to Darcey, his boyfriend, Lem—also known as Dr. Love, the world-renowned psychiatrist who's apparently become Alabaster Pen's resident shrink—used to treat Trevel as a patient. And, I guess Dr. Love is also responsible for Trevel coming here, and he might be harboring some bad blood over the matter.

The whole situation is odd. I've never actually met Dr. Love—I've seen him in the halls once or twice—but it's understood that he and Manuel Blanco are pals, which is a little shady. I guess Trevel was something of a gift, or a bargaining chip, to allow Dr. Love to stay onboard here now that he's fucking The Carver. *And rather unapologetically, I might add.*

I don't know what any of it means, but I *do* know that if Dr. Love is the reason Trevel is here, then I would assume Trevel is probably not a fan of the gorgeous doctor, and by extension, his boyfriend. *Felix*. And Felix is one of us now, despite how much Kang protests.

It's all becoming very Bloods versus Crips, the Capulets and the Montagues… Team Edward versus Team Jacob.

Oh God… Ren and his Twilight. He's gotten under my skin.

When we saw Kang talking to Trevel yesterday at dinner, it made us a bit nervous. Kang claims there's nothing going on between them, that they've exchanged very few words, and we're overreacting. At the same time, it's clear that he's upset about us welcoming Darcey into our group, which could be part of the reason he's been drifting.

As fun as it is to sit here and have sing-alongs like a bunch of goofballs around a campfire, at the end of the day, we're still in *prison*. And when you're locked up all day, every day, with nothing but time to sit and stew, it can be tough to let go of grudges.

With someone like Kang, no relationship to preoccupy his mind and body… I don't foresee him forgetting what Darcey did to his friend anytime soon.

He's tolerating him for us, which has gotta stand for something. Still, I can feel the rifts developing just beneath the shore.

Once we've hung up with Dash, I look around the room for Joy. She's usually pretty prompt in getting her phone back when we're done. But right now, she's in the back of the room with Velle, having a conversation that looks serious from where I'm sitting.

Attempting to take my mind off of all the drama, I turn to Felix. "So, how are things going with your man?"

Felix's lips slope into a smile that answers my question without words. "It's awesome. He's… *perfect*," he sighs dreamily, and I grin.

"That's cool. I'm happy for you guys," I tell him, and he bites his lip.

Kang scoffs, loudly, and Felix peeks at him, his smile slipping.

Ignoring Kang, I keep talking. "Does he see any other patients down there in the East? Or is it just you?"

"So far, it's just me," Felix replies. "But he thinks now that Trevel is here, the Warden might want him to start seeing him again…"

Felix's gray eyes take on a fraught darkness behind his black-framed glasses, troubled gaze setting on the tray of picked-apart food before him.

"Have they ever fucked?" Ren blurts the question with his standard lack of conversational finesse. I elbow him in the ribs, and he grumbles, "Damn, babe! I'm gonna bruise if you keep doing that."

"Rein it in a little," I hiss at him, then turn back to Felix. "Sorry. He has no filter."

Felix chuckles. "It's okay. No, they haven't fucked." I can't help noticing how Kang suddenly seems invested in the conversation he wanted nothing to do with a moment ago. "Lem was always straight before… before we met."

Felix's mouth twitches, and he tugs his lower lip with his teeth again. I'm telling you, this dude is the cuddliest, most precious sociopathic murderer ever. You just want to pinch his cheeks. Maybe from afar… *in case he decides to bite your fingers off.*

"See? I love that," Ren hums. "You're out here doing the Lord's work. Turning hot dudes to the dark side. Bless you, child."

Ren makes the holy cross motion, but wraps it up with a wrist-flick, and Felix laughs.

"If they've never hooked up, then why do you care if your man starts treating him again?" Kang butts in with a tone both curious and accusatory.

Felix's face lights up, clearly excited that Kang is actually talking to him for once without being insulting or threatening. "I don't know if I *care*, necessarily…"

"You do," Kang grunts. "I saw it on your face when Ren asked the question. It worries you…"

Felix swallows visibly. "Maybe a little…"

"What's wrong? You don't trust your *perfect* Doctor Daddy?" Kang sneers.

Felix's eyes narrow, his features sharpening drastically. In a blink, he looks much more *Carver* than cuddly, and it's giving me chills. Ren notices and rubs the goosebumps on my arm.

"Oh, I trust Lem emphatically," Felix murmurs. "It's Trevel Fenwick I don't trust."

Kang stares at Darcey for a moment, before lifting a shoulder like he doesn't care either way, though I think it's obvious he does. But I just don't know *why*.

"Is that dude even gay?" Ren chirps, pulling at a thread on my t-shirt sleeve while his eyes dart across the room briefly, toward Trevel. "When it comes to Brits, I seriously can't tell."

"I think he's Pan," Felix mumbles.

"He is," Kang says definitively. "He's Pansexual."

Ren squints at him. "How do *you* know?"

"He told me." Kang gives him a casually snarky look.

"So, let me get this straight." Ren leans in. "Out of the *limited words* you claim to have exchanged with that string-bean, at least two of them were him informing you of his sexual orientation?"

Kang blinks at him, then sits back, folding his arms over his chest. "It would appear so."

The two of them are having a staring contest, and I'm starting to feel unsettled again.

"Please tell me you don't actually like this guy," Ren scoffs.

"So what if I did?" Kang's head cocks. "Would that be a *problem* for you?"

"You've gotta be fucking kidding me…" Ren puffs, shaking his head.

"Lighten up, *Dad*," Kang grunts. "I'm not fucking the dude or anything. I just don't see why talking to him is such a big deal."

"He's not one of us, Byron," Ren hisses.

"You know who *was* one of us??" Kang snaps. "O'Malley. But this preppy little monster killed him. And now you guys are hanging out with him! Welcoming him into our group with open fucking arms… Like he just swooped in to take O'Malley's place!"

Kang is simmering, vibrating in a way that I can feel from across the table. Darcey is just sitting quietly, calm gaze framed by his glasses. Entirely unaffected by the drama he's caused.

I get where Kang is coming from. Loyalty is very important, to all of us. But I also happen to like Darcey. I know it's fucked-up, and we should be supporting our friend, who's been a big part of our lives for *years* now.

But Felix Darcey has no one else. Without us, he just sits alone down in the East Wing with his doctor boyfriend. He hasn't said it outright, but I know he appreciates us befriending him. I can't see taking that away just to honor the memory of a guy I'm certain wouldn't have batted an eye if we died.

Tension hangs over our table like a storm cloud as Joy finally stalks over to get her phone.

Goddamnit… We were so busy arguing, I didn't even think of using it! I could've been Googling things or playing Candy Crush instead of listening to all this Mob Wives bullshit.

"Everything good?" Joy asks us on a breath, stuffing her phone away.

"Yup," Ren grunts.

"Fan-fuckin-tastic," Kang mumbles.

Joy's eyes scan all of our faces, most likely picking up on the disgruntled mood. She stares at Kang for a few extra seconds before placing her hands flat on the table, leaning in. "You wanna know what we haven't done in a while?"

We all gaze up at her, and she lets loose a small grin.

Oh… shit. Rec time?!

It's been so long!

We haven't been down there since the day Dash beat the crap out of Ren. Kang's gone with Joy alone a few times to spar, but the rest of us haven't been allowed, especially with the lockdown. But I guess timeout is officially over.

Yeaaa! Thug life!

"For real??" Ren gasps.

"Hell yea." She straightens. "We'll go now. The whole bunch of you. Killer bee, you wanna join us for some mediocre recreational activity in a moldy basement?"

Felix peeks at me and Ren, then looks back to Joy, a tiny smile forming as he nods gleefully.

Kang does another one of his blatant scoffs, to which Joy cocks her head. "Don't be salty, gwiyeoun sonyeon. It's bad for your health." She winks at Felix.

"*Fine*," Kang huffs, standing up. "I can coexist…"

I show him an appreciative smile. "Thanks, fam. It means a lot."

"So long as you guys can do the same." He smirks, hopping over his seat and sauntering off…

In the direction of Trevel Fenwick's table.

"Is he fucking serious??" Ren snaps, shooting up out of his seat.

"Oh God…" I mumble, watching Kang strut right up to Trevel.

He's talking to him for a moment, a sly grin on his face as he glances over at us, gesturing in our direction. Trevel is just blinking up at him, studiously observing his face. Then he looks at us.

Ren is seething. My mouth is hanging open.

Felix waves.

"What the hell are you doing?!" Ren whispers-scolds him.

Felix shrugs. "Might as well play nice, right?"

"Are you sure you're a serial killer?" I arch a brow.

"Oh, yea. Big time." He pulls a charming grin, glancing at Trevel once more. "The best way to get people to drop their guard is to act like you're dropping yours."

Well, this is awkward.

We're down in the basement rec room, for the first time in like six months. Sure, it smells like mildew and rusty, old metal, and there are cobwebs everywhere. But still. We *should* be having fun, because at least it's a change of goddamn scenery.

And yet all I can focus on is the lurker in our midst.

You know how there are some people you click with instantly? You meet them one time—hell, even just talk to them online—and suddenly you're BFFs?

Yea, Trevel isn't one of those guys.

Ren was totally right to be skeptical when we met him in the showers. Trevel just brings this aura with him, like when you can feel a ghost in the room. He's too quiet, and he stares too hard, and he's just… fucking creepy.

I mean, the guy *is* good-looking. He's *extremely* attractive, in this slim, sharply-angled, severe European kind of way. He has that sickly-chic appearance, so you can't tell whether he's famous, or homeless. Like, he could be strutting down a catwalk in Versace, or overdosing in an alleyway with a needle in his arm.

But the fact that he's hot and Ren hasn't even *remarked* about it? Now, *that's* gotta tell you something right there. *The red flags are billowing.*

I have no misconceptions about the man I love. I know he's been trying real hard to kick his sex addiction, and quite frankly, he's killing it. But just because he's finally trying out monogamy for a change, doesn't mean he's no longer a highly flirtatious, raging nympho.

If a man is attractive, Ren has something to say about it. But the only even slightly positive thing I've heard him call Trevel is *Harry Potter's drug dealer.*

This field trip could have been a good opportunity to get to know the guy, but it isn't really working. I'm too busy watching him, wondering what the hell his deal is. And I'm not the only one. Joy also seems unsure of how to act around Trevel. Felix is just playing his timid monster game, hiding behind his glasses and overall inconspicuous appearance. Ren is actively giving off *Big Bitch Energy.*

And Kang is smitten.

Okay, maybe not *smitten.* It's not like the two are actively flirting or anything. But they've been chatting here and there, and the rest of the time is spent casting one another gazes that are suspiciously seductive, based on how *often* they happen.

Mostly, they seem like pals. That *click* we're not feeling with Trevel, Kang apparently is, like they're a pair of antisocial buddies, bonding over how much they dislike everything.

And unfortunately, once *our* friend, the buffer, runs off with Joy to begin their sparring, Ren, Darcey, and I are left standing around with the human version of an aloof Jack Skellington, making humdrum chitchat.

"Fuck it." Ren finally says when the awkward silence gets to be too much. "I'm playing, if anyone wants in."

He whips off his shirt and sashays over to grab the basketball, dribbling and darting up the court. My gaze lingers on my man for a minute, the way his muscles look while he's jogging and shooting... Jumpsuit pants sagging enough to show off the top of that perfect peach of a butt in his boxers.

God, he's fucking fine. I can't believe I get to be with that.

I'm wiping away drool, wondering if there's any chance of sneaking off into a dark corner somewhere so I can get inside that sweet booty, when a smooth voice with a British accent croons just behind me.

"Is he your boyfriend?"

Slanting my face to peek up at Trevel, I note the way his eyes are following Ren. He's already seen all of us naked, so I guess there isn't much surprise anymore. Still, it seems like he's actually noticing how drop-dead beautiful Ren is a little easier now that he's not speaking.

I have no idea what possesses me to say this. I've been adamantly denying it for months. But when this hot, ghoulish guy is looking at *my* Ren, asking me if he's my boyfriend, the only word my mouth is able to produce is...

"Yea."

Trevel nods. "How long have you all been an item?"

"Five years," I mumble. Again, easier than breathing.

"Wow." His lips twitch. "And he hasn't driven you mad yet?"

I chuckle. "Oh, every day."

He makes this tiny humming sound that I think is supposed to be a laugh, his eyes moving away from Ren, back to their host. *Kang.* He watches Kang and Joy kicking and punching at one another, blocking, advancing, like a graceful dance.

"What about him...?" Trevel's voice grows much softer. "It's *Byron*... right?"

I side-eye him, warding off my sly smirk. *Smooth, bro. We all know you know his name.*

"Mhm," I rumble.

His face slopes to look at me, violet eyes shining with intensity. "Is he... seeing anyone?"

Standing taller, I puff my chest as much as possible so it doesn't feel like he's towering over me. "Look, man... Byron is one of my best friends in the entire world. So I'm only gonna say this once... mess with him, and you'll answer to us. *Got it?*"

He blinks, sucking on his bottom lip for a moment. "That's not what I asked you."

My teeth grind. "He's not seeing anyone. He's straight... sort of." I pause and shake my head. *Shut up, idiot! Don't tell him anything.* "Whatever, the point is that he doesn't need anyone messing with him. So just tread lightly."

"I'm sure he can look after himself." Trevel tilts his head. "And from what I understand, he's not been thrilled with your partner lately." My gaze narrows. "They're usually quite *close*, isn't that right? He told me they've had bunches of sex... Was that before or after your *five-year* relationship started?"

Clenching my hands into fists, muscles stiffen all over my body, an instant fury burning so strong it's seeping from my pores.

Oh, I do not like this guy. Not one bit.

What a damn prick!

And why the hell has Kang been telling him all of this shit?? He said he barely spoke to the dude! Sounds like they've been staying up late, braiding each other's hair and swapping sex stories.

Trevel's mouth lifts at the corner, and *God*, I really want to bitch-smack that little know-it-all smirk right off.

Turning, I search for Darcey, needing a backup, *stat*. But I find him at the entrance to the rec room, greeting a large, strapping black man with immaculate dreads.

Oh, shit. Dr. Love is here.

"Baby, I thought we were gonna play." Strong arms wrap around me from behind, a warm, muscular body pressing into my back.

Ren drapes kisses along my nape while I hold his hands around my waist, spinning to face him.

"Not now. We've got a problem..." I tilt my head, nodding toward the doorway.

Ren is still evil-glaring at Trevel, but when he picks up on what I'm trying to show him, his face drops. "Oh, damn. That's—"

"Dr. Lemuel Love," Trevel growls, immediately storming over.

"I think this room is cursed," I grumble, taking Ren's hand and dragging him with me.

I have no idea what kind of drama is about to go down, but my stomach is all bunched up with nerves. Ren and I stagger up to Felix and Dr. Love, right behind Trevel, expecting to have to pull him off the good doctor.

"Holy mother of *God*, he's fine," Ren whispers by my side, and I want to scold him, but I'm too busy admiring the warm and fuzzies that come from watching this unlikely pair together.

Felix and Dr. Love look so different in *so* many ways. And knowing that Felix Darcey is a *serial killer* and Lemuel Love is a clinical psychiatrist only adds to list of blatant contrasts you'd think would make them the last two people in the world to be romantically involved.

But then there's the way they're looking at each other…

Felix is showing Dr. Love an eager grin, eyes all sparkly as he walks his fingers up the man's chest, subtly playing with one of his dreads. And Dr. Love's mouth is pleasantly curved, a possessive hand resting on Felix's waist.

They're lost in their own little bubble as Dr. Love whispers something to Felix that has him blushing and biting his lip. It's mesmerizing to witness, and I can't help wondering if this is how Ren and I look to outsiders who see us together.

The molecules dissolve, however, when Dr. Love looks up to see Trevel standing there with his arms folded over his chest. You'd expect some kind of visible reaction from the doctor, but no. The dude just stares, robotically blinking a few times at his former patient.

Jeez, he's more of a rock than Joy.

"Hello, Doctor," Trevel says quietly, his entire mood shifting to a palpable blaze of carefully compacted disdain.

"Trevel," Dr. Love rumbles, *zero* emotion in his tone.

And then they both go silent, just staring.

These two used to have conversations?? I can't picture it.

"Babe, this is Luthor and Ren," Felix chirps, tugging on Dr. Love's shirt. Either not picking up on the tension or just ignoring it as he motions to us. He leans into his side. "They're my friends."

Dr. Love peeks down at Felix for a moment, the fondness in his amber gaze returning, but only for the bespectacled little psychopath.

"Hi." I offer him a kind, if not strained, smile.

"So good to meet you, Dr. *Love*," Ren croons, fluttering his lashes while my eyes narrow at him. "That's a great suit. The color really brings out your eyes."

"Alright, take it easy," I mutter, and Ren winks at me.

Dr. Love's mouth twitches ever-so slightly. Blink and you'd miss it. "I've heard a lot about both of you."

Ren fawns while I smile at fondly Felix, who's practically bouncing, toying with Dr. Love's fingers as he whispers, "I have friends. No big deal."

"What are you doing here?" Trevel hisses, glaring at the doctor, who seems completely unfazed by his attitude.

"What are *you* doing here??" Ren snaps at Trevel. "I'd rather have him around than you." He aims another flirty grin at Dr. Love, nodding toward the court. "You play?"

"Actually, I do," Dr. Love replies stoically.

"Cool! We could play two on two," I gasp. "I call Dr. Love's team!"

"No way! It was my idea," Ren gripes.

I scowl at him. "No, it was *my* idea. And you're already good, you don't need him."

"If that's the rule, then we should just play couples," Ren huffs.

"I don't like sports…" Felix mumbles.

"Maybe another time," Dr. Love says, amusement etching his eyes. "I was actually here for…"

His voice trails as Joy and Kang wander over, sweaty and panting.

"What's up?" Joy addresses Dr. Love, more casually than I'd expect.

"We need to talk," he says, eyes shifting to Trevel once more. "Rook and Velle are on their way."

Right on cue, the clomping of combat boots alerts us to the arrival of two more large dudes, and in strolls Velle with Rook right behind him.

"Wow, gang's all here," Velle grumbles. But when his eyes land on Trevel, he frowns. "Where'd he come from?"

"This one invited him," Joy sighs, jutting her thumb in Kang's direction. "Don't ask."

Kang shifts, glancing at me and Ren for a moment before he inches away from us to stand closer to Trevel. And maybe I'm just being paranoid, but it feels like something is happening…

Like he's choosing this new, hostile presence over us.

Velle nods at Joy, flicking a quick glance at Dr. Love before stalking over to the corner of the room with Rook and Joy scampering after him. Dr. Love brushes his lips in Felix's hair then joins them, leaving the rest of us, the *prisoners*, to fidget in place wondering what the hell they're doing over there.

"What do you think they're talking about?" Ren whispers to me.

"I don't know…" My eyes linger on the group of them, the way they're huddled in a circle, talking about something that's clearly important and too confidential to be shared with us. "It's weird, right?"

Ren grabs Felix and drags him closer to us, peering briefly at Trevel before he whispers, "Do you know anything about this?"

Felix's lashes flutter, and he shakes his head.

"Is your man pulling the double-cross on The Ivory?" Ren cocks a brow.

Felix stares at us for a moment, then whispers, "I can't talk about it."

Ren and I share a look. "Okay, dude, you need to be really careful," I tell him quietly.

"Especially with this one around." Ren nods in Trevel's direction. "Something strange is going on… The Warden's been too quiet for too long."

"I'm sure Lem knows what he's doing…" Felix says, though his forehead lines and I can see that he isn't entirely confident in his words.

"Just watch your back," I advise, turning to Ren. "Did you know Kang told Trevel about you guys?" Ren's gaze narrows. "He's been fucking talking to him… A lot more than he's letting on."

Ren's jaw ticks, and he spins, stomping up to Kang. He grabs him by the arm and Kang whips around, shooting him an irritated look.

"May I speak with you for a moment, please?" Ren is seething, keeping his tone as calm as possible, but I can see it in his eyes, the blue flames of rage just beneath the surface.

"What is it?" Kang grunts, yanking his arm out of Ren's grasp.

"Getting awfully chummy with that prick, huh?" Ren snaps on an aggressive whisper.

"We've been over this," Kang grumbles. "It's none of your fucking concern. You don't own me. I can talk to whoever I want."

"Bro, we're just saying… Are you sure you can trust him?" I wedge in closer, taking on a calmer tactic than Ren's blunt-force approach.

Kang is visibly wound, muscles in his neck straining, fists balled at his sides. He leans in. "You two are un-*fuckin*-believable, you know that?"

"What the hell is your problem—" Ren starts barking, but I place a hand on his chest to shut him up.

"Byron… you're our friend. We're looking out for you, because that's what we do for each other." My eyes lock on his, trying to convey sincerity.

"Oh, really? Is that how it works?" He huffs. "Because it seems more like you only needed me to make each other jealous. It's the fucking *Luthor and Ren Show*, twenty-four-seven, three-sixty-fucking-five. You don't give a shit about me."

My heart is hammering in my chest, the pain of his words echoing in my brain as he gets even closer, stepping to Ren.

"You let Parker fucking *die* because you were too busy with your own narcissistic bullshit," he growls. "Where were you, Ren?? Off getting railed somewhere, obsessing about Luthor… "

Ren's eyes widen, brows zipping in visible pain and remorse as his shoulders slump.

"And you." Kang aims his wrathful glare at me. "How many cellmates have to disappear before you realize you're just as bad?! You can play innocent all you want, Luthor, but I *know* you. You're just as self-absorbed as he is."

My bottom lip trembles and I bite it.

"You two are so fucking toxic. *Both* of you. Egotistical, obsessive fucking junkies for this sick fucking game you involve us all in." He huffs an unamused laugh with a bite, shaking his head. "You deserve each other. And now you've got what you want. So don't try to pretend you care about anyone else… *Especially* not me. Because we all know it's a fucking lie."

I'm stunned into place, solid and trembling as Kang turns away from us. It feels like he just slammed his fist into my chest and ripped out my beating heart. My throat is so dry I can barely swallow, peering at Ren, watching him gnaw on his lower lip with glistening sadness in his blue eyes.

Bringing up Parker was a low blow. Seriously… What the fuck??

Kang marches back over to where Trevel is talking to Felix. I don't know what they're saying, but it doesn't appear unpleasant. In fact, Felix is smiling.

Kang takes Trevel by the arm, yanking him away. And I catch a pleased grin on Trevel's lips as they wander off together… *Close*. The closer he gets to Trevel, the further he gets from us, and it's wrenching painfully on my insides.

I can't believe he just said all that…

Does he really feel that way?

Am I a bad friend? Am I… selfish?

I still can't move, just staring as one of my best friends in the world confides in some *stranger*. My eyes shift to Darcey, only to find that his smile has evaporated, and he's glaring at Trevel with a calm so frightening, all the hairs stand up on the back of my neck.

This isn't right…

Trevel isn't just some weirdo, he's *bad* for Byron. I know he is.

He's here to stir the pot, and for whatever reason, Kang just doesn't see it.

Because he hates us.

We're toxic. According to him, we're both the problem….

Our relationship *is the problem...?*

Commotion snaps me out of my despondence, and I look up as Joy, Velle, Rook, and Dr. Love are stomping back over. Their walkies are going off like crazy, a bunch of voices blaring through at once.

Joy has hers in hand and she's barking into it. "Wait... hold on a second... *What* the fuck is happening??"

"Keep the goddamn lines clear!" Velle roars into his, twisting the nob on top. "Peters, what the fuck, man?? What's going on?"

Officer Peters comes through, garbled and frantic. "They're fucking *everywhere*... rushing the halls like they own the place..."

I hear Jasper shouting through Joy and Rook's walkies. "Back the fuck up, asshole! Who do you think you are?? *Velle!* Get the fuck up here now!"

"Peters... *Who??*" Velle snarls, eyes wide as he shares a look of severe unease with his partners.

"New guards..." Peters breathes. "A whole team of them. They say they're here on *his* orders..."

"Fuck..." Joy's face drops in horror as she switches off her walkie, cutting off the shouts of mayhem from just upstairs.

Velle grips his so tight, the plastic snaps in his fist when Officer Peters adds, "He brought them in... The Ivory."

CHAPTER TWENTY-FIVE

Luthor

When I was eight, my parents took me to watch the fireworks for the first time.

Fireworks have always been a family thing for us. Something we'd do together on all sorts of occasions. But that first time, on the Fourth of July, I remember feeling riddled with anxiety.

The crowds were too big and noisy, people everywhere. I was a stressed little kid, probably the first sign that social situations weren't exactly my *jam*.

Nonetheless, my parents assured me that once the show started, I'd calm down and have fun.

Yea, sure, Mom and Dad. There's no way the loud-as-fuck explosions in the sky will stress me out more.

Together, the three of us spread our blanket out on the sand and plopped down, surrounded by dozens, maybe hundreds of other families, there to enjoy the same thing. And I was understandably nervous, because I didn't know what to expect. I didn't like loud noises, or huge groups of people, and all I could focus on was the laughter of all the kids who were so much cooler than me. Less anxious than me… With their *friends*, sharing jokes, running around and being *free*.

All I felt was weighted to the ground with my fingers digging in to hold on for dear life.

But sure enough, on the first pop, everyone went silent. All butts were on the ground, gazes aimed at the sky, like a sudden blanket of calm had been draped over the half-mile stretch of beach.

It startled me, that first big *bang*. But when I saw the colored embers scattering through the air, I finally got it.

Wide eyes, mouth open to gust *ooh* and *aah*, I watched them light up the night, adrenaline melting into a hypnotized serenity. Some boomed, some fizzed, some sparkled, but they were all *loud*, *crazy*, and *beautiful*. Chaotic bursts of prismatic fire I just couldn't take my eyes off of.

That something so *dangerous* could become so exuberant; chemical reactions to thrill and dazzle.

Ever since then, I've loved watching fireworks over the ocean. Putting all of my racing thoughts on hold for the colorful explosions in the sky.

I try to channel it, when I'm feeling overwhelmed. When the anxiety is piling up, and too much is happening *too fast*... I close my eyes and imagine fireworks.

That's what I'm doing right now, with Ren's hand gripping mine, loud clomping footsteps coming from every direction as tense voices boom and metal doors slam. Leaning my body into his warmth, I let him guide my way while I focus on his energy.

My controlled chaos. My beautiful, scary flourish of flaming bright color.

"What the fuck is this?!"

I flinch at the roar of Velle's voice.

There are strangers *everywhere*. Filing through the halls between our row and the adjoining corridors. Big, dead-eyed dudes in uniform—*their* uniforms, which are distinctly different from those of Velle and his men.

I'm sure it's intentional.

"Yo, what the fuck is going on, man??" Peters huffs, rushing over with Jasper, their bugged eyes giving away extreme duress. "Where'd these pricks come from??"

Velle is death-glaring at the men storming his halls, but they're not paying him a lick of attention, and I can feel the rage coming off him in waves. I think he's seconds from Hulk-bursting out of his clothes.

"He didn't say anything to you?" Jasper asks him quietly, still eyeing the dudes who are wordlessly scurrying about.

"Is that a real question?" Velle hums, swallowing visibly. His eyes shift to Rook. "Get them back to their cells." Then he tells Joy, "Round up the team. We'll meet at the spot in twenty."

They both nod and everyone disperses. Joy, Peters, and Jasper go one way, Velle charges in another, and Rook stays with us, motioning for us to follow him to the row.

My pulse is pinging, my hand sweating where it's being comfortably strangled by Ren's fingers. I turn my head slightly, checking on Kang and his new bestie, Trevel, both of whom are watching the commotion with the same amount of perplexity as the rest of us. Kang's eyes meet mine for only a second before darting away fast. And my stomach falls even deeper.

When we left the rec room, Felix and Dr. Love headed back toward the East. *Honestly, they're probably safer down there than up here…*

Surrounded by whatever the hell this is.

"You," Rook growls at Trevel as he pushes open the door. "Hands on that wall. You move, I shoot you. Got it?"

Trevel doesn't respond. He just gives Kang a puzzled look while obeying Rook's orders, wandering over to the wall by the door and placing his palms flat on it. Rook brings us through, but we barely make it a step.

Three big guys clomp into the row. One goes to Kang, cuffing him fast and shoving him toward his cell. Another one grabs me, and the last grabs Ren. And they physically *pull* us apart.

"What the fuck?!" Rook barks.

"No, wait…" I gasp, clinging to Ren's hand as tightly as possible.

"Get off me, you fuck!" Ren hisses, fighting against the hold of the large man.

Rook gets up in the face of the guy who's practically dislocating my shoulder, hand falling to his Glock. "Let him go."

"Stand down, Officer Samuels," the guy rumbles.

Rook's face shifts in confusion. "How the fuck do you know my name?"

The guy's head simply cocks, a smug ghost of a smirk passing over his lips.

Everything is happening so fast, the sounds of inmates shouting from inside their cells ringing in my skull. Trevel is grabbed hard by the arms and shoved forcefully against the wall. A pained grunt flees his lips while he's cuffed aggressively behind his back, then yanked out of the row.

Despite Rook's barks of protest, the two guards holding me and Ren finally wrench us apart, cuffing us both behind our backs. And suddenly Ren is being dragged away in the direction we just came.

"Ow, Jesus… Not so rough, damn!" Ren grunts.

"Where are you taking him?? Where are they taking him?!" Panicking, I look to Rook, who has his walkie in hand. I think he's calling Joy.

Ren's eyes stay with mine as I tremble, being pulled in the opposite direction. *Away* from him. "Baby, listen to me… It'll be okay," he calls, feet skidding on the ground as the man drags him through the door. "I'll find you, no matter what, I promise!" His voice rises to a shout as he disappears out of sight. But I can still hear him yelling, "Lexington, I love you! Fuck you, you goddamn mouth breather! Let g—"

The shuffling cuts off when the door closes. I growl raggedly over my heart lodged painfully in my throat. "If they hurt him, I swear to God!"

Breathing heavily, I'm fighting against the man pulling me to my cell. He shoves me inside, slamming me up against the wall face-first, so hard my head knocks against the concrete.

Dazed, with my forehead throbbing, I peer into the hall. Rook's still out there, talking to Joy on the radio. His eyes are wide, but he's mouthing something to me. I think it's *stay calm*, or *just do what he says*, I really can't tell.

"Rook…" I cough. "Make sure Ren is alright. Don't let them… hurt him."

Sniffling, I force myself to keep it together as best I can, though I'm trembling head to toe. The dude who's been manhandling me is rifling through my shit, and I'm racked with sudden terror so insistent, my knees are shaking.

He's gonna find my computer. Oh God, oh fuck. I didn't hide it well enough.

I'm so fucking dead.

The more I watch him, though, the more it looks like he's just trashing the place, rather than actually confiscating anything. Still, he's making a goddamn mess, breaking what little I have in the first place. I guess eventually he gets bored, because he storms out of my cell, slamming the door behind him and marching off like a literal SS officer while Rook chases after him.

"Hey!" I yelp out into the hall. "I'm still fucking cuffed!" My voice joins the medley of hollers and wails from the other cells. "How the hell am I supposed to take a piss??"

"Yo, Luth??" Cooper says my name from the next cell.

"Yea," I sigh, fury and despair filling me like sand that weighs me until I'm on the floor.

"What the fuck is going on, bro?? Who are these fuckers?"

Manuel Blanco's new SWAT team, apparently.

"I dunno…" I whisper, resting my head against the bars.

Too much… This is too fucking much.

Kang hates me. Ren is gone… Who knows where the hell they're taking him, or if he'll be safe.

Manuel Blanco just pulled a power move. Brought in his own guys to completely undermine Velle.

A new regime has taken over Alabaster Pen. And from the looks of it, we've had it easy with Velle and his guards over the years.

They're the goddamn Powerpuff Girls compared to these new assholes.

"Fuck…" I squeeze my eyes shut while the screams echo off the walls.

I gotta get it done. No more fucking around…

But how am I supposed to work without my hands??

I need to figure out a way. I have to get Ren back…

My thoughts are spinning. Everything is cluttering up inside my skull, suffocating my every bit of logic. All I have left are emotions, and they're *awful.*

"Kang?!" I shout as loud as I can into the row. Even if he can hear me, I don't expect him to respond. "I'm sorry! I never meant to hurt you… You're so important to me, you gotta know that!"

Pressure throbs behind my eyes. I close them tight to will it away…

All of this uncertainty, this stifling unknown, is making it so I can't breathe.

Stay positive… You have to.

Velle, Joy and Rook will figure something out. They're good together. They make each other better.

Ren is alright… He has to be.

He's the only thing holding me together.

All these years, I've thought Ren made me weak; that he ruined me, tore me to pieces with his bare hands for his own amusement. *But that's not true…*

He makes me *strong*. If it weren't for him and all his issues, I'd still be that scared, lonely kid who used to cry himself to sleep missing his home, his bed, his *family*. He taught me how to survive this place, because he showed me that prison life can be more than just shuffling through one day to the next.

Ren made Alabaster Pen a place I actually *chose* to stay in…

Although right now I'm seriously regretting that brilliant fucking decision.

But honestly, it wouldn't have mattered. I could be offered a million more chances to leave, and I won't take them. Because *he's* here. And this is where we fell in love…

Toxic or not. Codependent, whatever…

It's always *us*, above all else. He's my *boyfriend*, and I love him.

We're staying together... Even if it means burning down everything else.

I feel like an idiot.

For every time I ever complained about how shitty things were here... For all the grumbling about the food, or the conditions, or the guards...

God, what a whiny bitch I was.

Things can *always* get worse. *That's the official slogan of Alabaster Penitentiary.*

Take your licks and like 'em, because you never know when the Warden will *poof!* Wave his magic wand of sadistic fuckery and rain a monsoon of new bullshit all over your worthless existence.

Sitting alone in the cafeteria used to be one of my least favorite things. But now it's taken on a whole new scope of misery.

The room is silent. *Yes*... it's actually *quiet* for once in Alabaster Pen, which has to be the most ominous experience of my life. I never thought I'd miss the shouting and raucous laughter of the idiots around me. But here I am, sitting quietly, staring at my plate of sludge, praying for one of Dirt's ground-shaking burps, or that high-pitched hyena laugh Simmons makes when he thinks something's really funny.

I miss the old days... Ren and Kang bickering about bullshit while Dash cackled and threw noodles at them. The time Ren tried telling us he blew Justin Trudeau—the Canadian Prime Minister—and Parker laughed so hard, milk came out his nose. Or when Landon made a joke about kissing me, so Ren pantsed him in the hallway.

I miss being with my friends, chatting and laughing and ragging on each other, bringing some light to this unbearably dreary place.

And I miss Ren. More than anything else, I fucking miss him *so bad*, it feels like my gut has been sliced open and my organs are being pulled out one at a time.

I miss his dazzling smile, and his delicious scent, his possessive touch, and his achingly sweet taste. I miss watching him push his dark, shiny hair back and wink at me like he fully knows exactly how damn beautiful he is. And his voice, whispering ridiculous, filthy things in my ear to make me squirm while we're sitting in a crowded room.

What I wouldn't give to hear those rumbly words right now, above all else.

But instead, all I have are memories that hurt, in a sea of silence.

The new guards have instituted a no-talking order. Meaning we're not allowed to speak, *at all*, anywhere outside of our cells. So meals, showers, and walking the halls in between are all done in complete quiet.

It's creepy as fuck, and so insufferably *boring*, it's like an all-new form of torture within these walls. And there's nothing we can do about it.

A few inmates backtalked when it started. And they disappeared. Who knows if they're in solitary, or the East… Or dead.

The Warden's guys are ruthless; vacant robots made strictly to follow orders. *A million times more terrible than Velle has ever been, even in his hay-day.*

Of course Velle is still *here*. His team, the familiar faces who have guarded us for years, are still around. But they're being constantly undermined and disregarded by the Warden's new army, making everything so very uncomfortable.

If tension was visible, it'd be like a thick smog in the air, clouding us, sucking the oxygen out of our lungs. The divide is palpable. It hasn't been that long, but it feels like a decade has passed already, and I just don't think I can stomach much more of this.

Accepting life here and surviving was all well and good when it was minutely tolerable. But *now*, I just don't see how I can keep this up.

Without Ren, I feel like I'm drowning.

Joy pops her head into the room, eyes landing on me before she casually strolls inside, as if she was specifically checking for me. The new guards, Equino, Pedroia, and Cruz—*I only know their names from the tags on their lapels*—are circling the room like sharks, shooting her looks that she shoots right back, striding nonchalantly over to me.

She drops her hand onto the table by my tray. Shooting me a wink, she pinches my cheek, then saunters off to grab food for the inmates in solitary. I'm able to smile just a bit, though it's definitely strained and sad, watching her leave without so much as a word.

Fuck, I hate this fucking place.

Waiting until the douche-roombas are far enough away, I slide my tray aside to reveal a small, folded piece of paper. I check on them one more time before opening it up to read.

He's doing fine.

Just that one line has me sighing out of relief as I read on.

Still in the East. A little tired, but he's cracking jokes.

He wanted me to tell you Happy Thanksgiving, and he looks forward to your stuffing.

Ew. I can't believe he actually got me to write that.

I chuckle quietly to myself, biting down on my trembling lower lip.

He loves you and misses you... I won't lie, he's really sad, but I don't want you to worry. We're looking out for him as best we can.

Just stay strong, lil Luthy. We're gonna figure this shit out.

Burn after reading.

LOL jk. No but seriously. You're gonna have to eat this note. Sorry, dawg.

Breathing out steadily, I fight back the tears, using every ounce of strength I can muster to push off the breakdown that's been wanting to swallow me up for weeks. I crumple the note into a little ball and soak it with juice from my Hi-C juice box, mushing it up into a puddle of sludge.

Because yea, no. I'm not actually going to eat it.

Dread has retreated just a fraction, knowing that Ren's okay. I've seen him only once since the day he was ripped from my hands. A couple of weeks ago, when Rook brought him up to shower with us, claiming the one downstairs was *broken*. It was simultaneously the best and worst moment of my life. Because I was so motherfucking *happy* to see him, it was like my heart was exploding. But also, we couldn't talk, or touch. We were left just *staring* at one another, mouthing things and shivering in need while we watched each other wash up.

The literal second I got back to my cell, I was jerking off so furiously, I came all over the place in less than a minute.

The thing is, the mess our lives have become is doing more than just depressing me down to my core. It's sparked a roar of determination within me. Maybe I work better under pressure, who knows.

But every waking moment I spend in my cell is now dedicated to solving this problem... And I'm fucking close.

So close I can *smell* it.

When our silent meal is finished, the assholes bring us back to our cells. I pass Kang in the hall, and it doesn't exactly surprise me to find him walking beside Trevel. The new guards broke everyone up into smaller groups, so I don't see him that often. Not that we could talk even if we wanted to, which I'm sure he still doesn't. But his eyes do linger on mine for a moment while we walk in opposite directions, and I don't see as much loathing as I did the last time we spoke.

Turning over my shoulder, I watch him disappear through the doors. As much as I dislike Trevel, I guess I'm just glad Kang has someone.

Going it alone is a real gut-punch.

Pedroia pushes open the door to the row and we all file through. But I pause when I see Velle coming out of Ren's cell with a bag. He gives me a brief look and a subtle nod before stomping past us, shouldering into Pedroia on his way out.

I smirk to myself while the big asshole seethes.

So funny that I used to see *Velle* as *the big asshole*. Sure, he's still a big asshole, but he's definitely the lesser of two evils. In fact, I'd go so far as to say I consider him a friend on some level.

If it comes down to us versus them, I'd side with John Chevelle in a New York fuckin' minute.

Back inside my cell, I wait for the sounds of the Warden's Gestapo to clear, then I get to work. I loosen the stitch in my mattress, digging inside for my device. Pulling it out, I smile fondly.

Hello, darling.

LOIS 2.0 is a real brick-and-mortar type machine, but she works. I've put my blood, sweat, and tears into this thing—literally—and I couldn't be prouder. She's my *baby*, born from nothing but spare scraps and my motherfuckin' wit.

I really am Dr. Frankenstein up in this bitch. 'Cause it's alive.

By only sheer luck, I managed to get all the pieces together right before the new guards arrived. I've done nothing but program for the last however many weeks. Hours and hours spent with bloodshot eyes, cursing and praying to the gods of technology that this would take.

When I saw my first blue screen, I burst into tears.

Naturally, that was just the beginning. And now, hundreds of hours of coding later, I think I've finally got it.

Something you might have noticed about me is that for a dangerously smart guy, sometimes I can be pretty freaking dumb. Not necessarily stupid, just *reckless*. But only when it comes to the people I love.

That time I fixed the servers in the East Wing? Yea, fixing the glitch took all of five minutes. The rest of the time was spent studying every square inch of the Alabaster Pen servers and their code, then programming a wireless driver, which makes for easy pairing—*the hacker's best friend.*

And here's something I'm sure *no one* knows… the servers for both control rooms are connected. They run on different bandwidth, but essentially, they're all one system. Meaning that anything I did in the East also works in gen-pop.

Pretty cool, huh?

I wasn't lying when I said I wouldn't disrupt the servers with the fixes I made that day. Because realistically, it wouldn't do me any good. Simply wiping them out wouldn't have helped me, not back then, and certainly not now.

What I *did* was drop a tiny bug in there to lie still and wait. So that in the event I ever got LOIS 2.0 up and working, which I have, my hibernating ninja parasite could wake up and infest the damn system.

Gazing at the screen now, I'm rippling with excitement.

I can't believe I actually did it.

Everything takes infinitely longer with this device than it ever did with original LOIS. By the time the lights turn off in the row, my back is cramped, and my ass is numb from sitting for so long… But I'm in.

I'm fucking in.

Locked onto the servers. In control of Alabaster Pen with the push of a few buttons.

"Holy shit…" I breathe, biting down hard on my lip. "I… am a fucking *god*."

Seriously. I want to jump up and *scream*, and happy dance like a brilliant madman. But I can't. I can't draw attention from the new guards.

As robotic as they seem, this device can't power them down. Maybe next time.

Still, I allow myself a few seconds to stumble to my feet and do the cabbage patch around my cell. *This is a million times more amazing than hacking into the Pentagon!*

Because with this, I can…

Slowly inching over to the bars, I go for my first official test, typing, clicking, and swiping. My eyes stay up on the camera in the corner of the ceiling as I hold my breath.

Here goes nothing…

Tap. The camera's red light goes black, and it slumps over, powered off.

"Yes!" I do a little hop, celebrating as quietly as possible. "Oh, man. So frickin' cool. Now for the coup de grâce."

My fingers work on the screen, sifting around through back-end controls.

"Please, please, please..." I whisper, grabbing the metal bar of my cell door.

And *click*. I push it open.

Oh my GOD, it works! I'm a genius! Fuck everyone!

I'm *hollering* inside, shaking so hard I almost drop LOIS 2.0 on the ground. My adrenaline is jacked through the roof as I peek my head out into the row.

Holy crap, I'm free. I'm literally out of my cell right now.

Okay, focus, spazz. You have very limited time to pull off what you're trying to accomplish here.

Stepping out into the row, I tiptoe like a kid sneaking to catch Santa Clause on Christmas Eve. The row is quiet and dark, nothing but snores coming from the other cells. But still, I need to be stealth. If one of these fools is awake and they spot me, it'll be all over.

Prancing past the cells, I stay light on my feet while making it quick, and by the time the door is in sight, I'm practically running. I make sure to disable the camera on the other side before pushing on the door to the row, which opens for me because I'm a fucking badass.

Closing it quietly, on the other side, I release a long exhale. Then I switch the cameras back on in the row, making my way through the halls. In the direction of the East Wing.

Turning cameras on and off takes a little more time than I wish it did, but it's the smart play because I can't have anyone in the control room getting suspicious. I'm not sure if the Warden replaced the guys in there, but I have to assume he's at least watching things more carefully now. And I'm not trying to get caught.

Not when I'm on my way to hold my man again for the first time in what feels like a fucking eternity.

Listening carefully as I go, I stick close to the walls, taking the long way down, past the rec room, in order to avoid solitary, since you need keys to get around down there. It takes nearly a half hour, especially pausing at every creak and thump I hear. This building is noisy as hell, and there seem to be some loud winds billowing outside.

I'm shivering, from nerves and the cold, creeping through hallway after hallway. I don't even really know where I'm going, but I just need to keep moving. Finally, I make it into the East Wing, and I'm frenzied, darting up and down the rows of padded cells, peering in each small window for any sign of dark hair and blue eyes.

But I don't see him anywhere.

Disappointment is creeping. *If I did all of this just to get to him and he's not even* here, *I don't know what I'll do.*

But at the end of the final row, in the last cell, I look through the tiny plexiglass window and my heart screeches to a halt.

Oh, baby…

Curled up on the floor in a straitjacket is my boyfriend. Eyes closed, dark hair hanging in his face. I feel like such a wimp, but I'm about to cry.

Ready to charge inside and attack him, I glance down at the door, dread crawling fast from my stomach all the way up my throat. There's a handle with a lock.

A fucking lock!?

Why?? Why on earth is there a goddamn motherfucking lock??

I growl out of frustration and devastation, ready to collapse.

"Lex?"

My eyes jump. Ren is wobbling to his feet and rushing to the door.

"Baby," I whimper, touching the window.

He's just *so* beautiful. So sad and happy and tired and fucking gorgeous, I can't even breathe.

"H-how are you here??" he sputters, and I can barely hear him through the stupid door.

"I… I had to come see you," I tremble out the words. "I miss you so fucking much, Ren. I'm *dying* without you. I got my computer working… I came all the way down here only to get stopped by a goddamn *lock*. Fuck, baby, I wanted to hold you…"

He sniffles, lips shivering and looking all pouty and delicious.

"I want to kiss you so bad," I whine. "This *sucks*."

"It's okay." He smiles at me. One of those stunning, dimpled model smiles I missed seeing more than the sun in the fucking sky. "Just being able to look at you and hear your voice is enough."

"No, it's not," I grunt. "I fucking failed. This thing is worthless."

I'm stubbornly tapping buttons while Ren chuckles. "God, you're so cute. I've missed the fuck out of you, my baby love."

"But it doesn't *matter*," I growl, grabbing the door handle. "Because I can't get in—"

The handle twists, and the door abruptly opens, bringing me with it. And it's so unexpected, I stumble inside the cell, crashing right into Ren. He loses his balance and we both topple over, falling onto the floor. I land on top of him, our shocked grunts turn swiftly to loopy giggles.

"What the hell…?" I look down at him, and he's beaming.

"Guess you're still a genius after all," he sighs.

"Yea, right," I huff, glaring at my device on the floor. "I had no idea the servers could override the locks. I wonder if it works like that in solitary too…?"

"Baby, no offense, but I don't give a good goddamn about any of that right now," he rasps, sitting up. "Get this thing off me so I can touch the fuck out of you. Please."

Chuckling and flushed, I undo the laces of his straitjacket, watching him stretch out his long arms. And then he lunges at me, grabbing my face.

Our lips are together in a flash, hungrily devouring, almost too fast. Our teeth are clashing, fervent moans escaping in between the furious sucking and tongues flicking harshly like our mouths are battling for pleasure.

"I love you so fucking much," Ren groans between my lips, pawing at me everywhere he can reach. He pushes me onto my back, pinning me to the floor.

"I love you too, sweet flame," I hum, fisting his silky hair while I roll him over and straddle him. "I'm never letting go of you again, I swear to God…"

"Are you finally gonna say it…?" He smirks, and I laugh softly.

Pulling from his kiss just an inch, I hold his jaw in my hands. "You're my boyfriend, Warren."

He lights up, an uncharacteristic flush in his cheeks as his lashes flutter.

"Mmm… I finally get a boyfriend when I'm trapped in a padded cell." He grins lazily. "Seems fitting."

I rumble, kissing his soft lips over and over. "Oh, please. You've been my boyfriend for years at this point. Since pretty much the moment I met you."

"Well, yea… I certainly saw it that way," he teases, holding on to my hips.

"I'm sorry I didn't." My voice grows serious. "I'm sorry I hesitated so much… Baby, if I knew this was going to happen, I would have—"

"Lex… Stop," he cuts me off with a whisper. "We're in prison. This was never going to be a picture-perfect love story. Especially with me being a total fucking train wreck and all. The fact that we're even here right now is nothing shy of incredible. So let's… savor it. Okay, baby? Let's have right now, because honestly, we just don't know what might happen outside that door. If we're going to wind up wishing for one more moment, then let's take advantage of the one we're *in*... The one your super-smart brain gave us."

I can't stop smiling, just like I can't stop kissing him, touching his face and his neck, sliding my hands up inside his shirt to feel that warm skin and all those muscles.

He's totally right. We *don't* know what'll happen out there. We don't even know how long we have in here. But if I have him *right now*, I'm going to make it count.

For all those times I wanted to kiss him, but didn't... For all the time I spent thinking about him, wishing I could get him out of my head, but knowing I never would...

Maybe it's bittersweet that we're finally here, boyfriends in love, with our future so vague. But such is the curse of falling in love in prison.

So right now, in this padded cell, with uncertainty just outside, I'll let his chaos settle me.

Like fireworks over the ocean.

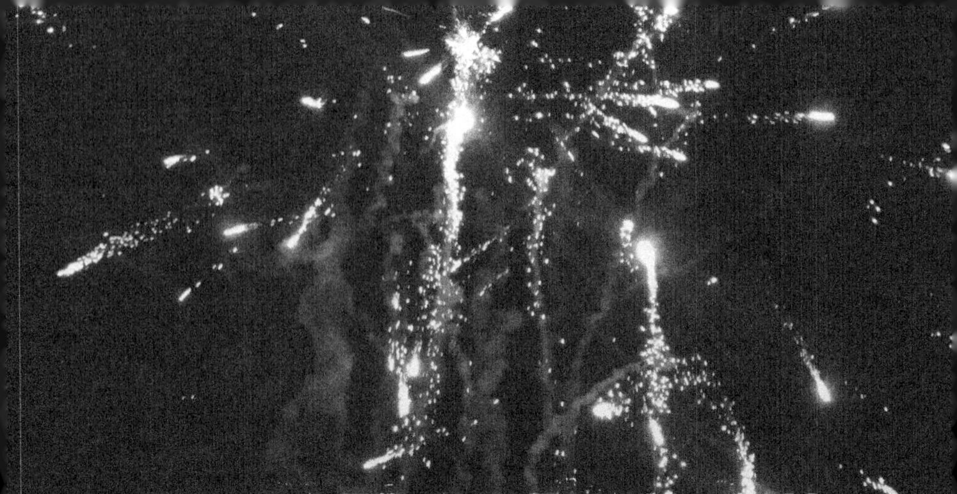

CHAPTER TWENTY-SIX

Ren

MY BOYFRIEND…

My… *boyfriend.*

Mine.

How am I so happy when I've been isolated down here for longer than I can even recall? How am I *floating* around this padded cell like a butterfly on the wings of a hummingbird?

That's probably the gayest thing I've ever said, and yet right now, it makes perfect sense.

Because I'm with Lexington, and he loves me, and he's *finally* my boyfriend.

All the rest of it is just background noise.

Especially while we're lying on the floor in our undies, making out like two sex-starved maniacs.

God, I missed this… I missed how hard he kisses me when he's all frustrated and greedy and wound-up. How we can never seem to decide which one of us is going to be the more dominant one. It's always a power struggle and I *love* that, because I spent so much of my life on my hands and knees with my face being stuffed into various pieces of furniture.

I still love that when Lex does it to me. But I also like being the one to pin him down when he gets all nervous and fluttery.

Starting out, he was on top, holding my hands down while he sucked and bit my lips raw. But then I flipped him over and straddled his hips. And now we're rubbing our cocks together while he squeezes my chest and plays with my nipples, and *dear Lord*, I could combust already because I just missed every single particle of him.

Slipping my hand between our writhing bodies, I grip his cock, massaging it with my fingers. Running up that long, thick shaft from his balls, feeling him throb at my touch, leaving a wet spot soaking through the material of his boxers.

"I love your cock," I whisper into his mouth, pushing my nuts down onto his until he groans.

"Yea?"

"Yea..."

"You make it so big and hard, baby," Lex purrs, sliding his hands down to cup my ass.

"Mmm... That pretty cock's been missing me, huh, gorgeous boy?" I bite his bottom lip, tugging it with my teeth, then swiping my tongue to soothe the sting.

He nods, fucking adorable, dreamy, green-eyed morsel that he is. "Every part of me missed every part of you."

He shoves my boxers down below my ass, his fingers teasing between my cheeks. So I yank his down too, exposing half of that perfect, pink dick.

"Tell me..."

"Mmff...?"

Moving my lips to his ear, I whisper, "Tell me every dirty thought you've ever had about me, Lexington." I suck on his earlobe, and he shivers. "Every wet dream, every filthy fantasy... Every urge you've had that made this big dick *weep*. I wanna know so I can arch your back and curl your fucking toes, beautiful. It's my official job... as your *boyfriend*."

"God, Ren, you're so fucking sexy." He squirms beneath me, spreading his legs. "You wanna drain me, don't you?"

I hum a raspy chuckle, sucking bruises on the sweet flesh of his throat. "Your orgasms are mine, love. *All* mine. It's only fair I make you shoot so hard it hurts."

"I love how good you make it hurt, naughty flame..." His finger grazes my hole and I'm clenching in hot, aching need already.

I know we should probably make this fast, but I can't help myself. It's been way too long. I want to draw this out, edge us both together so that by the time we reach the finish line, we're fucking incapacitated.

"Tell me," I breathe, making my way down to his chest.

Lex swallows, dragging his fingers up my back. "M-my… nipples. I love when you suck and bite them."

"Mhm… I'm well aware." I grin, lapping at the peaked flesh, swirling my tongue around before going in for a brutal suck that ends with it between my teeth. My fingertips tease his flinching cock. "Baby boy, you're already dripping all over the place."

He whimpers while I work on his nipple some more, moving from one to the other. My mouth is all over his chest, biting the curves of his pectorals as his fingers brush up into my hair and he gives my head a little shove.

"Clean it up," he whispers a command, such a soft, *Lex* way of asserting what he wants, I'm swooning and panting at the same time.

Nipping my way through his abs, I slurp the swollen, messy head of his cock between my lips, sucking out little pulses of his flavor while he whines and spreads his legs wider. Losing myself in working his dick deep into my throat just happens. It's the least laborious job I've ever had. I could probably suck his big, beautiful dick for *hours* and not get tired, which is really saying something, because it's quite large.

"Uhh… *Ren*." He yanks my hair in his fist. "You s-suck so deep… Swallow my cock, baby. Eat it whole."

"Mmm mm mmmm," I rumble on him with tears in my eyes, grinding my erection into the floor.

"If you're hungry… I think you should… go lower."

Peeking up at him, I crumble for the way he looks, biting his lip with his cheeks all blushed. I suck up his length, making sure to tease underneath his crown a few times, loving how his cock moves, lurching forward at the sensation.

"You want me to eat your ass out, gorgeous?" My gaze shines up at him, and his down at me while he nods slowly.

"Y-yes, please."

God, this fucking kid. His entire existence is gonna make me come.

Taking his boxers down, I swoop them off of his legs, kneading his thighs in my hands while I push them up and bend his knees. He gasps and I growl, kissing his inner thighs, his balls, his cheeks. *Everywhere*. Just *worshipping* him the way he deserves when he looks so goddamn perfect with his ass open and his feet in the air.

"My boyfriend wants a nice tongue lashing on his sweet little hole, huh?" I hum, making a trail of kisses from his balls, down his taint and in between his cheeks.

"Mmm... my boyfriend eats ass like an ass-eating rock star."

Rumbling chuckles, I spread him open wider, burying my mouth. Licking and licking, slow but ravenous, he's sloppy wet when I spear my tongue inside him as best I can.

"Unnghh... *fuck*, that feels so good." He clenches.

I bite the meat of his butt cheek, and he whimpers. "Relax, so I can get in deeper."

Muscles ease up for me, and I stuff my tongue inside, fucking his hole with it while reaching for his cock to stroke. His hands are still in my hair, on the back of my head, stuffing my face deeper, practically suffocating me. I'm fucking *obsessed*.

"*Ohh*... Oh, *fuck yea*... Eat this ass out, Warren." His hips are moving, writhing against my mouth while I go to town on him. "S-suck... suck my hole. Kiss it, lick it... *ohh God*, your tongue is *incredible*."

I'm barely even holding his legs open anymore. He's just lying there panting, spread-eagle, forcing my head between his legs and choking on desperate gasps. I might be losing oxygen to my brain myself, because everything is all hazy. But I *love* it, rutting into the floor over and over, my balls drawing up tight.

"Baby, I wanna fuck..." Lex pleads, hoarse and quivering. "I've been dreaming about sliding inside you..."

Pulling my mouth back, I suck in a much-needed breath. "How long have you wanted to put it in my ass?"

"From the moment I met you," he groans. "And every day since. I even brought lube..."

Chuckling, I bite my lip. "You came prepared?"

He grins and nods, sexy as fuck shy-boy energy. "Let's be real, there was no way we weren't fucking tonight."

The kid has a point.

Rustling through his pants, I grab the small tube, squeezing some onto my fingers. Then I toss it at him, crawling over his hips. "Make my ass wet."

Fisting his cock, I stroke the lubrication onto him while he sinks his fingers between my cheeks, painting my rim, then stuffing two in me at once. Slow, but *deep*. He doesn't stop until his knuckles meet my skin.

"*Uhhgod.*" My head drops back.

Lex pumps his fingers in and out, only for about a minute before I'm impatiently lifting off of them, propping myself over his dick.

"Apparently, I'm not the only one desperate to get this cock in you." He smirks, holding my waist while I lower onto his fat tip.

"Please… If I could live with my ass wrapped around your dick, I would."

Welcoming him in actually takes a minute; that's how fucking long it's been. I don't think I've gone this long without sex since I lost my virginity. But for some reason, the waiting has made this feel a million times better. I'm *quaking* in anticipation, and once the smooth curve slips inside, my entire body lights up.

"*Ohhfuckyeaa…*" I purr, eyes rolling back in my skull as I sit my ass down on his every inch of silky skin covering rigid stone.

His cock blazes inside me, stretching me so good I'm instantly shuddering, sweating and whimpering. My cheeks rest on his pelvis, his full, hot, throbbing length buried in my body. It feels so good, my dick is *leaking* all over his abs.

"*Ffuck…* my tight, perfect flame, you're so hot you're burning me up," he hisses, grabbing my cock, massaging it with all the slick precum. "*Uhh, Ren…* God, I love being in you."

"Mmm, baby boy." My palms slap down on his chest as I lift my hips and drop them back, swiveling on him and seeing stars. "You're so… *d-deep.* Fuck, I think you're in my stomach…"

"Good," he croaks. "Fuck me, Warren… Work my dick in that sweet hole."

A greedy growl leaves my lips as I collapse over him, kissing him fast, my movements becoming frantic. "Your mouth is so fucking filthy, I love it."

In seconds, I'm riding him like a fiend. Rolling my hips, sloping and grinding. Bracing myself on my knees, I grip his jaw while we suck each other's mouths numb, biting and licking, whining and grunting. My cheeks are slapping on him, the sound ringing through the small room with the rough breaths leaving us both every time I crash down. His cock is jamming almost violently at my prostate, so damn good in this position, I'm going cross-eyed.

"You like that, baby?" Lex groans while our bodies sweat together. "Does it feel good?"

"Mmmfuckyea, it's *euphoric.*"

I'm humping the literal life out of both of us right now, our bodies slamming together, rough sex that's somehow tender and sensual.

This is the fucking I've always needed. Exactly the way it is with him... More than just physically deep. It's an erotic, emotional profundity.

"Is my dick touching it...?" His voice takes on a curious rasp. "Your spot?"

"Uh-huh." I nod fast, squirming into him, riding him harder and harder.

"I... um..." His fingers graze up and down my sides. "I wish... I mean, I *think* I do..."

I kiss his shivering lips. "Lexington, I told you... tell me everything you want, baby, and I'll give it to you."

"I wish I knew... how it feels." He gulps.

My movements slow. "To be fucked?"

"Well..." His voice trails, cheeks redder than they've ever been in all the years I've known him.

"To have something in your ass...?" I nip his jaw. "Touching your prostate?"

"I dunno..."

Slowing down, I straighten, gazing down at the glistening gems in his irises. We all know I'm not one to do any kind of topping, but the thought of putting my fingers inside Lexington while I'm riding his cock has my balls thrumming with need.

Oh, I'll do it, you curious little thing. I'll totally finger that ass, no qualms whatsoever.

Grabbing the lube, I squeeze some onto my fingers. And Lex parts his legs immediately, already fucking eager for this.

Jesus, I had no idea he'd ever want me to finger-fuck him... This is beyond wild.

I reach behind myself, running my slick fingers between his cheeks.

His hole is quivering, eyelids drooping as he mewls. "Will it... hurt?"

"I'll go slow," I whisper, precum dripping from my cock at how incredibly sexy this is, how nervously excited he looks, and the buzzing pleasure of sitting astride him with his dick deep in my ass.

Teasing him at first, I get him nice and slippery. Then I gently nudge the tip of my middle finger into his hole. He's *unbearably* tight, all bunched up and anxious. So I use my free hand to caress him all over; his thighs, up his hips, then his abs and chest, onto his neck. He breathes out steadily, relaxing just enough for my fingertip to glide in.

"*Uhhh...*" he whines, squeezing my hips.

"More?" I ask him softly, and he nods.

"P-please…"

Holy fuck, this is already so hot.

My finger slides in deeper and his back arches. "*Ohhh*, fuck, Ren… *More.*"

Deeper still, I stuff it into the insanely tight channel of his ass, biting my lip as I wedge in up to my knuckle. Then I draw it back, and he purrs.

"Holy motherfffuck."

"Am I hurting you?"

He shakes his head. "N-no… no no, that feels… *so* good."

Alright then. I do it again, pushing my finger in deep, then pulling it back, working up a slow rhythm of finger-fucking his tiny hole while gradually jumpstarting my hips to ride his cock again. Not sure how it's even possible, but he feels ten times harder now.

"Umm… *uhh more,*" he pleads, dragging his fingertips over my erection where it's bobbing on his abs. He fists it and begins to stroke me. "Give me more, baby…"

"More fingers?" I ask, but I don't wait for him to answer, stuffing the index in with the middle.

"*Fuck yesss.*" He smacks his hand against my ass, squeezing me so hard I'm sure I'll have bruises.

I can't help the wicked grin on my lips as I work my ass on his cock and finger him deep, going absolutely out of my *mind* for how insanely hot this is.

"Lex, you're so greedy, baby boy," I croon. "Your ass is so tight it's swallowing my fingers right up…"

I curl them just a bit, and he sobs. "*Ah*… Oh God, I think I just came a little…"

I chuckle, doing it again. He shudders. "Yea, that'd be your prostate, beautiful. Does it feel good?"

"*Yes yes yes.*" His hole clenches my fingers. "Touch it again…"

I barely even notice how hard I'm fingering him, matching the thrusts of my hand with the tempo of my hips, chasing my own bliss with his cock all the way up in my body.

"*God*, Lexington… I can't believe how good it feels to finger-fuck your warm little hole…"

"Mmm-more," he pants, writhing desperately against my hand. "Deeper… fuck me *deeper*, baby."

"My fingers won't go any deeper."

His hand on my cock slows, and he releases his grip, brushing his palm over it in a tender caress. Gazing down at him, I find him chewing on his full bottom lip, staring at my dick with mischievous twinkles in his green eyes.

I tilt my head. "You want me to fuck you…"

It doesn't come out like a question, because it isn't one. I can tell just from the way he's looking at me, petting my dick like a kitten… His curiosity has reached an unhinged peak, and now he wants me to put my whole cock in him.

And honestly, while *I'd* never even considered doing it before, I don't think this is the first time *he's* thought about it.

"Are you mad…?" Lex blinks up at me.

An enamored grin sweeps over my lips. *He knows me so well.* "I'm a fucking bottom, baby." I lift a shoulder in a shrug, still rocking my hips on him. "I've never put my dick in anything other than a mouth. Well, actually, I *have* fucked a fleshlight before, and that was pretty cool. And when I was thirteen, I made a hole in my pillow and—"

"*Ren…*" he whines. "Stop talking. If you don't want to, it's fine. I don't care, I just love you…"

I pout. "And you wanna see how it feels to have a big cock in your ass…"

He shivers and groans. "Maybe…"

"You're so goddamn cute. I can't say no to you." I tug my fingers out of him, and he grunts.

"You don't *have* to do it…" He traces my abs coyly. "Your fingers feel amazing."

"Trust me, my dick will feel even better." I swivel on his cock a few more times to savor that luscious feeling. "Anything in the *world*, I'll do for only you, baby. You know that. But just be prepared for me not to have the slightest clue what I'm doing…"

His face lights up. "Oh my God, I get to take your virginity!"

I bite my lip. *He's right…*

Technically, I've never fucked anyone before.

Okay, this is cool. Now I'm excited.

Hopping off of his cock, he beams with a thrill. But as soon as I kneel between his legs and grab him by the hips, tugging him closer, his grin falls away and his eyes widen reticently.

"This is gonna hurt… isn't it?"

"Not necessarily." I lube up my cock, pushing slippery fingers around on his hole. "We got you nice and primed."

"Don't make fun of me if I make weird noises or look like I'm crying," he whispers, and I can't help but laugh.

"Baby, I'm a seasoned pro and the first time you fucked me, I melted into a puddle of goo in minutes. I'm sure you'll always be infinitely cooler than me when we have sex."

He grins. "Is that because you love me so much…?"

Melting over him, I kiss his lips, slowly grinding my cock against his. "I love you so, *so much*… I'm like a virgin with you, Lexington. It's all brand-new sensations."

"I love you, Warren," he breathes, kissing me slow, fingers combing through the strands of my tousled hair. "Let's lose our virginities together."

"I can't wait to put my dick in you for the first time." I fist my slick erection, aiming it up to his ass.

He's trembling from head to toe, and I get it. I'm shaking myself… I guess this is a big deal.

I might actually be… *nervous*.

We kiss ourselves up to it, rocking into each other until he's squirming and I'm about to combust. The head of my cock struggles against his hole, desperate to get in, but also not wanting to rush him. It feels good regardless. But eventually, he relaxes just enough, opening up for me. And I push my cock inside.

"*Uhhffuck*," he chokes, his dick immediately throbbing out a rough pulse of precum between us. "Ohhh God, oh God…"

"*Wow*… hot fucking damn." My forehead drops onto his shoulder as I stuff my cock in a little more. "How am I even moving in you? So, *so tight*, baby, Jesus… Holy hot *virgin ass*…"

"It b-burns a lot," he quakes.

"Want me to stop?"

"N-no fuckin way."

"Good," I growl, barreling into him even deeper.

His back arches, and he cries, face etched in lines of pain. But his legs are spread open wide, and he's gripping my ass, holding me close. Pulling me *deeper*…

"God, this is *incredible*. Your ass feels like burning hot bliss, baby," I groan, sucking on his throat while I give him inches and inches, forcing myself to go slow when my body has this instinct to just fuck into him as hard and deep as possible. "I can't believe this is how good it feels to fuck you… So snug and *perfect*. I never wanna leave this ass…"

"*Mmmmm*… *Ren*. B-baby, *fuuuck*, how d-deep is your d-dick?"

"Like halfway..."

"*Halfway?!*" he croaks, and I grin lazily with my head spinning. "Can't be... No way. You're t-touching my organs."

"You like it *deep*, dirty boy," I growl. "I know you do..." I thrust into him farther while he tremors and sobs. "My fingers weren't cutting it, huh? You needed a cock in here... *Begging* for me to slide in up to my nuts..."

"Ren... *uhhh, Rennn*... I'm... falling... *apart*."

Pulses of sticky stuff are flowing from his cock where it's growing harder, *thicker*, engorged and about to burst between our abs. Lifting myself up, I sit back, gripping his thighs so I can watch myself moving in him. It's officially the hottest thing I've *ever* seen in my entire life.

I might have just switched roles. I'm a top now.

Okay, let's not get carried away.

"Lexington," I hum his name, shoving in until I'm settled between his legs, with his balls resting on my pelvis. "Look at how big your dick is right now..."

His eyes are closed, head tipped back in obvious tortured bliss. So I reach up and grab his jaw, forcing him to look. His gaze is lidded, but still, he manages to peer down at his dick, all stretched and shiny, veins popping. He peeks up at me, pale skin flushed across every perfect inch of him.

And he whispers, "Fuck me, sweet flame. Move your big dick in my ass..."

"I'm so in love with you..." I gasp, drawing my hips back.

He whines a garbled noise. Then I thrust back in, and he groans out even louder. We're probably being too loud, but I have zero fucks to give.

This is nothing shy of heaven on earth.

I'm operating on nothing but instinct. I don't know how to fuck someone, but I know how *I* love to get fucked, so I just do that, stroking my cock in him, building a gradual tempo until before I know it, I'm drilling into his body, and his legs are wrapped around me. We're both sweating and panting, and he's jostling back and forth with how hard I'm pumping him full.

"*Uhh*... Baby, you're fffucking my... *spot*. Oh, right there. *Yes yes yes*," he rambles, abs clenching.

"Is my dick on that sweet spot, pretty boy?"

He nods fast, grabbing my hands and lacing our fingers.

"Is it *aching*?"

"Yea..."

"Want me to keep fucking it?"

"*Fuck yea*... Ren, your dick feels *so good* hitting me there."

"Good, baby."

He reaches for his dick, but I smack his hand away.

"I wanna touch it..." he whines.

"Not yet. Not until you're about to come."

"I *am* about to c-come."

"Oh, thank God... So am I."

Slamming into him over and over, my world begins to tilt on its axis. Everything is blurring, and I'm a giant ball of sensation, focused only on Lex. How beautiful he is, how tight and sweet, and fucking dirty. How insatiable he is for sex with me, in any form. Just like I am for him.

I love him so hard, and I'm loving *his body* so hard, I think my heart could stop beating and I'd survive solely on *him*.

"I'm gonna come in your ass, Lex..." I whimper, gripping and squeezing his waist, running my hands up to his chest to play with his nipples. "I'm gonna drain my big dick in this tight hole."

Snatching his hand in mine, I stuff his fingers into my mouth, sucking them rough and sloppy.

"Want me to finger your ass while you're f-fucking me?" he rasps, and I nod quickly.

Sitting up straight, he puts us nose to nose, until he's practically on my lap. Then he reaches around me, wasting no time driving two fingers into my ass.

"Ohhh, *fuck yea*, that's it." My head falls back. "One more..."

He pushes in a third, and the burning stretch has me weeping.

"God, you're so dirty," he whines, grinding frantically on my hips, like he's actually trying to ride me. It's goddamn *stupefying*. "So *perfect*. Make me come, sweet flame... Make me come on your big cock."

"Come on my big cock, baby..." I feel him tightening, tensing, his ass clutching me tighter and tighter.

I spit on his erection. "Jerk that pretty dick, love."

He shudders. "*Ffuck yea*... Spit on it again."

My chest flutters, a drunken grin forming on my lips. "And *I'm* the dirty one." I spit on his cock again and he fists it, tugging slowly while I ram my dick into him deeper and harder, spitting on his chest, rubbing it onto his nipples.

"I'm gonna come... I'm gonna fucking *come*, Ren, holy fuck, I'm... *ohhhgodyesss*."

"I'm coming with you... Mmmmfucking *busting* in your ass, beautiful boy..."

A spectacular explosion of mutual lust hits us both. Lex sobs, his dick spraying pulses of cum, shooting all over his chest while mine shoot into him. My balls contract, ass clenching hard on his fingers as chills rush through me. I keep stroking, spilling my orgasm deep inside him, filling his hole with wave after wave of thick spurts that rock me down to my foundation.

I never could have predicted this... How absolutely fucking *mind-boggling* it feels to come inside him, ass tightening and releasing, like it's trying to pull out every last drop.

"Lex... Lexington, oh my *God*, baby, suck it out. Suck my cum out, you sexy fucking thing..."

"It feels so good... You coming in me... *Fuck*, Ren, don't stop..."

"I won't stop..."

"Please, never, *ever*... stop..."

Even after the climax is done, I'm still pushing, and he's squirming while we both gasp for air. Lex is clinging to me like a vine, shaking and sputtering, his fingers finally tugging out of me.

And then he melts, slumped against my chest while I hold him, rubbing his back and his legs, grazing his thighs, down to his ass. Laying him on the floor, I sigh through a grin, curling up on top of him, sated and purring.

"What in the actual fuck..." he croaks, and I snort.

"That was insane... I can't even process it."

"No kidding." His fingers brush through my hair and down my back. "I feel like I'm on a cloud. Is this how you feel every time you get fucked? Because if so, I *totally* understand your sex addiction." I laugh. "No, really, Ren. I owe you a huge apology. All of your actions were fully justified."

Lifting on shaky arms, I gaze down at him. "This is just us, baby. It's never been this way with anyone else."

Lex blinks, grabbing my face and pulling my lips to his. We kiss it out slowly, for a while, just lying on the floor, wrapped up in each other. He moves his hips on my softening cock, and I slide out of him, touching the spot where my cum spills out. It's filthy, but somehow romantic, if that makes any sense. Because we love each other so *desperately* that even the most illicit, raunchy fucking somehow becomes beautiful.

And while I'd love nothing more than to lie naked with him forever, we decide to put our pants back on just in case. But the cuddling doesn't stop. The soft touches and sweet kisses, and hums of sheer bliss.

Our hearts beat together at the same pace. We're *finally* synchronized, on the exact same wavelength.

For the first time in years, after all the chasing, slowing down and speeding up, we finally made it. We're *here*, in unbreakable love.

"What are we going to do, Ren?" Lex asks, voice taking on a serious note.

"I don't know, baby…" I hum, playing with his hair, rubbing the softness against my palm.

He's quiet again for a moment before he rumbles, "If we could go anywhere, right now, where would you want to go?"

I think for only a beat. "I'd like to see where you're from."

"California?"

"Well, I've been to LA before. And San Francisco. But I mean specifically where *you* came from. I want to go to all of your places. The beaches where you watched fireworks. Your school… your house."

"You wanna come over my house?" I hear the smile in his voice, and my heart skips.

"I'd love to see your bedroom," I croon.

He chuckles. "It'd be great for one of our dry-hump sleepovers."

I laugh. And as it fades, I kiss his forehead. "Then let's go."

He peeks up at me. "Really?"

"Let's get the fuck out of here, while we still can. Because if they realize you're gone… Baby, if something happens to you, I'll completely fucking lose my shit."

"I can sneak back before morning…" he mumbles.

"I know, but that's not the point. Lexington. You don't deserve to be here. You never have. This is a place for heinous killers, for psychopaths and deranged fucking animals. People like *me*, not like you. Baby, you're so *good*. The idea of you rotting in here for one more second makes me sick to my stomach."

The seas of green in his eyes shimmer with emotion.

"You're too smart, Lex. You're a goddamn *genius*. You actually made that device, and it got you out… Don't stay. Keep going and never look back."

His brow furrows. "I don't like how you're saying this…" I simply shake my head. "Ren, I won't go… without you. I won't ever leave you here."

"But you don't *deserve*—"

"And neither do you," he cuts me off. "Nobody deserves a place like this. Well, maybe some people… I don't know, but *not* you. You might be fucked up, but you're also amazing, Warren Xavier. All the best things are a little of both." I run my thumb along his lower lip while he breathes, "If I couldn't leave you when Dash asked me to go, then I sure as shit can't leave you now."

My lashes flutter. "You could've gone with Dash…?"

"It doesn't matter," he says firmly, placing my hand over his heart. "This belongs to you. Yours belongs to me… We fucking belong *together*, Warren."

We both go silent for a moment, just staring at one another, eyes locked.

I'm always going to be more concerned with him getting out of here than me. But just because we've made it here in our relationship, doesn't negate all my issues. I'm still infinitely selfish, and the idea of living the rest of my life without him is like a jagged knife carving out my heart.

So I whisper, "Tell me what you're thinking."

He chews on his bottom lip. "Could we make it off the island?"

"I have no idea," I mutter, mind sifting through all the possibilities. All the things I know, and all the bullshit that's come up recently to throw a wrench in it. "The weather is terrible out there. I've been listening to the wind pick up for days. There's no more boat…"

"What about the ferries?" he hums. "The ones that bring stuff, like deliveries."

I nod slowly. "We could stow away on one. But if they realize we're gone, they'll stop them from leaving the dock."

"You think we could get a weapon?" My eyebrow cocks at him, and he chuckles. "We would need something, right? A gun or whatever, just in case…"

"I don't like the sound of that," I tell him. "If anything were to happen to you…"

I'm trembling just thinking about it, and he kisses my neck. "I know."

We both go silent again, brains running a mile a minute through all this internal noise.

"I should just go back for now," he whispers. "Regroup. Try to come up with a plan. We have an advantage, because they don't know about the device. It could give us some time to come up with something—"

"That's a great plan," a deep voice croons, and we both jump, scrambling up. "Never underestimate the element of surprise."

Manuel Blanco smirks at us from the doorway, arms folded over his chest.

Oh, fuck… Fuck fuck fuck.

Heart slamming up into my throat, I gape up at The Ivory, impending doom washing through me like a sickening wave of nausea. He's surrounded by two of his guards.

Lex lunges for his device, but the Warden barks, "Don't fucking move."

The guards pull their weapons, each aiming a gun at our faces.

Like a reflex, I reach for Lex's hand, lacing his trembling fingers in mine.

The Warden tilts his head at us, in that curious animal way. He's a goddamn snake, seconds from lunging to sink his fangs in, and I don't know how to stop it.

I need to protect Lex. Protect him at all costs.

He's all that matters.

The Warden's head does a subtle bob. "Get them out of here."

The guards storm into the cell, hauling us to our feet. I'm shaking so hard I can barely breathe, millions of thoughts swarming my brain at once, making me dizzy. My hand squeezes onto Lex's as tightly as possible while they try to pull us apart.

Lex has never looked more terrified, eyes wide, lips quivering with fear. The guards forcefully yank us, severing our connection. But I keep my gaze with him.

I tap my finger on my chest right above my heart, over the fireworks I inked on my skin for him. He notices what I'm doing, and I only hope he can hear my wordless message.

Meet me at the fireworks, baby. That's how I'll find you.

The guards cuff our wrists aggressively, and I'm just able to whisper, "I love you," before a bag is shoved down over my head.

Even without sight, the vision of my true love in tears haunts my mind.

Shuffling noises and grievous grunts echo.

"I'll find you, baby!" Lex shouts, his shuddering voice growing further away. "Don't fucking hurt him!"

"Lexington!" I cry, stumbling forward.

Something comes down in a hard *thwack* against my skull.

And it all goes dark.

Pain...

My eyes flutter open, but my vision is so blurry I can't see. Even if I could, though, it's so dark in this room. Pitch black...

Where the fuck am I?

My skull throbs, temples pounding a persistent ache. Lifting my hand to my head, I feel a sticky wetness in my hair I just know is blood.

The more I come to, the more I can feel that I'm lying on a bed, a stiff mattress basically the same cot-style as our bunk beds. When I shift, the metal creaks. And when I move my legs, I feel that one of my ankles is being held down... It's shackled. Loose enough that I can sit up, but I definitely can't stand.

Blinking over and over, I struggle to get my eyes to adjust, squeezing over the fog until I realize I'm in solitary. It's a cell I've never been in, though, because there's actually a cot in here. Still, the rest of it is familiar. Dark as fuck, not even any real light streaming in through the tiny window. There's a bit of a glow, but it looks like the lights are off in the hall.

"Power's out," the familiar voice rumbles, and my spine stiffens.

Fuck my life. He's still here.

"Tell your goon thanks for the concussion," I croak, rubbing my skull. "Fingers crossed for short-term memory loss."

The Warden hums, and I sit up straight, trying to pin down where he is in the room. I know it's probably not wise to be popping off smartass remarks, but it's my defense mechanism. Especially when I'm sure there's nothing I can do physically to get myself out of the heaping pile of shit I'm currently existing in.

"Warren, I know we haven't always seen eye to eye..." He shifts, and suddenly I can see him. His glowing halo of white hair is visible from across the room. "What with you burning down my business and all..."

"Don't forget all the hours you logged having your team of psychopaths poke me with hot needles and cook my brains out." I sit up straight.

Stepping forward, he comes into view. He's wearing his usual tailored suit, sans jacket. And his tie has been loosened, collar unbuttoned in a haphazard way. His ivory-white hair is sort of strewn about. He definitely looks a lot more disheveled than his usual dapper appearance.

As he grows closer, I gulp down a mouthful of nerves. He stops right in front of where I'm sitting, gazing down at me, irises as dark as the rest of the room.

"Call it even?" The corner of his mouth twitches.

I fake a huff of soft laughter, immediately losing my amusement to glare up at his face. "Where's Lex?"

"Relax," he sighs. "Your boyfriend is fine." I breathe out quietly, until he adds, "For now."

Launching up off the bed, I try to lunge at him, but I'm held back by the goddamn chain around my ankle.

Seething, my chest heaves as I snarl, "If you hurt him, I swear to *God*, I'll destroy you."

His shoulders move to display his smug little chuckle.

Ohhh, sweet Jesus, I wanna rip his fucking face off.

"Warren, honestly..." He leans in, putting his face in line with mine. "Did you think I would just let it slide? That adorable little genius hacked into my servers. Quite frankly, I'm as impressed as I am infuriated. But I told him what would happen if he tried anything..."

Fear lances up my spine. I'm shaking, *trembling*, mind suddenly fraught with worry.

"Where *is* he?" I growl once more, fists balling at my sides.

The evil prick checks his watch. "Right now? Still in one piece. But I can't guarantee he'll stay that way for much longer."

A guttural roar of wrath leaves my lips as I grab him by the throat, squeezing as tightly as possible. But he gets the jump on me, slamming me down onto the bed on my back. I hiss when he takes my wrists and pins them over my head.

"Don't make the mistake of thinking you can overcome this, Warren," he teems, mere inches from my face. "People don't change. You will *always* be a lying, manipulative whore."

I snarl out loud, fighting against his hold, but his body weight is keeping me trapped.

"This is where you belong," he whispers, a tone of pure malevolence. "On your back, waiting to be filled."

The Ivory presses his hips into mine, the hard shape of him brushing on my dick. A seething whimper escapes me, and I spit in his face.

His gaze grows even more sinister, dark eyes gleaming as he smacks me, hard, across the face. My cheek is stinging, chest heaving while I struggle and fight, refusing to give in.

I'm not letting this happen... I will not *allow this man to fuck me.*

"Is that any way to treat your favorite client?" he croons, tilting his head.

What...?

I blink, freezing beneath him.

And suddenly, it all makes perfect sense.

His dark eyes, his body... that voice.

My gaze falls to where his dress shirt is unbuttoned. He allows me to slowly lift my hand, pushing the collar open just enough to reveal the familiar tattoo on his chest...

The bird wrapped in barbed wire.

"It was you..." I whisper, gaping up at him in disbelief. "In the mask."

He stares at me, and my head is spinning.

He was Mask Daddy... The client at Edge who fucked me so... beautifully?

"Does this please you?" His lips lower to my throat, and he drops a delicate kiss on my Adam's apple as it dips.

I mean... No. It doesn't matter...

But there are flashes of tingling nostalgia sweeping through my extremities. That night brings me back... To the smell of smoke, and the vibrant flames. The anger, the rage, devastation, and festering pain... all replaced by a blaze of peace.

I barely even notice that The Ivory is still kissing my throat, his hips subtly rocking into mine.

"W-why...?" is all I can ask with this dazzling fog of perplexity sucking the air out of my lungs.

"You were always so beautiful," he breathes, barely audibly.

Chills sheet my exposed flesh.

Winds are whipping outside. I can hear them.

He releases my hands, and I don't fight. I *can't*. I'm just lying beneath him while he grinds his erection against my dick, touching me with the same passionate possession he did that night... In the dark VIP room. *Wearing a mask...*

Feeding me exotic fruit and sucking on my tongue... Fucking me and caressing my cock like he loves it.

It was *him*. He was the one who brought me to the peak of pleasure, not pain.

My hands slide down his sides.

"You were waiting for me..." he hums, sucking viciously tender on my neck. "Waiting for me to come back for you."

Thunder rumbles. It shakes the building.

I hear pieces of concrete hitting the floor across the room.

My heart rate is jacked, but I keep my movements slow and steady, sliding my hand between us to cup his cock. He shivers, thrusting into my hand. Hard as stone, it throbs in my palm.

The loud roar of winds and booming thunder rocks the foundation beneath this tiny bed. It's really dark out in the hallway…

"Why is the… power out?" I mutter, almost to myself.

But The Ivory is too busy humping my hand, whispering things I don't understand into my neck.

"Do you still *hate* me, pajarito?"

My free hand squeezes into a fist while the other keeps fondling his cock.

Boom.

More crumbling rocks scatter. The dull glow in the hall flickers out.

A noise and movement catches my attention. The door is open…

I can't see shit. It's too dark. But I can feel someone watching us. A shadow of someone out there…

"Si, papi…" Words come from a hushed voice I can't place. "Eres el diablo."

Who the fuck was that??

The Ivory stiffens. He lifts off of me, turning toward the doorway.

Boom.

A thunderous explosion rattles my bones.

Then something crashes, shaking the walls around us. It feels like an earthquake.

The ceiling splits.

And concrete falls like a wave, pulling me under.

CHAPTER TWENTY-SEVEN

Luther

Moments earlier…

"Where the f-fuck are we going?!" I shiver, stumbling over something on the wet ground. "I can't see shit… And it's freezing out here."

"For the last time, inmate…" The guard who's pulling me along growls, yanking my arm while cold rain pelts my bare skin. "Shut… *the fuck*… up!"

I know it's not the time, given this messed up situation, but I can't help smiling as I breathe ocean air deep into my lungs—only slightly obscured by the bag over my head. Still, I'm savoring it, despite how cold it is out here, the winds so strong they're pushing my body harder than the asshole with his hand on my back.

I haven't been outside in *five years*. Even with this obviously brutal storm raging, and the fact that I'm shirtless with a bag over my head, most likely being dragged to an untimely demise, I'm managing to enjoy the feel of the elements…

For what little time I have left.

After the Warden separated me and Ren—*and took my fucking computer, the prick*—one of his guys brought me to a dark room just off the East Wing. It had an exam chair in the middle of it, like that room Ren and I fooled around in that time. Only this room was much dingier, and it smelled like dried blood.

Not the best vibes.

I was shackled to the chair with a gag in my mouth for hours while they roughed me up. Honestly, I'm grateful they didn't go as hard as I'm sure they could have, I'm assuming because The Ivory told them to leave me alive.

So he could kill me slowly and painfully, just like he promised.

And when they put the bag back over my head and brought me outside, well... Let's just say there are no mysteries about what's about to happen to me.

They're going to toss me into Shark Bay.

It's not that I'm not afraid of death. I'm so scared I'm shaking while I shuffle in my shackles, feet sloshing through muddy sand and wet leaves. My heart is racing, and my teeth are chattering, from the fear and the cold rain hitting my exposed torso.

But more than all the worry about if it'll hurt, and the general abyss of the unknown that is the *afterlife*, my chest is caving in for one reason, above all else...

Ren.

My poor, beautiful, broken man... the first man I've ever loved. The first *person* I've ever loved, in any real romantic way.

Surely, he'll be beyond devastated if I die. And now *I'm* devastated thinking about him being devastated, because he doesn't deserve anymore pain. After everything we've been through, nearly five years of angst and tension, codependence, and obsession, and a lust that somehow turned into a fully *debilitating* love, we're finally to a place where we know *exactly* what we mean to each other. We're finally in a relationship, despite how unhealthy it might be at times.

So *of course*, this is the moment when I'm going to be killed.

Ren changed for me. Overcame his emotional hurdles enough to be the boyfriend I always secretly dreamed he could be, for *me*.

I mean, shit... He fucked me tonight. We crossed over a line into something so blazingly brilliant...

Me and my boyfriend... my villain with the perfect hero's disguise.

I don't want to leave him. I don't want to be wiped from this earth before I get to bask in the glory of his falling embers.

But I guess I don't have much of a choice. Because these men are dragging me in chains through what feels like woods, directly toward sudden death. I can hear the ocean waves crashing. We must be getting closer... Either that or this storm is just that aggressive.

A large bolt of lightning flashes, visible even from inside this cloth sack on my head, which is completely soaked through at this point. And only a second later, the thunder booms, rumbling the ground beneath our feet.

"Hey…" I grunt. "It's not safe to be out here in chains with lightning so close. We're in the middle of the fucking ocean."

"Won't matter for much longer," one of the guys mutters.

"Getting struck would probably do you a favor," the other guy adds.

"Right, because *you* have no metal on you." I roll my eyes behind my bag. "Idiots."

The guy dragging me stops walking. "What did you just say?"

"Hermano, leave it," the other guy grumbles at his pal.

Another flash lights up the darkness with a loud crack, like the sky just split down the middle. Thunder shakes beneath my feet, and I can't help it. I'm even more nervous now.

This storm is scary as shit.

Winds that must be at least forty miles an hour have the rain beating down so hard it feels like hail. Maybe it *is*. I have no idea where we are exactly, but I hear loud thumping sounds coming from somewhere nearby.

"Holy shit!" one of the guys shouts, and I feel his body brush past me.

"What the fuck??" I grunt, wobbling on my feet.

"Dios mío, was that a brick??"

"What's happening??" I gasp again, backing up slowly.

Lightning strikes once more, and I trip over a rock, crashing onto the ground. And when the thunder blares, another sound follows.

"Holy—"

That's the last thing I hear before a *massive* bang. A crash so loud, the ground shakes like an explosion. For a moment, I think a bomb was just dropped.

My default is to curl up into a ball and cover my head, but I don't have access to my arms. So I smush my face into the wet leaves and pray that I haven't been hit by shrapnel.

An oddly calm silence follows the monstrous sound. All I hear are the winds and the ocean. Trembling and unable to see, I lift my head slowly while someone next to me shifts.

"*Dios*…" one of the guards coughs. "Eduardo… está bien?" More shuffling. "Háblame! *Fuck fuck fuck*… Eduardo??"

"What the *hell* is going *on*??" I gasp, squirming on the ground to try to get this goddamn bag off my head.

"Shut up!" he barks. "Dios mío, *Eduardo*, por favor..."

Finally, the material catches on something, and I pull my head free. Blinking the fuzz from my vision, I balk at the sight of one of the guards knelt on the ground, cradling the body of the other guard. He's unconscious and visibly bleeding from the head.

I blink heavily, in shock. His skull looks split open...

Holy fuck, that's disgusting.

I'm gonna be sick...

My stomach rolls at the sight, and I look away while the other guard cries, clutching his clearly very dead friend. I have no idea what happened, but when I peek back over, I see a giant hunk of stone beside him covered in blood.

I gaze up. And all the air leaves my lungs in a horrified *whoosh*.

The prison... There's a big hole in it.

"Oh... my... God..." I whisper, gaping up at the destruction.

Alabaster Penitentiary has been smashed through. Probably not the whole thing, but a *diesel* fucking chunk of it is now nothing but rubble.

Remains of a giant structure are leaning to the right, as if the top half completely snapped off and fell... right onto the fucking prison.

That must have been the guard tower...

I'd heard about it, but of course, I've never seen it before. It looks like maybe it was struck, and the whole thing came toppling down, giant chunks of concrete, cement and rebar decimating nearly half the prison. It might have only hit one section... But the worn, crumbling conditions of the building did the rest of the work, like falling dominoes.

I can't even process what I'm seeing. I feel like I'm in a dream, or a nightmare, or some fucked up version of both.

This has gotta be a mirage...

There's no way that really just happened...

In an instant, my gut lurches up into my throat.

Oh my God, Ren... Ren was in there.

He could be hurt.

No. No no no, I have to go find him.

Scrambling, attempting to stand, I don't get far before tumbling back down onto my ass with a wet splat.

"Stay the fuck down!" the guard snaps at me, sniffling.

But there's no way. I *can't* just fucking sit here.

The love of my life was inside that building. I need to get to him. I need to help *him.*

My mind quickly rushes through anything and everything I could say or do to get this fucker to unlock my cuffs. Or, at the very least, turn his back long enough for me to make a break for it.

He has a gun, though... He could easily shoot me.

Think, Luthor. Think!

What would Ren do...?

"Hey..." I force my voice to remain even, calm and collected as I inch closer. "I was an EMT. I could help him..." The lie rolls effortlessly from my tongue, though inside I'm shivering.

The guard is solely focused on his friend, crying softly.

Slowly, I scoot closer. "Is he breathing? Let me check his pulse..."

"I said stay the *fuck back!*"

The guard whips in my direction, this time holding his pistol, aimed right at my face. Shaking almost violently, I stay frozen in place, gawking at him while rain sprays in my eyes.

"Okay, I'm sorry..." I whisper. "I'm not moving. I'm staying right here."

He wipes his face quickly on his sleeve, gun still pointed at my head. "This is your fault..." My brows shoot up. "If we weren't out here bringing you, he wouldn't have gotten hurt..."

"Hey, that was an act of *God*," I murmur.

"Well, here's a blessing you don't deserve." His hands tremble visibly as he cocks the gun. "You're going to die much quicker now."

Closing my eyes tight, I take a deep breath.

This is it...

"Ren, I love you..." I whisper, lips quivering. "I'm sorry..."

A flash blinds me out of nowhere, and I topple onto the ground again, rolling to protect myself. The guard screams, piercing the air with a loud, aggrieved yelp.

Then I hear a thud.

"Am I dead...?" I whisper with my face in the dirt.

Eyes creeping open, I peek in his direction. He's slumped on the ground, fucking *sizzling*. There's smoke coming from his body.

Holy shit, he actually got struck by lightning...

I can't believe it. I'm *stunned*. My heart is jumping so fast in my chest, I think I'm having a heart attack as I crawl closer to observe the damage.

It fried his hands bloody...

Okay, that is disgusting.

Tilting my face upward, I peer into the dark night sky, wondering if *God* really just struck this guy down to save my life.

Was that divine intervention...?

I shake my head... *No way. I'm a rational mind. I don't even know if I believe in God...*

But I *do* know that the chances of getting struck by lightning are like one in fifteen thousand. And the chances of getting struck by lightning *right after* someone warns you about getting struck by lightning... Now, that just seems highly unlikely.

So maybe someone is watching out for me...

I blink up at the sky, basking in the cool rain hitting my face, the breeze brushing my skin, the actual ground beneath my fingers. For the first time in five years...

"Thank you," I whisper.

Kicking back into action, I scramble over to the bodies. I'd like to get far away from this pile of corpses, but unfortunately, I need the keys to the cuffs and shackles. Getting them out of the dead guy's pocket with my hands behind my back proves difficult, but eventually I find them and manage to unchain myself.

Immediately, I'm on my feet, jogging in the direction of the giant hole in Alabaster Penitentiary.

I need a plan.

I can't just storm in there. If another one of the Warden's guys sees me, then I'm back to square one.

But I need to get Ren... I can't wait one more second. What if he's trapped, or hurt??

I'm really starting to freak out the closer I get to the prison. The place is fucked the hell up...

Is everyone alright? What about Kang?? Felix, Lem??

Joy, Rook, Velle...??

It's hard to tell how bad the damage is from where I'm standing, because *damage* is all I can see. It looks like the entire East Wing has been wiped out, maybe even into solitary... Or more.

What if the whole prison collapsed??

"Oh God, Ren..." I whimper, rubbing my face. "Where are you, baby? *Please* be okay... I need you to be—"

Pop!

My face jumps. Wide eyes stick to the sky, where green embers fizzle and fall through the darkness.

Thump… Pop!

There goes another one… It's blue.

My lips curl into a delighted smile, relief like strong booze warming me inside.

Thunk… Bang… Whoosh.

The sparkly white ones. My favorite.

"It's him," I gasp a chuckle, my feet bringing me in the direction of my fireworks.

It's Ren, I know it is. He's *alive.*

And it looks like he kept his promise.

Ren

Moments earlier…

Fucking motherfucker…

How many times can someone be whacked in the head in one day before they have to worry about serious side effects??

Sitting up is difficult. My entire body is heavy, my lungs tight. Sucking in a long pull of oxygen proves to be a bad idea, because the air is all dusty. I end up coughing hysterically while attempting to dig myself out of a pile of rubble.

What the fuck happened??

The whole damn ceiling fell down, almost right on top of me. Thankfully, I guess the cot flipped over and ended up protecting me from serious injury…

I wonder if The Ivory did that.

Peering around the dark room, I don't see him anywhere. There's some blood on the ground, but it could be from me. I have no clue…

I gotta get out of here.

By some minor miracle, I'm still clutching the key to the shackles in my hand, from where I pulled it out of his pocket. Naturally, I had no interest in touching his dick, but it was the only way to distract him enough to get the key. Though, he seemed pretty distracted already…

That voice…

"Eres el diablo..."

Who the hell was that??

It doesn't matter. There's way too much craziness to unpack right now... Especially after finding out that apparently, I've been fucked by the Warden in more ways than just his imprisoning me in this hellhole for years.

He was the Mask Daddy...

I can't believe it.

I actually had sex with The Ivory...

Jesus, I could use a cocktail right now.

Shaking it off, I use the key to unlock my shackles, freeing myself from the busted-up metal bedframe. I can't think about the fact that the number of people on this island I've taken dick from is still growing even after I've stopped sleeping around. I need to get out of here and find Lex.

I need to make sure he's alright. I have no clue where they brought him, but he could be hurt.

I'm coming, baby. Just hang in there...

Woozy and wobbling, I stand on shaky legs. It's so dark in here. All the power is out, nothing but a red glow in the hallway, maybe from some emergency lights or something. Climbing over a pile of concrete rubble, I tumble out into the corridor, looking around.

Jesus... This place is absolutely destroyed.

There's no way to know how much of the prison has collapsed. And quite frankly, I don't have time to worry about it. I have to assume the Warden put Lex in either solitary or the East Wing. So I check the rest of the cells in solitary first... A decision I wish I hadn't made.

There are dead bodies in two of them, both crushed almost beyond recognition. My panic subsides just a bit when I verify that neither is Lex. But the cell at the end of the row has completely collapsed in. I wouldn't be able to get in there to check unless I had a fucking excavator and half a day.

Fuck... Fuck fuck fuck, this isn't good.

Trudging through what used to be the hallways of the East Wing, I'm shivering, balking in all directions like I'm in some fucked-up nightmare. The place is in *ruins*. Water is leaking and dripping from broken pipes, only that dull red light illuminating the crumbled corridors, making the whole thing even more ominous.

Now that the building is split open, the wind is much louder. It's all I can hear, covering the silence of tragedy. I check as many cells in the East as I can, finding a few more bodies that, thank God, aren't Lex. But

I'm not relieved, not in the slightest. Because I have no idea where he is, and this place is too fucking huge, too much of a mess to keep wandering through rubble looking for him.

The longer I spend in here, the more likely one of the Warden's guys will find me. I need to get outside and use the signal. Maybe Lex had the same idea, and he's out there waiting for me right now…

Let's just hope I can find my stuff.

This is an epic disaster, but I need to keep moving. Velle told me he was stashing my things in Felix's cell, which apparently is more of an actual bedroom. I guess Lem made it for him so that Felix could live more comfortably in this prison.

Clearly, it pays to be dating your prison doctor.

The only problem is that I don't know where Felix's room is. Scouring the halls, I push open doors, praying none of the East Wing doctors or the Warden's new guards are in any of them, waiting to pop out and grab me. Most of these rooms are either locked, or the doors have been barricaded by rubble, but eventually I find one that's ajar, and I peek inside.

I can't see much, so I step in slowly, minding the stuff all over the floor. A shelf fell over, books scattered everywhere. Bending, I pick one up, reading the title.

"*Beneficial Brainwashing*, by Dr. Melvin Strange…" I murmur, tossing it back down.

The room looks kind of like a sparse dorm room, so I have to assume this is Darcey's place. Rifling around, I search and search through the mess, slumping onto the floor to check under the bed. There's a notebook with doodles all over the front cover…

Felix Love

Dr. & Mr. Love

Grinning, I push it aside. *Yea, this is definitely Felix's room. The little psycho is obsessed, it's so cute.*

Finally, my fingers brush over a strap, and I yank it out from under the bed. It's my backpack.

Yes! Thank you, Velle.

My chest constricts. *I hope he's okay…*

Being down here in the East for so long, away from Lex, has been torture. The *only* reason I was able to keep breathing was Velle, Joy, and Rook sticking their necks out for me. Delivering messages between me and Lex, bringing me food and supplies, assuring me that this mess would get sorted out.

I appreciate their help so damn much, but nothing has been *sorted*. In fact, the future of Alabaster Pen is more uncertain now than ever before.

But one thing I know is that I'm *going* to find Lexington. It's the only thing that matters. I need to find him so we can figure out what's next… together.

Checking on my things, I find everything I need in the bag, just like Velle promised. So I make my way back out into the wreckage, heading for the giant hole in the prison that leads outside.

Cold rain showers over my skin as soon as I jog through the broken halls, stepping out into the night air. The winds are aggressive, but I can't deny how good it feels to be outside, regardless of the fact that it's winter and I'm in nothing but jumpsuit pants. I guess I've been away from seasons for so long that they changed, because I remember this time of year being much colder. It is cold, yes, but I feel like it's actually warmer outside than it was in the prison.

Either way, I'm buzzing. The air is fresh and crisp, and the sounds of the ocean quixotic to my ears as I stumble across the wet ground, between trees, heading for the beach. I need open sky for my signal, but I should also stay a bit hidden, if possible, just in case someone else finds me before Lex.

At the edge of the woods, I drop to my knees in the sand, quickly pulling things out of my backpack. Huddling over it to make sure it doesn't get wet, I arrange the mortars in a line. Then I tear off a piece of paper from my sketchpad, rolling it up. In the side pocket, I find the match Jasper gave me.

One fucking match… Unbelievable. Even Velle wouldn't give me a lighter.

The thought makes me smile. *Honestly, I don't blame them.*

But this'll do.

Striking it inside the bag to protect it from the rain, I light the piece of paper. Then I take in a breath, using the flame to ignite the first mortar.

Please work… God, I hope it's not too wet out here…

Thump!

It shoots up into the air, then pops, green bursts flying through the darkness. I gaze up at it in awe, grinning before lighting the next. It goes off, loud and brilliant.

Come on, Lex. I'm right here, baby…

Lightning the last one, it booms in the night sky, sizzling white. My face darts all around, watching for any sign of movement. I don't see anything, and my heart is beginning to fall.

What if he didn't see them…?

What if he's already… gone…

Dropping my face into my hands, I rub the pressure from my eyes. I'm seconds from breaking down, the pain creeping up into my chest, making it hard to breathe.

"I can't believe you actually did it…"

My face whips, eyes widening as Lex rushes over to me. Smiling…

He's smiling. He's alive, and happy.

I'm weightless, floating to my feet just in time for him to attack me, folding me up in his arms.

"Thank God, you're alright…" I whimper, burying my face in his neck, kissing his wet skin over and over.

"I'm alright. I'm here," he whispers. "Baby…" He grabs my jaw, forcing me to look at him, the green in his eyes melting into me. "You gave me fireworks."

He beams, and I chuckle, kissing him fast, but gently. "I told you I would…"

"You did," he hums while our mouths move together, lips cherishing in tender nips and sucks. "You kept your promise, perfect flame. I knew you would."

"I love you so much, baby." My voice shakes, hands rubbing and caressing him all over, giving him warmth because he's so cold.

I bite his bottom lip, but he winces. Pulling back, I hold his face, looking him over, gasping as rage stiffens my muscles.

"It's not as bad as it looks," he breathes, circling my waist with his arms.

"No?? Look at what they did to you," I hiss, brushing my thumb over a split in his lip, touching some bruising and a cut by his left eye. My jaw strains. "I will end their miserable lives…"

"Yea… Already been taken care of," he huffs, and my head tilts. "We were outside when it happened… The guard tower fell down on the prison. Split one of the guards' heads open. Then the other got struck by lightning when he was about to shoot me in the face…"

I blink at him.

He shakes his head. "Am I hallucinating? I feel like this is… a lot."

"It is," I rasp. "It's fucking crazy. I was inside when it happened. The ceiling fell and almost crushed me."

Lex pouts, pushing my hair back where it's matted with blood. "We should try to check this… You might need stitches."

"Baby boy," I whine, kissing his wrist. I'm just so beyond relieved that he's *alive* and here. Maybe a little beat up, but that's to be expected with everything going on. "The important thing is that we're together."

He nods. "What do we do now…?"

We both turn to look at the prison.

"We can't go back in there," I mumble. "Chances are the Warden's guys are probably trying to round up the prisoners who are still alive before they escape."

"What about Velle…?" Lex shivers in my arms. "Kang, Felix… what if they're hurt?"

I shake my head. "I don't know, baby. I just… I don't think it's smart to go back there."

He pauses for a moment, nodding reticently. "You're right." His face shifts in the opposite direction. "What about the mansion?"

"Also probably not smart…"

"Then what do we do?" He hugs me tight, coiling around me. I think he's trembling more from worry than anything else. "If we stay out here, they'll find us. But there's nowhere else to go. Without knowing what's up with Velle, I just don't see how—"

"I have an idea."

Grabbing my backpack, I take Lex's hand in mine, pulling him into the woods. We run between the trees for a bit, on alert for any sounds or people. I don't see or hear anything, which is highly unnerving.

I just need to get Lex to safety. I have to get him out of here, because he doesn't deserve to be trapped on this fucking island for one more second. Regardless of all this mayhem, I'm determined.

We're gonna get off this rock.

If Dash could do it, then so can we.

"Where are we…" Lex's impatient question trails off when we reach the shore once more, only in a different spot. By the docks.

"That must be the Warden's yacht," I whisper as we get closer, keeping ourselves hidden behind a tree, just in case. "And the ferry that brings stuff over."

"There's no way we can get on one, though…" Lex mumbles. "They won't be leaving now. Not during a storm, especially after what just happened."

He's completely right. But I'm hoping one of them has a life raft or something we could grab. It'll be dangerous as hell, but we have to try, right?

I mean... What's the alternative?

We stand watching for a few minutes, and sure enough, the boats are crawling with people. I'm guessing they're the Warden's guys, staff, captains, and whatnot. They all seem pretty frantic, but it's obvious we'd never be able to get past them enough to hijack one of these boats.

"Look," I gasp, pointing at the yacht.

There's a small boat attached to the side of it, and because of the storm, it appears to have come loose a bit.

"We can grab that," I tell him. "It's probably not much, no motor or anything. But it'll have oars."

"And you think we'll be able to take that dinky little thing across ten miles of stormy ocean filled with sharks??" Lex gripes, shaking his head. His brows are zipped anxiously, fear sparkling in his eyes.

Grasping his hands, I hold them up to my chest. "I know it'll be tough... And really dangerous. But what other choice do we have right now, baby? Seriously, if you have another plan, I'm all ears."

He gulps, sucking on his bottom lip. "Have you ever sailed a boat before? I'm not, like... an outdoorsy dude..."

I can't help but chuckle at how adorable he is. *My sweet little computer geek.*

"I'm a rich kid who used to summer in The Hamptons. Of course I've sailed," I hum, and he grins. "Granted, that's not a sailboat... it's a tender or whatever, so it'll be more like canoeing." I gaze out at the waves for a moment. "The tide is low, which means the storm will be bringing us out."

Lex's lashes flutter. "Is that a good thing?"

"Oh yea. It means we won't have to fight to get away from the island. The waves will do most of the work. Then hopefully once we're out there, we can just cruise toward the nearest land."

Lex nods nervously. "Then what?"

I brush my fingers on his jawline. "Cali. That's the plan, right? We go there first, to your neck of the woods, and then we can figure out next steps... Like, Mexico, or..."

"This is crazy," he breathes, his face is lit up with frightened thrill. "I can't believe we're out here... I can't believe we might... get *out* of here."

His eyes fill with fast tears and he chuckles, then whimpers, dropping his face. My heart is cracked and withered, but still pumping to life because of my love for him.

He's been locked up for so long... so much of his young life spent behind bars.

He deserves to get out. He deserves to be free...

And maybe I don't, but I'm not leaving him. I'm going to get him off this island so we can have a real life together. Honestly, it never seemed possible until right fucking now, but here we are... Standing outside, in the rain, shivering together, hearts racing *wild*.

This is *real*. *We're* real, beyond the walls.

"We have to keep going," I whisper, kissing him softly. "We're gonna make it, baby. You and me, *together*. If Dash could do it, we can." Lex snorts a boogery laugh, and I smile, brushing his soft skin. "That kid's a disaster."

He smiles. "And we're not?"

I purse my lips, shaking my head. "Baby... we're supervillains. We can do *anything*."

"I love you," he whispers, holding my face, kissing my mouth with all his sweetness. "I love you so fucking much, Warren Xavier."

"I love you beyond all reasoning, Lexington Deon."

Pulling apart, our fingers locked, a burst of energy and determination flows between our gazes. We're really going to do this.

And I fully believe *we can*.

Waiting for the coast to clear, Lex stays behind to keep watch while I sneak over to the side of the yacht and untie the ropes for the tender, lowering it into the water. Thankfully, it's pretty dark, which should help us get out undetected. Though, it also means we'll have a harder time seeing where the hell we're going. But that's a risk we'll have to take. Fortunately, my backpack is stocked with emergency supplies. Some food and water, a flashlight, things of that nature.

After a few minutes, Lex scurries across the shore, joining me at the small boat. The waves are aggressive, already trying to pull us out before we're even ready. So we just hop in and hope for the best.

"I saw about four guys," Lex whispers as the boat sifts away from the shore. "Two inside the yacht. The other two ran off. It looked like they were heading for the prison..."

I nod, my eyes stuck on the yacht as we grow farther. "I don't see anyone, but we should get down, just in case."

Lying on my back, I pull Lex on top of me. He's shivering, his skin like ice. Rubbing his arms and back, I hold him close to me while the boat rocks, shifting so I can shield him from the rain with my body.

"Stop," he grumbles. "I don't want you cold and wet just so I'm not..."

"It's why I'm here, baby love." I kiss his lips. "To protect you."

"Mmf." He makes a sweet, sexy little noise that registers in my groin.

Pressing my hips into his, I grind slowly between his legs. "This will keep us warm…"

He chuckles in my mouth. "That's convenient for you."

Grinning, I kiss him deeper, writhing into him harder. And sure enough, the sexual tension and lust between us becomes a blaze, heating our bodies significantly.

My mind is reeling. I can't even fathom that this is reality… that we're actually escaping Alabaster Isle. *Together.*

I never thought I'd see the day when Lex Luthor Deon agreed to escape prison, with *me*.

How drastically things can change.

Peeling off of each other, we watch the island as it disappears out of sight. As elated as I am, there's some sadness in me, aching my bones like the chill in the air.

"I hope Byron is okay," Lex whispers my exact thought. "And Felix…"

"Velle, Joy, and Rook… they're badass motherfuckers," I hum, forcing myself to believe the words I'm saying. "I'm sure they made it. They'll be alright… They have to be."

"A big chunk of our lives happened in that prison," he whispers, squeezing my hand tight while the boat rocks. "Our relationship began there…"

I lift his hand to my lips, kissing his knuckles. "Here's to chaotic beginnings… And the beauty of what comes next."

He smiles, lighting up the sky like our fireworks.

Nestling him close, I clutch his body to mine as the waves pull us farther and farther out. For a while, we're just coasting. It's not smooth by any means, but part of me feels like the storm is bound to die down soon. Nearly an hour passes with Lex hugging onto me tight. I think he actually falls asleep for a bit.

But when the storm starts raging again, we're right back to hanging on with white knuckles.

Our tiny boat is jumping and soaring, each wave bigger than the last. And of course, the damn thing had no lifejackets in it…

I'm trying to stay calm, for Lex, because I know he's afraid. He hasn't been on many boats in his life, that much is clear. But regardless of my very limited knowledge of sailing, I can't deny that being out here in the middle of the ocean, without a clue as to where we're going or where we'll end up, is daunting. Even if I wanted to try to paddle us in a specific direction right now, I wouldn't be able to.

We're at the mercy of the waves.

The boat dives and crashes over another huge one, and Lex groans, clinging to my waist with his face buried in my chest.

"I think I might throw up..." he grunts while I rub his back. "This is why I don't do... boats. Motion... sickness.... *Oh, God...*"

I kiss the top of his head, all salty from the sea water. "It's okay, baby... I've got you. But if you need to hurl, that's fine. I don't judge. I ever tell you about the first blowjob I ever gave? In high school, I met this kid at a party... Threw up Southern Comfort all over his dick." I laugh nostalgically. "It was disgusting..."

"Ren, *please*," Lex whines, yanking out of my arms. "I'm gonna fucking puke..."

He lunges toward the side of the boat, gripping the edge as he leans over, gagging. I pout, rubbing his back in calming circles.

My poor baby... I wish I had some Dramamine to give him or something.

Unfortunately, the storm is getting worse. The boat is really flying, tidal waves lifting us and sending us down in an almost nosedive. My stomach is up in my throat, slamming back down fast like I'm on one of those big, swinging carnival rides.

This is getting too intense. My pulse is jacked as I grab onto Lex's waist, holding him steady as we bounce up and down.

"Baby, you might need to... come back and sit down," I call out over the crashing roar. "It's not safe..."

"I don't feel good..." he whimpers. "C-can I have some water, please?"

Exhaling, I brush my wet hair out of my face. "Okay, fine. But hold on tight, okay?"

He nods, and I let go of him for just long enough to grab my backpack and locate a bottle of water.

And in those five seconds, we're swept up by the largest wave I've ever seen in my life.

It has to be ten feet high.

"Lex!" I shout as our little boat careens vertically.

I dive for him, grabbing his hand.

Smash! We hit the water, the boat flipping on impact.

My body is instantly submerged in freezing cold ocean. Saltwater fills my nose and my lungs, burning my face. I'm tumbling, tossed deep and disoriented. But I think I still have Lex's hand...

Don't let go.

I manage to kick myself up to the surface, hauling air into my lungs as quickly as possible. I can barely breathe, muscles straining, lungs on fire. But I fight to stay up, pulling Lex with me.

"Lex!" I yelp, hoisting his body up against mine.

He's out cold.

"Fuck fuck fuck… Lex??" I smack his cheek gently. "Lex, wake up!"

The boat is a few feet away, upside down. Pushing to get to it, I swim with Lex tucked against me. I grab onto the wood, struggling to flip the boat back over, when another wave hits and sends me tumbling once more.

He slips out of my arms. I just can't hold him…

The tide is too strong.

Breaking through the surface, I breathe and scream, *"Lex?!"*

I don't see him anywhere. I can't see *anything* in the middle of this raging sea. I'm struggling to keep my head above water, and I can't fucking *find* him.

"Lex?!" I bellow again, searching frantically.

I don't see him…

I don't fucking see him anywhere!

"Fuck!" I roar, choking on salt like fire in my throat. "Lexington!! Where are you?!"

Diving under, I flail around, panicked. I can't see anything, it's too fucking dark.

He was unconscious… Was he even breathing??

Springing out, I yell so loud my voice disappears.

He could be anywhere, and I feel like I'm drowning inside and out. Terror pounds inside my chest, the storm creating a wrath in this ocean that I just can't fight through.

I swim and swim, screaming and crying.

Lexington!!

Where are you??

I can't breathe without you…

"Lex?!" my jagged voice echoes…

Just as one last giant wave sends the boat down on top of me.

CHAPTER TWENTY-EIGHT

Ren

It's all my fault…

"Fuck!" I startle awake, immediately launching into a fit of hoarse, painful coughs.

My mouth is so dry it hurts, an agonizing burn running from my throat into my stomach. I can't breathe and I'm shaking down to my bones, freezing cold and covered in sand.

Where am I??

I'm on a beach… It's daylight, and I look around, dazed and sore, my skull pounding…

I'm definitely concussed… There's no way I'm not.

I've been hit in the head like a fuckload of times today.

My brain is *throbbing.*

But visions are coming back to me. Realization dawning…

The prison. The fireworks… The boat.

Lex.

Where is he?!

Jumping to my feet, I stumble and crash back down, face whipping back and forth. There's tall grass all around me, low, calm waters leading into what looks like an inlet or something. Maybe someone's private beach…

Shit. I shouldn't be here.

But I don't give a fuck.

"Lex!" I try to scream, but my voice is too hoarse. Barely anything comes out, and I end up coughing for another thirty seconds straight.

Eventually, I manage to stand up, scrambling up and down every inch of the shore in search of Lex or our boat, or any sign that he's…

Gulp. No. No no no…

He's fine. He has to be. There's no other option.

By some minor miracle, I didn't die out there. I washed up on shore, alive. So he has to be alive too.

If I survived, and he didn't… Well, I'll slice my wrists open right here and end it all.

Fear racks me with shivers, the overwhelming nature of everything that's happened in the last twenty-four hours piling on top of me like I've been buried alive. Anguished sobs leave my lips, tears streaming down my cheeks while I shuffle around like a zombie… in search of my love.

My only fucking everything in the whole world… Lexington.

Baby, where are you??

Sniffling, I glance around, forcing myself to get it together and *think*. I'm obviously in New York. It's the only logical explanation, but where? New York is huge, and there are tons of beaches. Wandering a few more yards, I see some houses. They're not Hamptons houses, so this can't be Montauk.

Climbing up a dune to get a better look from higher ground, I spot the ferries.

Yea… This is Orient Point.

My eyes scan the area, but I don't see anything else. No sign of the boat.

No sign of Lex.

A distraught whimper leaves me, as I wander aimlessly, with no clue what to do or where I'm going. I'm just… lost.

"Hey… are you alright?" a male voice calls out, and I jump, peering over my shoulder.

An older man is walking a dog along the beach, coming toward me.

"Y-yea…" I grumble, wiping my nose. "You h-haven't seen a guy around here, have you? A kid with a shaved head…"

He stares at me like I'm insane for a moment before shaking his head. "No… You need some help? You don't look so good… You must be freezing."

"Never mind," I grunt, stalking away from him toward the road.

This isn't good. I can't draw any unwanted attention to myself.

I need to get cleaned up and maybe find a boat so I can go out and look for Lex. Or maybe I should call the hospital, or...

I hear the man speaking, and I turn again to find him on the phone.

Shit... He's calling the cops.

I take off running. Sprinting as fast as my tired legs will take me, following the road until I get to a neighborhood. Then I slink between some houses for cover. My mental state is frayed to shreds. I'm only fifty percent sure this is actually happening right now. For all I know, I'm in a coma in some hospital, having a terrible, awful fever nightmare. *Or maybe I'm dead...*

Fuck this.

Fuck fucking this.

This all my fucking fault.

It was my idea to get on that goddamn boat and try to escape during a storm that broke Alabaster Pen in half. What was I thinking?!

We should've just stayed, in our safe, comfortable little prison bubble, locked away from all the hassle and bullshit of the outside world.

No... They were trying to kill us. We could've died there just as easily.

This is just what I deserve.

I should've known this would happen...

I don't get a normal life, a relationship... Love.

Those things aren't meant for me.

I get pain, and torment, and despair.

I scratch the jagged scar on my wrist. *God, I just want to bleed right now...*

The sun goes down with me hiding, and not a single clue what to do next. Eventually, I break into a shed in someone's backyard and curl up into a ball on the floor.

"Lexington..." I sob, rubbing my eyes as sleep steals me. "Where are you, baby...?"

I'm startled awake again in the morning to sounds that remind me I need to keep moving. But with every step, the truth is following me like a raincloud of depression.

Lex might be dead.

He might be...

The hard truth to this devastating situation is I need to get the hell out of here. I've been here too long as it is. I need to disappear, and it kills me inside to think of going anywhere without Lexington. But I fight to stay determined, locating an old junkyard and slipping into a car that looks decent.

I have a long way to go to our meeting place.

That fucking voice in my head tells me it's *hopeless*. The voice I've ignored, stuffed down, locked up far away for months. But with Lex slipped from my grip, it's coming back. Fighting its way up harder, and louder.

He's dead.

You're chasing a ghost.

He's fucking gone, Warren... And it's all your fault.

"No..." I growl, holding the wires together, flicking them over and over like a match that won't strike. "He's not dead. He's *not*."

He is... You know he is.

You watched him die.

"No!" I shout, flinching at my stupidity. "Be quiet..."

The engine finally roars to life, and I breathe out of relief. Stuffing everything away, I slump into the driver's seat of the old Lincoln I just hotwired. A useful skill I picked up for literally no reason when I was a teenager, just because I felt like being an exhausting troublemaker.

I'll drive this thing for a while, across state lines at least, then I'll steal another. I'm going to drive across the country. I'll get to California, and I'll find Lex there.

He *has* to be there. I refuse to accept any other possibility.

At least it'll be warmer there...

He's dead.

You killed him.

Because you don't deserve love.

"Shut up," I sniff, shifting into drive.

Cruising up the road, I give the ocean one last glance.

He's not dead. He's alive, and he'll know...

He'll know to meet me in California, where we agreed we'd go.

Follow the fireworks, baby. I'll find you.

Fucking Dash.

That's all I keep thinking, every spare minute that I'm not hopelessly obsessing over the whereabouts of my boyfriend.

From the moment I set off on my cross-country drive, over the course of eight days, while I stole more cars, and food, and clothes, broke into more houses and slept cramped and shivering in the backseat, I've been scoffing at that crazy Russian brat.

He made escaping Alabaster Pen seem *so* damn *easy*.

The kid got out, cruised to wherever the hell he is, and just settled into his new life. Found his hot, growly soulmate without even lifting a finger, and they became an instant couple, buying a house, getting a dog...

Like a goddamn storyline about gay fugitives that was cut from *Love, Actually*.

Seriously... The universe just *gave* him his man; handed him over on a silver platter. And Dash wasn't *even* in prison for that long!

He was locked up for what... three months? If that??

God, it's so infuriating.

I know I'm not actually mad at Dash... I'm mad at myself, and the circumstances. I'm mad at The Ivory, and that storm, and whatever morons didn't stock that stupid fucking boat with lifejackets.

I'm mad at the world, but right now, I'm feeling stubborn, and helpless, and inadequate... So what better way to give myself some relief than blaming *Dash* for making us think escaping Alabaster Isle would be a piece of fucking cake.

I was in prison too long. I barely even remember how I used to behave before I was locked up. It took me almost the entire drive to California to work up the nerve to buy a cell phone, and still, I can't even remember how to use it.

I know I should try to call Joy, to find out if she's okay. Maybe they've seen or heard from Lex. But I *physically* don't remember how to Google things.

I know... It's ridiculous. It's as simple as typing something into a box, but I'm just staring at the screen like a flabbergasted old man.

Is this the online? How do I internet??

More troubling is that I'm finally in the Golden State, but I have no idea what to do next. I remember the name of Lex's town, Thousand Oaks, and I know he went to Berkeley, so I end up just cruising around that area for days, having a mini panic attack every time someone with a shaved head walks by.

I got here. I *escaped* from prison and made it all the way to the West Coast...

But it doesn't mean jack shit, because I have no earthly idea what to do next.

I was supposed to come here with Lex. We were supposed to be *together.*

Without him, outside of prison... I don't know who I am.

It takes me a while, but eventually, I figure out my phone well enough to look up Lex's address. According to Google, his parents, Marla and Dennis Deon, still live here in Thousand Oaks, so I'm guessing the house I've been parked across the street from for two days is the same one he grew up in.

I have no plan. I don't know what I'm doing, staring at his house all day and night. But it's the only thing I could think of doing. We had no official meet-up spot, but I've replayed our last conversations in my head thousands of times, and I just keep coming back to this.

When I said I wanted to see his bedroom.

My gut wrenches painfully at the memory... Holding him while he blinked those gorgeous shimmery green eyes up at me, touching me with soft caresses. It was all so perfect up until the moment the Warden showed up.

Our sated breaths, flushed, warm skin. The love in his gaze, and the honesty in his words.

"You're my boyfriend, Warren..."

"I'm never letting go of you again..."

Smacking my forehead down on the steering wheel with a painful thud, I squeeze my eyes shut.

What if he's really gone...?

I don't want to live in this world without him. I can't imagine breathing air into my fucking lungs, knowing he's not doing the same.

I just don't want to be alive if he isn't...

My chest is hollow, the weight of all this somber doubt and insecurity filling my limbs, crushing my shoulders down until it's difficult to even lift my head. But I manage it, just enough movement to slowly peek over at Lex's house again.

It's a cute house. Not huge, just average. It's not a grandiose palace of wealth and snobbery like my home in Manhattan was. It's exactly the type of place someone like Lex would have grown up in. I can almost picture him outside as a little kid, running around while his dad sprayed him with a hose in between washing his car.

Lex told me his dad loved his old Mustang he restored... It wasn't a hobby Lex shared, being a total nerd and all, but still. I know he loved his parents, and I know they loved him too. It's obvious, just from how sweet, and caring and well-adjusted he is.

The fact that his parents still live in the house they shared as a family, even after Lex was arrested, or *killed*, as far as they probably know… it shows that they don't want to erase him from their memory. If anything, they're clinging to him, just like I am.

I sit in this spot for a very long time, watching Mr. and Mrs. Deon come and go. It aches my heart how much Lex's dad looks like him. His mother is very pretty, but I see more of Lex in Dennis. The hair color, and the eyes. Honestly, if this is any glimpse into what Lex will look like in his forties, I'd be incredibly lucky to grow old with him.

He's definitely a DILF.

The thought brings a chuckle up my throat, but it gets lodged when reality hits. And I just continue to stare.

His parents look like nice people; down to earth, loving… normal. Pretty much the polar opposite of my parents. My parents would probably scoff at them, talk down to them for not being rich, like it makes them lepers or something.

Thank God those pricks are dead…

I could only imagine Lex and I trying to introduce our families. Beth and Kenneth Xavier's smug indifference being met by Marla and Dennis Deon's kindness.

Mom blathering about their latest trip to Saint-Tropez, Dad asking Dennis about his investment capital, while Lex and I snicker and hold hands under the table…

My lips twitch, loving the little picture I'm making in my head so much that my chest throbs and I whine from the pain.

It'll never happen… My parents are dead.

And Lex might be too.

This agony makes me want to jump out of the car and run up to Lex's parents. I just want to introduce myself… tell them that I'm their son's boyfriend, and that I love him very much. That he's not dead… At least, he wasn't. Not before, when we met. He was *alive*, and we fell in love, despite how terrible our surroundings were, and how much pain I put him through.

I need them to know that their son is a fucking *miracle*. I want to thank them for bringing such a beautiful soul into this world… Someone with the patience to deal with the chaos I am.

But it would just scare the shit out of them… Bring up more questions I can't answer.

God, I hate this so much. I've never felt more like a useless waste of oxygen than I do right now.

Being that I have nowhere else to go, I end up watching the house for longer than I intended. Enough that I learn their schedules. So when Mr. Deon goes to work, and Mrs. Deon follows only thirty minutes later, I make my first actual move in days, and climb out of the car.

Their neighborhood is pretty quiet during the day, but I still make sure the coast is clear before scampering over to the house. I find a tree in the backyard that's perfect for climbing onto the roof, and manage to jimmy open a window, maneuvering my way inside. Glancing around, I find myself in a bedroom. And I know immediately, without a second of thought, that it's Lex's.

The walls are painted hunter green, adorned with posters. Mötley Crüe and Superman… *Lex's favorites.* Wandering over to a bookshelf, I admire the collection of graphic novels, books, and memorabilia. A perfectly preserved comic with Lex Luthor on the cover staring right back at me has me gulping down my sadness like bile.

I can't believe I'm actually in Lexington's bedroom right now. I can't believe I'm here without him. It doesn't make any sense… It just feels wrong.

Everything in his room is pristine, not a speck of dust to be found, which only confirms my suspicions. His parents left it like this, because they love their son, and they miss him terribly.

I know the feeling.

Shuffling over to his bed, I sit down slowly, and before I even know what I'm doing, I'm horizontal. Curled up in a ball with an exhausted, melancholy sigh, I stuff my face into his pillow. And I can't even *fathom* that it still smells like him, but it does.

Tears fall from my eyes, soaking into the soft material.

"Baby, I don't know how to do this without you…" I shudder, pulling the pillow and hugging it against my chest, squeezing it tight. "There is no me without you, Lexington. *Please* come back to me…"

My sobs are quiet, but excruciating. I can't see or feel or hear anything but him. He's all around me and it's the most frustrating thing ever because I just want him for *real.* I want to lie here for as long as it takes until he finds me… But I don't think that's possible.

I don't have any fireworks to blow off this time. Who knows if that would even work again…

Sniffling, I reach for some items on his nightstand. There are a few books stacked up, some comics, and what looks like a sound machine. I snort a sad laugh.

My sweet boy loves his sleep.

I pick up an old iPod. Surprisingly, it still turns on.

Sticking one of the headphones into my ear, I press play on the first song… *Home Sweet Home* by Mötley Crüe.

I hug his pillow, listening to the song and bawling like a baby. Pretty embarrassing, but I can't even find it in myself to care. I miss him *too* much.

I'd give anything for him to walk in that door right now…

Smiling sadly, I pick up a picture of a younger Lex, maybe twelve or thirteen, with his parents. They're at a beach, but they're wearing Christmas sweaters.

Of course, being the East Coast kid I am, I can't process something like going to the beach in winter, but I have to admit, the weather is pretty nice here right now. It hasn't dropped below fifty since I arrived in California. I'm not sure if that's normal, but I have to appreciate it, being homeless and all.

My fingers brush Lex's smiling face before I flip over the photo. On the back, there's some handwriting. It's obviously Lex's, and I read it out loud…

"Fireworks at Sycamore Cove."

CHAPTER TWENTY-NINE

Luthor

4 years ago…

"It's just a little weird…"

"Why is that weird??"

"Because"—Ren cocks a brow at me—"you're eighteen."

"*Nineteen*," I correct him, and he grins.

"A distinction only an eighteen-year-old would be desperate to make." He smirks, and I roll my eyes, forking eggs into my mouth. "But my observation stands. Nineteen-year-olds don't listen to Mötley Crüe. It just doesn't happen."

I can't help but chuckle. "Why the hell not?"

"Because they were popular fifty years ago," Ren huffs.

"More like *forty* years ago," I grumble, sort of proving his point.

"Oh, I'm so sorry." He chuckles. "I know that an extra ten years makes a world of a difference." I laugh, shaking my head. "I'm just saying, even the older dudes I used to bone didn't listen to them."

"That's not exactly fair." My head slants. "When they were kids, radio hadn't even been invented yet."

I smirk wickedly, and he fakes a laugh. "You're *hilarious*, Lexington…" Ren purses his lips, blue eyes getting this twinkle about them that tickles my stomach.

It happens when I think he's flirting with me, which is often, I might add. It's no big deal, though. We're friends, that's it. He knows I'm not interested in more… *I think.*

He can flirt all he wants, it's not going to change anything. Ren's just an overly flirtatious guy. But it doesn't matter, because I like talking to him. I've really enjoyed having him around these past few months… Regardless of how judgey he can be about my taste in music.

"My dad listened to Mötley Crüe, okay?" I explain, fiddling with my fork. "He loves rock music in general. All of it, but hairbands are his favorite. I remember this one time when I was little"—my voice picks up as I chuckle at the memory—"we were blaring *Kickstart My Heart* and dancing around the room. He was Nikki Sixx and I was Tommy Lee."

The smile fades when I remember where I am.

I'm never going to see my dad again. These memories are all I have left…

"I can just picture you as a little kid bouncing all over the place." Ren taps my foot under the table with his, and my eyes jump. "You were probably so cute."

My lips quirk. "I'll take the Crüe any day over your fist-pumping club music." I imitate the techno beat, and he laughs.

"That's not all I listen to." He scowls over his amusement. "I also like whiny emo stuff…"

"Because you're so *brooding*?" Parker chimes into the conversation, and I cackle.

"I listen to straight-up gangsta rap," Toby says, fully serious.

We all stare at him for a second, Ren and I sharing a look. Then the three of us burst out laughing until Velle yells at us to shut up.

A few minutes later, we're throwing away our trash, getting ready to leave the cafeteria, when Ren nudges my arm. "I don't accept that we have nothing in common."

My smiles grows wide. It feels wider than it's supposed to, so I crush it as best I can. "Why is that a bad thing?"

He gives me this side-look, flashing a vivid blue emotion I can't read before he hums, "I thought friends were supposed to, ya know… share interests."

"They can," I murmur, thinking about my Fallout crew.

We're a bunch of total dweebs, I guess that ties us together. But Cyrus likes that indie electronic music, like M83 and Empire of the Sun… *Car commercial music.* Tony listens to country—*gag me twice.* And Reno won't admit it, but I'd hear him singing along to Miley Cyrus on the radio sometimes when we'd play.

"When you click with someone… I dunno, I think your differences can bring you closer," I tell Ren, walking beside him as Velle herds us out into the hall. "Gives you something to bicker about." I smirk, and he grins. "Keeps the spark alive, right?"

"Well, if you're looking for someone to argue with, then Lexington, my darling, I think we just officially became best friends." He winks at me, and I laugh.

The walk through the halls is tedious, one I've done hundreds of times over at this point. But when I'm walking next to him, something about it feels different. It feels *new*, every time. Waiting to see what ridiculous thing he'll say next, if he'll brush his arm against mine, or place his hand on my lower back when we walk through a doorway. Or spout one of those awful pick-up lines he seems to know way too well.

It's nothing more, I'm sure of it. Just a curiosity Ren brings with his endless dazzling tornado of a personality… But the thing is, I don't think I want to keep walking these crumbling corridors without it.

I like having him around. Ever since he got here, the monotony doesn't seem so… monotonous.

"Tell me more about you as a kid," he demands, rather than asking. Another characteristic wildly different from my own; that cocky boy swagger. "I like little Lex Luthor stories."

Chuckling, I slide my gaze to his for a second while I consider what to tell him. "We used to go camping."

"Yea?" His brow raises like he's interested, which sets an unusual fuzziness in my chest.

I nod. "There's this state park by the ocean that my parents love. They have fireworks all year round."

His steps slow. "Fireworks?"

"Yea," I reply, confused by the sudden roundness of his eyes. "It's a family tradition. Sycamore Cove was our favorite spot. Watching the colors pop over the ocean is—"

"I love fireworks," he says softly, a smile hijacking his lips.

"You do?" I can't help but mirror it, because of how absolutely *thrilled* he looks.

His chin bobs eagerly. "New Years in the city was awesome. And then they'd have them all summer in the Hamptons. Over the ocean…" He blinks and bites his lip. "Those are the best."

My mouth slopes. "So we do have something in common…?"

"It would appear so."

Ren grazes my fingers with his, and I give him a scolding look, to which he smirks wickedly.

Damn nuisance.

But I spend the rest of the walk back wondering what it would be like to sit beside him in the sand… and watch the sky melt.

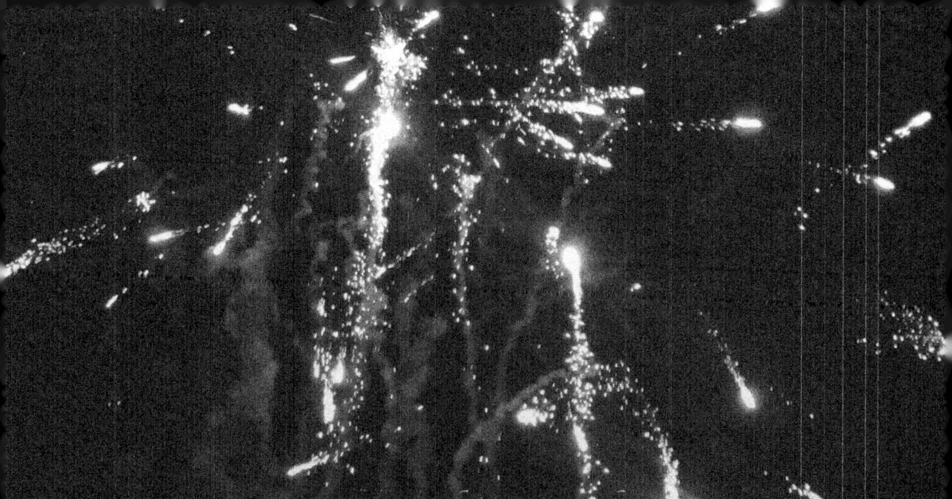

CHAPTER THIRTY

Ren

Today...

OH, HEY... WOULD YOU LOOK AT THAT.

I hate myself again.

Funny how easy it is to slip back into your default of sucking at life when you've lost your reason to live.

I've been in California for weeks. *Weeks*, all by my lonesome, with nowhere to go and no goddamn money. Not a single reputable skill to help get me by outside of prison...

Well, maybe *one*.

I don't want to think about it.

Every second I spend conscious, I'm considering ending it all.

This urge isn't just for pain anymore... The fresh new scars on my skin have given me that. I need something more permanent.

Maybe drugs... They'd be easy enough to find.

Or maybe I could throw myself off an overpass into oncoming traffic.

But it's still too uncertain. In this day and age, people are desperate to help you. With any of those attempts, I could wind up in the hospital with terminal brain damage, and I can't have that.

I don't want anyone to save me this time. I want to let go, *for good*.

I need a gun, so I can blow my goddamn brains out and leave this miserable existence behind.

Honestly, I *tried* to go the good route, I really did. I went into a few tattoo shops inquiring about jobs. But my guess is, because I have no employment history, no identification, and I look like a former model blacklisted for being too strung out, they all opted for the lie, *"We'll give you a call if anything opens up."*

Cool, yea. I won't hold my breath.

California is more expensive than New York, and a lot more aggressively indifferent to its homeless, which I didn't think was possible. I mean, technically, I *do* have a home. My stolen ninety-four Caprice Classic. It's got a roomy backseat, thank God for that. But after close-call number fifteen last week, breaking into people's houses to take showers and eat is no longer a sustainable way of living.

I'm broke. Out of options. And worst of all, I've been at Sycamore Cove every damn day waiting for Lex to show up, and he hasn't.

The voice is my head is too loud for even the strongest denier of reality like myself to overcome…

He's dead.

Lexington Deon is dead, *because of you.*

The love of my life slipped from my grip, and now, even if I had a goddamn choice, it wouldn't be one. I'm going to fucking kill myself, because I don't want to live anymore.

Not without him…

He was the only thing keeping me breathing in the first place.

I'm skulking around underneath the overpass, because I'm starving and exhausted, and I need some fucking money… Either to buy myself food, or a gun.

We'll see which one wins out with cash in hand.

I've watched plenty of young kids mulling about down here recently, getting into cars with strangers who drive away, only to return ten minutes later and drop them back off. So I think this will be a good place for me to do what I do best…

Because what does it matter when I'm all alone again, right?

I only have to stand here for five minutes before a car pulls up, and the window rolls down.

"Need a lift?" an older, heavyset guy asks me, smirking.

I cringe, glancing over his rumpled shirt and the cruddy state of his Honda Minivan with kids' lacrosse equipment in the backseat.

"I don't think you could afford me," I grumble.

He curses and drives off, and for the first time in weeks, I let a tiny smile slip.

The next three cars get the same scoffing sass. They call me a *prude*, and a *dicktease* as they peel away, and I just stand here chuckling, because I guess it's kind of funny when you think about it. I mean, I have a dollar twenty-five to my name and I'm turning married men away like guys selling water on the boardwalk for five bucks a bottle.

Look, just because I'm not in an upscale locale like The Edge, doesn't mean I'm going to give the goods away. I know what ten minutes of my time is worth. And I'm adding a surcharge for the fact that I really don't want to be doing this at all.

I call it the Bitch Fee.

"Are you a cop?" someone asks me, and I peer over my shoulder.

There's a kid with messy blonde hair standing there, opening a bottle of mouthwash. He looks pretty dopesick, dark circles under his eyes, which are a purely beautiful shade of brown and green hazel. They remind me of Dash…

Fucking Dash.

"Do I *look* like a cop?" I lift a brow.

He shrugs, taking a sip of mouthwash, gargling it for a moment before spitting it onto the ground. My eyes follow the blue liquid. "You've been standing over here for almost an hour, but you haven't gotten into a single car. If you're not a cop, then what the hell are you doing?"

"I'm holding out for the right score," I tell him firmly. "And you should too." My gaze glides him up and down, taking in his obvious definition, sharp jawline, perfect lips. "You're too hot to be handing that shit out to these chumps for a fistful of sweaty dollars."

He huffs, lips sloping in amusement. "You're not from here, are you?"

"No… I'm from New York. The land of opportunity." I grin, and he chuckles. "You a football player or something?? You're giving captain of the football team went on a bender…"

He laughs again, and I can't help how it warms me inside. He has a great smile, dimples and extremely straight, white teeth for a potential drug addict.

"You're a trip, new guy," he sighs. "Word of advice, though…" His voice trails as a new car pulls up. An Audi with tinted windows. *Not bad… A little sus, but there's potential.* "LA is a very different animal. Unless you plan on finding a sponsor to get you cleaned up, the streets are all you've got. Can't afford to be choosy."

The Audi rolls its window down, revealing a much more promising

John than the rest of these closeted husbands. The blonde kid gives me a look as if to ask, *You mind if I grab this one?*

I gesture with my hand. "By all means."

He shoots me a wink, opening the door and plopping into the car. "You're not in Kansas anymore, Dorothy."

"Be careful," I tell him quietly as the window rolls up, cutting off the sight of my mysterious new friend's hand sliding into the driver's lap.

The car speeds off, and I watch it go, my chest exponentially hollow.

I wish I'd asked him his name…

Not that it matters. I'm not here to make friends. I'm *here* because I have no other choice.

I fully understand what the kid was talking about. I could become a toy for one of the hundreds of *Producer Daddies* of Hollywood, brought out and trotted around at parties like a show pony. It would be more or less *exactly* what I did at Club Edge. I'm used to that line of work. I know I'd be good at it…

But I don't *want* to. Not after I fell in love, and experienced how blissful life can be when you have someone who actually *cares* about you to share it with. Lexington Deon ruined me for casual sex and whoring myself out.

Moments of wallowing later, my white whale shows up, in the form of white Bentley GT. The car slows to a stop, rolling the passenger window down to reveal a man in a suit with a cunning smile. He reminds me of Dom a little, in that you can just tell he's a shark waiting for the perfect moment to sink in those razor-sharp fangs.

"You're too pretty to be over here," he croons, then nods. "Get in."

Well, alright then. But only because you called me pretty.

Slipping into the car, I immediately melt into the soft leather seat as he drives away.

"So, whaddya need?" the guy asks. "Cash, drugs… both?"

Making myself comfortable, I turn on my heated seat. "Cash, mostly. But if you have strong drugs, maybe I'll take those too."

He peers at me while driving. "Looking to forget, blue eyes?"

That's so corny, I want to hurl. "This lovely *conversation* isn't necessary. I want a hundred for head. An extra fifty for swallowing. Fucking is negotiable, but I won't go below five, so don't even ask."

The guy's lips twitch. "You're a demanding thing, aren't you?"

"All worth it," I sigh, dead inside. "Satisfaction guaranteed."

The guy chuckles, cruising for a few minutes in silence before he pulls into a parking garage. I look around as he parks in a spot in the far corner, a bit secluded, but still.

"Where are we?" I ask, bemused.

"My office," he hums, turning off the engine and unbuckling his seatbelt. He turns to face me, grabbing my arm.

"Hey, what the hell??" I gasp as he lifts my sleeves, checking me for track marks, I guess.

"Oof..." He runs his thumb over the scars covering my wrist and forearm. *"Rough."*

Yanking my arm back, I pull my sleeve down, glaring at him. "Just tell me what the hell you want so we can get this over with..."

"Are you clean?" he asks, brushing my hair back with his fingers, scrutinizing me with a studious gaze.

"You'll have to be more specific," I hiss.

"When was the last time you were tested?"

My jaw clenches. "I resent that wording. People with STDs aren't *dirty*." He lifts a brow. "My *health* is fine, if that's what you're asking."

He stares at me for a moment, eyes falling to my mouth. "Alright, then."

Leaning his seat back, he opens his pants, and my heart lurches up into my throat.

Oh God, I can't do this...

Blinking hard, I shake myself out of it while he grabs the back of my head and pushes it into his lap.

This used to be so *easy* for me... But now it feels like pulling teeth without any nitrous.

I don't want to do this... I don't want his stupid dick in my mouth.

Why am I even here?? There has to be something else I could do... Anything.

God, Lex, why did you have to go and die on me?? Why did you have to leave me alone?!

You knew this would happen if you did.

My eyes are watering, tears streaming down my cheeks while I disassociate. Blood is rushing in my ears as I struggle to breathe, every muscle in my body clamped in displeasure.

No no no... No, I hate this. I fucking hate it.

I'm crying, and the guy either doesn't care, or he likes it because he's not stopping. I'm just slumped over like a hunched corpse, gagging and wheezing in pure misery.

Squeezing my eyes shut as tightly as possible, I think about Lexington...

My beautiful, sweet, shy boy.

I remember lying in a tiny, cramped bunk bed with him, kissing and touching, my heart so overflowing with emotion, I couldn't understand it. Of course, I *burned* for his hands on me, and his cock in my throat; the way he'd wrap his legs around me and caress my hair, shivering from head to toe with the new sensations I was giving him.

But it wasn't about how good it felt for our bodies. It was so much deeper than that.

I was in *love* with him from the second I laid eyes on him, and it was so confusing, it took me years to fully understand what it was. To finally grasp that we were inevitable, as more than just sex and fighting.

We were written in the stars.

From the moment we met, my heart leapt out of my chest and delivered itself to him. And despite how bruised and beaten and scarred it was, he took it anyway. He held it in his hands like a precious gift.

He *loved me back*, dirty, broken parts and all.

Lexington... I whisper in my mind with a heavy palm forcing my skull down. *I love you so much, baby...*

Wherever you are, I just hope you're happy... Happier than I am right now.

I have no choice but to imagine I'm with him...

Still using a proxy after all this time.

And twenty-minutes later, I'm deposited back on the street, with a hundred and fifty dollars and a gram of heroin in my pocket.

Emptier than I've ever been before.

"I'll look for you again," the guy says through the window while I stare off into space. "You're definitely worth the money."

Yea... I know.

He drives away, and I rush to the bushes, heaving my guts out.

I caved and used some of my money to get a motel room.

It's by the hour, so I'm only staying long enough to shower and sleep for a little bit. But when I wake up, I'm so depressed, I don't think a crane could pull me out of bed. My entire body feels like it's full of gravel, and every time I close my eyes, I see spores of black mold festering inside me like a disease.

I wish I could just lie here forever, but I need to get up. Regardless of how much it hurts, I need to go to Sycamore Cove for the fireworks. I haven't missed a show yet.

I'm fully aware that I'm torturing myself. It's been almost two months since we escaped from Alabaster Pen. I need to just accept the fact that Lex is dead, and figure out what I'm going to do next.

Either keep selling my body to random men for enough money to stay breathing. Or shoot myself full of that heroin and turn out the fucking lights for good.

It's pretty chilly out, so I bundle up as best I can with only two pairs of clothes, donning some worn sneakers and ripped black jeans I stole from the Salvation Army, and a hoodie I stole from Lex's bedroom. It says, *Talk nerdy to me*, with a cartoon of Albert Einstein pole-dancing.

It's my most prized possession.

I leave the hotel room quickly, knowing I owe them for an extra two hours that I have no intention of paying for, jumping into my beater and peeling out. I make the drive to Sycamore Cove, and because the universe seems content for me to drive off a cliff, love songs play on the radio the whole way there.

I'm in a fog of misery while I park and hop out, trudging to the beach as the sun disappears. It's dark, and I'm cold. But I'm *here*, no matter how badly it hurts.

Glancing around, I find the shore nearly empty as I plop into the sand and lie on my back, staring up at the sky.

I'm already whimpering, and the damn fireworks haven't even started yet.

"Just let me go..." I huff, tears seeping from my eyes. "I can't... *do this* anymore."

The first pop startles me. And as soon as I see the colors, I'm in a full-blown fit of convulsing sadness.

Why do I keep doing this to myself...?? Why do I keep coming here when all it does it make me miss him more??

He's gone, and I have to face it...

I'm all alone. And I deserve *to be.*

I deserve every single bit of this awful, wretched burn.

Movement comes into my peripheral, but I'm too tortured to care. The fireworks are thumping and booming, and I'm sniffling like a lonely loser, lying on the cold ground, wishing he was as dead as he feels.

But I can sense a body coming closer, encroaching on my personal space.

Come on, man… There's a whole beach available. Back the fuck off.

My glassy eyes slink over, brows furrowing at the shadowy figure fluttering a few feet away. It's obviously a guy, but he's also wearing a black sweatshirt, hood up, so I can't make out much of his features. Only that he's *staring* at me, shuffling like he might want to approach me, but he isn't sure.

"Can I help you…?" I mumble, sitting up slowly.

The guy stumbles over his feet, suddenly *running* right at me.

And as soon as he's close enough, the lights from the fireworks illuminate his face.

My heart stops.

Screeches to a halt so fast I actually cough.

"Oh my God, it's you," he cries, jumping on top of me.

No… wait…

What??

Arms curl around me, his body weight crushing me into the sand while I lie here in shock.

Holy… fuck…

"Is this… r-real??" I whine, quaking down to my goddamn soul.

He pulls back to gaze down at me, taking my jaw in his hands. And all I can see are shimmering green eyes filled with tears.

It's him. It's really him!

It's Lex. He's alive. He's here, and he's alive!

Oh my God, I think I'm having a heart attack…

"Baby, holy fucking shit…" he sobs, crashing his mouth to mine. "I found you! I fucking *found* you…" He's whimpering and whining, shuddering as he bawls into my mouth.

And my arms *finally* lift, pushing past the stunned lock in my muscles to wrap around his waist.

"Lexington…" I croak, crumbling to pieces. "Are you really here?? I'm… I'm…"

"I'm here, baby." He kisses the words onto my quivering lips. "I have you. I'm here. I made it."

"You… m-made it?" I grip his shirt in clenched fists, terrified of letting go for even one-second.

My lungs are collapsing, heart racing way too fast. I'm freaking out… *Beyond* freaking out.

I'm baffled, elated, nervous, scared, relieved, thrilled... *Way* too many things all at once. My body is shutting down.

Racked with tremors, I'm crying harder than I've ever cried before, holding on to my man tight, keeping him on top of me with our lips brushing while I sob into his mouth.

"Shh... It's okay, baby," Lex whispers, stroking my hair and my face, trying to pull back to give me space to breathe, but I won't let him. "Relax and breathe for me... I think you're having a panic attack, sweet flame."

My head shakes, and I cry even harder, hearing his voice call me that.

I thought he was gone... I was *sure* he was gone forever, and now he's *here*.

Maybe I really am dead... There's no other explanation.

Touching him all over, I take in the feel of him, desperate to convince myself this is real. The familiar shape of his body, his warmth and his smell and his voice... Those gemlike eyes and those soft pink lips.

It really is him.

He found me again, beneath the fireworks.

"I l-love you," I whisper on a jagged breath. "I missed you, and I *love you*, and I can't fucking believe you're here. Baby, I thought I'd lost you... I was sure I'd n-never see you again..."

"You can't get rid of me that easily, sweet baby flame." He smiles, and I'm breaking down.

I snort a sloppy laugh, clutching onto him for dear life. "Lexington..."

"Shhh, I know," he hushes me, soothing the burns in my soul. "Just breathe with me, Warren. I have you. I'm here, and I love you so, *so* much."

"You found me..." I hum, kissing him over and over. I'll never stop. *Never again.* "I'm never letting go of you again, not even for a second."

He chuckles, and my heart is soaring.

"I'm counting on it," he whispers...

While we lie beneath the colorful embers.

CHAPTER THIRTY-ONE

Luther

YES, YES, I'M ALIVE.

Hard to believe after everything that happened. Sometimes, I have to stop and pinch myself just to make sure.

But I *am*, in fact, alive. I don't know what it means, exactly… Surviving something so insane. Escaping prison only to almost drown, then still managing to make it across the country to find that the love of my life is *also* alive, and has been in my hometown waiting for me.

It's the ultimate improbability.

The universe, or God—*maybe they're the same thing*—must want me here. Which is a good thing, because I have no interest in leaving.

Not after everything I did to make it back to him.

When Ren finally calms down enough that I'm no longer worried he might pass out, we lie in the sand together while I tell him the story of my brush with death. Unsurprisingly, it's very similar to his. But instead of washing up on shore, I was rescued by a fishing boat.

The guys who found me brought me to a hospital, but because I had no ID, they couldn't identify me, which was a very good thing. As soon as I woke up, and felt well enough to leave, I snuck out of the hospital and immediately started hitching rides west.

I'm not proud of myself, but I did what I had to do, like stealing someone's phone at a coffee shop and using it to buy myself a bus ticket. I also used it to try calling Joy, but I wasn't able to get through.

I spent weeks worried sick about Ren, praying with every breath that he was still alive, and would be heading for California just like we'd planned. All of my logic and reasoning told me there was no way. He'd most likely died in that storm, and I was racing across the country for no reason… Chasing a ghost.

But I had to stay positive. I held out hope, no matter how bleak it felt at times. Because if *I* hadn't died in that storm, there was no way Ren had. He's a million times stronger than me.

He's a fighter, always has been.

So I channeled all of that energy, and used it to get myself back home in search of my man. But when I got to Cali, I was lost and hopeless all over again. Just because I was *here*, didn't mean I'd be able to track him down. It's a huge state… He could've been anywhere.

Then I went to my house.

It killed me not to see my parents. All I wanted was to run up to them and hug them… to show them I wasn't dead, and tell them how much I've missed them all this time.

But I couldn't. It wasn't safe. Even just being at the house was asking for trouble, so I only went inside for a few minutes to get some clothes and regroup.

And the moment I stepped into my old bedroom, I *knew* Ren had been there.

"How'd you know?" he whispers, nuzzling his face into my neck, kissing that spot he always does that gives me more chills than the cold in the air.

"The picture of me and my parents, here at the fireworks," I rumble, brushing his silky hair with my fingers. "It was on my bed, next to my iPod. When I turned the music on, it was playing *Home Sweet Home*… and I don't know how, but I just fucking knew it was you. You'd been there…" I pluck the material of my hoodie he's wearing. "Rummaging through my stuff, apparently."

Ren chuckles, wiggling in my arms. "I like your bedroom, by the way. It's very on-brand, you sexy fucking nerd."

Growling, I slope my leg over his to hold us closer together. "Leave it to you to escape prison and come all the way across the country just to break into my house and steal my clothes. You're such a stalker."

"I made out with your pillow too," he teases, and I laugh. "Seriously, though… your window is way too easy to climb in and out of. Your parents are lucky you had no interest in sneaking dudes into your bedroom until I came along."

"Are they…?" I rumble, running my hands down to his ass.

He nods, sniffing me.

The thrumming arousal in my veins subsides just a bit when the weight of the situation comes back into focus. "I'm sorry it took me so long to get to you, baby." I kiss his hair.

"Are you kidding??" He lifts his face to lock those iridescent blue irises on mine. *God, I missed them so much…* "You came back from the *dead*. Lexington, it was all my fault that we were separated in the first place. That plan was *so stupid*. You could've been killed… You almost were—"

"Stop," I demand gently. "It *was* dangerous, yes, but it worked. I only wish I'd found you sooner. I got here as fast as I could, but it wasn't fast enough, baby. I hate to think of how you've been struggling all these weeks…"

Ren's eyes are wide and sparkling with intense emotional trauma as he chews on his lower lip. I witness him swallow, brushing my fingers over his Adam's apple.

"Lexington… I fucked up," he whispers sorrowfully, brows zipped together. "I did something that I—"

Leaning up, I kiss him quickly, cutting off his words. "It doesn't matter."

His head shakes with our mouths hovering. "You don't understand. I'm *sick* over this, baby… I didn't want to, but I just… I couldn't… I *thought*—"

"Ren, I don't want you to say another word," I interrupt him once more, grazing his trembling lips with my thumb. "I'm telling you, I don't care. It doesn't matter, because it's in the past now. We did what we had to do to find each other. *That's* what matters, baby. It's the *only* thing that matters… Us. Together again, for good."

He whimpers a tired breath, blinking back visible tears while I kiss the sadness off of his mouth.

I'm sure I know what has him torn up, but I don't want to think about it. The mere fact that he's so tormented by this proves how much he's changed, from the man who hurt me intentionally all those years ago.

He's still the same Warren I fell in love with, my crazy friend who used to torture me with the sheer *mayhem* of him. But he's grown in one key aspect that I know will keep him as faithful to me as he can be…

He fell in love, too.

"Are you mine, Warren?" I touch his chest to feel his heart jumping.

"*Only* yours," he breathes, kissing me with fervor. "Forever. I belong to you *forever*, Lex Luthor Deon."

The truth in his words has me weightless. The way I can feel his honesty in his every movement, in his lips and his touch. He's done lying, because the entire truth is right here in front of us.

We made it through the storm.

Holding and cradling him, I rock him gently for a bit. Until the ocean breeze gets to be too much.

"Baby, you're shaking," I whisper. "We need to get out of the cold."

"All I've got is the car I've been living in, and, like, eighty bucks," he says.

"I hacked into some dude's Apple Pay, but using it to get a hotel is probably too risky," I tell him. "I have a plan, but it's late right now. The car will have to do for tonight."

"Hey… are you a Microsoft?" He grins huge, biting his lip. I lift my brows, waiting for it. "'Cause you're crashing at my place tonight."

I cackle out loud, and he beams. "Baby, wow. You did a nerd one."

He nods animatedly while I kiss him breathless.

Getting up slowly, at last, I brush the sand off of him while he tries to contain his obvious thrill. Then we walk, hand-in-hand, to his car.

Ren opens the door for me while I smirk. "Chivalrous. I like it."

"I try." He shrugs jokingly.

"It'd be sweeter if you weren't guiding me directly into the backseat." I laugh, climbing in.

He scoots in next to me and closes the door, grinning wider. "You knew what this was."

Chuckling softly, I grab him by the jaw for fast, hungry kisses, instantly pulling him on top of me. Sure, the state of our lives is pretty up in the air, but the most important thing is that we're back together. And it's been *way* too long since we've humped each other's brains out.

That's gonna be priority numero uno.

Ren grinds between my legs, his cock instantly just as hard as mine; like stone. Two massive, throbbing dicks, rutting into one another with obnoxious denim in the way.

"I love you," he purrs into my mouth, ripping at my clothes. "I missed you so bad, I'm probably gonna nut in like two seconds."

"Same," I rasp, shoving my hoodie off his shoulders. But I pause, blinking in amusement at the *Rick and Morty* t-shirt underneath. It's awfully familiar. "Man, you really raided my wardrobe, huh?"

"One of the perks of wearing the same size," he sneers, tugging it over his head.

"I guess I have a lot to learn about dating a guy…" I drool, tracing all the lines of muscle I've missed desperately. "It's definitely tighter around this delicious body."

"I lost some weight…" He pouts.

I pause to swallow down the gloom. I know it's obvious he hasn't been eating much recently. I'm sure I look like shit too… But none of that matters right now.

"You look gorgeous, as usual," I purr. "I'm the luckiest guy in the world…"

"I fucking love you, beautiful boy." He sucks my bottom lip into his mouth, nipping it, toying with my tongue until I'm dizzy.

"I love you more than *anything*, my sweet, perfect, sexy fucking flame." I open his pants, pushing them down enough that his cock pokes out. My fingers run up and down his length. "Oh, *hi*… I missed you terribly."

"You're talking to my dick, aren't you?"

I bite my lip, and he chuckles, yanking my pants down to pull mine out.

"Let them play," I rumble. "Look how much they missed each other…"

Ren growls, curling his fist around us together, stroking gently while I push my hips up to his hand. Frantically, we shuffle our pants out of the way as much as possible, the feel of his nuts rubbing up on mine making me weak.

"I wanna get naked with you." He trembles, biting and sucking on my mouth. "I missed you too badly to half-ass this. Only full ass right now…"

I chuckle, then hum. "'Kay…" Lying back, my eyes flutter shut while he undresses me like I'm a prince. "Anything you want in the world, baby."

Within seconds, we're both completely naked and Ren is straddling my hips, rocking his ass back against my cock.

"Do you have lube?" I ask him, hoarsely. He shakes his head. "Well…" I lift him by his hips. "I'll have to get you nice and wet with my mouth then, huh?"

He groans and nods, biting his lip while I scoot down. "Please do… I'm *aching* for you, Lex."

"Spread your legs and ride my face, baby," I command, gazing up while his cock bobs above my head.

"Hungry, gorgeous?" he whines, repositioning.

"Fuck yea." I grab his ass hard in my hands and he purrs. Holding him in place, I bury my mouth in between his cheeks, impatiently *starved*.

"Ohh... God, *Lex*..."

My tongue is in him in an instant, feathering over his hole before plunging as deep as I can get it. It only takes a moment before he's grinding on my face, holding himself up by the ceiling of the car, working his ass on my tongue.

"Mmm... mmm *mmmm*..." I groan into him while he bounces gently on my lips, opening enough for me to fuck my tongue in and out of his tiny, eager hole.

"Jesus, that feels so good..." he hisses. "I missed your mouth... I missed your tongue... *God*, I missed having *any* part of you inside me."

"I love this ass, baby," I croak, licking and licking, getting him nice and sloppy wet. "Is this my little hole?"

"All yours," he moans, hips writhing, suffocating me deep while I hold him open wide. His balls are rubbing all over my face, and he grabs his cock, jerking himself roughly above my head. "*Fffuck*, eat me, Lex..."

"You like how I eat your ass out?" I growl, my words muffled by his quivering heat.

"Y-yesss... Baby, suck on it."

"God, ride my tongue with this sweet little cunt..."

"*Fuck fuck fuck*, baby, your *mouth*..." he whines, tightening.

Pushing him off quick, he pouts like the stubborn, needy, sexy thing he is. But I bite my lip, giving him the loving sex eyes.

You know, the ones that say, *I love you so damn much, and that's why I need to destroy you with my dick.*

"Spit on me, baby," I rumble up at him.

And he does so, no qualms whatsoever. It's one of my favorite things about Ren. When it comes to anything sexual, you won't catch him hesitating. He's down for it all, which gives me the freedom to explore anything my lust-crazed former virgin mind could dream up.

Ren spits on my cock until it's dripping wet, then he climbs over me, pressing me between his cheeks. I hold him open while he holds my dick, pushing it against his tightness. Both of our chests heaving, hooded eyes locked as he fights the resistance.

"It's been so long, baby," he pants while working his hips.

"It's been a few weeks." I grin teasingly, and he scowls, face flushed.

"Not everyone goes twenty-three years without having sex." He bites his lip, smashing my crown into his hole.

"You're too *tight* for me, Warren," I croon.

"Mmm, but I want this big dick in my ass." He shivers, eyes rolling back as it finally starts to slip in. "S-so *bad*..."

"Then open up for me," I plead breathlessly, fingers digging into his cheeks. "God, I wanna fuck you... Open that hole so my dick can slide in."

"I want you fucking my ass, baby," he mumbles. "I want every... *inch!* Fuck *yesss*..."

The head bursts into him and we both groan out loud. He sinks down further on me, and my entire body is trembling.

"Mmm... *slow*," I croak. "Take me in nice and slow, sweet, scorching flame. Just like that..."

"Your cock is perfect," he gasps, palms flat on my chest. "So hard and hot and thick..."

When his cheeks make it to my pelvis, I hold him still, keeping him seated on me for many generous seconds until he starts to squirm.

"I wanna move..." he whines.

I graze my fingers along his aching length where it's resting on my abs. "Yea?" He nods fast, dark hair hanging in his eyes. "You wanna bounce on my cock, baby?"

"Yess, *please*, Lexington... Let me ride your big cock."

My head tips back, the ecstasy I'm already feeling just having him wrapped around me enough to draw my balls up tight. But I loosen my grip on his hips, allowing him to move, and he gradually lifts, gliding back down with a grunt.

"*Ffuck* me..."

My cock twinges inside him as he keeps going, building a rhythm of up and down, fucking himself slow and deep on my every swollen inch while his hard dick slaps against my stomach.

"Baby boy, I love you," he mewls, raspy and deep, sounding like he's falling apart already. "I *love* how your dick throbs inside me."

"Fuck, Warren, I've never felt what you give me." I push my hips up into him, and he sobs.

We're rocking together, grinding and pumping and clutching each other like we're holding one another to the earth. Dripping with sweat, windows fogged, I sit up so I can kiss him, grasping his face and sucking greedily on his lips.

"I love you," I gasp, stuffing my tongue into his mouth.

He meets it with his, grabbing my throat. "I love you more..."

"No, I love *you* more," I growl, biting his lip hard.

"*No*, I love—*ah!* Fuck, Lex..." He cries when I cup his balls and give them a rough squeeze. "Jesus, you're gonna make me come..."

I can't help rumbling an erotic chuckle as he bounces on my lap, riding my cock *hard*. So hard his head is hitting the ceiling. Reclining onto my back, I pull him with me, jerking his dick while he works me over furiously between his legs.

"Right there, baby... *Mmmfuck yea*, right *there*." His hole clenches. "I'm so fucking close..."

"Gonna need you to rush, sweet flame..." I grunt, fisting his hair. "I can't hold... on..."

"Don't hold on." His lips fall to my neck, where he kisses and sucks and bites my flesh. "Fucking *come* in me, Lex... Shoot it in deep."

"Ohh... *fuck*. Oh fuck, oh God..." The pleasure is whisking me away. Everything is all hot and swimmy. "I'm gonna come so hard inside you, Ren..."

"Come hard in me..."

"I'm coming... I'm fucking *coming* for you, baby."

Just as my dick begins to pulse, Ren shudders, his own cock spraying hot orgasm all over us while I fill him with mine.

"Lex... *baby*, fuck the cum out of me..." He pants and purrs and growls, fucking his whole body against mine, stroking his cock between our abs, slick cum smearing our skin. "Your dick is... so... fucking... *good*."

"You're so full right now." I bite his mouth, breathing out rumbling words while my balls tighten and release. "Feel this hot cum deep in your body, gorgeous."

"I missed you so much," he whines as we both quake, fluttering down from the heavens. "I love you... and I..."

Suddenly, he's crying into my mouth again, tears running down his cheeks as his cock throbs out even more, a full second orgasm. I can't even believe how incredible it looks.

"You're so goddamn beautiful," I whisper, my heart swelling almost painfully in my chest. "The way you come is just... *perfect*. You're mine, right, Warren? All mine, always...?"

"Yes," he croaks and sniffles. "*Yours*. Your boyfriend..."

A beaming smile takes over my face, and I kiss him gently; his lips, his cheeks, his jaw, licking away the salt of his tears while my own fall.

"*My* flame," I breathe.

Blissfully back in the arms of my *boyfriend*. The only one I'll ever have.

"Don't stop holding me, baby..." he hums, curling up on my chest.

"Never letting go of you. *Mine*."

In the morning, we go to a diner for pancakes while I get to work on my plan.

I'm not certain it's going to work. In fact, I have a basket full of doubts.

But what are we if not living proof that the impossible can be done?

Ren is gleefully eating everything in sight—using only one hand because we refuse to let go of each other—while I type away on his cell phone.

We ditched the car and the phone I'd stolen before we came here. Figured it was the best bet. Sever all ties that could potentially lead the cops our way.

It's been a long time since I've been on social media... Five whole years. So naturally, all my accounts are long deactivated. And interestingly, so are the ones that used to belong to the person I'm searching for.

He's unlisted anywhere on Google. The only shot I have at finding him is through the guys I haven't spoken to since before I was arrested.

Fortunately, their accounts are still active on Discord.

"Here goes nothing..." I mumble, typing out a direct message and pressing send.

"Kiss for luck." Ren grins, pressing a soft one on my lips.

"You taste like maple syrup," I hum, and he winks.

The phone vibrates. Checking the screen, my heart is in my throat.

DamnDatTony: Uhh... who is this?

I bite back a grin, typing.

ClarkKenteatsmyass: TONY!!! I missed you so much omg. Don't freak out, okay??

DamnDatTony: Dude I'm seconds from blocking you.

ClarkKenteatsmyass: It's Luthor...

A full minute goes by.

ClarkKenteatsmyass: Tony?

DamnDatTony: Is this some kind of sick joke??

ClarkKenteatsmyass: No… I wish. Look, I know I vanished out of thin air, but you gotta understand, it wasn't by choice. And not a day has gone by when I haven't wished I could talk to you and Reno again.

DamnDatTony: This is so fucked up… How do I know it's really you?

"Babe, selfie." I nudge Ren, and he looks up from his food long enough for me to snap a quick picture of us.

DamnDatTony: Holy fuck, it's really you… LEX LUTHOR IS ALIVE, WTF?!?!?!

DamnDatTony: Who's that you're with?

My fingers start typing, but I pause nervously, peeking at Ren.

"Let me guess, they're asking who I am, and you're freaking out because this is your first official *coming out* moment…" His blue eyes slink to mine, and he smirks.

"Please… Give me a little more credit," I mumble.

"That's exactly what's happening, isn't it?"

Scowling at him, I finish typing the message and send it. "There. See? I'm not freaking out."

Ren peers over my shoulder to read the text.

ClarkKenteatsmyass: He's my boyfriend. His name is Ren.

"Be still my heart!" he overacts, dripping with sarcasm. "That's the most romantic thing I've ever read!"

Growling, I roll my eyes, typing out more.

ClarkKenteatsmyass: I'm in love with him, Tony. I know it's strange because I didn't date guys before, but things changed when I met him. He's perfect, and crazy… and suuuper hot (obv). He's my reason for breathing, tbh.

Ren hums, kissing my jaw. "You're getting blown to smithereens later, sweet boy."

I smile while the phone buzzes repeatedly.

DamnDatTony: That's way tooo much to unpack bruh

DamnDatTony: I'm adding Reno to the chat

****LuckyShot has joined the chat.****

DamnDatTony: Reno! Luthor's back and he has a gay boyfriend!!

LuckyShot: *GIF of Homer Simpson disappearing in the bushes*

ClarkKenteatsmyass: Hiiiii Reeee!

ClarkKenteatsmyass: It's true… I have a boyfriend. He's reading this entire interaction over my shoulder so don't say anything bad about him

LuckyShot: Well……… I'm sure he's a lovely man

ClarkKenteatsmyass: He's actually pretty awful

Ren elbows me, and I grunt.

DamnDatTony: Hold up, so where have you been all this time??

LuckyShot: Yea, it's been years dawg.

LuckyShot: Were you off on a gay cruise meeting this homeboy and falling in love?

ClarkKenteatsmyass: In a way…

Ren laughs out loud.

ClarkKenteatsmyass: Guys, unfortunately I don't have much time to chat right now. I need your help…

DamnDatTony: Wow… he shows up after 5 years asking for shit.

LuckyShot: Typical

ClarkKenteatsmyass: When have I ever asked you chodes for anything??

No response, for many seconds.

LuckyShot: He's right.

DamnDatTony: Ok. You're totally selfless, Luthy. How can we help?

ClarkKenteatsmyass: I need to get ahold of Cyrus

LuckyShot: Why…?

LuckyShot: Because he's gay?

ClarkKenteatsmyass: Yea, exactly. It's a rule. Every gay guy must seek out every gay person they've ever met to discuss rainbow business, didn't you know that?

ClarkKenteatsmyass: *eye-rolling emoji*

"Your friends are stupid." Ren giggles at my side. "I love it."

ClarkKenteatsmyass: I just need his help and I can't find his info anywhere. Have you guys heard from him?

DamnDatTony: Not often, but he has a new Discord…

LuckyShot: It's ShyGuyCy

"Aww!" I squeal, immediately adding him as a friend and typing out a message.

ClarkKenteatsmyass: Good looks, fellas.

DamnDatTony: Lemme guess, you're gonna ghost again?

I smirk.

ClarkKenteatsmyass: No way, nay nay.

ClarkKenteatsmyass: Just give me a bit to get a good encryption going. And like the Terminator… I'll be back ;)

Peeking at Ren, I wink while he purrs in my ear, "*Come* with me if you want to live…"

A snorting laugh bursts out of me, and I grab his face. "There is no conceivable way I could love you more."

"*God*, the traffic here is horrendous," Ren gripes as we get out of the car, stretching our limbs.

"Says the guy from New York." I grin, thanking the Uber driver with a wave.

"New York traffic is like the Autobahn compared to this." Ren grabs my hand while we trudge up the walkway of the giant house.

"Hey, just be glad *we* didn't have to drive." I pull in a deep breath to calm my flinging nerves.

"That's true…" he sighs. "I can't believe your online friend you've never met in real life sent a car to pick us up."

"He's a good dude," I murmur, stopping in front of the door. "Just be polite, okay? I don't know what to expect, and we could really use a win."

"Who are you talking to??" Ren chirps. "I'm a treasure."

I roll my eyes, though I can't stop grinning. I've been all smiles for the past two days. Despite not knowing how *anything* in my life is going to pan out, I'm back with my boyfriend, kissing and touching and bickering nonstop. It's just the best, and quite frankly, it's difficult to see any of the negative with this one great big flaming ball of awesomeness in our arsenal.

We're out of prison, in the real world, together.

Everything else can suck my butt.

Holding my breath, I ring the doorbell, fidgeting in place. Ren's right… It *is* nerve-racking to be meeting an online friend in real life.

Especially when you're fresh out of prison and have completely forgotten how to act around people who aren't criminals.

Let's just hope Cyrus isn't horrified by us...

The door opens, and we're greeted by a tall, shirtless dude with golden hair, muscles for days, and brilliant ocean eyes.

I think we just opened the door to an Instagram model's feed.

Ren squeezes my hand.

"Holy crap, you're Tauren Vance," I murmur as realization dawns, and I freeze in my state of star-struck.

He smiles kindly. "You must be... Lex Luthor." His gaze narrows teasingly, and I giggle the uncoolest sound I've ever made.

"I love your tattoos..." Ren's head tilts, gaze sliding down Tauren's exposed torso, following the stars of ink disappearing into his sweatpants.

I elbow him hard in the ribs. "Sorry. This is my boyfriend, who has no manners..." Leaning into Ren, I whisper, "Behave. We're in the presence of greatness."

"I could *bow*..." He bites his lip.

Tauren simply chuckles and steps aside. "Please, come in. Cyrus and his brother are out back."

He guides us inside, and we follow like eager puppies. I knew Tauren would be here, given that Cyrus told me so when we were messaging. He lives with his stepdad and his twin brother now, after all the drama went down with his parents before I was locked up.

We didn't get into any of that, though. Basically, I just told him I needed help, and he gave me his address.

He's always been the sweetest dang human on the face of the earth.

But Tauren Vance... I mean, *wow*. The guy is a rock star to us tech nerds. His startup blew everyone's minds, and he became a billionaire at thirty-four. After which he sold the company to Amazon, and now I guess he travels the world with his stepsons as a super wealthy and almost unfathomably attractive genius.

Seriously... Goals. I mean, not the stepsons part. But the rest... The dude's an icon.

"Great place," Ren croons, heart-eyes aimed primarily at Tauren, which has me scowling.

"Should I muzzle you now, or...?" I whisper.

"Baby, you know who I am." He slopes his face in my direction. "I'm never not gonna notice hot guys. But no matter how much I tease, they'll never *ever* hold a candle to my sweet, fuckhot, big-dicked perfect boyfriend."

My cheeks flush, and I bite my lip while he kisses my neck. "Are you *lying*, Warren?"

"Never to you, my beautiful love."

I blink at him, beaming. "I believe you."

Tauren peers at us over his shoulder while we walk through the house toward the backdoor. "I didn't want to interrupt… That was highly adorable." I don't think I could possibly be redder. "But regarding the house, thank you. It's just a rental. We've been here for a bit, but we tend to move around a lot. I'm sure Cy will tell you."

We stop in front of the doors, and he turns to face us. "Honestly, I'm really glad you're here. The boys don't get to make many friends… Since we travel a lot, and all."

Ren and I nod, sharing a look before he pushes open the door, gesturing for us to head out back. It's a gorgeous view of Malibu, trees and ocean just a few yards away. There's a pool, but it's a little cold for that right now.

Ooh! Hot tub!

Glancing left, I spot two black-haired guys sitting side by side in reclining chairs. They're identical twins, a fact that's only apparent because I *know* it. Otherwise, it might be hard to tell.

One of them has his lip pierced and his fingernails painted black, all black clothes, hood up with a guitar in his lap as he strums beautiful music. And the other looks like his nerdy reflection, in a blue hoodie that says, '*Ask me about my cats*,' typing away on a laptop.

That one's obviously Cyrus.

Tauren brings us over, and they both look up at the same time, identical green eyes locking us with shockingly similar expressions.

"Hey! Oh my God, it's really you!" Cyrus jumps out of his chair, throwing his arms around me.

Smiling fondly, I hug him back, thoroughly warmed by this friendly greeting.

See? Online friends are *real friends.*

Releasing me, he peeks at Ren. "And this must be *Warren*." He gives Ren a hug, and Ren looks surprised by the affection. Cyrus pulls back, holding him at arm's length while he glances at me. "I've gotta say, I was only mildly shocked when you said you were coming over with your *boyfriend…*"

I chuckle, rubbing the back of my neck. "Yea, I know. I guess a lot can change in five years, huh?"

Cy's eyes fling to his brother, then to Tauren. "You can say that again. Um, guys, this is my brother, Colson."

The emo version of Cyrus nods at us and grumbles, "'Sup."

Tauren plops down next to him on the chair. "Don't mind him. He gets grouchy when he's in the zone."

The three of them share another look, and I'm getting some vibes that I'm trying hard not to fixate on. It's clearly not lost on me or Ren that Tauren's hand is resting on Colson's knee.

His left hand has a ring on it still... That's interesting.

Colson's wearing one too, though he has a few rings on, so maybe it doesn't mean anything.

My eyes are trying to be subtle while they search Cyrus's hands, landing on a ring on his left hand. I blink rapidly.

"Have a seat," Cyrus says kindly. "Make yourselves comfortable. Mi casa es su casa. You want something to drink?"

"Uh, that's—"

"On it." Tauren jumps up from his seat before I can finish, storming back toward the house.

Ren and I plop down on the same chair, Ren's arm slinking possessively around my waist. Colson is eyeing us pretty hard, and when our gazes meet, his darts away, focus back to his guitar.

"So... What the hell have you been up to for the last five years?" Cyrus asks, sitting cross-legged on his chair, giving us his full attention.

"Alright..." I sigh. "I'm just gonna dive right in. Remember how I helped you erase that video that time?"

Colson's face snaps back up.

"How could I forget." Cyrus purses his lips to cover up a smirk.

"And you agreed to owe me a favor in return...?" My brow arches.

Cyrus nods. "Mhm..."

"Well, I'm here to cash in on that." I straighten. "And if we're being honest, it might seem a little crazy. But I need you to promise you won't tell anyone we're here... Not that you've seen us or talked to us. As far as you're concerned, you haven't heard from me in five years, got it?"

"Already done." Cyrus nods. "No questions asked. You have no clue how much you actually helped me back then, Luthor. I'm eternally in your debt."

"That's sweet… Hold that thought." I grin. "So basically… we're escaped fugitives."

Cyrus chokes on nothing and starts coughing.

Colson's face lights up. "This just got a fuckload more interesting…"

"Hang on… *what now??*" Tauren barks, staggering over with a tray full of drinks like he's the butler.

"It's a long story." I rub my eyes. "I can't get into the whole thing right now, but I promise I'll tell you all the details. Essentially, we were in this awful prison, and we escaped. And we just need somewhere to crash for a few until we figure out our next move."

"Holy bananas…" Cyrus whispers, gaping at us.

"Alright, listen," Tauren growls. "You seem like sweet kids. But this doesn't sound safe in the slightest. I'm gonna have to ask you to leave."

"Hang on, let's just hear them out," Cyrus whines.

"Nope. Sorry." Tauren shakes his head assertively back and forth. "You two are my only concern, and I will *not* go to jail for harboring fugitives. Not a chance in hell."

"The cops won't be looking for us," Ren says. "It's not that kind of place."

We give the three of them knowing looks, and since they're all obviously smart, they piece together what we're not saying.

"Okay, well, I'm sure *someone* will be looking," Tauren argues. "And I can't have that."

"T…" Cyrus mumbles.

"Don't *T* me," he grumbles, arms folded over his chest like he's laying down the law. "It's my *job* to protect you both. End of discussion."

Colson clears his throat, standing up and padding barefoot over to Tauren. "May I speak with you for a moment?" The evil twin suddenly looks and sounds a lot more polite and subservient than one would expect.

Tauren's eyes lock with Colson's, some visible heat moving between them as they share a wordless conversation. Eventually, he nods, and the two of them stalk inside the house.

I'm *itching* with curiosity right now. Especially after the rumors from all those years back, about Tauren and Colson having a physical relationship.

But where does that leave Cyrus in all this??

I'm dying to ask, but I know it's not my business to pry, not when they've so graciously invited us into their home.

My boyfriend, however, has no problem doing it.

"Is your hot brother banging your hot stepdad?" Ren asks Cyrus, without an ounce of shame or social etiquette.

God, I love him.

Cyrus spits out his sip of water. "Uh… No. *No*, that's not…" He seems a bit flustered, and of course, he changes the subject. "Listen, don't worry about Tauren. We'll smooth things over with him. As far as I'm concerned, bros before… the law?" I chuckle, and he grins. "You're welcome to stay here as long as you need to. We're in Cali for a little while longer, anyway."

"How much longer?" I ask.

"Open-ended," he hums. "We kind of just go wherever the mood strikes, whenever it strikes us. Take as much time as you need. Plus, this place is huge. More than enough privacy."

"Good, 'cause we just got out of *prison*." Ren smirks. "The amount of fucking we need to do to make up for lost time could be considered rude when you're a guest in someone else's home."

I laugh, shaking my head.

Cyrus blushes, mumbling, "Trust me, I get it."

Ren peers at me.

Okay, yea. They're definitely both fucking the stepdad.

How does that even work?! God, I'm so curious!

Tauren and Colson return a moment later. Tauren is brushing his messy hair back into place and Colson is flushed with visibly swollen lips. He plops back down in his chair, shooting a wink at his brother.

Tauren purses his lips at us, then sighs. "Let me show you to your room."

Cyrus wasn't wrong. This house is ginormous.

I guess I'd expect nothing less from a damn *rental* acquired by Tauren Vance.

The three of them gave us a tour, then offered us something to eat, which naturally we accepted and scarfed down because we went years without a decent meal. I swear to God, everything tastes like heaven in my mouth compared to the gross food of Alabaster Penitentiary. Cyrus said we can go for tacos tomorrow, and I burst into tears.

It was a little embarrassing. Let's move past it.

They also gave us beer. And while it wasn't my first drink—*I partook at a few parties in college... Okay, I sound like a total nerd*—I also turned twenty-one in prison. I'm not exactly a drinker. But I was excited to try a delicious local microbrew while Ren stared at me, giggling.

And now I'm drunk.

We've adjourned to our new bedroom, upstairs, on the other side of the house. It's decorated nicely, modern and not too ostentatious. The view of the ocean from our window is gorgeous, and running my fingers along the comforter, I think I'm actually getting a hard-on from how damn soft it is.

Ren closes the door and locks it. And we stand there, gazing at each other. Smiles so wide we look deranged, eyes all lit up and shimmery.

I bite my lip, and he bites his.

I cannot fucking *believe* we're here. I still can't.

Ren and me... Together. Alone in an actual bedroom with an actual nice as fuck bed.

No bars, no chains, no guards waiting to pull us apart. No cold, musty prison air, or stiff mattress pads on rickety bunk beds. No toilet five feet away.

We have our own private en suite, through an actual *door*. Our own shower for only us to use. With a tub.

We can take a bath together!

Seriously, it's all so mind-bogglingly fantastic and unbelievable, I'm still on the verge of endless tears. It might take me weeks to get over this overwhelming flood of emotions. But I'll get there... I'm sure I will.

Right now, I'm just... basking in it.

"What... what should we do first?" I murmur, voice fluttering with excitement as I watch my boyfriend breathing heavily.

"Is that a real question?" He smirks, lifting his shirt over his head.

My pulse pings as I follow his lead, both of us stripping down naked and crawling into the bed. The sheets must have a thread-count of a million. I can't stop squirming my bare flesh around on their softness.

Ren nestles in, grabbing me by the waist and pulling until we're flush. Heads resting on the fluffy pillow, we just stare at one another; sky-high blue meets stormy sea green. I place my palm over his heart, the rapping calmer than it's ever felt in all the times I've touched him here.

"I always wondered how this would feel," I whisper. "To be in a bed with you... Outside of there."

"Me too," he hums, fingers dancing up and down my hipbone. "I used to dream about it."

"Me too." My voice is so low, it's but a rumble in my chest. "I wondered if it would be the same..." I swallow and he blinks. "If it was the prison holding us together..."

His eyes shine, not a single glimmer of doubt in there, despite my words. As if he's fully confident in us, and what we are to each other.

I love that about him. I love it so much it almost hurts, because he's never had a single wavering doubt that we'd end up together.

About *himself*? Sure. There's been a lot of doubt there. He was never confident in what he could be for me. But his *feelings* for me... Those were fragments of truth scattered among the lies.

A burst of flaming love to light up the night.

"And?" he breathes, lowering his mouth over mine.

"You were right," I confess. "I'm yours, firestarter. Beginning to end."

His smile brushes mine. "I've always been yours too, baby. You know that."

"Promise?" I trace the ink over his heart.

"Promise."

And he kisses me with possession.

No word of a lie.

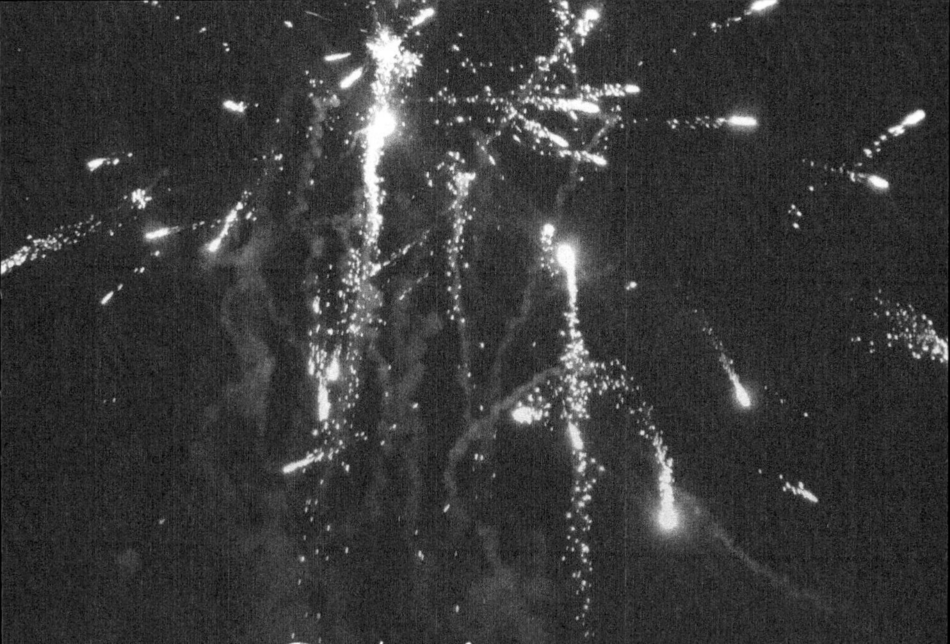

Ren's Epilogue

"Uhh… fuck… *Harder*, baby."

"You like it rough, sweet flame?"

"Mmmyeaa… Fuck it like it's yours."

Lex growls, biting the back of my neck hard. "It *is* mine…"

"Fuck yea, it is…" I groan, eyes rolling back while his hips smack against my cheeks. "Claim it. Show it who's—*oh God, right there*—boss."

My entire front is smashed against our bedroom window, and Lex is just pounding away at me from behind. Pulling my hair, sucking my shivering lips, driving that big, perfect cock in and out of my ass while my dick leaks all over the glass.

That's gonna be a difficult stain to explain to the cleaning lady.

I should probably just clean it myself…

"Jesus, baby, you're lighting me up," I cry, praying we're not fucking so hard that I might come crashing right through this window…

But then also barely caring because with that dick living on my prostate the way it is, I couldn't give a fuck less about plummeting two stories amidst shards of glass.

My boyfriend's dick is that *good.*

"I hope you're ready, naughty flame…" he grunts, gripping my throat and squeezing until my face becomes tight.

"R-ready…" I whine, wondering what'll happen if I come all over this window.

"Ready for a big load in your sweet ass," he hisses, pumping his cock almost furiously.

God, his mouth is just so filthy... I love it.

Hard to believe this kid was a virgin when I met him. An adorable, doe-eyed boy who'd only ever made out with girls. Now, he's fully aboard the gay sex train, saying things like, "That tight hole is so thirsty for my cum, isn't it, baby? You gonna suck me dry, you pretty little slut?"

My heart is racing, beads of sweat running down my back that he licks up like the ferocious fuckboy he is. For *me only*, of course.

"Lexington, you fffuck me so good... Fuck me open, baby... *God*, fuck that sweet spot, baby love."

"I'm gonna come..." he groans, slamming into me harder and harder.

I can feel his body stiffening. *He's about to blow...*

And my balls draw up in wait, because *God*, I love that feeling of him swelling up and pouring into me.

"Come in me deep, Daddy..." I purr, smirking because I know he likes when I say things like that right when he's about to come.

Sure enough, he grabs me by the hair, yanking my face so he can kiss my mouth roughly. "Don't come," he growls, then whimpers, his entire body shuddering. "*Fuuuck* yes, Ren, I'm coming. *Uhh* I'm coming in you."

"Come for me, babe," I whisper between his quivering lips.

"Don't come... *don't come, don't come*... God, I'm coming, but *don't*... you... dare... *come*."

A gasping chuckle leaves my lips while my muscles burn with the strain of holding back. Just feeling his cum unloading inside me is always enough to push me over.

But I have to obey his commands... I just *have* to.

I don't even have a choice. As much as I love pushing his buttons, when we're fucking, if he gives an order, it's like gospel for my body, whether I want it to be or not.

Lex fizzles down from his orgasm high, and I'm clinging to the window, knowing that a light breeze could send me spilling over the edge.

Lex pulls his cock out of me, spinning me around quick and falling to his knees. My eyes shoot open to watch as his mouth slurps over my slick, dripping head, his fingers gliding between my legs.

"Mmmff..." I grunt while he sucks me rough and deep, stuffing two fingers inside my ass to hold his cum in place.

He pops off with a sigh, licking and teasing my nuts. "I love this cock... It tastes so sweet. So big and hard leaking everywhere." He peeks up at my face. "You wanna come, don't you?"

I bite back a pout, nodding fast.

He pulls his fingers out of my ass, raising a brow. "You want me to swallow it all?" He stuffs them into his mouth, sucking off his cum from my ass, and my knees are *buckling*.

"Jesus fucking Christ..." I whine and grunt when he shoves his fingers back inside me. "Y-yes! *Please, Lex*... Beautiful boy, suck all my cum out into your perfect mouth."

"Mmm..." he hums, lurching his wet mouth back onto my dick to suck hard.

He bobs for only a few seconds before I can feel it rushing up, muscles clenching in my abs. His fingers reach for my prostate, and I choke out a strangled sound, my orgasm bursting out between his plush lips.

The way he sucks me in unlike anything I've ever experienced in all the *many* blowjobs I've had over the years...

He goes at me deep, sucking hard, but always keeping it slow. Like he's making out with my cock, tongue working forward and back, using it to massage my aching inches until I have no choice but to spill for him.

My ass clenches on his fingers, streams flowing into his throat while he drinks down every drop. And when he's sure I'm done, he slurps off, giving my crown a soft little kiss before standing up, pulling his fingers out of me at the same time.

"My cum is leaking out of you, filthy flame," he sighs, kissing my lips softly while I cling to him to stay upright. "Gonna be a sexy *mess*..."

"Carry me to the shower..." I yawn, sated and blissed out, arms draped over his shoulders, while I slump, exhausted, against his body.

He chuckles and hoists me up, carrying me, only sort of uncoordinatedly, to the bathroom. My legs are around his waist and we're both giggling like idiots, because I'm sort of bigger than him. Not by much, but still. It's funny when he carries me. I'm sure it looks ridiculous.

He doesn't set me down on my feet in the shower, but rather lays me down on the floor, immediately turning the water on so it sprays cold in my face.

"Ah! Jesus!" I scream while he laughs wickedly. "You bitch!"

"Who, *me??*" He bats his eyelashes, stepping inside the glass shower stall.

"You're an annoying idiot," I grumble as he helps me stand.

"That's not very nice." He faux pouts. "I just sucked a pretty magnificent orgasm out of you."

Pushing into his space, I back him up against the wall, both of us grinning and glaring. It's what we do. We like to fuck and fight together. Teasing is a second language, and we're both constantly trying to figure out which of us is in charge. Realistically, it fluctuates, and I love it that way. Gone are the days of being tossed around by giant, cocky alpha-holes.

I don't miss it one bit.

The way Lexington and I burn each other up is a million times hotter than anything I used to tell myself I liked.

I was always lying, anyway.

"Where'd you learn how to suck dick like that?" I narrow my gaze at his face, grabbing some expensive body wash and lathering it up in my hands.

"Where do you think?" He huffs, rolling his eyes. "From the only dude who's ever sucked my dick before… The one who's been consistently sucking me off for years." I grin, running my soapy hands across his wet skin. "I picked up a few things."

"Hmm… Tell me more about this mysterious cocksucker. He sounds hot," I tease, and he laughs.

"Well…" Lex sighs, leaning back and letting me wash him. "He is definitely hot. Fucking *gorgeous*, really. He's smart and sassy…"

"*Sassy?!*" I cackle.

"He's fun," he goes on. "So, *so* much fun. Definitely the coolest guy I've ever met. And he's loyal, and has a big heart." I lift my brow. "And even bigger dick."

"There it is."

He beams. "He's psychotically possessive… Crazy jealous… Just a real toxic fuckboy."

I giggle, biting my lip.

"But he's *amazing*. He's everything I never knew I wanted, and everything I've ever dreamed of having, all in one beautiful, messy, *perfect* package."

Lex's eyes are really shining at me, causing my hands to slow. My smile slips away, raw emotion taking over in place of the teasing. Because, yes, I know he's telling the truth, but there's something so vulnerable about the way we're standing here, naked, beneath the spray of water.

Like we've done so many times before, locked away in prison.

"He's my villain with the face of a hero," he whispers, touching my chest gently, tracing his name that I added to the firework tattoo over my heart. Then he takes my hand, moving it to my name on his chest, in the exact same spot. "And I want to be his… till death do us part."

What...?!

My heart slams fast, chills sheeting my flesh while I gulp down a mouthful of nerves.

Lexington Deon drops down onto one knee in the fancy shower, holding my waist while he peeks up at me, looking all shy and terrified.

"Warren Xavier..." he mumbles, voice shaking. *I'm gonna fall...* "Will you marry me?"

Holy, oh my God...

What in the name of...

"Yes." I shove the words out as fast as possible. My head starts bobbing up and down, pressure building behind my eyes. "*Yes...* fuck yes. I mean, *come on...*" He snorts, biting the inside of his cheek while I whimper and drop onto the floor before him. "*Fuck*, Lexington... *Yes*, I will marry you."

Our mouths crash together, kissing and laughing and crying like idiots. My heart is soaring through the air like a bird finally free of chains.

I can't believe this...

I can't even...

I'm about to pass out, I'm shaking so hard.

"Are you surprised?" he rumbles, and I laugh into his mouth.

"Uh, *yea*," I mewl, kissing him over and over. I physically can't stop. "What the hell?? I didn't see that coming at all..."

"I know." He beams. "I wanted to be the romantic one for a change."

"Please, you're always romantic." I sigh, still shivering while I touch his jaw. "Just the other day, for example. You brought me that cookie."

He snickers. "It was a Valentine's heart from Panera. Really not that serious."

"I thought it was very romantic," I swoon, and he pouts.

"I was going to wait until later, but I couldn't," he hums, touching my lips. "Not when you tee'd me up like that."

I chuckle. Then pause. "Wait... you planned to ask me later?? This wasn't just a spur of the moment thing...?" His face lights up, and he jumps out of the shower, scampering away. My face scrunches in confusion. "Lex...? Are you coming back?"

"Finish washing your ass and come here!"

"Okay, that's highly rude," I scoff. "If that's how you're going to talk to me as my husband, I might have to reconsider..."

"Just get out here, you nuisance!"

Rinsing off quickly, I strut out of the giant fancy shower, wrapping a large, super soft towel around my waist. This bathroom is literally the polar opposite of the showers at Alabaster Pen, which just makes showering together *so* much better. I mean, probably fifty percent of our relationship was spent showering together in that moldy fungus-ridden place. But *now* when we do it, there are no guards barking at us. No strangers washing their balls a few feet away. No angry rapists looking to fuck or fight.

We get to fuck *alone*, and take our time. We have warm water and expensive toiletries provided by our rich friends. Not to mention, the tub…

Damn, that thing is something else. We've only been here two weeks and we've gotten *very* good use out of it.

Sauntering around the corner into the bedroom, I stop short. Lex is holding something in his hand, and he grabs mine, pulling me closer.

"What… is that?" I whimper, blinking at it in shock.

"It's an engagement ring," he murmurs. "For you." Taking my left hand, he slides it onto my ring finger. "I found it on the beach. I think it's silver… Nothing special, but I wanted you to wear it."

My chest is caving in as I stare at the slender circle around my finger. "It's beautiful…"

"You really like it?" he asks, and I'm about to collapse.

He seems so *excited*, so nervous and thrilled at the idea of giving this to me.

My sweet, shy boy…

He wanted me to wear his ring??

"But what about you?" I gaze at it, mesmerized. "You don't get one?"

"When we get married…" he whispers, and I shiver, "I'll wear one too."

"So you're saying I'm the girl in this scenario?" I rumble, and he laughs.

"Well, *you* were the one wearing lingerie… I'm just saying."

"You're so *funny*, Lexington," I hiss, grinning as I tackle him onto the bed.

We end up making out for many minutes, until I can't help but suck his perfect dick, attached to his perfect body, because *he's* perfect… And mine.

Till no death that could ever part us.

The next day, Lex goes out shopping with Cyrus and Tauren, while I stay home, practicing tattoos on Colson.

These three guys have been the biggest lifesavers ever.

Cherry flavor too… The best kind.

Not only have they allowed us to stay here while we figure out what the hell to do with ourselves, but they've also been paying for literally everything we do, since neither of us can work. We're completely indebted to them. Mostly Tauren, since a majority of the money is his. But some of it is also Colson's. He's a pretty famous musician at this point.

Colson's a bit more of a social media personality, content creator type figure, since he keeps his identity a secret and doesn't show his face. But he makes beautiful music and releases albums online, which he's been doing for years now under the name CBV.

I know what it stands for, but I'm not telling. That's a story for another time.

When it boils down to it, Lexington's online pal, Cyrus, and his brother and stepdad have become our family. And at a time when we really needed it, maybe more than we even fully understood.

Things have been a little tough, not knowing what's going on back in New York. We still haven't been able to reach anyone on the island, which keeps us in a constant state of worry.

I know what you're thinking... *You escaped from prison, dumb dumb! Who cares what's happened in that shithole! Move on with your life!*

If that is what you're thinking, it's pretty harsh, tbh.

Not everyone on that island was evil. In fact, a lot of those people were also our family. They're people we got to know over the years, people we confided in, and relied on. People who stuck their necks out for us when they really didn't have to. Mainly Joy, Rook, and Velle.

And Byron...

It's a sore spot, honestly. The fight we got into before everything went down still haunts me. He was one of my best friends; my *only* friends, because I've never really had them before. I just feel like shit over it, and not knowing whether he's dead or alive aches inside my chest sometimes.

For the first time in years, I'm finally comfortable enough to talk more about Parker. And what Byron said, about me being selfish and not caring about his death... It weighs on me heavily.

Lex insists it wasn't my fault. That I did everything I could have done for the kid, but it doesn't stop me from hating the fact that he died, and I never even got to say goodbye.

So yea... as happy as we are to be *free* and in love—and *engaged*, now—things aren't exactly settled.

"This is gonna be the coolest tattoo of Ronald McDonald anyone's ever seen," I grin, running the needle through the flesh on Colson's shoulder blade.

"What?!" he barks, and I giggle.

"Nothing. Never mind. So, how's that new song coming along?"

"It's good," he says quietly. "I'm not sure about the hook… Gotta keep working on it, I guess."

Artists. Never satisfied with anything.

I like Colson a lot. He's a good kid, very different from his brother, and from Tauren. I can kind of relate to his sullen, emo boy personality, though he likes to wear that stuff on the outside too. It's just a different sense of style, but from what I understand, he's really come into his own over the years.

"This gun is awesome," I sigh, ogling the fine lines of the mountain I'm drawing on his back. "I don't see how I'll ever be able to pay you guys back."

"Psshh," he scoffs at me, and my grin widens. "Don't worry about paying us back. Money ain't no thang."

"Yea, that's because you have it," I grumble, chuckling.

"Hey, you told us your story." He peeks at me. "You were a spoiled rich kid growing up too. *And* your parents were fucking loser scumbags." He smirks while I continue to laugh. "We're a lot alike, ya know."

"That we are," I sigh, fiddling with the gun.

Suddenly, fingers are grazing the rough skin of scars on my wrist, blacked out by the excessive ink I cover them with. Gulping, I shift awkwardly.

Until he says, "I've been there, man."

I cock my head at him. "Yea?"

He nods. "I didn't do it that way… Not all the time, anyway. But I tried to end it once…"

A faraway look passes over his features, as if he's remembering something.

I'm just staring at him, my heart breaking a little. I know exactly how that feels… To be so out of control in your own head, while everyone else is walking by, chatting, laughing, interacting with you.

On the outside, you might look normal, but beneath the surface, it all feels rotten and heavy with so much sadness you just have to *get rid* of it, at any cost.

"How did you overcome it?" I ask him quietly, with more vulnerability seeping out in my tone than I'd like.

I know for a fact Lexington makes me happy. He fills me with light, gives me warmth and affection and love every single day we're together. But it's not right to rely on him to fix my issues, and I know it's probably not something he's even capable of doing.

These are things I'd need to work on *myself*, for me.

"Well, for one thing, I finally got some support." Colson sighs, and I pick back up tattooing him to distract from how much this conversation is affecting me. "I finally asked for help, because people aren't just gonna know what's on your mind, ya know? They're not psychics."

"Lex says psychics are swindlers," I mumble, and he laughs.

"Yea, Cy and Tauren say stuff like that too," he hums in amusement while I grin. "Anyway, I found an actual doctor, a *good* one, who wasn't a murderous fuckhead. I got on medication, and I learned how to manage it the right way. It's like Dr. Lonnie always says… Mental illness isn't your fault, but it is your responsibility."

Nodding, I chew on my lip for a moment, considering this. "I think it'd be… cool. To feel better, I mean. To actually know what's going on in my head and try to… like you said, manage it."

"What's stopping you?"

"Uh, hello…" I huff. "Escaped fugitive. No job, no real identity. It's not like I can just pop on over to therapy every week. I don't even know where we're going to be from one day to the next…"

But then something pops into my mind.

Dash… His Schizophrenia.

He said he's been managing it… With medication and doctors.

If he can do it, wherever he is, then I could do the same thing.

Lex and I could find a place together. I could do freelance tattooing… And tech stuff can be done from anywhere. We could make a life together… *Here*, on the outside.

It might not be normal like other people's, but since when have we ever been normal? We're misfits. We still are, prison or not.

Noises at the front door call our attention that way. In seconds, Lex comes scampering into the room with bags, Cyrus and Tauren right behind him.

"Did Ren tell you the big news?!" Cyrus squeals at Colson, doing a little hop.

Lex is grinning up a storm, biting his lip while Colson lifts his brows at me.

"I was getting around to it…" I murmur, purposely stifling my excitement so I don't seem like such a little girl.

"Don't leave me hanging in suspense, goddamn!" Colson huffs.

I glance at Lex one more time before mumbling, "We're getting married."

Cyrus cheers. Tauren laughs. Colson grins and claps. And Lex just looks so fucking adorably proud and joyous I can't even stand it.

I wanna eat his face off, I'm telling you.

"This calls for a celebration," Cyrus sings, turning to bat his eyelashes at Tauren. "Can we open the Dom, please?"

"On it," Tauren grumbles, tapping Cy's chin with his knuckles before he saunters off.

Their relationship, man... I'm still wrapping my head around it.

But if anyone could understand people like us, it's these guys. We're all fucked up in one way or another... The losers, the misfits, the weirdos.

Why not wear our scars on the outside, for the world to see?

After all, it's our pain that makes us what we are...

Invincible.

"Go," Cyrus swoons, shoving Lex forward.

He chuckles, stumbling over to me. "Hi, sweet flame."

"Hi," I hum while he takes my face in his hands, laying just the purest, most irrevocably loving kiss on my lips. "Did you miss me?"

"Every second I'm not with you." He grins.

God, we're so codependent. I love it.

Tauren returns with glasses, popping the bottle of champagne, and pouring us all some.

"I'd like to raise a glass," he says in that sexy brogue. "To Luthor and Ren, and their undying love. May you forever hold each other's hands through the chaos of life... Toss up your middle fingers, and tell the world to fuck off."

"Here here!" Colson and Cyrus shout at the same time, whooping and wailing and laughing.

Lex and I shake our heads, chuckling while we sip and bask in the freedom of *love*, beyond the walls.

"They're kinda crazy, huh?" I whisper, as he pulls me close and kisses my neck.

"My beautiful, forever flame... all the *best* things are."

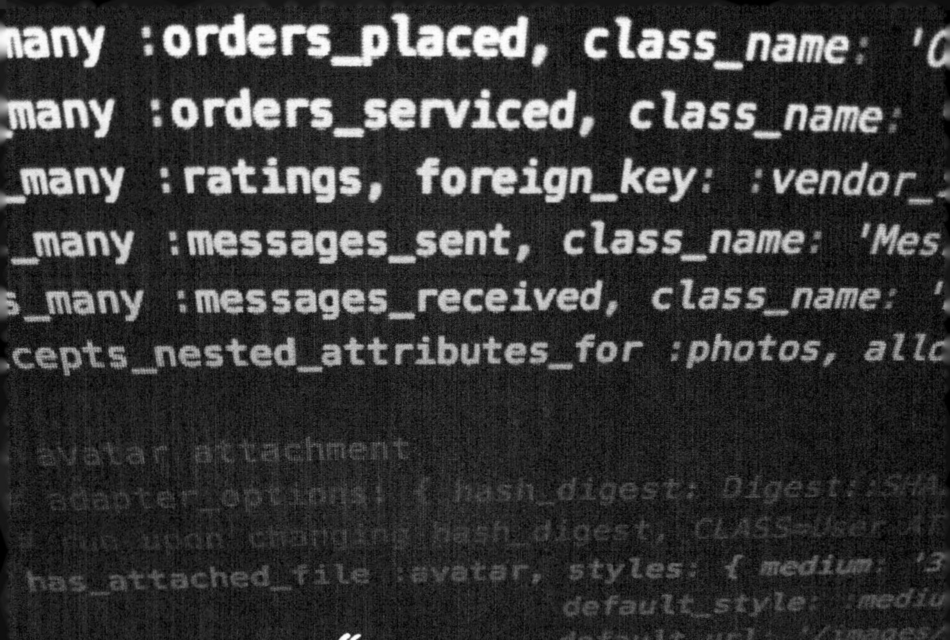

Luthor's Epilogue

STARTLING AWAKE, I SHOOT UP IN BED, SWEATING AND PANTING.

That was a crazy dream…

I glance around in the dark, trying to get my bearings. But all I see through the haze are concrete walls.

I feel the stiffness of a flimsy mattress beneath me.

I'm cold… *So, so cold.*

Blinking over and over, I see metal bars again…

No. No no no…

There's no way I'm back here. I got *out*, I know I did.

"Ren?!" I try to call to him, but my voice isn't working…

Nothing's coming out.

I can't breathe… I'm *suffocating*, beneath a freezing surface.

I'm underwater. I'm *drowning*…

"No!" I try to scream, but I can't.

I'm going under, sinking to the bottom like a stone.

The burn in my lungs kills. I kick and scream, trying to swim to the surface, but I'm not getting anywhere.

I'm… *dying*.

"Ren!"

Flinging around, my eyes reopen, and I'm in a different room. A room with white walls… In a different bed.

"Are you alright?" a voice asks… It's not familiar.

Someone leans over me. A person I've never seen before.

"Do you know where you are?" they ask me. I shake my head, confused. "You're in the hospital. You almost drowned."

"No..." I grunt. "That's impossible. I got out... I found him!"

"Calm down..." the nurse says. "You need to relax..."

No. Get away... This isn't real. I found him... I made it.

Nurses are holding me down while I struggle and fight. "Get off of me!"

"Bring him downstairs..."

That voice... It sounds like...

No... Not him.

Not The Ivory.

"You can't do this!" I kick and scream while large guards pick me up and carry me away. "I got out!"

They put me in a straitjacket. I can't move...

I... can't... fucking... breathe...

"Let me go... Ren!" I scream.

"Wake up..."

I hear his voice.

"Lexington... I'm *here*. Wake up, baby..."

Sucking air into my lungs, my eyes finally open *for real*, face flinging around. Ren is holding my arms down, blue eyes shining at me in the dark room.

"Where are we??" I gasp as his grip loosens, fingers brushing my hair away from my sweaty forehead.

"We're in California, baby," he says calmly, and I melt into the soft bed. "At Cyrus's house."

"Oh, thank God..." I breathe out my relief. Ren cuddles up next to me and I roll onto my side to face him. "I had a terrible dream..."

"Yea, I heard," he hums, swiping a tear from my cheek. "You were mumbling a lot of stuff."

Sighing a rumbly chuckle, I smoosh myself into him, and he immediately wraps me up. The way his big arms hold me and comfort me is unlike anything I've ever felt. I'm so safe when I'm with him. And now that I think about it, I've *always* felt safe with Ren. Maybe not emotionally safe, but definitely physically. He's been protecting me since day one... Against pretty much everything but himself.

"Are you okay now, beautiful boy?" He kisses my hair, tousling the silky strands with his fingers.

I haven't shaved my head in months at this point, so my hair is growing out a bit. I considered shaving it when we got to Cy's house, just to keep up with my look. But I like the way it feels when Ren plays with my hair. It's calming.

"Yea…" I sigh. "I'm good. It was just a nightmare. I've had a few since we got here."

"Me too," he mumbles, and I pull back to gaze up at him. "I've been thinking about them…"

I nod. He doesn't need to elaborate. I know who he's referring to.

Our friends. Our *family*…

Kang, Joy, Rook, Velle, Felix. Even Dash. We haven't spoken with him in a while, and we have no way of getting in touch with him. Joy's phone hasn't been working; believe me, I've tried.

We have absolutely no idea what's happening on that little island of misery that was our home.

"I've been *thinking*…" Ren says softly. "I feel like we should try to find Dash." I blink at him while he chews his lip. "He's our last remaining connection, ya know? There has to be a way to get to him…"

"Baby, I've tried." I rub my eyes. "I've searched high and low. There's no trace of him anywhere… It's a good thing. It means they're being safe."

"I know, but I just think it makes sense for us to go where he is." The way his eyes are shining tells me there's more to this than him missing Dash.

Tucking my face into the crook of his neck, I kiss his pulse gently. "Tell me what you're feeling, baby."

"I want us to go somewhere we can start a life together, Lex," he murmurs. "The way Dash did with Kemper. That should be our next move… Finding a place to settle. Somewhere we can actually *live*, not just stay breathing. We were breathing in the Pen… And now we're free. So what do we *do* with that?"

I can hear in his voice that this is important to him. So I put us face to face once more so I can see his blue flames while he speaks.

"I want to start… looking into getting help." He breaks our eye contact, nervously. "I want to work on myself, like Dash is doing. I think it's important, for us and our future. But also, for me."

Nodding, I hold back the loving smile as much as I can. Because I know this is hard for him, but at the same time, I can't help how proud I am of him for even suggesting such a thing.

He's so strong, and he's come so far.

"I can't wait to spend the rest of my life with you, Warren," I hum, kissing him softly.

"Are you sure?" he mumbles, and I chuckle. "It's probably gonna be really hard. I'm a total nutcase."

"You are," I tease. "But you're *my* nutcase. I think you're perfect, baggage and all." He breathes, grinning over my lips. "I promise, baby, I'll do everything I can to find Dash. We'll find a place to go where we can live… and get married." He beams, releasing a soft sound of excitement. "Where you can tattoo and go to therapy, and I can hack into things."

He laughs. "Not the Pentagon this time."

"Oh God, no," I scoff. "I want none of that mess."

We both chuckle, and he sighs. "Are you sure you're okay with all of this…?"

"All of what?"

"Leaving California… for good?"

"Well, I assumed we'd need to eventually."

He gives me a knowing look. "I just thought maybe you were hesitating."

Blinking at him, I watch his lips twist in that smug way he does when he knows he's right.

He's just so insufferable, I swear.

And I'm the crazy person who loves it more than anything.

"Okay, *maybe* I've been hanging onto the idea of being close to my parents," I grumble. "I hate being so close to them and not being able to see them."

"Then why don't we?" he hums.

I shake my head. "It's too dangerous…"

"I'm sure we could figure something out," he offers supportively. "At least just one time, so you can finally say goodbye."

The thought of it has my heart leaping. I would *love* more than anything to just see my mom and dad one last time.

And maybe I could introduce them to Ren… I'm sure they'd be all sorts of confused, about a lot of it. But they deserve to know that I'm alive, and that I'm in love.

They deserve to know my fiancé.

"I can tell by your silence that you're on board." He grins. "So it's settled. We'll find Dash, find our landing spot, and then arrange to see your parents before we go."

He kisses my lips, then rolls over, giving me his back.

I chuckle. "That's it? Conversation over?"

"Mhm," he breathes. "It's all settled. Now, big spoon me, baby."

"As you wish, princess." I curl up into him from behind, kissing his shoulder.

"I know I should hate that, but I won't lie... I'm feelin' it."

Rumbling content laughter, I close my eyes and drift back off.

No more dread in my head.

In the morning, Tauren brings Ren and Colson down to the beach to surf, while Cyrus and I stay inside like the big dorks we are, resurrecting an old bit of nostalgia.

"Alright, look here. The nukes have been dropped," Tony barks into my ear through the headset. "I expect to see you all rallying right now."

"But I'm hanging up posters in my house," Reno whines.

"I've got you, buddy!" Cyrus gasps, sitting next to me on the couch. "I'ma comin'!"

"Hang on. I'm too heavy," I grumble.

"Look at this noob," Tony jeers. "Been outta commish for a while, huh hot stuff?"

"You're one to talk. You never play this game anymore," Reno says.

"You're right," Tony sighs. "Why are we playing this again? There are, like, a million better games out there."

"Because! It's for old times' sake," Cyrus whines.

"Yea. Honestly, fuck the nukes," I huff. "Let's just talk shit like we used to. Remember when Cyrus ranted for forty-five minutes about the order of best Batmans?"

We all laugh, while Cyrus shakes his head.

"It's because the list is so obvious, and anyone who doesn't agree can suck my butt," he mutters.

"Bro, I'm not getting into this with you again," Reno replies. "And I'm *definitely* not sucking your butt."

"In what conceivable world is Keaton better than Bale, though?? Honestly," Cyrus starts up, and I'm wheezing. "No, seriously! I really want to know what your thought process is here."

"Um, my thought process is that Keaton is a legend," Reno argues.

"I'm not doubting that. I'm just saying as far as who brought Batman to life *the best*," Cyrus says with confidence, "Bale has to beat Keaton. It's just a fact."

"Luthor... This is all your fault," Tony gripes, and I snicker.

"I know, it's hilarious. You should see how red he's turning." I peek at Cyrus, smirking.

He shoves me. "I am not. I just happen to be very passionate about Batman, is all."

"Yea, no shit. This argument has been going on for, like, six years," Tony laughs.

"Come on, fellas. You can't count the time the debate was paused!" A familiar female voice suddenly bursts into our ears. "Just like you can't count on Cyclops to be unbiased about the Batman with the hottest growl."

Cyrus and I gape at each other.

"Leah?!" I gasp.

"The one and only," she croons.

"Oh, shit!" Tony shouts.

"The gang's back together! Ride or fuckin' die, bitches!" Reno goes off.

"Leah, holy shit!" My chest swells. "It's so good to hear your voice, man! How's it hangin'??"

"Always down to the floor, Luthy." She chuckles. "Long time, no talk… I wasn't sure you were still… active."

I grin. "Yea, some shit went down. But it doesn't matter. I'm here now."

There's some music playing through her mic that sounds a little familiar.

"Yo, Leez, what are you listening to?" Reno asks.

"CBV," she says, and Cyrus starts smacking me on the arm over and over. "He's one of my favorite artists."

"That's dope." I beam at Cyrus while he falls over onto his side.

"Yeaa… *uh!* That shit's a jam!" Reno is vibing. "Turn it up!"

"So, Luth… What's new?" Leah asks. I can hear a million unspoken things in those two words.

"Well… I'm… um," I shift. "I'm actually seeing someone."

Cyrus coughs, "Don't be a bitch."

"I'm engaged," I add, scowling at him.

"Oh my God, that's fantastic!" she cheers.

"Bro… excuse you," Tony grumbles. "You didn't tell us you were engaged!"

"Yea, when'd you pop the question??" Reno asks.

"Only a few days ago." I focus on making food and supplies in the game to avoid how much heat is rushing to my face.

"Congratulations," Leah sings. "Who's the lucky creature?"

My face breaks in two, and I whisper to Cyrus, "Love her."

"She's seriously the best," he hums.

"His name is *Ren*," Tony answers the question for me.

"Yes, and he's quite fetching," Reno adds.

"Ahh, I see," Leah says. "So this Ren, is he like us…? Or is he, ya know… Cool?"

Cyrus snorts.

"He's so stinkin' cool," I sigh, and they cheer.

"Oh yea! Luthor bagged a jock!" Reno exclaims.

"He's not a jock." I frown. "Even though, he *is* really good at basketball. But he's more like a… rich socialite."

"Living for it." Leah chuckles.

"But he doesn't act that way," I tell them. "He's more… Oh man, what's the word I'm looking for?"

"Sweet?"

"Genuine?"

"Dangerous?"

"Yes! All of those," I hum, and Leah cackles. "You can't describe Ren with words… He's just Ren."

"And you *love* him?" Leah asks.

I have to bite back my grin. "Yea… I do. Like, *too* much."

"So I guess you do know how to feel it then… huh?" I can hear the smile in her voice.

And a giant grin covers my face to mirror it. "I guess so."

"Well, we fully expect to be invited to the wedding," Tony says.

And now I can't stop thinking about this crazy wedding that'll probably never happen. With all of our friends and family… It's a nice thought.

I can dream, right?

"Okay, anyway, enough about Luthor's Prince Charming," Reno rumbles. "Back to this Batman list."

"Oh, Jesus…" Leah sighs, and we laugh while the two of them continue their six-year-long debate.

We're joking around and talking shit more than we're actually playing, and it feels just like old times. The sun begins to set, and we eventually say goodbye for now to our crew to set up for dinner.

I can see Ren, Colson, and Tauren walking back up from the beach, laughing. And it fills my heart with joy. And not that I want to think about it, but even if it all came crashing down right now, at least I'd have these memories.

The thing is, you have to stop and recognize when you're in the good times. Force yourself not to take moments of bliss for granted. Because the memories are great, but they don't hold a candle to the real thing, and you'll always wish you could get this back.

By some flick of cosmic fate, I got a second chance. To laugh with my friends, to have a *real life* and experience love outside of that tomb that held me for so long.

And I refuse to let it slip through my fingers again.

I'll savor every moment while I still can. Because life is too short, and freedom isn't guaranteed.

"I'll be right back," I mutter to Cyrus, grabbing my phone and slinking up the hall.

I shuffle into the study and close the door, placing a call to Joy's phone.

One last try... just to see.

It actually *rings*... My heart lurches up into my throat.

It's ringing for the first time in weeks. Unfortunately, no one answers. And I hang up disappointed. I'm just about to leave the room when the phone starts ringing in my hand, startling me.

It's Joy's number. *She's calling me back.*

I swipe so fast, I almost drop the phone. "Hello??" I don't hear anything at first, so I check the screen. "Hello?? Joy??"

"Hello, Luthor..."

My spine stiffens.

It's a male voice. Familiar... With a British accent.

"Why... why do you have Joy's phone?" I stammer.

"Let's not worry about that for right now," Trevel sighs, smugly, causing my fists to clench. "Where are you and Ren? Far away, I'm sure..."

"Listen, I don't want to do this with you right now." I rub my eyes. "Can you just tell me if Byron is okay??"

"Of course he's okay. He's with me now," he chirps.

My jaw strains. *Okay... I'm gonna need to perfect teleporting so I can go knife this motherfucker real quick.*

"What about everyone else...?" I ask, terrified of the answer.

"Boy, you two really ducked out just in time, hm?" He ignores my question and keeps blathering in that smug British tone that makes me all ragey and nervous. "It's almost as if... you *wanted* this to happen."

"What?" I grunt. "That makes no sense."

"Maybe not. But maybe that's how it seems to some of us..."

My head is spinning like a top from his crazy.

Now he's, what? Brainwashing Byron into thinking we blew the place up and left him for dead??

"What's your game, Fenwick?" I hiss.

I just don't understand what the hell he wants. *Why is he trying so hard to turn Byron against us?*

"You know, it's actually very simple," he hums. "I want revenge. I want to take everything away from the man who's taken *everything* from me..."

Dr. Love?

I gulp, worry coiling around my gut. I don't know Dr. Love all that well, but he seemed okay to me. More importantly, he's with Felix. So I'd say this asshole's vendetta puts The Carver directly in the line of fire.

Felix Darcey can handle himself, of that, I'm sure. But something tells me this dude isn't one for physical altercations.

He seems like a mindfucker of the highest degree.

"I know you're upset, but just try to see the bright side"—I push my newfound optimism on him—"if it weren't for Dr. Love, sure, you wouldn't be in prison. But you also wouldn't have met Byron. So... ya know. Silver lining."

Trevel chuckles. It doesn't sound very happy. "You're sweet, Luthor. And you know what? You have a point."

"Yea... See? It's all—"

"With Byron on my side, it'll be much easier to get what I want," he cuts me off. "Being that he hates little Felix Darcey *so* very much. He's practically foaming at the mouth."

"That's not really what I meant—"

"Things aren't going well on this island, Luthor," he mumbles. "Not for your people. The storm only made it worse... The place is in shambles, and The Ivory has Velle on the ropes."

Bile begins to rise up my throat. "What does that even mean? What's going on there??"

"Don't worry about it," he brushes me off flippantly. "Alabaster Pen isn't your problem anymore. Just focus on taming your wild boy. It's what you're good at, right?"

"Trevel, listen to me—"

"I'll tell Byron you said hello," he rasps, sounding like he's moving around. "He'll be glad to know you aren't actually dead. *Yet.*"

I'm growling a curse as he disconnects the call. "Fuck! You little twat!"

"Jesus, babe, what's going on in here?" Ren pushes the door open, gawking at me.

I immediately place another call to Joy's phone, but it's going straight to voicemail.

"That son of a bitch..." I seethe, calling over and over, though it's getting me nowhere.

"Who??" Ren grabs my shoulders.

"Fucking Trevel," I exhale, raking fingers through my hair. "I called Joy's phone, and he answered."

"Holy crap..." Ren's dark lashes flutter. "Is... is Byron...?"

"He said he's okay," I huff. "And that they're together now. Or that Byron is siding with him... I have no clue. Ren, I'm worried. He said a bunch of shit, about Velle and them being in trouble..."

"He's just messing with you, love." He pets my face in calming caresses. "He's an asshole."

"Yea, but why would he have Joy's phone...?"

Ren doesn't have an answer to that, and it's whipping up my nerves even faster.

I know it's crazy to be concerned about that island and the people on it... Ridiculous, preposterous, downright fucking *nuts*. The place is a pit of despair, a tomb where we lost friends. Good people *died* because of that hellhole, and against all odds, we managed to escape.

We should be running straight to a new life, and never looking back.

But at the same time, that place made me who I am. It brought me a love I never thought I could feel, friendship I was too afraid to let in.

It probably makes me a fucking moron and a half, but I feel tied to Alabaster Isle, on some deep level I don't even fully understand.

And I know Ren feels it too. I can read the emotions in his twinkling blue eyes.

"Maybe I can try to reach Lem..." I mumble, and Ren nods, pulling me closer to him by my waist. "Or Velle... Find out what's really going on over there."

"And? Then what...?" Ren asks, and I blink.

"I don't—"

"What if... What if they need help? What's the plan, baby?" His head wobbles. "I mean, are we really going to go *back*, after risking our lives... after *everything* we went through getting off that island?? Can you honestly tell me you think going back there is a good idea??"

"No," I mutter. "No, I can say with almost absolute certainty that it's a terrible fucking idea." He lets out a slow breath. "Listen, baby, I would never even suggest anything unless you're totally on board. We're a team. We move together, no matter what... Okay?"

He nods, showing me his vulnerability. And we're both silent for a moment, clinging to each other until he mumbles, "So, what do you think it is...? Like an uprising? Us versus them type shit?"

"I don't know," I sigh. "But I can't stand the idea of them being in danger. Joy, Rook, even Velle. I mean, as fucked up as they were, they're our family. And Byron..."

I shake my head solemnly, and Ren gnaws on his lower lip, clearly deep in thought.

"The Ivory has a weakness," he says softly, blue eyes widening.

"If it comes down to it, baby..." I push his hair back gently with my fingers. "*If* they need us..."

Ren blinks, then scoffs. "We're not heroes, Luthor."

"Nope." My lips curve. "Just villains with better disguises."

this is not THE END.

SNEAK PEEK of

SHADOWMAN

Alabaster Penitentiary, Volume 5

Byron

FEEL HEAVILY, OR FEEL NOTHING AT ALL.

Those are the two wildly different sides of my personality.

Sometimes I'm empty. *Dead* inside.

Lost like a shadow, existing only as a silent, lurking piece of someone else.

Other times, my heart races so fast, and my chest cinches so tight, I think my ribs could snap. My mind captures a thought. Traps it the way a child traps a butterfly in a jar, to ogle with wide eyes while it flutters about… Then ultimately dies from lack of oxygen because I forgot to poke air-holes.

Do I resent being like this?

Yes. Of fucking course I do.

It's not exactly *fun* to live each day not knowing how I'll feel the next. If I'll be stewing in a silent ache of emotions that make me want to scream and punch the wall until my knuckles are bloodied to the bone…

Or if I'll be a corpse.

But the thing is, *no one* knows about any of it. These are things that rest beneath my surface, and nobody *ever* gets that deep.

The world is full of narcissists. Human beings are inherently self-involved, which certainly enabled me when I was free. Before I got locked up, I adored how engrossed people were in their own bullshit.

It made it real easy for me to slink around undetected.

But here, in *Alabaster Penitentiary,* I find the lack of attention sort of… vexing.

I'm not saying I want everyone to be focused on me all the time, or even most of the time. It'd drive me nuts. But there are definite moment when I feel like I could slit my own throat in the middle of this cafeteria, and no one would bat an eye.

Do they even see me?

Or am I still completely... invisible?

Lifting my gaze from the plate of slop in front of me, I watch my friends. Luthor is talking about this device he's been working on for months. His body is turned, facing Ren, which would indicate that he's really only speaking to him. Not me.

And Ren is smiling—as he does when he's looking at Luthor. Full attention given, only occasionally breaking eye contact to watch Luthor's lips move.

Pouring over him curiously, I study Ren's face. Sparkling eyes the color of a bright blue sky, pointed nose, curved lips forming their signature smirk and framed by pretty-boy dimples. Jawline sharp, dusted in a dark stubble. *Almost time for a shave.*

Down my gaze travels, over the slope of his neck to his wide shoulders, biceps and torso plump with muscles you can't see when they're hidden by his shirt. But *I* know they're there.

His long arm is slightly extended, and I lean forward to see where his hand is, though I don't really need to. I already know it's resting possessively on Luthor's thigh, subtly grazing up and down.

Because Luthor *belongs* to Ren. He always has, even when he was acting like he didn't.

It didn't matter that Ren cheated on him. I knew from the moment it happened he would fall back under the spell of Warren Xavier. It was only a matter of time before they were like this.

Attached, in a state of constant fawning and obsessive desire that borders on psychotic.

Luthor's a genius—*literally*. The kid is so smart, he could probably work for NASA, or become the next Steve Jobs, if he wasn't locked away in concrete hell. So forgive me for harboring some resentment over his stupidity when it comes to our *friend* Ren.

Not that I think it's *stupid* for someone to want Ren... A lot of people do. I just feel like it was obvious Luthor would go back, and him claiming he *wouldn't* drove me a little nuts.

Maybe it's none of my business... I mean, it is *their* relationship. They can go about it however they want. Obnoxiously codependent... *Fine.* That's their prerogative.

But I've been caught in the middle of their toxic shit many times over the years, which is why sometimes I feel like I'm trapped on this carnival ride with them. For me, it was unintentional, but I think for them, especially for Ren, it was very deliberate.

It's just the way he is, I suppose. Another selfish soul with a one-track mind, compulsively aimed in only one direction. But that doesn't make it any less infuriating.

Deciding that I need to get up and move for a second before I explode, I stand with my tray. Luthor's eyes fling to me and he tilts his head, as if he's about to ask where I'm going. But Ren picks up one of his hands, affectionately playing with Luthor's fingers.

Attention effectively drawn back.

I roll my eyes, jaw clenched as I stomp away from the table. My brain is pinging receptors of many vivid emotions, all of which are bothering me immensely while I sullenly dump my food into the trash, tossing my empty tray into the pile with a huff.

This is all just so *annoying*. The way I'm filled to the brim with chaotic things that have no business being inside me. The itchy discomfort of feeling like I'm a child again, standing in the corner...

Watching.

Luthor is one of the very, *very* few people in this world I actually trust. I'd go as far as to call him my brother, which may be kind of weird, considering recent events. Nonetheless, he's been my friend since the moment I got here, and I don't like resenting him for things beyond his control. After all, it's not his fault his naivety and general sweetness made him easy prey for someone like Ren.

Glancing back over to the table, I scoff internally at their heart-eyes and hushed conversations.

Ren's such a jealous weirdo.

He had the nerve to imply that I might have a *thing* for Luthor. The other day, in the showers... He was messing with me about it. And he couldn't possibly be more misguided.

I mean, where would he even get that from??

Sure, Luthor and I did mess around a tiny bit. Just once. But I've also been consistently fucking Ren on and off pretty much since I got here, so it's really not a big deal.

And he was there too, with me and Luthor. *He* orchestrated the whole thing, as he tends to. One of his brilliant schemes to lure Luthor back in, using me as a pawn in his damn sexual games.

I guess I could tell him to fuck off when he suggests it... But it's very important to me that they understand how little I care.

I'm not gay. I'm not *interested* in men sexually. I never have been.

Yes, we're in *prison*, and the options are severely limited. Understandably, your hand gets old real quick. If someone's offering, I'll take it, because a mouth is just a mouth. A hole is just a hole, no matter how surprisingly good it feels. Maybe some more than others…

Whatever. The point is that it doesn't matter. Their mess isn't mine, and fooling around with them is just another way to pass the time in this boring fucking place.

Luthor is still just my friend, and I could fuck Ren a million more times without feeling a goddam thing. And now that he and Luthor are fucking, it's all irrelevant. Because I assume he doesn't need to use me anymore…

Which is *fine*. Since, you know, I never cared in the first place.

Ren got what he wanted, and he'll probably never even *think* about all the stuff we did together ever again. So… good.

I'm not thinking about it either.

Inside, my stomach is twisting and wrenching. Probably because I barely ate and I'm perpetually starving. A burn is making its way up my throat as I reluctantly wander back toward the table, dreading it and pretending I'm not. But I don't get more than a step or two before someone appears in my peripheral.

My face shifts, and I peer up at the figure, now standing right beside me. It's the new guy…

#102.

His irises shine down at me, and I'm instantly held still, just like when he came up to us the other day. It was the first time I saw him, this new inmate who popped out of nowhere with his peculiar eyes the shade of indigo. They're practically purple. *Very odd.*

And he clearly isn't shy with the eye contact.

"Hi, again," he hums quietly. I just blink at the lurching character, tall and slim, with messy black hair and a British accent. "You're Kang… right?"

I nod slowly, eyes flicking to my table, checking on my friends like a reflex. Ren wasn't shy about his distrust for this person when we met him in the showers. But he's one to talk…

He's a pretty untrustworthy motherfucker himself.

And it's irrelevant. Because he's not paying attention to me, anyway.

"Byron," I murmur to the Brit. "You're name was…"

"Trevel," he answers, though it was on the tip of my tongue. A unique name for sure. "Trevel Fenwick. Newest addition to this bloody nightmare."

I huff a small breath that's usually as close to a laugh as you'll get from me. I'm not one for flagrant laughter. *Not many things are all that funny.*

Unsure of what to say to the guy, or why he decided to come up to me in the first place, I simply stand still and portray my standard indifference.

"So how long have you been here?" He asks me, seemingly interested.

"Well, I'm #62," I tell him in a bored tone, though the way his intense violet gaze is zeroed in on my face brings an inexplicable need to fidget. "If that gives you an idea."

His head tilts curiously. "That must be a couple years, then? At least."

I nod again, pulse picking up, because his accent reminds me of someone…

Someone who meant a great deal to me.

I don't like it.

Trevel isn't put off by my surly silence. He lets out an exhale, unusual eyes drifting over to Luthor and Ren. "Those are your mates?"

I swallow hard. "Yes."

He purses his lips, offering a curt bob of his head. "I hope I haven't offended them somehow. The dark-haired one seemed to think I was up to no good when we met. Though, I can't say it's the first time someone's assumed that about me at first glance."

His shoulders move subtly, a rumbly noise coming from within his throat. A very modest chuckle, like mine.

"That's just Ren," I mutter. "It's how he is. He's crazy protective… of Luthor."

Trevel shifts his gaze back to me, cocking a dark brow. "Only him?" My lips part, but before I can speak, he adds, "I recall him moving *you* away from me as well…"

I can't help the scoff that puffs out of me. "Oh, yea. He'll definitely *act* like he's being a loyal friend. But really, he's just trying to control everything."

And manipulate me.

"You don't strike me as the type to be controlled," Trevel says almost curiously.

The comment makes me feel odd, but I push past it and remember myself. "I'm not." I huff, not missing the twitch in his lips. "But he bosses me around like I'm just some lovable sidekick. And yet when it comes to standing up for *our* friend who was murdered, he shrugs it off."

Shaking my head, I feel the palpable rise of heated anger in my veins when thinking about what happened to my cellmate… Before *and* after his death.

Trevel's forehead lines, casting orbs of deep purple at me. "Your friend was murdered?"

"Yea," I sigh. "By this preppy little shithead who calls himself *The Carver*. And now they're befriending the psycho. Inviting him to sit with us and shit, like it didn't even fucking happen. Totally spitting on our friend's grave."

This little tangent is kind of spewing out on its own, but I barely even care. Because now that I'm saying the words out loud again, I'm fuming on behalf of Kieran O'Malley, someone who meant a lot to me. Clearly, a lot more than he meant to Ren.

Something in Trevel's face has shifted. His already severe features have gone dark, a bit of mayhem in his eyes. It's pretty alarming.

But before I can try to inch away from it, he reaches out and places a hand on my shoulder. I flinch, startled by the fact that he's touching me. But he keeps it there, leaning in closer.

"Loyalty is everything," he whispers. Chills sheet my flesh. "I'm sorry about your friend."

Frozen, I stare up at him while I mumbling, "Thank you."

Trevel's chin dips, lips moving *too close* to my ear. "You might like the taste of revenge." Warm breath brushes it and my teeth set, gut flipping upside down. "I know I did. It's quite… sweet. Like honey."

My throat is so dry I can barely gulp as his hand sweeps off my shoulder, brushing down my back before pulling away. I only have one full second to stammer until the guards bark that it's about time to leave. My eyes flick toward the booming voice, and when they return to Trevel, he's already walking away.

What the hell was that?

My mind is cycling through his words as Luthor and Ren walk over to me. Confusion traces the fingerprints I can still feel on my shoulder.

As we leave the cafeteria, my gaze wanders cautiously to the mysterious stranger with the violet eyes. I'm unable to rid myself of this sensation… One I haven't felt in a very long time.

He can actually see me, can't he?

A fellow man in the shadows, perhaps.

Stay tuned for SHADOWMAN, coming in 2024!

A NOTE FROM THE AUTHOR

Goodness gracious, great balls of fire, amiriteee?!?!!

So, hopefully you're all *okay*. Maybe a bit shaken, but it's nothing we haven't been through together already. *Ha!*

Seriously, though. I just have to say, I'm so beyond glad that Luthor and Ren are together and happy, because literally *nothing else* in the world of Alabaster Pen is looking good right now.

Alright, enough fucking around, Nyla.

By now, you know how I wrap my books up here, explaining stuff, discussing details and providing insight into the inspiration for my borderline psychotic stories.

In this one, I'm absolutely certain I will be forgetting things. This *entire book* is an Easter egg hunt, chock full of little niblets, either from past books, or secrets to be revealed in the next two. I barely even know where to start, other than to tell you that this'll be a long one, since there's *so much* to cover. I'll try to keep it brief, but I think we all know that's not my strong suit.

(You're a rambler, Nyla. Just accept the fact that you over-write like a maniac and call it a day).

Honestly, I could have easily split this book into two. But that would've made me itchy. So here we are, with a 200k depiction of Lex Luthor Deon and Warren Xavier—*the Prince Harry and Megan Markle of Alabaster Penitentiary, if you will.*

I guess I'll start by mentioning the structure of this crazy behemoth. Interweaving flashbacks is a hard thing to sell, and I know a lot of readers are sorta critical of it. But when you're working with a timeline that spans over *many years*, you only have two choices—flashbacks, or big time jumps. And to be fair, I've seen complaints about both, so I guess it's a lose-lose (*lol*).

With *Fragments*, we had to do both flashbacks and time jumps, the *present day* following our timeline we've seen in the previous three books, and the flashbacks happening over the five-ish years from Luthor and Ren's simultaneous arrests, their prisoner-meet-cute, and the gradual development of what brought them to their uneasy state by the time Dash arrives.

Could I have pushed the present-day timeline back in *Fragments*, starting it *after* Dash had already gotten there? Sure. I considered it. But the overwhelming fact is that Dash winds up being a *huge* driving factor in

Luthor and Ren coming back together. The AP series was really *born* with Dash. That's why he's so important to me, and I make sure to mention him at least once every five minutes, no matter what's going on.

Dash's escape ignited the final *kaboom* with Velle and The Ivory in *Joyless*—yes, there were other factors, but this was a big part of it. It launches a chain of events, but most of all, Dash had poignant moments with both Luthor and Ren individually, so that by the time he escaped, our boys were ready to collapse into each other.

I've just gotta say, it is *immensely* satisfying to finally have these details about what Dash was really doing during all of his *Officer Kemper* psychosis moments out in the open. Didn't I tell you?? Questions. Will. Be. Answered.

I feel like I can finally breathe again lol. I've been sitting on these deets for a while.

For all the readers who were distraught over wondering *how* it was possible for Dash to fabricate all those interactions with Officer Kemper… *Fragments* shows you how. I don't want to spend this whole time talking about Dash, but I feel like this is really important (and like I said, I've been holding this in for *years*).

Dash is a very introspective character who, before his arrival in AP, was fumbling through his illness like a deep fog. I can't remember if I said this in the author's note of *Distorted*, but without treatment, Schizophrenia psychosis can be triggered easily, by things like stress, depression, etc. When Dash got to the prison, he was at his lowest. The perfect time for him to meet our darling little cupcake, Lexington Deon.

When Luthor says, "Living here is like living with a chronic illness. You find some way, *any* way, to live with it. To *live*… in spite of it," that, in essence, is the moment *Officer Kemper* was born. Of course, it's choppy. The way Dash remembers things isn't *exactly* how or when they went down—obviously. But there are bits and pieces of reality scattered in amongst the hallucinations, which we see from Luthor and Ren's sides in *Fragments*.

When Luthor tells Dash about Ren and the cock cage… *Yea*. That's where he got that from.

Um, hello! Callum Kade… The guy Ren lost his virginity to. There's your name. *Callum* Kemper.

The sex dreams Luthor was overhearing were Dash in psychosis, imagining his interactions with Officer Kemper, and probably the most unexpected of all these revelations… Dash *becoming* Officer Kemper and making out with Luthor.

A bit of a trip, if I do say so myself. But I absolutely I *loved* that scene.

We've known since the end of *Distorted* that *Officer Kemper* was a manifestation of Dash's subconscious. And the palpable shift, when he flips from himself into the *Officer* personality, had Luthor—*and me*—reeling.

There are no romantic feelings between Dash and Luthor, we know this. But from Luthor's perspective, never having hooked up with any guys other than Ren (and Kang… *hi yummy bromance threesome*), it was like something he *needed* to experience.

There are a lot of details in these interactions—*remember the wintergreen mints!!!* So *many*, in fact, that I could probably talk about it for hours. But I said I wouldn't turn this into a Dash retrospective… It's the *Luthor and Ren Show!*

As I stated in the foreword, *Fragments* is about so much more than just their love, though we definitely get it. The burning love between Luthor and Ren is alive and well pretty much from the moment they meet, and it survives and even thrives for years, despite all of the chaos, self-destructive or not.

But this book is *also* about the island as a whole, and two people on it who were profoundly lonely on the outside, coming into this prison where, for maybe the first time in their lives, they finally made *real* connections and found themselves.

In that spirit, let's delve into our boys. Beginning with Mr. Warren Xavier.

Ren was always going to be one of the more complicated characters I've written. I knew it from the moment I decided to give him a book, back when I was writing *Distorted*. And in all fairness to his lying ass, he actually wasn't as much of a nuisance as I'm sure he could've been. Something about his brokenness really resonated with me. His endless searching for anything to fill the void. His terrible parents and his experiences with Callum Kade. I found his voice *spilling* out, especially in his flashback chapters, before he gets to AP.

Just one of many messages from Ren as a character is that there is absolutely nothing *wrong* with loving sex. When it happens safely and consensually, it's a beautiful thing, and sex work is also a legitimate career. Sex workers deserve rights. Point blank. And honestly, as much as the internet can be a downfall to humanity sometimes, the rise of things like OnlyFans have really provided an outlet for people to explore safely. But the stigma still very much exists, and unfortunately, it also gets tied into the tragic realities of other topics discussed in the book. Like sex trafficking, sexually transmitted disease, etc. (As always, some resources will be provided following this.)

I'll get into what led to Luthor's arrest in a moment, but first I just want to touch on Ren and his job some more. While I know that Ren did enjoy working at Club Edge, the reasoning behind his love of rough sex with strangers, drugs, and the overall pain he felt he *deserved* just wasn't healthy. And that's the biggest point to sex work, is that it needs to be *chosen* by the individual, which sadly a lot of times it isn't.

The prologue—taking place the day Ren burns his house down—was the final straw for Ren. Something settled deeply within him after his last client—*um, yea... The Ivory*—at which point his psychological issues took over.

Was it disturbing? Hell yes. Was it *right* that he killed his parents and those people at the club? Of course not. But such is the dark side to the characters in this series, and Ren has a lot more darkness in him than we could even begin to discuss right now.

Dealing with Ren's sex addiction, and his instances of *cheating*, was understandably difficult, and emotional, for everyone involved. But hopefully, you were able to see through his actions and realize that none of the pain he caused was intentional for anyone other than himself. Whether it was the self-sabotage, or physical self-harm, nothing he did was ever meant to hurt Luthor, though he knew on some level he would. But that was all part of it.

Ren grappled internally, with the *I don't deserve happiness, I don't deserve love. I'm going to destroy everything because that's what I'm good at* type stuff. The arson was the ultimate cry for help, which is why he wasn't miserable being sent to Alabaster Pen. If anything, it was probably a good thing for him, though it also enabled him for a long time.

The self-harm and his suicidal thoughts were particularly rough for me. His internal pain ran so deep, and the thing to understand is that while this is *fiction* and a lot of it is embellished for entertainment, the real, *raw* struggles of human beings suffering from mental health issues, to me, are very important to depict.

Ren's actions toward the end, when he's alone in California, were devastating, yes. But the most pivotal moment was Luthor finding him, against all odds, and assuring him that *it didn't matter,* and it wouldn't change the way he sees this man, who he loves. It was a true sign of growth between the two of them. That they could accept each other and *love* each other, faults and all. Give up that toxic energy and just be there for one another, as friends *and* lovers.

But of course, we know that while it's a great notion, love cannot, in fact, cure mental illness. It can help, sure, but Ren needed to address his desire to get real help in the epilogue. And I'm proud as fuck of his strength and how much he developed as a character.

In moments like his talk with Dash in the showers—before they got into that fight—and in his loving support of Parker Freeman (*may he rest*), Ren really showed his heart and maturity. He's not the black-souled demon he makes himself out to be. He's just a human being with complex issues, and it's what I love most about writing these broken boys. Being able to give them the love they need and deserve in their partners who will accept them, no matter what.

Back to Club Edge for just a sec. It's an interesting piece of the story. We will certainly find out more about this business owned by Manuel Blanco—*one of many*—and about him having sex with Ren as *Mask Daddy*.

The tattoo of the bird wrapped barbed wire is a symbol—*remember the butterfly knife Felix uses to kill O'Malley in Brainwashed?* There was a bird wrapped in barbed wire on that, too... With the initials AA.

Who is AA, you ask?

insert smirky face

For now, I just need to address The Ivory's behaviors in the scene at Edge, when he's with Ren, and the way he behaves with him in the cell in solitary toward the end.

"Do you still hate me, pajarito?"

Oh, boy. I am *telling* you. There are millions of tiny puzzle pieces all over this entire series. You should definitely read each book more than once lol. You'll pick up new details every time.

I'll come back to the destruction of Alabaster Pen, but first, I do need to mention Luthor's arrest. It probably sounds bad, but despite how awful parts of that chapter are—the child sex slavery stuff, all based on real information, by the way—I can't help but love it. Not because of the terrible reality that these things happen every day, which they do. But Luthor being painfully *dedicated* to his friends is just so indicative of him as a person. He's unbelievably kind, loyal, and empathetic down to his bones. *The perfect shy nerd to accidentally hack into the Pentagon.*

Luthor's genius-level abilities got him into trouble, almost accidentally, and what I hope is that you were able to picture him all disheveled, with empty soda cans everywhere, staring at his screens and mumbling things about the government. Because that's totally the vibe I was going for.

Writing a hacker was fun as hell. In a series full of characters who are unhinged psychopaths, murderers, cops and Cartel capos, having the lone genius computer nerd made Lexington Deon into even more of a diamond in the rough.

There are so many things I loved about writing Lexington Deon. His shy, introverted personality, the way he loves his parents and his online friends, his dork-level humor, and the fact that he didn't even realize he had a sort of demanding sexual side until he met Ren.

Their constant shift was a role reversal I didn't plan whatsoever. A lot of things about their chemistry—and their sex—just happened while writing them. The "play-rough" sex scene is a perfect example. It was as *angry* as they could go, because their neediness for one another was too powerful. Luthor and Ren's is a chemistry that erupts in neediness and praise, and ultimately love.

Okay, I gotta move on, because honestly, I could swoon over them for days on end.

Let's get into the *action*.

It begins with the end of *Joyless*, and the tension between Velle and The Ivory. (Velle cashing in on the information Ren promised him will come up again.) Remember toward the end of *Brainwashed*, when Lem has Felix in the mansion and The Ivory calls him down to talk… He's is visibly less put-together than usual, obviously stressed, and speaking to his assistant about *vetting* someone. *This* is when Manuel Blanco is preparing to bring in his new crew of guards to take control from Velle and the team.

To a man like Manuel Blanco, power and control are everything. So you can almost guarantee that if he's quiet, it's the calm before the storm. There was no way he would allow Velle get away from him like that. Nor would he let someone take over what he sees as *his*.

But how about that first ever proxy scene between Velle and Ren?

I know some readers are reticent about sexual interactions with non-main characters, but I'm telling you, it's always important. And when it comes to Ren, it was to be expected. I mean, it's a prison full of horny dudes (and one chica). Do we really expect them *not* to be constantly humping?

Behind the scenes, while Luthor and Ren are falling in love, becoming friends with Felix and talking to Dash on the phone, rifts are happening.

In the rec room, Velle, Rook, and Joy have a little pow-wow with Dr. Love about the very idea that something dangerous is afoot.

And then, *bam!* In come the terror squad (lol).

In theory, it looks like Luthor's efforts, in building his computer and hacking into the servers, were used only to see his man one more time. But trust me, we haven't seen the last of his computer or his hacking, so don't you worry.

The interaction between The Ivory and Ren in solitary makes it seem as if Manuel Blanco has some kind of attraction to Ren. I'll go out on a limb here, and say it's *much* more complex than that. In fact, it almost seems like The Ivory's been playing the proxy game long before Ren started it... (wink).

Who was he really talking to when he said those words...? Pajarito?

And whose voice came from out in the hallway just before the ceiling fell??

I'm gonna tell you right now!

Kidding, obviously. I'm not telling. Yet. But I promise, it's *real* good.

Alas, we've reached the storm that rocked Alabaster Isle!

Picture this... Felix and Lem are at the mansion. In the garden.

Lem just proposed to Felix, and it was super sweet. Petals of yellow dahlias flutter in the wind... As a bolt of lightning strikes, the crack of thunder opening up the sky.

The end of Felix's epilogue introduces the storm, and the *Fragments* timeline picks it up with gusto.

The *storm* on Alabaster Isle is something I've had planned since the start of the series, coinciding with the arrival of Manuel Blanco's *army*. All of this drama comes to a head just as the biggest storm they've ever seen wipes out the guard tower, crashing right into the already deteriorating prison.

This is what I meant when I said that *Fragments* sets up the finale. *Shadowman*—Volume 5—will begin with Trevel's arrival in AP, so it's more accurate to say that *Fragments and Shadowman* together set up the finale.

The state of the prison and everyone in it is currently left up in the air. A cliffhanger for Velle and our guards, The Ivory and this mystery person in the halls, Felix and Lem at the mansion, Dash and Kemper's uncertainty down in Tulum (*The Vacation Crossover Story, which is a Patreon exclusive, actually touches on this for a moment*), and Luthor and Ren in California, devising a plan.

The *chaos* has only just begun...

Which brings us to Byron Kang and Trevel Fenwick.

As it stands, we don't really like either of them. Kang was a real jerk to Luthor and Ren, and Trevel is obviously a snake in the grass. But with Kang's sneak peek, we find that there's a lot more than meets the eye. Byron Kang is hurt, and confused, and it's definitely been going on for a while. His emotional turmoil has been building, and Trevel shows up just in time to give him a much-needed confidante. When Kang's bitterness has been dousing his relationship with Luthor and Ren in kerosene, Trevel becomes the match.

From the outside, it's difficult to see liking Trevel Fenwick—yes, he's gunning for Felix ands Lem. But just you wait. He's a character I'm very excited to provide more of.

Alright, *Jesus*... I need to wrap this up, because this is by far my longest author's note ever. But I'd be remised if I didn't give a quick shout out to my *Double-edged* fans!

How great was it to see the twins and Daddy T again?! Middle fingers up, right?!!?!

If you haven't read *Double-edged*, then Cyrus, Colson and Tauren are just random friends to Luthor and Ren. *(But if you're okay with a super taboo emotional journey, you should totally check it out, and see the quick cameo from* ***BerkeleysLexLuthor*** *that introduces the Cyrus and Lex friendship. All info on the book page.)*

Last thing. The mysterious blonde sex worker Ren was talking to under the overpass... Do you know who that was? *Any guesses?* I'll give you a hint. He's an old friend of Felix Darcey...

Come to The Ivory Mansion Spoiler group on Facebook for discussions ;)

Velle calling Luthor "Birdman" at one point, is a nod to Alcatraz—one of many, and won't be the last, especially where birds are concerned.

And, it wouldn't be a Nyla K book without endless DC references. Superman and Lex Luthor... Lex naming his computer Lois. I mean seriously. *So cute.*

What else can I say? Evil can be good. Heroes are villains.

And the love between these characters will persist, despite the world crashing down around them.

I hope I haven't broken your brain too much with all of this. But even if I did, I'm not exactly *sorry*. This series is my *Pulp Fiction*. My *Once Upon A Time In Hollywood*.

This mix of real-world, raw, human issues and desperately fictionalized drama has to be the most fun thing I could never have dreamt of doing, and I'm forever grateful that while sitting in my Brooklyn apartment during quarantine, I cocked my head and said, *"Hm… I think I wanna write a story about a prison."*

Gay romance Alcatraz.

Guantanamo, but make it hot, and queer asf.

Anyway, that's it for now. If you actually read all of this, and processed a quarter of it, you're my favorite kind of person on earth. You understand the assignment.

I said it before, and I'll say it again. We ain't in romancelandia no mo, toto.

Welcome to Alabaster Penitentiary, where the one rule is there are no rules.

I'll meet you back in the rubble. We'll get this bloody party started. ;)

RESOURCES

If you're thinking of harming yourself, please know that it's not the answer. You are loved, and no matter how dark it can feel at times, all life is a gift.

Dial 988, or visit 988lifeline.org if you need help.

For LGBTQIA+ resources and assistance, visit www.itgetsbetter.org
It does get better. Trust me.

For human trafficking/child trafficking resources, or to donate:
www.savethechildren.org/us/charity-stories/child-trafficking-awareness
This is an international, non-government operated organization.

End the HIV stigma, help spread awareness, and donate:
www.eltonjohnaidsfoundation.org

The Elton John AIDS Foundation is a bold organization, committed to more than just stopping the spread of HIV/AIDS. Read up on more above.

Find more information here: glaad.org

Find more about sex workers' rights here: sexworkersproject.org

ACKNOWLEDGEMENTS

I have to thank some people. Because finishing this book without winding up in an asylum myself took a lot of ears listening to me in the throws of a breakdown.

I struggled a lot getting my motivation back after my last release. My personal life was beyond hectic, my schedule was fuller than usual, and it seemed like 2024 had popped off fast. I wasn't ready.

Thankfully, I have the best readers in the world, and the most amazing support system of people who believe in me when I don't. Here they are.

First off, my fiancé, Patrick. The dude who's forced to share me with every single character in my brain, and when he complains even a little, gets his head chewed off. Babe, you've been driving me insane for eighteen years, so at this point, I'd say we're even. Thanks for putting up with me working myself into a ghoul on this book, coming to bed with the sun up, when you're waking up for work. You didn't do it silently by any means, but I know you do support me to no end. If I said this won't happen again, I'd be lying, but I'm seriously gonna try.

To my amazing team… Amber, my fantastic PA who listens to lengthy, neurotic voice messages of me freaking out, worrying and stressing all the livelong day. I am so beyond grateful for your friendship and your dedication, especially when you have your own stuff going on. And I'm so pumped I get to spend release day with you! And Karie, thank you for making awesome videos for me, managing my TikTok because I'd rather die than set foot on that app again, and just being a sweet, supportive addition to our little squad.

My editor, K… I think I almost broke us both with this one. Now we know, for the future… It is entirely possible to complete a 200k novel full of nothing but backstory, interweaving timelines, action and sex in three months. So long as you don't mind giving yourself ulcers and destroying your relationships. LOL. I'm barely kidding, but honestly, I couldn't do anything I do without you, you know that. You're a fucking crazy lunatic, just like me. Big Ren Energy.

To Mackenzie of Nice Girl Naughty Edits… You're such a superstar, it's not even funny. You have been such a huge part of my career as an indie author, but also this series in particular. Thanks for listening to me ramble, and being so flexible. You're a calming presence when I need it, and I'm so happy to call you a colleague and a friend.

The Flipping Hot Fandom! You guys, I swear… You're the reason I do this. I know I've definitely said it before, but I won't stop saying it. You're the most badass people I've ever encountered. Thank you so motherfucking much for your support, and sticking by me even when I have to get quiet for weeks on end because I'm locked up in a prison. But you guys love that prison! Which makes you just as fucked-up as me, and I'm living for it.

Ashlee O'Brien—Ashes & Vellichor. My cover designer and fellow perfectionist. You just get me, man. You do. Honestly, I couldn't be more appreciative of the work you do, especially on this series. You've elevated these books. QUEEN. That's it. That's your title.

Stacey from Champagne Book Design, as always, thank you for the brilliant interior formatting. I'm amazed you still wanted to work with me after For The Fans lol. You rock so damn hard. I absolutely love the work you do, on all my books. Keep slaying.

Thanks to Michelle Lancaster for the beautiful cover photo, and Andy Murray, the model who gave us some pretty Luthor vibes to drool over.

To Pink Flamingo Production for helping bring this series to life in audio!

All of my author friends who have supported me, either with DMs, or bitch-sessions, or sharing love for my stuff… Thank you for being amazing, creative, brilliant beings of light.

To the Inmates ARC Team, for all of your hype over this series. I'm so beyond excited to keep going with this sexy, dark, maddeningly intense world.

Anyone who's calls or messages I ignored while finishing this book… Thanks for understanding. I'm only just getting use of my brain back. And anyone I forgot because I'm so out of it… I love you!

Lastly, to the readers. To the fucking badass, fearless, incredible lovers of the hot, smutty, unique worlds I whip up… I think you're all just freaking amazing. I hope you loved Luthor and Ren, and I hope you're willing to foam at the mouth again until we return once more to the Pen. I've got awesome shit in store for you, and don't worry… It'll always be unapologetically Nyla K.

No matter what ;)

FLIPPING HOT FICTION BY NYLA K

Subscribe to my Patreon for bonus content, like *The Vacation* (PUSH/ Alabaster Pen, etc. Crossover), and more!

The Midnight City Series:

Andrew & Tessa's Trilogy
(MF Forbidden / Age Gap, celebrity romance, suspense. Read in order)
Midnight City (TMCS #1)
Never Let Me Go (TMCS #2)
Always Yours (TMCS #3)

Alex & Noah
Seek Me (TMCS #4 – Standalone / Spin-off, MF Friends to lovers / Angst)

Unexpected Forbidden Romance:

PUSH (Standalone, Taboo / MMF, bi-awakening)
PULL (Continuation novella!)
Trouble (Spinoff, MM, gay-awakening, second chance)
Audio for the Love Is Love books available now!

To Burn In Brutal Rapture (Standalone, MF Taboo / Age Gap)

Double-edged (Standalone, MMM Age Gap, Twincest – **BANNED by Amazon!** Can be found on Nyla's website, Google Play & Eden Books.)

For The Fans (Standalone, MM, Stepbrothers) Also available is audio!

Alabaster Penitentiary:

Distorted, Volume 1 (MM, prisoner/prison guard, dub-con, mindf*ck)
Audio available now!

Joyless, Volume 2 (MMF, prison guards, bi-awakening, second chance, kinky)

Brainwashed, Volume 3 (MM, doctor/patient, true crime)

Fragments, Volume 4 (MM, frenemies to lovers, jealous/possessive/pining) Audio coming soon!

Shadowman, Volume 5 (MM, bi-awakening) – Coming in 2024-2025!
Ivory, Volume 6 (The Finale)
Alabaster Pen is available in audio!

The Control Room, a FREE Alabaster Pen short!

Twisted Tales Collection:

Serpent In White (MMM, dark romance, drug cult, age gap, foster brothers, retelling of the Brothers Grimm's *The White Snake*)

Standalone Novella:
Unwrap Him by Nyla K (An Age Gap, Taboo MM) – Available across all digital retailers, and Nyla's website!

Join my Facebook reader group for discussions, giveaways, and all the best Nyla K madness!

Don't forget to share and leave a review! It means the world!

ABOUT THE AUTHOR

Hi, guys! I'm Nyla K… Author of Flipping Hot Fiction, which basically means all things unique & boundary-pushing! If you're looking for the same old story, you won't find it here. I'm the… *bad guy* ;)

I'm an awkward sailor-mouthed lover of all things romance, existing up in Maine—in our dream house in the woods—with my partner, who you can call PB, or Patty Banga if you're nasty, and our fur baby, Ziggy Stardust! When I'm not writing and reading sexy books, I'm rocking out to my various awesome playlists, cooking yummy food and fussing over my kitten (and no, that's not a euphemism). Did I mention I have a dirtier mind than probably everyone you know?

I like to admire hot guys (don't we all?) and book boyfriends, cake and ice cream are my kryptonite. I can recite every word that was ever uttered on *Friends*, *Family Guy*, and *How I Met Your Mother*, red Gatorade is my lifeblood, and I love to sing, although I've been told I do it in a Cher voice for some reason. I'm very passionate about the things that matter to me, and art is probably the biggest one. If you tell me you like my books, I'll give you whatever you want. I consider my readers are my friends, and I welcome anyone to find me on social media any time you want to talk books or sexy dudes!

Get at me:

info@authornylak.com
Visit AuthorNylaK.com for Banned books, Signed Books & Merch!
The Flipping Hot Newsletter!
Patreon: Where you'll find Nyla K UNCENSORED!
Instagram:@AuthorNylaK
Facebook: AuthorNylaK
Tiktok: @NylaKAuthor
Twitter: @MissNylah
(Misc uncensored content! NSFW!)
Goodreads: Nyla K
BookBub: @AuthorNylaK

Happy reading!

Printed in Dunstable, United Kingdom

82188656R00323